Helen Forrester was born in Hoylake, Cheshire, the eldest of seven children. For many years, until she married, her home was Liverpool – a city that features prominently in her work. For the past thirty years she has made her home in Alberta, Canada. She has travelled widely in Europe, India, the United States and Mexico.

Helen Forrester has written four bestselling volumes of autobiography: *Twopence to Cross the Mersey*; *Liverpool Miss*; *By the Waters of Liverpool* and *Lime Street at Two*. She is also the author of a number of equally successful novels: *Thursday's Child*; *The Latchkey Kid*; *Liverpool Daisy*; *Three Women of Liverpool*; *The Moneylenders of Shahpur*; *Yes, Mama*, for which she won the Writers' Guild of Alberta Award for the best novel of 1988; *The Lemon Tree* and *The Liverpool Basque*. In 1988 she was awarded an honorary D.Litt. by the University of Liverpool in recognition of her achievements as an author.

By the same author

Fiction

THURSDAY'S CHILD
LIVERPOOL DAISY
THREE WOMEN OF LIVERPOOL
THE MONEYLENDERS OF SHAHPUR
YES, MAMA
THE LEMON TREE
THE LIVERPOOL BASQUE

Non-fiction

TWOPENCE TO CROSS THE MERSEY
LIVERPOOL MISS
BY THE WATERS OF LIVERPOOL
LIME STREET AT TWO

HELEN FORRESTER

The Latchkey Kid

Mourning Doves

Grafton

HarperCollins*Publishers*
77-85 Fulham Palace Road
Hammersmith, London W6 8JB

www.harpercollins.co.uk

This omnibus edition published in 2004
by HarperCollins*Publishers*

ISBN 0 007 71203 0

Set in Times

Printed and bound in Great Britain by
Mackays of Chatham plc, Chatham, Kent

The Latchkey Kid

CHAPTER ONE

The ladies of Tollemarche, Alberta, were always wonderfully clever at disposing of their menfolk; so that these gentlemen, if not already in their graves, were encouraged by their wives to depart northwards in search of business, or, to escape from constant nagging, to conferences in Ontario or hunting trips in British Columbia. And it was surprising how frequently they found it necessary to motor down to Edmonton or Calgary.

The ladies' sighs of relief, as the sound of their partners' cars disappeared with distance, indicated that the gentlemen would certainly not be missed, as long as the flood of money engendered by the discovery of oil in Alberta continued to flow so gratifyingly into their joint bank accounts during the boom years of the 1950s.

Unhampered by demanding males, the ladies were free to control the city's social life, which burgeoned forth as a result of the suddenly acquired wealth of the inhabitants. The big oil strike near Tollemarche had been responsible for an upheaval in the existing order; and the fight for social status, before a fixed pecking order could be re-established, was a ruthless one, waged in every drawing-room, church hall and charitable institution.

In this war amongst the teacups, the worst sufferers were the children.

The ladies were not quite so successful in disposing of their offspring as they were of their husbands, though they did their best. It was difficult to do without children, because they were a necessary status symbol and a subject for conversation. The ladies, therefore, had four or five babies as quickly after marriage as nature would permit, and thus provided themselves with an indefinite number of conversational gambits.

The trouble was that after they were born, children had

to wait for six years before they could be sent to school and forgotten for most of the day. The ladies had several methods of dealing with this problem, or 'making them independent and self-reliant' as they called it. The easiest and most commonly used method was to ignore them as far as possible.

It is startling how quickly children discover that they are not wanted. Once a child could walk and had, through dire necessity, learned how to shed a wet pair of training pants and put on his snow suit, he would vanish into the street, not to be seen again until lunch time; once he was tall enough to reach the refrigerator door handle, the problem of lunch was also solved – he could get it himself.

Another method was called 'having activities'. This consisted of enrolling one's child in a private playschool, which sent a car to pick him up in the morning and deposit him back on his own doorstep in the late afternoon. After this, he could be hastily driven to a music lesson, followed by a painting or a dancing lesson. This type of day was guaranteed to exhaust even the most energetic youngster, and he would thankfully walk home, to watch television, eat his supper and put himself to bed.

Some people had baby-sitters of varying degrees of unreliability, mostly young girls in their teens, who were themselves expecting illegitimate babies and needed a temporary home, or elderly women lacking much strength to deal with children. All of them seemed to have in common a cold dislike of children and a determination to do as little as possible for their inadequate wages.

In these circumstances, a determined mother could be free to groom herself, hold office in this or that community activity, or find a job, in order to fulfil herself; though none of them seemed to be able to explain why acting as a bank teller or the secretary of a charity, for example, was more fulfilling than looking after their own children.

The perfectly kept living-rooms of Tollemarche homes were for visitors; the basements, despite their fire hazards, were good enough for the children; there they often slept and there, if the temperature went much below zero, they also played.

Conscientious parents, and there were some, viewed the situation with dismay. Public pressure was against them, and they often fought a bitter battle to maintain the kind of home life in which they believed.

It was into this world that Captain Peter Dawson, a Canadian army officer, brought his young Welsh wife, Isobel. She was the daughter of an old friend of his, who had married a Welsh lady and settled in Caernarvon. Both Isobel's parents had been killed in a motor accident, and Peter Dawson had obtained leave from his unit in France to attend their funeral in Wales. There he had met a distraught Isobel and her broken-hearted schoolgirl sister, Dorothy. He had helped Isobel sort out her father's tangled financial affairs and had fallen in love with her quiet, fragile beauty. He had pressed her to marrry him, though he was considerably older than she was, and she had accepted him at a time of great emotional exhaustion. Leaving Dorothy in the care of a great-aunt to finish her education, Peter had, at the first opportunity, brought Isobel back to his native city of Tollemarche. Isobel soon realized that she had not made, from her point of view, the wisest of marriages, but Peter was very kind to her and she did her best to make him happy.

She had been married only four years when her husband was murdered while serving as a member of the Canadian peacekeeping mission in Cyprus. He had had only one more year to serve before he could have retired into civilian life, and both he and Isobel had been looking forward to this. Her grief at his death was deep and sincere.

She had, as yet, no child to console her, and she had cabled her sister Dorothy to come from Wales to spend the winter with her. Captain Dawson's parents, themselves stricken, had no idea how to deal with their weeping daughter-in-law, and were thankful to leave her to Dorothy.

Sociable Dorothy, although only seventeen years old,

7

managed to infuse some sort of order into Isobel's shattered life, hoping that soon Isobel would decide what she would do in the future, so that she herself could go back home to Wales, which, from the vantage point of Tollemarche, seemed infinitely cosy and desirable.

One cool September Saturday, as the first snowflakes drifted quietly across the picture window, a white-faced, rather exhausted Isobel sat sewing in her living-room. On the following Monday she proposed to go back to the job she had taken to make it financially possible for Peter and her to buy their little home. She had told Dorothy that she felt that the steady routine of her secretarial work would, for the moment, be most helpful to her. She found it impossible to admit, even to herself, the relief which flooded her whole being at the idea that she was no longer bound to live out her life in Tollemarche.

She put her needle and thread neatly away in her sewing box, brushed stray cotton threads from her skirt and went to the window to draw the curtains, before preparing supper.

Across the road, two little girls who frequently came in to visit Isobel, eat toffees and gossip, were teetering uncertainly on the edge of the sidewalk. They had apparently exhausted all the games that a four-year-old could invent, and they were shivering in the wind as they considered exploring the world on the other side of the road.

'Sheila and Penny's parents must still be out,' Isobel remarked. 'I can't see Mrs Brent's car yet – I suppose she is still at the Lady Queen Bees' tea, and Mr Brent must be still at his curling club.'

Dorothy stopped laying the table for supper and stared at her sister, her blue eyes wide with disbelief. 'You mean those kids have been by themselves all the afternoon – just for the sake of a tea – or curling?'

'Certainly. Probably they couldn't get a baby sitter. Anyway, Sheila always has a latchkey tied round her neck, so they can get into the house.'

'There ought to be a law against it,' replied Dorothy emphatically, as she banged knives and forks down on to the table.

'There is – but it doesn't seem to be enforced.' Isobel sighed, remembering many an argument on child care which she had lost, being invariably defeated by the rejoinder that she had no children and, therefore, knew nothing about them. Her tone changed, and she said decisively: 'I'm going to come home with you, as soon as Pete's affairs are cleared up. Tollemarche was livable with Pete, but without him it will be intolerable. These empty women make me sick and their neglected kids break my heart.'

Dorothy tossed her head to clear her long black hair from her eyes, and grinned elfishly at Isobel. 'We could live together and paint London pale pink,' she said hopefully. 'Or Wales!'

Isobel smiled at the tall, rangy girl. 'Pink it shall be,' she said.

Dorothy went on with her work for a minute and then asked: 'Isobel, what happens to these kids, supposing they don't drop themselves over the railway bridge in sheer despair?'

'Well, some of them are chronically in and out of courts – they become pretty unscrupulous. Some, as you know, seek revenge – they riot, they take drugs and generally make damned nuisances of themselves. Some nothing can spoil, and they grow up into the nicest young people you can imagine.'

'Like Hank Stych, who rents your garage?' asked Dorothy, a hint of mischief in her eyes. She had already met this young man, when he had last come to pay his rent, and found him startlingly different from the Welsh boys of her acquaintance – a big, silent boy with disillusioned, almond-shaped eyes sunk above high cheek bones, a boy who had stared unblinkingly at her until she had begun to blush with embarrassment, so that she had felt stripped, not only physically but mentally as well. Finally, he had

9

held out a bunch of one-dollar bills to her, said 'Rent,' and without another word had vaulted over the veranda balustrade and loped down the path to the garage. Very odd, she had decided, and yet nice. 'Does he wear a latchkey round his neck?' she inquired.

'Hank?' Isobel looked thoughtful. 'Yes, Hank's all right – brought himself up like Sheila and Penny are doing.' She laughed. 'He's probably been promoted to a key ring by this time.'

'I like him,' said Dorothy, determined to show she could like the unusual.

Isobel's eyes were still merry. 'Better watch your step with him. Nobody ever told him where to draw the line, and he's not as innocent as he looks – he's got quite a reputation for wildness.'

Dorothy opened the oven to see how the dinner was coming along, and her voice was muffled as she tried to avoid the steam from the casserole she was peeking at. 'You were saying that he has written a wonderful book – and that it's going to be published?'

'Yes,' Isobel sounded anxious, 'and I am really worried about it. You know, Pete and I encouraged him like anything in his writing. What we didn't know for a long time was that this book is his revenge on his parents.

'Doll, you know that this province is known as the Bible Belt?'

Dorothy nodded as she closed the oven door.

'Well, by Bible Belt standards it's the filthiest book imaginable. What this town is going to say when it reaches here isn't hard to imagine. Olga and Boyd Stych are going to be blamed, because everyone will think they were agreeable to its publication. It will ruin Olga socially.'

Mrs Stych and her arch-rival Mrs Frizzell had both called to express their condolences to Tollemarche's most interesting widow. Dorothy had dealt with both of them, aided by Isobel's giddy young sister-in-law, who had explained the social nuances of it all by saying: 'That pair of grasping alley cats would tear the eyes out of anyone who managed to make the social pages of the *Tollemarche Advent* on a day when they should have been featured. They just want to be seen calling at the house.'

'I don't think Hank realizes how devastating it may be to his mother when his book comes out,' Isobel went on.

'Do her good,' said Dorothy laconically.

'Well, I feel guilty,' Isobel responded.

'Maybe people will be more careful of their children after they've read it,' suggested Dorothy hopefully, and then added: 'She's nothing but a social climber, anyway.'

'She's a coming lady in Tollemarche.'

'That ghastly, fat Humpty Dumpty of a woman?' exclaimed Dorothy scornfully.

Isobel nodded, her lips compressed, and then said: 'Yes, that ghastly, fat Humpty Dumpty is heading for a great fall, poor thing. And it is partly my fault.'

CHAPTER TWO

Mrs Theresa Murphy, the Mayor's wife, had, by dint of playing first violin in the local amateur orchestra, established herself as one of the cultural leaders of Tollemarche. On four Thursday evenings during the winter she could be seen, dressed in spotty black and glittering with rhinestones, sawing happily away on her violin through four public concerts, under the baton of Mr Dixon, the elderly English master from Tollemarche public school, who tried gamely to keep the rest of the orchestra in time with her, since he had long ago given up trying to keep her in time with the orchestra.

As the wife of the civic leader, Mrs Murphy had to do considerable entertaining in generous western style, but in this field she made no attempt to keep pace with Olga Stych or Donna Frizzell; she knew when she was beaten.

Since culture did not hammer quite so hard on Mrs Frizzell's door, she had more time to plan parties. Her annual garden party, for buyers of fleets of cars and trucks who dealt with her husband, was always a memorable occasion, reported upon in detail by the queen of the social columns of the *Tollemarche Advent*, a lady who could make or break a local hostess. Mrs Frizzell found it impossible to forgive Mrs Dawson's becoming a widow the same week as her party; a history of Mrs Dawson one night, and the remarks the following night of the lady secretary of the United Nations' Society on the role of the Canadian peacekeeping force in Cyprus, had meant that for the first time in years no report of Mrs Frizzell's party appeared, though room had been found for a report on one of Mrs Murphy's receptions.

Mr Frizzell's business did not seem to suffer from the omission. He did an ever expanding trade in cars and trucks under his big red neon sign, which proclaimed on one side

FRIZZELL'S GARAGE – YOU CAN TRUST MAXIE, and on the other FRIZZELL'S GARAGE – I GREW WITH ALBERTA. His critics agreed that he had sure grown with Alberta – just fatter and fatter!

Mrs Frizzell was the ruthless driving force behind his business. She nagged him northwards to the Peace River district, to establish garages there, and even as far as Fort McMurray, with instructions to buy land for future service stations. Then she went on with the lovely task of making herself the most important lady in Tollemarche.

Mrs Olga Stych, the wife of a consulting geologist, her next-door neighbour, dared to challenge her on this; and their homes, which had, until the commencement of building in Vanier Heights, been two of the nicer houses in the best district of Tollemarche, echoed their ambitions. They were filled with wall-to-wall broadloom and the finest imitation French Provincial furniture. Their L-shaped living rooms were graced by open fireplaces, with the latest shapes in petrified wood adorning the mantelpieces. Each owned a weird splotch of colour in a white and silver frame, painted and framed by a local artist. One had only to buy a Wedgewood coffee service or a piece of Bohemian crystal and the other would have the same the following week.

Through the six months of Alberta's bitter winter each lady tried to outdo the other in the number of coffee parties given and the number of charitable offices each managed to obtain. Through the summer, as the skyscrapers grew on Tollemarche Avenue, they boasted of the glories of their country cottages and the important people from Edmonton or Calgary who had spent a weekend with them at these summer homes. Theresa Murphy persuaded her husband to buy an entire lake and news of this purchase spoiled both Mrs Frizzell's and Mrs Stych's summer.

Each week the ladies spent anxious hours in Andrew's Beauty Salon having their hair tinted and set, still more anxious hours in Dawn's Dresse Shoppe or the Hudson's Bay Company store, adding more dresses and hats to their already over-extended charge accounts. Olga Stych's generous figure would be a nightmare to any dress shop, and her dresses were consequently always more expensive than Donna Frizzell's were. In despair, one day, of finding a well-fitting winter coat, she hastily counted up the amount of land around Tollemarche which her husband had bought up and decided he was worth at least a Persian lamb coat. This error proved to be nearly the last straw needed to break his credit, since he had raised every cent he could in order to invest in land for building. He protested to her hotly about this extravagance, but was quickly sent back to his rocks, cowering from her wrath.

. The third fall after the oil strike in Alberta came slowly in, while Isobel mourned her husband, quite unaware that she had mortally offended Mrs Frizzell by crowding her August garden party off the social page of the *Tollemarche Advent*. The glory of the Indian summer crept across the land with pale sunshine, golden leaves, deep-blue skies and treacherously cold winds. The publication day of Hank Stych's book went unremarked in Tollemarche, mainly because the only bookseller in the town had not had time to unpack his new stock, and book reviews were featured only once a month in the *Tollemarche Advent* and then only in an obscure corner of an inner page. The leaves fell thickly in the more established portions of the city, to the envy of residents in the bare new suburbs who were still awaiting paved roads and street lights, never mind trees.

Mrs Donna Frizzell looked despondently out of her picture window. The unfenced oblong of grass in front of the house and the narrow path to the sidewalk were full of leaves twirling in the wind. Mr Stych, during his last visit home, had already cleared the adjoining garden, and the Frizzells' leaves were gaily invading his once tidy lawn. Mrs Frizzell's lips tightened as she guessed what Olga Stych's remarks would be when she saw them.

That intolerable woman, she thought bitterly, had managed to become president of the Tollemarche Downtown Community Centre by a majority of a single vote, and Mrs Frizzell had had to be content with the vice-presidency, which office she declared gave her all the work and none of the authority. (She gave no credit to Olga Stych for her undoubted talents as an organizer.) To make matters worse, Olga was also the secretary of the Noble Order of Lady Queen Bees – a pack of overdressed snobs, groaned Mrs Frizzell, whose members set the standard for every social event in the city. Maybe, if she could squeeze a mink coat out of Maxie, it would help her towards the membership which always seemed to elude her by a vote or two, a vote strongly influenced, she feared, by Olga Stych. One day, she promised herself, if ever she got the chance, she would give Olga Stych her comeuppance.

In the meantime, since no amount of nagging would persuade Maxie to rake up the leaves or to allow her to employ a man to do it, she would have to do the job herself.

Mixed with the need to tidy up the garden was a desire to show her neighbours her new purple, slim pants and striped purple and yellow jacket. She therefore eased her thin shanks into these all too revealing pants, put a pair of gilt oriental sandals on her feet and hastily touched up the mauve polish on her toenails and fingernails. She peered anxiously into her six-foot-wide dressing-table mirror to see if any white hair showed after her last auburn tint, and found to her satisfaction that all her hair was the same improbable shade.

She went through the house door leading into the garage, seized a rake and plunged into the cold wind. She began to rake from the front of the house towards the road, then realized she had nothing in which to put the leaves. With an irritability caused as much by her slimming diet as by the lack of a box, she almost stamped down the stairs into the basement, which was comfortingly warm, and found a couple of cardboard boxes.

Working with feverish haste, for the wind was piercing through her elegant jacket and Gentle Curve bra underneath, she filled the boxes, staggered with them to a row of garbage cans in the back lane and dumped their contents into the bins. Her feet were icy cold in their open sandals when, on the fifth trip back to the front lawn, her patience was rewarded.

Mrs Stych drew up at the kerb in her new European car, bought, needless to say, from Maxie's arch-rival down in Edmonton. She heaved herself out and opened the trunk to display several large paper bags full of groceries. Mrs Frizzell hastily drew in her stomach, tucked in her tail, and posed with her rake, just as she had seen the Hudson's Bay Company model do when showing pants. A pair of University students passing by hastily averted their faces to hide their giggles.

Mrs Stych, however, did not avert her gaze. She peered over the bag of groceries clasped to her bosom and was almost consumed by envy. Five feet high and weighing one hundred and seventy pounds, a veritable Humpty Dumpty of a woman, Mrs Stych had no hope of ever being able to wear pants gracefully.

Mrs Stych ate with all the avidity of one who has known starvation. Her father, an immigrant from the Ukraine, had carved his pig farm out of raw bush. Her pregnant mother had pulled the plough when they broke a part of their holding for wheat and vegetables, and Olga's first memories were of carrying away stones from the furrows. They had known such hunger that even now Olga could not bring herself to throw away a single crumb and always ate whatever was left after a meal.

Looking now at her plump, well-kept hands, two heavy diamond rings worn above her unexpectedly old-fashioned wedding band it was hard to believe that her mother was a work-bent Ukrainian peasant who still wore a black kerchief over her hair and spoke little English.

Mrs Stych fixed her button eyes upon the elegant figure of Mrs Frizzell and bowled purposefully across the lawn. Her high, grating voice was caught by the wind and carried half a block, as she asked: 'Aren't Maxie able to do the leaves?'

'He's up at Grande Prairie, seeing to his new garage and car lot.' She smiled, showing an excellent set of artificial teeth, as she rallied her forces. 'Enterprising, that's Maxie,' she added, her eyes agleam with malice.

While she spoke, she remembered Maxie's grumble from behind his newspaper, the last time he had been home, when she had told him to do the leaves.

'Do 'em yourself,' he had said. 'You ain't got nuttin' to do while I'm away up the Peace, not now Joanne and Betty is married.' His pursed-up, babylike lips had quivered. 'I got no time, you know that.'

In the tirade which immediately followed, Mrs Frizzell had reminded him that she was a pillar of the community, all for the sake of his business. She was secretary of the Tollemarche United Church Willing Workers' Group, vice-president (not president!) of the Tollemarche Downtown Community Centre, a driver for Cripples' Transport, a member of the Car Dealers' Wives Society and, she would remind him, a member of the Committee for the Preservation of Morals. And, she would like him to know the Morals Committee had just succeeded in having D.H. Lawrence's books banned from the cigar stores.

Mr Maxmilian Frizzell had never read a book since leaving school and did not know who Lawrence was, so he put down the newspaper and took up the *Car Dealer and Garageman* with what dignity he could muster. The next morning he departed, thankfully, for the North, to see his new garage and a silent, obliging Métis woman of his acquaintance.

The leaves remained on the lawn.

The high heels of Mrs Stych's new, mink-trimmed bootees were now sinking into the Frizzell lawn and threatening to snap at any moment, so she knew she must be quick. She therefore ignored Maxie's undoubted enterprise, and asked: 'Any news from Betty yet?'

Mrs Frizzell brightened. She fell right into the trap, as she said: 'Yeah, she got a daughter in Vancouver General yesterday. Don't want me to go over yet. Her husband Barry's taking care of the other two kids – he's a real capable boy.'

17

'It must make yer feel old, being a grandmother for the sixth time,' promptly replied Mrs Stych, her face carefully arranged to indicate that it was a disaster.

Mrs Frizzell was not, however, so easily crushed. Scottish ancestors, one of whom had married a Cree, (who was, of course, never mentioned by any member of the family), had given her a physical and mental toughness which enabled her to fight methodically for anything she wanted badly. Now she wanted to squelch Olga. It had to be done, however, without giving too much offence – Mrs Stych was, after all, a Lady Queen Bee. Old at fifty, indeed!

She smiled sweetly.

'At forty-five, I don't mind. I married young and so did Joanne and Betty.' She lifted her lance. 'I'm just so glad they're settled with good, respectable boys for husbands.'

Mrs Stych winced. Mrs Frizzell had no need to remind her that her neat, conforming sons-in-law were far more popular in their home town of Tollemarche than Mrs Stych's own son, Hank.

Hank, when Mrs Stych thought of him at all, always gave her a headache. Consequently, she had done her best to ignore his existence. But Donna Frizzell never failed to remind her of his dragging progress through school, compared to Betty and Joanne's smart performances. Now, at nearly twenty, he was still struggling to pass his Grade 12 examinations in high school, having been assured by his father, the school, and society at large that the world held no place for a boy without his Grade 12. Mrs Stych could many times have wept with humiliation when Donna hastened to tell her of yet another minor car accident in which his ancient jalopy had been involved, yet another girl with whom he had once been seen who was 'in trouble'. For a boy who only worked part-time in a supermarket he had too much money, and this was another source of innuendo from Mrs Frizzell. Olga herself was far too busy to worry about what Hank was doing, but she wished Donna would mind her own business. And now she had pierced her again in this sore spot.

Mrs Stych clutched her groceries more tightly to her bosom and tried to heave her high heels out of the roots of the Frizzell grass. One day she would get even with Donna for this. Hank might be wild, but nobody had pinned anything serious on him yet. The Frizzell sons-in-law might wear halos, but when it came to financial success they were nowhere.

'Yeah,' agreed Mrs Stych, at the same time disinterring her high heels. 'They sure need to be good boys, being so hard up. Betty and Joanne must have a hard time managing.'

Mrs Frizzell had been feeling that victory in this verbal exchange was hers and had been preparing to leave the garden. Now, bent over a box, she nearly choked at this reference to her daughters' poverty. She jerked herself upright, just in time to intercept a charming smile from Mrs Stych, as she looked back over her shoulder on her way to her own front door.

Mrs Frizzell, in a red glare of rage, for a moment imagined Mrs Stych as a neatly wrapped bundle of well minced beef.

CHAPTER THREE

Mrs Stych had just set down the last of her bags of groceries on the kitchen counter and begun to unpack them, when there was the sound of a heavy truck drawing up outside her house.

'Mother!' almost wailed Mrs Stych. 'And the girls coming for bridge!'

She trotted into the living-room, where three bridge tables had already been set out, and peeped through the picture window.

Her mother was already clambering laboriously down from the seat beside the driver, displaying a lumpy mass of grey woollen stocking and woollen knickers in the process. Her brother was already changing gear, and as soon as the old lady was safely on the sidewalk the vehicle ground noisily forward, with its protesting load of smelly pigs, towards the market.

Mrs Stych felt a little relieved. At least that humiliating old truck would not be parked outside her door when the girls arrived. She could just imagine the scathing looks with which Mrs Josephine MacDonald, the president of the Noble Order of Lady Queen Bees, would have regarded it. Perhaps, she hoped guiltily, Joe would return to pick up her mother and take her home before any of the guests arrived.

The old lady's footsteps could be heard, ponderous and threatening, on the front steps. Mrs Stych vanished immediately into the kitchen and continued to put away groceries, as if unaware of her mother's arrival.

The porch door clicked as her mother slowly entered. There was the sound of feet being carefully wiped on the doormat, as once sharply requested by Mrs Stych soon after her marriage had taken her into polite circles. Two heavy farm boots were then heaved off. The door into the living-room was opened.

'Olga, where are you?' called her mother in Ruthenian, her brown, wrinkled face beaming. 'I have come for three hours while Joe is selling the pigs.'

Mrs Stych, untying her apron, bustled out of the kitchen and tried not to show her despair.

'Why, Mother!' she exclaimed, embracing the stout shoulders and implanting a kiss on her mother's cheek. Is it really necessary for Mother to smell eternally of hens? she wondered, and ushered her into the kitchen so that the unmistakable odour should not permeate her carefully prepared living-room.

Mrs Palichuk sank onto a scarlet kitchen chair and eased off her drab grey winter coat so that it draped over the back, retaining, however, the black kerchief which modestly veiled her hair. She was dressed in a clumsy black skirt and a heavy grey cardigan, and, in honour of the occasion, had put on her best apron, which was white and had been exquisitely embroidered by herself. It always astonished Olga Stych that her mother's horribly distorted hands, with their thick, horny nails, could produce such delicate embroidery and could paint with such skill the traditional patterns on eggshells at Eastertide.

Mrs Palichuk planted her stockinged feet squarely on the white and beige tiles of the kitchen floor, and looked around her. She enjoyed exploring the intricacies of her daughter's kitchen. The electric toaster which turned itself off when the toast was done and the electric beater enthralled her. She was happy enough, however, to return to her own frame house, built by her husband after their first five bitter years spent living in a sod hut. It was heated by a Quebec stove in the kitchen and she cooked with wood on another iron stove, and no cajoling by her widowed son, Joe, was going to make her alter her ways now.

'Expecting visitors?' Mrs Palichuk asked, speaking again in Ruthenian.

As usual, Olga answered her in English. 'Yeah,' she said, setting the coffee pot on the stove. She took out the

21

electric beater and arranged it to beat cream, while Mrs Palichuk watched, fascinated.

'Eleven for lunch and bridge.'

In her heart Olga Stych hoped her mother would take the hint and depart. Then she realized that the older woman could not go without Joe to transport her, and she wondered what in earth she was to do.

Dimly, Mrs Palichuk perceived that she was in the way, and it hurt her.

'I won't disturb you,' she said. 'I've brought my embroidery – I'll sit quiet while you play.'

Mrs Stych rallied herself. 'It's all right, Mother. You're very welcome. It's just you don't play bridge.'

'Oh,' said her mother with a sniff, 'I'll be entertained enough, watching your fine friends.'

Mrs Stych cringed at this remark. It was bad enough to have to produce a mother who smelled of hens, worse to have all one's guests disconcerted by the beady eyes of an old countrywoman. She said nothing, however, but continued her rapid preparations for her guests.

The back screen door slammed and a second later her son Hank padded silently into the kitchen. He was a tall youth with very broad shoulders and deep chest, a trifle plump like most North American boys, but giving an impression of great physical strength. His skin had a yellowy tinge and he had the same deepset black eyes as his mother and grandmother.

He unzipped his black jacket and flung it on a chair.

'Hi, Ma,' he said mechanically and then realized that his grandmother was also present. His face lit up. 'Hi, Gran,' he said with more enthusiasm, went across to her and embraced her with a bearlike hug.

Laughing and fighting him ineffectually, his grandmother roared pleasantries at him in a mixture of Ruthenian and broken English. At last he let her go, and, puffing happily, she straightened her kerchief and skirt. 'How's school?' she asked in Ruthenian.

Hank spoke no Ruthenian but he could understand the

simple sentences his grandmother used – more easily, in fact, than her garbled attempts at English.

He made a wry face and shook his head, his eyes holding, at that moment, the same merry twinkle as his grand-mother's, a gaiety missing from his mother's expression.

'He don't work,' said his mother disapprovingly. 'Always out somewhere. Did you do your homework last night, Hank?' she asked in a voice devoid of real inquiry.

He was very hungry and answered her query absently. 'Yeah, I did.' Then he asked: 'What's cooking, Ma?'

'Got the girls coming for lunch and bridge. Make yourself a sandwich.'

Obediently Hank got a plate, took two slices of bread from the breadbox, and, after rummaging about in the refrigerator, found some luncheon meat, a glass of milk and a cardboard cup of ice cream. His grandmother watched, her toothless mouth agape.

In all the desperate, toiling years she had been in Canada, neither her husband nor her son had ever made themselves a meal, except on one or two occasions when illness had confined her to bed. Yet here was her grandson fending for himself, leaning amiably against a kitchen cupboard and eating a self-made sandwich, while his mother gave infinite attention to food for women who should have been at home attending to their own children. It was with difficulty that she refrained from making a sharp remark.

After a moment, she managed to say through tight lips: 'Come out and visit us on Sunday.'

Hank looked uneasily at her. 'I can't,' he said. 'Got a date.' Then, feeling that the reply was too abrupt, he added: 'I'll sure come out and help with any work Uncle Joe wants doing on the next weekend.'

Mrs Palichuk smiled. 'I know you will. Come then, work or no work.'

He agreed, and lounged away to his room, from whence the sound of his portable typewriter could soon be heard.

'He don't really work,' said his mother crossly. 'That

typewriter used to go half the night. Now he don't bring it home from school half the time.'

Mrs Palichuk came to Hank's defence.

'He seems to be keeping up his piano playing,' she said. 'He was trying out the new one that Joe bought for his little Beth to learn on, and even I knew he was playing well.'

Olga grunted, and then admitted grudgingly: 'Yeah, he practises on our old piano in the basement. Does some at school, too, I suppose. But he won't try competing in the Festival – he's too lazy.'

'You don't give him enough time, you and Boyd,' said Mrs Palichuk. 'You never did encourage him. Always out gallivanting, and him home with a sitter or maybe nobody at all, for all I know.' She sniffed and wiped her nose with the back of her hand. 'You didn't even give him one of those fancy cookies just now,' she added in an aggrieved tone.

Mrs Stych glared at the exquisite collection of cookies she was arranging on a tray. 'He's too fat,' she snapped. Her voice became defiant: 'And what time did you and Dad ever spare for us?'

Indignation welled up in Mrs Palichuk. She closed her tired, bloodshot eyes and saw herself again as a young woman, buxom and pregnant, set down in wild bush country, her only asset a husband as young and as strong as herself. She remembered how, side by side, they had hacked and burned the underbrush, borrowed a plough and pulled it themselves, working feverishly to get a little harvest to last them through the first arctic-cold winter. In those hungry, freezing years she had borne and lost two children in the small sod hut in which they lived, before Olga, coming in slightly easier times, had survived. She had fed the precious child herself and carried it with her into the fields, watching it as she wielded a hoe or sickle, tears of weakness and fatigue often coursing down her dusty cheeks. A year later Joe had arrived, and the first doctor in the district had attended her in the first room of what was now a complete frame house. She remembered the doctor telling her, as gently as he could, that it was unlikely that she would have more children, and the shocked look on her husband's face when he heard the news. They would need children to work the land when they became old. Her husband had been kind, however, had kissed her and said the Lord would provide.

And the Lord had provided, reflected Mrs Palichuk. The farm was well equipped with machinery and did not need the hand labour of earlier years. Olga and Joe had been able to go to school, though they had plenty of farm chores as well. Olga, the brighter of the two, had clamoured to be allowed to go to college in Tollemarche, and both parents had encouraged her in this, hoping she would become a school-teacher; but she had met Boyd Stych and got married instead. It was not fair to say that her parents had had no time for her or for Joe; all four of the family had worked together, and, as the settlement grew, they had enjoyed churchgoing and Easters and Christmasses with their neighbours.

Her exasperation, added to her feeling of being unwanted, burst out of her, and she almost shouted at her daughter: 'Your father and I were always with you, teaching you to be decent and to work. Joe always makes time to play with his kids – he's got to be both mother and father to them – in spite of having to run the farm alone since your father died. You're just too big for your shoes!'

Mrs Stych was unloading savoury rolls and a bowl of chicken salad from the refrigerator and she kicked the door savagely, so that it slammed shut with a protesting boom. When she turned on her mother, her face was scarlet and her double chin wobbled as she sought for words.

When the words came, they arrived as a spurt of Ruthenian, the language of her childhood.

'I'm not too big for my shoes!' she cried. 'You just don't know what it's like living in a town – it's different.'

Mrs Palichuk wagged an accusing finger at Olga.

'Excuses! Excuses!' her voice rose. 'You were always good at them. Anything to avoid staying home and looking after Hank. How he ever grew up as decent as he is, I don't know.'

Arms akimbo, Olga swayed towards her mother.

'Let me tell you,' she yelled, 'Boyd and I are somebodies in this town, and mostly because I was smart enough to set to and cultivate the right people.'

'Rubbish!'

'It's not rubbish – it's true.'

Mrs Palichuk heaved her formidable bulk off the frail chair and thrust her face close to Olga's.

'And what good will it do for Hank, if it is true?'

Olga drew herself up proudly.

'His name will be in the Social Register,' she announced.

Mrs Palichuk was reduced to stunned silence for a moment. Then she roared, like a Montreal trucker stuck in a lane: 'You'll be lucky if his name's not on a tombstone – like his friend who killed himself.'

Olga's voice was as tremendous as her mother's as she screamed: 'Don't be ridiculous!'

Hank materialized silently at the kitchen door, some school books under his arm. He surveyed the two women, who were oblivious of his presence as they tore verbally at each other. With a shrug, he retrieved his black jacket, pinched a couple of cookies from the carefully arranged plate and drifted quietly away through the front door.

When he stopped to look back along the road, he saw two cars draw up in front of his home, one after the other. A sleepy grin spread over his face. The bridge-playing girls had arrived, a collection of overdressed, overpainted forty-year-olds. As the sound of their giggling chatter reached him on the wind, his amusement faded and gave way to loathing. There was Mrs Moore, the dentist's wife, mother of his friend who had committed suicide because life did not seem worth living; and there was Mary Johnson's mother looking as prim as a prune, not knowing that her daughter was no better than a streetwalker. Hank made a vulgar sound of distaste, shoved his hands in his pockets and continued on his way.

He remembered how, as a child, by dozens of small acts of perversity, he had brought his mother's wrath down upon himself, so that she did at least notice his existence. His father, being a geologist, was away from home most of the time, so that Hank could, to a degree, forgive his neglect. But his mother had nothing to do except care for him, and this she had blatantly failed to do. Instead, she had toadied to these ghastly, grasping women in glittering hats, women who themselves seemed to have forgotten that they had husbands and families.

As he had grown older, his anger had turned to cold bitterness, and creeping into his mind had come the idea of revenge, something subtle enough to humble his mother, make her realize that he lived, without killing her.

After long consideration, he had decided that he would try to write a book so outrageous that the Presbyterian élite of Tollemarche would ostracize the whole Stych family and thus put an end to his mother's inane social life. He had worked at the idea with all the intensity of youth, and now it was about to bear fruit. The book was, apparently, the kind of tale for which all young people had been waiting and its heavy sales in the United States had amazed him; the first hardcover edition had sold fast enough to surprise even his capable publisher.

He tried now to think with savage pleasure of the dismay likely to afflict his mother, once her female companions heard of it. He found, however, as he loped along, ostensibly to school, that he could not feel the same bitterness that he had done when he first started to write. Instead, he was glowing with hope of a future which, until recently, had seemed to him to consist solely of repeating Grade 12 over and over again in a remorseless, inescapable cycle of misery. Hank Stych, he told himself smugly, was a success.

CHAPTER FOUR

Mr Maxmilian Frizzell owned the biggest garage and car salesroom in Tollemarche. It took up half a block of Tollemarche Avenue and was gaily painted in red and white. Above its well-polished showroom windows an electric sign proclaimed to the world his slogan, YOU CAN TRUST MAXIE.

At the back of his premises he owned a used-car lot which faced on a less fashionable avenue, and here he sold second-hand cars, trucks and motorboats. His salesmen in the front showroom were sleek as well-fed cats, immaculately dressed in dark suits and ties, while the ones on the back car lot were chosen deliberately for their comfortably seedy looks; they leaned more towards coloured shirts and zippered jackets, and their haircuts were longer.

One Saturday morning, some two weeks after Mrs Frizzell's encounter with Mrs Stych, Mr Frizzell was seated at his office desk in a glassed-in area above the garage proper, from whence he could see all that was going on at both back and front of his property. He was going over his books and noting complacently that he was doing remarkably well.

He got up slowly from his chair to stretch himself and went to the window, overlooking the back car lot. It was busy, and all the salesmen were occupied. The autumn sun glinted softly on the pastel-coloured vehicles, most of which Mr Frizzell expected to sell before winter paralyzed the second-hand car business for four months. To one side of the lot was a collection of European cars and leaning over a snow-white Triumph was Hank Stych, talking to one of the salesmen. The salesman was just closing the hood, and Hank walked round to the back of the car and bounced it firmly up and down with his hands.

'Why does Van want to waste his time showing a car as expensive as that to a kid like Hank?' wondered Mr Frizzell irritably. Surely the man had enough sense to take him over to the other corner, where aged Chevrolets lay wearily beside battered Valiants, motorbikes and scooters.

The salesman and Hank, however, seemed to have reached some agreement and strolled towards the office, where fat old Josh presided over the financing section with the careful rapacity of a born moneylender.

Mr Frizzell shrugged his shoulders. Josh would soon cut Hank down to size. He dismissed the subject from his mind and decided to go down to the tiny lunchroom he ran for his employees, to get a cup of coffee.

His appearance caused a rapid scattering of employees who had outstayed their coffee break, and he sat down contentedly to munch a doughnut with his coffee. A few minutes later, Van entered, looking very pleased with himself.

'Sold that Triumph,' he called to Mr Frizzell.

Mr Frizzell stopped munching.

'Who to?'

'Hank Stych.'

'You're crazy!'

'Nope. He bought it all right.'

Mr Frizzell swallowed a piece of doughnut whole.

'How's he going to pay for it?' he asked, trying not to appear over-anxious.

'Traded in his jalopy, put a thousand down and the rest over six months.'

'Now I know you're crazy,' exploded Mr Frizzell. 'What the hell – '

'It's O.K., Boss. It's O.K., I tell yer. He wrote a cheque and Josh okayed it with the bank – phoned Hnatiuk, the manager, at home.'

Mr Frizzell slowly dunked the remains of his doughnut into his coffee. 'You're kidding?' he said without much conviction.

'No, I'm not. Ask Josh. Hnatiuk at the bank said he's

29

always had quite a good balance in his savings account – for a kid – and he's deposited quite a bit of money recently. He's got the money, all right.'

'Well, I'll be damned,' said Mr Frizzell, forgetting for a moment his Presbyterian upbringing. 'Where's he get it from?'

'Dunno. Ain't our headache.'

Van swallowed down a scalding coffee and got up. 'It's my lucky day,' he said cheerfully. 'Go see what else is cooking.'

'Sure,' said Mr Frizzell bewilderedly, 'sure.'

Hank drove the gleaming little Triumph out of the lot. She was a peach, he thought lovingly, a perfect peach, and all his, provided he was satisfied after giving her a run on the highway. He drove her carefully in and out of the busy Saturday morning traffic and wondered idly how he was going to explain about her to his mother, without saying where he got the money from. She was going to learn the hard way about the book, he was determined about that. His father wouldn't even notice the car, he thought, without much bitterness – too busy with his oil hunting. Probably wouldn't be home for weeks anyway.

Well, his book, his beautiful, shocking book, was published at last, and being bought by every kid in the States, so the balloon was bound to go up one of these days. Judging by the latest letter he had received from New York, care of Isobel Dawson, it was going to go up with a bang – there had been sufficient talk of banning it to make sure that everybody bought it, without any real danger that it would be banned from the bookstores. Maybe it might just make his mother realize he was alive. At any rate, everybody would think she had condoned his writing it and that should raise a fine storm for her. He clenched the steering wheel so hard that the car wobbled, and he hastily righted it. It would serve her right.

He had given up his Saturday job in the supermarket some time back, so today he would just drive and drive, drifting along the miles of highway toward Edmonton.

He stopped for a red light, prepared to make a right-hand turn as soon as the arrow flicked green. He knew the change would be slow, so he took out and lit a cigarette while he waited. He whistled mechanically at the back view of a girl waiting to cross the intersection, though of late girls seemed to have lacked their usual charm for him. The girl turned her head and half smiled at him behind her glasses. He knew her. Her name was Gail Danski, a prim-looking chick, but not so prim when you got her into a dark corner, as he had once discovered when taking her home after a school dance.

'Hi,' he shouted. 'Like a ride?'

She hesitated, and was lost.

She cuddled in close to him as they tore along the highway. Hank was fun, even if it did look as if he would never make Grade 12 and never earn much. He knew how to give a girl a good time.

'Where we going? Mother will be looking for me.'

'Let her look.'

She rubbed her leg against his.

Since it was obviously expected of him, he took his right hand off the wheel and put his arm around her shoulders. She laughed and took off her glasses, then gently slid her hand into his pocket.

'I haven't had any lunch,' she complained.

'We'll stop at a drive-in, and then what say about a nice, quiet park?' He might as well make hay while the sun shone, he told himself.

She giggled and looked sly. 'O.K.'

It was just too easy, he ruminated, as he bit into a huge hamburger at the drive-in. All you had to do was write about it afterwards, and you could make a real fast buck. Then he remembered the long, toilsome months when he had worked to perfect a style of writing, giving hours to his literature and language assignments, more hours to dissecting other people's novels. No, it was not that easy, he decided, smiling a little ruefully to himself, and there was a lot more hard work ahead.

His friend regarded him curiously over her hamburger. It was strange how Hank had a way of withdrawing from one's company at times, just as if he had forgotten one was there. Still, he looked fine when he smiled like that, almost handsome, with his wide mouth and perfect teeth.

'Wotcha laughin' at, Hank?' she asked.

'It wouldn't interest you, hon.'

It was midnight when he finally eased the Triumph to a stop in front of his parents' house and swayed gently up the steps. He could not, at first, unlock the door, though the porch light was on; the keyhole kept moving. He should not have had that last drink or that last kiss. That girl was unbelievable. Who would imagine that a thin, stuck-up-looking type like that could know so much? And yet, unaccountably, he had not been happy with her. Finally, he had felt sick at his behaviour and had dropped her off at her home with a feeling of relief that she was not the clinging type and perhaps he could avoid her in future. Girls like that were toys, and he was fed up with toys.

He found the keyhole, opened the door quietly, and crept into the living-room. His mother must have gone to bed. He went along the passage as silently as he could, and, safely in his room, flung himself on his bed without undressing. He felt dirty and his head ached.

He hauled a pillow out from under the bedspread and arranged it to ease his throbbing temples. He had had enough of this kind of game, he decided. Maybe he could settle down a bit now; quit high school, travel – and write. It would be good to get out of Tollemarche, out of Alberta, and see the world a bit. Suddenly, he was asleep.

He woke up only when his mother slammed the front door as she went out to church. He lay quietly, with a comfortable feeling of pleasant anticipation of the day before him, imagining his mother in her pale blue Sunday outfit getting her European car out of the garage and manoeuvring it down to the United church. Time was, he remembered, when she had attended the Greek Orthodox

Church, where he also had gone when small, but its splendour had palled when she had realized that more fashionable people belonged to the United Church. Hank chuckled, and then winced when he moved his head suddenly. Even God could be fashionable.

He got up, took a shower, combed his hair with care and put on a new black T-shirt. He ate a dish of cornflakes while wandering around the kitchen and then went out to look at the Triumph, still parked in front of the house. His mother would imagine some stranger had parked his car there. But the car was his and it was beautiful. He loved her like a woman and he ran his hands lightly over her as if she would respond to his touch. She was silent and acquiescent, however, so he climbed in and drove her round several blocks, just for the joy of it, taking the sharp corners so fast that her tyres shrieked in protest. Then he went slowly back to within two blocks of home, drove up the back lane and stopped before the old wooden garage which he had rented for so many years from Isobel Dawson.

As he entered the garden through the back gate, Isobel got up from in front of a flower bed where she had been planting bulbs. He was pleased to see her looking less pale than when he had last seen her, and she grinned at him with something of her old cheerfulness. She wore a shabby, tweed skirt and a turtleneck sweater which had shrunk slightly, making her look even smaller than usual. She had no makeup on and her long fair hair was twisted into a knot on top of her head. Hank could not imagine how she managed to look so elegant in such an outfit; the concepts of breeding and natural grace were unknown to him, and the quiet air of command she had scared him slightly. All he knew was that compared with the trollop he had been with the day before, she was like a princess, a very untouchable snow princess seven years older than he, who had recently lost her husband.

Fear of hurting her in any way made him abrupt. 'Got something to show you,' he announced without preamble. 'Oh?' she queried in her soft, clipped English voice.

Dorothy's voice held a distinct Welsh singsong, but years in London had worn away any trace of it from Isobel's speech.

'Yeah, come on outside.'

Still holding a trowel in one dirty hand, she followed his huge, droopy figure into the lane.

'My goodness!' she exclaimed. 'What a lovely car!'

She walked all round his precious beauty and admired its finer points. Finally, she came to stop beside him and looked up at him with a serious, troubled air.

'You know, Hank, the car is very nice indeed, but is it wise to buy it just at present?'

He was immediately defiant, his black eyes narrowed and his mouth hard.

'Why not? It's my money, isn't it? I can do what I like.'

She answered him gently, pushing a loose lock back into her bun as she did so.

'Yes, my dear, it is your money, and you really earned it. The car is lovely – but do you think you should flash money around yet – I mean, before the town knows how you came by it?' She stopped, then said: 'Look, come and have some tea with me before you start work. Have you seen any American papers?'

The endearment caught him by surprise and his face softened. He did not know of the English habit of using such affectionate epithets rather haphazardly, and he was impressed that she should consider him her dear.

'O.K.,' he said, considerably mollified, and followed her obediently up the garden path and into the kitchen.

The two women students who rented rooms from her had gone to church, and the remains of their breakfast lay on the table in the breakfast nook. Isobel looked at the muddle with distaste, then quickly washed her hands, put a kettle of water on the gas stove and assembled cups and saucers on a tray, while Hank ambled curiously around the old-fashioned kitchen. It had none of the clinical efficiency of his mother's, but it did remind him of his grandmother's kitchen out on the farm, with its prosaic line of battered saucepans which shared a shelf with a large bowl for making bread and a hopeful looking collection of cake tins.

There was cake, satisfying and fruity, and he sat on the edge of the chesterfield in Isobel's sitting-room and ate it appreciatively between gulps of strong, sweet tea from one of her best bone china teacups.

He liked this room, he decided. A man could put his feet up here without fear of being rebuked, and maybe he could even leave things about. Her desk looked untidy and a basket by the fireplace was filled with old magazines and newspapers. On a little table by the piano was a pile of much thumbed music.

He got up and went to the piano, sat on the stool and found that it revolved. He did a slow twist on it, laughing at her as he did so, then played a chord. She did not object, so he broke into a piece by Debussy and she listened attentively. After a few minutes, he became aware of Peter Dawson's portrait staring down at him from the top of the piano, and he stopped.

'I didn't know you could play,' she said. 'You are quite good.'

'Always got an A in music,' he replied, still contemplating the portrait. 'Paid for lessons out of my newspaper money.' He nodded towards the photograph. 'Sorry about Peter.'

She was suddenly tense and her voice came stiffly: 'Thank you.'

Seeing her quivering lips, he wished he had not mentioned Peter. What a clumsy lout he was! Desperately he wanted to comfort her, but how does a man comfort a girl crying for someone else, he wondered anxiously. 'You'll feel better later on,' he floundered. 'Lousy job – the army.'

She controlled herself with an effort. 'Yes, but I think he felt the peacekeeping mission was very worthwhile.'

He tried to change the subject. 'Funny to think you're a Canadian.'

She realized he was trying to lead the conversation away from her husband, to be kind and make up for his blunder. 'I suppose I am,' she said. She picked up a New York paper

35

from the pile on the coffee table. 'I wanted to show you this.'

He felt a little snubbed and was angry with himself. He took the paper from her, however, and after a quick glance at her set face, read the column she indicated which was headed 'Book Reviews'. He whistled under his breath.

' "*The Cheaper Sex* . . . a disgusting book . . . vulgar pornography . . . shocking," ' he read in a mutter, and looked at her sheepishly.

She had recovered herself and tiny humorous lines were gathering round her eyes.

'Now read this one,' she commanded.

He read aloud: ' "Delicate delineation of a boy's sensations on discovering physical love . . . powerful and evocative description of adolescent suffering in an unsympathetic society . . . the best to come out of Canada for years . . . " Aw, hell!' He slammed the paper down, his face going pink in spite of his efforts to appear blasé. 'Do you think it was a sick book?'

Isobel smiled and said: 'No, I told you it was a good book, and I was right. A lot of things which are thought rather wicked in North America are regarded as normal in Europe. The thing is that, in a day or two, the *Tollemarche Advent* will wake up to the fact that you wrote it. There will be headlines – and I don't think your parents are going to like them much.'

Hank's voice was sulky as he replied:'What do I care? I started to write it so as to shake them. They never cared about me, did they?'

'They are going to care now.'

'They're about twenty years too late. Anyway, I did finally send it under a pen name – Ben MacLean – mostly to please you,' he said defensively. Then he added, with a sudden burst of frankness, 'I reckoned the news would seep out anyway in time and cause them to lose plenty of sleep.'

'I think in a place as small as Tollemarche it will come out,' she agreed.

'Waal,' he drawled defiantly, 'let it come out. That's

36

what I originally intended. Now, I don't care either way, Isobel.'

The use of her first name did not imply familiarity, as it would have done in England, though she had never really got used to being on first-name basis with everyone; she was invariably disconcerted by this custom.

She leaned forward to pick up a cigarette box. When she opened the lid, it commenced to play a tinkling version of 'The Bluebells of Scotland'. She offered him a cigarette from it.

He was charmed by the tune and took the whole box from her while he listened; his face reflected an almost childlike absorption. This was the first time that he had been past the big covered back porch of her house, and everything was new and interesting.

'Say, where did you get that?'

'It belonged to my Welsh grandmother – she bought it in Edinburgh while she was on her honeymoon.' She enjoyed his obvious fascination with it and it reminded her of another suggestion she wanted to make to him.

'You know, Hank, if you really want to write for a living you should go to London and Edinburgh, go to Europe, too – perhaps try working for a newspaper or magazine. See something of life.'

'I've seen plenty already,' he snapped, his face suddenly hardening, though basically he appreciated the personal interest which prompted her suggestion.

She ignored his tone of voice and agreed with him.

'You have in a way – but you know, there are other places than the Prairies and Jasper and Banff – and, by and large, the world isn't very interested in books about Canada. You will need to branch out and –'

She stopped, anxious not to offend him. His presence kept at bay the pictures that danced through her mind, of Peter lying in the dust, her Peter who had, she realized suddenly, always had the same slightly defensive outlook that Hank had, of trying to forestall criticism.

'The Bluebells of Scotland' had also stopped, and he put

the box down slowly, his eyes turned thoughtfully towards her.

'Branch out and . . . ?' he asked.

'Acquire a veneer of civilization,' she said unexpectedly, with a brutal honesty possible only with someone she regarded as an old friend.

Impulsively she put her hand over his and said with passion: 'You are going to have to deal with a smart, slick world, quick to ridicule those who do not understand its manners – a world where you want friends, not enemies. You can't defy the world as you can your parents; you have to work with it a little – and be polite to it.'

The hand under hers clenched on the settee cushion, his face went red, and his eyes flashed such vindictive rage for a moment that she thought he would hit her, then he controlled himself, sitting silently by her on the settee, until she felt his hand gradually relax.

'Hank,' she said rather hopelessly, 'I didn't mean to hurt you.'

He slowly lifted the hand which had been clutching his, opened it and very gently implanted a kiss on its palm, and laughed when she gasped at the caress. She was too innocent, he thought.

'I kiss the hand which beats me,' he said melodramatically, and put it down firmly in her lap before he had any further ideas. 'Yeah, I know I'm a savage compared to your itsy-bitsy English world.'

She was still shaken that anyone should calmly kiss her when she had not been long widowed, but his remark stung her into retort.

'It's a very tough world,' she said defensively. 'English people are generally very well qualified and if you are not good at your work you'll soon go under, there.'

He had quite recovered his good humour, and said: 'O.K., O.K., what do I do now, ma'am?'

'It depends on whether you have any money left.'

' 'Bout five hundred bucks – from working in the store and from the articles you helped me to place.' He paused, and then said, 'I used the advance payment for the book to get the car.'

His eyes twinkled when she told him he was rich.

'When does High School finish?' she asked.

'In June next – but I'm quitting right now – I've had enough.'

She was still telling herself she should not be put out by a kiss from a youngster who did not realize what he was doing, and she tried to nod her golden head with an appropriate display of adult wisdom, as she said: 'Yes, you're wasting your time. Has your publisher asked you to go to New York?'

'Yeah, he has. Next week. Mostly about the film – and they want to talk about another book.' He pulled a crumpled letter out of his shirt pocket, opened it and handed it to her to read.

'Sent me a cheque for expenses, too.'

She was immediately businesslike and succeeded in putting some suggestions to him in her crisp English way, which banished from her mind again any other thoughts.

'What about asking Albert's to set you up with a really quiet-looking business outfit for New York? Take the clothes you have on with you, so that if he wants you dressed up as a teenager you have the proper clothes for that, too.' She paused, looking at him reflectively, and then asked: 'Don't you think you had better speak to your father about all this?'

Hank chuckled. 'I'd have a job. He's away up the Mackenzie in a canoe – with a prospecting party.'

'Oh, dear. Well, what about your mother?' She looked imploring, and he realized that her eyelashes were golden, too. She was a true blonde. 'Hank, you really ought to tell her.'

He withdrew his mind from contemplation of her eyelashes, and asked heavily: 'You kidding?'

'No.'

'I just hope the shock rocks her to her Playtex foundations.' He sounded malicious, and then, as Isobel made mild noises of protest, he went on in more conciliatory tones: 'Aw, I'll just tell her I'm going on a trip right now – an' don't you tell her.'

'I don't really know her. I've met her twice on formal occasions, but I am at work all day, so I don't often see my neighbours. And I don't intend to meddle in your family life – if you can't talk to each other, it's none of my business.' She smiled at him. 'You have always been a careful tenant in the garage. If you have a table and a typewriter in there, I don't mind. I've known you for years. I know you write under the pseudonym of Ben MacLean and wish to keep your literary activities secret, so I have never seen anything wrong in taking in your mail.' She leaned back against the settee, her eyes regarding him quizzically, and said: 'There. I've done my best to square my conscience for your sake. How's that?'

'And what about all the times I've asked your advice while you were doing your yard work?' he teased.

'Well – um – the students who live with me sometimes ask advice, too.'

'Oh, brother!' he exclaimed, looking suddenly troubled. 'They'll be coming back from church soon – and Dorothy, too – and I don't want you embarrassed.'

'Embarrassed?' She was surprised.

'Yeah. You know. Neighbours talkin' and that kinda thing.'

'Good heavens! One can be friends with men without that sort of gossip. What do they think I am – a baby snatcher?'

He was hurt to the quick.

'Not here you can't,' he almost snarled. 'And I'm no baby.'

She looked up at the six solid feet of him, at the huge, deep chest under his black shirt, at his bulging arm muscles. Then she raised her eyes to his cross, slightly plump face, its high Ukrainian cheekbones and sallow skin, now flushed with anger, and finally at the intelligent, black eyes, almost pleading to be told that he was a man.

She pitied him, and said, smiling gently: 'No, you have grown up in the years you've had my old garage, and you are very much a young man.' She hesitated, and then said very sweetly to comfort him: 'And it was nice of you to think of my reputation.'

He did not tell her that hers was the only female reputation he had ever given any thought to and that he did not know why he bothered. He just stood looking down at her for a moment, his eyes still pleading, and then abruptly he turned and picked up the tray and carried it into the kitchen for her.

'I guess I'll go and do some work,' he said heavily. 'I got the rough outline of another novel in my head.'

She forced herself to be cheerful. 'That's the spirit. You'll go from strength to strength, I know it.'

He felt happier. She could surely be real sweet when she tried, he ruminated. He saluted her, went through the screen door, vaulted the balustrade protecting the steps, and swaggered down the garden.

The Triumph was soon garaged, with its nose almost touching the back of his chair. He sat down at the old table by the window and put a new sheet of paper into the typewriter.

'*Mother and Son*', he typed, 'By Ben MacLean'.

CHAPTER FIVE

On Sundays Maxie Frizzell caught up with the various jobs his wife Donna required him to do. He sometimes thought it would be pleasant to lie in bed with his wife on Sunday mornings, now that there were no children to interrupt them, but Donna reckoned they should be through with all that kind of stupidity, so he was resigned to the sporadic consolation of his Métis up north.

Donna's latest demand was that he should extend the patio and then roof it over.

'I helped you by clearing all the leaves in the yard,' she told him half a dozen times, 'and I got a cold while I was doing it. Now just you get busy on that patio.'

Maxie made himself some coffee and took it out to the patio, where he surveyed the work to be done. He had already prepared the ground for the extension of the concrete flooring, and, since this was likely to be the last Sunday of the year when it would not freeze, the next job was to prepare the concrete mixture, which lay against the wall in a large bag.

He worked slowly but efficiently for nearly two hours, fearing that, if he did not finish the work quickly, frost would make it impossible for him to continue; then, tired and sweating, he went and sat on the front doorstep to rest.

Next door but one, new neighbours had recently moved in and a man was at work in the garden, slowly digging a flower bed, while a small boy pottered about trying to help him. They were both very fair complexioned, and they chatted sporadically to each other in a language foreign to Mr Frizzell, who imagined that they must be Dutch or German. He remembered his wife mentioning to him that some immigrants had moved into the street, and, because he knew that neither Donna nor Mrs Stych would bother to call on immigrants, he felt vaguely sorry for the newcomers' isolation. When the man looked up from his digging Frizzell lifted a tired hand in salute and the man gravely acknowledged it.

Closer to hand, the white Triumph was standing outside the Styches' house, and Mr Frizzell gazed at it uneasily. Though he did not like Stych much – too stuck up by far with his university degree and his oilmen friends – he hoped that Hank had not stolen the money for the car.

He saw Olga Stych go off to church an hour early and deduced that she must be helping with some small church chore before the service. Then Hank came out and drove off, and he cursed him quietly. That young so-and-so might easily have got his Betty into trouble, if he had not caught them in time. Children, he muttered fervently, were just a curse sent by God.

This reminded him that it was nearly time for church, so he heaved himself to his feet and went to make some more coffee, this time for Mrs Frizzell as well.

She was sitting up in bed, her glasses already adorning her gaunt face and her hair curled up tightly on rollers. She accepted the coffee with a grunt and told Maxie not to sit on the bed, because he had cement on his jeans.

He lowered himself gingerly to a gilt chair and stirred his coffee, the spoon circulating slowly until it finally stopped and he sat staring at it.

Mrs Frizzell drank her coffee quickly, then scrambled out of bed and proceeded a little unsteadily to the kitchen, her cotton nightgown drooping despondently round her. She took a roast from the refrigerator, put it into a baking tin, wrapped two potatoes in tinfoil and put both meat and vegetables into the gas oven. Having adjusted the heat and thus satisfactorily disposed of the problem of lunch, she went to the bathroom for a shower and then returned to the bedroom.

Maxie was still staring at a half cup of coffee.

'You sick?' she asked, as she struggled into her best foundation garment. Her body was still damp and the garment was too tight, so she was pink with exertion by

43

the time she had managed to zip it up.

'No.'

'You'd better shower or we'll be late.'

'Yeah.'

He got up reluctantly, put the cup down on the dressing table and walked slowly towards the bathroom. At the bedroom door he stopped. His wife was painting her eyelids green.

'You know Hank next door.' He made it a statement rather than a question.

Mrs Frizzell turned. She looked weird with one green eyelid and one veined pink. 'Sure,' she said.

'Has he been left any money by somebody?'

'Not as far as I know. She'd surely have told me if a rich relative had left him somethin' – I'm sure she would. Why?' she inquired, as, tongue clenched between teeth, she carefully finished her second eyelid.

'Nothin'. I just wondered.'

Mrs Frizzell stopped half-way into a bone-coloured skirt – bone had been last year's fashionable colour, according to the *Tollemarche Advent*.

'Maxie Frizzell! What do you know that I don't?'

He was sorry that he had brought up the subject and hastily departed for his shower, shouting that he would tell her while he was dressing.

By the time he came back she was ready, looking like a spangled Christmas doll, her bone suit augmented by a scintillating green, three-tier necklace and bracelet, a startlingly flowered green hat, tight, incredibly high-heeled shoes of shiny green, and her fox stole.

She was sitting tensely on the gilt chair.

'Well?' she demanded.

'Say, you do look nice.' He went over to her, holding a towel round his middle, and gave her a smacking kiss on the cheek.

She pushed him off irritably.

'What's this about Hank?'

He let the towel drop and dug around in a drawer for some underwear.

'Maxie, cover yourself! You're not decent!'

He ignored this and leisurely got into his undershirt.

'Hank,' she reminded him, her anxiety to know apparent in her rapt-attention.

'Well, he bought a Triumph off us yesterday.'

'So what?' She was disappointed.

'You don't get a Triumph one year old for cents.'

Mrs Frizzell digested this truth, and the import of it slowly became clear to her.

'That's right,' she said thoughtfully. 'Mebbe his father got worried about him driving that old jalopy – it weren't safe. He might have helped Hank buy a new one – he's making enough money.'

'His father don't hardly know he's born yet,' said Maxie scornfully.

'How's he payin' for it?'

'A thousand down and the rest over six months – plus his old wreck, of course.'

'Cash?'

'No, cheque – but it's good – Josh checked with the bank, called Hnatiuk at his home. Hnatiuk says his savings account has been in good shape for a boy this past two years.'

Mrs Frizzell licked her finger and smoothed down her eyebrows with it. This was truly a mystery. She pondered silently and then was suddenly alert. Hank must have done a robbery to have so much money – he must have – there had been one or two bad ones recently – a Chinese grocer had been shot to death, in one instance.

She was filled with excitement. She would get hold of Mrs Hnatiuk after church and see if she knew anything about it. No good asking Olga Stych; she'd just stick her nose in the air and say that Boyd was doing very well.

'Hurry up,' she said, as if the church service would be over all the quicker if Maxie got a move on. And then she

45

said: 'Mebbe he's one of that gang that has been holding up grocery stores.'

'Mebbe,' said her husband. 'I don't care what he's done. None of my business. The finance company will pay us and they'll soon squeeze the balance out of him.'

'For heaven's sake!' Such a scandalous-sounding mystery, and he didn't care. He didn't care about anything, except cars and trucks. A fat lot he even cared about being late for church and she trying to keep up a good style.

'For goodness' sakes, hurry up,' she exclaimed, standing up and folding her stole around her. 'I'll go get the car out.'

The Reverend Bruce Mackay, the patient and acquiescent minister, went on to 'fifthly' in his sermon, and Mrs Frizzell was sure he would never end. Mrs Hnatiuk, who was wearing a fast-looking white jockey cap, was only two rows in front of her and Mrs Frizzell did not know how to bear the suspense. The final hymn had eight verses, not to speak of a chorus of Hallelujahs at the end of each one; Mr Frizzell enjoyed this and sang in a pleasant tenor voice.

Across the aisle, Mrs Stych expanded her tremendous bosom to shout to the Lord in a wobbly soprano. Borne along by the music and the comforting sermon, she was happy.

It was over at last. The minister stood at the door and shook the hand of each member of his congregation, with a kindly word for each boy and girl. The children viewed him with wary respect, since, in spite of his air of benignity, he frequently exploded when faced with old chewing-gum stuck under the pews, the choir guardedly shooting craps during the sermon, and similar juvenile straying from the path of righteousness.

Mrs Frizzell eased herself – it could not be said that she exactly pushed – through the crowd so that she was next to Mrs Hnatiuk, while Maxie stopped to talk to clients.

Out on the pathway, Mrs Hnatiuk was surprised to find her hand gripped enthusiastically by Mrs Frizzell, who was normally so condescending, and her health solicitously inquired after. Mr Hnatiuk had taken one look at the approaching Mrs Frizzell and had dived for cover into a knot of other businessmen. Mrs Hnatiuk was cornered.

Mrs Frizzell circulated painstakingly through all the usual conversational openings, the weather, the forthcoming Edwardian Days Carnival Week, the coming winter and what winter did to the car trade, wondering how to get round to Hank's Triumph. She was unexpectedly helped along by Mrs Hnatiuk, who said: 'Ah, there's Mrs Stych. I just love her little car.'

'Yeah,' said Mrs Frizzell, with satisfaction. 'Maxie just sold her Hank another nice one, a Triumph.'

'My! They must be doing well,' said Mrs Hnatiuk. 'Three good cars in the family, counting Boyd's Dodge.'

'Maxie said Hank paid for it himself,' dangled Mrs Frizzell hopefully.

The fish failed to rise.

'Did he?' exclaimed Mrs Hnatiuk. 'He must be working at something good.'

'He's still in high school. Doing Grade 12 again.'

Mrs Hnatiuk's five little girls were still in elementary school and, consequently, she did not come into frequent contact with high school students. She was, therefore, unaware of Hank's reputation for being rather irresponsible. She said maddeningly: 'Say, that's a nice stole you've got. Mrs MacDonald's got a blue mink, but that one of yours is nice, too.'

Mrs Frizzell nearly screamed. Either Mrs Hnatiuk really did not know much about Hank or she was just being perverse.

'Where do you think he got the money from?' she queried.

'Who?'

'Hank Stych.'

Mrs Hnatiuk's pale blue eyes opened wide. 'From his father, I suppose. Where else?'

'He might have stolen it.'

Mrs Hnatiuk's eyes nearly popped out of her head. 'Do you think so?'

It was obvious that Mrs Hnatiuk was not telling. Mrs Frizzell mentally crossed her off her list of guests – she'd never really be anybody anyway – and abruptly made her farewells.

She moved down to the kerbside, smiling graciously as she elbowed her way through the crowd. Mrs Stych was having difficulty starting her little car, so Mrs Frizzell bobbed her flower-decked head down until her hawklike nose was level with the half-open window.

'How does Hank like his new Triumph?' she asked.

Mrs Stych ceased her frantic turning of the ignition key for a moment, and looked perplexed.

'Triumph?'

'Yeah. His new car.'

Mrs Stych pursed her heavily painted lips and looked at Mrs Frizzell as if she feared for Mrs Frizzell's mental health.

'He hasn't got a new one. You know he's not working yet.'

She gave the ignition key another desperate turn and the engine burst into song.

'But,' Mrs Frizzell began, 'he – '

Her words were lost in the sound of grinding gears, and the car leaped away from the sidewalk, knocking Mrs Frizzell's hat askew and leaving her mouthing furiously at nobody.

CHAPTER SIX

Hank was not in when Mrs Stych returned home from church. She made a cold lunch for herself and then left to visit her mother-in-law. Every Sunday afternoon she meticulously visited either her mother or her mother-in-law, these indications of filial affection being indispensable to anyone of her aspirations, with a public image to maintain. She never bothered to write to her husband while he was away, husbands being regarded as of very little importance, except as sources of money.

While Hank was, in his grandparents' opinion, too small to be left alone, the two grandmothers had insisted that he accompany his mother, and he had enjoyed wandering round the Palichuk pig farm with his grandfather or playing in a corner of the lounge of his Grandmother Stych's more fashionable home. He was the youngest grandchild, however, and as he grew to be a hulking, noisy ten-year-old, his aging relatives found him very tiring. After the death of Grandfather Palichuk, the custom arose of frequently leaving him at home. Even now, he remembered with a shudder the appalling loneliness of Sunday afternoon, spent trailing noisily around the streets with a group of equally neglected youths, returning to the empty home to eat his supper while the television set bawled commercials at him to fill the silence, until he heard the scrape of his mother's key in the lock.

Occasionally, his father was at home during the weekend. But he also felt that he should visit his mother. He had, too, a lot of paper work to deal with while in Tollemarche, and only rarely shared his Sunday supper with his son. He was a taciturn man who found it difficult to talk to a boy; but he did sometimes spare time to tell him of his travels in the wilder parts of Alberta, of encounters with grizzly bears, white water rushing through narrow gorges, being lost in unexpected snowstorms, in an unconquered wilderness totally alien to his suburb-bred son.

When Hank was fifteen, his best friend, Tommy Moore, committed suicide by quietly dropping himself off the railway bridge into the icy waters of the North Saskatchewan. He had threatened to do it for some time, but only Hank had taken him seriously and tried to dissuade him. Hank felt stripped of the only person in whom he could confide, and, for a while, considered following his example. Perhaps it was fortunate that at that time he discovered girls, and a year later met the Dawsons, who always seemed to have time to stop and gossip with him. He had by now forgotten the faces of many of the girls he had run around with, and Peter Dawson was dead, but there was still Isobel, the one steadying influence in his life.

From watching Isobel and her husband he had discovered that there was much more to sex than just taking a girl to bed or being uneasily married to a frigid, grasping woman.

Peter Dawson had been considerably older than Isobel and since he had only a few more years to serve in the army, had decided to establish a permanent home in his native town. It had taken their combined savings to make the down payment on a house in overcrowded Tollemarche and Isobel had declared that she could manage without a car. She therefore advertised the garage as being for rent, and at the same time got herself a job as a secretary to an insurance broker, to fill in the time until Peter should be at home permanently or a family should arrive.

When a younger and less sophisticated Hank had come quietly through the back gate in search of the garage, the couple had been busy planting a lilac tree. He had watched them silently as they lowered the little bush into the prepared hole, with considerable argument as to how the roots should be spread. It was a different kind of argument from any he had heard before; it was friendly and joking. When the earth had been finally pressed down round the tree roots, Peter Dawson had put his arm round his wife's tiny waist and they had surveyed their handiwork with obvious satisfaction. He had kissed her on the nose, and they had strolled around their small domain, debating what else they should do to the garden.

Hank had hastily retreated round the side of the garage, while they decided where to put a sand box for the child as yet unconceived, and then he had re-entered the gate, giving it a diplomatic slam behind him.

He had not had much hope that they would rent the garage to a teenager, since teenagers were regarded generally as being as reliable as something out of the zoo. Peter Dawson had, however, asked who his father was, and had then inquired if the family was any relation to Mr Heinrich Stych, who used to teach in Tollemarche Public School.

'Yeah – sure,' replied Hank. 'He was my grandfather.'

Captain Dawson was immediately more friendly.

'Well, that's great! He taught me when I was a boy. Of course you can have the garage. I don't think we will be needing it for a while.'

He asked what kind of a car Hank had and was very encouraging when Hank told him that he and his friend Ian were going to rebuild one.

Hank paid five dollars from his paper money as the first month's rent, and, later that day, he and several of his friends pushed a dowager of a car round from his back lane, where it had been dumped by a tow truck, into the Dawsons' garage. The Dawsons themselves had enthusiastically helped to heave it over a rut and up the slope to the garage.

Ian MacDonald and he had stripped down the old wreck and searched junk yards for spare parts. Mr Frizzell, before the unfortunate episode with Betty, had been prevailed upon to donate four old, though still serviceable, tyres; and finally the great day arrived when he backed it slowly out of the garage and drove it round to his own home in the vague hope that his mother might like to see it.

'I won't have that thing standing in front of the house,' she had said forcibly. 'Take it away.'

Crestfallen, he and Ian had driven to Ian's house, but Mrs MacDonald had gone to an art exhibition and Mr MacDonald to a service club meeting. Ian's kid sister, who was playing mothers and fathers with her friends in the crawl space under the porch, said it was marvellous, so they had to be content with this infant praise and with taking her and her mud-covered friends for a ride round the block.

Wrathfully indignant at his mother's lack of appreciation of his efforts as a mechanic, an idea which had long been in his mind, that of writing a novel, had crystallized. He would write a book which would cause a sufficient furore to upset both his parents thoroughly and make them realize that he was a person to be reckoned with. To do it, he had to have more privacy than his room allowed, and he had tentatively approached Captain Dawson, who was home on leave and was painting the porch, for permission to put a table and chair in the garage, so that he could work there.

Captain Dawson sensed that there was more behind the request than was readily apparent. He was used to handling a great variety of young men, and his piercing stare, as he considered the request, made Hank quail; he had a suspicion that Peter Dawson could make his wife quail at times, and in this he was right.

'Why can't you work at home?'

Hank decided that, in this instance, honesty was the only policy possible and had said frankly that he wanted to try to write a book. He did not feel he could write freely if the typescript was readily accessible to his mother.

The Captain wiped the paint off his hands and carefully avoided showing his amusement. He agreed that a mother's censorship would be very limiting, and, after consulting Isobel, who was enchanted with the idea, he said that the furniture could be brought in.

'You had better change the lock on the door,' she had teased, 'because I might be tempted to peep at the manuscript.'

He had gravely changed the lock and kept both keys. She had, however, through the months of work, taken a real interest in what he was doing, and he found himself confiding in her more and more. It was she who, when the manuscript was ready, had given him an introduction to Alistair MacFee, a professor of English at the university. Professor MacFee had read it had been startled by its undoubted merit, and had carefully discussed it chapter by chapter with him, suggesting how to improve it. Glowing with hope, Hank had gone back to the garage and pruned and polished. Then the professor and Isobel, both young and enthusiastic, had helped him to choose a likely publisher to whom to send it. The English firm which they first suggested returned the typescript. Undaunted, Hank sent it to a New York firm and they accepted it. He was so excited that he forgot about the revenge the book was supposed to wreak on his parents.

Now, *The Cheaper Sex* had been out in the States for some weeks, and it seemed as if everyone under the age of twenty-one wanted a copy. On the day of its publication, Hank had gone jubilantly to Isobel's back door, armed with an autographed copy for her and her husband.

He had found an ashen-faced Isobel, showing none of her usual gaiety or cordiality. She had written a receipt for the month's rent for the garage, which he had proffered at the same time, and had received the book with a watery smile. She had then wished him good luck with the sale of his book and had quietly shut the door in his face.

Bewildered and hurt at her lack of interest, too shy to ask what the trouble was, he had gone back to the garage completely mystified, and had spent the rest of the evening painting his jalopy electric blue.

When he finally went home, he saw the *Tollemarche Advent*. It informed him in letters an inch high that Captain Peter Dawson had been murdered in Cyprus.

His first instinct was to rush back to Isobel. Then he told himself that he was a nut who had written a book in her garage, and that he had no right to intrude.

As a way of showing sympathy, however, he had the following Saturday morning put on his best suit, which was far too tight for him, and gone to the memorial service for Captain Dawson in the nearby Anglican church. In total misery, he watched, from the back of the church, the stony-faced widow, flanked by her husband's mother, a surprisingly elegant woman in smart black, and his father, a retired Royal Canadian Mounted Police officer looking tired and grey, as they went through the formalities of the service. Absorbed as he was by the sight of a family in grief, a new phenomenon for him, he could not help observing, with some awe, the large number of military men present to testify to their friendship with the dead man. They sure looked smart, he thought, and from that moment he began to cultivate the straight, dignified bearing which was to be his hallmark in later life; only occasionally did he forget and relapse into his old North American droop.

His quick eye also registered with some interest that not one of the ladies present, as far as he could judge, belonged to his mother's circle. This quiet group of people looked so simple and unassuming that at first he could not think what made them interesting to him, and then he realized that they gave every appearance of complete sincerity. Like Isobel, they were what they looked, quiet people doing very necessary jobs and a that moment grieving for one of their number who had left them.

He thought that he left the church unnoticed, but Isobel saw him as she stepped out of her pew, and, as far as anything could penetrate to her at such a time, she was touched by his solicitude.

It had been apparent to Hank for some time that, in spite of repeating Grade 12 at school, he was likely to fail his exams again. French and Ukrainian, mathematics and chemistry bored him to the point of insanity; only in music and English could he hope to get decent marks. On December 28 he would be twenty years old, and he wondered bitterly when he might be allowed to grow up. He decided to consult Mr Dixon, his English teacher, who was also his counsellor and, therefore, knew more about him than did the other teachers.

Mr Dixon, friend of Mrs Murphy and conductor, in his spare time, of the amateur orchestra, had accidentally launched Hank on his writing career a few years earlier by encouraging him to enter an essay competition sponsored by a service club. The essay, on 'The Dangers of Smoking', had cost Hank a number of Sundays of hard work, and he estimated that he must have smoked at least eight packs of cigarettes while writing it, but to his astonishment it had won him a hundred dollars. He looked at Mr Dixon with new respect and, to that gentleman's delight, really began to work hard.

On the Monday morning after Isobel had advised him to accept his publisher's invitation to go to New York, he went to see Mr Dixon.

Mr Dixon could hardly believe his ears as Hank poured into them the story of the book and its apparent success. He immediately insisted that Hank should tell his parents, and warned him of the evils of leaving school without succeeding in obtaining the magical Grade 12, without which there was no hope, he insisted, of leading a normal life. Hank already had the feeling that his life was going to be anything but normal and was adamant about leaving school, but agreed reluctantly to tell his father when next he came home. The clinching argument that Mr Dixon made about informing his father of his literary success was that probably Hank would need help in investing discreetly the earnings of the book, and it was well known that Mr Stych was an astute businessman. Hank was the product of a boom town and knew that money earned money extremely fast; with luck, he could double and treble his capital by investment in Tollemarche.

Mr Dixon heaved a sigh of relief at having gained at least one point, and decided that the question of leaving school could be left to the parents and the Principal. Hank was grateful to him for his promise not to discuss either matter with anybody.

Hank went home to lunch.

His mother was in, seated at her kitchen desk and

gloomily going over the month's bills – her Persian lamb coat made the Hudson's Bay bill look enormous, and, at the rate she was paying it off, it would take until next Easter to clear it.

'Like a bologna sandwich?' he asked her, as he made one for himself.

She grunted assent, and he filled the coffee percolator, set it on the stove and then rooted around in the refrigerator for the ketchup, while he wondered how to approach the subject of his going to New York.

'Ma,' he said in a tentative tone of voice, his face going slowly pink with the strain of trying to communicate with his despondent parent.

'Yeah?' she queried absently. She would wear the Persian lamb to the meeting of the Symphony Orchestra Club tonight, even if it was a bit warm.

He thrust a sandwich on a plate in front of her. 'Ma, I'm going on a trip for a week.'

Mrs Stych swivelled round on her stool and forced herself to attend to her son.

'Y'are?' She sounded puzzled.

'Yeah. I'm going to New York for a week.'

He told himself that it was ridiculous for him to be nearly trembling with fear, wondering what form her explosion would take.

She frowned at him for a moment; then her brow cleared.

'With the United Nations Debating Club?'

Hank accepted the temporary reprieve thankfully. Darn it, why hadn't he thought of that himself? Undermining his mother's social prestige was one thing, having to tell her about the book himself was another.

Her face darkened again.

'Who's payin'?'

'I'm going to pay some. You know I got a bit saved. The rest they're paying.' He hoped she would not ask who 'they' were.

'Well, I guess that's O.K. When you goin'?' It was typical

56

of her that, although she regarded Hank as a child, she did not ask who would be supervising the group she imagined would be travelling to New York.

'Thursday. Be back next Wednesday.'

'O.K. Y' father will be coming by then.'

His legs began to feel weak and he sat down hard on a red plastic and chrome chair, while he held his sandwich suspended half-way to his mouth. He remembered Mr Dixon's persuasive arguments regarding telling his father about *The Cheaper Sex*, but he doubted if Mr Dixon knew what kind of father he had.

'That's good,' he said dully, putting down his half-eaten sandwich.

The book should have been in Tollemarche's only bookstore for several weeks; however, when Hank casually sauntered in and asked for a copy, old Mr Pascall said it had not arrived. It would probably come in the next shipment from Toronto.

Hank had no doubt that, sooner or later, old tabby-cats like the MacDonald woman would get wind of it and would give his mother hell about it. His mother would never get round to reading it and he hoped fervently that his father would not either. Anyway, he consoled himself, nobody in Tollemarche over the age of forty ever really read a book, though they talked about them.

He swallowed the last of his coffee and went to his room to inspect his wardrobe. He decided to put his two drip-dry shirts through the washer that night. His one decent pair of dark pants and his formal suit were too small for him. The rest consisted largely of T-shirts and jeans. Mind made up, he returned to the kitchen, picked up his zipper jacket and departed, officially for school, but in fact for the town to do some shopping. His mother, busy checking the T. Eaton Company's report on the state of her account there, did not bother to reply to his monosyllabic 'Bye.'

Albert Tailors, in the shape of old Mr Albert himself, took one look at him and channelled him to the Teens Room, which was festooned with guitars and pictures of pop singers. But Hank protested firmly that he wanted a dark business suit, three white drip-dry shirts, dark socks and tie, black shoes, a light overcoat and an appropriate hat. The clerk inquired delicately if it would be cash or charge.

'Cash,' snapped Hank irritably, and was hastily rechannelled into the men's ready-tailored department. The clerk stopped for a moment and whispered to Mr Albert, who, realizing that instead of selling a pair of jeans he really had a customer with money to spend, hurried towards Hank.

'I want a good suit. It must look real good. But I gotta have it now.'

Mr Albert humphed and measured.

The first suit was too loud, even Hank knew that.

'No. I want the kind of thing – the kind of thing these big oil executives wear.'

Mr Albert laughed, a trifle scornfully. 'It would cost about a hundred and twenty dollars at least.'

'So what?' replied Hank belligerently. 'That's what I want. I gotta go to New York. I wanna look right.'

Mr Albert's superior smile waned. He sent the clerk hurrying into the back room to get a dark grey suit which had just come in and then said: 'Going to New York? You're a lucky fellow.'

'Yeah,' said Hank noncommittally, as he examined himself critically in Mr Albert's big triple mirror. He was not pleased with what he saw. He tried drawing in his stomach and straightening his shoulders, as instructed by the physical education teacher. The result was better, but not his idea of a distinguished author.

He was soon eased, pinned and patted into the grey suit, the cuffs hastily turned up by the clerk, the back smoothed by Mr Albert. It looked weird over a T-shirt, but it undoubtedly fitted quite well, except for the length of the pants.

He gyrated carefully so that he could see himself at all angles. My, he did look different. The good cut made his shoulders look their proper width and reduced his generally plump look. He grinned at himself. He looked a man at last, not a school student.

Fascinated by this new vision of himself, he continued to stare. He would like Isobel and Dorothy to see him like this.

Mr Albert's voice came from a distance: 'You'll need a good white shirt with it, and a tie . . . ' Mr Albert considered ties. 'One in a quiet red, I think. And plain black shoes.'

Hank did not hear. He was still staring at himself in the mirror, seeing himself for the first time as a man, not a boy. In that moment, his uncertain struggle towards manhood was over. He had always been taught by women, with the exception of Mr Dixon, and ignored by his parents. Unthreatened by war service, he found, like his friends, that the only way to prove to himself that he was grown up was to chase and lie with innumerable young women. Some of his friends had married while still in high school, and all of them, married or single, were agreed that sex was a dissatisfying pastime. None of them had as yet discovered a deep, rewarding love.

Now Mr Albert, with more ability than Hank thought such an old fogey could exhibit, had shown him that he could look quite as dignified as Captain Dawson, not a bent peasant like Grandfather Palichuk or a rugged, outdoor type like his father, but a very respectable townsman called Hank Stych.

Hank was suddenly deeply grateful to old Mr Albert for taking him seriously. He glowed, as he came out of his trance, and said: 'I'll take it. Do you think you could find me a dinner suit as well?'

CHAPTER SEVEN

In the eyes of most Albertans, Tollemarche was a tourist centre second only to Calgary and Edmonton. In order to encourage the winter tourist industry, it had a winter fair featuring exhibitions of interest to farmers, and many winter sport events. Of recent years, the fair had been lengthened into a fortnight-long frolic called Edwardian Days, finishing two weeks before Christmas. The city dressed up in Edwardian clothes, shop windows showed displays of Edwardian families enjoying Christmas, the restaurants served such Edwardian delicacies as Oxford sausages and English beef-and-kidney pie, and the bars offered large glasses of white wine cup. The Tollemarche ladies, in bonnets and cartwheel hats, gave teas at which they coyly sipped at China tea flavoured with lemon and mint. In the evenings, skating parties were held under coloured lights and skates flashed under long skirts to tunes like 'The Blue Danube'. The climax of the fortnight was the Grand Edwardian Ball, which was the most important occasion of the whole winter, and thinking up suitable costumes for this event kept the ladies occupied for weeks beforehand.

The greatest complication about any ball is that one requires menfolk with whom to attend it. Most of the year, the matrons of Tollemarche regarded their husbands as nuisances better out of the house, but the ball was an occasion for which husbands, sweethearts, even brothers, were in great demand. Young women married to salesmen, for once, took an interest in where their husbands would be on the great day; the older men, who ricocheted between various business interests, were lectured steadily, any time they put in an appearance at home, on the necessity of being in Tollemarche at this time; and those males who were doomed to spend their lives in Tollemarche found themselves with intolerable lists of jobs to be done, from laying out backyard skating rinks to pinning up the hems on their female relatives' costumes.

While Mr Stych was canoeing back down a tributary of the Mackenzie, already dangerous with chunks of ice, to an appointment with a helicopter, Mr Frizzell was trying on his last year's brocade waistcoat and finding it too small; Mr MacDonald, Ian's father, was winding up a trying compensation case for his insurance company at Vermilion; and Mr MacDonald (oil) was trying to explain to his superiors in Sarnia, Ontario, why he must be back in a place like Tollemarche by the middle of December. In the ornate new council chamber, Mayor Murphy was trying to convince the city council that to be a real Edwardian Mayor he ought to wear mayoral robes, as they did in England; the newly extended hospital was bracing itself for additional accident cases; and Hank Stych stood in the airport at Calgary waiting for a local plane to take him north to Tollemarche.

Though he had found New York impressive, the people did not seem to him very different from those of Tollemarche. His publishers had been smoothly charming and undoubtedly a little surprised to find their backwoods author a careful, quite business-like man in a town suit, who would not sign anything until he had read the small print several times and understood it thoroughly.

Full marks to Isobel, Hank thought grimly; she had done a lot of homework trying to check what his rights were regarding serialization, filming and translation, and had primed him well. He had met the press at a cocktail party and had stood there answering impertinent questions with disconcerting honesty, a glass of ginger ale in one hand and a canapé in the other; when he could not immediately think of an answer he nibbled the canapé and viewed the questioner with cold button eyes. His childhood exposure to life in the streets of a western town, still so new that most of the people who had founded it were still alive, had left him with no illusions about people or their motives, and it was always for the motive behind the question that he looked.

Now, as he waited for his flight, he felt exhausted, as if he had been playing an enormously difficult game of poker for high stakes. And yet, in spite of the fatigue, he felt, good, as if for the first time in his life he had really stretched himself and grown up. He knew that basically he had enjoyed the careful battle of wits.

In his bag was a tiny music box in the shape of a windmill, bought specially from Macy's for Isobel, and a stuffed monkey for Dorothy to sit on her bed. He had also rather reluctantly bought a box of chocolates for his mother and a box of cigars for his father.

On the aircraft the stewardess brought him a copy of the *Tollemarche Advent*. The preparations for Edwardian Days were not yet featured on the front page, but an inner page had a half column on the redecorating of the main hotel's ballroom for the Edwardian Ball. He let the paper fall into his lap.

Up to now, he had always competed in the skating events and had escorted one of his classmates to the Teens' Square Dance, held well away from the elegant ball. Now he had a sudden ambition to go to the ball. Like Cinderella, he told himself with a grin. But there was more to it than that. Attendance at the ball indicated considerable standing in the adult world and he had a sudden savage desire to show his parents, who would be there, that he had made it on his own, without any help from them. The tickets alone were so expensive, not to speak of the need for a good costume, that they would realize that inexplicably he had had some financial success.

He considered taking Dorothy, but she was only seventeen, too young to hold her own in a possibly difficult encounter with the élite of Tollemarche. He wondered if he dared ask Isobel. She had been widowed for five months, very nearly. Did she go out now and, if so, with whom? He felt a pang of jealousy, which was intensified when he remembered the smart army officers who had been at her husband's memorial service. Had any of them made any approaches to her?

He brushed the newspaper angrily off his lap and told himself not to be a fool. She was seven years older than he was. She'd never look at him.

He arrived home at one in the morning. His mother was not yet in; presumably she had gone to a party. He made himself a cup of coffee and then, feeling deflated and not a little depressed, went to bed.

Isobel and Dorothy were battling their way against the wind down to the bus stop, the following morning, when they met Hank hunched up in his old black zipper jacket and a pair of earmuffs, which gave him a quaintly catlike appearance. He had his hands in the pockets of his jeans, which were, as usual, at least two inches too short, and tucked under one arm were one or two schoolbooks. His face was pinched with cold and he looked rather dejected, but he greeted them heartily.

'Hiyer, babe?' he said to Dorothy, and: 'Hi, Isobel.'

'Hello, Hank,' they said in chorus from the depths of the fur collars of their coats.

They were burning to know how he had got on in New York, and Isobel asked him.

'I'm rich, ma'am. I'm rich. Book's doing fine – going into paperbacks next year, and they confirmed about the film.'

'Oh, Hank, how exciting!' exclaimed Isobel, her face going even pinker than the wind had made it. 'Congratulations!' Then she noticed the books. 'Are you going to school?' she asked.

Hank looked guilty.

'No, but I haven't told Ma yet, so I came out as if I were going too school.'

'Hank, you are naughty,' Dorothy chided. 'It's going to be all over town – in fact, I can't think why it isn't already – and your mother will be the last to know.'

He turned up his inadequate collar and executed a dance step or two to keep his circulation going.

'So what?'

Isobel looked at Dorothy reprovingly. 'It's Hank's business, Dorothy.'

'Aw, don't be hard on her, Isobel. She just don't understand. Mind if I work in the garage today?'

'Not at all, Hank. Go ahead.'

'Thanks a lot. Seeya tonight, mebbe.'

He must have worked for a long time in the garage. When Dorothy came home from town, however, he was digging over the vegetable patch, despite its half-frozen state and the gently falling snow.

'You don't have to do that, Hank,' she said, as she came through the back gate. 'Isobel will get a man to do it in the spring.'

'And what do you think I am, honey?' He had stopped digging and was leaning against the spade, waiting, as if the answer was important to him.

Dorothy laughed. 'Oh, Hank, you are an ass.'

'Thanks,' he said dryly, his face taking on the blank expression it usually had when he was annoyed.

Dorothy was puzzled and did not know what to say, so she smiled and then started up the path to the back door, when he called her back.

'Say, Doll, I want to ask you something.'

She walked uneasily back to him, her legs in their tight pants looking like those of a young colt. 'Yes, Hank?'

He weighed her up for a moment, his wide mouth compressed and then asked: 'D'ye think Isobel would come to a ball with me?'

Dorothy decided she had better not laugh this time, though she wanted to, so she said cautiously: 'I don't know, Hank.' She wondered a little resentfully why he did not ask her to go, though she would have been scared if he actually had done so; she lacked a North American youngster's experience with the opposite sex.

'I mean, is she still in mourning? It's over four months now, and it'll be five before the ball comes up.'

Dorothy was thoughtful. 'No,' she said at last. 'She seems to be getting over it pretty well. She goes about a bit

64

– English women are a bit different from Canadians, you know, Hank.' Then she added in a confiding tone: 'Of course, she was not much with her husband really – and I think that helps – she isn't reminded of him at every turn, like an ordinary widow would be.'

'You're right.' He rubbed the end of his nose with one grubby hand in a puzzled kind of way.

'Why don't you ask one of your girlfriends?' Dorothy inquired, far too intrigued at this unexpected interest in Isobel to remember that she was supposed to be indoors starting to prepare supper.

'Not suitable,' said Hank flatly. Then, feeling that perhaps he was being rather uncomplimentary to Dorothy, he added untruthfully: I'd ask you, honey, only you're too young for this one.'

'Is it the Edwardian Ball?'

'Yeah.'

'Oh, Hank, I'd love to go,' she implored.

'Sorry, babe. You really are too young.'

Dorothy felt crushed, and said bitterly: 'Well, if I'm too young to go with you, I'm sure Isobel is too old.'

This sensitive point made Hank feel as if he had been returned sharply to the schoolroom, but he said unrepentantly: 'Nuts! She's just old enough to have dignity.'

'Well, no doubt she'd feel safe with you,' Dorothy said pointedly. 'You'd better ask her.' And she flounced up to the house, her long black hair swinging rebelliously down her back from under her red woollen cap.

Though rather demoralized by his conversation with Dorothy, he did ask Isobel. He came up to the house that evening, armed with the music box and the monkey. He had changed into a clean white shirt and tie, and his dark pants just fitted him, though Dorothy wondered if they would stand the strain of his sitting down.

Dorothy had already told Isobel of the conversation that afternoon, so she was prepared; but he found it difficult to get round to the real object of the visit. He presented the music box, which was received with every expression of pleasure by Isobel, and the monkey to Dorothy, who could not help laughing when she saw it, because it was so typical of a craze for stuffed animals amongst the girls she had met in Tollemarche.

When finally he did broach the subject of the ball, Isobel refused to take his invitation seriously and said he should take someone his own age. Anyway, Tollemarche would be shocked if she went, she added wistfully.

He caught the hint of wistfulness in her voice and made the most of it quickly.

'For heaven's sakes!' he exclaimed. 'Why should you care what a lot of old tabbies think? Ma and Pop will be going. And for sure you can come – if you feel up to it?'

He wondered suddenly if she had got any fun out of her marriage to Peter Dawson. He remembered him as a kindly man but not a very lively one.

'Perhaps you ought to make up a party with your parents,' Isobel said dutifully.

'Come off it,' he said, grinning suddenly. 'You know I want to shake 'em. And I'd sure see you had a lovely time,' he went on with almost too much intensity in his voice, so that he feared he might have frightened her off.

Dorothy looked at Hank with sudden interest. His eyes were on Isobel, who was staring at her hands, and Dorothy felt a wave of jealousy at Isobel's Dresden china beauty and her look of compliant gentleness. She had taken it for granted that if Isobel accompanied Hank to the ball, it would be a kind of aunt and nephew relationship, but now she wondered.

Isobel looked up and laughed herself, her nose wrinkling up like a child's. She obviously had not noticed anything out of the ordinary, and Dorothy told herself not to be a fool imagining things. Maybe it would do Isobel good to be dragged out by someone she would feel at home with, and a man of her own age would cause much more of a stir in the neighbourhood.

'You should go, Isobel,' she said generously, swallowing her own disappointment at not being asked. 'Dress up in ostrich feathers, or whatever Edwardians wore, and have some fun. It would help Hank out – and probably nobody would recognize you anyway.'

Hank was not slow in taking his cue. 'Sure. You can be disguised,' he said hopefully. 'Lots of people go as well-known Edwardian characters – everybody wears Edwardian dress.'

It took them an hour to convince her that it would be all right to go, that she would not be disloyal to Peter; but, finally she agreed that she might as well indulge the boy.

Dorothy had an inspiration as to who they could go as, and for the rest of the evening they amused themselves digging through an old encyclopedia to find pictures from which to copy costumes.

CHAPTER EIGHT

The Ladies of Scotland League was holding its fall tea in the auditorium of a large store on Tollemarche Avenue. The decorations committee had spent the morning spreading tables with brown, yellow and green linen cloths and pinning gold-sprayed autumn leaves to each corner of them. Branches of fir, complete with cones also sprayed with gold, had been laboriously pinned to the walls. Brown and white bunting swathed the edges of the small stage.

A small table by the door had been spread with a green cloth embroidered with the insignia of the League, two thistles crossed above the initials L.S.L., and here, armed with white name cards and a bristling collection of pins, sat Mrs MacPhail, a determined young newcomer from Hamilton, Ontario, who had managed to obtain the post of secretary because none of the older members felt like undertaking so much work. Her hat was an aggressively red felt and she peered out from under its big brim like a shrew ready to attack. Beside her sat the treasurer, a formidable figure of some sixty years of age, in a pink gauze turban which did little to soften her high, bald forehead or her arrogant expression. She wore a matching crepe dress, which draped across her large bosom and red neck, and a mink stole was hung negligently over the back of her chair.

Anybody who had hoped to get past these two ladies without paying her dues would have been squelched by a look; and the pile of dollars in front of the treasurer grew as the number of white name cards in front of Mrs MacPhail diminished.

At one end of the hall, a long table, embellished with a lace tablecloth, had been laid with silver coffee-pots at one end and silver teapots at the other, a mass of flowered cups and saucers round each. In the middle of the table was a formal arrangement of chrysanthemums, flanked by white candles in silver holders. Two very old ladies presided over the tea and coffee pots; they were the oldest members of the League, having travelled out to Tollemarche district with their parents in covered wagons before the town itself existed. They therefore received the doubtful honour of pouring out for some two hundred ladies, regardless of the fact that it was a very arduous and tiring task.

Mrs Josephine MacDonald, president of the Noble Order of Lady Queen Bees, was also vice-president of the League and stood with the president in the receiving line, just beyond the treasurer's table. Mrs MacDonald was a Calgarian by birth, and her husband had been moved north by his firm to run the huge refinery that was now the pride of Tollemarche. She regarded the Tollemarche ladies as being outside the pale, and had treated them with such blatant condescension that they had quailed, and had sought her goodwill by voting her hastily into offices in those organizations in which she had deigned to take an interest. Today the president, Mrs Macpherson, in between gracefully shaking hands with each new arrival and presenting her to Mrs MacDonald, decided that she was nothing but a vulgar upstart, and she trembled with suppressed irritation at having to stand in the same receiving line with her. Why, there had been Macphersons grinding flour in the Tollemarche district sixty years ago, and it had taken her years of hard infighting to reach her present exalted rank; now this woman was, after only twelve months of residence, her vice-president. Mrs Macpherson bit her blue lips with her artificial teeth and looked down her beaky nose at the bland, well-powdered face beside her. Hmm! Nothing but paint on a piece of lard.

The piece of lard opened its lipsticked mouth in a thin smile at the next arrival, and Mrs Macpherson hastily recollected her duties, her black, old-fashioned hat bobbing in unison with her white bun, as she spoke to Mrs Frizzell. A nice girl, Donna Frizzell, real nice.

'May I present Mrs Frizzell,' said Mrs Macpherson to Mrs MacDonald.

69

Mrs Frizzell flashed a dazzling smile at Mrs MacDonald, showing no sign of the resentment against the lady, which she shared with Mrs Macpherson, while Mrs MacDonald inclined her head slightly in acknowledgment.

'We've already met,' they said in chorus, as they shook hands demurely.

'Well, now, isn't that just fine,' said Mrs Macpherson, a note of acerbity in her voice.

No other arrivals were awaiting attention, so Mrs Frizzell paused to speak with Mrs MacDonald, while Mrs Macpherson checked with the treasurer that all was well in the finance department.

'I didn't know you were Scottish,' said Mrs MacDonald, her bright smile looking rather fixed.

'Not me,' said Mrs Frizzell. 'It's Maxie that's Scotch. His mother came from Glasgow.' She enjoyed the opportunity of impressing the president of the Lady Queen Bees. 'He belongs to the Bonnie Scots Men's Association. He did a real funny Address to the Pudding last Robbie Burns Night.'

'Indeed,' said Mrs Mac Donald, delicately checking with one finger that her hat was still on straight. 'He must be a charming person.'

Mrs Frizzell looked a bit doubtful, and then said yes, he was, especially when he got going. She became aware that her beige Sunday suit was looking a trifle out of fashion, compared with Mrs MacDonald's burnt-orange outfit, and this confused her still more. Everybody seemed to have bought a new dress for the occasion, and she had hardly finished paying for her suit.

She searched for a new subject of conversation. 'Will you be going to the Edwardian Ball?' she asked.

'Naturally. Bobby expects to make up a party from the works and we shall come along for an hour or two.'

Mrs Frizzell wished mightily that she could infuse into her own voice just that inflection by which Mrs MacDonald conveyed that she was doing Tollemarche a special favour by coming to the ball. She was dying to ask Mrs MacDonald what she would be wearing, and then thought better of it. Probably the party would come in plain dinner dresses, just to show how far above such things they were.

She shifted the rather heavy, though small, paper bag which she was carrying, and said: 'I guess I'd better get some tea before all the cookies go. See you at the ball, if not before.'

'Right-ho,' said Mrs MacDonald unexpectedly. She had picked the word up from an English film shown on television and thought it charming.

Mrs Frizzell looked a little startled, and retired to the tea table with what she hoped was a stylish bow.

'Afternoon, Donna,' said a small ancient voice behind her. 'Coffee's at the other end o' the table.'

Mrs Frizzell, engrossed in thoughts of buying a new dress, as well as her costume for the ball, which was being made by a dressmaker and was as yet unpaid for, jumped and turned round.

The old tea pourer, Donna's one-time school-teacher, peered up at her through rimless glasses. 'Yer getting nervy, Donna. Should go to bed earlier. Always told yer mother you never went to bed early enough.'

Donna felt again like the girl who had been made to spit her gum into the wastepaper basket. Her depression deepened. Somehow this tea was not turning out to be the delightful social event she had hoped for, full of contented tittle-tattle and scornful criticism of all who were not Scottish and United Church. These Scotch women were tough and sure could make a person feel small.

Mrs Frizzell giggled nervously. 'I'm too busy these days, Miss Angus. Can I have a cup of tea please?'

'Yer can,' said Miss Angus, lifting the heavy silver pot with a shaky hand and slopping some into a cup. 'Sugar and cream's there. Help yerself.'

Mrs Frizzell fumbled with handbag, parcel and gloves, and finally managed to pick up the teacup as well, and to serve herself with sugar.

'Wottya got there?' asked the indomitable old voice.

Donna's face blenched a little under her makeup. She

knew Miss Angus had never liked her much; in fact, it was doubtful if Miss Angus liked anyone very much. Donna remembered with sorrow the number of humiliations she had endured from her in school, and the thought of exposing the contents of the parcel she was carrying to such a merciless judge unnerved her.

'Some books,' she finally murmured into her teacup, while she tried quietly to increase the distance between her and the tea pourer.

'Books? Never knew you to read a book yer didna hafta?' Miss Angus sniffed. 'Has Maxie taken to reading? Wottya bought?' Her voice rose commandingly. 'Lemme see.'

Other ladies standing nearby were beginning to take an amused interest in this interchange between the domineering retired school-teacher, who had ruled many of them when they were young, and Donna Frizzell, who could tear a character to pieces in three minutes with her sharp tongue.

'You're busy pouring now,' said Donna desperately. 'I'll show you after and explain about them.'

'Explain?' The old busybody from the back streets of nineteenth-century Glasgow was immediately alert. 'I got time now. Most people have had their first and aren't ready for their second. Come on. Let's have a look.' It was an order.

Mrs Frizzell clung to the paper bag.

'Not now,' she protested. 'I'll explain to you about them later on.'

She would never be allowed by Miss Angus to explain in front of the other women, she felt angrily. Miss Angus would have a field day, happy to emphasize her own high moral principles at the expense of an unloved member of a younger generation. The old devil! No wonder she had never got further than teaching in a one-roomed schoolhouse.

She bent forward to return her teacup to the table. The paper bag slipped, she grabbed it and it tore open at the bottom, spilling its contents onto the empty teacups near Miss Angus and turning some of them over with an attention-drawing rattle.

Several more ladies looked round sharply at the tea table, as Mrs Frizzell tried to snatch her purchases back. But Miss Angus slapped her wrist sharply with a teaspoon, as she picked up a paperback with her other hand and examined it closely. She looked paralyzed for a moment. The female depicted on the cover was stark naked.

'*Butterfield 8*' she read out in a clear, schoolmarm voice. She picked up another, while Donna watched like a terrified rabbit. '*Striptease!*' she exclaimed. '*Love of an Ape Man!*' She clawed for the one hardback in the collection and picked it up. '*The Cheaper Sex* by Ben MacLean.' Her face paled at the sight of the dust jacket on this one. 'Donna Frizzell, I thought better of you!' she thundered.

'But Miss Angus, the Society for . . . '

'I want no explanations. Take this pornography off my tea table!'

'Miss Angus, I . . . ' began Mrs Frizell in anguish.

Miss Angus bellowed like a slightly cracked version of Gabriel's trumpet: 'I said take them away, woman!'

Some of the ladies looked appalled, and others giggled. Mrs Frizzell snatched up her property, tried wildly to wrap the books in the remains of the paper bag, dropped one of them, picked it up and fled to the cloak-room at the back of the hall, followed by the titters and sniggers of not a few ladies who, knowing the reason for her purchase of the books, could well have rescued her from her predicament, but saw no reason to do so. There may be honour among thieves, but there did not appear to be anything similar among social climbers.

In the cloak-room Mrs Frizzell stood in a whirl of used paper towels, like a panting snowshoe hare in a snowdrift. A slow tear ran down her cheek, smudging her green eye shadow. Added to her humiliation was the knowledge that some of her friends, who had seen the incident, could have helped her but did not do so. She put the books down on the vanity table and with trembling fingers opened her handbag to find her face powder. Hastily she dabbed around her eyes, trying to stop the green rivulets running down her face. Her car was parked at the side of the store, and she would have to walk through three or four departments before she could reach the outside door.

She thought she heard someone coming down the passage, so she grabbed two paper towels and wrapped them round the offending literature. The footsteps continued past the cloakroom door, and she relaxed. When all was silent, except for the distant buzz of conversation from the tea, she crept out and almost ran down the back passage, as fast as her high-heeled shoes would permit. Her mind in turmoil, her thoughts entirely on escape, she hardly drew breath until she reached the sanctuary of the tall displays in the bedding and linen department on the ground floor and saw the safety of the store's side door beckoning to her. Thankfully, she allowed the revolving door to take her in its firm embrace and deposit her in the hall.

She stood for a moment, her eyes closed, trying to collect her thoughts, while she struggled to put on her gloves. Those cats and that old tabby, Angus; she could murder them.

The door of a car banged outside. Her eyelids flew up like window blinds wound too tightly.

Swaying gracefully up the steps on heels even higher than Mrs Frizzell's came Mrs Stych. She was dressed entirely in black except for white gloves, and her tall hat, together with the high-heeled shoes, gave her the height she otherwise lacked. Her dress, cunningly draped around her plump figure, made her look almost voluptuous; and over her shoulders was carelessly thrown her Persian lamb coat, which made Mrs Frizzell's eyes glisten with envy. Even her pearls looked real, thought Mrs Frizzell grimly, her thoughts for the moment diverted from her own nightmare frame of mind.

There was no way of escaping Mrs Stych, so Mrs Frizzell

waited while her neighbour pushed through the swing door. ' 'Lo, Olga,' she said mechanically and moved to pass out of the same door; but Mrs Stych wanted to show off her outfit.

'Hello, Donna,' she greeted her with enthusiasm. 'You been to the tea?'

Donna nodded assent.

'Wotcha going so early for?'

Mrs Frizzell made an effort to sound normal. 'Got a meeting of the Committee for the Preservation of Morals tomorrow night,' she said. 'Got to make a report to them – and I haven't prepared it yet.'

'Oh,' said Mrs Stych, moving slightly towards the inner revolving door so that the Persian lamb swung out in all its glory. She paused, however, before going through the door. 'What's that you've got wrapped up in lavatory paper? One o' the clerks'd give you a paper bag.'

Mrs Frizzell was just beginning to feel like someone recovering from near drowning, when this remark sent her under again. She shut her eyes tight for a second behind her spectacles, got a grip on herself, and said firmly: 'Some books for tomorrow.'

'Ah-ha,' responded Mrs Stych, a sly look dawning on her face. 'Betcha have fun reading them before you make a report.'

This was too much for Mrs Frizzell. She had been mortified enough. She could bear no more. She put her hand to her mouth, uttered a mourning cry and ran through the swing door to her car.

There was a parking ticket neatly tucked under the windshield wiper.

CHAPTER NINE

Boyd Stych unlocked the front door and slung his knapsack into the corner reserved for the coats and hats of his wife's visitors, clumped through the lounge in his heavy, laced boots and shouted not very hopefully: 'Hi, Olga, I'm back!' Since Mrs Stych was at the Ladies of Scotland's Tea, there was no reply.

Boyd unzipped his sheepskin jacket and flung it on a kitchen chair, opened the plaid shirt he was wearing and scratched his chest wearily. He was a tall, thin man with knotty muscles and a thin, high-cheek-boned face, his chin at the moment covered with ten weeks' growth of beard. From under fierce black brows a pair of hazel eyes looked out calculatingly at the impersonal kitchen, made spotless by the ministrations of a Dutch cleaning lady.

Although he had hardly expected anything else, he was annoyed that his wife was out. She was always out. He was tired after the long drive home, preceded by an even longer, freezing-cold canoe and helicopter journey. Thank God, that was the last time he would have to do it; after this he would go as an executive, by aircraft and helicopter only. He wondered how Olga would take the news he had for her, and decided grimly that she would not like it.

He wanted to have a shower and to change his clothes, before unloading the car; so he plodded slowly upstairs to his bedroom, leaving a trail of greasy, sweaty garments wherever he went. He remembered, just in time, not to shave – the beard was needed for the Edwardian Ball.

Mrs Stych was singing as she came up the garden path. As far as she was concerned, the tea had been a success. Her Persian lamb coat had overshadowed the treasurer's three-year-old mink, and her hat had caused a sensation. She had heard about Donna Frizzell's frightful taste in literature, and, though she was herself a member of the

Society for the Preservation of Morals and knew why the books had been purchased, she saw no reason to save her neighbour any humiliation, and had expressed suitably shocked surprise. It was gratifying to her to see that woman taken down a peg.

Her song was cut short when she saw the filthy knapsack sitting on the new, pink broadloom and making a smudge against the blush pink wall. Her eyes followed muddy boot tracks across the lounge, through the dining alcove and into the kitchen.

'Boyd,' she shouted. 'Wotcha want to make a mess like that for?' But only the sound of the shower in the distance answered her.

Sniffing crossly, she went upstairs herself and lovingly hung up the Persian lamb in the clothes closet. Then she sat down on the bed, took off her hat and eased her patent leather pumps off her rapidly swelling feet. The relief was great, and she sat massaging her toes for a minute while she looked at the collection of dirty underwear strewn over her genuine-colonial bedroom, and shuddered. Men were horrid, dirty creatures.

The horrid, dirty creature in her life, still bearded, but feeling much better after his shower, came striding into the room, tying a bathrobe as he came.

'Hi, Olga,' he said.

She looked up at him and said sulkily: 'Wotcha wanna make such a mess for?'

'Aw, shut up,' he replied. 'What about a kiss for your long-lost husband?'

She looked mutinous, then lifted a pouting mouth to his and squeaked protestingly as he pushed her backwards onto the bed and on top of her new hat. But Boyd did not care about new hats or new frocks. He had been ten weeks in the bush, a womanless bush, and Olga Stych had to put up with the fact.

She was far too quick-witted to complain and endured silently, but she managed to extract a promise of a new hat and a new dress from him, before getting up an hour later to

77

tidy herself and prepare supper. Neither of them had mentioned Hank.

Hank, school-books under arm, arrived, however, in time for supper. He said 'Hi' slightly nervously to his father, who grunted acknowledgment from behind the *Tollemarche Advent*.

Hank relaxed. Everything seemed as usual. Evidently the school had not communicated with his parents. He was unaware that a harassed Mr Dixon, caught betwen Hank, his parents and the school authorities, had disclaimed any knowledge of Hank's whereabouts, except to say, when asked by the school secretary, that probably Hank had the flu – there was a lot of it about.

As he tackled his cold meat loaf and salad, Hank thought he had better show some interest in his father, so he asked the back page of the newspaper if it had had a good trip.

'Yeah,' Boyd said listlessly, and then, with more animation, as he realized that this might be a good moment to break his news to his family, he added: 'Yeah, I did.'

He dropped the newspaper onto the kitchen floor, looked with distaste at his plate, and began to eat. Mrs Stych brought her plate to the table, picked up her fork and toyed with her food. She had eaten too many cookies at the tea and was feeling nauseated in consequence, but told herself wrathfully that it was Boyd's disgusting ways that had done it. Tomorrow, she promised herself, she would go down to Dawne's Dresse Shoppe – she'd make him pay. Wrapped in her own thoughts, she did not at first hear what her husband was saying and only became aware of his monologue when Hank said: 'Say, Dad, that'll be good.'

'What'll be good?' she asked suspiciously.

'Dad isn't going to have to go away any more – he's been made vice-president – gonna sit in an office all day right here in Tollemarche.'

Mrs Stych went pale as the full implication of this burst upon her. 'Not go away?' she stuttered.

'No,' said her husband cheerfully, 'and am I glad! Had enough of going on trips. Big business – collar and tie – that's me now.'

Mrs Stych's mouth dropped open. A husband always under her feet! A man who came home every night – and slept with her! Why, it was almost indecent – she might even have a kid. She would never be free. This had never happened to her before, and she was dumbfounded that, in the course of a few seconds, her life could change so much.

'Well?' he asked huffily, 'aren't you pleased?'

She said hastily: 'Oh, yeah. Yeah, I'm pleased.' But she looked like a Protestant faced with the Spanish Inquisition. She went slowly to the refrigerator, took out a block of ice cream, cut three slices off it and put them into glass dishes, then plonked the dishes on the table, during which time a new idea came to her.

'What sorta salary?'

'Pretty good,' he said. 'We'll be able to leave here and buy in Vanier Heights.'

She sat down and stared at her ice cream. Vanier Heights – that would be something. That was where Mrs Mac-Donald (oil) lived and she knew two wealthy doctors there already. She looked at her husband with renewed interest. Maybe she would manage after all. Maybe she could manage him, if he was the price of a house in Vanier Heights.

Although Hank was obsessed with his own problems, he was well aware of what was going on in his mother's head. He knew her too well, and he flushed, embarrassed by his own thoughts, and dug into his ice cream. He felt suddenly sorry for his father.

His mother licked her spoon reflectively, and said: 'Vanier Heights would be real good. We could sure entertain up there.'

Hank was just about to say, in order to irritate his mother, that it was in another school district and he would, therefore, have to change schools, when he remembered that he was no longer at school, and shut his mouth. Being out of school gave him a wonderful feeling. For two days now he had sat in Isobel's garage during most of school hours and planned his new book. Twice, when he had run out of ideas, he had driven the little Triumph out of the district to a coffee shop where he was not known, and had sat drinking coffee and talking to the men next to him at the counter, surprised to find himself accepted as a member of the grown-up world. One man had asked him what his job was and he said that he was an author. This had caused such abnormal interest that the next time he was asked he said that he worked in a garage.

One afternoon he had shared a pot of coffee with Dorothy, at her invitation. She was to stay with her sister until Isobel decided definitely whether to remain in Tolle-marche or return to England, and occasionally she became a little bored and was glad of Hank's lively company, though to her annoyance, he treated her as if she were a ten-year-old.

The day before his father's return, he had driven out to a lake some ten miles from the town; it was deserted and half frozen, and he had walked round it, finding that the fresh air cleared his head and that ideas came fast in the silence of the woods. The characters for his book began to emerge as persons and to walk beside him. Now, all he wanted was to get back to his typewriter and put them on paper before they faded. First, however, he had to ask Isobel if he could alter the lighting in the garage, so that he could see better at night.

The meal was finished, his father had returned to the newspaper, rather deflated at his family's lack of appreciation of his vice-presidency, and his mother had finished her ice cream and was rising from the table.

'Hank, now you can just do these dishes for me tonight. There's a meeting of the Queen Bees in an hour, and I've got to get into my robes.'

Hank made a face at her plump back disappearing through the kitchen door and reluctantly began to transfer the dishes to the sink. His father had put down his newspaper and was looking at her, too. He looked old and forlorn, in spite of the ferocious beard, as if he had hoped for something and been disappointed. Hank was so used to being deserted by his mother that he did not think it odd that she should go out on the first evening in ten weeks that his father had been able to spend at home. But he did see that his usually tough, self-sufficient male parent was, for once, looking as if he needed bolstering up.

As he turned on the hot-water tap and got out the dish detergent, Hank abandoned the idea of going back to his garage. 'Looks as if we're going to have a bull session, Dad.'

His father looked almost grateful.

'I guess so,' he said, and then roused himself. 'Here, I'll dry for you.' He took up the dish towel. And when Mrs Stych returned, looking like a fat Christmas fairy and complaining that she could not fix her wings, he was able to pin them onto her dress without rancour and to tell a thoroughly bawdy joke, which made Hank explode with laughter and his wife look outraged. 'Boyd Stych,' she shouted, 'you're disgusting!' He smacked her gold-black-striped bottom, and sent her, fuming, out to her little car.

'Any beer in the house?' asked Boyd, as soon as the car engine had started up and it could be assumed that Mrs Stych was on her way.

'Sure, there's some in the cold room downstairs.'

Boyd's face brightened. 'Say, let's have some. You go down and get it, while I make a fire in the living-room. This place is like a morgue.'

Hank was delighted, though at the same time a little suspicious of his father's prompt response to his friendly overture. The old man had never suggested before that they have a drink together; maybe it was all part of that new world he had entered when he stood in front of Mr Albert's mirror in his new suit. He loped down into the basement, dusted off half a dozen bottles of beer and brought them up, found glasses and an opener and took them into the living-room on a tray.

His father, an expert woodsman, had already got a fire going, and the room had lost some of its pristine newness and was looking much more cosy. The wood crackled and hissed, and Boyd drew the brass firescreen across it to stop the sparks from flying out at them. Together, they heaved the oversize coffee table, with its burden of unread art books, out of the way, and pulled up chairs. Mr Stych opened two bottles and handed a glass and a bottle to Hank.

'Ever drunk beer before?' he asked.

Hank did not know how to reply. The Alberta liquor laws laid down that no minors might drink, but it was not difficult to obtain beer or liquor, and he had often drunk himself silly. His silence made his father laugh.

'O.K., O.K.,' he said, 'I won't ask.'

Hank grinned sheepishly. Now, he knew, was the time to tell his father about *The Cheaper Sex*, while he was in such an extraordinarily amiable mood. He would have to be told; any day now it would dawn on Tollemarche that it had spawned its first successful author, and he could guess the kind of jokes his father's colleagues were going to make when they found out what kind of book he had written. He could not, however, think how to start, and the silence deepened.

'How's school?' asked his father, in a sudden valiant attempt to re-establish the frail line of communication.

'I've quit,' said Hank absently, and realized a second too late what he had said.

'You've what?'

He was committed and could only stumble on. 'I've dropped out – I couldn't stand it any more.'

Mr Stych sat up in his chair and glowered at his son. What, he wondered indignantly, had Olga been thinking of to countenance this?

'Are you crazy?' he demanded in horrified tones. 'Where you going to be without Grade 12? You have to go to university.' He looked his offending offspring up and down with angry eyes. 'Just what do you think you're going to do?'

Hank's face went blank. 'I'm gonna write,' he said stubbornly.

His father put down his glass with a bang, so that the beer slopped over on the side table. 'You'll do no such thing,' he shouted. 'You'll go right back to school on Monday morning and finish Grade 12. I'll have no dropouts in my family – we got enough hippie types hanging around. Never heard of such a thing.' He paused to take breath before continuing his tirade, and Hank said hastily: 'Listen, Dad, you don't understand.'

'Understand? I understand all right, and if you think you're going to live off me for the rest of your life you're mistaken. You get your Grade 12, and then you work your own way through university, same as I did.'

With a painful effort, Hank swallowed his own anger. He had either to get his father to listen or otherwise he would have to just walk out. He itched to do the latter, but common sense prevailed; he had seen how uncomfortable were the lives of other guys who had done that, either to marry too young or go it alone. A home was a sensible base for operations. He held up one hand in a conciliatory gesture to try and calm his parent, who by this time was striding up and down the room behind him.

He did his best to infuse good humour into his voice as he said: 'Hold it, Dad. I got fifty or maybe seventy thousand dollars earned, and I need advice about investing it. Believe me, I really need advice.'

Mr Stych stopped in his tracks at the mention of such a sum of money, as Hank had hoped he would, and looked at the boy as if he might have gone dangerously mad.

'Now what are you trying to tell me?' he asked, his mouth twisted in bitterness. He'd always known Hank was no good. Always bottom in phys. ed. and always hated baseball. What could you expect? he asked himself. Just trouble, nothing but trouble. Now the kid was sick in his head. Seventy thousand bucks – that was a good one!

83

'Now listen, Dad, just sit down and listen. I've got a real long story to tell you.'

Mr Stych stopped his perambulation and regarded his son with a puzzled frown. What was the kid getting at? He looked all right; in fact, he had improved. He was definitely tidier, and he had an oddly adult air of authority for a kid still at school. Of course, he was growing up a bit. Mr Stych sat down again and drained his glass.

'All right,' he said with an air of resigned patience. 'What is it?'

He nearly fainted when Hank began: 'You know I rent a garage from a young widow lady.'

Not a young widow at his age, for heaven's sake. Why hadn't he stuck to Grade 12 girls? Hastily, he reached for another bottle of beer and opened it, while Hank droned on: 'So I entered an essay for the No Smoking essay competition . . .'

With agitated fingers, his father felt in his shirt pocket for a cigarette, but he had forgotten to bring them from the kitchen. Hank tossed a packet over to him, and he had lit one before he realized that he had not known that his son smoked.

'. . . Isobel read it and sent me to Professor MacFee – an English Professor – with it, and they both helped me to send it to a publisher in London. I did – and it came back. So I sent it to another in New York, and he took it.'

'Who's Isobel?' asked Mr Stych, trying to catch up with the tale.

'The widow,' replied Hank, with more than a trace of impatience in his voice, and then continued: 'And it's selling so fast that I don't know what to do with the money. We're getting forty thousand dollars for the movie rights, and the serial rights – the first ones – are already sold in the States.'

Mr Stych looked as if someone had struck him. Forty thousand dollars! His no-good slob of a kid was talking of having forty thousand dollars. His heavy black eyebrows made him look fearsome as he glared unbelievingly at

Hank. 'You're kidding?' he said finally.

'I'm not, Dad. Ask Mr Hnatiuk at the bank if I haven't got real money. He's been real good. Dealt with me himself, and never told anybody so far as I know.' He took a nervous sip from his glass. 'You can see the letters from New York, if you come over to Isobel's. I been to New York only a short while back.'

Boyd ground out his cigarette. 'Christ!' he said, some of the anger evaporating. For the first time in his life, he really looked at his son, weighing up this product of the first six months of marriage before disillusionment set in.

Hank said earnestly: 'So you see, I sure need advice. I mean, I want to spend some, but I want to invest some, too. And you know about these things, that's for sure.'

His father was looking at him keenly now. Mellowed by two bottles of beer, he was convinced that Hank was telling the truth; his mind was already going to work considering how to double that forty thousand. Money fascinated him. Like a great many others in Tollemarche, he had made it his goal and his God. People who made money demanded respect; people who had none were just trash to be trampled underfoot, no matter what other gifts they had. He licked his lips.

'Sure, Son, you do need advice. You can lose money pretty fast by bad investment.'

Though his face showed nothing of his amusement, Hank laughed inwardly. Money and talk of money got you attention. He sighed with relief.

Boyd was silent for a moment. Then he asked: 'Have you told your mother?'

Hank went cold right down his back and into his feet. 'No,' he said. 'She don't even know I quit school.'

Boyd approved of this, and nodded his head in agreement.

'You're right not to tell her,' he said dryly.

A log in the fire broke and fell, sending out a shower of sparks. Hank silently drank down his beer, and hoped he had made the right move in telling his father. Anyway,

Isobel had been keen for him to tell both his parents, and her advice had been sound all through. He knew his father had a fair reputation as an astute businessman as well as an able geologist, and he hoped uneasily that they could deal honestly together over the money.

'If I had that much money and it was the first real money I had ever made,' said the businessman at last, 'I'd put a quarter of it in government savings bonds, and with the rest of it I'd buy as much land or property in and around Tollemarche and Edmonton as I could lay my hands on.' He looked at his son's face illuminated by the firelight. The boy was watching him anxiously. 'Do you expect to make any more like this?'

'Sure,' said Hank, with all the confidence of youth. 'I'm writing another.'

'Well, if you do, you could buy a business, or you could buy growth shares on the stock market. Myself, I'd buy a business.'

'Not me,' said Hank firmly. 'I'm gonna write. And I want to travel a bit. Maybe get a job on a newspaper or a magazine for a while. Feel my way around. Get some experience.'

Boyd leaned back in his chair and lit another cigarette. He had much to think about. In a place like Alberta, with that much capital and a good deal of know-how, which he himself had, the boy could be quite wealthy before he was forty. And amazingly enough, he expected to earn more. For years, he and Hank had exchanged only a few words, but now they began to talk, drawn together by the magic of money; and Hank was surprised and flattered to find that the elder man was entranced by his sudden success.

To Hank's intense relief, at no point did it occur to Boyd to inquire what the book was about. He did not even ask its name.

Mrs Stych came in at half past one, her wings bedraggled from the weight of her coat. She had gone on from the Noble Order of Lady Queen Bees' meeting to a party given by one of the members, and was by now tired, cross and a little tipsy. On the way home, the car had had a tendency to wander from one lane to another on the road. And now Mrs Stych stood rather dazedly inside the front door and wondered if she was in the right house.

The lounge was a mess. The coffee table had taken flight to one side of the room, and two chairs had been drawn up close to the fireplace with their backs to the chesterfield. The fireplace itself was filled with grey ash and cigarette butts. On every side table were empty beer bottles sitting sadly in rings of beer; two empty glasses decorated the mantelpiece, and the piece of petrified driftwood which usually graced it had been shoved to the back, to make way for some empty plates which looked as if they had held meat and cheese.

Mrs Stych's senses reeled. This was what happened when a man was loose in the house. He must have had some friends in. Her nose wrinkled at the smell of beer, and she kicked off her mink-trimmed bootees as if she were kicking Boyd.

She trailed around the room picking up beer bottles, looking oddly like a bee with broken wings. She removed eleven bottles, and then felt sick. The Ladies of Scotland's cookies, followed by meat loaf, succeeded by the Lady Queen Bees' angel cake buried under cheese dips and rye on the rocks at the party, would daunt the strongest stomach. She fled up stairs to the bathroom.

Her Dutch cleaning lady would be coming round in the morning – let her do it, thought an exhausted Olga a few minutes later, as she shakily bathed her face under the cold tap; Boyd could darn well pay her more housekeeping to cover the extra hours of work.

With some difficulty, she unzipped her gold and black dress in the bathroom and then trailed into the bedroom, self-pity and too much to drink tending to make her weep.

Boyd, with most of the bedding rolled tightly round him, was snoring contentedly. Rather than wake him by pulling the clothes off him and having to face the likely consequences, Mrs Stych put her housecoat over her nightgown, got a spare blanket out of her old hope chest, and eased herself down beside the chrysalis which was her husband. She slept immediately.

In his dreams, Boyd Stych made a million for his son out of forty-storey apartment blocks, and was chased by a flying book the name of which he could not see.

CHAPTER TEN

When Mrs Frizzell arrived home from the tea, Maxie Frizzell was already in, since it was early-closing day. He was sitting in the breakfast nook, a copy of the *Tollemarche Advent*, open at a page of advertisements dealing with cars, spread out in front of him, a cup of instant coffee in his hand. His overcoat and fur hat were neatly hung up in the hall and his overboots reposed on the boot tray in the back sunroom. Maxie was no believer in courting trouble – his wife nagged enough without adding to it.

He looked up when Donna Frizzell came in through the back door, and was startled to see that her hat was awry and her makeup smudged beyond repair. Unbelievable as it seemed to him, she almost looked as if she had been crying.

He got up as quickly as the tight fit of the table in the breakfast nook would allow. He'd bet twenty dollars she'd had a fender bender and that the car looked like a concertina.

'Had an accident, Donna?'

'No. Only another parking ticket.' She sniffed as she put down the parcel of books and took off her gloves, and sniffed again as Maxie sank back on his bench, relieved that his beautiful black Cadillac was intact. He looked at her uneasily, however. Something had happened. Donna was far too tough to cry, he reckoned, and yet it looked suspiciously as if that was what she was about to do.

He turned the page of the newspaper and then asked carefully: 'Anything wrong?'

She sat down on the bench opposite to him and looked at his fat baby face, which was now showing some concern. Then she put her head down on the table and wept unrestrainedly, the feathers of her hat dipping unnoticed into his coffee.

He was bewildered and did not know what to do. 'For

heaven's sakes!' he exclaimed, shocked to find that his wife, usually acidly in command of herself and of anyone else who came near her, could possibly be reduced to tears.

'What happened?' he asked warily.

He was answered by another loud sob and a gesture towards the untidy parcel which she had brought in. He again eased himself out of the narrow space of the breakfast nook and went over to the kitchen counter, looked at the parcel and looked at his wife, who was now almost hysterical. He decided that he must be courageous and investigate, so he unwound the paper towels, picked up the books one by one and read their titles. He guessed they were for the morals group, since neither he nor Mrs Frizzell ever really read a book, and he put them down again, still mystified.

He was fond of his wife in an absent-minded way, especially when she was not nagging at him, so he took a Kleenex out of the kitchen box and went back to her, saying rather hopelessly: 'Here, have a Kleenex.'

The sobs lessened and a hand was extended, into which he pressed the tissue. She sat up with a gasp and blew her nose hard; then, since he was close, she rested her aching head against his ample stomach. He put his arm around her shoulders, as he had not done for many years.

'Oh, Maxie,' she said, 'it was real bad.' For once her voice was faint.

She took off her hat and laid it on the table, and he saw with a sense of shock that her hair was white down the line of the parting where the tinting had grown out. She lifted a lined face to him, and he reached over for another Kleenex and smoothed the wetness away, so that she was almost without makeup. He could not remember how long it was since his wife had leaned on him, and he found it pleasant to be the one in charge of the situation.

In a rallying tone of voice, usually reserved for meetings with his salesmen, he said: 'Here, I'll make you some coffee and you tell me what happened.'

He busied himself with the electric kettle and a jar of

instant coffee, and in a moment or two put the hot drink in front of her. She was grateful to him for his solicitude and the tale came slowly out.

He listened anxiously because, in such an isolated community, any slur on his wife's character could have its effect on his business. The eleventh Commandment, 'Thou shalt not be found out,' was all-important.

When she had finished and was stirring a saccharine tablet into her coffee, he sat silent for a while, his little eyes half closed, his pursed lips showing that he was thinking hard. The refrigerator hummed its usual little tune to break the silence and Donna drank her coffee.

Finally, he said: 'What you need is publicity.'

Donna looked at him, aghast. 'Publicity! My goodness! Publicity! I've had enough of *that!* I've never been so ashamed in my life.' Her voice was hoarse with indignation.

'Yeah, I mean it. Listen, why don't you ring up the social editor of the *Advent*, and tell her about your meeting tomorrow. Complain that the Committee is not getting the coverage it ought to have for the work it's doing. Just tell her the names of those books and I tell you she'll be right over.' He glanced at the offending literature. 'Seems to me you've got a man-sized job on, judging by that lot.'

Mrs Frizzell immediately saw the relevance of his advice and began to look more like her normal self. 'Yeah,' she said thoughtfully, 'we do work hard.'

Maxie went on: 'Y' see, everyone who was at the tea will keep reading the social pages for the next day or two to see that their names are in the report of it; and, with luck, inside that time, on the same pages there'll be a report about your Morals Committee – then they'll know why you had the books, and old Miss Angus will be put in her place.' He, too, had suffered under Miss Angus's overbearing rule when he was at school, and he did not mind trying to make her look foolish.

Mrs Frizzell's face brightened. 'I'll have to ask Margaret first,' she said. 'She's the secretary and does the publicity.'

'Let her ask the *Advent*. It'll sound more official.' He

said this in his firm business voice, not his usually listless home voice, and she accepted his direction as readily as one of his mechanics would have done.

Mrs Frizzell felt a reluctant admiration for her husband swelling up in her. He was not quite such a dumbhead as one would think. Her name would probably appear in the newspaper twice within two days, since she was to deliver the main report to the Morals Committee; and that should really impress both friends and enemies.

The feathers of her hat were again sitting in the dregs of Maxie's coffee, so she hastily retrieved it and looked mournfully at the damaged plumage. 'I sure need a new outfit,' she said absently and without hope.

'Well, go and buy one,' Maxie said expansively. 'We're going to hafta give a big coffee party for the auto buyer from Henderson and Company, so make it a nice one.'

Mrs Frizzell swivelled round to face him. 'How much?' she asked distrustfully.

'What about a hundred dollars?'

Mrs Frizzell was immediately suspicious. To get so much sympathy and then to get a handout as soon as she asked for it, was unnerving. What had he been doing?

She regarded him steadily for a minute with eyes still bloodshot from crying. But he was beaming at her innocently, glad to see that she was feeling better.

'O.K.,' she said, a note of doubt in her voice. 'Is the garage doing all right?'

'Sure. That's why you can have a hundred dollars.'

She breathed a little more easily. He needn't think he was going to be allowed to wander. He had married her and he was going to stay married, and no nonsense about other women and buying her off with unexpected handouts.

She clicked her false teeth together, and announced with something of the normal snap in her voice that she was going to call Margaret right now. Then she would glance through the books she had bought, because she had to make a report on them. And would she ever roast that bookseller, old Mr Pascall!

The telephone call was made, and Margaret, heard amid the distant screams of children quarrelling, gushed that it was a darling idea and she would telephone the *Advent* herself, since she knew the women's editor well. Mrs Frizzell had carefully cultivated her, too, but she let it pass, while Margaret complained that all four children had the measles and that she was going to have to leave them alone if the babysitter did not come soon; she was not going to miss the dance at the Pinetree Club for worlds, and was dear Donna coming?

Dear Donna said virtuously that she had to write her report, and disentangled herself from the conversation before she was asked to babysit.

She disinterred two frozen TV dinners from the big freezer in the basement and put them into the oven to heat. Then she settled down at the dining-room table with her book purchases, which she had picked at random from the shelves of Tollemarche's only book store and from the racks of one of the cigar stores. She had also a sheet of paper and a ball pen, ready for action.

Before looking at the books, she wrote: 'The teenagers of Tollemarche must be protected from obscenity and smut.' That should shake the audience to attention, she thought, as she picked up the first book.

She ran through the first few pages of each of the paperbacks, her mouth falling open as she read. Really, the ideas that some people had! Sex and sin were, to her, synonymous, and she wondered how on earth she was going to convey tastefully to her audience how much sin was in these volumes.

She pushed her glasses back up her nose, clamped her mouth shut firmly, and picked up the hard-backed novel, which had cost six dollars and fifty cents of the Committee's small funds.

On the front of the jacket a naked young girl was spread languidly on her stomach on a seashore, nothing of her anatomy being left to the imagination. Embarrassed, Mrs Frizzell turned hastily to the back, where rave notices from several New York papers greeted her. She opened the back of the book, and found a heading on the fold-in part of the jacket which announced that this section was 'About the Author'. This time her mouth fell open so fast that she nearly lost her top dentures. It was unbelievable, yet there it was, clearly printed: 'The author, aged nineteen, was born in Tollemarche, Alberta, where he still resides . . .' This was followed by four or five lines about the book being a miraculous first novel, etc., most of which Mrs Frizzell failed to take in.

She leaned back in her chair whistling softly under her breath, then remembered that it was vulgar for a woman to whistle. She drummed her fingers on the Canadian maple table instead. It surprised her that Mr Pascall had not used for publicity purposes the fact that the author was from Tollemarche. Then she realized that books were really only a sideline to his stationery business; he sold more birthday cards than books. Even the advent of the university had not done much to increase his sales, she considered shrewdly, since she could not recall seeing a single bookshelf in any of the homes of university staff which she had visited. Probably the old man would announce in his window the book's importance to Tollemarche, next time he changed the display. Or perhaps he wouldn't, she amended, since the exhibition of the jacket itself would be enough to send Tollemarche into an uproar of complaints.

As far as Mrs Frizzell knew, apart from a book on local fish written by an ardent fly fisherman on the university staff, this was the first book to come out of Tollemarche. And it had been written, apparently, by some boy just out of high school, for heaven's sakes.

'Oh, Maxie,' she called. She knew that Maxie was acquainted with the bulk of the male population of Tollemarche, because anyone looking for a car sooner or later strolled through his car lot.

Maxie withdrew himself reluctantly from the excitement of the football game he was watching on televison. 'Yeah?' he queried.

'Do you know anybody in town called Ben MacLean? A boy?'

'Nope. Lotsa MacLeans. Nobody called Ben. Why?'

Mrs Frizzell did not answer. She went to the telephone table, took out the directory and looked up the name MacLean. There were indeed lots of MacLeans – nearly the whole Clan MacLean, as far as she could judge. Irritably, she slammed it down and went to wash and change, while she considered how she could trace this mysterious boy, this disgusting boy, this juvenile delinquent. Her Committee would teach him a lesson, she promised herself venomously, as she powdered her face.

Of course, all the Committee would want to read the book.

Well, they could wait; she must go through it thoroughly first. It was surely part of her duty to find out what finally happened to the seductive female spread out on the front cover.

CHAPTER ELEVEN

The Committee for the Preservation of Morals was to meet at the house of Mrs Murphy, the wife of the Mayor. It was a large split-level home, with unexpected staircases going, it seemed, in all directions, their wrought-iron banisters standing out against the pale-yellow broadloom which covered both stairs and floors throughout the house. The picture windows, thought Mrs Stych, were larger than any other picture windows in Tollemarche, and the huge brick fireplace in the living-room was festooned with real antique brass ornaments, ranging from a warming pan, top left, to a set of horse brasses, bottom right. The two square yards of broadloom devoted to the open hallway were almost blocked by a large bamboo plant, made of plastic, which waved majestically over a little fountain cascading water over two plastic shell-shaped basins which miraculously never overflowed.

Mrs Stych noted carefully all the '*day*core', as she called it, while she removed her coat and gave it to Mrs Murphy to hang up. Soon she would herself be in the market for a new home, and, though she and Boyd could not hope to out-do a contractor like the Mayor building for himself, she could pick up a few ideas and have them incorporated into their new house in Vanier Heights. She knew that in a couple of days' time Boyd's promotion would be announced by his company in the newspaper, underneath a studio portrait of him, and she held her head high as she swayed gracefully into the living-room. Since a few ladies who had been at the tea would also be at the committee meeting, and, anyway, Boyd had messed up her best black afternoon dress, she wore now a pretty gown in green wool which she had picked up in the last sale at Eaton's. As it was after six o'clock, and, according to her much thumbed book of etiquette, a lady might glitter after that hour, she wore long *diamanté* earrings. The result was, in the eyes of the ladies present, very glamorous indeed, and they were nice enough to tell her so. She simpered, and took her place on one of the enormous chesterfields flanking the fireplace, sitting next to Mrs Moore, the dentist's wife, mother of Hank's dead friend Tony. Mr Moore had recently discovered how lucrative preventive dentistry could be, and Mrs Moore was dressed accordingly.

Mrs Murphy had moved a coffee table to the centre of the room and grouped four chairs round it, for the use of the officials of the committee. She was a large woman, flushed with the exertion of constantly having to answer the door, and she still showed in her black hair, grey eyes and lovely skin, traces of her Irish forebears. She found the responsibility of being the Mayor's wife almost too much for her, and was in a constant flutter for fear she forgot something in connection with the entertainment of the steady procession of guests, important to Tollemarche, who filed through her home. She need not have worried, however, for her good nature and naturally hospitable manner covered up any small deficiencies in deportment.

Tonight she was to chair the meeting, so she left the front door unlocked for any late-comers, and, having seated the nervous little reporter from the *Advent* in a position where she could see and hear all the ladies present, giving her at the same time a hastily written list of the names of those expected to attend, she called the meeting to order. As she raised her little hammer to tap on the table, she wondered suddenly why the *Advent* had actually sent a reporter – they usually depended on the publicity secretary to supply them with a report. However, the recording secretary was waiting with the minutes of the last meeting, and Mrs Murphy announced her.

Donna Frizzel, angular in dark brown, sat as secretary of the committee, with the president, chairman and treasurer, while the lesser fry made their reports. She had a thin, satisfied smile on her face, which not even a few smirks and elbow nudgings among those ladies who had been at the tea could banish. She wished that the *Advent* had sent a more experienced reporter. This girl looked as if she was on her first assignment, as she sat with pencil poised over her shorthand notebook. However, she would probably be very careful over names, and that was what Mrs Frizzell wanted.

Mrs Stych's mind wandered as the voices droned on and the current film at the local drive-in cinema was condemned. She was thinking about a telephone call which she had answered just as she was about to leave the house. The call had been for Hank, and had been from one of his classmates, who said that he just wanted to inquire how Hank was. Mrs Stych, in a frantic hurry, had said that he was out but that he was fine, just fine. The caller had sounded a little bewildered, but had said that he was glad to hear it and would telephone again sometime.

Now Mrs Stych was puzzled. Why hadn't the stupid boy said he would see Hank in school in the morning?

The treasurer, in sharp, clipped tones, was listing the committee's various expenditures and was bringing to the attention of the members the fact that there was only twenty dollars in hand. Mrs Stych forced herself to attend, and the little reporter's pencil sped across the page.

Finally, Mrs Frizzell rose to make her report. She hitched her skirt down surreptitiously, cleared her throat, arranged her sample books in a neat pile in front of her, and then, fixing her audience with an angry glare, she began.

'The teenagers of Tollemarche must be protected from obscenity and smut!' she announced dramatically.

There was an immediate murmur of approval, though some of the ladies looked longingly at the lavishly laid tea table just visible in the dining alcove.

'They must be defended, it appears, from their own neighbours!'

It was as if an electric shock had gone through the gathering. Heads snapped round towards Mrs Frizzell. From their neighbours?

98

Mrs Frizzell's voice sank. 'Yes,' she hissed, 'from their own neighbours.'

She picked up *The Cheaper Sex* with the tips of her bony, scarlet-nailed fingers.

'This!' She paused for effect. 'This shameless piece of pornography was written in Tollemarche by one of our own teenagers. Undoubtedly his parents must have known about it, and that makes it doubly shameful.'

Twenty-four pairs of painted lips let out long-drawn gasps and then broke into speech. Questions poured towards the chair, and Mrs Murphy banged her gavel so hard on the coffee table that it left a mark, which distressed her so much that she forgot for a moment why she was hammering and stared sadly at the dent in the wood.

She recovered herself quickly, however, and cried: 'Order! Order, please! Ladies! One at a time. Mrs Davis.' She gestured with her gavel towards a doctor's wife, whose elaborately casual tweed suit proclaimed her husband's earning power.

Mrs Davis had been a nurse and her cold, crisp voice rose above the clamour. 'We should like to know who wrote the book and who published it.'

The voice had the effect for which Mrs Murphy had hoped. There was immediate silence and eager attention.

Mrs Frizzell surveyed the gathering exultantly. She wished passionately that she knew who Ben MacLean was. But this was her moment, she felt. She would never again have so much rapt attention focused upon her, and she stood silent, until one lady, younger than most of those present, started to rummage in her handbag for a cigarette.

'The name of the author is . . . Ben MacLean, the publisher a firm in New York.'

Conversation immediately broke out again, while each lady tried to recollect all the MacLeans that she knew. Mrs Murphy banged with her gavel, rather more cautiously this time. 'Ladies, please!'

A thin streak of a woman bobbed up at the back. 'What are we going to do about it?'

The voice of the doctor's wife rose above the hubbub. 'Have you read the book?'

Silence again. Everyone looked expectantly at Mrs Frizzell.

Mrs Frizzell went a little pink. She hesitated, and then said: 'Not all of it. I – er – um . . . '

Several ladies turned sharply on Mrs Davis, who was far too efficient in everything she did. 'Be reasonable, Hester. She wouldn't like to read a thing like that.'

'How else would she know it's a thing like that?' retorted Hester, unabashed.

'The first chapter was enough,' snapped Mrs Frizzell indignantly, glad that she did not have to explain that she did not give much time to reading.

Mrs Murphy snatched the opportunity to ask Mrs Frizzell to proceed with her report, which she did, outlining the story as far as she knew it and using as many euphemisms as she could. The name of the author was evidently a pseudonym, but it was hoped that the committee would take steps to find out who he was, would decide what should be done to clean this canker out of Tollemârche, and would take more steps to curb their local bookseller's and cigar stores' choice of books. She omitted to mention that, when they last made representations to the bookseller, Mr Pascall, he had said that he stocked the books he could sell; and if the ladies wanted him to sell better books they should take to buying them and reading them, instead of watching televison all day. Then he might be able to improve the quality of his stock.

Mrs Frizzell, having run out of steps, sat down.

'What are we going to do about it?' asked Hester Davis again, through a haze of cigarette smoke.

Handbags were snapped shut, legs were crossed and uncrossed, ladies leaned forward confidentially to their neighbours, ostensibly to confer, though a number got fits of giggles and had to hide their faces behind their hands. Mrs Frizzell gazed into space and Mrs Murphy smoothed back errant curls from her damp forehead. Almost all the ladies silently decided to go downtown the next morning and buy a copy of *The Cheaper Sex*. Each justified her interest in such a vulgar book by telling herself that in these matters one must be able to judge for oneself.

The little reporter realized suddenly that she had a real story for her editor and went pale with fear as she remembered that lady's ruthless slashing up of her last offering, the report of an insignificant wedding. She shivered and watched Mrs Frizzell apprehensively as the buzz of conversation continued.

Mrs Murphy threw the meeting open for discussion since discussion was already in full flood and refused to be dammed, and wondered if the coffee, left on a low gas in the kitchen, had started to perk yet.

A blonde lady, with bouffant hair above a heavily lined, over-powdered face, addressed the chair. Why, she asked, didn't they form a small subcommittee to inquire into the identity of this young author, and, when they had discovered it, they could report back to the rest of the members, and they could then discuss what action should be taken.

This suggestion met with immediate approval. The ladies were thirsty and wanted something to drink. Agreement on this suggestion would bring the meeting to a close, and most of those present would not have to do anything at all about the wretched book.

The motion was formally put to the meeting and seconded. The blonde lady, Mrs Johnson, whose daughter Hank regarded as little better than a streetwalker, found herself appointed chairman of the subcommittee, and she asked if Mrs Stych and the president, the hawk-faced wife of a real estate man, would serve with her.

Mrs Stych protested coyly that she did not know enough about books to be of any use, while she wondered privately how she was going to fit this new commitment into her already overcrowded schedule of social events. What about Mrs Frizzell? she suggested hopefully. Mrs Davis pointed out tartly that Mrs Stych was not at present serving on any of their other subcommittees, and that she must do something to help. Mrs Stych snapped back that all the ladies present must be well aware of the multitude of offices she held in the charitable organizations of Tollemarche. The ladies murmured reluctant agreement, since most of them had at one time or another tried to oust her from at least one of the appointments which they themselves coveted.

With a delicate sniff in the direction of a slightly cowed Hester Davis, Mrs Stych enrolled herself as a sleuth in search of an author.

The date of the next meeting was agreed upon, as a delicious odour of coffee began to permeate the room, and the ladies rose expectantly and looked towards the dining alcove.

Mrs Murphy had made brownies again, and the faces of some of the ladies fell. Mrs Stych, however, nibbled appreciatively at one of the chocolate morsels, while Mrs Johnson, who had no real idea how to trace an author, outlined a plan of campaign so huge that it would have confused an entire army staff, never mind Mrs Stych.

Did Mrs Johnson spell her name with a *t*? asked the little reporter.

Mrs Johnson said 'No!' indignantly, and Mrs Stych woke up and checked that the girl had her name down correctly, too. She began to take an interest in the Sleuthing Committee. She felt that having her name mentioned more frequently than ever in the social columns was highly desirable for the wife of a company director. She smiled dazzlingly at the little reporter and hoped that she would be referred to as 'charming'.

CHAPTER TWELVE

The women's editor of the *Tollemarche Advent*, having found nothing about Ben MacLean in the office files, decided that the quickest source of information regarding Tollemarche's first author would probably be Mr Pascall, the bookseller. She therefore telephoned him.

Old Mr Pascall saw no reason why he should make life easy for a gossiping female and made her hold on, while he sold two ballpoint pens and a packet of rubber bands.

'It's some high school kid called Henry Stych,' he finally wheezed down the telephone. 'Salesman did tell me sumpin' about a kid from here writing it but I forgot.

'Professor MacFee was in the other day – asked me to order him a copy. Told me the kid's name was Henry Stych. I asked him why the kid didn't use his own name, and he said maybe he thought Ben MacLean sorta sounded better.

'Want me to order you a copy? I sold the two I had.'

The editor ground her teeth. 'No, thanks. Which high school?'

A small girl was messing about with the birthday cards in Mr Pascall's shop. He felt he had wasted enough time on the editor, and replied with asperity: 'How should I know? There're only two high schools, aren't there – public and separate. Ring 'em up, can't you?' He slammed down the receiver and fled to the rescue of his birthday cards.

The editor put the receiver slowly back on to its rest.

Stych! That was interesting. She wondered if the boy was any relation to Mrs Olga Stych. Very thoughtfully, she turned to the telephone directory and looked up the name. Seven Styches were listed. She checked her file again and found that Olga's husband's first name was Boyd. There was no mention of any children.

Olga Stych had a vicious tongue and would not hesitate to use it, if she was mistaken in thinking there was a

103

relationship. It would undoubtedly be wiser to establish the young author's identity and then, if he proved to be Mrs Stych's son, perhaps have a quiet word with the boy first. Since the book seemed to be one that would cause some controversy, she had better proceed with caution.

Her mind made up, she picked up the receiver and dialled the number of the separate school.

The separate school had no Henry Stych on its roll, and the school secretary was left in a state of agonized curiosity at the *Advent*'s interest in such a person.

The principal of the public high school happened to pick up the telephone himself.

Yes, he knew Henry Stych, and, yes, he knew of *The Cheaper Sex*; he had confiscated a copy of it from a Grade 10 child only this morning. Henry Stych had *what*? Written it? Ridiculous!

The editor said she felt sure her information was correct, and could she have Henry's address and telephone number?

The principal was immediately cautious and warned her that the boy was under age. He suggested she should contact the father, Boyd Stych, and he gave the parents' home telephone number, feeling that she would soon trace it anyway.

Deeply concerned, he pressed the intercom buzzer and asked Mr Dixon, Hank's home-room teacher, to report to him without delay.

Mrs Stych had just got up and was still in her dressing-gown when she answered the telephone call from the *Advent*. Hank and Boyd had found their own cornflakes and coffee and had long since departed.

The editor asked for Mr Henry Stych. Mrs Stych faltered for a moment and then realized that she meant Hank.

She said gaily: 'The story isn't about Hank – it's about my husband, Boyd.'

The editor knew nothing of the story of Boyd's promotion, about to be featured in the financial section, and she said firmly that it was Henry she wanted.

Mrs Stych did not want to offend the queen of the social columns by arguing with her, so when that lady went on to inquire when the newspaper could send a photographer, Mrs Stych said in her most gracious tone of voice that the whole family would be at home that evening any time after six.

She rang off, happy that the *Advent* was taking such an interest in Boyd's directorship, finished her coffee and went to take her morning shower. It was only then, with the water trickling down her plump back, that an uncomfortably cold premonition seemed to trickle down, too. Had the Editor really meant Hank, and, if so, what had Hank been up to?

She pulled herself up firmly. If Hank had done something particularly dreadful, either Donna Frizzell or some other nosey parker would have been on her doorstep by now to tell her about it. It *must* be about Boyd.

As requested by Mrs Johnson of the Committee for the Preservation of Morals, she drove out to the library, with the intention of asking the chief librarian for information about Ben MacLean, but when she arrived he had gone out for morning coffee. His languid part-time assistant could not have cared less about books or authors, local or other; she supposed that there was a copy of the book in the new-fiction section.

Mrs Stych sailed majestically to the bookcase indicated, and found the offending volume almost immediately. She had not looked at Mrs Frizzell's copy, so this was her first glimpse of it. Before picking it out, she looked over her shoulder to make sure that no one was looking at her. There was only one person nearby, an elderly gentleman immersed in back copies of the *Edmonton Journal*, so she slipped the book out.

The sultry female depicted on the front shocked her. What a position to lie in – it was indecent! No wonder Donna had been upset. She read the summary of the story and the gushing praise of the New York critics, quoted on the jacket. Finally she turned the book over and read the brief notes about the author; and her deep unease of earlier that morning returned, but she crushed it down.

She read the first two pages and felt a blush rise from her palpitating bosom up her neck to suffuse her face. For heaven's sakes, did girls really do such things? Fancy the library allowing such a book on their shelves! She hastily returned it to its place, and in a state of some agitation went back to her car and sat there until she felt calm again.

She started the car with a jerk and hit the bumper of the car in front. Flustered, she reversed, and the groceries she had bought en route fell off the back seat and flopped to the floor. Damn that book! With painful care she eased the car out of its parking place and into the flow of traffic.

The cover said a high school boy. But what could a kid know about such goings-on as were chronicled in the pages she had read? What *did* a present-day high school boy know?

It came to her as a shock that, although she had an excellent opportunity to be acquainted with high school children through her son, she did not know any of his friends. With a burst of self-pity, she mentally reviled Hank for never talking to her or telling her what he was going to do. He never brought his friends to the house and she had never known where he spent his spare time. What *did* he do, other than ride around in his jalopy and sometimes help out in the supermarket?

As she manoeuvred the car through the traffic, the cold feeling which had menaced her earlier returned to plague her.

She tried to brush aside memories of the eager, tiny child that Hank had been, a child who had adored his ugly, heavy-footed Ukrainian grandfather, a child who had screamed with rage at her when she had thrust him into the arms of an unknown babysitter or had forced him to play alone in the basement, until he became a silent, morose schoolboy. Meanwhile, she had pursued personal aggrandizement at his expense, a whisper of conscience hinted, until he had learned that he was nothing but a nuisance to her.

The memories persisted, until she had worked herself into a peevish bout of self-pity, which was not improved by her discovery when she reached home that Hank had not shovelled the snow off the front walk before leaving for school. The snow would certainly invade the tops of her boots when she stepped out of the car, and she swore softly in Ruthenian as she retrieved the groceries from the floor of the car and turned to carry them into the house.

She had just slammed the car door by hooking it with one foot, when Mrs Frizzell, with a similar brown-paper bag of groceries, came round the nearest corner on foot, having been to the local store.

'Mornin', Olga,' she shouted as she scuttled towards her, a pair of rollers in the front of her hair sticking out like devil's horns from under her woollen hat. 'Where've you been?'

'Library,' said Mrs Stych shortly as she staggered through the snow towards her house.

Mrs Frizzell's face brightened. 'About the book?'

'Yeah,' replied Mrs Stych with an involuntary shudder. She suddenly recollected that she was now the wife of the director of a large company, and drew herself up with what she hoped was some dignity; but she only succeeded in looking more than ever like a pouter pigeon. 'Librarian had gone to coffee.'

'I'd like to know who wrote it,' said Mrs Frizzell wistfully.

Mrs Stych put her nose in the air, and said: 'We shall have the name in a day or two.'

Mrs Frizzell surveyed her neighbour speculatively. Olga seemed to be more patronizing than ever today. She was now looking round at both their houses distastefully, though the houses looked the same as usual, snow on the roofs, snow a foot deep over the yards, snow poised on every twig and leaf, a cloud from the central-heating chimney hovering calmly over each residence.

Mrs Stych had temporarily forgotten about Hank. 'I'll be glad to leave this house,' she said carefully.

Mrs Frizzell's nose quivered as she caught the scent of change.

'Leave it?'

'Yeah. Probably next fall. We're going to build in Vanier Heights.'

The effect of this announcement on Mrs Frizzell was all that Mrs Stych could have desired. The bounce went out of her as if she had burst. Envy sprang into her hard little eyes and gleamed maliciously. She stood rooted to the sidewalk, her mind a whirl of dislike. Vanier Heights? She could have cried. Why hadn't Maxie thought of building a new house there, the old stick in the mud?

She took two or three large breaths over the top of her bag of groceries, while Mrs Stych watched her stupefaction with complacency. She had, however, underestimated Donna Frizzell's powers of recovery. Between gritted teeth, Donna asked innocently: 'Isn't that a bit old-fashioned? We are thinking of buying a small estate outside the city, three or four acres, so that we could have a real nice ranch-type bungalow – and keep some riding horses.' The last was an inspired idea, a riding horse with an acreage to keep it on being quite a status symbol.

Mrs Stych licked her lips. 'Oh, no!' she drawled, determined not to be outdone, as she moved towards her front door. 'We wouldn't like to be far from town – we like culture – and horses smell so.'

Mrs Frizzell reminded herself that murder was not civilized.

Not trusting herself to speak, she right-wheeled and made for her own front door, which now looked hopelessly out of date and shabby. She would get to work on Maxie just as soon as his presence at home should coincide with hers; she had not seen him since returning from the tea, except when crawling wearily into bed.

'Let him just show his face,' she muttered darkly.

CHAPTER THIRTEEN

While his mother and Donna Frizzell sparred in front of their respective homes, Hank laboured in Isobel Dawson's garage. The day was overcast and it was becoming difficult to see what he was typing, so, about noon, when imagination began to fail him, he walked up to the house to inquire from Dorothy whether Isobel would mind if he had better lighting installed in the garage, provided he paid for it. The door was opened unexpectedly by Isobel herself. She was in a housedress and held a duster in her hand. She greeted Hank cheerily.

Hank looked nonplussed, and then asked, rather foolishly: 'Aren't you at work?'

'No. The boss went to Calgary and gave me the day off.' Hospitably, she opened the door wider. 'You'd better come in, it's cold out there.'

He entered gratefully. A strong smell of floor polish pervaded the house and the kitchen was in chaos, its furniture piled in the middle and a vacuum cleaner cord snaking round it to a hidden plug.

She apologized for the muddle and ushered him into the living-room. She gestured towards the chesterfield. 'Sit down. What can I do for you?'

He sat down, feeling somewhat shy in the midst of so much domestic activity, while she knelt and lit the gas fire. 'Canadians are always cold in this house,' she remarked in explanation. 'I don't keep it so hot as they keep theirs.

'Well?' she asked, as she got up off her knees.

Pretty legs, thought Hank, as he explained about the lighting in the garage.

Instead of giving the immediate agreement which he had expected, she said: 'Let's have some coffee. We'd better talk the whole thing over.'

Though he was a little surprised, he smiled and said with

alacrity that he could just use a cup of coffee, and he lounged after her as she bustled around the kitchen. She was unlike anybody else he had ever met and secretly he found her intriguing. Today, dressed like a housewife, she looked more human than usual, less distantly dignified. He wondered how he had found sufficient courage to ask her to the Edwardian Ball, and then remembered that it was her air of calm dignity which had made him anxious to take her to impress his parents.

'Where's Dorothy?' he asked.

'She's gone for a skiing lesson – she wants to learn before going home.' She wondered idly if Hank was interested in Dorothy, and the idea made her feel a little forlorn.

She lifted a cup and saucer in each hand, and he took one from her. His fingers touched hers and his heart gave a jolt, but she seemed perfectly in command of herself and had apparently felt nothing, so he told himself not to be a dope, and carried his coffee back to the chesterfield. He stirred it silently, as she settled herself in a rocking-chair opposite to him.

When he looked up at her, he found her regarding him with a troubled frown over the rim of her coffee cup. It seemed to him that in her gentle gaze there was more than a hint of despair, and it grieved him.

'The thing is,' she said, after a moment's hesitation, 'that I am going to sell this house.'

Hank nearly dropped his cup, as his brand-new writing world splintered into pieces around him. 'S-sell?' he stuttered.

'Yes,' she replied, her voice trembling a little. 'I'm going home.'

Hank was thoroughly disquieted. He was still young enough to feel that the present was permanent. Shut up in her garage, his work approved of and praised by her, comforted by Captain Dawson's and her advice, which had in all respects proved reliable, he had felt a safety and confidence unknown to him before. Even now that his father was aware of his activities, it would not be the same;

only she knew the appalling effort he had made, only she had read the manuscript through and appreciated the clarity of his prose and the honesty of his outlook. He had expected that any change in his routine would have been of his own making, not hers.

She was waiting for him to make some reply, and he said slowly: 'I guess you must be homesick, now Captain Dawson isn't here.'

'Well, yes. He wasn't here very much, as you know, but we were looking forward to the end of his army service and then we would have settled here.' She looked sober, and then added: 'I might as well go home – there's nothing to keep me here. My in-laws have other children, and it's always easier in one's own country.'

'I guess your parents will be glad to see you,' he remarked.

'They're dead. They were killed in an accident just before I was married – Peter was my father's friend.'

'Peter must have been a lot older than you?' ventured Hank.

She was not offended at the personal question, but her voice held a trace of surprise in it as she said: 'Yes, he was. He was at school with my father. You see, Father was actually born in Alberta – his parents came here from Wales – but when he was a young man he went back to visit, and fell in love with my mother and with Wales as well, and stayed there.' She smiled and ran her finger around the top of her coffee cup. 'Father always kept in touch with Peter and he planned to come and see us when he got leave from France, where he was stationed. As it turned out, he only came for the funeral.'

Hank was interested. He had heard of girls marrying a father substitute, but he had not met one before. He did not wish to make her unhappy by any further probing after such a flow of confidences, so he just asked her which city in England she came from, this being a question all immigrants were accustomed to.

'I don't come from England – I'm Welsh, from Caernarvon.'

He failed to realize the difference and his blank expression made her smile. 'Wales and the Welsh are quite different from England and the English,' she said. 'Being Welsh is a bit like – well, like being a French Canadian. I'm going back to my old employers in London, though.'

'I suppose I'd better find another garage,' he said rather hopelessly. Without asking if he could smoke, he quickly took out a cigarette and lit it, and then belatedly offered her one. She was amused at his blunder, but took one from him. He remembered to offer her a light.

He put his coffee cup down on a pile of English magazines, got up and stretched himself. His T-shirt was too small for him and came out of the waist of his pants. The pants themselves were too tight and too short, exhibiting a generous stretch of hairy legs. Isobel stifled a strong desire to laugh.

'I presume you're dressed for school,' she said.

He looked down at himself. 'Yep.'

'Does your mother know about the book yet?'

'No!' he snapped. 'Dad does.'

Isobel asked cautiously: 'Has he read it?'

'Jeepers, no. He don't even know what it's called. Never even asked me.'

He wandered towards the piano and very gently turned the picture of Captain Dawson face down on the top of the instrument. 'Goodbye, fella,' he muttered, but Isobel fortunately did not hear him.

'Do you think he'll mind that it is a rather controversial book?'

Hank sat down on the piano stool and struck a chord. 'It's too late to mind,' he said. 'He should have done a bit of minding years ago.'

'I think you ought to tell your mother.' Isobel's voice was almost imploring. 'She has a right to know, before anybody else tells her.'

Hank broke into the 'Cornish Rhapsody', playing with

112

such savagery that the little room was flooded with the storm of it. For the first time, Isobel felt a little afraid of him, as all the suppressed fury of a rejected child came pouring out in the music. She sat quietly, however, until the music found its way into calmer waters and then came to an end.

He spun round on the stool so that he could face her. 'Not bad, eh?' he asked, some of the tension gone from his face.

'You are very good,' she said, some of the nervousness receding from her. 'Do you practise much?'

'Most days. Used to practise in the school.' He grinned. 'That left the evenings free to go out, except near exam times.' It dawned on him that he had not had a date for weeks, and his first one would be with her at the Edwardian Ball. Must be going senile, he decided.

'Say,' he said, 'you'd better tell me more precisely about what I am to wear to this ball. We gotta make a hit – let 'em know we've arrived.'

Isobel's face looked suddenly young and animated. 'I'll get the book with the picture in it. I think it'll be fun. I haven't been to a ball since I came to Canada.'

Hank looked at her aghast. 'Honey,' he said, without thinking, 'it's time you started to live it up a bit.'

CHAPTER FOURTEEN

Boyd Stych, looking strangely civilized in a dark business suit and neatly clipped beard, was informed by his wife, when he came home, that the *Advent* was sending a photographer and a reporter to see him this evening and he was not to litter up the lounge – she'd just tidied it.

He grunted guardedly, as he heaved off his overshoes. Though he knew the press would be sending a photographer to take a picture of him for the financial pages of the newspaper, he suspected that their main interest was in Hank. It was not going to be possible to keep from Olga the information that her son had suddenly become quite a well-to-do youngster, though he had warned Hank on no account to tell her how much he had made out of his book. Boyd believed firmly that all women were incurably avaricious and was certain that, once Olga knew about the book, she would try to squeeze most of the proceeds of it out of Hank; and, to his credit, he was determined that this should not happen.

He dropped his briefcase on the chesterfield, and Mrs Stych snatched it up crossly and took it into his den, while he went to the refrigerator in search of ice cubes for a drink. Should he talk to her now, he wondered, or let Hank do it?

'Where's the rye?' he shouted.

'In the bar in the basement – where else?' came the sharp reply.

He went downstairs to the rumpus room and rummaged behind the tiny bar, and, after digging through a seemingly endless collection of empty pop bottles, came up with half a bottle of rye and some ginger ale. He felt he needed a drink – this could be quite a trying evening. Perhaps it was fortunate that he had no inkling of how trying it was going to be.

As he took an eager gulp from his glass, he decided that

Hank ought to tell his mother what he had been doing. He rationalized his cowardice by telling himself that, after all, it was Hank's headache, not his.

He wondered idly what sort of tripe Hank had written. Some sort of adventure story, he supposed, which would film well. He must ask him.

Hank drifted silently in through the back door and deposited a pile of school books on the kitchen table and a fair amount of snow on the kitchen floor from his moccasins. He quickly got a corn broom, went out to the back porch again and brushed his footwear clean; then he used the same broom to sweep the snow from the kitchen floor into a safe hiding-place under a scatter rug. No point in drawing fire, he argued, as he put the broom back into the closet.

As he took up his school books again and moved them into his bedroom, he wondered if his father had told his mother about his leaving school. Boyd had not promised to do this, though he had said he would go to see the principal to straighten out the question of his leaving. This promised visit to the school, mused Hank, would be his father's first since he had graduated from it twenty-five years earlier. He had had to ask Hank the name of the principal and what courses he had been taking, since he had never bothered to inquire about these before. So much for parental interest in education, Hank muttered.

He went to the hall table, where the postman usually desposited any mail, in the hope that there might be a letter for him, though most of his mail came via Isobel. He was agreeably surprised to find one from a friend who had joined the Mounties a couple of years previously. It was full of amusing anecdotes about his life as a policeman. For the first time, Hank did not feel a pang of envy at his friend's being already at work; he felt he was doing better than any young policeman could hope to do.

Olga heard him singing in the bathroom and shouted that supper would be ready in a few minutes.

'Put a clean shirt on and comb your hair,' she called.

'Somebody's coming this evening from the *Advent* to see your father.'

Hank stopped singing in mid-bar. Almost certainly, they'd be coming to see him, too. Jeeze, the balloon was about to go up!

'D'yer hear me, Hank?'

'Yeah, Ma.' And he began to hum a funeral march.

The terrible bitterness against his parents that had led to his writing a book meant to shock them had faded into indifference; yet there lingered in him an understandable vindictiveness. He knew he would be happy if, in some way, it taught his mother a salutary lesson, but he could still quail, like a little boy, in anticipation of the violence of her wrath.

At dinner, the hastily prepared steak was tough and Boyd complained about it. Next time Olga bought steak, he said, he would cook it.

Olga Stych was immediately biting about men who dressed up in aprons and fancy hats, and thought they could cook over a smelly barbecue.

'I suppose all the months I was up North you reckoned I had a chef along with me,' snarled Boyd.

Hank hastily finished the store-bought cake which followed the steak, and went to his room. He thought he might as well look over his skiing equipment, instead of listening to his parents snapping at each other. If his mother was already as irritated as she sounded, he decided that the evening would be full of squalls.

He sat down on his bed while he threaded new laces into his boots, and then paused, one lace suspended in his hand, as he wondered suddenly why the wire service had not given the *Advent* any news about him. Then he realized that any such news would be about 'Ben MacLean' and that they would not connect it with him. He chuckled to himself. Probably the paper didn't even have wire service, and if it did, he'd bet a dime that anything which had come in about the book's author had simply been buried in the chaos then reigning in the newspaper office.

The *Advent* had survived for years with a staff of four, plus occasional help from the owner's wife with the reporting of weddings and similar social occasions. Its circulation had grown enormously as immigrants flooded into Tollemarche, and it had expanded into the shops which flanked it on either side. Now, new offices were being built for it on the other side of the road, but they were not quite ready, and meantime, the new publisher from the East and his editors functioned in an atmosphere of such utter confusion that it is doubtful if an efficiency expert could even have fought his way in through the door. Donny O'Brien, the ancient typesetter inherited from the original *Advent*, swore each day that it was only by the grace of God that the paper ever got launched in the taxi which delivered it to the newspaper boys.

Only the queen of the social columns, recruited a couple of years previously from Calgary, sat calmly at her desk, her silver-tipped fingers delicately feeling the pulse of the city's social life. Other editors might make a slip, but let her so much as spell a name wrong and her telephone would blare, and some outraged lady would correct her with withering sarcasm.

She was delighted when the story of Hank fell into her lap; an interview with his mother would fill half a column nicely. Her pleasure was, however, short lived. Like all good stories unearthed by such lady editors, it was snatched away from her, and, barring wars and acts of God, as Donny O'Brien reported to Mr Pascall, the bookseller, it would be a front-page headline on Monday. It was, therefore, no quiet lady columnist to whom Mrs Stych opened the door that evening, but an eager male reporter keen on a front-page story.

He shot through the door almost as soon as it was opened, closely followed by a small, bald-headed individual carrying what looked like a suitcase.

'Hank Stych!' he hailed a startled Boyd, who had half risen from an easy chair, scattering the papers on which he had been working. He wrung Boyd's hand. 'Say, this is great for Tollemarche – really put us on the map.' Then, turning to his companion, he said: 'Pose him against these drapes, Tom.'

Tom hastily opened his case, took out a tripod and set his camera up in the middle of the lounge, while Mrs Stych watched, open-mouthed. Neither visitor had taken the slightest notice of her.

The reporter was saying to Boyd: 'Say, let's have a picture with you reading the manuscript.'

Mrs Stych felt a sudden constriction in her stomach.

The reporter consulted his notes. 'We hafta have a picture of a Mr Boyd Stych as well.'

Tom nodded agreement, and went on rapidly assembling his camera.

Boyd found his voice. 'I'm Boyd Stych.'

The reporter looked up quickly, took in the fact that Boyd's Edwardian Days beard was streaked with grey, and said: 'Say, I am sorry. I sure thought there was a writer hidden behind that beard of yours.'

Boyd hastily bent down to rescue his papers from being trampled. 'The beard is for Edwardian Days,' he said primly.

'Oh, sure, it's a beaut. All ready for tomorrow, eh? You just might win the prize for the best one, at that,' the reporter replied, fingering his own scanty side whiskers.

Mrs Stych listened to this conversation with slowly growing horror. The cold feeling she had experienced that morning crept over her; she remembered the library book, and, with a feeling of panic, recollected Hank's trip to New York. Behind them, she envisaged the faces of the Committee for the Preservation of Morals, as she had last seen them, glistening with almost sadistic anticipation of the crushing of the young author and of giving Mr Pascall and the cigar-store merchants their proper comeuppances.

'I think I'm going to vomit,' she muttered to no one in particular, and sat down with a plop on a new imitation Italian chair, which received her with a reedy groan.

Boyd was calling up the stairs for Hank to come down,

and she watched silently, as if at the movies, while he emerged from his ground-floor bedroom, walked past her without looking at her, and held out his hand to the reporter, who winced as he felt its grip.

'Hi,' said the reporter, wondering if his hand would ever recover.

'Hi,' said Hank. He stared with some scorn at his would-be interviewers, who were some inches shorter than he was. He seemed to fill the room with his contempt for the people present.

'Say, that sure was some book you wrote,' remarked the reporter, to fill the silence. 'Haven't read it myself yet, but I'll get around to it – I sure will.'

Hank's expression was cynical, as he gestured to the man to be seated.

Mrs Stych was thankful for the chair under her, as she felt the colour drain from her face. The lounge rocked in front of her. How could he write such things? she wondered dumbly; how could he know so much about sex, so much about sin? Sin was sex; pride, avarice, gluttony had no place as far as her life was concerned. Only sex was really wrong, only fallen women really burned.

Out of the corner of his eye, Hank could see her stricken face. He felt no pity. When had she ever shown him pity? This was really going to rock her and it would do her good.

'Yes,' he told the reporter, it's called *The Cheaper Sex*.' In response to a further query, he added irritably: 'Sure it's about sex – what else would it be about with a title like that?'

The reporter said soothingly that their reviewer, Professor Shrimp, had given it a lotta praise, and the review would probably be in the arts section, next to the film shows, on Monday.

Mrs Stych whimpered softly and the reporter glanced at her curiously. Queer old bag. What did she think of it?

Mentally, Mrs Stych felt as if she were writhing in her death agonies. The Subcommittee appointed by the Morals girls! How could she face it? And worse, how was she going to face the whole organization when it met? Some of the

Morals group were also Queen Bees, some were Daughters of Scotland and strict Presbyterians; the United Church itself – how could she attend it now? It would be all over town that her son wrote pornography. She would never, never, she cried inwardly, as she clutched her handkerchief to her mouth, be able to face the girls again.

Boyd was surprised at the name of his son's book, but, unlike his wife, he had not read any of it, and he supposed that Hank had deliberately chosen a titillating title to help sales. He, therefore, continued a subdued conversation with the photographer, not feeling it in the least necessary to introduce his wife to either visitor.

The reporter snapped a rubber band over his notebook, told Hank he would have rung him about the details of the book but he had not been able to get through. Hank said that was O.K., and the photographer surged forward. The photographs were taken, while Mrs Stych leaned back in her chair, her eyes closed, and chewed her handkerchief savagely; and the camera was quickly returned to its case.

'Must be proud of Hank and Boyd,' said the reporter, pausing on his way to the front door to speak to Mrs Stych for the first time.

Mrs Stych opened her eyes slowly and looked at him as if he had gone mad. Then, with a great effort, she managed to nod her head in vague agreement.

Proud? Mrs Stych wrung her hands behind the reporter's back, and wished passionately she could run home to Mother on the pig farm; she longed suddenly for the smell of hens and milk, for a place where nobody had to keep up appearances or be other than what they were. Why had she ever come to town to get herself an education? Why had she married a dirty type like Boyd, to spawn a boy like Hank, who had never been anything but a damned nuisance to her?

She glared at Hank as he stood by the front door ready to open it for the paper's representatives, and tried not to scream while these gentlemen put on their boots again.

In twenty seconds more they were gone, to the sound of

spinning wheels on the ice and grinding gears. And she was left with the shattered remains of all that she had found dear in her life, and two extraordinarily sheepish-looking men.

She suddenly regained the initiative of which shock had left her temporarily bereft, and shot from her chair like a well-punted football. Arms akimbo, her face still white under her heavy makeup, she snarled: 'Will one of you please explain what's been going on behind my back?'

The silence was painful.

She rounded on Hank and screamed: 'You great, dirty slob – wotcha done?'

CHAPTER FIFTEEN

When Boyd was a child of eight, he and his father had had to sit out a tornado while visiting a German friend who had settled in Kansas. Boyd was reminded of the howling noise of that fearful storm by his wife's tantrum.

He and Hank were upbraided, reviled and screamed at, until, without uttering a word in retaliation, Hank took his jacket out of the hall alcove and strode silently out of the front door, followed by a shriek from his mother that he was as disgusting as his father; like father, like son.

Gone to his widow, ruminated Boyd enviously, and wished he had a friendly widow, too.

It had taken him only a few moments to discover, from his wife's tirade, that Hank's book was not quite so innocent as he had imagined; however, any book that made so much money was a good book, in his opinion, and he had defended Hank hotly.

Hank had made no attempt to defend himself. He had stood quietly swaying himself on his heels, an almost derisive expression in the curl of his lips as he smoked a cigarette, his very silence provoking her to further abuse.

He used to do that when he was small, remembered Boyd; it had been unnerving, wondering what he was thinking about while you shouted at him. He had never cried when he was struck, and Boyd felt with a desolate pang that probably the boy was wiser and braver than he was. It was only too apparent, as Olga tore into him about the disgrace she would suffer, that, like a hippie, he cared nothing for the kind of life his parents led; he did not share their values or ambitions. His quiet retreat through the front door had somehow emphasized his scorn.

The crack about his being disgusting like his father, had hurt Boyd. It was apparent from his wife's continuing rampage that much pent-up animosity against her husband was coming out, and the crash of a glass ornament warned him that there was probably more to come.

He knew that she had not enjoyed his homecoming or the renewal of a sexual life; throughout their married life he had been at home for only a few weeks at a time, and she had been free to make her life as she chose. She had chosen, he reflected aggrievedly, to ignore him as far as possible.

The directorship, for which he had struggled for years, represented to her only a house in Vanier Heights. Didn't he or Hank matter to her at all? He stroked his beard and then scratched irritably through it. He knew the answers to his questions very well; all too many men were relegated to the position of drone – and they resented it; they showed their resentment all too often by despising women and taking the attitude that such inept creatures should be allowed to play while men ran the world and did anything in it which was worth doing. He had taken this attitude himself, but was finding it very uncomfortable to maintain, after his long years of quiet in the bush, untroubled by anything worse than wind or weather. He laughed ruefully and his wife whipped round at him.

'You laughing at me?' she demanded belligerently.

He looked up at her, as she swooped towards him like a sparrow hawk. Her face was distorted with rage, a horrible clown's face painted red and white, her body a red tub supported by nyloned legs.

He jumped up and shouted at her sharply: 'Oh, shut up!'

'I won't!' she yelled.

He slapped her soundly across the face twice.

She shrieked at the sting of the blows, which left a red mark down one side of her face. Then she was silent, staring at him with horrified eyes. He had never struck her before. The horror gave way slowly to self-pity, the blue eyes filled with tears and she began to weep, the tears making runnels down her heavy makeup.

'For Pete's sake!' he muttered moodily, and shoved his hands in his pockets and went to stare into the empty fireplace.

'You don't understand,' she sobbed. 'You never did understand anything.' She fumbled feverishly in a fancy box on the table for a paper handkerchief. 'How I am going to face the girls at the ball tomorrow? It's all right for a man; men are used to smutty books and vulgar jokes – women don't go for things like that.'

She collapsed on the chesterfield and tried to bury her face in one of the stony little cushions that decorated it.

Boyd frowned down on her. 'Don't you tell me that! Bet that Pascall sells more of Hank's book to women than he ever will to men.'

He hoped that he was right in this belief. For the first time, he considered seriously his own situation with regard to his son's career, both present and future, and he felt uneasy. He could visualize the sniggers of his subordinates. A new director, responsible for a large section of the company's business for the first time, was not in a particularly enviable position; there were men equally as bright and considerably younger, poised ready to pull the mat from under him as soon as they saw an opportunity; Hank could be their chance. He picked up the piece of ornamental driftwood from the mantelpiece and tried to stand it upside down, while he considered this, and his wife's sobs slowly diminished. He felt miserably lonely.

He became aware that Olga was quiet at last, exhausted beyond words. He turned and looked down at her.

Her face was still turned into the cushion, her dress twisted tightly round her generous curves, the skirt hitched up and exposing her plump, well-shaped legs. He smiled suddenly at her tiny feet encased in shiny, high-heeled pumps. Olga had always loved clothes, and he wondered for whose benefit she dressed; probably for that godforsaken bunch of old hags, the girls. His face clouded again at the thought. This was not the way he had hoped life would be when he had married her. He had believed that a country girl like her would find him wonderful, a college man with great ambitions. Their life was going to be different from those of the married couples around them, he had promised himself.

He wanted badly to creep into her arms and be told he had done marvellously well, that she had put on her red dress and her new pumps specially for him, for his seduction. His loneliness, far worse than anything suffered in the empty north country, overwhelmed him and became intolerable.

He took a hesitant step towards the chesterfield. She did not move, though she must have heard him, so he sat down tentatively beside her. She whimpered and wriggled further into the chesterfield's cushiony depths. If he was to get anywhere, he told himself reluctantly, he would have to do the comforting.

'What are you going to wear tomorrow night?' he asked, with a burst of sheer genius.

She slowly looked round at him, her eyes wide with surprise and doubt, the wretched book forgotten. 'Oh, Boyd,' she breathed, 'just wait till you see it!'

He half turned and put his arm round her recumbent form.

'Is it real pretty?'

'Yeah,' she sighed, still eyeing him distrustfully, 'it's real nice.'

Boyd began to feel better and not a little smug. It was just like the books said – all a man needed was a good technique. He let his hand wander a little, and got it petulantly pushed away as she heaved herself out of the clutches of the chesterfield's upholstery, and sat up on the edge of it. Her face was still sulky and she still sniffed occasionally as she put her feet to the ground.

Patiently, he tried another tack: 'Like a snack?' he asked.

Something of the sulkiness vanished and she wiggled her feet down more firmly into her shoes. There was a suggestion of enthusiasm in her voice when she replied: 'Yeah. I would.'

She rose and tottered, like a child still uncertain of its balance, to the refrigerator and swung open its massive door. Merely viewing its contents made her feel better. A barbecued chicken and a ham, both provided ready to serve by the local supermarket, made her mouth water. She opened the small freezer at the top, and four different types of ice cream, some frozen cream cakes and some ready-to-bake cookie mixes promised further consolation.

Boyd followed her out and, without being told, put some coffee on to percolate. He also got out rye bread and mustard. She always wanted the same things after a fight – ham on rye with mustard, followed by vanilla ice cream with walnut topping, a large slab of cake and coffee. Well topped up with these, thought Boyd as he hunted for the bread knife, she would be in a much more amicable mood, and then he might get somewhere with her.

CHAPTER SIXTEEN

Hank breathed with relief the icy, sweet air outside his parents' house. The night was beautiful, with a clean-swept sky filled with newly polished stars. Low on the skyline, just above the housetops, a red glow marked the reflection of neon signs in the centre of the city and he could hear the steady roar of traffic crossing the old river bridge towards it. The road in which he stood was, however, deserted, its avenue of leafless trees eerily quiet under the high street lamps. His mother's voice came faintly to him through the double doors of the house. He pitied his father, though he knew him to be physically and mentally tough and well able to take care of himself.

He stood shivering on the step, uncertain what to do. He smiled wryly to himself. *The Cheaper Sex* had already done very well what he had originally intended it to do – draw his parents' attention to his existence. It was obvious that during the next few weeks they were going to waste a lot of their valuable time thinking about him. But now he was older he did not care very much whether they were interested or not. He was far more concerned with consolidating his new-born reputation as a writer by producing another book of equal merit as fast as he could. He knew that, like a canoeist, he must ride the current while he could, finding a way through the rapids of life and somehow transforming his experiences into a story that rang with the honesty of his first book. Standing in the cold in front of the house, he realized suddenly that this was his ambition, to mirror life truly, so that people laughed when they saw their own image through his eyes.

His ears were getting numb, warning of frostbite, and he clapped his hands over them. He could not go far without mittens or earmuffs. His first idea on coming out had been to go and see Isobel and Dorothy, and then he had been overcome by unaccustomed shyness. Now he decided he would go and get the car out and possibly call on his old friend, Ian MacDonald, now in his second year at the university; it seemed a long time since they had so light-heartedly rebuilt his jalopy in Isobel's garage.

He stuffed his hands into his pockets and, to keep himself warm, jogged the short distance to the garage.

The curtains had not been drawn over the back windows of Isobel's house, and he stood looking into the lighted rooms for a moment before unlocking the garage door. He chuckled as he saw Dorothy in her bedroom carefully pressing her hair to a fashionable straightness, on the ironing board with the electric iron; her contortions in an effort to reach up as far as possible were as complex as those of a cat trying to reach its middle back. Two students were seated in the kitchen, drinking coffee and laughing over some joke. He waited, hoping to see Isobel, but she must have been in the front of the house. Finally, he unlocked the garage and went in.

The white Triumph, its hood up, awaited his command; the gas stove in the corner roared in its usual muffled fashion. The typewriter on the desk seemed to float like an iceberg in a sea of paper, but he felt too tired to work. He opened the doors of the garage and then got into the car preparatory to backing it out. He sat for a moment, however, slumped in the driver's seat with the ignition key in his hand and no lights switched on, while he went over his mother's bitter words.

His fatigue was overwhelming. He told himself ruefully that too much had happened to him in the previous few weeks. He felt as if he had been blasted, in that time, right out of boyhood into manhood, as if he had been called up for the army and sent to war. And he had not done badly, he felt, especially as he had had to manage in New York without a lawyer or an agent to help him. 'You had nothing to lose but your chains,' he muttered and laughed a little.

What should he do in the immediate future? he asked himself.

Home was becoming untenable, but he dismissed the idea of taking an apartment on his own; living with his mother had been lonely enough. He toyed with the idea of going to stay with Grandmother Palichuk and his uncle, then realized that, once they understood the tenor of his writings, they would try to persuade him not to produce another book. And the new book was growing healthily; soon he would like Isobel to read it, and confirm his opinion that it was as good as his first one, or better.

Isobel! He swung the key ring fretfully round on his finger. Hell! Isobel was going home to that weirdo place in the U.K. from which she came. It struck him suddenly that he did not know how he was going to live without her. He stared blankly through the windshield at his piled-up desk. He knew that even if he had been able to finish his first book, he would never have had the courage to submit it to a publisher; the only other person to whom he might have turned for advice, Mr Dixon, the English teacher, would never have condoned its content. Captain Dawson was gone, and now Isobel was going. He heaved his huge shoulders against the seat back as he considered, rather hopelessly, the emptiness of his life in the near future.

He told himself not to be a fool. He had friends like John MacDonald, Ian's cousin, who was still plodding through high school, and Ian himself, of course; and there was Brett Hill, who had left school to become a flower child and now lived in comfortable squalor in a hut by the river, spending most of his life in a haze of marihuana. The majority of the boys with whom he had gone through school had left last year, and had been either at work or in university for some months past. He had got left behind to do this crazy Grade 12 again, left in a limbo of those really too old for school, too unqualified for work.

God, what a world!

Well, he did not have John's sticking power or Brett's enjoyment of drugs. What he wanted was to work amongst men, strong-minded men who knew where they were going, like his publishers in New York. My, they were tough, but so had he managed to be. All he needed was experience, he decided, and to get out of this goddam town, away from nagging schoolmarms, hysterical mothers and browbeaten fathers. He could try getting a job with a newspaper or magazine in Toronto or, maybe, Montreal – his French could be worse. He could afford to start at the bottom and do anything, just anything to enable him to be an adult.

Tomorrow he would go into action. And tomorrow he was certainly going to attend the ball with Isobel. His first intention had been simply to spite his mother by showing her that he could circulate alone in her world; now he wanted to give Isobel a good time. It would give him, he realized, great satisfaction to show her off in that old cats' paradise. Do her good to have a whirl for once; being Peter Dawson's wife must have been pretty boring and being a widow must be even worse.

As he turned on the car lights, the side door of the garage opened and Isobel entered carrying a table lamp.

He rolled down the car window, and she said, with surprise: 'Hello, I didn't expect to find you here.' Then she lifted the lamp to give him a better view of it. 'Do you think this would give you a better working light?'

'It'll do just fine,' he said. 'Thanks a lot.'

She put the lamp down on the desk, after carefully clearing a space amongst the papers. She wrapped her cardigan closely round her: she was shivering. 'Gosh, it's cold in here.'

Her voice quavered with the chill, and he opened the car door. 'Get in,' he said. 'You'll freeze.'

'It's O.K. Just came with the lamp. I must go back to the house.'

'Aw, come on,' he wheedled, 'stay a minute. I wanna ask you sumpin'.' He looked so like a small boy asking a favour that she complied, easing herself round the car to the opposite side and climbing in, her teeth chattering. He leaned over her and shut the door and rolled up the window. She looked very small and frail beside his huge bulk, and he heaved a rug from the back of the car and cautiously tucked it round her, then turned on the car heater and the headlights.

'That better?' he asked.

Her smile was impish above the plaid blanket as she nodded.

They were very close together in the tiny car, and Hank found himself unexpectedly scared. He was not sure what kind of behaviour she would expect from him, and hastily advised himself to play it cool, even if she was insulted because he made no advances to her. For her part, Isobel had been used, like most English women, to working in close proximity to men, and had crawled in beside him with as much thought as if he were a child of ten. Now, with the warmth of his body slowly penetrating the blanket and his face turned towards her so that he could see her, she was not so sure of herself. His face, in the faint light penetrating the interior of the car from the garage's ceiling light, looked sad, like the faces of Red Indians who hung about the centre of the town; they, too, had a Mongolian cast of feature, and the hardness of their lives gave them an air of grim melancholy. Her eyes moved compassionately over his face; he had their quiet dignity, too, she ruminated, in spite of his hunched-up carriage.

His heart was beating like a tomtom, but he asked her with a grin: 'What you thinking about?'

The golden eyelashes immediately came down to veil her eyes, and when she opened them again, she was her usual quiet, distant self. 'Tomorrow's dinner,' she said flippantly.

'You're having it with me,' he reminded her.

Her eyes twinkled. 'So I am,' she said. 'That will be very nice – though I don't know what my in-laws will think of me, gallivanting round the town.'

'Let 'em rot,' said Hank with heat. 'You can't stay locked up all your life.' Then, to change the subject, he asked: 'What do you think of my beard?' He fingered the wild scrub which, like most Tollemarche men, he had been nursing along for the past ten days.

'It looks ghastly,' said Isobel frankly. 'Perhaps the barber, when he does your hair for the ball, could trim it into some sort of naval shape – show him the picture I gave you of the man you are supposed to be. I think, if you add an artificial moustache, it would help.'

Hank felt deflated. He was proud of the amount of beard he had been able to cultivate in so short a time. Isobel sensed this, and said comfortingly: 'I am sure the barber could make a beautiful job out of it.'

He sighed with mock resignation: 'O.K., I'll go see him. I have to have an English-style haircut anyway.'

Her eager face with its small, pointed chin was turned up towards him. Could a widow be so innocent as to expect him to be unmoved when she was so close to him that he could smell her perfume? he wondered. Sure, he was scared of her, but that was because he did not want to offend her; it did not stop him wanting to kiss her.

His sudden silence bothered Isobel. She asked: 'What did you want to ask me?'

'Waal, I wanted to ask you sumpin' – and, oh yeah, I wanted to tell you sumpin', too.' His Canadian accent sounded to her almost like a Midwest American accent, and yet it had small nuances of sound that made it different. Although Alberta was too young to have acquired an accent of its own, its beginnings could be detected among those born in the province – a certain harshness of voice, a certain slowness of articulation not unpleasant to the ear, which mirrored the calm doggedness of people used to living in a climate which would daunt the bravest at times.

'You did?' Isobel's voice was gently encouraging.

'Yeah, the *Advent* sent a man tonight to see me – and Ma nearly hit the roof.' He chuckled. 'She'd read a bit of my book somewhere, when she didn't know I had written it – and she sure was mad at me!'

He produced two crumpled cigarettes out of the change pocket in the front of his jeans, and handed her one. He leaned over her and lit it with a lighter retrieved from the same pocket. For a moment after the cigarette was alight he held the flaming lighter still before her face, examining her with doubting, narrowed black eyes. She regarded him steadily through the flame, her expression anticipatory, waiting to hear what he had to say. Her calmness irritated him, and he snapped the lighter shut and slumped back into his seat again.

A little sulkily, he went on: 'When we go to the Pre-Edwardian Supper tomorrow, you know it's O.K. to wear your costume? People wander round town all week in bustles and fancy waistcoats – and they will all next week.'

'Thanks, I intended to do so. The town really looked Edwardian when I was down there this morning – all trailing skirts, bonnets and beards.' She stopped and then said shyly: 'Are you quite sure you want to take me? I – I – er – I'm a bit older than you are, you know.'

'Waddya mean? What's age got to do with it? I've asked you, haven't I?' The black brows knitted together, and Isobel was amused to see something of Mrs Stych's well-known hot temper flash out of his eyes. 'I want *you!*' he added passionately.

She was pleased, and said: 'Well, thank you. I would enjoy it very much. My brother-in-law expects to be at the ball – he was a bit shaken when I said I thought I would be going – he wasn't very keen about it.' She hesitated and twirled the wedding ring on her finger. 'You know, this will be the first time I have been anywhere, except to work, since – since Peter was killed.' Her voice failed her.

A twinge of jealousy ripped through him, but he managed to address her very gently while he stared through the windshield, his whole body tensed as he hoped that she would not change her mind.

'Oh, yeah. I forgot that – I guess you haven't. If you feel you shouldn't come, it's O.K. by me.' He turned towards her and said earnestly: 'I can understand about it.' Inside, he was promising himself furiously that if the old biddies at the ball said anything to hurt her, he'd kill them, just kill them.

Her gratitude showed in her face. 'Thank you, Hank, you're a dear. I do want to come.' She stopped, feeling that

133

this was a turning-point in her widowhood, a modest launching into a new life, a point which had to be reached sooner or later. She had not expected that the invitation to the ball would include dinner with Hank, but she told herself firmly that Peter had no need to be jealous, and then added, with sudden insight, that whatever feelings she might have for Hank were immaterial, since she was so much older than he was. That Hank might have any feeling other than gratitude to her did not suggest itself to her.

In the quietness that followed, Hank wondered how she could possibly look so beautiful when she had no makeup on and her hair was scraped back in an unfashionable ponytail. 'You must get pretty lonely,' he said suddenly.

She jumped, and recollected that she should have returned to the house long before. She smiled at him. 'Sometimes I do, though Dorothy has been so good and helpful since she has been here.'

'Well,' he said determinedly, 'we'll have fun tomorrow – it's a promise.'

'Fine,' she replied, as she started to open the door. 'By the way, what time shall I be ready?'

To have his convenience considered by a woman was a shock to him. He managed, however, to say quite casually: 'I'll pick you up about seven. O.K.?'

'Yes, I'll be ready. Bye-bye.' She slipped out of the car, closed the door carefully, and, with a wave of her hand, left him.

Only when she had gone did he remember that she had made no comment about his mother's behaviour, and this seemed to put the occurrences of the early part of the evening into better perspective for him; they were really not worth talking about.

Dreamily, he switched on the ignition and backed out of the garage. An indignant hoot warned him that he had nearly hit another car moving down the back lane, and this brought him back to reality. His fatigue and depression had almost vanished, and he drove off happily in search of a barbershop, outside the town itself, which would probably still be open.

CHAPTER SEVENTEEN

The sky was overcast and the wind moaned softly through the bungalow-lined streets, as Hank brought the Triumph round to Isobel's front door at seven o'clock the following evening. He remembered, from a lesson he had had at school called 'Making the Best of Oneself', that it was bad manners to toot his horn to call a girl from her house, so he squeezed himself carefully out of the driver's seat, giving a sharp yelp when he caught his fingers on a collection of brooches pinned to a wide ribbon strung over one shoulder of his evening suit and tied at his side, and went up the wooden steps to ring the doorbell. He had not bothered to wear an overcoat, despite the cold weather, but he did have overshoes on, and they stuck out quaintly from under his immaculately pressed black trousers. In his hand he held a florist's box, and while he waited for the door to be answered, he pressed more firmly to his upper lip a grey moustache of generous size.

Dorothy came to the door, and did not immediately recognize him. Then she said: 'Good heavens! Come in. Isobel is nearly ready.'

Isobel was in the living-room, having a five-tier imitation pearl necklace clasped round her neck by one of her student boarders, who started to giggle when she saw Hank.

Hank had eyes for no one but Isobel.

'Do I look that bad?' she demanded, as he stared at her.

'No,' his voice was enthusiastic. 'I should say not! You look the real goods.'

Her waist had been firmly laced in to give her a correct Edwardian hourglass figure, and her tiny bosom pushed up. A discreet amount of padding at the rear gave her a Grecian bend of charming proportions.

She laughed, while Dorothy handed her a borrowed fur

coat to put over her shoulders. 'I think you look very nice, too,' she said shyly. The barber had cut his beard in British navy fashion, and he looked so English in spite of his Slavonic cast of feature that she felt suddenly as if he were a fellow countryman, and her behaviour became more relaxed in consequence.

Hank handed her the florist's box. It was opened and all three girls admired the Victorian posy of tiny roses which it contained, while Isobel worried privately that he was going to too much expense on her behalf.

Dorothy helped her down to the car, so that she would not spoil her train or silver slippers in the snow, and then stood a little forlornly at the door watching them drive away. She had an uneasy premonition that one or other of the couple was going to be hurt; not even Peter had ever looked at Isobel, as far as she knew, the way Hank had looked at her when he came into the living-room.

The snow had been cleared from the front of the Palace Hotel and a red carpet laid across the sidewalk to the main door. It was a popular place for dining, and cars of every description were drawing up before it to deposit ladies, and then being driven round to the parking lot at the back of the building. Hank did the same for Isobel.

She did not, of course, know any of the ladies standing waiting for the return of their escorts, since she had never moved in Tollemarche's fashionable circles. She let down the train of her dress, however, and, holding her gorgeous nosegay, swept regally through the door of the hotel into the palm-decorated foyer, the commissionaire having opened the doors for her.

Though a few people in the foyer were wearing cocktail dresses or lounge suits and there was a sprinkling of plaid shirts and cowboy hats, most people were clad in elaborate Edwardian evening ensembles. Isobel could not help marvelling at the amount of money and attention to detail lavished on these clothes. But her own costume also caused a stir, and it was apparent from the amused look on the other patrons' faces that the character she had tried to create was recognized. She was pleased, because the dress had been concocted out of three old wedding gowns bought from second-hand clothes shops – or, rather, economy shops, as they were called in Alberta.

Hank arrived quicker than she had hoped, having done a fast sprint round the building. He had shed his overshoes and looked very distinguished. His appearance beside her caused a burst of laughter, and two cowboys, already merrily drunk, clapped and roared appreciation.

When the restaurant's hostess had dealt with Hank's request for a table for this busy evening, she had at first said she did not have one available, implying by her lofty manner that the hotel did not cater to shaggy teenagers. Hank had been determined, however, and she had finally promised one, mentally seating them in an ugly corner by the service door. The old Chinese who owned the hotel, however, had that morning gone through the list of his prospective patrons, as he always did, and had recognized Hank's name. Mr Li probably knew more about the residents of Tollemarche and their visitors than anyone else, and he had seen Hank's real name given in the columns of the *New York Times*. Here, in his opinion, was a local celebrity, and his hostess was surprised when he carefully rearranged the parties she had booked, so that Hank was at a very good table where everyone could see him; Mr Li wanted to make a regular customer of such a successful young man.

Hank was jubilant at being placed where they could see and be seen, and were not deafened by the orchestra. Only three tables away, the Mayor was entertaining a noisy party of out-of-town guests, with a flustered Mrs Murphy trying to keep the horseplay within bounds. Further down the room, the MacDonalds' oil refinery group were ordering a dinner of the more unusual Chinese dishes and casting occasional supercilious glances at their more rowdy fellow townsmen. Several gentlemen ogled Isobel, much to her amusement and Hank's annoyance. Hank was immensely proud of her, and he dredged up for her benefit everything he had ever heard or seen about good manners when escorting a lady – all the half-digested columns of Ann Landers, the dancing lessons of the physical education teacher at school, the behaviour of the New Yorkers whom he had observed with his usual concentration, came to his aid.

Isobel, though pleased, was surprised. Hank's behaviour to her had always been good by Tollemarche standards, but she had not hoped for such courtesy in more sophisticated surroundings. She set out to entertain and amuse him, and readily chose a dinner so that he was spared the agony of coping unaided with a menu, which though written in English, was enormously long; and he was able to say that he would have the same as she did. The problem of wines did not arise, since many restaurants were not then licensed in Alberta, so he did not have to admit that he was under age and could not drink.

While they were waiting for their steaks, she asked: 'Did your parents know you were going to the ball?'

'No.'

She was mystified. 'Why not? How on earth did you conceal the fact?'

He shifted his water glass around uneasily and did not answer her first question. 'Waal,' he said, 'you know I got my haircut real late last night – and I haven't seen them since.'

Her puzzlement deepened and was apparent from her expression. He explained: 'I came out early, before they were up, and didn't go home for lunch. I picked up my suit from the cleaners, and while I was dressing Ma was out – and Dad hadn't got back from the Holyrood Club.'

She was really bewildered now. 'But wouldn't your mother want to know if you had lunch all right, and what you were going to do this evening while she and Mr Stych were at the ball?'

'You nuts?' The tone was incredulous. 'Heck, no! Got my own lunch. They'd think I was going to the Town Square Hop for teens I guess.'

138

Isobel smiled up at the waiter as he placed her steak before her. 'It doesn't sound very friendly to me,' she said flatly, when the man had gone.

Hank impaled his steak on his fork; it was still sizzling from the charcoal fire on which it had been cooked. While he cut into it he grinned at her from under his false moustache. 'Friendly?' he queried. 'Is anyone friendly with their parents?'

'I was.'

He was sobered, and began to eat. He had actually had no lunch and was miserably hungry. After a couple of mouthfuls, he said reflectively: 'I think things are different in England. Read a lotta English books. The life just isn't the same.'

'I suppose so,' said Isobel circumspectly. She wondered if Peter's young life had been like Hank's. Until that second, she had never considered what his early life might have been like – it had always seemed too far away to be important. He had always been grown up to her, never young – more like her father. And with that thought came such a burst of self-revelation that she found it difficult to go on eating calmly, and only iron determination kept her placidly balancing bits of steak on her fork and eating them.

She remembered the frighful stripping away of all her ordinary life by the sudden accidental death of both her parents, of the terrible feeling of responsibility for Dorothy, so much younger than she was. She remembered the funeral and the tall, capable soldier friend of her father's who had come to attend it and had dealt so well with lawyers and with her fat, harassed uncle, who was one of the executors of her father's will. She had been happy to replace her father with another father figure, who had become her husband. She realized desolately that though he had been immensely kind to her, she had never really known him.

I must have been mad, she thought. But common sense answered her back sharply. Not mad, it said. He was a kindly, decent man and you were not unhappy with him. If sometimes you hankered for a better physical relationship, you loved him well enough to be faithful to him.

'Anything the matter?' asked Hank, who had been watching the play of expressions across her face. Then he leaned over to place his hand over hers, and said softly: 'I guess this outing must be pretty hard on you.'

His effort to understand her situation touched her, and she fought back sudden tears to say: 'Oh, no, Hank. Everything is lovely and I am truly grateful to you for dragging me out. Everyone is so merry – and the dresses are fabulous.'

'Fine,' he said, with a sigh of satisfaction, as he looked round the crowded restaurant. Then he asked: 'Do you like Alberta?'

She grasped at the new subject eagerly: 'Yes, I do.' She paused reflectively. 'It's breathtakingly beautiful. But I don't think I could go on living indefinitely in Tolle-marche.'

Hank was watching a sorely inebriated building contrac-tor who was trying to heave the evening shoes off his girl friend's feet. When, with a final flurry of nyloned legs above the table top, he got them off, he proceeded to fill them with rye from a bottle under the table and drink a toast to the assembled company. 'I guess,' said Hank, 'Tollemarche is a bit raw for you.'

Isobel also had watched the incident of the shoes, and admitted that it was so.

'I think you'd like Edmonton better,' said Hank. 'It's really going places now, with orchestras and theatres and stores like we don't have up here.'

'Yes, I've been there,' replied Isobel, now completely in control of herself, 'and it is fun.'

'Sometimes go down myself to see a show.'

'Do you?' asked Isobel, trying not to sound too amazed.

He grinned. 'Sure,' he replied. 'Gotta get an education for myself somehow.'

The waiter brought coffee and dessert and they lingered over them, talking of plays and playwrights. Nobody knew who they were, except Mr Li, and they were left in peace.

'Why do you hafta go back to England?' asked Hank.

'There's nothing to keep me here. And, you know, Hank, I'd like to live a little.'

'Holy cow! You could live here – or down in Edmonton. Waddya mean "live"?'

'I mean to feel alive – to be in the middle of things. Alberta is on the edge of the world and nothing touches it, except the faintest ripples of what goes on elsewhere.'

'Humph, I'd have thought that was something to be thankful for.'

She nodded her head, making her tiara flash like a halo. 'Yes, it is, really. If one is afraid of poverty or war, there's a lot of comfort here. But you see, Hank,' she went on more passionately, 'life isn't just a matter of being comfortable. One wants to try one's strength and see what one can do – and I really long to hear an expert talk about his work, to argue politics, to look at fine pictures, plays, books, and discuss them.' She stopped and clicked her tongue irritably. 'I don't know how to make you understand.'

She looked hopefully at him. He looked very mature in his beard, which, with the hair at his temples, had been rubbed with talcum powder to give it a greying appearance. One day he will really look like this, if he cares to make the effort, she reflected; and I believe he could become a great novelist, too.

He grinned wryly, and said: 'You could teach up North – you'd find it a real struggle up there – and the Eskimos are the world's greatest experts on arctic survival! But there wouldn't be any theatre shows.'

Isobel laughed. 'You're right – but it would be more isolated even than Tollemarche.' After a moment, she added confidingly: 'You know, when I first came here I used to feel sure that if I walked along the highway for any distance, I would drop off the edge of the world – it was so flat and empty.'

'I guess I can understand that.' He thought of the miles of waving wheat, with nothing on the skyline but a couple of grain elevators thrusting their white fingers to a cloudless blue sky, and he thought of the pure, white beauty of the same type of scene in winter – hundreds of miles of snow and the same polished blue sky. To someone used to a crowded, small island perhaps it was frightening. 'It's beautiful,' he said stubbornly.

'Of course it is,' she agreed.

There was silence between them, and then he said: 'Remember you said I should go get some experience somewhere else? Since Ma is so mad and you are going away, mebbe this is the time to do it.'

'I think it would be a good idea, just to have a better idea of what the outside world is like. Do you want to work or just to travel?'

'Jeeze, I dunno. I'd hafta work on my book all the time, anyway.'

'Well what about taking a hiking holiday through Europe first? It wouldn't cost so much, and then – '

His moustache fell off with shock. 'Hike?' he interrupted, horrified. 'You mean walk?' He hastily retrieved the moustache from the saucer of his coffee cup, and clapped it back on again.

She burst into laughter, partly at the moustache and partly at his typical North American aversion to using his legs. 'Yes, I really mean walk. If you walk you will have the chance of talking to all kinds of odd people. You can meet and walk with other young people, from youth hostel to youth hostel.'

He said vigorously: 'I'd drop dead after the first day – you'll have to allow me a car.'

'Oh, come on now, you wouldn't die – you'd lose pounds and really toughen up.'

He looked at her beseechingly: 'I sure would slim – dropping pounds one by one across Europe – don't you feel sorry for me? I couldn't do it – unless you came with me,' he added with sudden inspiration.

'Oh, Hank, don't tease. You know I've got a job waiting for me. I have to earn my living – my pension isn't going to be enough.' She leaned towards him eagerly, her lips parted and her tiny hands gesturing. 'But you go, Hank. You'll be glad you did. Britain, France, Germany, Holland, they are all wonderful in their infinite variety. You haven't seen a single piece of good architecture yet, not a single good painting, never talked to a person whose family has lived in one place for five hundred years. You haven't seen a thoroughgoing slum yet. You can't realize what a war can do to a country and its people. Go, Hank, and see it all – you'll understand a lot of things much better afterwards, and be a better writer in consequence.' She stopped and began to blush, ashamed of her impassioned outburst.

He was impressed by it. 'Say, you do take things seriously, don't you?' he marvelled. 'Even me! Sure, I know I need to see things. And if you think I ought to foot it, I will – but don't expect my feet to enjoy it.' Then he added defiantly: 'I've seen the Empire State Building. Have you?'

She chuckled. 'No, I haven't. No desire to see the States at all – I think Quebec would be much more fun – you might do a bit of exploring there, too. You've got quite a lot of Canada to see yet.'

'O.K. You're the boss. You're the first person I've ever met who cared what I did, anyway.' He sighed. 'Do I have to hike the whole two thousand miles or so to Quebec as well?'

'It wouldn't be a bad idea,' she said with a twinkle in her eyes, and then, as he groaned in mock horror, she added: 'But I think I'll let you off that.'

'Thanks, pal,' he said dryly, and signalled for his bill.

CHAPTER EIGHTEEN

Mrs Stych was far too busy getting ready for the Edwardian Ball to recollect that she had not seen Hank since he had marched out of the house the previous evening. She had spent the afternoon at the hairdressers, and was now standing in front of her Stately Castille dressing table pinning a scarlet flower coquettishly over one ear.

'Boyd,' she called, 'you ready?'

Boyd came into the room, fastening a red and gold brocade waistcoat. 'My, are we ever dressed up!' he said sardonically. Not even two helpings of ice cream with walnut topping had melted Olga's resistance to him the previous evening, and he was feeling irritable.

Despite the appropriateness of her gorgeous costume, Olga was not feeling her usual confident self. Late the previous evening she had announced that she would not attend the ball, just to be sniggered at by the whole town. But Boyd, more for his own sake than for hers, had persuaded her that she ought to attend, notwithstanding the possible reactions of the girls to the publication of Hank's book. Otherwise, he said, it would look as if she was ashamed. Secretly, he felt that it was essential for the promotion of his business that they be seen at all Tollemarche's big social functions. He had, therefore, helped Olga to lace herself into a formidable pair of corsets and then to struggle into a magnificent red satin dress, heavily trimmed with black lace. He had also heated some soup and made sandwiches for their supper, as there was not time, in her opinion, to eat dinner out.

With great care, she now placed on her head a cartwheel hat of black velvet trimmed with dyed ostrich feathers, and examined herself in the mirror. She picked up a long-handled, frilly parasol and a black velvet handbag, and posed with them. The skirt of the dress was caught up at the hem and pinned to the waistline with a flower to match the one in her hair; this left one silk-stockinged leg bare to the hip, in true dancing-girl style, and Mrs Stych felt she looked very daring. She smiled satisfiedly at her reflection.

Behind her, Boyd turned away to hide a smile. The fact that she was so fat made her look much more like the dancing girl she was trying to portray than perhaps Olga would have wished; gold miners had liked their women fat.

Olga felt more content than she had during the whole previous twenty-four hours. With a costume like this, the first prize at the ball would certainly be hers.

'You supposed to be Klondike Kate?' asked Boyd.

Mrs Stych smiled slyly at him out of the corners of her eyes. 'Yeah,' she said, regardless of the reputation of that hardy lady of the Klondike gold rush. ''Cept I couldn't face wearing high laced-up boots – I'm wearing my black pumps instead.'

Boyd allowed that the black pumps looked real nice.

He picked up one of his wife's old gilt necklaces from her open jewel box and draped it across his waistcoat to represent a watch chain. Then he struggled into a high-buttoned black jacket. 'Did you get me a buttonhole?' he asked.

Mrs Stych looked at him in shocked reproach. 'Why, Boyd, I thought you'd surely get flowers for both of us, seeing as you are home all the time now and aren't just coming in at the very last minute.'

Boyd realized the justice of her remark and also that an explosion was imminent. Living at home, he reflected angrily, had its hazards.

'O.K., O.K.,' he said quickly, 'I just asked. I wasn't sure if you would want a corsage with that outfit. If you do want one, we can stop at Bell's Flowers and get one. I can get a button-hole, too.'

The threatening glow of rage in Olga's eyes died; she gave him a sour look, but said only: 'We'll do that.'

Her husband muttered that he would go and start the car, and for the moment she was alone. Her thoughts reverted to Hank and his diabolical book, and she felt sick with fright at the thought of all the slights she might have to face at the ball. Yet she could do nothing about it; Boyd was right that if she stayed at home it would look as if she was ashamed.

She sniffed. She'd show them if she was ashamed or afraid. She opened the fine louvre-board doors to the closet, took out her Persian lamb coat and draped it round her shoulders. Absently she stood stroking its silky lapels; few women in the town had a better coat than this, and it would be paid for by April thank goodness. She lifted her nose in the air, so that her double chin did not show so much, and, with the same bravery with which her parents had faced their first fierce winter, she went out to smite the enemy; in this case, to outdo the girls with the glory of her coat and costume.

In keeping with the period they were trying to reconstruct, many citizens of Tollemarche travelled to the ball at the Donegal Hotel in vintage cars, and many of these were now parked along the side of the street on which the hotel stood. Whether they would ever start again after prolonged exposure to the winter storm which was obviously blowing up, was problematical, but many of the owners felt it was worth paying a fee to Tommy's Towing Company afterwards, just to enjoy the envy of those who did not own such treasures.

The Mayor, who had triumphed over the city council with regard to mayoral robes, had solved the starting problem by sweeping up to the hotel in a well-preserved closed carriage, which had been salvaged from the back of the old Hudson's Bay factor's house and then refinished. The two horses which drew it did not quite match, despite a quick application of boot blacking over the lighter spots of one of them, but the general effect drew cheers from passing carloads of merrymakers.

Mayor Murphy beamed as he handed down his plump wife, who wobbled unhappily in a gown of bright purple velvet, and then helped down two saturnine gentlemen

146

from the Montreal Mortgage and Trust Company, who were visiting the city to buy land on speculation. His coachman, a Cree Indian brought in for the evening from a nearby reserve, was disguised in a black top hat and neat black uniform. As soon as the Mayor was safely inside the lobby, he turned the carriage round and headed for the fire station, where the horses and he would keep warm with the firemen on duty until such time as the Mayor should telephone for him. As the first snowflakes of the storm hit him, he hoped that the firemen had some beer tucked away at the back of the hall.

Olga Stych did her best to control her palpitating heart as she made her way to the cloakroom of the Donegal Hotel, while Boyd went to park the car. She put her hand on the knob of the door marked WOMEN, but was unable to make herself turn it. What would they say? What *would* they say? But it was no good – a new arrival behind her forced her to open the door and walk in.

The place was a mad-house of waving plumes, raucous voices and cigarette smoke.

' 'Lo, Olga', and 'Hiya, Olga,' greeted her on all sides.

Mrs Stein of Dawne's Dresse Shoppe, wearing her grandmother's wedding dress and veil, was squeezed out of the crowd round the mirrors and up against Olga's hefty bulk.

'Say, you look fine,' she said, appraising the scarlet dress with a professional eye through heavy horn-rimmed glasses. 'A real scarlet woman,' she joked. 'Did Mary Leplante make it?'

Mrs Stych felt as if twenty years had been taken off her age. Her enormous bosom swelled to dangerous proportions in such a low-cut gown, as she answered proudly: 'Yeah, Mary made it.'

So the girls were not going to let the book make any difference. They were wonderful! They sure were. She linked her arm into that of Mrs Stein. 'Come on,' she said with gay condenscension, 'let's go find the boys!'

Before leaving home, Olga had glanced quickly at the

front page of the *Tollemarche Advent*, which the paper boy had just flung on to the step as she came out. She had seen on the lower half of the front page, under the heading 'Local Boy Makes Good', an almost unrecognizeable picture of Hank. She was too rushed to read the columns underneath and had left the newspaper lying on the boot tray just inside her front door. Now, she did not pause to consider that, throughout Tollemarche, few of those attending the ball would have stopped to read the newspaper on such a night; it would have been left to languish until Sunday gave time for its perusal. True, the eight o'clock news on the local radio station had also mentioned Hank, between a war and a dock strike, but nobody really listened to the news, anyway. Unconscious of this, however, Olga felt like a reprieved felon, and her relief was so great that she quite dazzled Boyd's fellow directors by her vivacity.

The ballroom was filled with the sharp smell of chrysanthemums, specially flown in from British Columbia for the occasion. Potted palms were grouped round the stage, on which sat a large dance orchestra in full evening dress. Around the sides of the ballroom and in the balcony above were set tables covered with stiff white cloths, for six or eight persons; each table had a vase of roses, also from British Columbia, and a pair of small, shaded electric lamps to light it. Like many of the hotels in Alberta at the time, the Donegal's dining and ballrooms were not licensed, but this did not deter their patrons. Into the iced ginger ales went large measures of rye from bottles kept discreetly under the table and, similarly, gin was being dumped generously into the lime juices of tittering ladies. Some of the parties were already very merry, and it was apparent that some people would have to be carried to their cars before the night was out.

At the door of the ballroom stood one of the members of the Chamber of Commerce, dressed in a white wig, knee breeches and a yellow satin coat. He had volunteered to be the major-domo of the evening; as people arrived, he took their names and announced them in a loud bass. From him, the guests proceeded to an interminably long receiving line, made up of the Mayor and Mrs Murphy, the president of the Chamber of Commerce and his wife, the president of the Edwardian Days' Committee and his daughter, he being a widower, and several very ancient inhabitants, both male and female, whom the committee had agreed it would be easier to include than exclude, most of the ancient inhabitants being both rich and sharp of tongue.

'Mr and Mrs Maxmilian Frizzell, Mrs and Mrs John MacLeod, the Right Honourable Frederick Shaeffer and Mrs Shaeffer, Professor Mah Poy and Mrs Mah, Dr and Mrs Stanilas Paderewski,' roared the major-domo, warming to his job and being careful to keep his voice clear by taking an occasional quick nip from a friend's bottle.

The bustles and fancy waistcoats, the trains and evening suits, flowed slowly past the reception line and down three thickly carpeted steps to the ballroom floor or, if they felt they were past the age of dancing, climbed complainingly to their tables in the balcony.

In a quiet moment, the major-domo took out a pocket handkerchief to wipe his perspiring face, while he remarked to the Mayor that he deserved a city contract as a reward for enduring a wig in this hothouse. The Mayor smiled noncommittally. It would take more than a hint like that to land the office furniture contract for the new city hall; a contract as big as that should be worth something. He fingered his new chain of office, and then, looking past the would-be contractor, he laughed.

Standing waiting to be announced was a dignified woman in a lavender dress embroidered with pearls and sequins. She was made taller by her hair, which had been tightly waved, powdered, and piled on the top of her head. Her big tiara sparkled in the soft light, and a five-tier pearl necklace shimmered delicately over a high neckline of boned lace. She wore across her breast a wide blue ribbon tied in a knot at her hip; a large brooch on the ribbon suggested an order of some kind. In her white-gloved hands she carried a nosegay of roses and a silver fan. She was accompanied by a distinguished-looking man in full evening dress, whose hair was cut English style, whose beard was neatly trimmed in naval fashion. He, too, sported a sash across his chest decorated by a row of medals and two star-like brooches, and below his white tie hung an elaborate enamelled cross; all the medals had been won for skiing or swimming, but nobody noticed the fact. What was noticed was the authoritative air of the pair of them as they advanced unsmilingly towards the major-domo.

The major-domo grinned at them; this was going to be fun. No couple whom he had announced up to now had managed more appropriate costumes. Very quietly, he went over to them and edged them behind a potted palm, whispering hastily into their respective ears. They nodded agreement, and he caught a page-boy and gave him a message for the orchestra. After a moment or two, the conductor raised his head and nodded towards them. The major-domo took up his position again and cleared his throat, while Isobel and Hank advanced slowly towards him, doing their best to maintain their grave dignity, though Hank's moustache was quivering dangerously.

The orchestra brought its current piece of music to an end, and sounded a great chord. Conversation ceased immediately and everyone, including the receiving line, looked round expectantly.

'Their Royal Highnesses, the Prince and Princess of Wales,' roared the major-domo.

The ballgoers looked up in silent astonishment, and then a ripple of laughter went through the crowd, and they began to clap, while Hank and Isobel acknowledged with the faintest of condescending nods the ironic bow of the quick-witted Mayor and the bows and curtsies of the rest of the receiving line, all of whom rose to the occasion admirably, except for a deaf, old lady at the end, who announced crabbily that she did not know what the major-domo was about, talking of 'fences and bales'.

Hank and Isobel moved to the top of the steps and bowed

to the applauding crowd. To some of those present they brought back happy memories, and there was not one person there who did not recall the opening exercises in the little red schoolhouses across the province, when they had stood to attention in front of a picture such as Hank and Isobel now presented, and vowed to be faithful to the flag and to George V and his consort, Queen Mary. Some were nonplussed at the couple being announced as the Prince and Princess of Wales, but their brighter neighbours hastened to remind them that in Edwardian days, the old king, Edward VII, would be reigning.

'Who are they?' was the whisper that ran round the room between the claps. Even the major-domo could not remember having seen them before, and came to the conclusion that they must be some young married couple who had recently come into the town.

Mrs Stych looked cursorily at the Princess, did not know her and turned back to her rye and ginger ale; she barely glanced at the Prince. Boyd thought he knew the turn of the shoulder on the man, but could not place him. He, too, went back to his drink.

The Mayor was not going to betray the fact that he did not know someone in the town who was rich enough to spend forty dollars on tickets for the ball, so, as he and Mrs Murphy moved towards the dance floor to open the ball, he slapped Hank heartily on the back, and bellowed: 'Have a good time.'

The orchestra struck up a waltz, and Hank and Isobel made for her brother-in-law's table, which they had been invited to join; on the way, they passed the table of Isobel's employer, a heavy dark-jowled man, who rose and caught her hand as she went by. 'Happy to see you here, Isobel,' he said.

She smiled and, with a lighter heart, went on to her table. Some people in Tollemarche were evidently going to be pleased that she was in circulation again.

Joanne Dawson, in a tight, low-necked dress of salmon pink, had already consumed two gins, and greeted them effusively while Dave Dawson, a quiet, tired-looking man about thirty-five, pulled out a chair for Isobel.

Isobel introduced Hank to them, and he said politely: 'How d'yer do.' He sat down slowly, eyeing Joanne's rather daring costume with an unblinking stare. She was dressed as a chorus girl, her full skirt hitched up to show tight-clad legs and hips, the low neckline leaving little to the imagination.

'Too much cleavage,' decided Hank. 'No class.'

Dave wore dinner clothes of the period, and Hank knew instinctively that he and Isobel would get on very well together. Hank felt an ill-bred lout beside him, and he wondered how Isobel endured him; he decided he did not like himself very much, and this detracted for a little while from his enjoyment of the masquerade.

'You looked just fine up there on the steps,' Dave said to Hank. 'In the half light, you looked just like old Georgie.'

'Thanks,' said Hank, warming to him. He checked that his moustache was still in place. 'Hope I don't lose this,' he added while Joanne giggled shrilly.

'Say, what are these?' he asked, pointing to some tiny, pink cards with pencils attached to them which were lying on the table.

'Ladies' programmes, stoopid,' said Joanne amiably, leaning on her elbow unsteadily towards him. 'Here, give one to Isobel,' and she pushed one over to Hank.

Hank looked it over, mystified. 'Wottya do with them?' he demanded.

Isobel took it from him. 'See,' she said, 'it contains a list of all the dances. In the old days each girl had one, and the gentlemen came up to her and booked dances with her by writing in their names. It was the job of the M.C. or the host and hostess to see that, as far as possible, all the cards were filled.'

'That's easy,' said Hank, taking the card back from her firmly. He wroted his name across the whole column of dances.

'Say,' protested Dave, 'give us a chance.'

Hank looked at him with mock lordliness. 'I'm the Prince of Wales, remember.' Then, good-humouredly, he passed the card to Dave, who wrote his name against a foxtrot before supper and a waltz later in the evening.

'What about poor little me?' demanded Joanne, with a pout. She regarded Isobel as a drip, and had no intention of spending the evening tied to their table. She was, however placated when Dave wrote his name all over her card, and Hank wrote his name in the spaces of the dances which Isobel would dance with Dave.

She greeted with squeaks of joy the approach of two gentlemen dressed in Edwardian suits and white stetson hats, and made each of them sign his name on her card. Isobel, suddenly nervous of possible censure of their recent hero's widow being at a ball, kicked Dave under the table, and whispered 'Prince and Princess'. He was a quick man and, with exaggerated deference, introduced the visitors to Hank and Isobel, murmuring: 'Their Royal Highnesses, the Prince and Princess of Wales.'

'Let's dance,' said Hank, and dragged her unceremoniously to the edge of the ballroom floor. He stood tapping his foot impatiently in time to the music, while she carefully anchored the train of her dress by a loop hooked over her little finger.

He whirled her out on to the floor at the fast pace demanded by a Viennese Waltz, and was surprised to find her following him effortlessly.

'Say, where did you learn to dance?'

'In England – most English women dance.'

'Ballroom dancing, like this?'

'Yes.'

'I thought they were all swingers.'

Isobel laughed. 'Most of us can dance modern dances as well.'

'Can you?'

'Well, I haven't danced more than a couple of times since I was married, so I'm probably a bit out of date, but I think I could make a fair showing even so.'

He grinned down at her wickedly. 'Mebbe we'll go to a night club sometime and get back into practice. What say?'

'Maybe,' she said cautiously. 'I think more people in England dance than people here.'

He considered this while he negotiated a corner, in which the city editor of the *Advent* appeared to have got stuck with his partner. The partner was saying: 'Now, Joe, one-and-two, one-and-two, one-and-two. Now, turn!'

'Don't you have any fundamentalists?' he asked.

'I don't think there are many. We're mostly heathens.' She added, a little breathlessly: 'When your book is published in England, it won't cause half the stir it is going to cause here.' Then, after being twirled neatly out of the way of the Mayor, she remembered the reporter's visit to Hank the previous evening. 'What does the *Advent* have to say about you today?'

'Haven't had time to look yet. I don't care, anyways.'

He pulled her a little closer, so that she could feel the warmth of him. 'Enjoying yourself?' he asked.

She looked up at him and her face was alight with gaiety. My God, she's really beautiful, he thought. She just needs bringing out. He held her close, and did a dashing double reverse turn with sheer exuberance, much to the discomfort of at least half a dozen other couples who were already finding such a fast waltz rather exhausting and were thrown into confusion by Hank's lively variation.

Dave Dawson was honestly glad to see her flushed face so bright when they returned to the table. She had been the subject of several anxious consultations in the family, who felt responsible for her future and yet found her supercilious English manner very trying. Only Dave's and Peter's father, himself once an immigrant, had understood how profoundly different was her life in Canada compared to her childhood in North Wales and her business life in London. Her mother-in-law was a Canadian who had failed to adapt in Britain and persuaded her husband to emigrate. Had Peter lived, thought Dave, probably Isobel would have settled in, but he had not been surprised at her decision to go home. Now, as he watched her while he drew out Joanne's chair, he wondered if the talented boy who had brought her to the dance might not persuade her to stay in Tollemarche.

Dave was not the only person who watched her with interest. From across the empty floor, Olga Stych, her eyes glazed with horror, had just recognized her son and was saying in a furious voice to her husband: 'Who's that bitch he's with?' She half rose, prepared to sail across the floor to the attack, but Boyd leaned solicitously over her and pressed her back down into her chair with bruising fingers.

'Shut up,' he said in a whisper. 'Remember where you are! The other directors are here.'

She recollected her hostess manner and smiled up at him sweetly; then, turning so that her hat hid her from the curious eyes of their guests, she muttered: 'The impudence of him!' Her bosom heaved as she glared at Boyd from under the safe shadow of her hat: 'You gotta deal with him, Boyd. You really have.'

CHAPTER NINETEEN

Isobel danced the whole evening. Occasionally, Hank had to yield her up to other gentlemen; her employer politely claimed a dance, and one or two friends of the Dawson family visited their table, were introduced and, with varying degrees of good manners, asked for dances. Prompted by Isobel, Hank dutifully asked their ladies for dances, and pulled faces at Isobel over their shoulders whenever they passed on the floor.

By the time the buffet supper in an adjoining room was announced, they were both hungry again. They found themselves the centre of a rowdy party, made up of acquaintances of Joanne and Dave, and as soon as Isobel had collected a plateful of food, Hank found himself conniving with Dave to edge Isobel out of the crowd and back to their table by the dance floor, where they ate quietly together.

Isobel, well aware of the conspiracy, said: 'Thank you, Hank.'

'Think nothing of it,' Hank replied. 'They're not your type. Dave said to tell you he thought he'd better stay with Joanne.'

'I think I'm being spoiled tonight,' Isobel teased gently.

Hank looked bashful. 'I wouldn't know about that, but I sure know the kind of company you should not be in.'

'Well, bless you!' she said, laughing, as they got up to dance.

The city editor of the *Advent*, who had been the original owner of the paper until he had sold out to a syndicate about six months previously, could remember the days when he had helped to set the type himself, and he felt tremendously important when he was asked to judge the costumes at the ball, aided by Mrs Murphy and the wife of the president of the Bonnie Scots Men's Club.

Towards the end of the evening, after a suitable roll of drums from the orchestra, he announced a grand parade of everyone desiring to compete. There was considerable good-natured shoving forward of some competitors by the more shy, and finally almost everyone made the circuit of the dance floor. Twelve were picked out and asked to parade again, among them a simpering Mrs Stych, two Mississippi gamblers tossing a die between them, Hank and Isobel, a prospector whose gold-panning equipment was carried on a donkey which seemed to be slightly inebriated, and an assortment of ladies in fairly genuine-looking Edwardian fashions.

The twelve finally stood in line in front of the judges, who conferred earnestly together, Mrs Murphy being anxious not to accidentally upset one of her husband's political associates by not giving a prize to the Mississippi gamblers. The back legs of the prospector's donkey began to sag, and Isobel was certain they would lose to such a gloriously wobbly donkey.

The judge stood up.

'First prize, a beautiful set of luggage donated by Pottle's Best Brewed Beer, to Their Royal Highnesses, the Prince and Princess of Wales.'

Cheers and claps broke out as Hank and Isobel advanced towards the judge. Behind them, near the orchestra, Mrs Frizzell clapped her hand to her mouth in shock as she recognized Hank. The orchestra behind her made her jump as it suddenly burst forth with a few bars of 'God Bless the Prince of Wales'. 'Bless him!' she sniffed, 'H'mmm!'

'Who are you?' whispered the judge. 'They'd probably like to know.'

Hank looked at Isobel. 'O.K.,' she murmured.

'I'm Hank Stych and this is Mrs Isobel Dawson.'

The judge, with a startled look at them, wrung both their hands and announced who they were, while Mrs Stych went slowly purple with rage.

Just wait till he gets home, she swore to herself. She'd teach him to run around with the widow of Tollemarche's hero, and go to balls meant for adults. Just because he had written an indecent book didn't mean he could invade her world and behave indecently with a woman only widowed six months. She'd teach him!

She turned and glared at that hussy of a Dawson woman.

The hussy did not remember who she was and stared back with queenly coldness, thinking that Canadians did not know how to lose gracefully.

The announcement of Hank's name had little effect on anyone present, except his parents and Mr and Mrs Frizzell. It was doubtful if anyone connected him with his parents. The announcement of Isobel's name, however, gave rise to a fair amount of interested whispering behind hands and fans.

The second prize went to the prospector and his donkey, amid hurrahs from a lively party in a corner. Unfortunately, the back end of the donkey sat down suddenly and had to be undone from the front end and carried off.

Mrs Stych accepted a set of records of Barbershop Singers, courtesy of Mollie's Milk Bar, for the third prize, and was congratulated by the judge, who realized the relationship, on the success of her family in the competition. She was past speech by this time and smiled at the judge glassily, as she withdrew to her table. She hardly heard the congratulations of the Frizzells, who seemed to think she had designed Hank's and Isobel's costumes as well as her own. When her voice returned to her, she said loudly that she needed a drink. Boyd presented her with this, with an alacrity which betrayed his apprehension.

He had spotted Hank during the second dance, and had examined at leisure the pretty girl with him. He had realized that she was not Canadian and that she was probably older than Hank. Was she Hank's widow woman? he wondered. He had watched her tiny, graceful figure as she danced, and had suddenly become nervous for his son's future. She had 'real nice girl' written all over her, he reckoned – the kind of girl one talked only marriage to – and he did not want his son to marry yet.

158

He looked at Olga, who was downing her drink steadily. He'd got married too young, he reminded himself desperately, and had had almost immediately a mortgage tied round his neck, as if he were a dog with a registration tag on its collar.

He began to consider how to persuade Hank to leave Tollemarche for a while, before Olga nagged him into a state of such perversity that he would marry the girl just to spite his mother.

CHAPTER TWENTY

They were leaving the ballroom after the last waltz and
Isobel looked back at Mrs Stych, who, clutching her prize,
was talking to a distinguished, grey-haired woman in a
black evening gown.

'I didn't realize that lady was your mother, until she
won a prize – she looked very pretty,' Isobel remarked
kindly.

Hank looked at her sardonically. 'Yeah,' he said. 'And
she sure was mad at our getting first prize. Come to think
of it, she was mad because I came at all.'

Isobel laughed. 'Wasn't that the idea?'

'Sure.' He looked as pleased as a tiger after a kill.
'She'll have quite a time explaining to the girls how I came
to be there -- and with you.'

'Really, Hank, you're dreadful.'

'Well, you won't come to any harm from it – you'll be
away from here.'

'I suppose so – though I feel very guilty.'

He stopped, while the crowd milled round them
towards the exit. 'Listen, honey. I could have gone
through all the business of introducing you to her, saying I
was taking you and what we would wear, and all I would
have got for my pains would have been a real earful.' As
he spoke, he shouldered back anyone who pressed too
close to her, so that she was not ruffled by the passersby.
Then he asked abruptly, 'Would you like to meet Dad?
He's over there, by the pillar.'

She moved round so that she did not appear to be
straining to look, and saw a tall, thin brown man, very fit
looking. In repose, his face appeared hard and a little
cunning. He caught her eye and stared back at her; a
glimmer of a smile showed, as if they were sharing some
secret joke. Then it seemed to her that a shadow of

anxiety passed across his face, if such a man could possibly be anxious about anything.

'Waddya think of him?'

'He looks very nice,' she said politely.

'Don't kid me, hon. He's as tough as they make them – and you know it.'

'One can be tough and nice,' she countered, drawing her handbag closer up her arm.

'O.K. Wanna meet him?'

'Perhaps tonight wouldn't be the best night, Hank. Some other time.' This would probably be the last time she would go out with Hank, and she felt there was no point in getting involved with his parents.

'From what you tell me, Mr Stych seems to be taking a lot of trouble on your behalf to see that the money you've made is properly invested,' she remarked to Hank, as he tucked a blanket round her in the car.

Hank was silent while he tried the ignition key in its lock. The engine coughed into life immediately.

'Making some money was the first thing I ever did that pleased him,' he finally replied.

'Hank, Hank,' she said reproachfully, 'what shall I do with you?'

'Well, I could suggest a few things,' he responded promptly, which silenced her.

In the station wagon parked next to them, a childish howl arose. Some child, put to bed in a sleeping-bag in the back of the car, had awakened, presumably cold and hungry. Isobel winced. Had his parents done that to Hank when he was small – or had they just left him in an empty house? she wondered.

The storm was now in full blast, and they crawled carefully through the shadowy mass of vehicles moving round them.

'If this continues till morning, think I'll go up to Banff and ski for a coupla days. Give Ma time to cool off.' He laughed. 'Don't want her to burst a blood vessel.'

'Good idea. You have been shut up too long.'

'So long as I'm not shut up in that factory of a school, I'm fine.'

He stopped at a red light and looked at her with laughter in his eyes.

'Can't imagine you still in school,' said Isobel frankly. 'I can't understand why you didn't just take off years ago.'

'There's a lotta pressure from all quarters here to keep you in school. Education's just become a fashion. They tell you you can't even run an elevator unless you got Grade 12.'

'You can go into the police force if you've got Grade 10 – and the Mounties will take you with Grade 11,' countered Isobel.

Hank chuckled. 'Sure. They don't want their police to be brainy – how'd they get away with what they do, if the police had brains?' His voice was hard and cynical. Then he changed the subject. 'Say, if I come to Europe, can I come and see you?'

'Of course. Both Dorothy and I will love to see you.'

He said practically: 'I'll get your address from you, before you leave.'

The thick snow muffled the sound of the approach of the car to Isobel's house, and when he stopped he did not immediately get out to open the door for her, but sat looking moodily at his hands on the steering wheel.

She gathered up her fan, posy and handbag. 'It's been a wonderful evening, Hank, and I'm really grateful to you for dragging me out.'

He turned eagerly towards her.

'Yeah, it was fun, wasn't it? We'll do something else together soon.' He added baldly: 'I'd expected it to be a dead bore – I just wanted to take a rise out of Ma.' His voice was husky. 'But you're fun – you're lovely.' He put his arm round the back of her seat. 'Isobel,' he said urgently, and then stopped.

She was afraid of what was coming. Remember, he's too young, an inner voice warned her, and she said in her most comradely voice: 'Yes, Hank?'

'Stop being so bloody friendly,' he exclaimed angrily, and leaning half over her, kissed her hard, holding her firmly round the shoulders so that she could not escape it.

For a moment she yielded to him. She had not been kissed by a man since her husband had left for Cyprus, and this strong, healthy youngster aroused feelings in her that no kiss from her husband had ever aroused. Then she began to struggle.

'Hank, please – please, Hank.' She felt desperately unhappy and pushed at his chest, so that he finally let her go, though he did not take his arm from around her shoulders.

'Isobel!' he pleaded.

'Hank – you mustn't, you know.' She laughed unsteadily and thought what a fool she had been to enter into this masquerade. She felt she could not trust herself, and said in a formal tone of voice: 'I must go in.'

His face looked heavy, sulky. He silently climbed out of the car, and paused, the snow whirling round him, letting the icy air cool him, before he walked round the car and opened the door for her. He had not had the slightest intention, when the evening commenced, of making love to her, but now he realized that he wanted her passionately.

She climbed out, and silently he picked the rug up from the seat on which she had been sitting. With a quick flick, he swung it over her head and shoulders.

His voice was trembling, as he said: 'I'm sorry, honey,' and he looked as forlorn as a flag on a windless day, as he held the rug round her with one great fist.

She smiled gently at him, her eyes soft below their golden lashes. 'It's all right, Hank. It was mostly my fault.' The snow was coming through her shoes, and she began to shiver. 'Would you like to come in for a drink? I think Dorothy will still be up.'

'No, thanks. I'd better get home.' He still held the rug close under her chin. 'You'll still be here when I get back from Banff?' he asked.

'Yes – I'm leaving next Sunday. Dorothy will stay a few

days longer to tie up a few ends for me – but I have to start my London job.'

He hardly heard what she said. He stood looking at her as if mesmerized, watching the snowflakes land on her hair and cheeks, to melt into gleaming droplets. She was so different from anyone he had ever met before, and, though he had often talked to her before through the years he had known her, he wanted now to talk to her for ever.

'Like me to carry you up to the house?' he asked mischievously. 'Your feet'll sure be wet otherwise.'

'Oh, Hank! Don't be an ass – I won't melt. And thank you very very much for a lovely evening – all of it,' she added. She was quite steady now.

'Aw, come on – I'll behave – I promise.' And before she could reply he had picked her up like a baby and was carrying her quite carefully, despite her laughing protests, up to the front door. Before he put her down, he put his cheek against hers for a moment and then very gently kissed her again. Then he put her down quickly.

'See you,' he said. 'Thanks a lot for coming. 'Bye.' And he tore down the steps and got his Triumph on the move again, so fast that she had hardly got her key into the lock before the protesting machine was shrieking round the corner on two wheels.

'I'm mad,' he told himself, as he closed the garage door, and opened the trunk in order to put in his typewriter and manuscript to work on in Banff. 'I'm plumb crazy.' He stopped, with the lid half closed. 'I'm in love.' He snapped it shut. 'I've always loved her – ever since I first saw her.'

He put up the collar of his evening jacket and dashed the two blocks to his home, as if trying to get away from more than the storm.

He felt he could not face either parent that night, so he prised open the window of his ground-floor bedroom and hauled himself quietly in through it. Carefully he slid shut both the inner and storm windows. He could hear angry voices, muffled by distance, and was thankful he had not tried to unlock the front door and come in that way.

He took off his wet jacket and shook it.

The room was very untidy. He had not made his bed before going out in the morning and it was still in the same muddle in which he had left it. His pyjamas lay on the floor, with yesterday's T-shirt and socks, and a half-read novel, face down, lay on top of them. He was glad he was going to Banff – at least in the motel his bed would be made for him.

From the back of his clothes closet he pulled out a zipper bag, and quickly crammed into it some sweaters and underwear, the novel, and his transistor radio – he'd need the latter on the road, for weather reports. His ski boots were with his skis in the basement, and he decided to get them on his way out in the morning.

Slowly and thoughtfully, he stripped off his clothes and then lay down on the unmade bed. He would sleep for about four hours and start for Banff about six in the morning, before the traffic on the highways got heavy. He told himself he was nuts to set out on a journey of hundreds of miles in the middle of a storm, but he had a great urge to pit himself against the elements, get away from cloying, sickening Tollemarche, and think.

He closed his eyes firmly – better sleep. He hauled a blanket over his nakedness, though the room was warm, but sleep did not come. All he could think of was a tiny queen in a coronet decorated with snowflakes.

'Jeeze!' he moaned miserably.

CHAPTER TWENTY-ONE

While most of his congregation were dancing at the Edwardian Ball, the Reverend Bruce Mackay of Tollemarche United Church was preparing his Sunday sermon. He sat before his desk in his shabby basement den, trying to concentrate on a safe, comfortable theme, while his two sons practised drumming on a tin tray in the kitchen overhead. Above them again, he could hear his wife running the bath water for his younger daughter's nightly scrub. She shouted to the eldest of his children, Mary, aged fourteen, to come and help her put the younger ones to bed.

The noise was excruciating, his bald head throbbed, and the platitudes which usually flowed so easily from him refused to come. He was always very careful, in preparing his sermons, to wrap up well, in fulsome and flattering phrases, any unpleasant home truths which he wished to bring to the attention of his overfed, overdressed congregation. He had an uneasy feeling that a minister who was too unpleasantly honest could find his flock behaving uncommonly like wolves, and it might be difficult to get another pulpit if he wanted to move. It was, therefore, important to find subjects to talk about with which the congregation was in some degree of sympathy; but how one could do this with such a thundering racket overhead, he did not know.

He went to the basement stairs and called to the boys to be a little quieter.

There were moans of protest that they were never allowed to do anything they wanted to do; and this blatant untruth tried his spirits sorely.

'Just for a little while, boys,' he wheedled, holding down his temper with an effort. 'You could do your drumming later on.'

'Aw right,' came the sulky response.

He returned to the neat wooden desk, which he had made himself, and settled down to try again. Within a minute the silence was broken by irregular, sharp thuds in the kitchen, accompanied by excited shrieks. The plumbing groaned and gurgled as the bath water was emptied down the drain, and Mrs Mackay's voice reached a crescendo.

He leaned his head on his bony, capable hands. He could feel his temper rising, and he wished that for once, just once, he could stand up and preach hell and damnation to the filled pews of his fashionable church.

Most of the time he was able to control his inward rage, but he felt now that if there was not some quiet in the house soon, it would explode. All the suppressed bitterness at insufficient money, poor housing and an unruly family would spill out, and it would continue to erupt in ever lessening bursts for several days, until he was left exhausted, abject in his repentance, to pray for forgiveness from both God and tear-stained wife.

The bumps and bangs increased and were accompanied by shouts and screams; a fight had evidently broken out between the boys.

A new sound added itself to the general pandemonium, the sound of hysterical weeping, cries of denial and the outraged voice of his wife. Two sets of heavy feet could be heard clomping down the basement stairs. Mary, pushed by her infuriated mother, stumbled into the room. Her fat face was red, her glasses awry, and her drab, brown hair hung in rats' tails to her shoulders. Her well-formed bosom heaved with her sobs under a pullover which she had long since grown out of.

Mrs Mackay's plain, unpainted face was livid. She still wore a damp apron over her crumpled cotton slacks, and her hands were scarlet from immersion in bath water.

The minister looked up crossly at this sudden invasion; his headache was so bad that he could hardly see who had arrived. 'Whatever is the matter?' he asked.

Mary turned and made a dash for the stairs, only to be

caught by the arm by her mother and be swung back to face her father again. She began to shout defiantly at her mother through her tears.

'You've no right to take it from me. Janice lent it to me – it's her book – and I can read it if I want to.'

'What *is* this all about?' He held his voice down by sheer effort of will, but he still sounded testy. 'I'm trying to write my sermon.'

Mrs Mackay looked at her husband beseechingly. She was obviously in deep distress, though trying to keep calm. With shaking hands, she drew from her apron pocket a battered copy of *The Cheaper Sex*, and flourished it close to his face.

He took it from her and adjusted his glasses on his nose so that he could read the title. Mary stood paralyzed with fright. Upstairs, the boys ceased their fighting and crept down to see what was happening. Their smaller sister was already seated on the middle step, surveying with cold interest the distraught Mary.

'*The Cheaper Sex*,' he read in a deceptively quiet voice. Then, reproachfully, he added: 'Mary, this is not the kind of book you should be reading.'

'Not the kind of book!' cried Mrs Mackay, a note of hysteria in her voice. 'Just look at the picture on the front and then take a look at the first chapter.'

Mary said nothing, but allowed a hopeless sob to escape.

There was silence, while Mr Mackay turned the pages. He went very white.

'Mary!' he exclaimed, and there was such genuine sorrow in that single word that Mary burst into a flood of tears again.

'I want to know about love and things, and Janice lent it to me and she's read it and so have the other girls and why can't I?' The final words came out in a doglike howl.

The Reverend Bruce Mackay felt like Job for a moment. He closed his eyes, remembering Janice, the daughter of the town's leading hardware merchant, brassy and aggressive like her father. She was in Mary's class at school, the class beauty with a diary full of dates. She patronized the plain Mary unmercifully and he was sure she would have got a satanic pleasure out of lending this book to Mary.

His wife's voice intruded upon his thoughts.

'Be quiet, Mary,' she was saying sharply. Then to her husband she said in a tense voice: 'It was actually written by somebody in Tollemarche.'

Mr Mackay's eyes popped open: 'What?' he exclaimed, his mouth open in astonishment.

'That's what it says on the inner flap.'

'Good gracious!'

'Well? Aren't you going to do something about it?'

He shut the book with a sharp plop, and sighed. He was bubbling with anger, but still his voice was calm. 'I will,' he said, 'leave it to me.' He looked up at the open staircase and the three interested spectators seated there. 'Boys, go to bed now. Elsie, kindly take our little Donna and put her to bed, too.' He turned to Mary and she could see the rage dancing in his eyes. 'Mary, you are to stay here.'

Mrs Mackay saw the wisdom of disposing of the younger members of the family, and in brisk tones she repeated her husband's orders to them and herded them before her up the stairs.

Reluctantly and with many backward glances at the weeping but still defiant Mary, who continued to stand in front of her father, they went upstairs to bed. They all knew their father's terrible temper and even Donna, who hated her overbearing sister, felt a sneaking pity for Mary.

Mr Mackay sat down in his chair, closed his eyes and prayed aloud for spiritual guidance and for calmness of spirit. He felt he had, by holding the book, touched something defiling; and he was nauseated at the idea of his innocent Mary reading such a book. Her agonized cry that she wanted to know about love had passed him by. He did not consider how she was supposed to obtain a knowledge of sex in a household where there was no mention of its existence, where there was not even a cat to have kittens and where babies had arrived, neatly bundled up, from the hospital, with a tired and harassed mother, who had gone to fetch them.

Mary's sobs reduced to a sniffle as he prayed, and she looked apprehensively at him over a soaked paper hand-kerchief.

'Amen,' said her father, and after a pause, added: 'You may sit down, Mary.'

She sat down uneasily on the only other chair in the room.

'I will take charge of this book. I shall return it to Janice's father.'

Mary was terrified. 'Oh, no!' she exclaimed, 'he'll kill her!'

'I doubt it,' replied her father dryly, 'but she will get what she deserves.'

Mary began to worry about what she herself might be thought to deserve.

It began as a quiet talk on maintaining the decencies of life, and that included reading only good books.

'What about television?' asked Mary, now sufficiently recovered to consider laying a few red herrings.

The daily injection of murder, sadism and sex admin-istered by his television set to his children had bothered the Reverend Bruce Mackay for years. He had discovered, however, that if he turned the set off, the children merely wandered off to the homes of their friends, and watched it there; a number of sermons on the subject had failed to produce any parents capable of turning their sets off, too. He therefore endured the presence of this servant of Mammon in his house, where occasionally he managed to insist on censoring the programmes his younger children wanted to view; he had given up battling with Mary.

Mary had picked the wrong red herring. It reminded him of all his frustration at arguments lost with his ugly, rebellious daughter. He lost control of his temper, forgot he was a priest, and flew into a passion.

Mary quailed. She often baited her parents, driving them to the limits of their endurance and then retreating. But this time there seemed to be no retreat, no placating her father in any way. Her courage, already badly sapped, left her, and she sat on the wooden chair unable to move for sheer terror of her raging parent.

She had set out to read the book because she had hoped to learn the secrets of that dreadful sin, Sex, which everyone verbally disapproved of and in practice tolerated comfortably wherever it was exploited, be it in advertisements or on the street. She wanted facts about it and found herself denied them at every turn. Apparently gluttony, sloth, pride, envy and avarice were not nearly so serious, and, judging by her father's present mental state, neither was anger. She now realized, as she quivered in her chair, that sex must be truly deadly; otherwise, there would never have been such a fuss.

The Reverend Bruce Mackay had now reached a stage where he could not trust himself not to strike her, so he pointed to the staircase and told her to get out and stay out. No television, he roared, no pocket money, no desserts, no treats of any kind for a month. One chapter more of the Bible was to be read every morning, and Psalm 37 was to be committed to memory and recited to him on the last day of the month.

She forced her trembling legs into action and fled up to her bedroom which she shared with her little sister. She wept fiercely and silently until at last, still in her clothes, she slept.

Mrs Mackay heard her husband's voice raised in anger and later heard Mary go up to bed. She knew better, however, than to intrude upon her husband at such a time or to interfere between him and Mary by going to see the girl when she came upstairs. She argued, as she crawled into bed herself, exhausted from her long day's work, that she must show a united front with her husband in their disapproval of Mary; she could not own, even to herself, that she was just too tired to care what Mary's punishment was to be.

The book lay on top of Mr Mackay's sermon notes.

Distastefully, with the tips of his fingers, he flicked it open. Despite his best intentions, he began to read.

Hours later, he closed the book and read the notes about the author. It was unbelievable that Tollemarche could give birth to such a book. Its brutally truthful description of life amongst young people in the town went unappreciated; it dealt with a boy's sex life, and that was enough.

Inwardly burning, he went up to the kitchen to make himself a cup of coffee to calm his nerves, before he attempted to finish writing his sermon. On the kitchen counter lay the evening newspaper and he scanned the headlines while he waited for the water to boil.

The story of Hank leaped out at him. He felt as if he were being crucified. The son of members of his own congregation! Only then did he realize how deeply he had hoped that the author would prove to be some atheist from the university or, perhaps, a Roman Catholic. Dumbly he turned to page twelve, where, page one informed him, there was a review of the book.

The reviewer praised the book's honesty, clarity, tight plot and use of regional background. He hoped the author would continue to speak for the younger generations.

The minister was dumbfounded.

He slammed the newspaper to the floor, snatched up his cup of coffee and marched downstairs again to his desk. Breathing deeply and with most unchristian hatred in his heart, he tore up his sermon notes, took fresh paper and began to write.

CHAPTER TWENTY-TWO

Boyd Stych refused to be roused in time for Sunday morning church. When Olga shook him by the shoulder and told him crossly that he should show himself sometimes at church, he snapped at her and pulled the bedclothes over his head.

She put on a mutlticoloured striped duster and, closing her eyes as she passed her mirror so that she could not see her bleary-eyed morning appearance, she tottered into the kitchen to have breakfast alone. The moment Hank showed his face, she muttered, he would get his comeuppance from her, even if his father didn't care enough to give it to him.

She made herself some coffee, heated and buttered two large iced buns, and settled down to read Saturday's newspaper as she ate.

As she spread out the newspaper, she thought about the ball the previous night. She had enjoyed it until Hank came along and spoiled it. She had felt honoured to meet again Dr and Mrs LeClair. Dr LeClair was the president of Boyd's firm and normally did not stir far from his office in Montreal. He had decided, however, to venture into the wild and distant West because of the sudden upsurge in business in Tollemarche, and had extended his stay over a couple of months except for an occasional journey by jet back to Montreal to check on his vice-presidents' efforts to keep that end of the business going.

Mrs Stych sighed. Mrs LeClair sure was ladylike, so slim and elegant, with a lovely, snarly French-Canadian accent in which she had discussed her main interest in life, the care of exceptional children. Mrs Stych was painfully aware that her Ukrainian accent sounded heavy beside it. She had done her best, however, to express her admiration for anyone who could work with such unprepossessing children. She had not, thank goodness, had to introduce Hank to her. At least he had had enough sense to stay away from their party.

Hank's photograph stared up at her from the newspaper's front page. She thought it made him look older than he was. Under it was a fairly accurate history of his life and the news that he had written a daring and forward-looking book, reviewed on page twelve, which was proving a best seller and would be filmed shortly. The movie rights had been sold for – Mrs Stych gasped unbelievingly. It must be a misprint – Hank's lousy book could not be worth that much! Even if you took a zero off the sum mentioned, it was still a lot of money – more than a down payment on a house in Vanier Heights. No wonder Hank had been acting up, she sniffed to herself. Still, money or no money, she'd soon take him down a peg.

Five minutes later, when getting up to refill her cup, she saw a note scrawled on her kitchen blackboard. It said: 'Gone to Banff – back Saturday. Hank.'

Mrs Stych nearly screamed aloud. That was the way he had always been. He could duck out of bad situations quicker than a boxer in the ring. But he need not think he could escape this time, she promised herself. She'd teach him.

She sat down again and turned to the review on page twelve. This had been written by a young professor at the university and was full of praise. Everything that Hank had written was perfect.

This was too much for Olga Stych. It was a dirty book and she felt like sitting down right then and writing a letter of protest to the editor. Then she remembered how nice the girls had been the previous evening; they had proved themselves very kind by not mentioning it. Perhaps it was better not to draw more attention to the matter.

While she drank her coffee and perused the professorial effusion, fifty other ladies in fifty other kitchens were also catching up on the local news by reading Saturday's paper over their morning coffee. Many of them had attended the meeting of the Society for the Preservation of Morals, or had heard, from someone who had attended, about the terrible book which had been written by a Tollemarche student still in high school. Now, as it dawned on them that the author was Olga Stych's son, they chuckled and smirked almost fiendishly. A few of them positively purred like cats full of mice, as they realized that at last they could get their own back on Olga Stych, the woman who had cut so many of them out from senior offices in the many social groups, charitable and otherwise, in the town. Now, at last, they could challenge her unrivalled leadership of the aspiring coterie of Tollemarche matrons. Mrs Frizzell after the first shock of discovery, felt nearly ecstatic.

Into the ears of those husbands sufficiently awake to understand, they poured the shocking news, but in general all that penetrated to their alchohol-dulled brains was the fact that Olga and Boyd Stych's boy had made a pack of money out of a dirty book.

What, the ladies inquired rhetorically of these gentlemen, had Olga and Boyd Stych been doing to allow the publication of such a book? They must be out of their minds!

A few husbands, between groans about headaches, muttered that a man who allowed his son to accept a sum that big from a film company could not be out of his mind. They just wished their boys could make money like that.

The ladies were united in expressing their horror at such sentiments. Men, they said, had no culture, they were all sex mad and all they read were girlie magazines in the cigar store.

These were old bones of contention being dug up again, and, as the men all *did* read girlie magazines in the cigar store, they all clapped their mouths shut like well-sprung screen doors.

Mrs Stych was a few minutes late for church, owing to her detailed perusal of the newspaper, and she slipped into her usual pew near the front of the church, under cover of the first hymn. The florid female with two children, who usually shared it with the Stych family, was already seated, and she turned to stare at Olga with her mouth open as she braced herself for a top note. Mrs Stych hastily found her place in the hymn-book and joined in the final verse.

There was a rustle of closing books, and Mrs Stych smiled brightly at Margaret Tyrrell, the secretary of the Committee for the Preservation of Morals, who, with her husband and mother-in-law, was in the pew across the aisle. Margaret looked embarrassed and gave close attention to the arrangement of her skirt as she sat down. She did not seem to see Mrs Stych.

Puzzled, Mrs Stych turned her gaze upon the Reverend Bruce Mackay, who, strangely, proved to be looking straight at her. Did she imagine it or did he really mean to look so malevolent? She wondered if he disapproved of her hat, which was an expensive creation of Persian lamb and violets, to match her coat.

There was an abrupt quietness amongst the congregation and Mrs Stych felt as if every eye was upon her. Then, to her relief, the Reverend Bruce Mackay cleared his throat preparatory to addressing the Lord, and Mrs Stych relaxed.

She was totally unprepared for the blow when it came some three-quarters of an hour later. The minister mounted to the pulpit and put down his notes before him. He paused dramatically and then brought his fist down on the edge of the pulpit with a thwack which gave him the immediate attention of his audience. The published title of his address that morning had been 'Work in the Mission Field', so they were unprepared for such an assault on their nervous systems.

Mrs Stych was jolted, too. This tirade had nothing to do with foreign missions, but at first she did not connect what he had to say with herself. Then his outraged comments began to penetrate. She and Boyd were being preached at in a fashion which had gone out fifty years before. They were being held responsible for the work of their son – as if anyone could be responsible for what one's children did!

They were being held up as people who had allowed their son such licence that he was now in a position to damage minds younger than his and create a society of loose-living reprobates. Parents who filled their lives with empty social events to the detriment of their children's training were more of a menace to society than the delinquent child himself. The angry minister did not name the particular parents he had in mind for, indeed, he was saying to a whole group what he had been longing to say for years. However, not a single worshipper was in doubt about whom he spoke, and all eyes were turned again upon Olga Stych, and it seemed as if even the artificial violets on her hat were beginning to wilt under the collective glare.

Some of the eyes gleamed with satisfaction. Olga could be insufferable, and she was getting a good old-fashioned talking-to. Mrs Frizzell, her face inscrutable, was inwardly rejoicing, and promised herself the satisfaction of cutting Olga dead as soon as they got out of church. That two of the Stych family had won prizes at the ball rankled like a festering wound.

Mrs Stych had patronized the Reverend Bruce Mackay casually for a number of years, and had thought him a dumb, acquiescent mouse. Now it was as if the mouse had clawed her like a cougar. She could feel the colour go from her face, while the two children in the pew sucked their sweets noisily and regarded her with cold eyes; their mother's eyes, a quick glance told her, were equally icy.

She was too shocked to feel anger at Hank – she had for the moment forgotten that he was the instrument of her destruction. She knew only that her life was collapsing around her; the carefully built façade of importance and prestige, of money and influence, came tumbling down. All that she had striven for – to improve herself, to get away as far as she could from her father's pig farm, to become a leader of Tollemarche society – was swept away as if by an avalanche. She could feel the animosity which flowed around her like a cold fog. The silence, except for the accusing voice from the pulpit, was profound; not a handbag clicked, not a shoe shuffled.

At the end of twenty minutes he had finished. With firm fingers he folded his notes and put them back into his pocket. As he stared out over the congregation, he knew that they were with him, and he was thankful for it. A bitter lesson had had to be taught and he felt himself to be God's instrument to teach it. He hoped sincerely that many of the women facing him would realize that his sermon had applied to their vapid lives, too.

He announced the final hymn, and dumbly Mrs Stych stood up. She did not sing, however; her throat was too dry. For the first time in years, she wished passionately that Boyd had been with her to sustain her with his masculine strength. She had no hope that he would sympathize or understand what she was going through, but he might at least have felt some indignation at the clerical condemnation of his lack of parental responsibility; it would have put him on her side.

The service was soon over. Mrs Stych sat down suddenly, fearing she was going to faint, and the florid woman and her two sticky children pushed past her to get out, without even her usual smile and 'Hiya?' The minister raced round to the front door in order to be in time to shake hands with each member of his flock, and only when the great building was practically empty did Mrs Stych rise and go out by the side door. Being a late arrival, she had had to park her car down a side street, and now she was glad of it. She crept home through snowy streets under skies as leaden as her spirits.

Not one woman, she realized with a pang, had slipped into her pew to sit with her and comfort her. Presumably this was going to be the time for paying off old scores, and Olga quailed as she realized how many old scores there were.

CHAPTER TWENTY-THREE

Olga arrived home from church earlier than she usually did because she had not stopped to talk on the church steps, and she could hear Boyd in the basement, chatting with a neighbour as they played pool. Boyd had installed the table on an earlier visit home, mostly as a status symbol, and had then discovered that he enjoyed the game.

It was symptomatic of Olga's distressed state of mind that the Persian lamb coat was dumped with hat, gloves and handbag on the living-room chesterfield, and not immediately hung up in her clothes closet.

The telephone rang just as she was patting her hair back into place in front of the hall mirror. She could clearly hear Boyd swearing in the basement, and she called that she would answer it.

An excited Ruthenian babble greeted her. Grandma and Uncle were pleased Hank had written a book. Had she seen the paper? Was she coming out to visit them today? Please bring a copy of the book, so one of Joe's kids could read it to her and translate it for her. The newspaper picture was nice; could she have another copy of it? Who had been on their phone all morning? She had not been able to get through until now.

Olga forced herself to think. Of course, the grandmothers would want to read the book, and she felt she had reached the end of her stamina when she realized this. She determined to make Hank face his grandparents – she had enough battles of her own to fight.

'We haven't got any copies yet, Ma,' she stalled. 'Hank will have some soon, and he'll give you a copy.'

'Where's Hank?' demanded the cracked voice in the telephone receiver. 'Put him on. I want to tell him I'm proud of him.'

'He's gone to Banff,' said Olga thankfully.

The babble at the other end dwindled in disappointment.

Olga made a valiant effort to sound normal. 'I'll come and see you next week, Ma.'

'Well, bring Hank and bring his book.'

Mrs Stych made her farewells and leaned her head against the wall, as she dropped the receiver on its cradle. The telephone immediately rang again.

'Mrs Stych?'

'Yeah?'

An eager young feminine voice said: 'I just wanna tell Hank I think his book is real sharp, Mrs Stych. Is he home?'

'No,' said Olga shortly. With a voice like that, the girl could not be more than fifteen.

'Oh,' the voice was deflated, forlorn. 'When he comes in, just tell him Betsy called.'

'I will.' Olga put down the receiver quickly. The Reverend Bruce Mackay's remarks about influencing a whole generation began to have some meaning for her. 'But it's not fair to blame us,' she thought defiantly. 'We didn't write it.'

The telephone rang again. This time the voice was male and belonged to Tom in Grade 12, but the tenor of the conversation was similar. Mrs Stych began to feel sick.

She could hear Boyd showing his visitor out of the back door and promising that they would have another game next Sunday. He came slowly back in, looking pleased with himself, and saw her with her hand still on the telephone.

'That damned thing has rung all morning,' he said irritably. 'Hank this and Hank that – I couldn't sleep – I took the receiver off for a while – the kid must know the whole darn town. And where is Hank, anyway? He must have got up real early.'

'Gone to Banff,' said Olga briefly. 'Musta gone for skiing.'

'Better get some dinner,' said Boyd, opening the refrigerator. 'Suppose you'll be going to see Mother this afternoon?'

Olga was reviewing this engagement with Grandma

Stych with trepidation; she was not sure how much the old lady would know about Hank's book. She attended a different church, but she would have read the *Tollemarche Advent* – everybody did.

She said dully to her husband, 'I suppose I'd better go – she'll be expecting me. Get out that cold roast beef and some tomatoes.'

Silently they prepared and ate their meal, interrupted only once by another telephone call, this time from the local radio station's morning commentator, who said she would telephone again when Hank returned.

'Might as well come with you to see Ma,' said Boyd, wiping his mouth on his paper table napkin. 'Have to look through some papers tonight – might as well get out this afternoon.'

Normally Mrs Stych would have disliked this intrusion into a feminine visit, but today she was so dismal that she was grateful for any human interest.

'O.K.,' she muttered. 'We'll go right away.'

The visit was uneventful. The old lady was interested that Hank had published a book, but why, she asked, had he chosen such a vulgar name for it?

Olga's heart sank. This was it. This would be where Grandma would blow up.

Boyd was lighting a cigarette. Without a flicker of an eyelid, he said calmly: 'You have to have names like that nowadays for books, otherwise they don't sell.'

Olga looked at him in silent admiration.

Mrs Stych Senior tut-tutted and said she didn't know what the world was coming to. Olga hastily agreed, and equally hastily asked if Grandma had planted any tulip bulbs this year.

Grandma Stych was launched safely on a new subject, and Olga leaned back to listen, too wrapped in depression to talk much more. The old lady's English was almost perfect, her grammar painstakingly correct. She had a slightly Scottish burr to her accent, learned from the Scottish woman recruited to teach her by her father when they had first landed in Tollemarche; and Olga, remembering the hours when Hank had sat at her feet playing with toy cars, wondered if this was where he had learned English well enough to enable him to write.

Olga watched her husband as he talked about getting their lot fenced. He, too, had tried to get away from the Old World ties of his parents – he was more agressively Canadian than a Nova Scotian – and she could see that some of his mannerisms still offended his mother.

They had trouble getting the car to move when they were ready to go home; the back wheels spun and dug hollows in the packed snow of the driveway. A fuming Boyd had to push, while Olga turned the ignition key and accelerated. A friendly passerby lent his shoulder to that of Boyd and between the two of them they got it rolling down the slope to the road. Since Olga was in the driver's seat, she continued in it and drove them home. Boyd put down her unusual silence to the need to concentrate on driving over such treacherously ice-covered streets.

After supper, he retired to his den to look at the work he had brought home from the office. He assumed that, as usual, Olga would go to practise with her Sacred Song Chōrus Group, but, later on, he was surprised to notice that she was still moving about overhead.

Mrs Stych had intended to go to her practice, but, as the time for it drew near, her courage began to ebb. Most of the members would have been in church and would have heard the Reverend Bruce Mackay deliver his harangue, and Olga wanted to find out first what position the girls would take, after they had had time to talk the scandal over amongst themselves, before she laid herself open to snubs.

She stood in the middle of her sitting-room, which looked just like a picture in Eaton's catalogue, and wondered how to occupy herself. She was shocked to find herself chewing at her long scarlet fingernails, and hastily decided to tidy up the cupboards and drawers in Hank's room. She had not done this for years and was motivated by a sneaking curiosity to know what he had in them.

The girls made their decision sooner than she had expected. Soon after the chorus could reasonably have been expected to finish its practice, the telephone rang. Olga extricated herself with difficulty from the back of Hank's clothes closet, which she had found cluttered with several different sizes of ice hockey armour, indicating the different ages at which he had attempted to play the game. Provoked by yet another telephone call, she clicked her tongue irritably as she trotted down the passage and lifted the receiver.

It was Mrs Jones, the secretary of the chorus, a lady whom Mrs Stych did not know intimately. She was a pompous, narrow-minded woman, whose children were left to run wild and unattended in the streets as soon as they could stand, a lawless rabble dreaded by small children and cursed by shopkeepers. She did not ask Mrs Stych to resign; she ordered her to do so.

The chorus, she said, was united in feeling that Mrs Stych could not be considered a suitable person to assist in singing sacred songs, since she must have assented to her son's writing that dreadful, obscene book. And, if Mrs Jones might say so, it showed a shocking state of affairs in the Stych home.

Mrs Stych was stung into retort by the gross injustice of Mrs Jones's remarks.

'I suppose,' she said, her face aflame and her voice icy, 'you will also be asking Mrs Braun to resign, because her son stole a car recently, and Mrs Donohue, because of that bond scandal her husband was involved in?'

Mrs Jones gasped, and Olga slammed down the receiver in the hope that it would hurt her ears.

She stamped back to Hank's room and continued her rummaging. She had a morbid desire to see if she could exhume anything of his writings from it, but there was nothing – not a slip of paper, not even a book with a sexy looking cover; just his usual collection of classics in sober bindings. Two of them were *A Thousand and One Nights* and *The Decameron*, but Mrs Stych had never read these and knew only that they were very old books, so she dusted them and put them back unopened. The dust was thick on a few of the volumes, because she had always left this room to the mercies of her cleaning lady, who had not been very thorough.

Hank was expected to make his bed and keep the place tidy himself; this he had failed to do, and his shelves and drawers were in a chaotic mess. Mrs Stych decided that this was something else to take up sharply with Hank on his return.

Finally she shook out her duster and dropped it down the laundry chute. Because she could not think of anything else to do, she went to bed.

This, she reflected, as she lay in the dark, had been one of the most miserable days of her life. None of the girls, she recollected dismally, had telephoned, and she wondered if they all felt as Mrs Jones did. She also wondered bleakly what she was going to do in the future, if they all did take the same attitude.

CHAPTER TWENTY-FOUR

The next week was a frantic and unhappy one for Mrs Stych.

Mr Dixon, the English teacher, telephoned on Monday morning and asked if he could speak to Hank.

'He's up at Banff, skiing,' said Mrs Stych shortly, for the twenty-second time. She was tired of Hank, sick of the disturbance he had caused her. In a moment of startled self-revelation, she was aware that she had regarded him as nothing but a trial and impediment to her since the day he had been conceived; she had made every effort not to have any more children, so that she could give all her attention to her own ambitions. Her sudden sense of guilt increased her irritation.

Mr Dixon's faded voice became a trifle more enthusiastic.

'I wanted to congratulate him, Mrs Stych. His choice of subject was unfortunate, but it is not every young man who can write so well. I feel that I have had some success with him, if I may venture to say so.'

'Mr Dixon!' exclaimed Olga, her voice quivering. 'Wotcha sayin'? You shoulda stopped him. You musta known what he was doin'. Why didn't you stop him?' She snorted. 'The school should do sumpin' about boys like him.'

Mr Dixon's resentment of lazy parents flared up. He remembered that when he had advised Hank to tell his parents what he was writing about, the boy had refused. Mr Dixon had been aware for some time that Hank was writing a book of which his elders might not approve. He had got wind of it through stray remarks of Hank and his friends' and it had worried him very much. No amount of kindly counselling had been able to break through Hank's pig-headed hatred of his parents, thought Mr Dixon, or make

185

him try harder to study his other school subjects. Now this woman was trying to tell him he was responsible for her son's behaviour.

He spoke coldly. 'Parents do not seem to realize, Mrs Stych, that schools have little hope of curbing young people if their teaching is not reinforced by the home.' He paused, and then added: 'A novel is an effort to show some order in life and find meaning in it. Judging by Hank's novel, his experience of life cannot have been very happy, Mrs Stych. We should perhaps remind ourselves that the whole of Hank's young life has been spent in his home at Tollemarche.'

'Mr Dixon!' cried Olga indignantly. 'Are you suggesting that he learned those things at home?'

She was still speaking when Mr Dixon said: 'Good-bye, Mrs Stych. I will speak to Hank another time.' The receiver went dead.

Mr Dixon was not without courage, and he grieved for many of his pupils, some of whom got into far deeper trouble than Hank would ever do. He sat for a while after his conversation with Olga Stych, his hands folded on his desk, wondering what one unimportant bachelor schoolteacher could do to help. Even some of the women teachers on the staff, he knew, had children who were not adequately cared for – apparently two pay cheques were more important than caring for one's children.

There was a small knock on his door, so he closed the books he was using to prepare a lesson, and said resignedly: 'Come in.'

A tall, lank-haired girl entered. Her eyes were black-rimmed in her white face. She clutched her books for her next class to her stomach, and looked at him entreatingly.

'Mr Dixon, could I talk to you about something? I don't think my counsellor, Miss Simpson, will understand – a man might understand better.'

'Oh, good grief,' he thought to himself, 'not another pregnancy!' And even as he said: 'Sure, come in,' he was thinking that the tart-tongued Miss Simpson would think

186

he was trespassing on her ground if he dealt with this girl and would demand an explanation. Miss Simpson could be very trying.

Still, he could lend an ear. He could give a little time to these youngsters, time that nobody else seemed able to spare.

Mrs Stych, that redoubtable socialite, that ardent hostess to the socially prominent, had time to spare. It began to hang very heavy on her hands, and every day seemed to make matters worse.

The secretary of the Committee for the Preservation of Morals telephoned to say, in her girlish, gushing voice: 'Olga, you must understand. It just won't do to have you on the committee. I mean to say . . .'

Mrs Stych resigned; and Margaret Tyrrell got rid of a dangerous competitor for the post of vice-president next year.

The Lady Queen Bees were even more crushing. The chairman wrote and demanded her precious Queen Bee medal back within three days. The Queen Bees could not tolerate even the merest breath of scandal, she stated peremptorily.

Boiling with rage, yet feeling that she had no alternative, Mrs Stych dropped the medal into an envelope and got Boyd to post it for her.

She had been president of the Community Centre; and two members of the executive committee, both suave real-estate salesmen who found the Community Centre a convenient source of information about houses likely to come up for sale, called upon her and smoothly explained that many members were uneasy at her continuing in the presidency; there was a general feeling that she and Boyd must have condoned the publication of Hank's book. Neither man had seen a copy of the book, but they both assured her that neither of them had any special feelings about it; they were just unfortunate that they had been given the unenviable task of explaining the Community Centre's quandary to her. They hoped that she would not take it amiss, and that she would not hesitate to call upon them to sell her home when she moved to Vanier Heights.

Mrs Stych ventured to argue that the responsibility was not hers, but she was no match for two salesmen, so eventually she agreed to resign.

Mrs Frizzell, who was the vice-president, rejoiced, as she was immediately installed as president.

The Ladies of Scotland did not communicate with her, and, remembering Miss Angus's denunciation of Donna Frizzell's taste in literature at the last tea, Mrs Stych kept out of their way, feeling that her fate would be much the same there.

Usually the Stychs gave an at-home at Christmas. They announced the date and time of it on the Christmas cards they sent out, and could usually expect about a hundred guests to flow through their living-room in the course of the evening. This year, Mrs Stych decided, they would not hold it. She also decided that she and Boyd would not attend two coffee parties to which they had earlier been invited. Boyd received this information with relief, as he was very busy at work.

Despite the cold-shouldering from which she was suffering, all those ladies connected with charities in the city sent special appeals to her, to Boyd and to Hank. Money was money, after all, they told each other.

Boyd remained untouched by the general disapprobation. His long absences from the city meant that he could not conveniently hold any office in service club or other community endeavours, and his friends were old ones who had gone to school with him.

None of his colleagues had read a book since they left university, and, though they had heard of Hank's book through their wives, the only thing they remembered about it was the mighty sum paid for the film rights, and this was enough to reconcile them to anything.

Only in the emerging world of polite society in Tollemarche, a world ruled by women, a tooth-and-claw world, was its impact felt, just as Hank had originally planned that it should be. Mrs Stych's rivals found it a priceless opportunity to displace a woman who had been rapidly becoming a very influential lady in the city.

During her fortnightly visit to the supermarket, the shoppers she knew seemed suddenly blind and had a tendency to vanish down the other end of the aisle just as she entered it. Even Mrs Stein of Dawne's Dresse Shoppe, where her charge account was one of the largest, left her to a young, careless girl who did not understand the needs of a forty bust.

Feverishly she checked her engagement diary. The church tea and bake sale was to be held on the following Saturday and she had promised to contribute two cakes to it. With her finger on the entry, she considered whether she should prepare the cakes. The Reverend Bruce Mackay loomed before her, shaking a menacing forefinger, and she cringed. A report of his attack on obscene literature had been featured in Monday's *Tollemarche Advent*, and Mrs Stych's double chin quivered with horror at the thought of facing him again. The Lord would have to do without cake.

The diary showed that she was due to go curling the following day with some of the girls; it was a good team and they had done well the previous winter.

Mrs Stych loved curling and felt she could not forgo this pleasure without putting up a fight. She dialled the captain of the team.

The telephone was answered by the captain's six-year-old daughter, who said her mother was out and she did not know when she would be back.

Mrs Stych inquired where Chrissie and Donald, her elder brother and sister, were.

'Gone skating,' said the small voice laconically.

Mrs Stych asked the child to request her mother to telephone back about curling the following day.

'Oh, Mother doesn't want you on the team any more,' said the child with devastating honesty. 'She's asked Mrs Simpkins to play instead.' There was a sound of munching, and then the child continued. 'She says Mrs Simpkins doesn't play so well, but she has to 'tain the moral character of the team. What's moral character, Mrs Stych?'

Mrs Stych was rocking unsteadily on her high heels. Her face was pale. She swallowed and said quite kindly: 'I'm not sure, honey. I guess . . . ' She sought for words. 'I guess it means being truthful like you are?'

'Am I truthful? Say, thank you for saying so, Mrs Stych.'

'Is your baby-sitter with you?'

'I don't need a sitter. I just come in from school. I'm big enough to manage now.' She sighed. 'I gotta a door key hanging round my neck. And I'm eating a cookie – listen!' And there was a crunch as small teeth went through a cookie.

Mrs Stych, never very good with children, felt out of her depth, so she said: 'It's been nice talking to you, honey. See you.' She rang off.

She went and sat down by her picture window and thought about the little girl to whom she had been speaking. She had left Hank like that, with a key hung round his neck, as she tore from one social event to another, assuring herself that she was the busiest woman alive and that one must keep up one's interests; otherwise, what would one do when one was widowed?

Now look where she was! She wondered what the little six-year-old would be doing in the empty hours after school ten years hence – and she shuddered. Hank had written in uncomprising terms about what they did.

She watched idly as a taxi drew up outside Mrs Frizzell's house. Betty from Vancouver had evidently come on a visit with the new baby. Her eldest boy, a three-year-old, stood in the wind, waiting for his mother to pay the cabbie. His parka was unzipped and his hood thrown back, despite the cold. He turned and clumped up the path to his grand-mother's front door, and Mrs Stych nearly passed out. It could not be – it couldn't! A tiny, wooden-faced replica of Hank! She opened her eyes and looked again. A second look only confirmed her horrid suspicions.

Olga Stych closed her eyes and prayed fervently that Donna Frizzell would not see the likeness. A feeling of consternation swept through her. What else had Hank embroiled himself in?

CHAPTER TWENTY-FIVE

Hank fought his way back from Banff in a near blizzard, spending fifteen hours on the road in a determined effort to return before Isobel left. He arrived about midnight, having telephoned from Edmonton to say that he was on his way.

Sandwiches, cake and a warm welcome from both Isobel and Dorothy awaited him. In the privacy of the porch he kissed Isobel good-bye, leaving her pale and shaken, and promised himself privately that his tour of Europe would be short, so that he could spend a lot of time in London or Llan-whatever-it-was with Isobel. Without her, he knew after stern self-examination in the silence of the Rockies, he might as well be dead.

He had no desire to meet his parents that night, so he ploughed through the snow round the side of the house to the window of his room, which his experienced fingers quickly forced open. He pushed his bag in first, then clambered in himself, bringing enough snow with him to ruin the wall-to-wall broadloom.

His parents upstairs did not hear him, but Mrs Frizzell saw him through her bathroom window and, with a smug smile, promised herself the pleasure of spreading the news around Tollemarche in the morning that Hank Stych had been out so late that he had had to climb through his bedroom window to avoid his father.

She saw herself telling the story to Mrs MacDonald, with appropriately significant pauses, to suggest with whom she thought Hank had spent the evening. That young Mrs Dawson, thought Mrs Frizzell sourly, might queen it at the ball, but she was no better than the rest of them in leading Hank astray. The widow of Tollemarche's hero had no right to go out with any other man, never mind a boy. How Mrs Dawson Senior could endure her as a daughter-in-law was beyond Mrs Frizzell's comprehension.

Her malevolent contemplation of the probable relationship between Hank and Isobel was broken by the return of Mr Frizzell, aggressively drunk, from the Bonnie Scots Men's Association. He had just missed hitting another car, on turning into their street and was raging about careless young drivers.

Mrs Frizzell agreed that teenagers were plain crazy.

A cry from one of the bedrooms made it necessary for her to break the news to Maxie that Betty had brought the three children for a visit.

He cursed, and she was glad she had not told him how a nearly hysterical Betty had dumped them on her, with the news that her patient, law-abiding husband had left her and had gone to the United States to join the army. He had expressed the hope that he would be killed in Vietnam, and Betty had now returned to Vancouver, ostensibly to consult a lawyer friend. Mrs Frizzell had a horrid sinking feeling that the lawyer might be more than a friend and that the children might be with her for some time.

She shut the door so that she would not hear the baby's howls and went to bed. Tomorrow she would get a baby-sitter. No child was going to stand between her and the gratifying number of offices opened up to her by the fall of Olga Stych.

Unaware of the gaze of the witchlike female next door, Hank divested himself of his wet clothes and went to bed, still throbbing with the strength of feeling roused in him by Isobel. She was perfect; and he smiled as he remembered his farewell to her – he hoped she would remember it until he could see her again.

The scratched recording of bells, which served to call the faithful to the Tollemarche United Church, woke Hank on Sunday morning.

He lay in bed listening to it, while he recollected painfully that Isobel would be on the plane going eastward, having been seen off by her in-laws. He was back where he had started years ago – alone.

193

He told himself scornfully that he had a host of girl friends – and realized emptily that he had not called any of them for weeks. He knew every fellow in the neighbourhood, too, but mentally dismissed the lot of them as a pack of immature nincompoops; he had been through so much in the past few months that he felt old beside them.

He turned on his transistor radio and flicked hopelessly from station to station; every one had a preacher on it, busy saying how fast the world was travelling to either extinction or eternal damnation.

The Bible Belt, my God! It was time he got out of it.

He went through his mail, which had been delivered to Isobel's house. From an epistle from his publisher, he realized that he would need to go to Europe via New York.

He trailed off to the bathroom, turned on the shower to cold and stepped under it. The water was icy and he yelped and hastily turned on the hot tap as well.

Through the roar of the water, he heard his mother's sharp voice call: 'That you, Hank?'

He stopped scrubbing. He had imagined that she would be at church.

'Yeah, Ma,' he shouted.

She realized the impossibility of carrying on a conversation over the noise of the shower, which sounded like a miniature Niagara, so she went back to her breakfast coffee and buns, fuming silently.

On realizing that his mother was at home, Hank's first instinct had been to take refuge in bed again. But he was very hungry, so he put on a pair of jeans and a battered T-shirt, and, still drying his head with a towel, proceeded to the kitchen, from whence came the welcome odour of coffee.

'Don't dry your hair in the kitchen,' snapped Olga promptly. It was easier to squash people if you started by catching them in a genuine wrongdoing. She shifted her chair round to get a better view of him and glared at him distastefully.

'Why don't you get a better haircut – you look real foreign like that.'

He hastily plastered down his George V haircut with his hands, and looked at her speculatively. She had not yet dressed or made up, and she looked untidy and haggard, her face hard and unfriendly.

Silently he returned to the bathroom and replaced the offending towel. He stood for a moment, his hand on the towel rail, considering how to deal with his mother.

He thought of taking an apartment. An apartment home, based on seventy thousand dollars carefully invested, was a different proposition from a single room maintained by a schoolboy out of his earnings as a part-time grocery market clerk. If ever he came back from Europe – and he was beginning to wonder if he ever would – he would take one of the new apartments being built in the city, and, if his second book was a success, he would find a Japanese servant to look after him. He decided that he would pack up all his personal possessions before he went away, and store them in a corner of the basement.

Cheered up, he returned to the kitchen, opened the refrigerator door and was just taking out two eggs, when his mother put down the Saturday's *Advent*, which she had been reading, and addressed him.

'And just how long do you think you're going to live here for free?'

He was paralyzed with shock, the two eggs in his hand, and the refrigerator starting to hum because he still held its door open. The unexpectedness of this angle of attack had caught him unawares, and he did not know how to deal with it. He had been ready for upbraidings, but not this.

He had always taken the same attitude as his fellow students, that if his father insisted upon his staying in high school he could not earn much, and his parents must, therefore, be prepared to maintain him in food and lodging. He had managed to provide his own pocket money and clothes by doing odd jobs after school and, more recently, by his writing, since his fifteenth birthday. Now

195

his mother was challenging this basic assumption.

He swallowed and carefully closed the refrigerator, after replacing the eggs. He turned guiltily towards her. The fact that the situation had changed on his leaving school and having money in plenty had honestly escaped him.

She saw that she had hit him on a tender spot and she was glad. She would teach him that if he thought he was adult enough to attend the ball, he was adult enough to maintain himself entirely. She would wear him ragged, she vowed.

Her smile was thin and sneering as she waited for his reply.

Hank sought for words. He was dreadfully hurt. The merest reminder would have been sufficient to make him produce his pocket book. This was tit-for-tat with a vengeance.

Finally, he stuttered: 'Of course I'll shell out for keep. I just forgot, that's all.'

'I should think so,' she said sourly.

He hadn't finished speaking to her. He drew himself up straight, till his six feet of height towered over her, and she flinched at the totally disillusioned, sad eyes he turned upon her. Mr Dixon's remark that his life could not have been a very happy one flashed through her mind.

'Look here,' he said in a dangerously quiet voice, 'you and Father wanted me to make Grade 12, not for my own sake, but because it would be a disgrace to you both if I didn't. I had no choice but to take my board from you.' He took a long breath, and years of pent-up resentment poured out. 'Neither of you cared what happened to me. You were so busy with your stupid teas and bake sales, and Dad with his trips to the North to get away from you. The cars got more care than I ever did! I'm sorry I didn't go years ago – I would have gone if it hadn't been for Grandma Palichuk, I think.'

He paused to gather up his self-control, which was slipping fast. 'Well, I don't want to be a drag on you any more,' he nearly shouted. 'I'm going to New York and then to Europe and I doubt if I'll ever come back.'

He felt for his wallet in his hip pocket, drew it out, sought through it for twenty-dollar bills. He flung the six that he had on to the table in front of her.

'I left school about a month ago. Here's my rent. I'll pay again before I go, and I'll eat out.'

The sum was more than double that which she could have expected from a lodger in similar circumstances, and she sat staring at it, trying to be happy that she had crushed him, while he turned on his heel and went back to his room.

He flung himself onto his rumpled bed. The pain inside him was so intense, he did not know how to bear it. In his calmer moments, he had long since realized that children in Tollemarche were more endured than loved, now that they were no longer needed as unskilled labour on the farms; and he had often said bitterly to his fellow sufferers in Grade 12 that rats nurtured their young better than Tollemarche mothers did.

He had, as a small boy, made excuses to himself for his mother's neglect, and he had endowed her with feelings of affection which, he told himself, she had no time to express because she had a lot of work to do. As he matured, he realized that most of her activity was busywork, and to think that she loved anyone was just a dream on his part. He had become desperate to finish school, so that he might acquire financial independence, yet such was society's indoctrination, he was convinced he could not function at all without that magical Grade 12.

Now he had disproved this fallacy and was financially well launched. He had, too, a degree of emotional emancipation. And he hoped he had Isobel.

The knifelike pain eased and he became calmer. He told himself to stop being a fool. He had hit his mother with the aid of his book and she had merely done the natural thing and hit him back. Fair enough. What he needed was a good breakfast – and tomorrow, a travel agent.

He found a faded car coat and some earmuffs, rescued his boots from the corner into which they had been tossed

197

the previous night to drip mournfully on the rug, and carrying them in his hand, tiptoed to the front door.

A pile of letters addressed to him had been flung carelessly on the top of the boot shelves, and he gathered them up as he went out. He sifted through them in the privacy of his car. They were mostly congratulatory letters from his fellow students, but one was from his Ukrainian grandmother in her own language, with a scrawl from his uncle at the bottom of it. He said that he and Grandma and his young cousins all wanted to see his book, but most of all they wanted to see him, to tell him how proud they were of him. He was to come down to the farm as soon as he returned from Banff.

He decided that at this moment the smell of pigs and hens would be nicer than even the best breakfast, and he swung the car out of the garage and headed for the highway, hoping that the snowploughs would have cleared as far as the farm.

He wished wistfully that he had been born to Uncle Joe's wife. She had died, of course, but his grandmother had a wonderful, primitive motherliness which permeated the whole contented existence of his cousins.

Grandma, he thought, had done her best to spare her daughter the intolerable work load which had turned her own hands into revolting claws. She and her silent peasant husband had decided the girl was smart, had sent her to Tollemarche to high school and then to college.

He smiled grimly to himself. Tollemarche must have seemed wonderfully sophisticated, with its college, schools and churches, its homes with bathrooms and its many small stores; a handsome Ukrainian girl would feel she could better herself there. And Boyd Stych, just graduated from the University of Toronto and about to join an enterprising firm of consulting geologists, would have looked like a film star to a girl from a Ukrainian pig farm.

He drove fast along the road, set high above the surrounding country. He could see for miles across the bleak, snowy land, unbrokenly smooth except for an occasional windbreak of trees sheltering a cowering farm-house.

Where a letterbox nailed to a post marked the entrance, he turned into a cart track leading to the farm. He wished he had Isobel with him; he felt she and Grandma would get along together very well; they were both of them honest and practical – and, yes, gentle.

As he drew up between the barn and the back door, he suddenly remembered that he had not seen his father that morning. He would never have gone to church without being dragged there by his mother, and yet he was sure he had not been in the house.

He dismissed the question from his mind, as the door opened and his cousins came tumbling out to greet him and to admire the Triumph, which they had not seen before.

CHAPTER TWENTY-SIX

Olga Stych heard the front door close after Hank and her triumph at his humiliation slowly evaporated. Boyd had gone out early to see Mayor Murphy immediately upon his return from Mass, about purchasing a lot in Vanier Heights. He expected that these negotiations would be protracted, since the demand for serviced land was heavy and Mayor Murphy could name his own price. Without the presence of either man, the house was so quiet that even the creaking of its wooden frame seemed unnaturally loud. The snow outside and the double windows muffled all sound from the road, and Mrs Stych shivered and pulled her robe around her. Perhaps she should have gone to church and faced the supercilious stares of her erstwhile friends, rather than endure the emptiness of the house. The memory of the dislike in Hank's eyes as he left her battled in her mind with earlier memories of him as a frightened child left uncomforted.

She told herself she must be getting old to feel sorry for a great hulking brute like him. Next week she would give a dinner party for Boyd's more senior colleagues – that would keep her busy.

Making herself move briskly, she took a shower and made up her face. She tried on her new artificial eyelashes, sold to her by Monsieur de la Rue in his new Lady Fayre Beauty Boutique. He had sworn that they were just as becoming to mature beauties as to their daughters, and now, as she fluttered them cautiously in front of the mirror, she felt sure he was right. She added a further touch of blue eyeshadow and then put on her black dress, so that she would be ready to visit Grandma Stych in the afternoon.

Garbed in full visiting regalia, she felt much better, and began to consider that perhaps she had accepted her social eclipse too readily. Boyd had pointed out that they ought to cultivate some of the senior university staff, who were increasing rapidly in number and importance in the city. There were also one or two Canadian Broadcasting Company staff now resident in Tollemarche, not to speak of several new businesses being established with their concommitant executives. Perhaps, she pondered, it would be possible to drop the old Tollemarche residents almost as fast as they had tried to drop her.

Boyd had said: 'Those girls of yours don't really care a hang about Hank's book – or maybe the Reverend does – but nobody else. They are getting at us.'

Mrs Stych had been incredulous. 'Us?' She had squeaked.

'Yeah. Us. Y'know, the new pecking order in this town isn't yet quite clear – and we have been doing a bit too well. Hank's book is a good chance to put us back where we belong – way down.'

'Wotcha mean – pecking order?'

'Well, every town has a pecking order – like the hens in your Ma's back yard. Ours was fixed for years – Scottish Presbyterians at the top, Métis Roman Catholics at the bottom, the Indians nowhere, and everybody else in strictly acceptable order in between.

'Now, since the oil wells were discovered, so many new people have come in that it's all upset. Ukrainians and Germans, like us, have more money than some of the old Scots who've been here two generations. You can see I'm right – we have an Irish Roman Catholic for Mayor, with money in his wallet. Where was he fifteen years ago? Or even five?'

'We been here two generations,' Olga had said stubbornly.

'It doesn't mean the same thing. As far as the big people were concerned, we didn't exist until the past ten years. I tell you – now, I own more real estate in this town than the chemical plant does – more'n Tyrrell or Murphy even.' Then he added in a rueful tone, 'Except I don't have a lot in Vanier Heights.'

201

Mrs Stych ruminated over this conversation as she carved a store-cooked ham for Boyd's and her lunch. Apart from any entertaining they might manage to do to re-establish themselves, there were a number of public functions which they could attend, where it might be productive to show themselves; there was the Amateur Ballet Show, a full-evening-dress affair, and public lectures at the university – quite big people went to those.

She had just poured a commercial dressing over a quartered lettuce to go with the ham, when there was a heavy banging at the back door as if someone were kicking it.

She put the bottle of dressing down slowly, and considered what the new yellow paint on the back door must be looking like after such treatment. Indignantly, she marched to the door, yanked it open and peered through the glass of the outer screen door.

A small head in a snow suit hood was leaning against it at the level of the lower ledge, and a small foot in a rubber overboot was systematically kicking it. She pushed the door open, nearly toppling the owner of the head and foot.

'Just waddya think you're doing?'

She glared down at the peaceful face of a three-year-old boy, who, finger in mouth, stared unafraidly back at her.

He pointed a finger towards the house next door. 'Mummy says please come.'

'And who is Mummy?'

'She's my Mummy,' said the low-pitched voice patiently.

'Well, who are you?'

A note of irritation was noticeable in the child's voice, as he replied: 'I'm Michael.'

The cold wind was penetrating Mrs Stych's dress.

'Well, what do you want?'

Exasperation at adult stupidity brought a sharp answer: 'Mummy wants you!'

In an effort to stop the conversational circle being repeated, she asked him where he lived.

'Next door.' And he again pointed to the house of her immigrant neighbours, whose acquaintance, of course, she had never sought.

'And Mummy wants me?'

'Yeah, she burned herself and she can't feed Henny and she wants you to come.'

'Oh!' Mrs Stych was immediately attentive. 'Is anything on fire?'

'Only Mummy,' was the tranquil response.

'For Heaven's sakes!'

Mrs Stych snatched from its hook on the back of the door the coat which she usually wore when emptying the garbage, and whipped it over her shoulders. Without waiting for the child, she ran across the back of the unfenced lots, her golden house-slippers filling with snow as she went. She flew up the steps of the next house, struggled with the springs of the screen door, and then burst into the kitchen.

There was nothing on fire in the spotless kitchen, but a woman with one hand and arm wrapped in a tea towel and clutched to her chest ceased her agonized walking up and down and turned to her thankfully. Her round, flat young face was tear-stained, and it was clear that she was in great pain.

'Dank you, dank you for coming so quick,' she exclaimed gratefully, her guttural pronunciation of the words not helped by her laboured breathing. 'I haf burnt me.'

'Show me,' said Mrs Stych abruptly, as Michael pushed slowly in through the back door. He carefully took off his boots and placed them in the boot tray.

'It was the kettle – I somehow drop it and try to catch and the boiling water spill.'

She slowly unwound the towel to reveal a badly scalded right forearm and hand, on which big blisters were already forming.

Mrs Stych said tersely: 'Better get a doctor.'

'We haf no doctor, and if they don't know you doctors say go to the hospital.'

Mrs Stych nodded agreement. Doctors were in such short supply that it was unlikely that even her own doctor would come to a new patient; he would just direct them to the emergency department of the nearest hospital.

'I'll get out the car and take you up to the hospital.'

'Dank you – but I know not what to do with the children – I cannot leave them – my husband is in Toronto at a conference.' Despite her efforts at controlling them, she was nearly in tears again as she wrapped her arm once more in the tea towel.

'Lock 'em in a bedroom,' said Olga. 'They'll be all right.'

She looked quickly round the kitchen. Michael, his snowsuit half off, was watching his mother fearfully, and in a high-chair sat a slightly older child at which Mrs Stych stared in astonishment. It must have been about four years old, but its head wobbled and rolled erratically and its eyes stared emptily at her. Its tongue protruded from its mouth and it slavered slightly.

The mother saw her look, and said defensively: 'She is retarded. She cannot feed herself. She hungers.' She gave a faltering sigh. 'How could I lock them in a bedroom – alone?'

Mrs Stych felt physically sick at the sight of the retarded child. Since this immigrant woman seemed to think it was made of china, she would have to get more help from somewhere.

'Have you got a friend I could call?'

'Nobody close here – we are very new, you understand. In Toronto we know many people.' She moaned, and Michael ran to her with a whimper. She put her good arm round him lovingly and soothed him in a foreign tongue.

Mrs Stych felt cornered.

'O.K.' she said. 'Got any baking soda?'

'Ja,' and she indicated a cupboard.

Mrs Stych was not sure that she was doing the right thing, but she made a solution of baking soda and cool water, soaked a soft cotton pillow-case in it and wrapped this round the injured arm.

The mother gave a sigh of relief.

'Better,' she said thankfully.

'Now,' said Mrs Stych, with the firmness of desperation, 'I'm going to call Mr Frizzell, who lives over the other side of me, and ask him to take you to the hospital. I'll stay with the kids.'

'Their dinner?'

Mrs Stych looked at the little monster in the high-chair. 'What do they eat?'

'Stew is in the oven. Will you feed my Henny?' The voice was imploring.

Mr Stych licked her lips. 'Yeah, I guess I can.' Her voice was full of reluctance.

She went to the telephone and called the Frizzells' well-remembered number. Mrs Frizzell answered.

In a lofty tone, Olga asked for Mr Frizzell.

'That you, Olga?'

'It is.' Mrs Stych sounded frigid, and Mrs Frizzell was daunted as well as mystified. She called Maxie.

Mr Frizzell might be fat, but in a crisis he proved a wonderful help. He was also thankful to escape from three wailing grandchildren. He had his car at the front door inside three minutes.

The harassed mother cuddled Michael to her, and told him in her own language to stay with Auntie from next door and she would return before the big hand of the clock had gone round once. She kissed Henny, told Mrs Stych she was very kind, and, still in her pinafore, departed with Mr Frizzell.

A perplexed Mrs Stych was left with the slobbering little girl in the high-chair and with Michael, whose lips were trembling as he tried not to cry.

She found a casserole, ready for eating, in the gas oven. Aided by Michael, she found the necessary utensils and poured out glasses of milk for the children. Her repulsion for Henny was so great that she decided that she would give

Michael his meal first, in the hope that the mother would have returned by the time she was ready to feed Henny. Michael announced, however, that he could feed himself while she fed Henny.

He showed Mrs Stych a small baby spoon with which he said his mother fed the child, so Mrs Stych mashed up a small plateful of food, stuck a paper serviette under the child's chin, and tried to stuff a spoonful of dinner onto the protruding tongue. It dribbled down Henny's chin and she began to cry.

'She doesn't like anyone to feed her, except Mummy and her lady at school,' announced Michael. He was managing to tuck his own dinner into himself, though a fair quantity was getting plastered down his front and on his hands.

Mrs Stych did not answer. She was too busy holding down Henny's wavering hands, while she tried to get another spoonful in. Henny continued to dribble and blubber at the same time, while Michael climbed down from his chair and came to stare at her.

He put his sticky hands on Mrs Stych's elegant black lap. 'I'll show,' he announced, and climbed up on her knee, completely ruining her dress. 'Mummy showed me.'

He did manage to demonstrate roughly how to insert the spoon, and, without a word, Mrs Stych made another attempt.

Henny swallowed.

As pleased as if she had won a lottery, she followed it with another spoonful, and said to Henny: 'That's good'.

Henny stopped crying, and slowly and wearily Mrs Stych shovelled down most of the helping. At the end of half an hour, Henny refused to take any more, and Mrs Stych assumed thankfully that she was full.

She was a little pleased at her success. She wiped Henny and Michael clean and did the best she could, with the aid of the dishcloth, to the front of her dress. Michael called her Auntie and began to chatter to her. He got out his toy box and showed her each tiny car and teddy that he owned, while she washed the dishes and put the casserole back into the oven, to keep warm for the mother.

'What's your full name?' she asked Michael.

'Michael.'

'And what else?'

'Michael van der Schelden,' he said.

'Where does your father work?'

'University, 'course.' He ran a small truck round himself.

Mrs Stych wiped her hands dry and looked around the kitchen.

Michael glanced up at his sister. 'Henny wants a new diaper,' he said shrewdly, and Mrs Stych nerved herself for another ordeal.

She felt very squeamish and thought at first she would wait until Mrs van der Schelden returned. It wouldn't hurt the kid to stay wet for a while, she reckoned.

Then Michael said: 'She'll get in an awful mess if you don't hurry.'

With a sigh, she decided that probably Mrs van der Schelden would not be able to do the job when she did come back, as she would be bandaged up, so she asked Michael to explain to her how his mother did it.

Michael took her into a bedroom, bare except for a chest of drawers and a double bed. The wooden floor had been polished to a high gloss, and, when she opened the chest of drawers, neat piles of children's clothing and of diapers were revealed.

At Michael's direction, she spread a plastic crib pad on the bed, took the child out of the high-chair and laid it down on it. Henny dribbled down the back of her dress during this operation, but Mrs Stych was so absorbed in her efforts to get the child on the bed without dropping it that she did not notice this further spoiling of her new dress.

She took a large breath to steel herself against vomiting, and cleaned and changed the little girl, who watched her with what seemed to be a faint gleam of intelligence. She did not cry.

'Henny naps after lunch,' announced Michael suddenly, omitting to say that he was supposed to nap, too.

It occurred to Mrs Stych that Henny might be able to walk, so she put her carefully down on her feet, holding one hand firmly in case she collapsed. Held like that, she could balance herself and did walk in a shambling fashion. She looked up at Mrs Stych and gave a chuckle. Mrs Stych managed a thin smile in return.

She led her, on Michael's instructions, to a large cot in another room, lifted her over the rail and gently laid her down. The child was acquiescent, so Mrs Stych covered her, pulled down the window blinds and left her.

She suddenly remembered that Boyd would be home for lunch, so she telephoned him.

He had just come in and was in a very bad temper as a result of Mayor Murphy's refusal to sell him a lot in Vanier Heights. He wanted to know where the hell she was.

She told him what had happened, and he listened dumbfounded as she described what she had done with Henny, only interjecting an occasional 'You did?' as if he hardly believed her. Finally, he told her to stay where she was until Mrs van der Schelden came home.

Mrs Stych then rang Grandma Stych, to say that she did not think she would be able to come that day. Once again she described her morning's adventure, and Grandma Stych quavered her approval. Olga had done just what she would have done herself and had been most neighbourly.

Mrs Stych began to feel that she had been very noble. Then, as she walked slowly back to the kitchen, she began to think what coping with Henny twenty-four hours a day might be like.

'Why doesn't she put her in a home?' she wondered.

At half past two, Mr Frizzell returned with the accident victim. Mrs van der Schelden was feeling much more comfortable after some sedation. She clutched a small bottle of pills in her good hand.

The kitchen seemed suddenly to be full of pleasant, cheerful people. Mrs Stych felt better than she had for some time.

'You sit down quiet,' she said to Mrs van der Schelden,

'and I'll make some coffee. I've kept the dinner hot, and you should eat a bit if you can. You like a cup, Maxie?'

Maxie said he could just use a good cuppa cawfee – he was kind enough not to mention that he had had no lunch – and Mrs Stych busied herself with the coffee percolator. 'After you have this, you just go lie down a bit and rest yourself. I'll watch Michael.'

Tears filled Mrs van der Schelden's wide blue eyes. 'You are both so kind,' she said with feeling. 'Here we have felt so alone. Now I know I have good neighbours. How can I thank you?'

Mr Frizzell leaned over and patted her shoulder and said it had been real nice meeting her.

He turned to Olga. 'The intern said we should send for her husband. He says she mustn't put her hand in water for a while yet.'

Olga nodded agreement, and said to Mrs van der Schelden: 'We could phone him.'

'Ach,' said the young wife, 'that would be good. Then I say not to fear, just to come.'

'Have your lunch first,' said Mrs Stych in quite a motherly tone.

Michael had been chattering non-stop to his mother in Dutch while this exchange had been going on, and she suddenly grasped what he was saying. She looked up admiringly at Mrs Stych. 'How clever to feed and change Henny and get her to sleep. She not like anyone to touch her except her teacher or me.'

'Yeah?' Mrs Stych queried. 'I didn't have no trouble with her.' She put a small dish of casserole in front of the mother, with a plate of hot buttered toast. She then poured coffee for all of them. 'What kinda school does she go to?' she inquired, and then added baldly: 'Why don't you put her in a home?'

'Oh, we could not put her in a home!' the mother exclaimed passionately. 'We all love her.'

Mrs Stych, remembering the slobbering child, looked at Mrs van der Schelden in blatant disbelief.

The Dutch woman continued, as she fed herself awkwardly with her unhurt hand: 'We haf started on our own, a school for children like her, just some mothers together. We read how to help the children and we try everything to teach them. We teach Henny to hold a spoon. One day we will teach her to put it in her mouth. She walk better now – in the university comes a physiotherapist. He has much interest and try lots of new ideas. Soon we raise funds, have a real school like in Edmonton.'

Maxie, who had been quietly sipping his coffee during this exchange, now asked: 'How do you staff the school? What kinda people teach?'

'All volunteers,' replied Mrs van der Schelden, flourishing her fork. 'They gives days and days of work for little Henny and the others.'

Mrs Stych, hearing this, felt a little less noble than she had done earlier; it was evident to her that, for some unknown reason, Maxie was interested in this school.

The call to Toronto was put through, to Dr van der Schelden, and he promised to take the first flight home. Mrs van der Schelden was persuaded to go and lie down, a small boy called for Michael and they went out to play; on his mother's instructions, Mrs Stych made sure his hood was firmly tied and his mittens pinned to his sleeves, so that he could not lose them. Mrs Stych thought this was fussing unnecessarily – Hank had got by without any such attention – but she attended to the child's clothing without demur, anxious to appear gracious before Maxie.

Maxie said goodbye and departed. Mrs Stych was feeling rather weary herself and thought she might now go home. Then it struck her that someone would have to prepare the evening meal and feed the revolting Henny again. She pondered for a moment, and then put her head through the bedroom door to say she was going home but would return at five o'clock to help with the evening meal.

Mrs van der Schelden protested that she could manage, but this only served to strengthen Mrs Stych's resolve to return, so she just said: 'See you 'bout five,' and paddled back through the snow to her own house.

'God! You must have had quite a time!' exclaimed Boyd, emerging from behind a pile of graph paper on the living-room chesterfield.

Olga's black dress was a sticky mess, her makeup was hopelessly smeared and she had lost the eyelashes from her left eye. Her new gilt slippers were soggy with snow.

'Not too bad,' replied Olga abstractedly. 'Going back round five.' She turned her back to him. 'Unzip me,' she ordered.

Boyd obliged, glad that she had not asked him about his interview with Mayor Murphy.

She went upstairs, took off the dress, looked at it without a pang, and put it ready for the dry cleaners.

She was still thinking about the glimpse she had had of a different outlook on life, when she lay down on her bed and closed her eyes. She had not rested for more than a few minutes, when she realized abruptly that she was very hungry – she had forgotten to have lunch.

As soon as she felt rested, she got up and washed her face, found an old cotton housedress and put it on. From the back of the closet she retrieved a pair of flat-heeled summer shoes and slipped her feet into them. The gilt slippers lay in a dismal pool of melted snow. She picked them up and dropped them into the metal wastepaper container.

She found that Boyd had kindly put a plate of ham and lettuce ready in the refrigerator for her, and she sat down at the kitchen table and ate it absently.

CHAPTER TWENTY-SEVEN

'Tomorrow I think Henny cannot go to school,' remarked Mrs van der Schelden to Mrs Stych, as that lady patiently pushed Henny's evening dish of Pablum into her. 'It is a pity. She make good progress. Nobody else go from this part of Tollemarche – and me, I cannot drive at present.'

Mrs Stych thought of the appallingly empty Monday hovering over her, with only the throb of the washing machine for company.

'If you can help me dress her, I'll take her, and I could bring her back, too,' she offered on impulse.

Mrs van der Schelden protested that she could not allow Mrs Stych to do so much. Mrs Stych had already been so kind.

Olga was moved unaccountably by the near-affection apparent in Mrs van der Schelden's expression as she said this. Nobody had looked at her like that for years.

'Sure, I can do it,' she said firmly. 'I'll go to the stores in between.'

Monday morning was grey and icy. Mrs Stych had forgotten all about Hank and did not see him. He did, however, sleep in the house, eating breakfast at a coffee shop in the town before going to see a travel agent. The only sign that Boyd had left of his presence was an empty cereal dish and coffee cup in the kitchen sink.

Remembering the fate of her black dress on the previous day, Mrs Stych put on a pair of slacks and a car coat.

Henny was accustomed to her special seat in the van der Schelden's ancient Chevrolet, so it was decided that Mrs Stych would use their car instead of her own. The car was cold and Mrs Stych's fingers were clumsy on snowsuit zippers and seat buckles. Henny made protesting noises, and her arms and legs flapped wildly as she struggled to return to her mother. Mrs Stych did finally get away, however, with Henny slumped angrily down in her seat, slobbering and howling alternately.

Mrs Stych had been given the address of a church hall which had been lent to the embattled group of mothers, and she was thankful when, after crossing the river in a heavy flood of construction trucks serving the contractors building a new bridge, she found the shabby hall tucked behind an ugly red-brick church.

Henny, by this time, had given up her complaining, and Mrs Stych unbuckled her and lifted her out onto the sidewalk. It had been finally agreed that she would deliver Henny to the supervising mother, with Mrs van der Schelden's apologies for her own absence and the promise that Henny's father would collect her later in the day.

Henny staggered uncertainly around on the sidewalk, like a puppy searching for its mother's milk, while Mrs Stych locked the car. Feeling uncomfortably responsible for the child's safety, she ran to her and caught her hand. She guided her up the pathway to the open door of the hall, and, when Henny teetered uncertainly at the top of the basement steps that led down into the building, Mrs Stych picked her up and carried her down.

She pushed open the inner door and found that school was already in session. There seemed to be seven or eight ladies present in the gloomy basement room, with about double that number of children. Mrs Stych stood uncertainly in the doorway, holding Henny in her arms, and a grey-haired lady in a smock hastened towards her.

'Mrs Stych!' she exclaimed, her husky voice and her accent unmistakably French-Canadian. She grasped Mrs Stych's elbow and propelled her in a friendly fashion into the middle of the room.

At first Mrs Stych did not recognize her, her wispy, unset hair and bedraggled smock acting as a disguise. Then she was shocked to realize that she was faced with the wife of the president of Boyd's firm, whom they had entertained both at the Edwardian Ball and at the West Enders Club, to which Boyd belonged. Then she had been exquisite in black, hand-woven silk and real pearls; now she looked as if she had been on her knees cleaning a house for hours past.

'Good morning, Mrs LeClair,' Olga finally managed to stutter, as, still in her high-heeled snow boots, she found herself the centre of attention. She was still clutching Henny to her ample bosom and was finding her extremely heavy.

She put the child down, and another lady promptly came forward and greeted Henny in soft, clear tones, as she knelt down to help her off with her snowsuit. Mrs Stych, despite her confusion, was interested to see how the lady took one of Henny's hands and guided it to the pendant of the zipper, pinching the tiny fingers firmly over it. Henny made no real effort to help in the unzipping, but allowed her hands to be guided. The lady did the same with the little boots, and here for a second Henny did show some interest before her bobbing head turned away.

'Ladies,' announced Mrs LeClair, the French rasp of her voice carrying to the rafters, 'may I introduce a new helper, Mrs Stych – perhaps I should say Olga – the wife of one of my husband's colleagues.'

The mothers murmured a greeting, and Mrs LeClair turned to Olga. 'Let me show you where to put your coat. I presume Mrs van der Schelden was unable to come?'

'She couldn't,' confirmed Olga, and then began to add: 'I'm not supposed to stay – ' But Mrs LeClair had already started off towards a door marked WOMEN and did not hear, so Olga trailed after her rather helplessly, anxious not to offend the wife of the company's president.

Mrs LeClair led the way into the cloakroom.

'I did not know zat you are interested in exceptional children,' she remarked, turning her intelligent brown eyes upon Olga, who automatically had begun to take her boots off.

'Well,' said the floundering Olga, 'I – I don't know anything about them – I didn't know there were so many.'

Mrs LeClair clasped her hands together in a gesture passionate enough for a prima donna about to strike high

C. 'It does not matter. We none of us know much. I have worked with them in Montreal, and when Father Devereux here mentioned this group to me, I came to see if I could help during the little time my husband and I are staying in Tollemarche.' She smiled. 'We pooled our experience, and, by taking turns in caring for the children, we give the mothers a small respite.'

Mrs Stych gathered her wits together and opened her mouth to say that she would not be staying to help, having promised only to deliver Henny, but she did not stand a chance of getting a word in, now that Mrs LeClair was securely mounted on her hobby horse.

'Of course, we all read everything we can. One husband is a doctor and he is going to bring a new physiotherapist from the hospital, and they will try to think of new ways in which we can teach these poor children as much as they can absorb. We have also written to other groups to ask about their experiences.'

Tears came to her eyes as she went on: 'If you only knew, my dear! So many children are kept indoors, because their parents are ashamed of them, and some, which we have not been able yet to gather in, we are sure are thoroughly ill-treated. I dream – I dream . . . ' she raised her clasped hands towards the ceiling, 'of building a beautiful school in every major city, designed especially for them.'

Mrs Stych came to the conclusion that if she was not to offend such a dedicated and important lady she had better stay, so, with a sigh, she removed her coat and hung it up.

'Why don't they put them in homes?' she asked.

Mrs LeClair's eyes flashed.

'And leave them like vegetables to rot?' she asked. 'No! Not as long as I have strength to fight for them. They are all capable of love and they respond to love. I encourage these mothers! I say to them to work on! They can accomplish much if they try.'

She opened the swing door with a flourish, and passed through it so fast that Mrs Stych was nearly brained by its backward swing, as she followed her.

Mrs Stych looked around her cautiously.

Some of the children looked quite normal, and were sitting on the floor playing simple games with bricks and marbles. Henny was on a mattress, having her legs exercised and obviously enjoying it. Two youngsters lay in Karrycots and their attendant mothers were laying out mattresses on which to put them. One child sat on a mother's knee and was looking quite intelligently at a picture book. The mother was pronouncing very clearly the names of the objects depicted in the book and then trying to persuade the child to say them after her.

Mrs Stych was acutely aware that she was wearing slacks, her makeup was not good and altogether she was not looking her best, but she soon realized that she did not know any of the women present, except Mrs LeClair. She wondered where they came from. Four of them, in cheap slacks and blouses, worn without foundation garments, were obviously not of her social circle, but some of the others looked as if they might have money. They all had in common a look of intense fatigue.

She did not have long to ponder about the status of her fellow workers. With firm, bony fingers Mrs LeClair clasped her elbow once more and shot her into the kitchen attached to the hall.

'Sixteen small glasses of milk, and a biscuit for each child. Eight – no, nine coffees, please.'

Despite a subdued resentment at having been caught up so ruthlessly to help, Mrs Stych managed her best receiving-line smile for the benefit of Mrs LeClair, and said: 'Sure, I'll soon fix that.'

As she waited for the water to boil for the coffee, she thought about the pile of washing waiting to be put into the machine at home. She remembered that, had she stayed at home to do it, all she would have heard throughout the day would have been the slosh of the water in the washer and the hum of the dryer, interspersed with commercials if she had turned on the radio. Any telephone calls would almost certainly have been for Hank or for Boyd. The front door bell would have been unlikely to herald anyone but a collector for charity.

If she had been less tough, she would have wept with self-pity. As it was, she felt that she might just as well stick around to please Mrs LeClair, as face such a dull and empty day alone.

To get all the children to drink their milk proved a slow task, and Mrs Stych's coffee was left to get cold on the kitchen counter, as she struggled to get small fingers to grasp their glasses. All the mothers were anxious that the children should learn to feed themselves. They were not sure how to go about this, but they repeated the same movements every time they tried, and they had succeeded in getting some of the children to grasp their cookies or sandwiches, and two boys could drink from a glass.

A ripple of rejoicing went through the patient helpers when it was whispered that Henny had picked up her cookie and had, moreover, aimed it for her mouth. She had had to have help to actually eat it, but this tiny effort on the part of a single child gave new impetus to the day's work.

Mrs Stych was bewildered that such a small movement could be construed as a victory, but she managed to murmur politely that it was just wonderful.

The mothers, after discovering that she herself did not have a subnormal child, received her assistance with every demonstration of gratitude, and several of them expressed wonderment that she should be so good as to interest herself in their problems.

She helped fairly willingly to prepare a simple lunch from ingredients brought by the mothers, after which some chidren were taken home, and three other mothers arrived with a total of five or more children among them. All the time, Mrs LeClair, drawing on her experience in Montreal, trotted up and down the hall, encouraging, organizing, instructing. Her hair grew wilder, her hands became grubbier, as the dust from the floor rose, and she looked like some demented female from skid row, rather than the wife of a man making enough money each year to buy the

217

whole church hall. One mother said wistfully she wished Mrs LeClair could stay in Tollemarche long enough to get the school on its feet.

In the afternoon Mrs LeClair asked Olga to learn from another mother the principles of patterning. Mrs Stych was informed that when the brain had been damaged so that the child could not control its limbs properly, it was sometimes possible to teach another part of the brain to take over, if the limbs were exercised several times a day in the pattern of behaviour normal to them. The task, even to help one child, was a stupendous one, more than a mother alone could hope to achieve; sometimes in large families, it was possible to recruit enough people to take turns at exercising the child, but in most cases outside help had to be found.

'Twenty-four girls from Tollemarche Composite High School take turns coming to our home,' explained the mother who was teaching Mrs Stych, 'to put Beth through her exercises.'

Mrs Stych was astonished. 'High school kids!' she exclaimed.

'Sure,' the mother confirmed, as she smiled down at the golden-haired Beth, and then said to the child: 'You've got lots of friends, haven't you, honey?' She bent and kissed the smiling face, as she continued: 'When we started, she lay on her back and propelled herself along with wriggles. Now she can crawl on her tummy.'

The mother looked down with such obvious adoration at Beth that Mrs Stych felt embarrassed. She had never felt like that about Hank.

Mrs Stych was invited to try doing the exercising. The child at first whimpered at her touch, but Mrs Stych was very careful and she soon submitted more cheerfully to the manipulation of her legs, arms and back.

Many years before, Olga Stych had been a bright Ukrainian country girl doing her first year in college, the only Ukrainian in her class. Her teachers had told her that she had brains and should use them, so Olga had had a dreamy ambition of becoming a doctor or a lawyer, a Portia or at least a Florence Nightingale. Then she had, from many acid remarks and much cold-shouldering, learned that a Ukrainian was an ignorant, peasantlike clod. She became ashamed of her Ukrainian surname, and it seemed her Greek Orthodox Church connections were fit only for the illiterate. To struggle towards a profession with the two strikes against her that she was both a woman and a Ukrainian would be too hard, she decided. She therefore concentrated on finding a husband who was not a Ukrainian.

No Scottish boy would look at her: they could look much higher for a wife – theirs was the kingdom, thought Olga bitterly – and when Boyd Stych had offered himself, it had seemed a good compromise. And he had really loved her, thought Olga wistfully, as she bent Beth's small legs in the direction they should go.

Now, as Olga warmed to the work, she began to think, as she had not thought for years, about Boyd, about the children round her, even, rather painfully, about Hank, and she forgot about that very important personage, Mrs Olga Stych.

By half past three Mrs Stych was ready to drop dead with fatigue. Her blouse was stuck to her back with sweat and she guessed that there was not a scrap of makeup left on her face. The mothers were dressing the children, and a graceful, expensive-looking blonde had dressed both Henny and her own child in their heavy winter clothes. Mrs Stych thankfully rescued her car coat and boots from the cloakroom.

She took Henny by the hand to try to get her to climb the steps to the front door.

'Ah, you have the idea, Mrs Stych,' exclaimed Mrs Le-Clair, pouncing upon her as she waited for Henny, who, hampered by her snowsuit, was making a not very successful try at climbing the steps. 'Always make the child do as much as it can.' She patted Mrs Stych's arm. 'You will come tomorrow, of course. We need all the help we can get.'

'Well . . . .' began Mrs Stych, trying to make a determined stand.

Mrs LeClair clapped her on the shoulder. 'Ah, I knew you would! You will feel so rewarded.'

Mrs Stych opened her mouth again and managed to commence: 'But . . . ' when Henny, stranded on the second step up, began to howl, her head winding to and fro like that of a serpent.

Mrs Stych bent and set the child's hands firmly on the third step, and laboriously she climbed another. By the time she had got the rhythm of climbing, Mrs LeClair had darted to the other end of the hall, to assist a mother with a Karrykot.

Mrs Stych's lips narrowed to a thin line. She was not accustomed to people rushing off when she wished to speak to them. If Mrs LeClair had no time for her, she had no time for Mrs LeClair; she would not come tomorrow – nobody was going to make her work like a slave for a pack of crazy kids.

Henny allowed herself to be buckled into her car seat without demur. Mrs Stych climbed in beside her and glanced down at her in disgust.

Quite unexpectedly, Henny looked up at her and laughed like a young baby. The empty face with its slightly protruding tongue looked for a moment no different from that of any other tiny girl, and Mrs Stych hastily looked back at the road.

Dr and Mrs van der Schelden greeted Mrs Stych and Henny, on their return, like long-lost kissing cousins. Dr van der Schelden was a huge, fair-haired man and he nearly wrung Mrs Stych's hand off as he thanked her for all she had done. Mrs Stych felt so guilty about her dislike of Henny that she blushed and said hastily that she had done nothing at all.

She took gratefully the chair offered to her – she had not felt so tired for months – and accepted the hot coffee pressed upon her by Dr van der Schelden. It was very pleasant to be made a fuss of, and her face gradually resumed its normal colour.

'Mr Frizzell took me to the hospital again,' reported Mrs

van der Schelden, 'and sat with Michael in the waiting-room while the doctor look at my hand. He also is so good.'

'Yes,' said Dr van der Schelden. 'He has also suggested that he gets together a committee of interested businessmen, to raise funds for a proper school for Henny and the other children. Do you think he could do it?'

Mrs Stych assured him sourly that Maxie could do anything he set his mind to.

'Would it not be wonderful, Mrs Stych?' asked Mrs van der Schelden, patting Mrs Stych's hand gently.

Mrs Stych agreed that it would be, and wondered privately what the hell Maxie had in his head to suggest such a thing. Anything Maxie did always benefited Maxie in the end.

On the doorstep, her conscience pricked her and she said: 'I'll take Henny again tomorrow – your husband will have a lot to do for you and Michael.' Maxie Frizzell was not going to be allowed to outdo her.

Mrs van der Schelden's wide blue eyes moistened. 'Would you do so? That would be so kind,' and before Mrs Stych could stop her, she had put her arms round the elder woman's shoulders and kissed her.

Mrs Stych could not remember when another woman had last kissed her; they had toadied to her, deferred to her, tried to squash her, fought to keep her down, all with the sweetest of smiles over their teacups, but nobody had kissed her with warmth and gratitude before. Her face was still pink as she walked slowly through the snow across the adjoining lawns to her own front door and let herself in.

On the Frizzells' front lawn, a baby-sitter and two of the Frizzell grandchildren were making angels in the snow, and Mrs Stych was reminded uneasily of Hank.

221

CHAPTER TWENTY-EIGHT

Mrs Stych felt better after she had taken a shower, put on a loose red housecoat and a pair of red mules, and combed her hair. She felt too tired to paint her face. She did, however, go down to the basement and set the washing machine going with its first load of sheets; then she prepared a supper for Boyd and herself. Brown-and-serve meat chops were soon slapped into a frying pan and frozen chips put into the oven to defrost.

She laid the table in the breakfast nook for two people, and wondered where Hank would eat. A pang of conscience struck her – perhaps she should not have bawled him out quite so hard. Fancy if he had been like one of those kids she had been working with! What would she have done?

She squirmed inwardly as she answered her own question. She knew she would have repudiated him and put him in a home. As she worked, she uneasily compared the care given to Mrs LeClair's exceptional children with that given to the children in her own circle.

'It's ridiculous,' she told herself defiantly. 'So much fuss spoils kids – it isn't good for them – they gotta learn to be independent.'

Absorbed in her own reflections, she did not bother to greet Boyd when he came into the kitchen, grey and tired. He went straight to the refrigerator to get himself a glass of rye.

He eyed her tentatively over his glass, surprised to see her arrayed in her best housecoat. He reminded himself that he had yet to tell her that Mayor Murphy would not part with one of his lots in Vanier Heights, because he was waiting for the price to rocket even higher. He slumped down in a chair and finished his drink quickly, after which he felt strong enough to say 'Hi' to his wife.

'Hi,' she said back.

'Where's Hank?'

'Dunno.'

'Didn't see him this morning. Mebbe he'll be in for supper.'

She looked at him, and her lips curled. 'I doubt it,' she said.

'Why not?'

She took the potato chips out of the oven before she replied. Then she said carefully: 'Said he'd eat out.'

Boyd sensed that something was wrong. He spun the ice cube round and round in his empty glass. The rye was warming him, and he felt better.

'Something happen?' he asked, pouring a little more rye onto the ice cube. He guessed that Hank was doing one of his usual fast retreats from an unpleasant situation. Presumably Olga was still mad about the book. He watched his wife out of the corner of his eye as he drained his glass again. Her face had hardened, and he felt an unexpected pity for his son.

'I just told him he must pay his board now he's working.'

Boyd ran his tongue round the tips of his teeth. It was not an unreasonable request for a mother to make. He wondered, however, how she had approached the subject.

'What did he say?'

She put a plate of chops and chips in front of him, following it with a knife and fork and a bottle of ketchup. He put down his glass and picked up his fork, still watching her.

She filled the coffeepot and put it on the stove to percolate.

'Said he'd pay rent and eat out,' she said as laconically as she could, under his distrustful gaze.

Boyd slowly laid down his first forkful of chop and said in a shocked voice: 'Now, Olga, he's not some student boarding with us. That won't do.'

Mrs Stych brought her plate to the table and sat down. 'That's what he wanted, that's what he got.'

Boyd stared at her. He had never taken much interest in Hank. He had been away from home so much that he had, in fact, frequently forgotten the boy's existence for months at a time. But this upset his sense of propriety. It savoured of his grudging his son food from his table, which he did not. It offended his sense of western hospitality, a hospitality which demanded that even strangers be fed like fighting kings and his bulging refrigerator kept full for the use of the family.

His wife was looking mutinous, so he said heavily: 'I'll talk to him when he comes in.'

'You'll have to be quick,' she snapped. 'Says he's goin' to Europe soon.'

He knew that the smallest spark would light the fires of temper and she would start a tantrum, so he tried to eat his dinner.

The long evening he and Hank had spent together, when Hank had first told him about his literary success, had established a friendliness between them, quite separate from any fatherly feeling which Boyd might reasonably be expected to harbour for the boy. Boyd had first been amazed, and then had felt a sneaking admiration for a youngster who could defy a whole town and its heavily paternal school board, and make a small fortune out of it. He knew that Olga had lost some friends through Hank's choice of subject, but he had no desire to see the boy bullied out of the house because of it.

Olga ate her dinner and then retired to the basement, to sulk over the washing, leaving Boyd to wash the dishes.

A stony-faced Hank came home about nine, to find his mother had gone to bed. His father was, however, sitting smoking in his den, with the door open. He got up as Hank came through the living-room, and stood at the door of his room.

'Hi, Son,' he said tentatively; and, in spite of his own preoccupation, Hank noticed the weary droop of the elder man's shoulders and his general air of anxiety.

'Hiya, Dad.'

'Come in here. I want to talk to you.'

Hank was immediately on guard, but went in and took the chair indicated by Boyd.

'What happened between you and your Ma this morning about board money?'

Hank relaxed, and told his father what had occurred. Finally, he said: 'Honest, Dad, I just forgot. I'm not mean. Only she didn't ask so nice.' He grinned sheepishly. 'Guess I'm not altogether used to being independent.'

Boyd laughed. 'It's O.K. I'll fix it with your mother. You had better pay something – you have to get used to standing on your own feet – and one day you'll be having to make your wife an allowance.' He changed the subject. 'Your mother said you're going to Europe?'

'Yeah, thought I'd travel around for a while. I got a book coming along just fine. Feel I oughta see sumpin' before I settle down?'

Boyd sat silent. He had gone away from home to university at eighteen, so he supposed Hank would be all right. He remembered he had promised to help Hank invest his earnings, and thought he had better mention this.

'Do you want me to do anything about the money you've got, while you're away?' he inquired.

'Sure, Dad. Not all of it's in yet, of course.'

'Do you like to give me power of attorney?'

Hank had been considering this for some time, but his distrust of both parents was so great that he had not been able to convince himself that this would be a wise move. Boyd could see that his question was causing some confusion to Hank, though he fortunately did not realize why.

The boy stirred uneasily. 'Think I'd sorta like to sign everything myself. I'll be in London, and stuff don't take so long by air mail.' He hastened to add: 'I think your advice was great – and I wanna do just what you suggested – but I'd have a better picture of how I stood if I signed everything myself.'

'O.K.' said Boyd. 'I'll fix it – you give me an address.

225

Would London be where Mrs Dawson has gone?'

Hank flushed crimson and Boyd had to laugh, despite his anxiety that the boy might marry too young.

'O.K., O.K.,' he smiled, 'I won't ask. Just be careful what you do. She's a real nice girl and you have to give a girl like that a square deal. She's no Betty Frizzell.'

The colour which had suffused Hank's face drained as rapidly as it had come. Boyd's idle remark had hit a raw nerve; Mrs Stych was not the only member of the family who had noted the appearance of Betty's eldest boy. Hank had seen him and had felt thoroughly sick; he wondered how he could have gone near such a girl, and he wondered, too, how he could ever approach Isobel after the kind of life he had led up to now. He felt like crawling on his knees to her; he could understand how men could humble and humiliate themselves before women to gain their forgiveness.

'You don't have anything to worry about, Dad,' he said, his expression so desolate that Boyd began to worry about him as he never had before.

Two days later Hank left for New York, on his way to London. He hardly spoke to his mother and did not bid her goodbye. She was surprised to find after he had gone that he had cleared his room and packed all his possessions into cardboard boxes, which he had transported into the basement storeroom; stacking them neatly in a corner, so that she could hardly complain that they took up too much space. His bedroom looked like a hotel room, without a personality.

She told herself she did not care; he was nothing but a quarrelsome interruption in the mainstream of her life. Then she remembered that her life's mainstream had dried up. No amount of attendance at public functions or entertaining new people could put her back into the exalted position she had previously enjoyed. The real residents of Tollemarche had rejected her out of hand – and all because of Hank. Suddenly, in the horrifying vacuum her life had become, she was thankful for Henny.

When, after his conversation with Hank, Boyd had climbed the stairs to their bedroom, he had found Olga lying awake in the middle of the three-quarter bed they shared, staring at the gilt stars on the ceiling. The bed had a hollow in the middle where she had for years slept by herself, and she had absent-mindedly crawled into it.

While he was getting undressed, he thought he might as well tell her about his interview with Mayor Murphy.

'About that lot in Vanier Heights,' he commenced, his voice muffled as he removed his undershirt. 'Murphy won't sell.' His stomach felt constricted and he wondered if he was starting an ulcer.

His wife's voice was listless when she replied: 'Well, we gotta home, so we don't have to worry. Mebbe a riverside lot, one of those you got down by the creek, would be nicer.'

At first he could not believe his ears. 'You don't mind?'

'Why should I?' She sounded as if she was not really attending to his words.

He was stunned. He had expected a tirade lasting most of the night, and she was not even really interested; he wondered if she were well.

Thankful for small mercies, he got into bed and she reluctantly moved over to make room for him.

He usually smoked a last cigarette before turning over to go to sleep, and Olga watched with disgust the cloud of smoke that soon obliterated the gilt stars.

'What did you do today?' he asked.

Olga was immediately more alert. 'I worked with Mrs LeClair,' she announced smugly.

'Our LeClair's wife?'

'Yeah,' she said, half turning towards him, and she went on to tell him about her day with Henny.

'You should go again,' he said, quick to see the advantage of a closer association with his company's president. LeClair had holdings in a dozen first-class mines in Canada. With tips from LeClair, Boyd saw himself rising into the tight inner circle of businessmen who, working closely with their American associates, had made themselves millionaires.

He lifted himself on one elbow, so that he could see her face to face. 'See here, Olga,' he said confidentially, 'you've seen how difficult the LeClairs are to get to know personally. They've always kept themselves to themselves. They're mighty hard to really get to know – you get to know her real well and we're made.'

Olga, who had just been about to say that nothing would induce her to spend another day with those horrible kids, changed her mind. Anything that was in her self-interest was to be considered carefully. She stared thoughtfully at her husband, and then said: 'I suppose I could go again – they sure need help.'

'Sure you could, honey,' he wheedled, and bent and kissed her.

So Henny found herself again escorted by Mrs Stych, a Mrs Stych who seemed a bit easier to get along with than she had been on the previous day.

CHAPTER THIRTY

Olga Stych was, at best, no child lover, and the pupils of the
School for Exceptional Children at first sickened her, with
their grotesque movements and occasionally repulsive
looks. Without encouragement from Boyd and bullying by
Mrs LeClair, she would never have returned to help in the
school; but once having got a little accustomed to the idea,
she found that it at least filled her empty days and made her
forget the many snubs she received. The children's mothers
were very impressed that a lady whose name had appeared
so often in the pages of the *Tollemarche Advent* should be
prepared to spend so much time with them, and they did
not seem to associate Hank with her at all.

Perhaps because Olga was able to look more coldly at the
children than their closely involved mothers, she was able
to see each child as a living problem which had to be solved.
For years she had not used her brains or her organizing
ability for anything more intelligent than arranging teas,
spring 'fayres' or the affairs of the Community Centre. But
now, faced with the quiet despair of the mothers at the
school, she began to consider seriously what long-term
plans could be made to help both parents and children.

She had long conversations with Mrs LeClair regarding
similar schools which she had seen elsewhere, and Mrs
LeClair introduced her to the Baptist minister in whose hall
the school met.

Olga was thankful to help the minister organize some
Christmas celebrations for the children and their parents,
while Mr and Mrs LeClair went home to Montreal to spend
the holiday with their family. In spite of having Christmas
dinner with Grandma Palichuk, the festival without the
children would have been so bleak and lonely that Olga
shuddered at the very thought of it and pressed a not
unwilling Boyd into helping her decorate the church

basement with tinsel and balloons. It was, however, a visit of Mr Frizzell to the school early in the new year which really galvanized her into action.

Mr Frizzell, who wished to stand at the next election for alderman on the City Council, had for some time been looking for an organization with which he could not only identify himself but be identified by. The Bonnie Scots and other service organizations to which he belonged were all very well, but he did not get much personal publicity out of them. He wanted to start something new, so that when he tried for a seat on the City Council, people would say: 'Yes, he's Maxie Frizzell, that wonderful man who started thingumabob'. All he needed was a thingumabob, and he felt that in the School for Exceptional Children he had found it. One Tuesday morning, therefore, when business was at its quietest, he rolled gently into the church hall, with the same friendly unobtrusiveness which made him such a superb salesman.

The noise level lowered considerably as he entered, and startled mothers looked up. Mrs LeClair, whose time in Tollemarche was nearly ended, flew forward, and Olga Stych exclaimed: 'Why, Maxie, what you doin' here?'

With a look of disarming candour on his round face, he told Mrs LeClair that he had become interested in the school through the improvement in the behaviour of Henny van der Schelden, and he had come to see how it had been achieved. Mrs LeClair, fluttering like a hummingbird, showed him around and introduced him.

When they had got as far as Olga, who was composing an appeal for funds, while supervising two children playing with bricks, she left her appeal and the children for a few minutes and circulated with them, eyeing Maxie suspiciously as he expressed interest in all he saw. This was her new domain, she thought savagely, and no supercilious Donna Frizzell was going to be allowed to muscle in on it.

Maxie Frizzell, to his credit, was genuinely touched by the mothers' efforts to help their children and each other, with only makeshift equipment and inadequate, unsuitable accommodation. Surely, he thought, these kids, ignored by the school board and every other government department, deserved a better break than they were getting. He had thought of the school as just another stepping-stone towards a seat on the City Council, but as he began to realize the suffering of parents and children and was informed that there were many more children in the city in an even worse state, the quick, shrewd mind that had won him a small fortune in the rapid growth of Tollemarche was put to work to consider the basic needs of better accommodation, paid help, and an organization that would involve the doctors of the city.

Mrs LeClair was explaining her impending return to Montreal and her worry that the school might disintegrate when she left, since the mothers involved could not be expected to undertake the full organization and running of the school.

'I'm not tied down with kids,' said Olga firmly, her black eyes narrowed while she tried to get under the fence before Maxie. 'I can give time to it.'

'Wait a minute, wait,' cautioned Maxie, seeing his fine new project slipping out of his hands before he had even got started on it. 'Suppose we try and get a committee together, maybe with some of the kids' fathers. We might be able to sponsor a fund drive – rent a house, pay some skilled help or somethin'.'

'Don't try and start too big,' warned Mrs LeClair, as she accepted a cup of coffee from one of her helpers and offered it to Maxie.

When the three of them were holding wobbly paper cups of coffee, she said: 'Let's sit down with some of the mothers and talk about it.'

From that talk in the dusty church basement grew the Tollemarche Exceptional Children's School, with Mr Maxmilian Frizzell as president and Mrs Olga Stych as director of the school. As the months went by, it began to endear itself to the citizens of Tollemarche. Every car that went out of Maxie's booming car lots had a pamphlet in its glove compartment describing the work being done. Physicians of every kind were pestered for advice. A group went down to Edmonton to see the work being done there. Mrs Stych imbued the mothers with enough courage to get them to hold a tea in the school, so that interested persons could see the children at work. Parents who had been ashamed to show their subnormal children in public gained enough confidence to bring their offspring out of hiding and ferry them rapidly to the school, where they discovered that they had plenty of company and were given a degree of hope that their children might be more trainable than they had imagined.

Olga worked as she had never worked since her college days. She forgot to nibble, and over the year lost fifty pounds in weight. She was so busy that, at one point, three months went by without her adding anything to her Hudson's Bay charge account; she had no time to spend money on clothes. She was happier, too, when she had time to think about it, and this was reflected in her relations with Boyd. At last she had something worthwhile to talk to him about, and he became interested enough himself to volunteer to drive some of the children to picnics and other small outings. Olga spent little time at home, but her Dutch cleaning lady continued to keep the house spick and span, and in the evenings the couple frequently shared the chore of cooking the evening meal. It could not be said that they fell in love again, but a warm friendliness grew up between them, now that the house was no longer cluttered by a mass of bridge-playing, tea-drinking women. Olga's hot temper tended more and more to be directed towards people who thought her exceptional children were only fit for a kind of human junk yard, or towards officials in Edmonton and Ottawa who had never given them any thought before.

Of course, all this activity did not go unnoticed by the girls. Mrs Stych, in the course of her new occupation, never ran into any of her old cronies, but Mrs MacDonald told Miss Angus that she had seen Olga Stych running – actually running – down Tollemarche Avenue. Olga was wearing dreadful, flat-heeled shoes and her petticoat was showing below her skirt.

Miss Angus replied tartly that Olga Stych always was a fool, and poured another cup of tea – Miss Angus without a silver teapot in front of her would have had no reason for existence.

Margaret Tyrrell, when she went to be fitted for a new frock at Dawne's Dresse Shoppe, was told by Mrs Stein that Mrs Stych's clothes were hanging off her because she had become so thin, and it was Mrs Stein's opinion that only someone with cancer could slim so fast. A rumour, therefore, went round that Olga Stych was dying of cancer, and some of the girls' consciences smote them at the way they had treated her. Olga, however, continued to live and to feel extraordinarily well.

Donna Frizzell finally got wind of what Maxie was doing, and she held forth shrilly on the way he was wasting his time – time was money, and he should be on his car lot, not playing around with a lot of idiot kids. And that Olga Stych should not have anything to do with kids – look how her son had turned out.

Maxie was diplomatic enough not to point out that his three grandchildren still occupied the spare room, and nobody knew where either of their parents were. Betty was not much credit to her parents. Donna did not let her grandchildren interfere with her life much – she left them with a baby-sitter most of the time, and this worried Maxie more than he liked to admit. However, to stop the uproar, he suggested that she needed some more clothes and doubled the amount she could have on her Dawne's Dresse Shoppe account. Donna's complaints dwindled to a grumble.

Mrs Murphy, the Mayor's wife, her three chins trembling gently as she tried to keep track of the city's pecking order and at the same time see that her husband ate three meals a day, asked her priest about the new school and, particularly, about Mrs Stych's work there.

The priest was very old and it is not too certain that he

fully understood what she was talking about, but he answered that, for sure, 'twas the work of God that was being done there and it should be supported by all good Catholics.

'But,' quavered Mrs Murphy, 'it was Olga Stych's son that wrote that terrible book – and she must have known about it, Father.'

' 'Tis perhaps a penance that she is doing,' said the old man, his wizened face peering up from between hunched shoulders.

Mrs Murphy nodded agreement and immediately took out from the sideboard drawer a tattered notebook and added Mrs Stych's name to the list headed 'Do-gooders,' so that she got asked to the right Murphy dinners.

The person most astonished by Olga's new interest was Hank. His father wrote to him from time to time regarding his business affairs, and told him what his mother was doing; and, though Hank never wrote to Olga, a large box arrived one day at the school from London, England. It contained a number of very helpful books on mental retardation. It did not contain a copy of Hank's second book; this he sent privately to his father, and, after reading it, Boyd decided not to mention its existence to Olga; the distilled bitterness of the story might have really hurt her.

235

CHAPTER THIRTY-ONE

In the late fall, nearly two years after Hank had left for England, the great bridge across the treacherous North Saskatchewan River was to be completed, and the City Council was hopeful that a royal princess, on a tour across Canada, would condescend to stop at Tollemarche and open it.

'She can't just stop here and cut a ribbon,' expostulated one lady alderman, who was worried because she did not know how to address a princess. 'She'd have to stay overnight – it's too far for her to travel onwards the same day – unless she went back to Edmonton – and that bunch down there will surely monopolize her, if they get the chance.'

The other aldermen looked at her scornfully. One of them said firmly: 'We'll keep her out of Edmonton – there must be some way of filling up a day here.'

His eyes wandered round the council chamber, and alighted on the sole member of the Edwardian Days Committee who happened to be present. 'I know – she can drive through the city, have a civic luncheon, open the bridge and drive over it, and in the evening the Edwardian Days Committee can organize a dinner and ball for her.'

The Edwardian Days Committee man was nearly stunned at having a princess thrust at him, but recovered sufficiently to bat the ball back firmly to the Council: 'Who's going to pay?' he asked darkly.

Amid the flurry of discussion, a voice said: 'There'll be the Lieutenant-Governor and his wife, maybe the Duke, and ladies-in-waiting and equerries.'

The Edwardian Days Committee representative reeled with horror – he could not imagine what an equerry was.

Alderman Maxie Frizzell saw his opportunity and seized it. 'That leaves her with most of her afternoon unaccounted for – '

236

'She could rest,' interposed the lady alderman.

Maxie froze her with a look. 'I think she should spend the afternoon at the Exceptional Children's School – we really got somethin' to show her.'

The Council received the suggestion with relief. It was agreed upon immediately, and Maxie grinned to himself. He had never, in earlier times, dreamed that he would consider a child being taught to go to the bathroom by itself a great victory to be boasted about, but he knew it was. He wanted more money for the school, and nobody could give it publicity like a princess could – publicity meant money.

The Princess, with her usual kindliness, had the request added to her already overloaded schedule.

On a golden fall day, therefore, an astonished Olga Stych, accompanied by a triumphant Maxie Frizzell, found herself, in a plain black dress covered with a white apron, curtseying to a princess. When she took the royal hand, she was acutely aware that not even two layers of cream the previous night had lessened the roughness of her own hands, which had been long neglected. She knew she looked dowdy in comparison with Donna Frizzell, who stood forgotten in the background amid a bevy of minor officials, but she had not had time to buy a new dress for the occasion and had fallen back on an old black one which did not hang too loosely on her. Donna was looking gorgeous in raspberry pink wool worn with a pink georgette turban and hair dyed shocking red; her hard, thin face, however, was frozen into such an expression of envy that it was obvious that she should have been dressed in green.

The Princess did not seem to notice the shabby dress, and, indeed, all she saw was a very tired, capable-looking woman, whose long black hair was dressed in neat braids round her head, helping a blank-faced little girl to present her with a bouquet. The Princess had inspected many charitable institutions during her long life, but she felt very moved by the quiet patience of these Prairie women, who, she was told by the Lieutentant-Governor, had begun the school knowing nothing of the care or training of subnor-

237

mal children. Perhaps it was because they were so isolated that they were evolving methods which were beginning to attract attention from all over the continent.

The Princess spent over an hour going quietly from child to child, escorted by a group of nervous officials, helpers and, of course, Maxie Frizzell.

The children had been lovingly dressed for the occasion, and nobody cried or wet his pants during the visit. It must be admitted that some of the mothers standing quietly in the background, holding those children unable to walk, let the tears course down their faces as they watched. They knew that the Princess's visit would benefit the school immensely, and they appreciated what Olga and Maxie had done for their children. They had often said to each other that Olga need not have come to their rescue. She didn't have a retarded child – her own boy was so brilliant that the whole world had heard about Tollemarche, just because it was his home town; yet she never spoke about him, never rubbed it in.

After all the cars were gone, the children dismissed for the day, an exhausted Olga sat on the veranda steps to rest for a minute in the mild sunshine, while she waited for Boyd to come and collect her. She would go home and lie on her bed for a while, after which she and Boyd would attend the ball given for the Princess.

She leaned her head against the balustrade and closed her eyes, remembering the last ball she had attended, the Edwardian Ball to which Hank had taken Isobel. She could bear to think of Hank now.

For a long time, she had felt so furious with him that it was as well he was separated from her. She had blamed him for all her woes, hated him for not saying goodbye, for never writing to her. Then, as she became more involved in Henny's school and had seen that there was another Tollemarche, one of suffering, of always having to face doctor's bills, of tenacious love of children, of love for marriage partners, a Tollemarche that did not care a hang for social success – it was too busy trying to stay alive – she had begun to see herself for what she was, a grasping, selfish woman. This had made her angrier still, and she had plunged still deeper into the work she had undertaken, working off her self-hatred in her fight for recognition of the needs of the very helpless.

Boyd came silently up the path and stopped half-way to view the picture that his wife made as she dozed in the sun, her hands folded in her lap, her face tranquil.

'My! She looks more like her mother every day,' he thought; and he was happy – he liked his mother-in-law. Here, waiting for him on the steps, there seemed to be again the country girl he had married, a girl who seemed to have made a very special niche for herself in the hearts of the people of Tollemarche.

'Hiya, Olga,' he called cheerfully, 'got news for you.'

Olga's eyes popped open.

He was waving a letter, and he came up the veranda steps and sat down beside her. 'It's from Hank.'

The letter was addressed to both of them and invited them in friendly terms to attend his wedding to Isobel Dawson in a month's time. A formal invitation from Isobel's aunt was enclosed.

Olga put the letter carefully down in her lap. She remembered the tiny, fair-haired girl at the Edwardian Ball, and asked Boyd cautiously: 'Wotcha think of it?'

'I think it's great,' replied Boyd firmly, having spent half the morning, while trying to deal with his work, in thinking out what attitude he should take. 'She is older than he is, but she's got something he needs. She must have, seeing it's lasted this long.'

Olga fingered the letter uneasily. She said in a low voice: 'Y'know, Boyd, I know now I never gave that kid a square deal' – she hesitated, as though she found it difficult to drag out of herself what she had to say – 'and, y'know, I often feel sorry about it. I coulda done a lot better.' She picked up the engraved wedding invitation and turned it over. 'I guess he turned to her just because she showed an interest in him – like I never did.' Her voice, her weary, drooping eyelids, indicated a quiet, bitter sadness. 'Mebbe she's just kinda kind. Wotcha think?'

Boyd patted her hand uneasily. 'Well, he hasn't done so badly,' he comforted her. 'And, y' know, it's my belief she's not doing so badly regarding a mother-in-law.'

'Waal, I wish Hank would feel like that,' she replied with a small sigh, 'but I guess he never will.'

'Aw, I don't know,' said her husband, as he hunted through his pockets for a cigarette in a manner very reminiscent of his son. 'You be real patient with this Isobel of his – like Grandma Stych was with you – and, you'll see, he'll come round.'

A slow smile spread over Olga's face. 'Yeah, I never thoughta that – she was always patient with me. I never thought of it before. You're so right – I'll try.'

A new idea occurred to her, and she said: 'It was sure funny this morning, watching Donna Frizzell as I was talking to the Princess. It made me realize that I'd sorta arrived socially – that Princess didn't make no point about me being Ukrainian or anything like that – she was just kinda nice to me, and so was everyone else.'

Boyd put his arm round her. 'You've done really well, honey, and I'm proud of you – and what about a mink coat for the wedding?'

'Oo, my!' she exclaimed. 'That would sure be nice.' She paused, and then said: 'Provided there's enough in the bank to buy Isobel and Hank something real handsome as well.'

'There is,' said Boyd dryly. 'Believe me, there is.'

MOURNING
DOVES

This is a novel and its characters are products of my imagination, its situations likewise. Whatever similarity there may be of name, no reference is intended to any person living or dead.

I gratefully acknowledge information and advice regarding the Hoylake and District War Memorial from Mr J.T. O'Neil of Hoylake, Mr R. Jones of West Kirby, and Mr K. Burnley of Irby; help regarding costume from Mr Richard Brown, Victoria Public Library, Westminster, London; and information regarding flora of the area from Mr J.T. O'Neil of Hoylake and Miss Jemma Samuels of Wallasey. The background information which they supplied was invaluable, and I thank them all.

To Stephen and Lauren, with love

PROLOGUE

11 NOVEMBER 1995

The cenotaph stood on its great concrete plinth at the top of Grange Hill. To reach it meant a long climb for aged veterans and decrepit widows. Nevertheless, in this fiftieth anniversary year, a larger number than usual had turned out for the Remembrance Day service. Now the last wreath had been laid, and the parade had been formed up and was marching slowly down to the village.

As the voices faded away, Celia sat in her wheelchair, waiting with Rosemary, her West Indian carer, and her godson, Flight Lieutenant Timothy George Woodcock, DFC, until the narrow path down to the road was clear of people, and the wheelchair could be manoeuvred down.

Coming straight off the distant snow-topped mountains of North Wales and the estuary of the River Dee, the wind was cold, and, despite the blanket Rosemary had tucked round her, Celia was shivering.

She did not weep. Crying never helped anybody, she would say tartly. She had, however, a keen sense of inward loneliness, and she remembered suddenly her sister, Edna, friend and partner in so much of her life – ever since 1920.

What a year that had been. A year of final realisation that the men killed in the First World War would never come back, and neither would the safe, predictable life of 1914. Millions of ignorant, untrained women had had to remake their lives and find work to maintain themselves. I was one of them, considered Celia, as she sat patiently in her wheelchair and looked out across the misty

9

landscape of the Wirral. And I suppose that, in some ways, I was lucky.

She was, she knew, the oldest person to attend the service, one hundred years next week; and she was probably the only person in the district with truly clear memories of the First World War, of life before it began and of its aftermath.

Her luck had not held. The names of five members of her family were listed on the cenotaph, and every year she made the effort to come to lay a family wreath, gorgeous with huge plastic poppies and black satin ribbons, at the foot of the memorial. From the wreath dangled an old-fashioned black-edged card, which said,

IN TENDER MEMORY OF MY SONS, PETER, PAUL AND BERTRAM TREMAINE, KILLED IN ACTION IN WORLD WAR II, AND OF MY GRANDSONS, MICHAEL AND DAVID TREMAINE, LIKEWISE KILLED IN ACTION IN THE FALKLANDS WAR. NEVER FORGOTTEN.

As they waited, Timothy George also felt the cold and longed for a warm fire and a whisky and soda. A pity Bertram's wife could not be here, he thought; but, after her sons, Michael and David, had been killed, there was nothing to keep her in the Wirral, and she had gone south to live with her own mother in Devon.

Celia had remained, alone, in the red-brick Edwardian house which she and Alec had bought on their marriage.

It was strange to realise, Timothy ruminated, that, to most of the parishioners, both the First and the Second World Wars were forgotten wars, forgotten sacrifices. Except in special anniversary years such as this one, the crowds around the cenotaph grew smaller each year.

The flight lieutenant sighed. He supposed that Celia and he were, by now, simply walking history, not that Celia could walk very far; she was quite frail. This would probably be the last Poppy Day for her – and probably the last for many of the men like himself, some in uniform and some in shabby macintoshes, all with glittering collections of medals pinned to their breasts – and for the pitiful little bunch of widows and elderly spinsters, each with a red poppy in her buttonhole.

As he had glanced at the huddled old women, he had felt uneasily that even today there were some elderly women who were still not very good at managing life alone.

Their husbands, sons and lovers had died in the Second World War. Theirs was the second generation of women to be widowed by war or left without hope of marriage.

His own brother's name and also the names of Celia's brothers were on the Roll of Honour in the glass case on the cenotaph in Liverpool Cathedral. His brother, Eric, had been shot down by a sniper in Normandy during the Second World War, leaving a pregnant wife. His little nephew, he considered, had been fortunate to have been brought up by a kindly stepfather, considerably younger than his mother.

The wars had created a dreadful double generation gap, he thought grimly, and judging by the mismanagement in the country, the gap had not yet been closed.

He had for years held the notion that nobody had been able to fill the empty spaces left by the fathers and grandfathers who had died – or had been so wounded or exhausted that they were too weary to do anything much, once they had returned to civilian life. He remembered how tired he had been himself; it had been an enormous effort to start again after he had been demobbed.

Rosemary shook his arm, and said, 'I think we can go down now.'

He jumped, and then grinned agreement. In the comparative silence now surrounding them, the cold wind whined and the artificial foliage of the wreaths rustled faintly in reply, like distant voices calling.

Before they moved her, Celia turned to glance once more at the wreaths and then upwards to the bronze soldier in battledress who stared out over the sands of the estuary.

She remembered three little boys who had built a sand castle on the seashore, and how they had squabbled about who should place a paper Union Jack on its summit. She felt a sudden terrible pain go through her. Years later, they had followed that Union Jack and had gone gaily off to war and never come back. And in the Falklands War her two grandsons had done the same, for reasons that she could never understand.

'Goodbye, my dears,' she whispered, as the wheelchair began to move. 'See you soon.'

She took out a paper handkerchief and firmly blew her nose. One must never give in. Edna and I certainly never did.

Chapter One

❧

MARCH 1920

Was it really as small as that? Had that weed-covered quarter-acre ever held a formal flower garden, a lawn at the side of the house and a vegetable garden?

Louise Gilmore glanced up in despair at the house itself, one of a semi-detached pair. Sharp shards of glass stood upright in the frame of the broken hall bedroom window. She remembered how Gracie, her father's housemaid, used to shake her dust mop out of that window – regardless of who might be standing below on the front step. When the family came to spend their holidays in the house, one of the maids had always come with them; it was usually Gracie, who hated the isolation of the place, the steady boom of waves on the sea wall, and the sand which constantly sifted in from the surrounding dunes.

Now, Louise noted hopelessly, damp brick beneath the windowsill indicated that rain had soaked into the wall. The front sitting-room window had had a piece of board nailed over it, and the front door had lost most of its shiny black enamel; what remained was bubbled from the heat of many summers.

There was no garden gate. Only the wooden gateposts remained, and the encroaching front hedge had nearly obliterated them, too.

As a result of the death of her husband the previous Saturday, Louise had been terrified by the dire warnings of his executor, Cousin Albert, and of his lawyer, Mr Barnett. She had, they said, been left almost destitute and must, in order to raise some money on which to live, sell their beautiful Liverpool mansion immediately.

It was essential that she find speedily some other place to live in, so she had, that morning – only the day after her husband's funeral – dragged herself out of her bed and, with her younger daughter, Celia, made the tiring journey by train out to Meols, a small village on the Wirral Peninsula.

They had come to inspect a small – small from her perspective – summer cottage which had been in the family for years and had been rented out for most of the time. Cousin Albert had suggested that it would make a suitable retirement home for her, into which she could move almost at once.

She lifted her mourning veil from her face and flung it back over her black bonnet, then stepped on to the path leading to the front of the house. One of its dull red tiles had heaved and she tripped on it and nearly fell. She shivered, her breath coming in sobbing gulps.

'Be careful, Mother!' admonished her twenty-four-year-old spinster daughter, Celia, who was following closely behind her. 'Hold your dress up. You'll get it all muddy round the hem.'

Equally as scared as her mother, Celia was more snappish than usual. She herself was clutching her wide-brimmed black hat with one hand and holding down her own ankle-length skirt against the buffeting sea wind. She had sand in one eye and it was running tearfully from the painful irritation. She looked worn out.

Louise's lips tightened. She did not reply to Celia, as she lifted her black satin dress and petticoat an inch so that they did not draggle in the damp puddles on the dirty path.

Sometimes Celia could be very trying. Wasn't it enough that, only yesterday, they had stood by the grave of dear Timothy, her husband, who had shared her bed for thirty years? What was a bit of mud on the hem of one's skirt compared to losing him?

To add to her misery, Cousin Albert Gilmore, sole executor of her husband's will, had told her, upon his arrival, that Timothy had left heavy business debts, an announcement which had sent a frightening chill down her back. He had said that to keep up her fashionable home in the village of West Derby on the outskirts of Liverpool on what remained of her dowry would be impossible.

Cousin Albert had been completely heartless, she felt, not to give her some time to mourn, before unloading such cruel facts upon her.

Cousin Albert himself had, at first, not known what to do. He had, on Sunday, been telephoned by Mr Barnett, and he had arrived from his home in Nottingham on Monday. He had gone straight from Lime Street Station to see Mr Barnett in his office, and, warned by him, had gone on to Timothy's office to interview his chief clerk and to look at his files and account books.

What he had found was a financial disaster, which would, he thought in quiet rage, take him weeks to sort out. He berated himself for ever agreeing to be his cousin's trustee. He was, therefore, not in a very good temper and, when he arrived at Louise's house, he was, in addition, rumpled and hungry from his journey.

He had paid off the taxi at the driveway entrance and, carrying his suitcase, had puffed his way up a slight slope round a fine bed of laurel bushes to the imposing front steps. He pulled a huge brass bell handle and fidgeted fretfully until the door was opened by a frightened-looking parlourmaid.

Close behind the maid came Celia, wringing her hands helplessly, and whispering, 'Oh, Cousin Albert, I'm so glad you've come!'

'Yes, yes, my dear, I've come.'

He plonked down his small suitcase, and took off his black bowler hat to reveal a tumble of snow-white curls. He handed the hat to the maid and then peeled off his heavy black overcoat and pushed that on to her, too. He gave Celia a light peck on one cheek, and asked abruptly, 'Where's Louise?'

'In bed.'

'And your father?'

'He's laid out in the downstairs front sitting room.' Her voice quivered, and she added with evident anxiety, as she pointed to a closed, white-enamelled door, 'Mother wanted him buried from home, so I sent for the undertaker in West Derby. The undertaker thought that that room would be most convenient for visitors to come into, so I agreed.'

'Quite right, child. Quite right. When's the funeral?'

He looked around the hall. Seeing a door open, he remembered the family breakfast room and made straight for it, hoping to find a fire where he could warm himself. Celia fluttered after him.

'Tomorrow – at ten o'clock,' she told him, as he thankfully turned his back to a good coal fire and let the heat flood over him.

He had no feelings about the loss of his cousin, only a sense of irritation. He knew that it would be his duty to deal quickly with the affairs of a pair of tear-sodden women, who must change their way of life immediately. He also knew that he must make sure that grasping creditors could not lay hold on Louise's own modest assets. Timothy's clerk had assured him that she had not jointly signed with Timothy anything in connection with the business, which was a relief. At least she had, according to what Timothy had once told him, her dowry in the shape of the rents from six working-class houses in Birkenhead, for what little they were worth, and, in addition, this very fine house.

But he had been a lawyer himself, and he knew from bitter

16

experience that moneylenders could be quite ruthless and, occasionally, dishonest in their seizing of assets. Like any good Victorian gentleman, he was aware of his duty to any of his family, and nobody was going to strip his cousin's widow of her assets, if he had anything to do with it.

This rectitude did not prevent his being judged by Celia and her mother as inhumanly abrupt and callous with them, when, the next morning, Louise was persuaded to get up very early and get dressed in order that she might receive the many callers who would come to pay their respects to the dead before the funeral.

On the day of his arrival, since he felt that time was of the essence, she had also had to face, after a late lunch, the sad truths discovered earlier by her husband's trustee.

'You will need money from somewhere on which to live,' he had announced baldly. 'You will certainly have to sell this Liverpool house, and do it very quickly.' He sighed when he saw her shocked expression, but went on firmly, 'Whatever you get for it can be invested in an annuity to give you a modest income on which to live.'

Albert had gazed reflectively at the lovely embossed ceiling of her large upstairs drawing room, normally used only for big parties, and added, 'It's a valuable property in a good district – so close to the countryside – so it should fetch a good price.'

In his opinion, it was little less than a miracle that Timothy had long ago had enough sense to put the house in her name, so that it could never be seized to settle his business debts. Timothy had always taken the most appalling financial chances, he reflected. Of course, he had made a lot of money, though his luck, it seemed, was running out just before he died.

Albert had, therefore, very early the next morning, while Louise dealt with her visitors, been to see an estate agent and arranged for the house to be put on the market immediately; because she owned it, there was no need to wait for

Timothy's will to be probated before doing this. With the money it fetched, he had decided, he would buy the annuity for her from a reputable insurance company, which should just produce enough to keep her and young Celia in genteel poverty. In the meantime, they would just have to manage on the rental money from her Birkenhead houses – or take a small loan from the bank, which could be repaid from the money received for her home. Though he was not her trustee, he assumed that Louise would expect him, as the only man in the family, to undertake these financial arrangements on her behalf. Women were, in his opinion, quite helpless; he would present his very sensible plans for her future to her and, undoubtedly, she would accept them.

Before Timothy's sad demise, Louise had had no idea that she bore the burden of owning the Liverpool house, and the information had increased her bewilderment and her terror of being left alone. Timothy had always done everything, as a good husband should; all she had had to do was balance the housekeeping accounts, entertain his guests charmingly and be kind to him in bed.

It had been scant comfort to her when Cousin Albert, when talking to her on his arrival, had warned, 'My dear, you will probably have to manage without a servant. However, since there will be only you and Celia, a very small house will be quite appropriate, and I am sure you are an excellent housekeeper.' He had smiled at her with as much benignity as he could muster.

Louise moaned into her black handkerchief. Did he not realise that he was tearing her whole life apart? It was too much to endure.

He had watched her weep for a few moments, and then had leaned forward to pat her hand and remind her, as Mr Barnett, the solicitor, had earlier reminded him, that she also owned a little house, really a cottage, on the other side of the Mersey River. 'Your father's summer home – by the sea – in Meols, near Hoylake,' he had encouraged.

'When your sister Felicity died, she left it to you. Remember?

'Mr Barnett tells me that he recollects that it was let for years. I understand, however, from the agent, Mr Billings, whom I phoned today from Mr Barnett's office, that there is no one living in it at present.'

He heard Celia take a quick intake of breath, and he glanced over to her. Pale-blue eyes stared back at him from a dead-white face. She looked scared to death.

He continued in a more cheerful tone of voice, addressing himself partly towards her. 'After being let for so long, it will almost certainly require renovation – but that is soon arranged. You've probably seen it, Celia?'

'No, I haven't,' she muttered.

He stopped, wishing heartily that he had not been left the unpleasant task of telling these stupid women what they must do; he felt too old and tired to be bothered with them. He went on heavily, 'When Mr Barnett told me about it, I had thought of selling the cottage on your behalf, instead of this house. But it would not fetch much – I hope, however, that it won't need too much to make it a very comfortable home for you – and you must have an income from somewhere to live on, which only funds from this big house can provide.' He reminded himself that, after the funeral the following morning, he should make a quick trip out to Meols to check that the cottage was indeed habitable.

Louise had temporarily forgotten the cottage; she had not seen it since Felicity had died ten years before. Though the day-to-day care of her property was done through Mr Billings, dear Timothy had always kept an eye on it for her, including that which had been settled on her by her father at the signing of her marriage contract. The thought made her weep ever more heavily into her black handkerchief.

*　　*　　*

Now, as she looked at the cottage, she despaired. What would happen to her in this awful place? How could she bear it? And to add to her distress, her scandalous elder sister, Felicity, did not seem to have done much to keep the building up during her ownership of it. She remembered that, when the property had passed to her, Timothy had insisted on letting it, because, he said, it was too shabby for family use. Perhaps it was the tenants who had left it in such a mess.

How devout churchman Timothy had condemned Felicity's way of life. He would not hear of Louise having anything more to do with her. All because Felicity had dared to live in the cottage with handsome Colonel Featherstone, a scarred veteran of the Matabele and Boer Wars – without marrying him. As a result, Timothy had always insisted that she might have a bad influence on the children. He had even frowned when Louise bestirred herself enough to say defiantly that she must occasionally write to her only sister, no matter what she had done. And Timothy must have known very well that, if she married a second husband, Felicity would automatically lose the army pension left her by her first husband, dear Angus, killed at Rorke's Drift during the Zulu Wars. But Timothy had always insisted that shortage of money was no excuse for Sin.

Only her father had understood Felicity, she thought, as she sniffed into her handkerchief. Felicity had died childless, but, sometimes, when her own elder daughter, Edna, had grown up, she had seen in her some of Felicity's sprightliness and brave defiance of convention.

She would have been glad to have Edna with her now, but the girl was married and far away in Brazil.

When, before setting out for the cottage, cold dread of a future without a father or brother or son to care for her had consumed her soul, Louise had at breakfast wept openly in front of fat, elderly Cousin Albert.

Harassed Celia, at twenty-four far too old for marriage, had pressed a glass of sherry on her. Mother was so set in her ways, so difficult to deal with if her normal routine was upset, that Celia knew that if any action had to be taken, it would be she who must, somehow, take it.

She felt despairingly that she had no idea of business matters; Papa had always kept such information in his own hands. In consequence, she had become numb with fear as Cousin Albert explained to her her late father's financial circumstances.

The loss of her father, however unloving, had reopened her grief over the loss of her brothers, Tom and George, during the war, and her stomach muscles were clenched as she did her best to keep calm.

The more she considered her mother's and her own circumstances, the more terrified of the future she became. With no male to protect them or earn a living for them, what would happen to them? And still worse, what would happen to her when her mother died? She had nothing of her own; she had been her mother's obedient companion-help ever since she was fourteen. She was totally dependent upon her.

She also felt a profound unease about Cousin Albert himself. Was he altogether trustworthy? She did not know him well, but he struck her as a manipulative man, a man with little idea of kindness or humanity – though her father must have had some faith in him to make him his executor.

Immediately after the funeral was over, Albert had had a private discussion with Timothy's solicitor and old friend, Mr Barnett of Barnett and Sons.

Elderly Mr Barnett was himself trembling with fatigue and grief, because the AND SONS of his practice no longer existed; one had died while a prisoner of war and the other had succumbed to trench fever in the horrors of 1916. With difficulty, the old man had single-handedly kept the practice going for his sons while they were at war. Now, he knew he would never enjoy a peaceful retirement; to keep himself, his wife and three daughters, he must continue his practice until he dropped. It was no wonder that he found it hard to concentrate on what the pompous Mr Albert Gilmore was saying, and that he agreed to everything suggested in connection with Mrs Louise Gilmore's affairs.

After lunch, Albert took out his gold hunter watch and announced that he would go again to Timothy's office to do some more work, would stay one more night and then, the next morning, catch an early train back to his Nottingham home. 'Mr Barnett will have the will probated and will do a further check in case there are any, as yet, undiscovered assets,' he told Celia.

'My dear Louise,' he continued paternalistically to the tear-soaked widow, 'I shall be in constant touch with Mr Barnett – fortunately, I have a telephone – and, in a few days' time, I'll be in touch with you again by mail. In the meantime, you should go out to Meols – that is the nearest railway station – to look at your cottage there.' He tucked his watch back into his waistcoat pocket. 'Mr Barnett will oversee the paperwork regarding the house for you. An estate agent may come tomorrow to evaluate it.'

He carefully did not mention to her that, since her present home and its contents already belonged to her, she had the right to refuse to sell it. Nor did he tell her that that afternoon he would pay a quick visit to the cottage to check that it looked repairable. She must face reality herself, he felt defensively.

Albert did not want any argument about the sale either. He dreaded dealing with women – they were so volatile and so lacking in common sense, and physically they revolted him. Better by far to persuade Louise to sign a quick agreement with Mr Barnett that he should arrange paperwork of the sale.

That evening, after Cousin Albert and Mr Barnett had dined with her, she had signed the agreement to sell without even reading it.

It never occurred to her that she was signing away her own property, that she was free to make her own decisions. She was certain that men always knew best.

Terrified, white-faced Celia's instinct that something was wrong was, therefore, correct. Albert Gilmore's intentions were, however, of the best. He was simply convinced that women were totally incapable of running their own lives, a belief certainly shared by his late cousin, Timothy. With money coming in every month from an annuity and with Celia to care for her, he could comfortably forget Louise.

Now, buffeted by a brisk sea breeze, Celia and her mother stood in front of a dwelling which looked as shabby as a house could look without actually falling down.

'Built in 1821,' Celia said without hope. 'See! There's the date above the front door. No wonder it's shabby – it will be a hundred years old next year.'

A wave of pure panic began to envelop the younger woman, as her mother sniffed into her handkerchief, and wailed, 'What are we going to do, Celia? We can't possibly live here. What is Albert thinking about, suggesting such a thing? Couldn't we buy another house?'

Her daughter shivered, and tried to muster some common sense. She replied, 'Well, probably this is the cheapest roof we'll ever find, Mama, even if we have to have it repaired. Mostly, I suspect that Cousin Albert wants us resettled quickly, because he doesn't want us to live with him.'

Her mother turned back towards her, and with a sigh, inquired, 'What did you say, dear?'

Celia had bent down to pick up two hairpins which had fallen out of her untidy ash-blonde bun. Her voice was muffled, as she replied, 'I think he may wish us to begin a new life together without delay. He may fear that we expect him to invite us to live with him – he has a big house – I remember our going to visit him once, when I was little.' She straightened up and pushed the pins into her handbag. 'But he hasn't offered us a home, Mother – and I don't think he should have to. It is not as if he were your brother – then he'd have a duty towards us.'

Her mother responded with unexpected acerbity. 'Well, he is your father's trustee until the estate is settled. He might at least have stayed long enough to help us, instead of leaving us in the hands of a solicitor – and an estate agent who has had the insensitivity to come in the day after the funeral, and run around our home – with a tape measure!'

'The estate agent is concerned only with selling our house, Mother. He came to see it this morning only because Cousin Albert wants it sold quickly. He did apologise for intruding on us, remember. And the house is enormous, Mother, with seven bedrooms and three servants' rooms. Too much for just two of us.'

Her mother's puffed eyelids made her eyes look like slits in her plump face, as she replied pitifully, 'I don't want to sell it, Celia. It's our home. And, what's more, I don't like the agent – so officious and totally lacking in delicacy or compassion.'

Celia wanted badly to cry herself, but she put her arm round her mother's waist, and said gently, 'Try not to grieve, Mama. This little house is yours, too, remember – you can do anything you like with it. We can probably make it very pretty.'

Celia gestured towards the shabby front door facing them. 'I suppose Cousin Albert imagines we can arrange for the renovations ourselves?' She paused, as she tried to think clearly.

Louise continued to cry. At Celia's remarks, however, her petulant little mouth dropped open. She could do anything she liked with this miserable cottage? What rubbish! Men always looked after property.

'How can I get it done up? I have no idea how to proceed, and where would we get the money to do it?' she wailed.

Celia had to admit that she did not know either. She responded firmly, however, by saying, 'Perhaps we can find someone in the village, a builder, who could at least advise us about what it would cost.'

Then another frightening thought struck her, and she asked, 'Did Cousin Albert say what we were to do about money until the house is sold? We would have to pay workmen, wouldn't we?'

Albert had not mentioned immediate financial needs, except to say that he had himself advanced the money for dear Timothy's funeral.

Her mother closed her eyes. She had no idea what, if any, money she had to draw on for the time being. It was all too much. She was trembling with fatigue and bewilderment at the sudden upheaval in her life. She wished heartily that she could follow Timothy – and simply die.

It really was most inconvenient that Timothy should have a heart attack before he had even reached his fiftieth birthday – and die in his office. What a fuss that had caused!

As if she could bear anything more, when they had already lost both their sons, George – her baby – in the dreadful sinking of the *Hampshire* in 1916. Drowned with Lord Kitchener, she had been told; as if that made it any the less painful to her. And big, strong Tom, her eldest and the pride of her soul, killed on the Somme.

Her terrible frustration at their youthful deaths still haunted her. There was nothing she could do to express her love of them. She could not give them beautiful funerals to mark the family's grief at their passing. They had left no wives or children to be comforted. They did not even have graves which she could tend in memory of them. All she could do was weep for them.

And her own two brothers, who could have been so much help to her in the present crisis? Both long dead, Peter from yellow fever while serving as an administrator on the Gold Coast, and Donald, a major in the 43rd, killed in a skirmish in the Khyber Pass just before the war broke out. The Empire had cost an awful lot of men, she thought, with sudden resentment against governments as well as against poor Timothy.

Celia patiently repeated her question about money, and her mother mopped her eyes and responded mechanically, 'I suppose he thinks I'll find it out of my own small income – my dot. There may be a little money in the bank which is mine, and I still have most of my March housekeeping.'

'Do you have any idea how much is in your banking account?' Celia knew that her grandfather had settled on her mother a dowry – a dot, as such a settlement was popularly called – of rental housing in Birkenhead. It was doubtful whether the income from their small rents would be enough to tide them over, never mind pay for extensive repairs to this dismal house.

'I don't know how much. I will have to ask the bank manager – and Mr Billings.'

'The agent who collected the rent for this cottage and manages your Birkenhead property?'

'Yes, dear. Cousin Albert says I am lucky that, when I married, your grandfather made quite sure that that property always remained mine.'

At the mention of Mr Billings, some of Celia's fear receded. Mr Billings would surely know how to deal with house repairs. He might know how they could obtain credit so that they did not have to pay immediately.

As she searched in her leather handbag for the key to the house, handed to her by Cousin Albert, who had found it, neatly labelled, in Timothy's key cupboard in his office,

26

she said with false cheerfulness to her mother, 'Let's go inside. It may not be so dreadful as we think. Then, instead of going directly back home to Liverpool, we could pause long enough in Birkenhead to see Mr Billings; he'll know something about house repairs, I'm sure. We can take a later train back to Liverpool.'

'Well, I suppose,' Louise whispered wearily, 'since we are here, we might as well look at the inside.'

As Celia slowly turned the big iron key in the rusty lock, Louise paused to look round what had been the front garden, and sighed deeply at the sight of the foot-high weeds. She sobbed again into her large, black mourning handkerchief, one of the same set of handkerchiefs she had used when crying for her lost boys.

Celia's hand was trembling as she put the big key back into her handbag, before pushing hard on the stiff door to open it. What will become of us? she fretted. What shall we do?

Nineteen twenty was supposed to be a year when, two years after the war, things would settle down and life return to normal. Mourning was supposed to be over, your black dresses put away. But you can't bury grief as quickly as you can bury men, she thought bitterly.

At best, life was proving to be totally different from that of 1914, when during a gloriously hot August, Europe was plunged into war, and life's main preoccupation became the casualty lists.

Added to the death of her sons, her poor mother now had this burden of comparatively early widowhood, a penurious one, and the loss of her superbly furnished home.

As she pushed hard at the reluctant door, she thought for a moment of herself, and she saw no hope of a decent future anywhere.

Chapter Two

ℰ∾ℰ

As the door swung open to reveal a tiny vestibule, decayed autumn leaves rustled across a dusty tiled floor. Facing them was an inner door, its upper panels consisting of a stained-glass window with an elaborate pattern of morning glory flowers.

In an effort to cheer her mother up a little, Celia exclaimed, 'Wouldn't that be pretty if it were cleaned?'

'Mother loved it,' Louise said abruptly. Because her nose was so swollen from weeping, she sounded as if she had a heavy cold.

Using the same key, Celia unlocked the pretty door and hesitantly opened it. She had never been in the cottage before, and did not know exactly what to expect.

A very narrow, gloomy hall was revealed. It was poorly lit by a window at the top of a steep staircase to her right. To the left of her, two doors led off the hall. At the back was a third door. The lower half of all the walls was painted brown; the upper half looked as if it had once been cream. It was, however, very dirty; every corner was hung with cobwebs, and dust clung to them. Dust lay thickly on the wooden banister of the stairs, on the bare wooden treads, and on the ridges of the door panels. Under their feet fine sand, blown in from the dunes at the back of the house, crunched faintly on reddish tiles.

Celia quickly flung open the two doors and they glanced in at tiny rooms which looked equally dirty and depressing, their fireplaces choked with ashes, the bare wooden floors grimy and littered with bits of yellowed newspaper. The light from the windows, filtering through gaps in the boards hammered over their exterior, did little to lift the general air of dinginess.

Determined to be brave, Celia said to her mother, again steeped in melancholy, 'They've both got fireplaces – and quite big windows.'

Louise did not reply. She was past caring.

She did, however, follow Celia, as the younger woman approached the door at the end of the hallway, which she presumed correctly would lead into some sort of a kitchen.

A very rusty range had been built into one wall. With a long-handled water pump at one end, a sandstone sink was set below a filthy casement window positioned high in the house's end wall. Through the window Celia caught a glimpse of the straggling tops of hedges which she supposed marked the edge of the property.

Cautiously she pressed down the pump handle. It gave a fearsome squeak, but no water came out.

Her mother stared at it, and then said heavily, 'It has to be primed and it's probably rusted inside.' After a pause while she dabbed at her reddened nose, she added, 'There's a well at the bottom of the garden.'

Celia was appalled. The kitchen was awful, filthy beyond anything she had ever seen before. How on earth could one ever get such a neglected house clean – without a couple of skilled charwomen? But Cousin Albert had said no servants.

She realised with real shock that, if they did come to live in it, she herself would have to clean it. Her mother would not dream of doing an unpleasant job while she had a daughter to push it on to, and Celia had no idea even how to start.

She swallowed, and opened another door. 'This must be the pantry,' she said. 'Phew! How it smells!'

Because there was a sudden scuffle of tiny feet in its

confined space, she hastily slammed the door shut again. 'Ugh!'

'Mice!' her mother burst out. 'Oh, Celia!' She hastily gathered her skirts up to her knees, as if expecting an immediate invasion of her petticoats by the tiny intruders. Tears ran down her face.

'It's all right, Mother. It's all right! I don't think any came out.' Celia turned back to the hallway, and suggested heavily, 'We'd better have a look upstairs.'

There were three small bedrooms, and, in addition, a very tiny room at the front, over the hallway, which Louise said, with an effort, had been her elder sister's bedroom when they were children. It was in the latter that the window had been broken. Rain had got in and damaged the plaster. Under their feet brown linoleum squelched as they trod on it, indicating that there was water under it.

'Pooh!' exclaimed Celia. 'This room reeks of damp.'

Her mother blew her nose, and said very wearily, 'The floorboards have probably rotted.'

Celia nodded. She wondered, with a shiver, if they would ever have enough money, never mind enough strength, to put this tiny house into some sort of order. Cousin Albert must believe that it was possible, she decided.

In fact, Albert Gilmore had not thought the matter through very well. His main goal was to avoid having to take the two bereaved women into his own home in Nottingham, where he dwelled very happily with an obliging man-servant. He did not want them there even temporarily – they might be hard to dislodge.

He hoped that they would agree to settle in the cottage, or, alternatively, go to live with Louise's elder, married daughter, Edna, and her husband, Paul Fellowes, something he had not yet suggested to either lady – he felt that the latter idea must come from Paul and Edna, and was, in his opinion, a decision of last resort. In the meantime, he had pressed on Louise the idea of the cottage as a suitable home.

Paul was an electrical engineer, a director in his family firm which had grown hugely during the war, because of the international reputation of its engineers and their innovative approach to new problems. He had just completed managing a lucrative seven-year contract for the wiring of an entire city in Brazil. He and Edna would, according to Louise, sail for home this month. Once he was resettled in England, considered Cousin Albert, Paul Fellowes would certainly be able to afford to take in a couple of women, who would probably make themselves useful in his house, as such women always did.

On the other hand, he pondered, if they would agree to live in the cottage and were very careful, they should be able to manage on the rents from Louise's six houses in Birkenhead. The rents, in addition to the annuity which he proposed to buy for them from the proceeds of the sale of the West Derby house, should be enough for two women to live on.

He knew from his talks with Mr Barnett and with Timothy's chief clerk that there would, almost certainly, be nothing left of Timothy's estate. The man owed money everywhere, probably because much of his basic income had come from investment in railways, which, now that the war was over, were not doing very well. Had he lived, he might have been able to pull through a difficult period, but now there was no hope. His few assets must be liquidated to meet his debts.

He trusted that Paul Fellowes would, when he returned to England, help him with the paperwork necessary to wind everything up. Paul should soon receive his letter, sent to Salvador, Brazil, informing him of his father-in-law's death and asking him to break the news to his wife.

It was possible that the couple had already sailed for England before the letter's arrival. In that case they would receive the news from a telegram, which he had dispatched to Paul's father at their company head office in Southampton. Edna's last letter to her mother had mentioned that they expected to dock in Southampton and spend a few days with Paul's parents before coming north to visit her own parents.

As Louise and Celia struggled round the overgrown garden of the cottage by the sand dunes, Louise mentioned how relieved she would be to see Paul and Edna.

Celia agreed. She had almost forgotten what the couple looked like. She had never had a great deal to do with her elder sister, and she had met Paul only three times, so she was not particularly hopeful of being comforted. Their presence would, however, add a sense of stability to Louise in her shattered state, for which she would be grateful.

If Paul returned quickly enough, thought Celia, he would, at least, be someone to consult about the cottage – if he had any time; she had always understood from her father that businessmen never did have much time to spare for the affairs of women.

Standing in the cottage garden after the stuffiness of the house, it was a relief to Celia to breathe clean, salt-laden air, and, despite its total neglect, there was a healthy smell of damp earth and growing things.

At the bottom of the garden, they inspected an earth lavatory.

'It's utterly disgusting!' Celia exclaimed. 'Did you really use it?'

'Yes,' Louise admitted. 'It wasn't something we looked forward to. It was your father's main objection to continuing to come here for holidays.' She began to whimper, as she recalled with anguish the handsome water closet which Timothy had had installed in their West Derby home.

'Perhaps we could get a proper bathroom put in here,' Celia suggested doubtfully, as she shut the door firmly on the obnoxious little hut. Though she had long since learned that, to survive, she must bow her head and do whatever her parents decided, even her broken spirit had, on inspecting such primitive sanitary arrangements, begun to feel a sense of revolt.

After several days of being confined indoors, the fresh air was reviving Louise, and she looked around her, and sighed. She replied quite coherently, 'I don't think we could put in a water closet, without piped water and drains.' Then she exclaimed with something of her normal impatience, 'What a mess! I can't imagine what kind of a tenant must've been living here. Mr Billings must have been very careless about his selection of one.'

Celia contemplated the jungle of weeds and sprawling bushes round her. 'Did he pay the rent? The tenant, I mean,' she asked practically.

Her mother shrugged. 'I don't know. Your father took care of these things.'

Celia turned to stare at the back of the house. The roof looked all right, no slate tiles missing and the chimneys were all intact, as far as she could judge. Her eyes followed the ridge of the roof, and she remembered suddenly that there was another house attached to theirs.

'Do you own the house next door, Mother? I can see that the other side of the hedge has been trimmed, and there are curtains in the bedroom windows – and smoke is coming from the chimney. Someone must live there.'

Her mother looked up. 'No, I don't own it. My father bought this house simply as a summer cottage, rather than as an investment, and when he died he left it to your Aunt Felicity.'

Anxious to encourage her mother to take an interest in anything, Celia asked, 'Who does own it?'

'A Mr and Mrs Lytham bought the other side. I used to play with their children.' Louise's expression softened, and she added wistfully, 'We had some lovely times, playing in the sand dunes and paddling in the sea. I wonder what happened to them?'

Celia forced a smile. 'How nice that must have been.' Then she looked at her brooch watch. 'Perhaps we had better lock up, Mother, and go to have a talk with Mr Billings. He could advise us about repairs.'

Her mother nodded and they retraced their steps to the house, ruefully brushing down their long skirts. Even Celia's ankle-length, tailored skirt had caught in the undergrowth and had burrs and bits of leaves and seeds clinging to it.

Celia locked the back door and they walked slowly and dismally through the house, leaving muddy tracks behind them.

While Celia turned to secure the inner front door, Louise proceeded slowly down the front steps. She suddenly let out a frightened little cry, 'Oh!'

Celia spun round.

Standing in the middle of the red-tiled path was a tall thin man. As the women stared at him, he raised his cap and bowed. 'Good afternoon,' he greeted them politely.

Chapter Three

❦

Confronted by a man, both women were suddenly acutely aware of how isolated the cottage was.

Walking down the lane to it, they had passed only one other cottage, a squat little dwelling with a thatched roof. It had, Louise told Celia, been lived in for centuries by a family of fishermen. Now, they stared uneasily at someone who seemed to have sprung from nowhere.

'Good afternoon,' responded Celia nervously, while her mother stiffened, as she catalogued the man as no gentleman, despite his courteous greeting. The lanky man's grey hair was roughly cut and framed a lined, weather-beaten face. He wore a striped union shirt without a collar; a red and white cotton handkerchief was tied round his neck. His wrinkled, old-fashioned moleskin trousers, held up by a worn leather belt, were stained with dried mud.

As he looked down at her, Louise's silence did not seem to disconcert him in the least. His faded blue eyes held the hint of a smile, as he said, 'You must be Mrs Gilmore. The gentleman as was here to take a quick look at the cottage for you said as you would be coming. He come out late Tuesday. Nearly dark, it was.'

A quiet rage against Cousin Albert rose in Louise, blotting out all sense of fear or grief. So, during his stay with her, he had not spent all his time in Timothy's office checking over with the clerk just exactly what the financial situation was; he had also been out here, planning to condemn her to live in this awful place. He knew precisely what it was like.

With sudden understanding she realised how she had been manipulated. Albert and Mr Barnett had made her sign away her present home.

It was so unfair. They should have explained to her what she was about to do. Consulted her. The fact that the outcome would probably have been the same did not make any difference. She had not been asked what she felt about moving out here.

Could she not have sold this horrible cottage and bought another tiny house in a decent, civilised Liverpool street?

No time had been allowed her to recover from her bereavement, she raged; there had been no understanding that she was distraught with grief.

She was healthily furious, not only with Albert and Mr Barnett, but also with Timothy.

Timothy might have had enough sense to tell her that she owned their home, when he had originally transferred it.

Unless he had not trusted her? What a dreadful thought!

That was it. He must have felt, like Cousin Albert, that she was not capable of dealing with the ownership of such a valuable property; in transferring the ownership to her he must simply have been ensuring that no creditor of his could ever seize his home.

Men were like that, she felt with sudden, bitter understanding of the helplessness imposed on women.

She drew herself up to her full height, and replied frigidly to the stranger. 'Yes, I am Mrs Timothy Gilmore.'

'And the young lady?'

'My daughter, Miss Celia Gilmore.'

The man smiled down at the tiny younger woman. Framed by untidy blonde hair, her face had the whiteness of skin never exposed to sunlight. Her loose, black-belted jacket and full skirt were relieved only by a white blouse.

A tiny gold cross and chain glittered on a blue-white throat. A wide-brimmed black hat, worn squarely on her head, did nothing to improve her looks. A proper little mouse, her mam's companion-help, he judged her, but probably amiable enough to be a good neighbour. 'Nice to know yez, luv,' he said warmly.

Celia smiled nervously in return. She sensed that the old man approved of her. It felt nice; she rarely got approval from anybody. As her mother's patient shadow, she was usually barely noticed.

Their visitor pointed an arthritic finger at the house next door, and, as if taking it for granted that the ladies would be moving into the cottage they had just inspected, he said, 'I'm your neighbour. Me name's Eddie Fairbanks. Was head gardener to the earl till he sold the family home to be a nursing home for wounded soldiers. Proper kind to me, he was. Served him forty years I did, ever since I were a lad of ten, so I was close to retirement, anyway. He give me the cottage rent free for me lifetime and me wife's lifetime – 'cos, he said, I designed one of the best rose gardens in the north for him, and he loved roses. He hoped the servicemen would enjoy the garden. He lives in London now.' He paused to take a breath, while the two women stared at him. Since they did not say anything, he went on, 'My Alice passed away six years ago, so I manage by meself.' He paused again, as if expecting some response from Louise, but when there was none, he asked, 'Would you like a cuppa tea? The kettle's already hot. That house must've been cold when you went in – with the wind, and all.'

'No, thank you,' Louise replied stiffly. Tea with a gardener? What was she coming to?

Celia, however, caught her arm and, smiling unexpectedly prettily at the old man, she said, 'Mother! It would be so nice to get acquainted with Mr Fairbanks. He might be able to tell us more than Mr Billings would.'

'Ha! Old Billings?' interjected Mr Fairbanks. 'In Birkenhead, eh? He hasn't taken much care of the place for you, has he?'

Celia replied ruefully, 'No, not by the look of it.' She turned her head to smile up at her mother. 'A cup of tea would be lovely, Mother.' She gave Louise's arm a warning little tug. In their desperate situation, a male neighbour could be very helpful.

Louise was still inwardly steaming with rage, but out of courtesy she reluctantly agreed. She said to Mr Fairbanks, 'Very well. It is very kind of you.'

She made herself smile at the man, and he said, obviously pleased, 'That's better, Ma'am. This way, if you please.'

He led them down the path and round the wild, ragged front hedge. At the halfway mark, it suddenly became a neatly trimmed privet, and he led them into a front garden boasting a few daffodils and other small spring blooms. Near the house wall, sheltered from the cold wind, a blaze of red tulips stood tall and straight as an honour guard. The front window was neatly draped with lace curtains, and the front door stood open, giving a glimpse of a flowered stair carpet.

They entered through a lobby similar to the other one next door, though it lacked the stained-glass window in the inner door and the tiles were covered by a large doormat.

They carefully wiped their feet as they went in, and looked down the passageway with some curiosity.

It had the same brown paint with cream upperworks as the house they had just been in. It was, however, spotlessly clean, and the hall runner was thick cream wool with a lively Turkish pattern in dark reds and greens. Celia looked at it and hesitated to step on it.

'My shoes must still be muddy from the garden,' she said doubtfully to the old man.

'Don't worry, luv. The carpet cleans up fairly easy.' He

38

smiled at her and at her mother behind her, and gestured towards the colourful stair carpet. 'Alice and me, we hooked all the carpets in the house. Pure wool, they are. They sponge clean something wonderful.'

Murmuring polite amazement at such industry, the ladies were ushered into the back room, where a good coal fire glowed. 'Come in, come in and warm yourselves.'

He eased a rather bewildered Louise into a battered rocking chair, and told Celia to take the chair opposite, which was a low nursing chair with a padded seat and back, its velveteen worn with age.

As she sat down, she wondered how many babies Alice had fed while seated in the armless chair. She spread her skirt comfortably round her, and, a little sadly, thought how good it must feel to have a baby at the breast and be cosy with it by the fire. Then, as Mr Fairbanks hurried to get his best, flowered cups and saucers out of a corner cupboard and set them on a table in the centre of the little room, she almost blushed at her wickedness at harbouring such an idea.

Her duty was to her mother; she had been taught that in childhood, and, anyway, at aged twenty-four she was on the shelf – too old to think of marriage and babies.

Edna had been the pretty one, who had been groomed for marriage and had gone triumphantly to the altar with Paul Fellowes, a good solid match. Her father had, however, been worried when a besotted Edna had insisted on following her husband out to Brazil, though she was pregnant with their first child. Her daughter had survived being born in a hot climate, only to die of dysentery at the age of two. There had been no other children, and Celia often wondered why. Her friend, Phyllis Woodcock, had told her ruefully that babies arrived every year.

Edna was lucky that Paul was still alive. Had it not been for the contract in Brazil, he would surely have volunteered for the army at the beginning of the war, and it would have been remarkable if he had managed to survive until the conflict ended. She wondered if he had felt any regret at not being able to come home and fight – or had he thankfully made the business contract with Brazil, an allied country, an excuse not to have to sacrifice himself for king and country?

The latter was such an ignoble thought that she immediately turned her attention back to her mother.

Louise was sitting silently, her eyes half-closed, as the fire warmed her frozen feet. Her sudden spate of rage was draining away, and she felt dreadfully tired. She longed to lie down in the cosseting safety of her own bed.

After a few minutes, she roused herself sufficiently to take off her gloves and allow the heat to warm her hands. While Mr Fairbanks bustled into the kitchen to fill the kettle, Celia whispered to her, 'When do you think Paul and Edna will dock?'

Before replying, Louise waited for Mr Fairbanks to push between them to place the kettle on the hob, and turn it over the fire. It soon began to sing, and Mr Fairbanks said cheerfully, 'It won't be long, Ma'am.'

Louise acknowledged his remark with a condescending nod, and then, as he vanished in search of milk and sugar, replied to Celia, 'I really don't know. Albert thought it would be within two weeks. He thought it very likely that they had sailed a day or two before ... before ...' Her lower lip began to tremble.

Celia's voice was very gentle, as she suggested, 'So that it is possible that they will not receive his letter – or your letter to Edna?'

'Yes, dear.'

'That's what he said to me. In any case, once they get word in Southampton, I am sure they will take the first train up here.'

'Yes, dear.'

It was Celia's turn to sigh. 'I wish they were here. Paul

would know what to do about everything.' She felt like adding, 'And he would know how to deal with Cousin Albert, so that at least we would know more exactly what our financial situation really is.' She restrained herself, however, because she could see that her mother was crying silently to herself.

Louise's tears had not gone unnoticed by Mr Fairbanks. It was clear that Albert had told him the reason for Louise's coming to the cottage, because he said soothingly to her, as he rescued the puffing kettle and took it over to the table to fill the large earthenware teapot, 'Don't grieve, Ma'am. A good cup of tea'll set you up.'

He stirred the pot briskly, put an ancient knitted tea cosy over it, and asked, 'How much sugar, Ma'am?'

'Two, please.'

'And you, Miss Celia?'

'The same, please.' Really, he was being immensely kind, Celia thought, just like a grandfather would be. Both sets of her grandparents had died when she was small, and she had little recollection of them, except of veined wrinkled hands producing bonbons and popping them into her mouth, and being hugged and kissed. Her mother might not be getting much comfort from their encounter with Mr Fairbanks, but she herself was.

Before giving them their tea, Mr Fairbanks went back to his corner cupboard and produced a largish bottle.

'Would you be liking a drop of rum in your tea, Ma'am? It might help you a bit, like . . .'

Louise glanced up at him. For a moment she was shocked out of her misery. 'Oh, no, thank you. I couldn't possibly!' A gentlewoman drinking rum like a common sailor's wife? Brandy, perhaps, but not rum!

Celia, however, saw the sense of his suggestion, and she said, 'Have a tiny bit, Mother. It would give you strength. And we have yet to get to Birkenhead, to see Mr Billings

– and then go home – it will take all your strength.'

Louise faltered. The remaining part of the afternoon stretched before her like a long staircase hard to climb, and she was so tired, so dreadfully tired.

Mr Fairbanks smiled at her encouragingly, 'It won't do you no harm, Ma'am.'

She was persuaded, and she did cheer up, though she drank her two cups of tea with her nose wrinkling up in distaste at the odour of the rum.

Eddie Fairbanks did not offer rum to Celia. As a single lady she shouldn't be drinking anything but wine, and he didn't have anything like that in the house.

Warmed and comforted and a little drunk, Louise relaxed enough to ask the old man if he knew what had happened to her childhood playmates, the Lytham family, who used to live in his house.

He did not know where the family was, he said. He knew only that the leasehold of both cottages had run out, and that the Lythams had not renewed theirs, but that Celia's grandfather had come to an agreement with the earl to renew his for another hundred years. 'Because the houses are very well built, and your granddad probably wanted to keep his in the family for holidays.'

It was obvious from Louise's expression that she had no idea what was meant by leasehold, so Celia asked, 'What exactly does that mean? I've always wondered.'

Mr Fairbanks picked up his cup of tea, and took a sip. 'Well, you see, luv, nobody round these parts owns much land. Nearly all of it has belonged to the earl since time began. If you want to build on land round here – or farm it – you can persuade the earl to give you a long lease on it – these cottages had one for fifty years – and then you can build on it. However, at the end of the lease, you have to pay the earl to renew it; otherwise the land – and the buildings that you have built on it – revert to him, and he can rent them to somebody or pull them down.' He put his cup down neatly in its saucer, and then added, 'And what's more, you'll probably find that Mr Billings 'as been paying a ground rent to his lordship's agent each year on your behalf.'

Louise asked, 'Can we sell the cottage, if we want to?'

'Oh, yes, Ma'am, if someone is prepared to buy the lease from you. But you'd have difficulty getting a good price for it – they're a bit isolated – it's a fair walk to Meols railway station, and your cottage has bin proper neglected, if I may say so. And in winter the wind comes in from the sea something awful. The gentleman that came to look at it brought Mr Parry, the estate agent from Hoylake, along with him – and that's what he said. Neither house is worth a great deal.'

Louise felt a little comforted. At least Albert had considered selling the cottage, before he had condemned her to it.

For her part, Celia swallowed hard. Pay an earl for the right to live in a house that belonged to you, but you probably could not sell? What other money problems that they knew nothing about lurked amid the present turmoil of their lives? What other financial demands could they expect? She felt faint with fear, unreasonable fear that Cousin Albert might have deserted them, leaving them penniless. He had made it clear that the price of their Liverpool home would be used as the foundation of their income, and certainly not to buy another house. Once he had sold it for them, would he be honest and hand over the money? Celia felt sick with apprehension.

Her mother must have had similar vague fears, because she said rather desperately to her daughter, 'Perhaps we should go to see Mr Billings now, Celia.' She rose carefully, to hand her cup to their host, and thank him quite sweetly for his hospitality. He was a mere working man – but he was male and he knew things that she did not. Like Celia, Louise began to view him as a possible pillar of support, like a good butler would have been, had she been fortunate enough to have one in her employ, instead of a giggling fool of a parlourmaid.

Chapter Four

Eddie Fairbanks insisted on walking with the ladies down the sandy lane to Meols Station, and waiting with them until the steam train chugged in. He recommended that, instead of changing to the electric train at Birkenhead Park Station, they should get a cab from that station to Mr Billings' office. 'Being as it's getting late, and his office is nearer to Park than it is to Birkenhead Central.'

They took his advice, and were fortunate in catching small, rotund Mr Billings just as he was putting on his overcoat ready to go home.

As the ladies were ushered in, after being announced by his fourteen-year-old office boy, he resignedly took off his bowler hat again and hung it on the coat stand, then went to sit at his desk. As the women entered, he half rose in his chair and smiled politely at them.

The office boy sullenly pulled out chairs for the forlorn couple. Because of their late arrival, he would be late home and his mother would scold him. He returned to the outer office to sit on his high stool and depressedly contemplate the beckoning spring sunshine which lit the untidy builder's yard outside.

Louise had retired behind her mourning veil, and Mr Billings eyed her with some trepidation: widows could be very tiresome, particularly a real lady like this Gilmore woman; they never understood what you told them. Since she showed no indication of an ability to speak, he turned his eyes upon her companion, a thin sickly-looking woman, dressed in mourning black. She must be the daughter. He smiled again.

'Good afternoon, ladies. How can I help you?' he inquired politely of Celia. Then, before Celia could respond, he added, 'May I express my condolences at your sad loss. Very sad, indeed.'

There was a murmur of thanks from behind Louise's veil, and Celia blinked back tears. They were not only tears because of the loss of her autocratic father, but tears for herself because she had little idea of how to deal with business matters – and Mr Billings represented a solid weight of them.

With what patience he could muster after a long, trying day, Mr Billings waited for one of them to speak, and, after a few moments, Celia nervously wetted her lips, and explained about the need to get the cottage at Meols into liveable shape.

While he considered this, Mr Billings brushed his moustache with one stout red finger and then twisted the waxed points at each end of it. He said slowly, 'Oh, aye, it needs a bit of doing up if you're going to live in it yourselves. It was rented for a good many years to a Miss Hornby after your auntie died; she was crippled and she never did aught about aught. When she died, Mr Gilmore saw no point in doing repairs on a place he didn't use – and the rent wasn't much. So I had the ground-floor windows boarded up – they being expensive to replace if they were broken by vandals. And that's how it's been for a couple of years now.'

He clasped his hands over his waistcoat and leaned back in his chair.

Celia told him about the broken bedroom window and asked if he could recommend a builder who could repair it quickly, and anything else that needed doing, like new floorboards in the hall bedroom.

He immediately wrote out on the back of one of his

business cards the name and address of a Hoylake man, Ben Aspen, who, he assured Celia, was as honest as the day. 'I'll get my own man to put a new windowpane in for you tomorrow – I got a handyman I keep to do small repairs. Later on, you can tell Ben Aspen what else you want doing.'

She was greatly relieved and thanked him, as she carefully put the card into her handbag.

'Don't mention it, Miss,' he replied, as he turned to her mother, to address the daunting veil. 'Seeing as how you're here, Ma'am, I'd like to speak to you about your property in Birkenhead.'

Louise sniffed back her tears and lifted her veil sufficiently to apply a black handkerchief to mop up under it. 'Yes?' she fluttered nervously.

She jumped as Mr Billings shouted to his young clerk, still fidgeting in the outer office, 'George, bring the Gilmore file.'

Muttering maledictions under his breath, the youngster got down the file and brought it in and laid it in front of Mr Billings. When he was dismissed he bowed obsequiously to the ladies as he passed them.

They ignored him.

'Now, let me see.' Mr Billings rustled through an inordinate number of pieces of paper, while Celia watched anxiously.

'Humph.' He leaned back in his chair again, and addressed Louise. 'Now, yesterday afternoon a Mr Albert Gilmore come in. Said he was your trustee – when he said it, I thought for a second that you was passed on as well as Mr Gilmore. Anyway, he says that I'm to send the cheque for your rents to him, like I always sent them to Mr Timothy Gilmore – prompt each quarter day.'

Celia drew in her breath sharply, and opened her mouth to protest, but, seeing her expression, Mr Billings continued, 'Yes, Miss. That was my reaction, too. Them houses belong to you, Mrs Gilmore – according to my notes, they're your dowry, and, therefore, they aren't part of Mr Gilmore's estate; and so I tell him – and he was really put out. But I said to him as it is one thing to send the rents to your hubby, Ma'am, for which I have had your written permission these many years – in fact, my father had it before me – but another to hand them over to a stranger I don't know.'

He straightened up and looked at Louise, rightly proud of his personal rectitude.

Both Louise and Celia gasped at this information, and Celia felt sick, because it tended to confirm her poor opinion of Cousin Albert. It did not occur to her that Albert merely wanted to check that Mr Billings handed over the correct sum each month.

Louise was so shaken that she actually threw back her veil, to reveal a plump, blotched face, which might have still been pretty in happier circumstances. 'But he has no right,' she faltered.

'Precisely, Ma'am.'

Mr Billings smiled knowingly at her. 'But it so happened, Ma'am, that I was a trifle late making up me books this quarter and didn't do your account till this morning. One tenant, Mrs Halloran, being late with her rent – she owed five shillings – I held back to give her a chance to get up to date before I reported to Mr Gilmore that she was in arrears. I read your sad news in the obituary column, Ma'am – and I'm proper sorry about it, Ma'am – so I held the cheque back until I heard from you. I'd have written to you in a few days, if you hadn't come in.'

He fumbled in his waistcoat pocket and brought out a key ring. Then, selecting a key, he got up and went to a small safe at the back of the room. He took out an envelope and handed it to Louise.

'There you are, Ma'am. A cheque for three months' rents in total. Mrs H. paid up, and there was no repairs this quarter – it's less me commission, of course. All rents up to and including last Saturday, payable to you today, Lady Day, as per usual, Ma'am.'

Louise looked up at him with real gratitude. She was not sure how to cash a cheque, but she did know that it represented welcome money. In her cash box at home, she had a month's housekeeping in five-pound notes, which Timothy had given her, as he usually did on the first of each month; beyond that she had no idea what she was supposed to do about money. Behind her expressions of woe a deeper fear of destitution had haunted her as well as Celia.

Her thanks were echoed by Celia, who hastily added that they would, as soon as the cottage was habitable, be leaving their home in West Derby, Liverpool – it was already up for sale – and that she or her mother would let him know, before the next quarter day, which would be Midsummer's Day, exactly where he should send the next cheque.

He was a kindly man, and, as he gently clasped Louise's hand when they took their departure, he felt some pity for her. Women were so helpless without menfolk – and there were so many of them bereaved by the war. They had the brains of chickens – and it appeared to him that these two already might have a fox in the coop.

He said impulsively, 'If I can be of help, dear ladies, don't hesitate to call on me.'

Though Louise only nodded acceptance of this offer, Celia, whose stomach had been clenched with fear ever since her father's clerk had come running up the front steps with the terrible news of Timothy's sudden death, felt herself relax a little. She longed to put her head on the little man's stout shoulder and weep out her terror at being so alone. Instead, she held out her hand a little primly to have it shaken by him and apologised for keeping him late at his office.

Exactly how does one cash a cheque, she worried inwardly, and she wished passionately that Paul and Edna were in England to advise her.

Chapter Five

They were exhausted by the time they returned home, and were further alarmed by the notice hooked on to their front gate. It announced that This Desirable Property was For Sale. The estate agent, in response to Cousin Albert's instructions that he wanted a quick sale, had not wasted any time.

Louise immediately broke into loud cries of distress, and it was with difficulty that Celia and Dorothy, the house-parlourmaid, got her into the sitting room. The pretty, formal room, ordinarily used for teas and at homes, still smelled faintly of hyacinths and lilies, despite having been carefully aired after the funeral, and Celia felt slightly sick from it.

While Dorothy fled upstairs to her mistress's bedroom to get a fresh container of smelling salts, Celia laid Louise on the settee. She carefully removed her bonnet and put cushions under her head.

Then she kneeled down by her and curved her arm round her. 'Try not to cry, Mother. Everything will be all right in the end. Please, Mother.'

Louise shrieked at her, 'Nothing's going to bring your father back – or my boys! Nothing! Nothing!' She turned her back on Celia, and continued to wail loudly. 'My boys! My boys!'

'She'd be better in bed, Miss.'

Startled, Celia looked up. Winnie, the cook, had heard the impassioned cries, and had run up from her basement kitchen to see what was happening. Now, she leaned over the two women, her pasty face full of compassion.

'This isn't the right room to have her in, Miss. What with the Master having been laid out here, like.'

Celia herself, frightened by the faint odour of death, would have been thankful to run upstairs to her own bedroom, shut herself in and have a good cry. Instead, she rose heavily to her feet.

'You're quite right, Winnie. Will you help me get her upstairs?'

'For sure, Miss.' She turned towards a breathless Dorothy, who dumbly held out the smelling salts to her.

Winnie took the salts and said above the sound of Louise's cries, 'Now, our Dorothy, you go and fill a hot water bottle and put it in the Mistress's bed. And put her nightgown on top of it to warm.'

Dorothy's face looked almost rabbitlike as her nose quivered with apprehension. She turned to obey the instructions, but paused when the cook said sharply, 'And you'd better put a fire up there. It's chilly. You can take a shovelful of hot coals from me kitchen fire to get it started quick.'

The maid nodded, took a big breath as if she were about to run a marathon, and shot away down the stairs to fetch the hot water bottle and the coals.

As Celia and Winnie half carried Louise up the wide staircase with its newel post crowned by a finely carved hawk, the widow's cries became heavy, heart-rending sobs.

'She'll feel better after this,' Winnie assured Celia. 'A good cry gets it out of you.'

Dorothy stood at the bottom of the staircase, hot water bottle under one arm, in her hands a big shovel full of glowing coals, and waited for the other women to reach the top. The shovel was heavy and she dreaded setting the stair carpet alight by dropping a burning coal on it.

Have a good cry? And what had she in her fancy house

to cry about? Her old man had probably left her thousands, and not much love lost between them. And here she was howling her head off and the house up for sale, and never a word to her maids as to what was happening. Proper cruel, she was.

Would she turn Winnie and Ethel and herself off as soon as the house was sold? And, if not, where would they be going to live?

As her coals cooled, Dorothy's temper grew. She plodded up the stairs after the other women, handed the hot water bottle to Winnie, and then skilfully built the bedroom fire, while Winnie and Celia partially undressed the sobbing Louise, removed her corsets and eased her huge Victorian nightgown over her head.

Behind the blank expression on Dorothy's pinched, thin face, anger seethed. Winnie must ask the Mistress what was to happen to them. She must! If they had to find new situations, they should start now. Although there was a demand for good domestic help, the big mansions in the country were being closed down in favour of London apartments, and their domestic staffs dismissed; in consequence, a lot of competition faced a middle-aged house-parlourmaid like herself. And it was always difficult to find a considerate employer. She sighed. She had not felt that Timothy and Louise were particularly considerate, but she had become accustomed to them. Ethel, the maid-of-all-work, was young enough to try for a factory job, but she herself was in her forties – getting really old – and Winnie must be nearing fifty – it would be hard for her to get another job of any kind.

She took fresh lumps of coal from the fireside coal hod and laid them on top of those she had brought up. She ensured that they had caught and that the fire was beginning to blaze and then swept the hearth. Then she got slowly to her feet, and picked up the shovel.

As she contemplated her future, she began to feel sick. She berated herself that she had not saved some of the good wages she had earned in an ordnance factory during the war years. She had spent like a king until the factory closed down at the end of the war, and then she had come to work as a house-parlourmaid for the Gilmores, because domestic work was all she was skilled at.

She turned from the fireplace and paused to stare at the scene before her.

Seated on the side of the bed beside her mother, Celia held a small glass of brandy to Louise's lips and encouraged her to sip it between sobs. Winnie had folded back the bedclothes ready for the sufferer to lie down.

Nice woman, Miss Celia – but that useless, you'd never believe it. No spirit. Never had any fun, the Master being so difficult to please, especially so, Winnie said, since he lost his son with that Lord Kitchener, and then Mr Tom in France, poor lad.

Her own father had been a bit of a cross, she remembered, and not past beating her if she did something he didn't like – but when he had work, even if he was fair wore out by the end of the day, he could make the family laugh and they'd have a neighbour or two in and do some singing, with a drop of ale to drink by the fire. Old Gilmore had done nothing but complain, complain – and order you around as if you were muck.

She wondered if Celia's sister, Edna, was like her. She had never seen her, but she had heard she was a real beauty, and at least, it seemed, she had had enough sense to get out from under her old man by getting married.

Winnie impatiently glanced back over her shoulder and said, 'Get downstairs, Dot, and look to the soup for me. Give it a stir. I'll be down in a minute.'

Dorothy nodded, and went sulkily down to the basement kitchen, carrying her shovel carefully so that she did not drop a bit of ash on the stair carpet, which, every morning, she had to brush, from cellar to attic.

* * *

Louise finally cried herself to sleep, and an exhausted Celia was persuaded by Winnie to put her feet up on the old chaise longue in the breakfast room at the back of the house, while the cook put together a dinner tray for her.

'The Mistress didn't tell me what to make for dinner, so I made this nice thick soup, but I've got some cold beef, if you feel like something more. And the bread come out of the oven only a couple of hours ago.'

Celia nodded wearily, and said that the soup sounded lovely. When it was brought to her, she drank it slowly while Winnie stood and watched her anxiously.

When Celia's bowl was finally empty, Winnie removed it, and then hesitantly inquired if Celia could tell her what was going to happen to them all. 'Seeing the For Sale sign was a proper shock, Miss,' she explained. 'And Dorothy and Ethel is all upset. They're asking me what they should do.'

'You should all start looking for new situations,' Celia answered her frankly, though she did her best to hide her own sense of despair. 'I know Mother will be glad to keep all of you on for a week or two, while we sort out the house, and decide what to take with us – we are going to live in a cottage in Meols, which Mother owns.' She paused, and then said rather helplessly, 'We have no choice but to sell this place quickly, Winnie. And we shan't be able to afford servants.' She looked up at the shocked elder woman. 'I shall, personally, miss you terribly, Winnie, after all the years you've been with us, especially through the war.'

Winnie took a big breath, as she tried to control her own sense of panic. She inquired, 'Things must be very bad, Miss?'

'In a way they are, Winnie, though not as bad as they might be. Mother's lucky that my Aunt Felicity left her this cottage by the sea.' She sighed and fiddled with the fringe of the woollen shawl that Winnie had put across her legs to keep them warm. Then she said in explanation, 'Father had heavy business debts. We can't afford a servant – I'm hoping that we shall be able to have a daily cleaning woman – because I don't think I shall be very good at keeping house!'

She smiled faintly at the stricken cook, who, despite her own sense of despair, noted that poor Miss Celia was taking it for granted that she would have to run the house – and she probably would have to. And she so small and sickly-looking.

'How long do you think we've got, Miss?'

'Well, I haven't consulted Mother yet. Mr Albert Gilmore, who was here for the funeral, told us that the estate agent felt he would have no trouble selling this house. When it is sold, I suppose that we shall have to set a final date when we have to leave it – to suit the new owner. But we will have to let you go very soon.' She looked up imploringly at her old friend, as if to ask forgiveness.

Winnie's stout chest heaved, but she replied woodenly, 'I understand, Miss.'

'The other house has to have a few essential repairs done – and we have to get it cleaned – it's filthy at present.' She bit her lower lip, and then added quickly, 'I think that Mother can pay you all for this week – and, I hope, for another week. Tomorrow I'll talk to her, and we'll try to make a timetable of some sort, to help you.'

'It's good of you to be so honest with me, Miss. Can I tell the others?'

'Of course. There is so little time. You should all start looking for other situations immediately.' She stopped to consider the appalling upheaval facing her, and then added heavily, 'I'll ask Mother to write references for you tomorrow – and if one of you wants to go for an interview on a day other than your half-day, will you arrange it as best you can between yourselves?'

'We will, Miss. Thank you, Miss.'

Winnie bent and picked up the tray.

To Celia, her perceptions heightened by her own fears, the cook looked suddenly old as she turned slowly and went out of the room. She watched Winnie quietly close the door after her, and then she began to shake helplessly.

She clasped her arms tightly round her breast, and rolled herself over, so that her face was buried in the feather cushions which had propped her up. She began to sweat and her teeth chattered uncontrollably, as her fear of the scary world she was having to face and her sense of having betrayed an old friend overwhelmed her.

'Oh, God,' she whispered in desperation. 'What's going to happen to us? Heaven help us.'

She rolled again, to curl herself up in sheer terror into a tight foetal ball.

With what was left of her sanity she begged to die.

But she knew from experience of these attacks of panic that death did not oblige so easily. So in the unnatural silence of the home she was about to lose, she lay as still as she could, and prayed incoherently for release from the blind fear that engulfed her.

After a little while, her breathing became more normal, and she began to mutter very slowly, as she always did, ' "The Lord is my Shepherd; I shall not want." ' She hoped that, if she could concentrate well enough to recite the psalm right through to the end and was comforted by King David's immortal words, the seizure would ease.

It had always worked before when she was terrified, even when she was a child and had first realised that she was being brought up differently from her sister.

Because of her parents' special interest in Edna's well-being, she had always believed that their neglect of herself indicated that there must be something wrong with her. Had she some deficiency in her which they were hiding from her? Something weird which would one day spring out and send her mad – or, at least, make her a useless invalid, like a neighbour's daughter who had been confined for years to a wheelchair by an attack of infantile paralysis?

This childhood dread, implanted by careless, selfish parents, had fed upon itself until, in her confused, early teenage years, it became an overwhelming terror, which periodically swept over her like some mighty wave whenever she felt threatened.

Frightened themselves by these seizures, her parents had firmly put them down to that popular female complaint, hysteria. It was the height of vulgarity, an effort to draw attention to herself, they said. They had slapped and beaten her at such times, then locked her in her bedroom, until she saw sense, as they put it.

The panic would eventually wear itself out, and, exhausted, she would drag herself out of her bed and knock on her bedroom door to plead tearfully to be let out. She invariably promised that it would not happen again, but, sooner or later, it invariably did.

Now, in adulthood, she had slowly realised that she was probably quite normal. But Church and custom reinforced her parents' declaration that it was her duty as a good churchwoman and devoted daughter to care for them when they grew old. They had often made it clear to her that she was too stupid to be capable of doing anything else.

Sundry aged aunts and cousins at various times nodded their grey heads sadly over her and agreed that, since she was so plain and lacking in vivacity, she could not hope to marry. It was better she be the companion of her own dear mother than be faced with the horrors of having to earn a living at something dreadful, like being a companion-help in a strange household.

She had been devastated as it slowly dawned on her that she had simply been kept single and poorly educated for Timothy's and Louise's own convenience, not because they loved her and wanted to keep her by them. Her plaintive request during the war that, like many other women, she be allowed to nurse was met by a threat from Timothy to leave her penniless; nurses didn't earn anything, he assured her. With two servants deserting the family in favour of working in ordnance factories, Timothy was not about to allow a useful daughter to desert as well. Such was the class distinction that it never once occurred to Celia that she could do precisely what the servants were doing – earn in a war factory.

Though hopelessly cowed by her parents, she carried under her subservience a terrible bitterness. This week it had been added to by the realisation that, at his death, her father had indeed left her nothing. She was now entirely dependent upon her mother's whims.

Once she had understood that she was sane and not particularly unhealthy, she had not had a terror attack again. Like many other middle-class women, she sadly accepted that there was no escape from home. As a result of the war, marriage must now, in any case, be discounted – there were barely any men left for pretty girls to marry, never mind plain ones; they had died, like George and Tom, for the sake of their country; their names would be inscribed on one of the new war memorials going up all over a country which was already finding the wounded survivors an expensive nuisance.

'You can't marry a name on a war memorial,' she had complained pitifully to her only woman friend, Phyllis Woodcock, whose husband had proved to be too delicate for call-up.

Phyllis, who was not very enamoured of the married state, muttered agreement. Like Celia, she had been warned in her youth that, for a single woman who left home, there was no way for her to earn a living except by being a governess or, if one was uneducated, face a fate worse than death by joining the crowds of ladies of the evening all over the city. These sinful hussies were there for even the most innocent, honest women to observe, and it was whispered that they died of horrifying diseases. Just what ladies of the evening did to come to such untimely ends, neither Celia nor Phyllis were quite certain, but both of them were sufficiently scared not to want to try it.

Once when he came home on leave, George had told her cheerfully that someone had to keep the home fires burning while the men were away, and this had been a small comfort. The walls of the West Derby house became to her at least some sort of defence against the unknown.

She bowed her head and, with her mother and a group of elderly females, rolled bandages and knitted socks and Balaclava helmets for the troops. Her mother did a lot of organising of sales of work and big balls at the Adelphi Hotel to raise money for the Red Cross, which, for Celia, meant endless writing of letters and running hither and yon on small errands for her mother. She became accustomed to the invisible walls of her prison and to being her mother's obedient shadow.

Now, however, the sudden crumbling of the relative safety of her imprisoning walls had frightened her so much that panic had set in again; that open gates might lead to greater freedom for her to do something for herself did not occur to her; long-term prisoners do not always try to escape when the opportunity offers – and Celia was no exception.

' ". . . and I will dwell in the house of the Lord for ever." '

The muttering ceased, and she lay still. If she remained very quiet, she comforted herself, God would give her strength. He had to, because there was nobody but herself to look after Mother until Paul and Edna arrived to help her.

Chapter Six

❧

Soon after six o'clock the next morning, young Ethel, sleepy and irritable, clumped into the breakfast room. She swung a heavy coal scuttle into the hearth and followed it with a clanking empty bucket in which to carry downstairs yesterday's cold ashes from the fireplace. The room was dark, except for a faint glimmer of dawn through a crack between the heavy window curtains.

Suddenly awakened, a bewildered Celia sat up on the chaise longue.

At the sight of her, Ethel screamed and clutched her breast dramatically. 'Oh, Miss! You give me a proper fright! Haven't you been to bed?'

Celia swallowed, and pushed back her long tangled fair hair, from which all the hairpins seemed to be missing. She laughed weakly as she swung her feet to the floor. 'No,' she told the little fifteen-year-old. 'I was so tired that I fell asleep here on the sofa.'

Rubbing her hands on her sackcloth apron, Ethel came over to stare at her. She thanked goodness that it was only Miss Celia there, not the Missus. She had not bothered to put on her morning mobcap to cover her own untidy locks, and the Missus would have been furious to see her without a cap.

'Are you all right, Miss?'

'Yes, thank you, Ethel. Would you light one of the gaslights? I think it will still be too dark to draw back the curtains.'

'I were just about to do it, Miss, when I seen you.' Ethel drew a box of matches out of her pocket, and went to the fireplace. After striking a match, she stood on tiptoe to turn on one of the gaslights above the mahogany mantelpiece.

There was a plop as the gas ignited and the room was flooded with clear white light. Dead match in hand, Ethel turned, for a moment, to stare at her young mistress, before beginning to clear out the ashes. In her opinion, Miss Celia was taking her father's death proper hard and looked real ill with it.

She began to hurry her cleaning, so that she could return to the kitchen to gossip with Dorothy about it.

Celia sat on the edge of the chaise longue, absently poking around the cushions in search of some of her hair-pins, while her eyes adjusted to the bright light.

As she rose unsteadily to her feet, she noticed the silver card plate from the hall lying on the table in the centre of the room. It held a number of visiting cards. Dorothy must have brought it in the previous evening, and it had lain neglected because of Louise's collapse. Now Celia quickly sifted through the cards.

They indicated that the vicar's wife and two of Louise's women friends had called. In addition, there was a card left by her own friend, Phyllis Woodcock, who had been too far advanced in her fourth pregnancy to come to the funeral. She had scribbled a note to Celia on the back of her card to say that she would try to visit again tomorrow, after the midwife had been to check on her state of health.

Dear Phyllis! Childhood playmate and still her friend, despite her brood of awful children and her whining husband.

Tomorrow is today, thought Celia. God, I must hurry. See to poor Mother, talk some sense into her – about the maids, about the cottage, about what furniture we should take with us, what we should sell. How did one sell superfluous pieces of furniture? Go to Hoylake to see Ben Aspen, the builder recommended by Mr Billings – would he need money down or would he send a bill later on? Go to see Mr Carruthers, the bank manager, about what one did to cash the cheque from Mr Billings. Did Mother know how to cash a cheque?

After she had done all that, Celia remembered, there was the enormous task of writing letters of thanks for masses of flowers and in response to black-edged missives of condolence. Her father had been a well-known businessman and churchman, but, nevertheless, the interest engendered by his unexpected death had amazed Celia.

'He must have known everyone in the city!' Celia had exclaimed to her exhausted mother, who, on the day before the funeral, sat with that morning's mail, still unopened, in her lap, while Dorothy added yet another floral tribute to the pile surrounding her father's body in the sitting room, and Cousin Albert greeted the vicar and his wife at the door.

Louise responded wearily, 'He did. We did a lot of entertaining.'

'We did,' Celia agreed, remembering the long and boring dinners, which involved so much work. She herself often helped Winnie and Dorothy on such occasions, by doing the complicated laying of the table and overseeing, from the kitchen, that the right dishes for each course were lined up, ready for Dorothy to carry upstairs. She herself rarely appeared at the parties.

Now, with her father safely in his grave and Cousin Albert back at his own home, she stood, for a moment, balancing herself against the table and looked shakily at the visiting cards. Through her tired mind rolled unusual words, like dowry, annuity, bankruptcy, land ownership. How could she deal coolly and calmly with visitors, when her tiny world was in such chaos?

Paul! Edna! Please, dears – please come soon, she prayed.

She feared she might sink again into her panic of the previous night.

But Ethel was making a great dust as she cleared the ashes from the fireplace, and Dorothy was pushing the door open with her backside, as she carried in her box of brushes and dusters and her Bissell carpet sweeper. 'Mornin', Miss,' she said mechanically, as she saw Celia.

To calm herself, Celia took in a big breath of dusty air and replied gravely, 'Good morning, Dorothy.'

She went slowly out of the room and up the stairs. Her legs dragged, and she could not make herself hurry. Better leave Mother to sleep and then give her breakfast in bed, she considered. Before she wakes, I could make a list of things we must do, and, after breakfast, get her going on the more urgent ones – like seeing the bank manager.

Upstairs, she shivered as she stripped off her clothes still damp from the perspiration of the previous night. She hung up her black skirt to air, and left the rest in a pile on her undisturbed bed for Dorothy to take away to be washed.

Looking down at the smelly garments, she realised dully that she did not know how to wash clothes properly, and she wondered if they would be able to employ a washer-woman. Even during the war, when they had had to manage the house with only Winnie living in, they had been able to find women to do the washing and clean the house; they were usually army privates' wives, living on very small army pay, who had children whom they did not want to leave alone for long. They had been thankful to come in by the day to earn an extra few shillings.

As she washed herself in the sink of the jewel of her mother's house, the bathroom, which glittered with white porcelain and highly polished mahogany, she remembered the earth lavatory of the cottage. Such primitive sanitary arrangements meant that they must take with them the old-fashioned washstands with their attendant china basins, jugs, buckets and chamber pots; she recollected that three rooms in their present home were still equipped with these pieces of furniture. And there was a tin bath in the cellar – they would need that, with all the work that it implied – heating and carrying jugs of hot water upstairs to a bedroom, and afterwards bringing down the dirty water, not to speak of the dragging up and down of the bath itself, all chores that she herself would probably have to attend to.

While she brushed her hair and then tied it into a neat knot to be pinned at the back of her neck, she wondered resentfully whether, in addition to all the usual jobs her mother expected her to do, she was going to spend her whole future trying to deal with the domestic problems of the cottage.

Later, when she was dressed, the last button of a clean black blouse done up and a black bow tied under her chin, she paused to look at herself in the mirror, and made a wry face. She looked pinched and old. She was drained by the fears besetting her, acutely aware of her own ignorance. Even Ethel, struggling to make the fire go in the breakfast room, was not as helpless as she was. At least Ethel could make a fire and could probably cook a meal on it if she had to.

Why haven't I learned to cook? she asked herself dully. Or even watched Mrs Walls, when she comes in on Mondays to do the washing? Or looked to see in what order Dorothy does the rooms, so that she doesn't redistribute the dust? And as for making the cottage garden look decent, I don't know how to begin.

The answer was clear to her. As a single, upper middle-class lady, she was not expected to know. Her job was to run after her mother, be her patient companion, carry her parcels, find her glasses, help her choose library books in the Argosy Library, make a fourth player at cards if no one else was available, write invitations and thank-you notes – and be careful always to be pleasant and never give offence to men, particularly to her father. And when her parents were gone, she would probably do the same for Edna – tolerated in her brother-in-law's house, either because Edna had begged a roof for her or, on Paul's part, from a faint sense of duty to a penniless woman.

'I wish I were dead,' she hissed tearfully at the reflection in the wardrobe mirror, and went down to the breakfast room to find a pencil and make a list.

Chapter Seven

❧

While Dorothy and Ethel finished cleaning the breakfast room, Celia, list in hand, went down to the basement to talk to Winnie.

On seeing her young mistress, the cook hastily rose from eating her own breakfast at the kitchen table. With the corner of her white apron, she surreptitiously dabbed the corners of her mouth.

'Don't get up, Winnie. Finish your breakfast. I just thought I'd have a word with you, before Mother rings for her tray.'

Winnie sank slowly back into her chair and picked up her fork again. She looked cautiously at Celia, who had walked over to the kitchen dresser and taken down a cup and saucer. The girl looked as if she were on the point of collapse.

'Would you be liking a cup of tea, Miss?'

Celia laid the cup and saucer down in front of the cook, and then pulled out another kitchen chair to sit down on. 'Yes, please, if you can spare it from your pot.'

'To be sure, Miss.'

While Celia slowly sipped a very strong cup of tea and Winnie finished up her egg and fried bread, both women basked in the warmth of the big fire in the kitchen range. Ethel had made it ready in anticipation of Winnie's beginning the serious cooking of the day as soon as she had finished her own meal.

The heat was very comforting, and some of Celia's

jitteriness left her. 'I was wondering, Winnie,' she began, 'if one of you could come out to the Meols cottage with me and help me clean it. I think it will take more than one day. Could two of you manage, here, to look after Mother? I think I may have to be quick about making arrangements, and we can't move anything from this house until the other one is clean. Mr Billings, the agent, will be going out there today to make sure it is watertight.'

At the reminder of the impending demise of the household, poor Winnie's breast heaved under her blue and white striped dress. Her response, however, showed no resentment. She said helpfully, 'Oh, aye, Miss. Our Dorothy would be the best one to take – and you'd need to get the chimneys swept, no doubt.' She paused and ran her tongue round her teeth, to rid them of bits of egg, while she considered the situation. 'Anybody living nearby will put you on to a sweep, I'm sure. And you'd have to take brooms and brushes – and dusters and polish with you, wouldn't you?'

In twenty minutes, Winnie had a cleaning campaign worked out. She inquired whether the water in the house was turned on.

Feeling a little ashamed at how low they had sunk, Celia admitted that there was only a pump that did not work and a well of uncertain cleanliness. She said hopefully, 'I think Mr Fairbanks from next door would let us take water from his pump for a day or two. He's very nice.'

'Would he? That would be proper kind. A friendly neighbour's worth a lot.' Winnie heaved herself out of her chair and began to clear the table. 'You'd better get a plumber to fix the pump, hadn't you? You could ask him what to do about the well. He'll know – and I'll put together some lunch for you.'

Celia began to feel that her life was regaining some sense of order, and she looked gratefully at the cook. 'You're wonderful, Winnie,' she said with feeling, as she took her empty teacup to the kitchen sink ready for Ethel when she came down to the basement kitchen to do the washing up.

At that moment, Dorothy, carrying her brooms, bucket, dustpan and brush, and carpet sweeper, pushed open the kitchen door. She was bent on snatching her breakfast before she had to serve Louise and Celia their meal. Winnie told her immediately that she would be spending the next day in Meols, cleaning Miss Celia's new home.

Dorothy opened her mouth to protest, and then decided that it might be a bit of a change. She nodded assent, and said, 'Yes, Miss,' to Celia very primly, as if being whisked out to Meols was something that happened regularly to her. Then she hung up her dustpan and brush in a cupboard, and picked up the carpet sweeper again to take it outside to empty it into the dustbin. She unlocked the heavy back door and trotted into the brick-lined area outside.

As she opened the flaps of the carpet sweeper and shook out the dust, she could hear, very distantly, Ethel singing 'The Roses of Picardy', as she scrubbed the front steps, and she began to regret her agreement to go out to Meols. Out there, it would likely be scrubbing, scrubbing all the way, she considered sourly, as she clicked the sweeper shut. Why hadn't she suggested that Miss should take Ethel instead?

Before leaving the kitchen, Celia turned and gave the cook a quick hug. 'I don't know what we're going to do without you,' she said.

Winnie forced a smile, and wondered what she was going to do without the Gilmore family, whom she had served for over fifteen years. All through the war, I stayed with them, she considered dolefully, when I could have earned much more in a munitions factory – I was proper stupid. I could have saved something to help me now.

A bell in the corner of the kitchen rang, and she turned to see which one it was. 'Your mam's awake,' she shouted after Celia, who was running up the kitchen stairs. 'Will you tell me when she's ready for her breakfast?'

'I will.'

As Celia went up the second staircase to her mother's bedroom, she smiled slightly. Things were already changing. Winnie would never have referred to her mother as 'your mam' if her father had been alive; and, at the sound of the bell, Dorothy would have had to climb the two staircases to inquire directly what it was that Madam required.

Considering her flood of tears the previous night, Louise managed a remarkably solid breakfast. Celia, who did not want any, sat on the bed beside her, patiently wondering how to discuss their problems with her without causing yet another collapse into tears.

Finally, Louise laid her empty cup down on its saucer, and sighed. 'Put the tray on the side table for me, dear,' she ordered.

Celia did as she was bidden, while Louise crossed her hands over her stomach and stared disconsolately out of the window at a fine March day. She took no notice when Celia pulled out of her skirt pocket the list she had made earlier.

'Mother,' she said tentatively, 'because Cousin Albert thinks we may have to move quickly from here, I've made a rough list of what I think we must do at once.'

Her mother turned to look at her, her pale, slightly protruding blue eyes showing no sign of tears. There was, however, a total absence of expression in them, and Celia wondered if her mother was feeling the same sense of unreality that she was, as if she were a long way off from what was happening, that this wasn't her life at all; she was merely watching a play.

'Yes, dear?' Louise's voice was quite calm, though she sounded weary.

Celia gathered her wandering thoughts, and began by saying, 'I thought we'd better see, first, how much money we have access to.' She paused, feeling that it was vulgar to consider money when they had just been bereaved. But they had to live until the house was sold, so she added firmly, 'I suppose that dear Papa gave you the housekeeping at the beginning of the month?'

Louise gave a sobbing sigh, and said, 'Yes, dear. I hope I can make it last through the first week in April.'

'Then there's the cheque Mr Billings gave you yesterday. How do we get money for it? Do you know?'

'Your dear father always paid it into my bank account, and when I wanted to pay for a special dress, or something, for either you or me – or gifts – personal things, I wrote a cheque. I'm sure Mr Carruthers would show us how to put Mr Billings' cheque into my account.'

'Is there anything in the account at present?'

'I don't think so, dear. Your dear father got me to write a cheque on it for him about three months ago. It was a loan.'

Celia felt an uncomfortable qualm in her stomach at this disclosure. She wondered what else her father might have done, which would further imperil their limited finances. She suggested that if Louise felt strong enough they should pay a call on the bank that afternoon, to which Louise agreed.

'Did Papa have a solicitor for his affairs, Mama?'

'Well, he had Mr Barnett, of course, who came to the funeral, dear. As far as I know, he did any legal work in connection with your father's business. He's supposed to be supervising the sale of this house, remember?' Louise moved restlessly in her bed. 'But Father didn't use his services very much, because he was expensive. He even wrote his will himself; but Cousin Albert says that it is perfectly valid. He said it was witnessed by Andy McDougall and his chief clerk.'

Celia knew of old Mr McDougall. When he had attended the funeral, he had looked as ferocious as his reputation held him to be, and with him there had been another old gentleman, who could well have been his chief clerk. She recollected vaguely that he was a corn merchant and had a small office, similar to her father's, in the same building. She had noticed Cousin Albert talking with them after the funeral, probably because, as Albert had told her, he needed, first, to satisfy himself of the authenticity of the witnesses' signatures to the will.

'Do we need a solicitor, Celia?' The question held a hint of anxiety in it.

Celia chewed her lower lip. 'I don't really know, Mama,' she confessed. 'But this house belongs to you – and it's a handsome house – it must be worth quite a lot.' How could she say that she did not trust her father's cousin very much – she had no real reason to feel like this, except that he was being very domineering and he had apparently tried to collect the rents which Mr Billings had refused to hand over to him.

She said slowly, 'I think that you should have a legal man to make sure that you receive what is yours.'

Her mother gave a small shocked gasp, and Celia hastily added, 'Well, laws are funny things, and it is difficult for us to know what we are signing – we can read it – but understanding is something different. Did you understand the papers that you signed for Mr Barnett and the estate agent the other day?'

Louise was frightened. 'Not really; they both said they gave them permission to sell the house and for the agent to charge me a commission for doing it. Should I have had a solicitor of my own? Albert said I should sign – and he was once a solicitor himself.' She looked helplessly up at Celia.

'Try not to worry, Mama. The papers probably are all right.' How could she say to her mother that it was Albert

72

Gilmore himself about whom she felt doubtful? She finally replied carefully, 'I know he was a solicitor. But he's looking after the will – which is Father's affair. You don't have anybody. Perhaps there should be someone who is interested only in your affairs.'

'Yes, dear. I see.' Louise was trembling with apprehension as she began slowly to get out of bed. Her huge, lace-trimmed cotton nightgown caught in the bedclothes, and momentarily a fine pair of snow-white legs were exposed to the spring sunlight pouring through the windows.

She hastily hitched her gown more modestly round her, but not before Celia had the sudden realisation that, though her mother always appeared old to her and her face petulant, she was extremely well preserved, with a perfect skin and luxuriant hair.

She might marry again. And, if she did, where would I be? she asked herself fearfully.

She swallowed hard. She had enough to worry about without anything else.

She said carefully, as she moved out of Louise's way, 'Perhaps Mr Carruthers at the bank could recommend a solicitor to us. We could ask him.'

As Louise nodded agreement, they both heard the front door bell faintly tinkling in the kitchen.

'I think that will be Phyllis. She left her card yesterday when we were out, and said she would come again today. There are some cards on the tray for you, too. Will you be all right, Mother, if I go down? We could walk round to the bank this afternoon. Phyllis won't stay long.'

Louise was already on her way to the bathroom and in the distance they could hear Dorothy running across the hall to answer the front door. Over her shoulder, Louise agreed resignedly, and then said in a more normal voice, 'Really, Phyllis should not be walking out in her condition.'

'Times have changed, Mother. Ladies-in-waiting go about a lot more than they used to do.'

'A true gentlewoman would not!' The remark sounded so much more like her mother's usual disapproval of Phyllis that Celia was quite relieved. Louise had disapproved of Phyllis ever since she had first appeared at the front door, when she was nine years old, to ask if Celia could come out to play hopscotch. In Louise's opinion, the daughter of a carriage builder – a tradesman – was no companion for the granddaughter of a baronet and daughter of a prominent businessman in commerce. The girls had, however, clung to each other. Both were lonely and shy, great bookworms, and were over-protected – Phyllis because she was a precious only child and Celia because she was to be kept at home as a companion-help. Neither was allowed to mix very much with other children.

Celia let her mother cross the passage to the bathroom, and then ran lightly down the stairs, to be enveloped – as far as was possible – in her friend's arms.

Chapter Eight

❧

With a toddler clinging to her hand, Phyllis greeted her friend tenderly. 'I'm so sad for you and for Mrs Gilmore. It must be terrible for you.'

'Thank you, dear. How are you?'

The inquiry did not need a reply. Phyllis was her usual untidy self. Her hair below her wide-brimmed beige hat was threatening to fall down her back at any minute, and her face was drained of colour, except for black rings round her tired eyes. Her long black skirt, which had dog hairs on it, half-covered her swollen ankles. To disguise her pregnancy, she wore an out-of-fashion cheviot cape of her mother's which barely met across her swollen stomach.

Phyllis simply grimaced in response to Celia's mechanical inquiry, and then shrugged as if to convey that her wellbeing was of no consequence.

Celia went down on her knees to ask the toddler, 'And how's little Eric today?'

Eric turned away from her and buried his grubby, marmalade-smeared face in his mother's skirt. Celia smiled and patted his flaxen head as she got up again.

'Come into the breakfast room. There's a good fire there. Dorothy hasn't done the sitting room yet.'

Phyllis sighed with relief as she sank into Louise's favourite chair. It was upholstered in faded green velveteen and was armless, which allowed space for the stout or pregnant to spread their skirts comfortably around them. She remarked with feeling, 'I shall be thankful when my little burden arrives.'

'It can't be long now, can it?' Celia asked. Though Phyllis had explained to her how dreadfully vulgar were the things a husband did to you which led to having a baby, Celia had never liked to inquire how long it took the baby to grow.

'Any time now, the midwife thinks. This morning she advised that I should stay close to home.' She shifted uneasily in her chair, and then went on, 'You always get hours of warning, though, so I thought I should squeeze in a visit to you. You and Mrs Gilmore must be absolutely devastated.'

Celia nodded. She did not know how to explain what she was feeling, because after her little talk with Winnie in the basement kitchen she had sensed in herself a stirring of relief.

She had realised suddenly that she was not grieving for her father so much as she was upset at her own lack of competence in dealing with the disarray he had left behind him. He had been very hard to live with; and she had to admit that she had not, in the past week, missed his hectoring voice criticising some alleged fault in her behaviour.

To cover her confusion at Phyllis's remark, she glanced round to check on little Eric.

She saw that he had discovered one of the household cats asleep on what had been Timothy Gilmore's chair. He was nuzzling into the animal's long black fur. It seemed to be tolerating him quite well, so she asked Phyllis if she was comfortable in the chair in which she was sitting. Having been assured ruefully that she was – as far as it was possible to be comfortable in her situation – Celia asked, 'How many babies do you want to have, Phyllis?'

Phyllis laughed. She said cynically. 'I don't have any say in the matter. They simply come.'

'Does it hurt?'

'Yes – and it makes you so tired afterwards and you want to cry a lot. And husbands don't like that, of course.' Phyllis winced under her breath and straightened her back.

Celia drew a stool towards the fire, so that she could sit close to her friend. 'Perhaps, when Mr Woodcock progresses in his career, you will be able to have a nanny as well as your maid?' she suggested. She leaned forward to tug at the bell pull hanging beside the fireplace, to call Dorothy and ask her to bring some coffee.

Phyllis slowly drew off her black gloves, as she replied, 'I hope so.'

Long ago, she had, when Celia had asked her, told her frankly the basic facts of sexual intercourse and that it was a right of a man to demand it of his wife. Poor Phyllis had gone into her marriage totally ignorant of what it implied, and had been so shocked and her husband so clumsy that she had never enjoyed it. She endured it as best she could – and the babies came, and her husband grew ever more irritable and hard to live with. Neither she nor Celia, therefore, had any idea that intercourse could be pleasurable. It was popular to coo over babies and forget what went beforehand.

Celia did not know the details of Phyllis's marriage, but she did understand that her friend was worn out and unhappy, and she had long since begun to think that marriage was not quite the happy state that girls were told it was.

If one had an income of one's own, she had considered, it would be pleasanter to remain single – except that one could not have a baby, and she herself would love to have just one, like little Eric.

Phyllis returned to the reason for her visit. 'How is Mrs Gilmore?' she asked.

'She seems more herself this morning, a little less exhausted.'

'I was horrified to see the For Sale notice on your gate. Does Mrs Gilmore really want to move?'

Even to Phyllis, Celia did not feel able to talk of financial problems; it was not the thing. So she said abruptly that the house was far too big and that they were going to renovate a summer cottage that they owned, in Meols. 'The sea air, you know – Mother thinks it will be good for both of us. My Aunt Felicity left the place to Mother. Father didn't like it, so it has been let for a number of years. It's vacant now.'

Phyllis's dejected expression lifted a little. 'How lovely to be able to live by the sea,' she responded longingly.

'You'll have to bring the family to visit us, once we're settled in,' Celia replied with a sudden glint of enthusiasm. 'Sea air would do you a world of good.' She suddenly saw an advantage to living in Meols. She could really give some relief to Phyllis by inviting her out for the day, with the children.

A sullen Dorothy arrived in response to the bell, and Celia told her to bring a pot of coffee and some biscuits and a glass of milk for Eric.

Celia's ring had interrupted an anxious conning by Winnie and Dorothy of the Situations Vacant column in *The Lady*, a magazine devoted to the interests of middle-class families, which included a constant search for competent, cheap domestics.

Back in the kitchen, while she assembled the tray, Winnie glumly closed the magazine. 'All the best jobs is in the south. Nothin' up in the north here at all. We'd better look in the evening paper when it comes.'

'Oh, aye,' Dorothy agreed, as she quickly measured coffee beans into the grinder and turned the handle vigorously. 'I were thinking I might try for a waitress's job. You get tips then.'

'That's all right if you've got a home to go to. If you

haven't, you've got to find a room somewhere – and that'll cost you.'

'I suppose.' Dorothy whisked the ground coffee into a pot and poured boiling water over it from the kettle kept simmering on the hob. She stirred the coffee and clapped the lid on the pot. Then, as she paused to let the grounds settle, she asked, 'Do you know where the Missus is? I want to do her bedroom.'

'Lying in her nice warm bath, I'll be bound – and no hot water left for washing the tiles in the hall. You take the tray up, and I'll put the big kettle on the fire again.'

'Ta ever so.'

As Dorothy moved a small side table closer to Celia and then set the tray down on it, she took a quick look at Phyllis's face. Very close to her time, she reckoned knowingly, and this was confirmed by Phyllis's face suddenly puckering up as the ache in her back became sharper.

If I were her, Dorothy thought, I wouldn't be sitting here drinking coffee; I'd be on my way home, I would. It was not her business, however, so she withdrew discreetly, to descend again to the kitchen and share her thoughts with Winnie.

Chapter Nine

As Ethel clumped through the hall on her way to the kitchen to get a bucket of clean hot water with which to wash the tiles of the front hall, she heard a high shriek from the breakfast room, followed by the sound of some-one bursting into tears. She paused uncertainly, wondering if the Missus and Miss Celia were having a row. Then she remembered that Mrs Woodcock had come on a visit while she had been wiping down the front railings and she won-dered if the lady had, perhaps, fallen over the Old Fella's footstool – and her expecting.

She put down her bucket, wiped her hands on her sack-cloth apron and ran across to the breakfast-room door. Clearly through it, she heard Miss Celia's agitated voice say, 'You mean it's coming?'

Mrs Woodcock replied tearfully, 'Yes, dear. The water's broken. Could you ask Mrs Gilmore to come – quickly? Please!'

In response to this urgent request, the bell in the kitchen jangled distantly. Ethel tentatively opened the door, to peep round it.

Mrs Woodcock was writhing and whimpering in the Mistress's chair. She was gasping, 'I'm so sorry, Celia. I'm so sorry.'

In order to remove her visitor's wide-brimmed hat, Miss Celia was trying to take out Mrs Woodcock's hatpins, which were pulling at the poor lady's hair as she turned and twisted.

Thumb in mouth, Eric was staring at his mother. Then he let out a frightened yell and ran to her, to clutch at her skirt and try to climb on to her knee.

Dorothy came running through the green baize door at the back of the hall. She inquired of Ethel in a low voice, 'What's up?' She crowded close to the little kitchen maid, her nose twitching nervously as she peered at the breakfast-room door.

Ethel stepped back from the door and turned to her eagerly. 'I think Mrs Woodcock's baby's coming,' she replied in an excited whisper. 'Shall I run up and tell the Mistress?'

Dorothy paused for a moment, her hand on the brass doorknob.

'Holy Mary! Are you sure?'

'Sounds like it.' Ethel pointed a thumb at the half-open door. They could both hear Phyllis's frightened little gasps and Miss Celia's ineffectual reassurances.

'Oh, aye. Go and tell the Mistress – quick.' Dorothy pushed the girl aside and, feeling a little scared, entered the room. She nearly tripped over a cat which shot out and across the hall.

Celia was bent over her friend. She looked up and exclaimed through white lips, 'Oh, Dorothy! Thank goodness you're here. Ask the Mistress to come down. Mrs Woodcock is in great distress.'

Eric, pushed away by his mother, was sitting on the hearth rug. At the sight of another strange woman, he began to shriek in good earnest.

Over his noisy protest, Dorothy replied calmly, 'Ethel's gone for her, Miss. Here, let me take the little boy.' She bent down and swept the child up into her arms. ''Ere, now. You just be quiet – and your mam'll be fine.' She spun round and picked up a Marie biscuit from the coffee tray, then walked him over to the window. She pointed out a couple of pigeons roosting on the back wall and gave him the biscuit to eat. In thirty seconds, she had reduced his howls to small sobs.

She wiped away his tears with her apron and told him he was a good, brave little boy, and, in a minute or two, his Auntie Dorothy would take him down to see the tom cat in the kitchen.

Over her struggling friend's head, Celia looked at Dorothy with amazement; she had never seen her before as anything but an automaton who cleaned rooms and waited at table, and said dully and mechanically, 'Yes, Miss,' or 'No, Miss,' in response to whatever was said to her.

Wrapped in a camelhair dressing gown, knitted slippers on her feet, Louise came running into the room, twisting her wet hair into a knot as she came. 'That fool of a girl said . . .' Then, as she saw the little tableau by the fireplace, she realised that the message Ethel had blurted out was true.

She had been feeling helpless and deserted as she lay crying in the cooling water of her bath. But when Ethel had knocked frantically at the bathroom door and poured out her message, she had instinctively responded to the call for help.

Now, faced with Phyllis's obvious desperate need and the necessity of saving her fine old Turkish hearth rug from being ruined by having a baby born on it, she entirely forgot her grief.

She said calmly to Celia, 'Find Ethel and send her for Dr Hollis.'

Celia fled.

Phyllis lifted a woebegone face, flushed with shame, to Louise. 'I'm so sorry – oh – I've ruined your chair – the water's broken.' She gave another little moan. 'I'm having a midwife, Mrs Fox from Green Lane – if I could get home, I could send for her.'

There was a tartness in Louise's voice, as she responded,

'I don't have a carriage to send you home in, my dear. Timothy would never have a carriage – said they were more nuisance than help.' As she spoke, she was pulling back the stool on which Celia had been seated, to clear a path to the door, so that they could move Phyllis upstairs.

'To order a cab would take precious time,' she went on. 'I don't think we should chance it. But don't worry.'

The tearing, familiar ache which enclasped Phyllis's waist eased for the moment and she protested quite coherently, 'The pains don't seem to be coming very fast yet. Surely I could reach home all right, couldn't I?'

For reasons which Louise could not analyse herself, she was reluctant to let Phyllis go.

The sudden crisis had jolted her out of her own grief, diverted her mind. She was loath to face again a long day which, she knew, would otherwise become filled with problems which she did not know how to deal with. Childbirth was familiar – at least she knew from experience how to deal with that, she told herself.

With a sense of power and new-found energy, she said gently, 'Don't chance it, Phyllis. The baby might be damaged, if you gave birth in a cab. We'll try to get you upstairs and on to a bed.'

With all her normal authority, she turned to Dorothy, who was jigging round and round to make the child in her arms laugh and was having some success with him. 'Take the little boy down to the kitchen – Eric, is it? And ask Winnie to come up, please.'

Making a great game of Eric riding a horse, Dorothy galloped out of the room. Before Louise turned back to her stricken guest, she actually smiled briefly at such an amusing display from her parlourmaid.

Celia had already found Ethel in the kitchen, placidly emptying more hot water from the kettle into her bucket. She hastily instructed the young girl to take off her apron and run – run – for Dr Hollis. Then, a little breathlessly, she explained to a startled Winnie what was happening.

'Well, I never!' Winnie exclaimed with interest. She wiped her hands on the towel tucked into her waistband, and then stood with arms akimbo, as she considered the situation. 'Do you think it'll be born here?'

'I don't know, Winnie – I don't know much about these things. Mrs Woodcock seems in great pain.'

'Well, of course, you don't know, Miss Celia. You being a single lady, like. I'll put the kettle on in case.' She seized her largest kettle and went to the sink to fill it.

'Mrs Woodcock is all wet, Winnie – and the hearth rug and the chair are soaked.'

'Oh, dear.' The cook looked knowingly at her young mistress, as she hung the kettle on a hook over the roaring fire. She was about to say something more, when Dorothy clattered down the stairs, with a giggling Eric bumping on her shoulder.

'Missus wants you – now. There's a right to-do up there.' She jerked her head towards the staircase. 'And this young man wants to see Tommy Atkins, don't you, pet?'

Tommy Atkins, long, thin and black, was curled up on Winnie's rocking chair. At the sound of his name, he pricked up one ear and half opened a green eye, perhaps suspicious that he was about to be dumped in the cellars to deal with a mouse.

Winnie was already taking off her blue and white striped kitchen apron, to reveal a spotlessly white one underneath. She looked a little grim, as she said, 'Oh, aye. Miss Celia just told me.'

Feeling that Eric was better left with Dorothy, who had obviously captivated him, she said to Celia, 'If you don't mind, Miss, you'd better come up as well. If we got to move Mrs Woodcock, like . . .' She stumped up the stairs and Celia followed her, her thin white hands folded tightly against her stomach, as she tried to quell the panic within her. She dreaded to think what might be happening to

Phyllis – and yet the situation held a morbid fascination for her. Could a baby really arrive like Phyllis had told her they did?

When they hurried into the breakfast room, Phyllis was still sitting in the ruined chair. To Celia's relief, she did not appear to be in pain.

Louise was patting the pregnant woman's shoulder comfortingly, as she said briskly to Winnie, 'Celia will have told you of Mrs Woodcock's condition. Do you have an old oilcloth tablecloth downstairs?'

To Celia's surprise, Winnie did not seem particularly mystified by the question. 'Er . . . Yes, Ma'am. There's one on the table I keep the bread bin on. I could wipe it down for you.'

'Good. Open up the spare room bed and lay it on the mattress. Then get some of the old sheets from the sewing room and put them over it – in a pad, if you understand what I mean. Tuck them in well.'

Winnie smiled widely, showing a gap where a front tooth was missing. 'Yes, Ma'am. We'll have Mrs Woodcock comfortable in no time.'

'There's one basin on the washstand – better get a couple of tin ones from the kitchen as well. And tell Ethel or Dorothy to make a fire in the bedroom – it'll be too cold for a newborn baby.'

Showing a surprising turn of speed, Winnie went to do as she was told, while Phyllis wailed, 'I'm putting you to so much trouble!'

'No, no, my dear. You can't help it.' Louise sounded calmer than she had at any time since her husband's demise, and Celia realised with astonishment that all the women were thrilled with what was happening, including the usually lethargic Ethel, who had not even stopped to take off her sackcloth apron before sprinting off to get the doctor.

*　　*　　*

With infuriating leisureliness, the doctor's wife received Ethel's breathless message, panted out in her dark hallway.

'Doctor's still doing his morning surgery,' she told the little maid, and, as if to confirm her words, an elderly lady accompanied by a young girl came out of a back room, followed by the cheerful voice of Dr Hollis. 'Now, remember, three times a day – and plenty of rest.'

The old lady smiled faintly, but did not respond, and Ethel and Mrs Hollis made space for her to get to the front door. 'Goodbye, Mrs Formby,' Mrs Hollis said courteously to the patient, as she closed the front door after her.

She turned back to a fidgeting Ethel. 'Do you know how fast Mrs Woodcock's pains are coming?' she inquired, and before Ethel could reply, she continued, 'I don't think Mrs Woodcock is one of our patients, is she?'

Ethel was sharp enough to realise the inference of the last remark. It meant, who will pay the doctor's fee? She liked Mrs Woodcock, who was always polite to her, so she answered stoutly, 'I don't know about the pains, Ma'am. But she's a real friend of Miss Celia, and it were Mrs Gilmore herself what sent me here.'

'I see.' The reply appeared acceptable, because Mrs Hollis said she would ask the doctor to step round immediately surgery was over. In about an hour, he should be there.

'Thank you, Ma'am.'

Full of excitement, her need to find another job completely forgotten, Ethel opened the doctor's front door and sped down the steps.

Chapter Ten

❧

Immediately upon her return, Ethel was entrusted with the job of taking Eric home. At first, Eric objected strongly to being taken from Dorothy and the comfortable security of the Gilmore basement kitchen. He remembered that his mother was upstairs and he shrieked that he wanted her. Fortunately, from the distant confines of the spare bedroom Phyllis could not hear him. If she thought about him at all, it was with the confident expectation that he would be properly cared for in her friend's house, and would soon be delivered safely back to Lily.

Ethel carried with her a note from Louise to Lily, Phyllis's cook-general, explaining what was happening, and asking her to feed the children their lunch and tea, and to make sure that Mr Woodcock's dinner was ready for him when he came home from work. It was possible, Louise advised her, that Mrs Woodcock would not be home for a couple of days. She added that she would arrange for Mr Woodcock to be informed, at his office, of his wife's predicament.

While Louise hastily scribbled a note to Arthur Woodcock, Phyllis sat on the edge of the wooden chair in the spare bedroom. Winnie helped to divest her of her sodden clothes and then slipped one of Celia's huge cotton nightgowns over the young mother's head.

'Arthur's going to be awfully cross,' Phyllis whimpered to Celia. She gave a small shivering sigh, and then winced as a roll of pain commenced.

Startled, Celia looked up at her. 'Why?' she asked. 'It's his baby, too!' She had been inspecting the soft pad of old sheets Winnie had contrived in the middle of the bed, and now she shook out and spread over it another clean sheet and a light blanket to keep her friend warm. She was surprised at Phyllis's remark; it contradicted all that she had learned from the many romances she had read. Didn't men love their wives for producing their children?

Phyllis gritted her teeth and waited for a spasm to pass before she said hopelessly, 'Oh, he'll be cross about everything. For my being such an idiot as to get caught like this – and having to help Lily care for the other little ones. He always gets angry if his routine is upset, and Lily will have her work cut out with three children and the house to look after.'

Winnie interrupted the exchange, to get Phyllis into bed before the pain increased. She smiled benignly down. 'Don't you worry about your hubby, Ma'am. You just concentrate on the baby, and relax as much as you can between your pains. You'd be surprised how men can manage, if they have to.'

But Phyllis knew her husband too well to hope for anything other than constant complaints and weak bursts of sudden rage, and she closed her eyes to try to stop the tears rolling down her cheeks.

Celia gently folded the bedclothes over her friend, and bent to kiss her. When she saw that Phyllis was crying, she took her handkerchief out of her sleeve and wiped the tears away. Then she hesitantly kissed her again. Though she was quite frightened at being so close to a birthing mother, she said cheerfully, 'Winnie's right. Mother will talk to Arthur, I'm sure. She's just gone downstairs to write a note to him – Ethel will take it to his office – and she can write today to your mother, if you'll give her the address, to ask her to come like she did for the other children. If we post a letter soon, she'll get it by tomorrow afternoon's post.'

Phyllis conjured up a small smile. Her mother would certainly come and would run the family like a general conducting a battle – and Arthur would hate her more than ever. And take it out on Phyllis the day her mother left.

Winnie had gone to look at the old clock on the mantelpiece to check the timing of the recurrence of Phyllis's pangs of pain. As Louise bustled back into the room after dispatching Ethel, Winnie said to her, 'The baby will be a while yet, Ma'am. Shall I make some tea? Miss Celia could sit with Mrs Woodcock while I do it; and you could get dressed before the doctor comes.'

Louise had forgotten her own bedraggled state. She glanced down at her dressing gown, and laughed. 'Yes, indeed, I must, mustn't I?' She hastened off to her own bedroom, saying to Phyllis as she went that she would send Ethel to Arthur's office as soon as she returned from delivering Eric to Lily.

The laugh surprised and pleased Celia. Though childbirth was not a normal thing to her, it obviously was to her mother; and a sense of normality was what they all needed. As Winnie pushed the bedroom chair towards her, so that she could sit by the patient, she took Phyllis's hand and squeezed it.

'Is there anything I need to do for Mrs Woodcock?' she asked Winnie, hoping that she herself would not faint if the baby came while the other two women were out of the room.

'If the pains are sharp, you just hold Mrs Woodcock to comfort her until they pass. If they start to come close together, pull the bell immediately and I'll run up. But she'll know, won't you, Ma'am?'

Phyllis nodded. She knew only too well from experience, and, in her despair, she wondered how she could endure being racked by childbirth almost every year of her life.

As it happened, Celia was not left alone with Phyllis,

because Dorothy came up with buckets of coal and wood chips and yesterday's newspaper tucked under her arm, to make a fire to warm the room for the arrival of the new infant. She had reluctantly relinquished Eric to a buoyant Ethel, who was undeterred by Eric's howls and flying little fists. She picked him up and held him firmly against her shoulder, as she ran down the front steps.

As Dorothy expertly built the fire, she realised that she was enjoying the unusual morning. 'Young Eric went off quite happy with Ethel, Ma'am,' she told Phyllis. She paused while she screwed up the newspaper and laid loose balls of it in the fire grate. 'She comes from a family of thirteen, so she's fine with children. Lovely little fella, he is,' she added.

Phyllis nodded, and then gave a long, slow moan. God help me if I have to go through this thirteen times, she thought.

Celia leaned over and put an arm round her. Phyllis's face was contorted; then, to Celia's relief, she relaxed, and said in her usual soft tones, 'Thank you, Dorothy, for managing him so well.'

'It were nothin', Ma'am.' Dorothy was acquainted with Mrs Woodcock's Lily and knew all about Arthur Woodcock's relations with his wife. Both maids had lost sweethearts in France and had little hope of marrying. They were agreed, however, that it was better to be single than have a nit-picking husband like him. She picked up a pair of bellows lying in the hearth and blew the struggling fire until the coals had caught thoroughly.

As she tidied up the hearth, and with a polite bob towards the bed, went slowly down the stairs to the kitchen, her mood changed. If her Andy had survived the second battle of the Marne and come home last year, she could have been hoping for a baby now, even though she was middle-aged. Andy would have made a great dad, like the old man who was his dad, she thought wistfully.

Pity they'd waited so long, though seven years' engagement wasn't that long. After all, you were supposed to save before you could marry. Not that she had saved when she had been working in the ordnance factory. Easy come, easy go.

As she washed the coal dust off her hands in the pannikin in the kitchen sink, she smiled and shrugged her shoulders at the memory of the good times she and Andy had had when he had come home on leave.

Forget it, she told herself. You could have been stranded now, with a young baby to bring up alone. It was going to be hard enough to find a new, decent place without a child. With one, she wouldn't have a hope.

A bell on its spring near the kitchen ceiling rang suddenly.

She grinned wryly to herself as she dried her hands on the kitchen roller towel. Miss Celia getting into a panic, no doubt.

Winnie was busy pouring hot water into a big breakfast teapot. As she laid the pot on the tray she had prepared, she chuckled. A similar thought had occurred to her. As Dorothy quickly took off her enshrouding sacking apron which she used for rough work, the cook said, 'It won't hurt Miss Celia to see a birth – it's probably the only chance she'll get! And any woman ought to know what to do. Here, take the tray up to them.'

Dorothy's small mouth quirked into a smile of agreement. 'Oh, aye, if she does, she's going to be proper shocked. She don't know nothin' about nothin'. I'd bet on it.'

Years later, after another war, looking back on that day, Celia had smiled. She had been terrified. But in a few hours, she had learned so much about women, she considered; that they could organise in a crisis, work through it together, be brave under suffering. And, further, that you did not know what friendship meant until you had faced crises together.

It changed for ever her ideas of what women could do, without men to tell them what incompetent fools they were. They had, of course, sent for the doctor – male – but, unlike her father, he had actually approved of their efforts on Phyllis's behalf.

Chapter Eleven

Because she had no idea at what point in the proceedings the baby would arrive, Celia had rung the bell when a much sharper pang had struck Phyllis; instead of a moan, she had suddenly cried out.

By the time Dorothy had navigated two flights of stairs with the tea tray, Phyllis was more relaxed and was whispering an apology to Celia for being such a coward.

Dorothy put down the tray on the dressing table, and inquired if Madam would like a cup of tea.

Facing for the moment only an awful ache round her waist, Madam said with a sigh that she would, so Celia propped her up a little with an extra pillow and held the cup while she sipped. Dorothy filled another cup and set it down on the bedside table near Celia.

Since Phyllis did not seem threatened by another immediate spasm and Celia's face was an unearthly white, the maid tried to reassure Celia by saying, 'Don't fret, Miss. You drink your tea, too. It'll be a bit yet afore the baby comes. The pains come quick when baby is actually on its way. Winnie's got the kettle on for when the doctor comes, and she's going to make a bit of lunch for everyone.'

The reminder that the doctor would be coming was a comfort, and Celia felt a little better. In fact, Louise had only just finished her toilet, when he arrived.

While Celia and her mother retired to a corner of the room, he did a quick examination of his patient, then pulled down her nightgown and neatly replaced the sheet and blanket over her. He assured the struggling mother that the baby appeared to be positioned correctly and that he did not expect the delivery to be difficult.

Phyllis told him that she had arranged for Mrs Fox, the midwife, to help with the delivery, but that she had been caught unexpectedly in dear Mrs Gilmore's house, and that Mrs Gilmore had sent for him.

'Excellent. Excellent woman, Mrs Fox,' he said, as he picked up his hat. 'She has a telephone by which she can be reached – the chemist next door to her is very obliging in this respect. I'll phone her as soon as I get back to the surgery.' He patted Phyllis's hand, and when Louise came forward, he told her, 'I doubt if Mrs Woodcock will need my services, but I expect you have someone you could send for me, if Mrs Fox feels it necessary?'

All the women were reassured by the doctor's visit, and, when warm, friendly Mrs Fox rolled quietly into the bedroom, her tiny slippered feet making no sound on the carpet, despite her vast bulk, Phyllis greeted her with pleasure before suddenly arching her back and emitting a sharp scream.

Shocked, Celia spilled some of Phyllis's second cup of tea as she hastily put the cup down on the bedside table. She looked imploringly at Mrs Fox as she straightened herself up. Phyllis's eyes were closed, and she was taking small, quivering breaths.

'Don't leave me, Seelee,' Phyllis breathed and sought for Celia's hand, which she clutched tightly. Only Celia understood how fretful and awkward Arthur was. She would understand how Phyllis was dreading going home to face his constant nagging, when she would be at her weakest after the ordeal of childbirth; the presence of Celia in his home had never deterred Arthur from humiliating his wife by picking at her whenever he was annoyed. Even if Celia did not understand the root causes of it, her friend had seen enough to understand her terrible underlying unhappiness.

At the use of her childhood nickname, Celia was almost moved to tears. She gulped and said, 'Of course, I won't, dear.'

Mrs Fox approached the bed and glanced down at Celia's left hand. No wedding ring. No wonder the woman was looking as scared as a mouse before a cat. Probably hadn't got the faintest idea of what was happening. She leaned forward and wiped the thin perspiration off Phyllis's forehead and her closed eyelids. The lids were not crunched tight with pain, so she said, 'That's right, Ma'am. Rest yourself in betweens. I'm just going to take a look to see how things are. Just lift your knees up and apart a bit.'

As the bedclothes were lifted back and Phyllis's night-gown flipped up, Celia politely turned her eyes away and concentrated them on Phyllis's face. Phyllis opened her eyes and smiled wryly up at her, while the midwife probed and pressed with her hands, and then carefully sponged her with surgical spirit. The midwife said quietly to Louise, 'Her time's too close to give her an enema to empty her bowels.'

'Stay with me!' Phyllis begged her friend again. 'It's not as bad as it sounds. I'll make an awful noise, but if you'll hold on to me, it'll feel easier.'

With her face as white as a newly donkey-stoned door-step, Celia assured her that she would never leave her.

Louise intervened with a protest that it was not suitable for a single woman to remain in a birthing room. 'My dear Phyllis, it simply isn't the thing at all.'

Phyllis looked at her with wide uncomprehending eyes, and Louise turned to her daughter. 'Celia, you must leave!'

Winnie, peering over Louise's shoulder, her expression genuinely concerned, added, 'You may faint, luv – and we'll be too busy to deal with you.'

Celia cringed, and then as Phyllis's grasp of her hand

tightened, she found the courage to say coldly, 'I shall be quite all right, Mother – Mrs Fox.'

Mrs Fox did not rise to the appeal in Celia's voice. It did not matter to her who was present, as long as they kept out of her way.

Celia faltered, and then, as Phyllis groaned, she said quietly, 'No. I want to be with Phyllis.'

Louise's voice was frigid, as she said sharply, 'Celia. You are being most disobedient. Please, leave the room.'

Outraged at being ordered about like a child, in front of a servant and the midwife, Celia said, 'I won't.' She loosened her friend's hand, turned her back on Louise and very carefully slipped her arm under Phyllis's shoulders. Phyllis put an arm round Celia's neck and clung to her.

Louise was red with anger; Celia had never defied her like this; she would not have dared, if her father had been alive. She took a step forward, as if she might pull her daughter away, and Mrs Fox, for the sake of her patient, put a restraining hand on her arm. 'Let them be, Ma'am. Let them be, if it helps Mrs Woodcock.'

Breathing hard, Louise stared at the midwife. 'It's most improper,' she protested.

'It may be, Ma'am, but this is not the moment to argue. Will you be so kind as to step back, so that I can deal with Mrs Woodcock.'

Rebuked, Louise stepped back, and Winnie persuaded her into an easy chair by the fire. 'Best to leave it, Ma'am,' she advised.

'It's scandalous, Winnie!'

'Nobody will know, Ma'am, if you don't say nothin'.'

Sitting rigidly in the chair, Louise closed her eyes. Suddenly she turned her head into the curve of the chair's padded back and began to cry softly into her black handkerchief.

Frightened to death by what she had done, nevertheless Celia stood by her promise. She would not shift. Phyllis became rapidly far too absorbed in her own struggle to take much notice of any argument. With Celia, she concentrated on Mrs Fox's instructions, both of them shifting position as needed.

With a groan so deep that Celia had never heard anything like it before, a tiny, perfect person was finally expelled and the cord was cut and tied. And, to Celia's astonishment, the baby immediately cried out.

Phyllis relaxed in Celia's arms. Her smile was so triumphant that it was as if she had not gone through what was, to Celia, an appalling operation.

The baby was quickly bundled up in a warm towel, while water to wash it was poured into a bowl by a smiling Winnie, and Celia glanced down to see what was happening.

Phyllis's legs were still spread. Mrs Fox had pushed sheets of newspaper under her buttocks and, with a tin bowl in her hands, seemed to be waiting. In fact, except for hearty yells from the baby, everyone was very quiet.

Phyllis's tired body heaved suddenly. It seemed to Celia that there was an awful lot of blood as the placenta came clear. She had never heard of an afterbirth. She believed that something dreadful was happening to Phyllis and that she was bleeding to death.

In a blaze of fear for her friend's life, she fainted.

Chapter Twelve

❧

Celia came round to find herself sitting on the floor, leaning against Phyllis's bed. Winnie was kneeling by her, one plump arm round her. She was chuckling at her, as she wiped Celia's face with a cold, clammy face flannel.

At the same time, Louise was standing by her and scolding her. 'It's disgraceful. I told you to leave the room,' she was saying. 'Birth is not a pretty sight. Single women are not supposed to watch it – it's like a guttersnipe gaping at a street accident.'

Winnie squeezed Celia gently, and said to Louise, 'Now, don't take on so, Ma'am. Miss Celia's a brave little lady, and Mrs Woodcock is her dearest friend. Of course she wanted to help – and I think she did.'

'Indeed, she did help,' came Phyllis's voice from above her head. 'Are you all right, Seelee?'

The sound of her friend's voice, clear, though a little weak and sleepy, was a great relief. Whatever she had witnessed was evidently something quite normal. The women round her were calm and undisturbed; in fact, as she gazed at them it was astonishing how happy everyone looked; even her mother's scolding voice did not sound as acidic as she had expected it would be.

'Come and see the baby,' urged Winnie as she helped Celia up. As she staggered to her feet, however, Celia's first thought was for Phyllis.

The young mother lay with eyes closed, great black rings round them in marked contrast to an ashen face. Mrs Fox was bathing her and there was a strong smell of disinfectant from the bowl of water she was using. As she sponged, she threw each piece of rag that she used into another bowl. Mrs Fox had never yet lost a patient to childbed fever and she was taking no risks with this one. The precipitous arrival of the baby had not given her time to assemble boiled sheets, boric lint, and so on. Disinfectant and her own well-scoured person had to be the barrier against infection.

Celia laid a shaky hand on Phyllis's narrow wrist. 'Are you all right?' she asked.

Phyllis slowly opened her tired eyes. She smiled. 'Yes,' she said, and then, with more animation, 'A little boy!'

'Congratulations,' Celia said mechanically. 'I'm sure Arthur will be pleased.'

A shadow passed over Phyllis's face. 'I hope so. Do have a look at him.'

Winnie had turned and picked up the new infant out of the drawer, which, with a bolster pillow in it, had been pressed into service as a temporary cradle.

'Isn't he loovely!' she exclaimed, her plain face transformed into beauty as she looked down at the tiny baby. 'Here, luv, you hold him for a minute.' He was thrust into Celia's arms.

He was so light! So tiny! So helpless! She automatically closed her arms tightly round him, and felt a surge of protective love for him. She was aware of no one else, simply this tiny scrap of humanity and herself. It was the beginning of a lifelong devotion to her godson.

'Bring him to me,' whispered Phyllis.

With a sudden sense of guilt, Celia turned and reluctantly laid the little bundle on his mother's chest.

'What are you going to call him?' she asked.

Phyllis's eyes turned towards Louise, who was handing a clean nightgown for the patient to Mrs Fox. 'Well, if Mrs Gilmore doesn't mind, I'd like to call him Timothy

George. I'll have to ask Arthur if it is all right, of course. When I asked him the other day about names, he said let's wait to see if it's a boy or a girl.' She did not add that he had seemed unable to face the advent of another child.

Her father's and her dead younger brother's names.

Celia saw her mother's face soften. 'How very sweet of you, my dear,' Louise said, and bent to kiss the weary mother. She sighed. 'Since Edna lost little Rosemary, I have begun to doubt if I shall ever have any grandchildren. I must say that it would be so nice to have the names perpetuated.'

Phyllis gripped her hand. 'You and Seelee have been so good. I can never repay you.'

Mrs Fox came forward to help Phyllis into the clean nightgown.

She muttered a little anxiously that Phyllis must rest now. She took Timothy George away from his mother and then slipped the starched nightie over her patient's head. In the distance the front doorbell rang.

'I wonder if that is Arthur?' Phyllis's muffled voice came through the fine cotton.

Chapter Thirteen

✧✦✧

The women waited expectantly. Mrs Fox fussed around her patient. She told her she should sleep for a little while and then have some hot soup. Winnie smiled down at Phyllis and said she had a pan of soup simmering on the kitchen fire.

But Phyllis ignored them, as she watched the door eagerly, and her face fell as only the dragging footsteps of Dorothy were heard along the passage. Arthur was obviously not going to ask the bank manager, under whom he worked as accountant, if he could leave a little earlier, so that he could come to see her. She supposed, despondently, that he would come when his day's work was finished rather than break his perfect record of never having taken time off, except for statutory holidays. She began to cry weakly and noiselessly; it had been the same with the arrival of all her children.

When Dorothy opened the bedroom door, after knocking politely and being told by an impatient Louise that she could enter, the reason for her slowness and for the whiteness of her face was immediately apparent.

On the small silver tray that she carried lay two telegrams.

She proffered them to Louise. 'The boy's waiting on a reply, Ma'am. I asked him into the hall.'

After a war in which a telegram almost always announced a death or, at best, someone missing in action, the very sight of a small orange envelope was terrifying;

two of them at the same time was enough to paralyse Louise. She could not make herself take them off the tray.

Mrs Fox was the first to recover. She moved a chair swiftly under Louise, and said gently, 'Sit down, Ma'am.'

Staring at the tray as if it were a cobra about to bite her, Louise mechanically did as she was told.

Already very shaky, Celia was fighting against fainting again. She made herself move towards her mother and put a protective hand on her shoulder. 'It really can't be anything very much, Mother,' she half whispered. 'The war's over.'

Winnie broke in. 'Maybe Miss Edna and Mr Paul has landed,' she suggested.

'Of course,' responded Louise with immediate relief. She took the envelopes off the tray, and said, 'Thank you, Dorothy.'

While she slit the first envelope, the others relaxed and muttered about being so silly over telegrams.

She read the missive aloud.

> 'Darling Mother stop so sad about Father stop meet me Lime Street Station London train arriving 1.30 pm Friday stop all my love Edna stop'

Louise laughed in relief. 'Quite right, Winnie,' she told her beaming cook.

As she opened the second envelope, Celia queried, 'I wonder where Paul is. Edna sent the telegram.'

The answer to her question was in the second telegram, sent by Edna's father-in-law, Simon Fellowes.

Louise's voice faltered as she read it out.

> 'Regret to report passing of my son, Paul, from influenza stop died aboard ship stop buried at sea stop devastated stop our condolences to you in your loss stop letter already in the mail stop'

'My God!' Louise let the telegram flutter into her lap. 'I thought the flu epidemic was finished.'

'I seen one or two cases recently.' It was Mrs Fox's cool voice as she read the telegram over Louise's shoulder. 'It's lucky your daughter didn't get it, Ma'am. When it strikes it tends to take everybody in the prime of life.'

Louise nodded agreement. Edna alive – but widowed – and still so young – it was too awful to contemplate. 'It's too much!' she cried. 'I can't bear it.' She began to rock herself backwards and forwards like a demented child.

'Don't, Mama. Please, Mama.' In tears herself, Celia clasped her mother to her.

Gone was the woman who had so efficiently organised the baby's birth – Louise was again wrapped in her own grief, crying with a depth of despair which had not occurred even when her husband's body had been brought home.

'Let her cry, Miss. She'll be better afterwards,' Winnie whispered.

'Poor Mrs Gilmore! Poor Edna!' Propped up on one elbow, Phyllis was staring at the stricken group of women at the foot of the bed. She stretched out her hand towards them. She turned her gaze towards Celia. 'Celia, dear.'

Winnie was saying, 'I'm so sorry, Ma'am,' while Dorothy stood transfixed, silver tray in hand, only her nose quivering, as she tried to gather herself together.

'Wh-what shall I tell the telegraph boy, Ma'am?' she finally stuttered.

Fighting her growing panic as, in a flash, she saw all the implications of this further death in the family, it was Celia who picked up Edna's telegram from her mother's lap and said swiftly, 'I will come downstairs, and write a reply for him. One of us must meet Edna tomorrow.'

Her mother muttered almost gratefully, 'Thank you, dear.' She had stopped rocking herself when Celia had embraced her, but, sitting on the stiff wooden chair, she looked lost and broken while hopeless tears ran down her face.

Winnie stepped forward and issued an order herself. 'Dorothy, go and get the Master's brandy from the dining-room sideboard, and pour a glass for everyone.' She emphasised the word everyone, to make it clear that she included Mrs Fox, Dorothy and herself.

Clinging to the banister, Celia walked carefully down the long, red-carpeted staircase to deal with the patient tele-graph boy.

The youngster was standing in the hall with his hands behind him like a soldier ordered to be at ease. He knew better than to sit down on one of the four red velvet chairs set stiffly against one wall; they were not intended for the lower orders.

He was used to white-faced women with trembling hands, trying to find pencil and paper, and he immediately brought out both from the breast pocket of his grey uniform.

'Oh, thank you,' breathed Celia with relief, as she addressed a loving and sympathetic answer to Edna, care of her father-in-law, and another of condolence to Mr and Mrs Fellowes themselves.

After he had carefully counted the number of words and she had paid him for its transmission, from the change purse in her skirt pocket, the telegraph boy paused and looked hopefully at her.

Celia was puzzled and then realised her omission.

A tip! That was it. She produced another silver threepenny piece and pressed it into his hand. He grinned and picked up his peaked cap from the hall table. She watched him cram it on to his head, as he ran down the steps to his bicycle.

As she slowly closed the heavy front door after the boy, she felt again a terrible sense of despair, made worse by a threepenny piece handed to a patient boy. The small silver coin represented her own inadequacy: her ill-preparedness for dealing with even the smallest problem, never mind coping with a distraught mother and with poor Edna, the loss of her father and her home.

Her father had always done the tipping. A small item in the perplexing world into which she was inexorably being pushed. But she knew it was important if she was to get service. She must remember to take some change with her, if she went to the station to meet Edna. Porters had to be tipped.

As she went back upstairs, her shock gave way to realisation of how much she had been depending upon Paul's arrival. His loss would mean that she and her mother had no one to lean on but Cousin Albert. Edna had, at least, her father-in-law to turn to for advice.

In the bedroom, the baby was crying healthily, Mrs Fox was packing up, after downing a thimble-sized glass of brandy proffered by Dorothy, and Phyllis was lying down again and staring at the ceiling.

'Where's Mother?' Celia inquired of Mrs Fox.

'Your Winnie took her to lie down and drink her brandy in her bedroom.' Mrs Fox glanced in the dressing-table mirror, to make sure that she had pinned her wide-brimmed black hat on straight, and then picked up her shawl to wrap it round her shoulders. 'Mrs Woodcock must sleep now. If she wants the baby by her, make sure you put it back into its cradle when she falls asleep – you don't want to overlie it, do you, Mrs Woodcock?'

Phyllis smiled weakly. 'No, of course not. Dorothy is making me some tea and biscuits – I mustn't have brandy. Then I'll sleep. Celia, you should drink your brandy, though; it's on the dressing table. You must be feeling awful.' She turned to the midwife, to thank her in a weak voice for easing her pains so skilfully.

'You're welcome, Ma'am. It wasn't a difficult birth, was it, Ma'am? I'll come back this evening to take a look at you. If you don't feel right, Miss Gilmore'll phone me, won't you, Miss? I've left me number on the chest of drawers – it's really the chemist next door. He'll send his boy to tell me quick enough, though.'

Celia had no idea where she was going to find a phone from which to make such a call, but hoped her mother might know of one. And there was always Ethel – she loved being sent out with a message. She nodded agreement, and, with a smile and a half-bob, Mrs Fox departed.

Immediately she could be heard going lightly down the stairs, Phyllis said, 'Bring Timothy to me, dear. Poor little thing, crying his head off!'

Very carefully, Celia did as she was told, and then sank down on the bedside chair. With his head on his mother's breast, the baby was comforted and fell asleep. The room was at last quiet.

Though she was crooning softly to young Timothy, Phyllis saw that Celia was trembling almost uncontrollably. She repeated to her, 'Drink your brandy, Celia.'

Celia got up and, while still standing, she gulped it down. It made her splutter, and Phyllis laughed. 'Not as fast as that!' she said. 'Slowly!'

Feeling even more stupid, Celia nodded and sat quickly down on the chair again.

After a few quiet minutes, she asked, 'When will Arthur come to see you, do you think?'

'About five o'clock, I expect – when he's finished work. He'll probably get a carriage or a taxi to take me home.'

Celia was shocked. 'Surely you shouldn't be moved yet? I'm sure Mother wouldn't mind if you did your whole ten days' lying-in here. We're not going to move yet.'

'Oh, I'll be all right. I only stayed in bed for two days after Eric. Arthur couldn't stand the disruption.'

'He shouldn't give you babies then!'

Phyllis was silent. Celia had accidentally hit squarely on the problem which lay between herself and her husband, a fear of intercourse which seemed to produce babies every year. She did not know how to solve it. She had never heard of birth control.

She swallowed hard and then changed the subject by saying, 'Edna is going to need all your help, Celia – with no child to console her.'

The brandy had helped Celia. She was feeling steadier, and fractionally more optimistic. She said, 'Yes. Yes, she will.' Then she added, with a sigh, 'I hope she will be more of a comfort to Mother than I am.'

Phyllis was too tired to do any comforting herself. Her eyes drooped. Celia gently took Timothy from her. He whimpered, and she instinctively held him close to her and rocked him for a while before putting him down in his improvised cradle. Then, after tucking the bedclothes closer round Phyllis and putting a little more coal on the fire, she went out into the passage, closing the door behind her.

She stood for a moment leaning against the closed door and staring at the rich jewel colours of the carpet. Then she shut her tired eyes.

Poor Paul. To escape the war and yet still be taken. It was true that the Spanish flu had gone through the younger members of the population like some mighty scythe. It had killed the remains of the same age group which had died as a result of battle. You only had to look at the crowds in the streets of Liverpool, she thought helplessly; there were lamentably few male faces between the ages of, say, sixteen and forty, and not that many young women – Celia had been luckier than two of her women friends, in that she herself had survived an attack of it.

She shifted her feet uneasily. In the richly furnished, silent hall, she had a dreadful feeling of being quite alone, and she wondered why she should be alive when all her potential friends, never mind the ones she actually had had, were dead.

She shivered with sudden cold, and straightened herself up. Then slowly, with dragging footsteps, she went along the hall to her mother's bedroom, and tapped on the door.

Chapter Fourteen

❧

Impeccably neat in a black jacket and pinstriped trousers, Arthur Woodcock arrived on foot precisely as the Gilmores' grandfather clock in the hall struck a quarter past five. He had taken his usual bus from town.

He handed his black bowler hat to Dorothy and asked to see his wife. Dorothy showed him into the sitting room. It was her own decision; she did not want dear Mrs Woodcock made unhappy by an unfeeling husband, she told herself. She smiled at Arthur, and said politely, 'I'll get Miss Gilmore. The Missus is a bit upset.'

'Humph.' He did not inquire why Louise was upset – he presumed it was from the disorganisation of her day. Well, she wasn't the only one – he would be late for his tea, thanks to his wife's stupidity.

When Celia came into the room, he rose from his chair. Celia looked even more lachrymose than she usually did. Her nose was red, as were her eyes, her hair was disarranged – and she still had on her apron.

She tried to be cheerful for him. 'You've a lovely new son,' she told him, as she held out her hand to him. 'And Phyllis is fine – she's sleeping at the moment.'

'Good.' He shook her hand. 'I'm sorry that you have been so inconvenienced. I've ordered a taxi to come here at half past five to take us home.'

Celia's eyes widened. 'Oh, you can't move her yet. She must rest – and it's not wise to take the baby out. Mama would be quite happy for her to have her ten days' lying-in with us. We would see that she had complete rest. Mama says it is vital for her health that she rest,' she finished eagerly.

'That's most kind of you. She can, however, rest at home. May I go up to see her?'

Confused by his arbitrariness, Celia said, 'Yes, of course.' She wished her mother was with her to insist on Phyllis's staying. Her mother was, however, still on her bed, weeping to Winnie that she could not go on.

As Celia led the way up the stairs, Dorothy again answered the front doorbell. On the step stood a heavily moustached male, wearing a stiff peaked cap. He was wrapped in an old overcoat and innumerable scarves.

'Taxicab for Woodcock,' he announced. Behind him stood one of the new-fangled hackney carriages; as Dorothy told Winnie afterwards, 'making a noise somethin' awful'. In fact, the vehicle was the pride of the cab driver; its boxlike body, its engine gently pulsating under a brass-trimmed hood, were the latest in rapid local travel. It bore no comparison to the old hackney carriages drawn by horses, and the driver did not want it to be kept waiting. 'Now, 'urry up,' he admonished Dorothy. ''Aven't got all day.'

Dorothy told him primly to wait in the hall, while she told the Mistress of his arrival. The man took off his hat to expose a very grubby-looking bald head and stepped inside.

Meanwhile Celia quietly opened the bedroom door for Arthur.

Arthur marched straight over to his sleeping wife. He shook her shoulder, and announced that he had come to take her home.

As Phyllis stirred and opened her eyes, Celia said anxiously, 'I've told Arthur that we all hope you will spend your lying-in with us – it would be a pleasure to us.'

'I am afraid that will not do,' Arthur said primly. 'The other children need you.'

'Lily can . . .' Phyllis began rather desperately, but nothing she or Celia could say would move him. And the decision was precipitated by the arrival of the taxi. 'I've no clothes to put on,' was her last protest.

Arthur lost his temper. 'Did you walk round here like Lady Godiva?' he asked.

Shocked, Celia interrupted to say that Phyllis's clothes were in the wash.

When he asked what had happened to them, neither woman answered him. If, after three other children, he did not understand childbirth, they were much too shy to explain it to him.

He asked if he might borrow the blankets off the bed to wrap her in, and added sarcastically, 'I suppose her shoes are fit to wear?'

Totally out of her depth, Celia rang the bell for Dorothy, who fumed as she clumped upstairs again, past the waiting taxi driver who was muttering in the hall because he was being kept waiting, and the taxi outside was consuming petrol at an awful rate. She was sent for Phyllis's shoes, at that moment lying in the kitchen hearth to dry. Her dress and a black petticoat had been hung to dry over a clothes horse by the same fire. Her underwear had been put in the wash house in the back garden, ready for the attention of the washerwoman when she came on Monday.

Celia glanced around her desperately, unwilling to enter the argument going on between man and wife. 'I'll get Mother,' she said and ran down the passage to Louise's bedroom.

Her mother was lying quietly on the bed, and Winnie was seated beside her gently patting her hand, and saying that everything would get sorted out after a while and then she would feel better. The cook looked up as Celia ran in.

Celia told her that she could not cope with Arthur, who was insisting on moving his wife. 'Please come, Mama,' she pleaded.

Winnie interrupted to suggest that Arthur could come to Louise. When Louise protested that she could not receive a man in her bedroom, the cook pulled another quilt over her.

A furious Arthur was brought in and was amazed to see her recumbent. The surprise cooled him down sufficiently for him to ask, 'Are you well, Mrs Gilmore?'

Louise said, 'I've just heard that Edna has lost her husband. I am afraid it caught me at a weak moment.'

'My condolences. In that case you will be thankful to hear that I am taking Phyllis home in a taxi, which has' – he looked at his watch – 'already been waiting for nearly ten minutes. So much expense! So much bother, simply because Phyllis did not stay at home as she should have done.'

Louise immediately forced herself to sit up and say that having Phyllis in the house was no bother at all. She should stay.

While Louise did her best to persuade the irritable young man to give his wife time to recover, Celia went back to Phyllis, who was sitting on the side of the bed in her bloodstained nightgown.

Horrified, she ran to her. 'Phyl! You're bleeding!'

Phyllis smiled weakly and asked for a fresh napkin of some kind. 'It's all right, dear. Don't be afraid of the blood. I shall be bleeding off and on for a while yet.'

'I'm sure you should rest, Phyl. Tell him to go to blazes!'

'I have to live with him all my life, Seelee.'

It sounded like a death sentence to Celia, as she delved into a chest of drawers to get yet another clean nightgown, a winter vest to go under it and a winter woollen shawl, and then went to the airing cupboard for a clean towel to stem the blood. She did, however, understand Phyllis's remark. It did not do to quarrel with men. They held the purse strings.

Silent and disapproving, Louise, Celia and Winnie eased the drooping little mother into the taxi. Dorothy held the baby, swathed in towels and shawls contributed by Louise and Celia, and then laid him in his father's arms. It was the first glimpse of his father the child had had. He opened his tiny mouth and howled. It did not endear him to his angry parent.

Chapter Fifteen

That evening, though an exhausted Louise was reluctant to discuss their position, Celia insisted that they go through her list, which had lain neglected in her skirt pocket all through the momentous day of little Timothy's birth.

'Everything is too, too awful, Celia,' the older woman sobbed.

Celia really pitied her mother. But fear of the future outweighed pity, and she said firmly, 'I'm so very sorry to bother you, Mama, but if we can get ourselves a little organised, we may feel better.' She did not mention that she was afraid that, tomorrow, Edna might bring with her a whole host of additional difficulties for them to cope with.

Still lying on her bed, Louise pleaded, 'Let me rest for a little longer. We could talk after dinner.' She looked appealingly at Celia, and begged, 'I don't know how to bear it all, Celia.'

'Of course you don't, Mama. It is all so heartbreaking for you. Rest a little longer. I'll get Dorothy to bring some wine up with your dinner.'

She herself felt she had been so racked that she had no more strength. She arranged the warm quilt over her mother and kissed her gently. Then she went down to the kitchen to arrange for dinner on a tray to be sent up.

Celia snatched a quick meal in the dining room, and, later on mother and daughter went painstakingly through

Celia's list of the things they had to do. It was obvious that Louise was doing her best to cooperate.

Celia felt that she was being quite brutal in her treatment of her mother and she herself longed to go to bed, but she knew that there was nobody else to take charge of the situation. There was a limit to what she could achieve in one day, she thought wearily, and tomorrow Edna would have to be met and comforted and her plans inquired about.

Edna and Paul had never had a home in England. At the time of their marriage, Paul had been preparing to go to Brazil. They had stayed in Southampton, therefore, with his parents during the months of preparation that were necessary, before his company finally sent him out to supervise a seven-year contract to provide electricity for a rapidly increasing population in Salvador and its environs. As a result, Edna had no house of her own to return to, and Celia wondered if, now she was widowed, she expected to live with her mother. She did not bother Louise with this likely problem. Louise was already distressed enough.

After some persuasion, Louise tremulously agreed that she could, the following day, manage to go, alone, to see the bank manager, the bank being only a short distance away. She would pay in Mr Billings' cheque and inquire exactly how much money she had. She would also ask Mr Carruthers about getting a solicitor of her own; they had agreed that they did not want Mr Barnett to look after them. Meanwhile, Celia would take Dorothy out to the cottage and get her started on cleaning it. She would then go into Hoylake village to see Ben Aspen, the building contractor recommended by Mr Billings, about repairs and redecoration. She would take a train direct from Hoylake to Liverpool to meet Edna.

'Whatever will poor Edna think, if I don't meet her, Celia?' Louise asked in dismay.

'The trouble is, Mama, that we don't know exactly how

much time we have, before we have to move – Cousin Albert said the estate agent believed he could sell this house quite quickly, and neither of us has any idea what he means by quite quickly. It could be next week.' She sighed. 'And the expense of running this house is very great – coal, gas, servants, gardener, not to speak of feeding the five of us. I doubt if we can last for a month financially, unless Mr Carruthers can spring some nice surprise on you.'

'I know, dear.'

'I'm sorry that I can't go to the bank for you. It is not my account – it is yours, and I imagine they will surely need your signature on something. If you don't go tomorrow, everything will have to wait until Monday – and we will have lost a whole weekend.'

'It really is too bad. Are you sure, Celia?'

'I am sure.' She would go insane, she thought, if she did not reduce the number of things on her list – the load was too great. 'Until we know exactly what money we have, Mother, we can't even buy a new broom.' Her nerves were in shreds and she was not being very diplomatic.

Louise burst into tears, as she agreed. 'I wish Tom or George were here,' she cried. 'They would have been such a support.'

At this mention of her strong, laughing younger brother, who had sailed off so lightheartedly to face the German navy, and Tom, big silent Tom, Celia felt a physical pain, a tug at her heartstrings. How could God be so cruel as to take them both? And then, when the slaughter seemed over, it was strange how the Spanish flu epidemic had swept away millions more of the strong, like Paul.

Where was God in all this? As she had done earlier, she felt a terrible sense that she was spinning alone in a great void.

And then there was beautiful Edna. It was really hard on her. No husband, no father, no child.

In response to her mother's cry, Celia said simply, 'Yes,

the boys would have helped. They were the nicest brothers any girl could have.' Her small frame trembled with her efforts to contain her own grief, to attend only to what she was doing, and, above all, not to panic.

She decided to leave until the next evening the question of what furniture they should take with them and what should be sold; to go through it all would take hours, possibly days, and she had a feeling that her mother would defend every bit of it from the horrors of its being sent to the auction room; yet much of it was so large that the removal men would never get it through the cottage's front door, never mind up the narrow staircase.

She tucked her grieving mother up in her bed and told her to try not to worry about anything; she would feel stronger in the morning. Then she went slowly down to the basement kitchen.

She found all three servants, themselves tired out by the unusual day, sitting quietly round the fire, drinking cups of cocoa before going to bed. Their conversation stopped immediately she opened the door. They put their mugs down on top of the fender and stood up.

Celia was embarrassed at having intruded on them at an hour in their long day which was one of the few they had of their own. She said shyly, 'I'm sorry to disturb you.'

Then she quickly went on to ask if, the following morning, Winnie and Dorothy would put together some basic cleaning materials that would be needed at the cottage. 'There's an old straw trunk in the attic,' she told Dorothy. 'We could put everything into it. If the leather straps have rotted, you could cord it up.'

Though resentment welled within her, Dorothy said, 'Yes, Miss,' in her usual dull fashion. She did not want to do anything more, once she had cleared Miss Celia's dinner things from the dining room. Now she would have to go all the way up to the top of the house and root around the dusty attics to find the trunk Miss Celia meant – she would never have the time in the morning. Yet Miss Celia looked so ghastly that she could feel only pity for her.

As Dorothy hunted through the contents of the house's enormous attics for the straw trunk, Celia crouched by the dying fire in the morning room, and planned exactly how she would manage the next day. 'To begin with, I'll send Ethel down to the stables to order a taxicab to take us to Central Station to catch the electric train,' she decided. 'Though it will be more expensive, it will be quicker than going by bus.'

'Miss Celia looks real ill,' Dorothy opined to Winnie, as early the next morning, they packed clean rags, a bucket and ewer, soap, scouring powder, rust remover, a bottle of oil for hinges, black lead for the fireplaces, a big black bottle of pine disinfectant, broom heads, and a dustpan with its appropriate hand brushes.

After they had corded up the trunk, they slipped a couple of the brooms' handles under the rope, so that the whole bundle could be carried between them.

'Oh, aye,' Winnie agreed in response to Dorothy's remark. 'It's all too much for her – what with Mrs Woodcock's baby, and now Miss Edna. I'm going to pack you both a lunch and you take care of her, Doll, and make sure she eats.'

She turned to Ethel, who was wearily working her way through the washing up of the breakfast dishes. 'Ethel, luv. Go down to the cellar and look on the tool shelf. I'd better put in a hammer and nails and some screws and screwdrivers – and a pair of pliers. Bring up what you can find.'

'Holy Mary, Winnie! What are we supposed to be doing out there? Rebuilding the place?' Dorothy interjected. 'I'm not going to undo all them knots, so we can add tools to that lot.'

'Don't be daft. I'll put them in the little shopping basket. But a place what has been empty so long is sure to lack a nail or two, and there's no man to be putting them in for her. She'll have to learn to do it herself.'

Celia took her mother's breakfast tray up to her bedroom, since Dorothy was packing the straw trunk.

Immediately she had wakened her and had drawn back the thick velvet curtains, she asked Louise, 'Could I have a little money from the housekeeping, Mama, please? For the fares and anything extra Dorothy may need for the cottage.'

She had never asked her mother for money before and she hardly knew how to phrase the request. She had received three shillings a month as pin money from her father, the same amount as Ethel earned, and she still had the current month's payment in her locked dressing-table drawer. In view of their sudden straitened circumstances, she had earlier been conscience-smitten as to whether she should give it to her mother or keep it. Then she had been caught up in a fear of making a mistake during the difficult days ahead. Suppose I get off at the wrong station, she had agonised – or get on the wrong train. If I have no money of my own, I won't have a hope of sorting myself out, of being able to buy another ticket or take a bus. I'm so stupid.

Her mother rubbed the sleep out of her eyes and looked at her daughter doubtfully. She sighed, as she said, 'Celia, I'm so tired. I hope we'll be able to manage.' Then she looked about her bewilderedly before telling her daughter, 'Bring my cash box to me – it's in the centre cupboard of the dressing table.'

It was quite a heavy seventeenth-century mahogany box, originally meant to house a Bible, and Celia lifted it with care on to her mother's lap. As Louise sleepily fumbled for her keys in her dressing-gown pocket, Celia stroked the polished wood and said, 'I've always thought what a lovely box this is.'

'Humph. I brought it with me when I married your father – like a lot of the furniture in this house, it came from my grandfather's home.'

Her mother paused to yawn, and then realising that Celia was interested, she went on, her voice still heavy with sleep, 'My grandfather was a widower for years. He lived alone, except for a couple of servants to care for him.

'As you may remember, Felicity and I were the only children left, after my brother died in India, so, on my own marriage, my parents, in their turn, were left alone in a large and very empty house. My grandpa was getting very frail by that time, and he gave up his home and came to live with them.'

She yawned again, as she opened the box and scrabbled about in it. 'Grandpa was very fond of me and he told me I could have anything I wanted of his furniture, provided my mother did not want it.' She looked up at her daughter, and smiled at the recollection. 'Mother thought the stuff was dreadfully old-fashioned, but I was young and I thought it was very fine and delicate-looking – and dear Timothy, your father, though he had an excellent pedigree, didn't have much money when we were first married, so we were both grateful for the offer.' Her mouth quivered as she mentioned her late husband. Then she swallowed, and after a moment, continued, 'Later on, we had everything reupholstered and refinished.

'Then when your other grandfather died, he left us his picture collection, as you may possibly remember. I think the pictures are rather gloomy, but your father liked them, so, of course, we found space for them.'

Celia glanced round the bedroom. 'You always did have lovely taste, Mama. And you mean to say that all this stuff goes back to Georgian times – the Regency? That it is all antique?'

Her mother glanced up from her box. She was pleased by Celia's unexpected compliment. 'I suppose it is. It's certainly very old indeed. But it has been well looked after.' She picked out a note. 'Here is a five-pound note, dear. It's a lot of money. Don't lose it, and don't spend what you don't have to. But I imagine you may have to pay Mr Aspen something on account.'

'I'll be careful, Mama.' She folded the note and stowed it in her own deep skirt pocket. 'Do you have any small change, Mama – for tips? For porters. Edna's bound to have a lot of luggage. And Dorothy and I have to carry all the cleaning stuff out to the cottage. I think that, at Meols Station, I will have to get a porter to help.'

'Yes.' Her mother took her change purse from under her pillow; Celia had crocheted it for her as a Christmas present, because one could no longer buy such a purse in the shops – housewives now used leather ones. She pulled back the rings of it, to delve amid the sovereigns in the pocket at each end, and finally gave Celia some silver sixpences.

Celia's hand automatically closed on the coins, but she did not thank her mother. Her mind was elsewhere. 'You know, Mama,' she said thoughtfully, 'we shall have to sell a lot of furniture, because we have far too much for the cottage.'

'I know. Don't remind me.' Louise's voice was suddenly full of reproach, as if it were Celia's fault that her well-kept furniture would have to go.

'Some of it may be more valuable than we know. Do you know anybody who could say what it is worth?'

'Celia, you really do have the most dreadful ideas. How can I take someone I know round the house to ask them that?' There was a hint of a sob in her voice, as she complained, 'It is bad enough that I will have to let that dreadful estate agent take perfect strangers round the house.'

'Sorry, Mama.' Celia was too exhausted to follow up the subject further. She herself longed to crawl back into bed and simply rest. But then there would be nobody to look after Mama or Edna.

She lifted the cash box off her mother's knees and put it back where she had found it. Then she said, 'Perhaps, tomorrow, Mama, when you are less tired, you could look round the house and see what you want to keep. Remember how small the rooms of the cottage are.'

Louise lay back on her pillows and pulled the bedding up round her chin. 'I'm not likely to forget it,' she responded huffily.

Celia bent and kissed her and went thoughtfully downstairs to have her breakfast. For the first time in years, she really looked at the furnishings of the upper and lower halls and the staircase. Two huge chests of drawers on the first-floor landing, each with an oil painting carefully centred above it; three charming watercolours on the staircase wall; and, in the front hall, two Russell engravings, six chairs, a large hall table, two occasional tables, a hope chest, a barometer, a large hat stand, innumerable vases, candlesticks, trays, a fireplace complete with brass pokers, in one corner a huge china pot with drooping dyed seed pods in it, a brass gong on a stand – and, near the front door, a grandfather clock, which showed the times of sunrise and sunset, and struck the quarter-hours as well as the hours. And of course the carpets – they, also, were probably valuable.

There was enough furniture in the halls alone to fill the biggest room in the cottage chock-a-block, she realised with a sense of shock.

Before entering the dining room to ring the bell for her breakfast to be brought up, she paused and smiled at the beautiful old face of the clock. It had been her friend ever since she could remember; its firm sprightly striking had comforted her through nights when she had lain terrified in her bed or had been shut in her room by angry parents; it reminded her when she was supposed to do her routine tasks of the day, and now, suddenly, it reminded her of her stiff, unbending father carefully winding it up each Sunday morning. He, too, had loved that clock, she guessed – the thought made him suddenly more human to her.

She smiled again. She must remember to wind it on Sunday. She would never part with it, she decided. It might just fit into the back of the hall in the cottage. She must take a tape measure to see if there was room. And she had better take pencil and paper to write down the measurements of the rooms. And a big apron to protect her tailored skirt from the dust.

I'll never manage to remember everything, she told herself hopelessly, as she went to the side of the dining-room fireplace to pull the bell rope again. Dorothy was slow in answering this morning.

I've never had to remember so much in my life. I've just done exactly what I was told to do – no more, no less – bits of things, and be reminded about them – like Dorothy. Only, Dorothy knows more than I do.

As Dorothy rushed into the dining room with the breakfast tray, Celia seated herself at the huge table, and the harassed maid dumped the tray in front of her.

Dorothy stood back, panting a little, as she said, 'Ethel didn't have time to light the fire in here this morning, Miss. What with me getting ready to go to Meols, like – and she having to run down to the stables to order the taxicab for you. She done the one in the breakfast room, though – ready for the Missus getting up.'

Celia assured her that it was quite a warm morning, but that she should ask Ethel to have a good fire in Miss Edna's bedroom by evening. 'Could she manage to clean the room?'

'Oh, aye. She's quite smart, is Ethel. Which room would it be, Miss?'

'Of course! You never knew my sister, did you? The back bedroom with the roses on the walls was always her room. The room we put Mr Albert Gilmore in when he was here. Ask Mrs Gilmore what bedding to use.'

'Yes, Miss. I'm to be ready in half an hour, Miss?'

Celia was cracking her boiled egg. She did not want it, but she knew she must eat something. 'Yes, please,' she replied mechanically to Dorothy's question, and then she asked, 'Have you had your breakfast?'

Dorothy was grateful for the unexpected inquiry. 'Oh, aye. Had it an hour ago, at six o'clock.' She smiled, as she went out of the room. She was certain that the Missus would never have bothered to ask such a question.

Chapter Sixteen

❧

Dorothy had been both excited and scared to find herself riding in a taxicab, a mechanically propelled vehicle which actually did not need a horse to pull it! She had seen cars and lorries in the town – but to be really riding in a car was a thrill indeed. She had never crossed the river by anything but a ferryboat before, and it was with similar excitement that she trotted beside Celia down a long passage and steep staircase to the underground electric train. She was glad that she had agreed to accompany Celia. What a wonderful morning!

The guard stored the clumsy trunk in the guard's van at the back of the train, and, when they had to change to the steam train at Birkenhead Park, he called a porter to transfer the trunk to the other guard. Celia shyly parted with sixpences as tips and all the men looked quite happy.

At Meols, the porter was busy with a series of first-class passengers and took no notice of their beckoning fingers. So, between them, they lugged the straw trunk down the long sandy lane from the station to the cottage, and thankfully dropped it on the doorstep. They were giggling and gasping like two schoolgirls who had been racing each other.

'I bet we been quicker than waiting for that porter to finish with the snobs,' Dorothy said unthinkingly, as Celia found the key for the door.

Celia smiled to herself; she had bought third-class tickets for the sake of economy; they had always gone first class when her father was alive. Was one really a snob if one bought first-class tickets? she wondered.

As they inspected the ground floor of the interior of the cottage, Dorothy followed Celia very closely and very quietly. It was Dorothy's opinion that one should be careful of ghosts in a house left long empty. They did not, however, seem to disturb anybody – or anything.

They slowly climbed the stairs and went into the front bedroom, which was about as big as Louise's dressing room in her present home.

Dorothy folded her arms across her stomach and considered the grubby, forlorn-looking little room. Her nose wrinkled. 'Where'll I start, Miss?'

Celia laughed, but it was not a happy laugh. 'I don't know, Dorothy,' she admitted. 'I must go into the village to see a man who does repairs, and try to find a sweep to sweep the chimneys. So don't bother about cleaning windows today – the sweep is bound to spread soot, no matter how good he is.' She looked around the stuffy room, and said, 'I noticed, as we came in, that Mr Billings has had the glass replaced in the single room over the hall – and he's taken the boarding down from the downstairs windows – so at least you can see to work.'

'Suppose I start with all the hearths, Miss – get them clear so the sweep can work,' Dorothy suggested, as she slowly drew the hatpins out of her big black hat. 'Then I could give the whole place a good sweep with the hard broom we brought. Get rid of the litter, like?'

Celia gratefully agreed to these suggestions. 'The single bedroom doesn't have a fireplace, so you could clean that room thoroughly. If the linoleum on the floor looks very damp, you could pull it up in strips and throw it out; I think we shall have to buy new. Then scrub the wooden floor underneath with disinfectant. When it dries we can see if we have to replace the planking.'

As they moved out of the bedroom and down the precipitous little staircase, Dorothy nodded. 'You said the pump didn't work. Where would I get water, Miss?'

'I'm going to ask Mr Fairbanks, next door, if you could draw a few bucketfuls from his pump.' She sighed. 'That's another person I have to find – someone who will say whether the well is usable – and will mend the pump.'

Since there was no clean place on which to lay it, Dorothy stuck her hat back on her head, rather than putting it on the hall floor while she struggled with the knots of the rope round the trunk. She laid the broom handles on one side, and pulled off the lid. Very carefully, she took out a neat brown paper parcel and handed it to Celia. She smiled up at her, and announced, 'Lunch!'

The deep lid of the trunk made a clean receptacle in which to deposit hats, coats, gloves, purses and the precious food. Both of them shook out the sackcloth aprons, which lay on top of the cleaning materials, and wrapped them round their black skirts.

They looked at each other, and, for no particular reason, they laughed. 'We look as if we're going hop-picking,' remarked Dorothy. She was glad to see Celia laugh, and she said, 'Would you like to go and see the fella next door about water, while I begin on the living-room fireplace?'

Celia agreed.

Feeling very shy, she walked down the tiled path, the sand squeaking under her boots, round the high privet hedge with its new green buds, to Mr Fairbanks' nicely varnished front gate. Before opening it and entering the garden, she hesitated nervously, and then, before her courage failed her, she unlatched it and hurried up the path.

She knocked timidly at his black-enamelled front door. As she looked at it, she wondered if she would ever reduce next door to comparable orderliness.

From his front room window, Eddie Fairbanks had seen her coming, so the door was opened immediately, and she was greeted like an old friend. In her sackcloth apron, she looked even smaller and frailer than when he had first seen her, and he said warmly, 'Come in, Miss. The wind's cold this morning.'

As he led her into the cosy back room which she remembered from her previous visit, and sat her down in the same nursing chair, she was shivering, partly from chill and partly because she had to deal with a man alone in the privacy of his own home.

While she settled herself in the chair, he turned the hob with its black kettle on it over the fire. 'Will you be having some tea with me?' he asked.

His amiability gave her confidence. She smiled quite sweetly at him, and said not just now, because she had to set the maid to work and then go to Hoylake and from there to Liverpool to meet her sister, who was coming up from Southampton. And would he be so kind as to let her maid draw some water from his kitchen?

'Oh, aye. When she's ready for it, she should come and tell me, and I'll carry it in for her. Would she be liking some tea?'

'I'm sure she would. She had her breakfast awfully early.' What an old dear he was, she considered, as he looked kindly down on her. She stopped shivering.

While weighing her up, he rested his shoulder against the mantelpiece and waited for the kettle to start singing. She looked so careworn that he said cautiously, not wanting to offend her, 'I think – I think you'd better have a cuppa before you go to Hoylake, Miss. While I make it, you go and tell your maid what you want done and that she's to come over when she wants some water. Then both of you come and have a quick cup. How about that?'

She hesitated, and then said, 'Very well. You are most kind.' She found it strange to be treated with consideration – only harried Phyllis seemed to treat her similarly – or Winnie, when Louise was out.

When she told Dorothy about the invitation, Dorothy

said promptly, as she continued to rake out the cinders and ashes from the front room fireplace, 'That'd be nice. But you open that lunch right now and eat some of it – sandwiches – because otherwise you won't have time.'

It seemed odd to be given an order by the house-parlourmaid; Winnie was the only servant who had ever ventured advice, and she usually addressed herself to Louise.

Celia took out a sandwich and hastily consumed it. As she brushed the crumbs off her black blouse, Dorothy got up from her knees to take the bucket of ashes outside, and said, 'There's a packet of biscuits. You take it and you can eat them on the train, to keep you going. There's lots else for me.'

'Are you sure?'

Dorothy grinned at her. 'Winnie told me that I had to see that you eat – so you better had, or I'll be in trouble.'

'That's very nice of both of you.'

There was something quite different about this morning, she considered, as the pair of them tramped round to Eddie's house. I am not only doing different things, but people are behaving differently, too. This thought stayed with her as, twenty minutes later, she set out for Hoylake.

She had been armed by Eddie Fairbanks with the name of a sweep, which would save her time hunting about when she reached Hoylake village. 'Go and see this chap before you go to see Ben Aspen,' he advised. 'Ben'll keep you talking for hours, if you don't watch. If you tell him you must catch a train, it will help to stop the flow!'

She smiled, as she hurried through the sandy lane and then on to the tarmac main road. Ben Aspen must be quite a well-known character.

Chapter Seventeen

❧

While en route to the sweep's house, she found the notice board of a plumber on a cottage gate. A plumber might know about wells and pumps, she thought, and promptly knocked on his door.

At both his house and that of the sweep she found herself dealing with their wives. Both of them laboriously wrote down with the nub of a pencil on a scrap of paper her name, her address and the address of the cottage.

Once the plumber's wife had taken the address of the cottage, she said, in surprise at Celia's request that her husband should look at a well and a pump, 'There's mains water down there. What you need is to have it connected and turned on, and have a modern set of taps put in. And there was a sewer laid down as well, as I remember.'

Celia was doubtful that a woman would know about waterlines, so she responded, 'Mother only said it had a well.'

'Well, I never! Well, let Billy come and look at it for you. Tomorrow morning, aye?'

As she turned away from the door, Celia was suddenly wild with hope. If the woman was right, a colossal load of work would be saved. With running water, they could have a water closet – if there were drains nearby, of course – and even, perhaps, a bath with taps. That would make Mother happier, though it might cost a great deal.

I don't care what it costs, she thought. I really don't want to spend my life carrying big ewers of water up and down stairs for Mother's bath. I don't want to try to keep a stinking earthen lavatory from smelling because she will perpetually complain about it – or even one with a bucket, which has to be emptied and the contents buried each day; I doubt if I have the strength even to dig a hole.

She had rarely felt such a strong sense of revolt – but as her father's affairs had been dealt with, she had watched with growing apprehension. Because Cousin Albert had left Louise alone, to deal with her domestic affairs, and Louise had done nothing, all the responsibility was being pushed on to herself. There was no one else, now Paul had been taken by the flu – and to the best of her limited ability, partly out of a sense of self-preservation, she was indeed tackling the situation.

As she waited for the sweep's wife to answer her knock, she felt angrily that it was not that her mother was truly incapable – the birth of little Timothy George had proved that she had plenty of energy, despite her bereavement, when she was interested enough to use it.

The sweep's wife, a waif with a baby at her breast, promised that her Henry would be there that afternoon. She kindly directed Celia to Mr Aspen's domain across the railway bridge at Hoylake Station. 'And follow the lane, like you was goin' back to Meols. You can't miss it.'

Hanging on to her hat, Celia battled her way up Market Street against a salt-laden breeze, climbed the pedestrian bridge over the railway, and turned into a country lane where a freshly green hawthorn hedge, curved landwards by the sea winds, sheltered a few violets and one or two primroses.

A few more minutes' walk took her to a fenced compound with two huge gates which were wide open. To her left, just past the open gate, lay a small shed marked OFFICE.

Celia had never in her life faced, alone, so many strangers in one day, and she was surprised and relieved to find herself again talking to a woman instead of to Ben Aspen himself.

Behind the office counter stood a handsome, fair-haired woman about her own age. Her snow-white blouse with its black bow tie made her look plumper than she probably was. Her tanned rosy face was surrounded by carefully arranged tendrils of golden hair; the remainder was swept into a large bun at the nape of her neck and secured by a big black bow of ribbon.

On seeing Celia, a pair of cobalt-blue eyes twinkled amiably, and the woman picked up a pen and dipped it into a bottle of ink. She held the pen poised, ready to write, as she asked, 'Can I help you?'

Celia explained her business, that she had been sent by Mr Billings and needed some painting and small repairs done to a cottage.

'Me dad's got someone with him, but if you'd like to have a seat there, I'll go and tell him you're waiting.'

She went outside, and, as Celia sat gingerly down on a dusty bench, she heard her calling across the yard to her father. Through the office door, she observed stacks of wood in neat piles, wheelbarrows and ladders, sacks and boxes the contents of which she could only guess at, a mountain of discarded old bricks and rolls of tar paper.

Near to the office door stood a car and by it lay a big tarpaulin, as if it had just been removed from the vehicle. Though the car was dusty, the sunlight caught its brass and black enamel and made it look new. A boy about eight years old wandered in through the gate, and surveyed it. With great care, he drew a round smiling face in the dust on the door.

'Alfie! Leave it alone!' shrieked the lady clerk, as she came running back to the office. 'You know you mustn't touch anything in Grandpa's yard. Come here! Better not let Grandpa see you near that.'

She turned to Celia as she came up the office step. 'I'm

sorry, Miss. Father won't be a minute. They was just getting the car out of the barn before you came. They want to sell it.' She paused before entering the office, to look at the car, her expression stricken. 'Me hubby built it,' she explained. 'He loved mechanical things.'

Celia nodded and said, 'He must be a brilliant mechanic.' Then she added shyly, 'I'll only take a few minutes of Mr Aspen's time.'

The boy had followed his mother into the office. He paused to stare at Celia. She smiled at him and, after a moment, he grinned back. 'Have you just come from school?' she asked, trying hard to appear friendly.

He nodded. 'I come to have me dinner with Granddad and Mum.'

His mother seemed a little confused by this baring of her domestic arrangements, and said sharply, 'Now, Alfie, don't you go bothering the lady. Go in the back room and start your dinner. I'll be with you in a minute.'

As the boy wandered round the counter and disappeared through a doorway, his mother said to Celia, 'Me dad's short of men at the moment, Miss. So I'm filling in in the office.'

'That's very clever of you,' Celia replied with genuine admiration.

'Well, needs must. I learned a lot from me hubby. He was me dad's clerk of works, and he always kept the books and did the estimating and ordering for Dad – he could estimate, real accurate – he were a first-class builder's clerk. That's how I met him, 'cos he was working for Dad.' She paused, and to Celia she suddenly looked old. She said flatly, 'He died at Messines Ridge in 1917.'

'Oh, how terrible!'

'I thought I'd die myself,' the woman admitted baldly. 'But I'd got young Alfred to think of – and me dad needed help – working for him has kept me going. Dad wants Alfie to have the business when he retires. It does mean that

Dad'll have to continue to work a lot longer than he would've done though.'

Celia's heart went out to the woman. She said compassionately, 'You have my deepest sympathy.' Then, feeling that her remark was too formal, she added, 'I think you are being very brave.'

The woman made a wry face. 'There's a lot like me. You're not married?'

'Me? Goodness me, no.' Celia shrugged her shoulders and made a small deprecating gesture with one hand. 'We did lose George, though, at Scapa Flow, and Tom in France – they were my brothers.' She looked down, and then out at Ben Aspen who was coming across the yard. 'I do miss them,' she said sadly. She turned her eyes back to the clerk, who was knocking sheets of paper into a neat pile on the desk. 'But it's not like losing a husband, I am sure.'

'I don't know, Miss. It seems as if everybody lost someone, doesn't it? And I worry about Alfred growing up without a dad – though his grandpa keeps him in line.'

'I am sure you do worry.' Celia rose from her dusty bench, as Mr Aspen himself came up the step, and took off his bowler hat.

Celia's first thought was that she had never seen quite such a huge white beard – it stuck wildly out in all directions, nearly obliterating the old man's face. A red nose peeped through an unkempt moustache. Huge white eyebrows bristled above eyes identical to those of his daughter. A pair of very red ears made brackets round the whole. He wore a brown velvet waistcoat over a striped shirt, and his baggy trousers were held in at the knee by pieces of string tied round them.

His voice was very deep, like that of a younger man. 'You wanted some repairs, Ma'am? Betty here said Mr Billings sent you?'

Very diffidently, afraid she might make a fool of herself, Celia explained that she needed someone capable to look over the cottage to see what repairs were necessary – chimneys, downpipes, etc. The structure needed its external woodwork painting, and, in addition, she went on bravely, she would like to know what it would cost to paint the interior – just plain white would do – something inexpensive.

Ben scratched his bird's nest of a beard and looked her over. Not much money, he deduced – but a lady. 'You know Eddie Fairbanks, by any chance?' he asked. 'He lives in a cottage, which I think is the one next to yours.'

'He's the tenant of the other house – they are semi-detached. Mama and I met him when we went over our house earlier this week.'

She waited, while he thought. He said finally, 'Oh, aye, I know the property all right, though I've not been down there for a while. Trouble is I'm short of skilled men, especially them as can estimate.' He turned to Betty, who had stood quietly by her counter, while he dealt with Celia. 'Do you think you could take a look, Bet, and do the estimate? I can tell you what to look for.'

Betty's expression which had been rather sombre lifted considerably. She smiled at Celia, and said, 'I think so. When would you like me to come?'

'Tomorrow afternoon? I've a plumber coming in the morning.'

'We're not usually open Saturday afternoon. But in the morning, you could talk to the plumber while I go round the place. I wouldn't be able to give you a price until I've had a chance to work it out, anyway – it would be Monday for that.'

Considering his reputation for talk, Ben Aspen was quite quiet. He confirmed Betty's promise of a price by Monday, and, as Celia left him, politely said good afternoon to her.

As she turned at the bottom of the office steps, she saw him go through the office, presumably to join his grandson for lunch. She heard him say heavily, 'I'm sorry to sell the car, Bet. But we'll never use it – and it'll deteriorate. It's already sat there five years.'

Before she went out through the great gates which opened on to the lane, Celia stopped to put on her gloves, and looked back into the builder's yard. The car gleamed outside the office door, but her eyes were on the barn at the back of the yard.

Its doors had been flung wide open and a boy was slowly sweeping it out – it looked as if it had a stone floor. It must have belonged to a farm at one point, she deduced. It looked weather-beaten, but the car which Betty said had been in it showed no sign of rust, so it must be fairly watertight.

There was plenty of time before the arrival of the train for Liverpool, so she walked leisurely back to the railway station. She found herself enjoying the country view. To her left, she looked out over a small ploughed field. Beyond it was open land, incredibly green already, leading her eyes to misty, low hills. She basked in the quietness, broken only by the distant sound of sawing from the direction of Ben Aspen's yard and the chatter of sparrows in the hedges. She felt relaxed, at peace, for the first time since her father's death.

At the sight of the railway station, she was quickly brought back to the fact that she had another onerous task to fulfil, before she considered anything else, and she dreaded it. She must meet her elder sister at Lime Street Station. More grief. More comforting to be done.

She thrust other considerations out of her mind, while she went into the little red brick station to buy a train ticket to Liverpool.

She and Edna had never been very close. Edna had been sent as a boarder to a finishing school. After she was twelve, Celia had been withdrawn from Miss Ecclestone's Day

School for Young Ladies to help her mother at home, her place in life already decided upon by her parents. The explanation given to the little girl was that she could not learn much more at Miss Ecclestone's and that she was too delicate to be sent away from home. The fact that she and Edna had gone through the usual cycles of ill health together did not occur to the child – they both had had chickenpox, measles, mumps and the dreaded scarlet fever at about the same time, when these diseases swept through the neighbourhood. Influenza, colds and gastritis had struck both of them no more than other children.

The very idea that she was delicate, something wrong with her, something that her parents had not divulged to her, still fed her panic attacks as she grew older.

At the finishing school, Edna had learned to dance and to paint with watercolours, to deport herself with dignity and some grace, to play the piano and to make polite conversation. She had learned a smattering of French, and more arithmetic, history and geography than Celia had. She copied the attitude of her mother towards Celia, regarding her as stupid, disobedient to their parents, an irritating younger sister who was always crying about something.

At the coming-out dance which her mother arranged for her, Edna met Paul Fellowes, the son of one of her father's friends. He was a self-assured, handsome man ten years older than she was and already well established in his father's company. Six months later, she became that magical person whom every girl dreamed of, a fiancée with a diamond ring on her finger. She flaunted the ring at every opportunity as a symbol of her supreme success.

After a two-year engagement, which both the Fellowes and the Gilmores felt was a respectable length of time, in 1912 Celia found herself, as chief bridesmaid, walking behind her sister up the aisle of the Church of St Mary the Virgin amid a gaggle of other young women, all giggling behind their bouquets of yellow roses and maidenhair ferns.

She was so consumed by jealousy of her sister's success that she was incapable of enjoying the ceremony or the reception at their house afterwards, and, for some time, she was referred to by those who had been present as 'that sulky sister of Edna Fellowes'.

For months, Celia pestered her mother about when she would give a coming-out party for her. There was, however, always some reason why it could not be done, the final argument being, towards the end of 1914, that so many families were in mourning that it would be inappropriate to give such a party while the war lasted. A crushed Celia conceded defeat.

As she sat in the Liverpool train, Celia remembered all this. She wondered how she would feel when she met her sister. Edna's experiences were so different from her own.

At least I'm not jealous any more, she considered with a faint smile. Edna lost her little Rosemary and now she's lost her husband. I need a sister at the moment and, other than Mother, I must be the only person in the world who really does need her.

She hoped wistfully that sophisticated, elegant Edna would be as brave as Betty appeared to be. It would certainly help.

Chapter Eighteen

❧

When, at Birkenhead Park, Celia changed from the cosy warmth of the steam train to an unheated electric train, she helped a young woman with two tiny children on to the latter, and the shivers of the children led to a polite conversation. The little family reminded her of Phyllis, who was far more of a sister to her than Edna had ever been, and of new-born Timothy George. Her morning had been so full that she had given no thought to the struggle her friend was probably having.

I should go this evening to see how they are, she reminded herself. With Edna to care for, however, and her mother's probable complaints about her desertion of her during the day, it seemed doubtful if she would get the opportunity.

She sighed. Though she felt she had done quite well that morning, it had tired her. She had made an enormous effort to express clearly and concisely to the people she had met exactly what she wanted them to do; now she prayed that the hope of tap water that the plumber's wife had given her would be realised.

I hope everything works, she thought anxiously. That the sweep and the plumber will come, as promised, that Dorothy and Mr Fairbanks got along together, and that Mr Aspen's daughter gives me a modest estimate.

Her eyelids drooped with fatigue and, as the electric train sped through the tunnel, she began to doze.

She awoke when the train stopped at Central Station

with its usual sudden jerk, and the lady with the children smiled and said she hoped she felt better after such a nice nap.

A little bewildered, Celia helped her fellow travellers on to the platform, and then quietly followed them out of the station, up steep stairs and sloping passages until she found herself at street level.

She paused uncertainly at the station gate. Outside it, heavy drays lumbered past her, interspersed with cars driven by chauffeurs. Innumerable cyclists and pedestrians darted in and out between them.

'Are you lost, duck?'

Celia jumped. Leaning against the stone gatepost of the station lounged a woman with a highly painted face beneath a purple veil draped round a purple hat.

A fallen woman! No one, except actresses and fallen women, made up their faces. Disconcerted, Celia simply looked at her.

The woman laughed. 'Are you lost?' she inquired again.

Celia swallowed, and said in a small scared voice, 'I have to go to Lime Street Station, and I am not quite sure where it lies from here.'

The woman took her by the elbow and pointed her in the right direction. 'Go up here and turn left. Five minutes' walk. You'll find it.'

Losing some of her fear, Celia said politely but shyly, 'Thank you very much.'

The woman laughed again. 'Go on with you, luv. You're a nice girl. You shouldn't be hanging around here.' She gave Celia a little push, then leaned back against her pillar again.

Somewhat shaken, Celia took the route indicated. Amid the hurrying, indifferent crowd of pedestrians, she felt vulnerable and afraid. She had never walked alone in the city centre before and the fact that a fallen woman, as she called her, had actually addressed her had unnerved her.

It was with relief that she reached the huge entrance of Lime Street Station. Here she had, once more, to stiffen her resolve before she could waylay a porter to ask which platform the train from London would arrive at.

Without stopping his rapid scuttle towards a train already in, he told her. When she went to the platform that he had indicated, her entrance was barred by a ponderous, bewhiskered ticket inspector, who demanded her ticket.

Flushing nervously, she told him she was meeting her sister travelling on the train.

'You need a platform ticket, Miss – or you could wait here for her.'

'Where would I purchase a ticket?'

The man looked down at her superciliously as if she were sorely lacking mentally, and said, 'At the ticket office, of course – or from the machine over there.' He pointed to a red-painted machine against the far wall.

Confused and flustered, she looked at the machine and decided that modern machinery would be too much to face, and she went to the ticket office, where, for one penny, she received a grubby grey ticket. The porter at the gate gravely punched a hole in it and gave it back to her. She walked through to the platform and began to calm down.

The train was just coming in.

Hoping to find good tippers, porters were running beside the first-class carriages ready to help with luggage. People meeting the train engulfed Celia, who, being small, was soon elbowed away from the train itself. Doors swung open. Men and women descended and were captured by porters, some of whom had trolleys on which to transfer steamer trunks carried in the luggage van at the rear of the train.

At the back of the crowd, Celia sought frantically for Edna, hoping to see her standing in the doorway of one of the carriages. She stood on tiptoe, and a man's voice behind her said, 'Wait for a minute or two, Ma'am, and the crowd will clear.'

She turned, and nearly knocked a man off his crutches. His blue hospital uniform failed to disguise his fragile thinness. Not much taller than she was, incapacitated by his crutches, he certainly did not need to be pushed and shoved by a thoughtless crowd.

Celia conjured up a smile for him, and stepped to the side of him, as she replied, 'That sounds very sensible. I am looking for my sister.'

'I come out to meet me mate. He's bein' discharged from a military hospital in London – they can't do nothing more for him.'

Celia's sympathy was immediately aroused. 'Is he very badly hurt?' she asked.

'Well, they've patched him up, he says. His shoulder were smashed and he lost an ear as well. A bit scarred and his hearing'll never be the same. And he can't use what's left of his right arm.' The man's expression was suddenly bleak, and Celia realised that he was much younger than he had first appeared to be. Eighteen or nineteen, she guessed.

'And you?' Her tone was gentle.

'Me?' He looked down at his crutches. 'I'll be throwing these away soon, I hope. They say I'll limp always. But I'll be able to walk, thanks be.'

'Good. Where did you serve?'

'Messpot, Ma'am.'

Mesopotamia. Another place of death, another name for sorrow nowadays. 'I'm glad you got back here safely,' Celia said with feeling.

'Thank you, Ma'am.'

As the wounded man had forecast, the crowd was, indeed, thinning. When a large trolley of luggage was pushed away by a straining porter, a tall, elegant woman in black with a black veil over her face was suddenly revealed. She gestured imperiously to a porter, who came to her immediately.

Celia had not expected to have difficulty in recognising Edna. It had not occurred to her that almost every woman on the train would be dressed in mourning and that a number of them would be veiled. The gesture to the porter was so completely Edna, however, that she smiled again at the wounded soldier, said she hoped he would find his friend, and pushed her way purposefully through a loose group of children, her normal diffident good manners forgotten, in her fear of missing her sister.

'Edna,' she called and ran the last few steps towards her.

Edna said to the porter, 'I have luggage in the van.' Then, at the sound of Celia's voice, she swung round and said, 'Oh, Celia! Where's Mother?'

Celia stopped. How do you kiss somebody with a thick veil over her face, when no attempt is made to lift it and greet you?

Edna settled it by saying, 'We have to go down to the luggage van. I have three trunks.' The porter turned his trolley and walked briskly towards the end of the train, followed by Edna. Nonplussed, Celia dodged between passengers going the other way, and followed her.

The porter was given Edna's name and climbed into the van to search for her luggage. Edna turned back to Celia. 'You didn't answer me. Where's Mother? Is she ill?'

Bewildered and hurt by her sister's indifference, Celia straightened her hat, which had been knocked awry during her struggle in the crowd. Before she answered, she had to search for words.

'Mother is not feeling very well, as you can imagine,' she managed to say. 'We are having difficulties about Father's estate, and she had to go to the bank this morning. So I volunteered to meet you.' She tried to smile at the veil.

'I see. I would have imagined that a bereaved daughter was more important than a bank.' She called up to the porter in the van. 'Not that one – the green leather one behind it.'

Celia began to tremble. The fear of a panic attack, there on the station, almost brought one on. Edna was right, of course. She was more important – but the situation was hard to explain in one or two words on a busy station.

She took a big breath, while Edna scolded the porter for not lowering the expensive trunk down on to the platform more carefully. Then she said, 'Well, things have been terribly complicated for Mother and me. I'll explain it all when we are in the taxi.' At the same time the train made a big chuffing sound, as it prepared to reverse itself away from the platform.

'What did you say?' Edna asked, her voice like a schoolmistress demanding a response from a mumbling child.

Celia made another effort and repeated her remark. A second and a third trunk were added to the first, with sharp admonitions to the porter to be careful. Then Edna ordered the long-suffering man to find them a taxi, which he did.

After he had heaved two trunks on to the luggage platform beside the taxi driver, the porter pushed the third trunk into the wide passenger section. Because Edna was fiddling for change in her handbag, he gave Edna's hat box and small jewel case to Celia to hold.

Edna pressed some change into his hand. He touched his cap and said resignedly, 'Thank you, Ma'am.' Celia guessed that she had not tipped him enough. He then held the taxi door open so that the ladies could step in.

As the taxi jerked forward, Edna gave the driver her mother's address. Celia closed her tired eyes. She hoped her Mother would not be hurt by Edna's distant manner.

Edna settled herself in her seat and threw back her veil. Celia felt the tiny movement and opened her eyes. She half-turned to look at her sister.

She was shocked.

A gaunt, yellow visage had been revealed. The hazel eyes,

though still quite beautiful, were sunken in black sockets, the chin was long and bony, like their father's had been. The skin was yellow and wrinkled, like that of a much older person. Deep lines between the heavy black eyebrows added to the woman's general air of irritability. As Celia stared at her, she sensed, however, a terrible exhaustion behind the irritability.

'What are you staring at?'

'You have changed quite a lot,' Celia replied honestly. 'I suppose I have, too.'

'In the awful climate which I have endured for the last seven years, one expects to change.' Edna drew off her gloves, to reveal hands equally yellow and shrivelled, though still slender and still graced by the magnificent engagement and wedding rings which Celia had, long ago, envied so much. 'One gets fevers so often that they weaken one.'

Edna leaned back in the taxi seat and gazed out at the bustling, black-clad pedestrians in Lime Street, many of them holding black umbrellas to protect themselves from a sudden drizzle of rain. After the brightly clad, motley crowds of Salvador and Rio, they looked like participants in a huge funeral. Seeing them, Edna felt so filled with anguish that she did not want to face the remainder of her family.

It had been bad enough dealing with Papa and Mama Fellowes' grief at the loss of their only son and their concern for her widowhood. As if she cared a hoot about Paul – a domineering man, a selfish man at best, a bully determined that she should bear more children.

That, she thought, had been a fight to the finish, because, after Rosemary, she was not going to go through the loss of another child; he had been furious and had taken a Brazilian mistress. She had wished him dead many a time, so that she could be free to be honestly and openly in love with his secretary and occasional translator, Vital Oliveira.

Dear patient Vital, a small man, a nobody but infinitely lovable. Her whole body longed for him.

Amongst the Fellowes family, her despondency and tears had been assumed, naturally, to be for Paul, not from having, perforce, to say goodbye to an almost equally distraught Vital. Both were sufficiently realistic to know that it was highly unlikely that they could ever arrange to be together again, and it had hurt – God, how it had hurt – to part, with that feeling of finality.

Paul was for the first part of their residency in Salvador often away from home, as a great dam was built to create power for electricity. Vital coped with his correspondence and records at the city end of his work. For Paul's convenience, he lived in the same great house.

Without any knowledge of Portuguese, Edna had been left in Salvador to run their home as best she could. It was Vital who at first translated her orders to the servants, who saw that they did not cheat her, who found her a doctor to supervise her confinement. He brought her an English/Portuguese dictionary, for which she thanked him gratefully, and he recommended a teacher.

Rosemary died when her father was away from home. It was Vital who, silently in the background of her distress, kept the house servants in order, found a gentle nun to sit with her and himself arranged the funeral.

They became the best of friends, and later, secret, desperate lovers. A scandal would have finished Vital and ruined Edna. Both realised that they were financially dependent upon Paul. And it was a miracle that they were not found out, Edna thought. There must have been suspicions, but intrigue was part of the society, and there were other love affairs which were politely overlooked. And, anyway, Paul and I were English Protestants; there was little understanding of us.

But old Conchita, the housekeeper already installed in

the house when she arrived, had known. She had seen Paul strike his wife on one or two occasions, and slowly she had been moved to protect the young mother.

Edna smiled grimly. To protect her, Conchita could lie with incredibly fast ingenuity. Small and modest in her black dresses, she looked the epitome of integrity – but she resented Paul's high-handed manner with his Portuguese staff – and Vital, who also suffered from this, was the son of a friend of hers. She had been a great help to the lovers.

The answer to Edna's passionate prayers had come in Paul's death on the way home. She had had no option but to come home with him. A single word out of place and Vital would have lost his job with the company and his excellent reputation as a reliable and gifted employee.

Be careful what you pray for – prayers are not always answered in the way you imagine they will be, her nanny had always cautioned her.

How right Nanny had been. She was free, but it was unlikely that she and Vital would ever meet again.

Unaware of the turmoil in the mind of her sister, Celia had expected to deal with tears and hopelessness, and anxious questions about her mother's mourning. She had no idea what to say to this wizened shell of a woman. As they edged their way up the hill towards West Derby, however, she felt she should say something about Paul.

'Both Mother and I were so sorry to hear about Paul's sudden passing. We both feel dreadful that you should have lost him. Mother sends her fond love to you.' She paused, and then added, 'And you have my love and sympathy, too.' The last words seemed stiff and formal to her, but she did not know what else to say.

Edna's barely visible lips tightened. 'Thank you,' she said equally formally. 'It was sudden – quite a shock.' She stared woodenly ahead of her. She had managed to contain her feelings in Southampton while the Port Authorities, all male, had discussed over her head her isolation as an influenza contact. She had, later, done her best to comfort Paul's parents.

At Lime Street, she had hoped to be met and comforted by her own mother, even if Louise did not know the exact reason for her grief. Instead, she was face to face with her younger sister, and pride would not permit her to give way in front of her.

'Was it really Spanish flu?' asked Celia.

'The ship's doctor said it was. All the passengers on the liner were terrified that they would get it. I was quarantined in my cabin, and none of them would come near me. The Health Authorities in Southampton would not let us dock until all the passengers had been examined. They wanted to send me to an isolation hospital for a few days.'

'How awful! Did anyone get it?' Celia began to relax.

'Not to my knowledge. I suppose most of the world has already been exposed to it. I told them that. Finally, I asked them to send for my father-in-law – and he came in his car to fetch me. He promised that he would call the family physician before allowing me to mix with anyone – so they let me go.' Edna's voice expressed considerable satisfaction at her winning of the battle with the Health Authorities, and Celia was suitably impressed.

'Why Paul, I wonder?'

'Oh, Paul? He met all kinds of people in his work and socially. He could have caught it anywhere. In Salvador people get a fever and die and nobody knows what it was that took them. Only something like cholera is quickly identified.'

It seemed a step forward to Celia that she was managing to get Edna to talk to her. 'Why didn't you come home from such an unhealthy place?' she inquired.

Edna considered her answer to this query, before slowly replying, 'Well, I did not want to come home alone. Paul was general manager of the whole project, as you know –

and my father-in-law is a party in the consortium that did the development. Paul felt he must see the work to an end; and he did finish it to schedule.' Edna absently twiddled her rings round her finger. 'If we had come home before the war ended, he would probably have been conscripted, in spite of his age. And then he would have lost his life, anyway.' She bit her lips, as she condemned herself as a great liar.

'He might have done,' agreed Celia soberly, and then she added, 'Dozens of people died, too, in Liverpool from the flu – and they were often the remaining young people in a family. It was tragic.'

'No doubt.' Edna sounded remote, uninterested.

Celia felt shocked at such an indifferent reply, and then reminded herself, more charitably, that Edna would be as wrapped up in her own grief as their mother was.

It seems that only I don't have that privilege, she considered with pain; I mustn't weep for Tom or George or express the terror I feel at Father's death; I have to keep on going – but going where?

It's like walking into a fog.

She felt her sister sigh, and she glanced at her. On the yellowed cheek lay a solitary tear. Poor Edna! Celia took one of her hands in her own, and was surprised when Edna clasped her hand tightly for the rest of the journey.

Chapter Nineteen

For most of the taxi ride through the crowded streets of Liverpool, they sat silently side by side. The thin yellow hand clutching Celia's told her clearly that Edna was more upset than she appeared, but, as they approached West Derby, Celia felt that she must warn her sister that she was not alone in suffering grief.

'Mama is still dreadfully upset,' she began. 'It is barely a week since Papa passed away, you know.' She wanted to cry out, be gentle with both of us – please. We are suffering like you are. But she was nonplussed by her sister's lack of any kindly demonstration of feeling towards herself, so she said no more.

Did Edna care twopence about her father's death, she puzzled? She had, after all, been separated from her family for seven years, and had been in boarding school before that. Had she, perhaps, forgotten that it was her sister who was sitting beside her, someone to whom she should feel free to express her sorrow for the loss of both father and husband?

In response to Celia's warning, Edna said impatiently, 'Yes, I know. Papa Fellowes told me. And Mother wrote to me at Southampton.' Edna stared out of the taxi window. 'It is difficult for both of us.' That it might be difficult for Celia still did not seem to occur to her, for her next remark was, 'Papa was a very trying man.'

Celia was shaken that her father's favourite daughter should make such a shocking remark, especially when he was dead; it was certainly not the thing to criticise the dead. From Celia's point of view, Papa had provided everything for Edna, good clothes, education, a fine wedding and a dowry – had even introduced her husband to her. What more could he have done? She felt resentfully that she herself would have been grateful if he had done any one of these things for her. 'Whatever do you mean?' she asked.

Edna's answer shocked Celia even more. Her sister said, 'I wondered if she was thankful to be widowed. A lot of women are. And Mother had to manage Father very carefully.'

'Oh, no, Edna! Mama is quite broken-hearted. And even more so because she is going to lose her home.'

'What?' Edna turned so quickly towards Celia that she hit her knees on the trunk which had been heaved into the back of the taxi.

With her right hand, Celia was steadying on her lap Edna's hat box and jewel case, as well as her own heavy handbag. At the explosive query, she shot a startled glance over the pile at her sister. 'Didn't Mama tell you?' she quavered.

'No.'

In a trembling voice, as if her late father's financial position were her fault, Celia explained as best she could.

Edna sniffed. 'Nonsense. I don't believe it. Cousin Albert has made a mistake.'

Not wishing to quarrel in front of a taxi driver, Celia muttered, 'We will talk about it when we get in. I am sure Mama will explain it to you.'

'Indeed, we must talk about it. I have come up here in the expectation of being welcomed home!'

'Well, of course you are welcome. Where else would you go?' Celia responded indignantly. At the same time she wondered what Edna would think of the cottage, and she shuddered.

At the thought that she might have to share the cottage with Edna, as well as with her very critical mother, she felt suddenly sick.

During her long day, she had begun to think of the little house as being the beginning of a more open life for herself, despite the work it represented. She felt that everybody she had met that day had been very nice to her and had treated her as a person in her own right. Putting the cottage in order was proving to be a refreshing experience.

As the taxi drew up, Dorothy opened the front door. Her mother, looking exactly like Queen Victoria in her widowhood, came out on to the top step, and looked down at them, with the same woebegone expression as Queen Victoria exhibited in some of her photographs.

Edna left Celia to deal with the taxi driver and the luggage and ran across the pavement and up the wide, gracious steps. Her mother held out her arms to her and she was embraced. They turned and went inside.

By the time Dorothy, Winnie and Ethel had helped the taxi driver to get the heavy trunks up the steps and into the hall, Celia had taken the boxes that had been on her lap upstairs to Edna's bedroom. She then came down to pay the driver and tip him. She knew from her father that a man who tipped the proper amount received service from the lower classes – woe betide him if he tipped too little. The driver seemed pleased by the amount she gave him, touched his cap to her and went slowly down the steps. She shut the door after him, and, with the other women, surveyed the luggage.

'We'll never get them up the stairs, Miss,' said Winnie, already resentful that she and the other maids had been totally ignored by Edna as, with Louise, she had gone straight into the sitting room to be warmed by the fire and divested of her hat and jacket. Winnie had been the cook in the house when Miss Edna was a girl; unlike Dorothy and Ethel, she knew her. She even knew her favourite desserts, and had, that afternoon, made a magnificent apple pie with egg custard for her.

Celia noticed Winnie's forlorn look and guessed the reason for it. She realised suddenly that Edna had treated her, too, exactly like a bad employer would treat a servant. She was reminded of Edna, as a young woman, ordering her to fetch and carry for her, without thought or thanks – exactly as her mother did.

She took off her own hat and coat, and said wearily, 'Leave the trunks where they are, for the moment, Winnie. If we can't get them up the stairs, they could be unpacked down here. The empty trunks won't be too difficult to move.'

'Thank you, Miss. Shall I send up the tea tray?'

Celia was so demoralised that she felt that she must first ask her mother, so she peeped round the sitting-room door to inquire.

The two women were already deep in conversation, and Louise barely turned her head when she answered, 'Yes, bring the tea.'

The three servants were bunched by the door leading to the basement steps. Older than the other two, Winnie was still panting from her exertions with the trunks, and Dorothy was sullenly silent. Only Ethel's eyes sparkled with interest at the arrival.

Celia passed on her mother's instructions, and then said gently to Dorothy, 'I'll come down later on and hear how you got on in Meols.'

'Yes, Miss.' Dorothy sounded exhausted, and Celia had a sudden desire to hug her and tell her everything would eventually turn out all right. But one did not hug maids, so she turned and went slowly into the sitting room. She shut the door, and then took a seat a little away from the fireplace which was blocked to her by the other two women.

Her mother was weeping softly into her black handkerchief, while Edna lay back in her armchair and listened, with her eyes closed, to the story of the house and how awful the cottage was.

Celia thought of the warm comfort of Eddie Fairbanks' back room, and, when her mother paused to wipe her eyes, she interjected with some determination, 'I think the cottage can be made very pretty – and this morning I learned that piped water is probably available – you know, Mama, we never went into Mr Fairbanks' kitchen – he may already have had his pump replaced by taps.'

'Really?' Her mother looked up from her hanky in surprise.

'I should hope there is at least clean water there.' There was scorn in Edna's voice. 'I've had enough of bad water these past seven years.' She slowly heaved herself upright in her chair as Dorothy knocked on the door, and then brought in a tea tray heavy with scones and homemade cake. 'How many bedrooms has it?'

Edna's question confirmed to Celia that she probably expected to live with them, and the tiny hopes and dreams which had begun to grow while she was in Hoylake fell to ashes. She had a strong suspicion that Edna would never tolerate closeness with humble people like Mr Fairbanks or Betty or Ben Aspen who had been so civil to her; in Celia's mind had been planted a timid hope that these people could become her own kind and helpful friends. She knew her mother would never approve – but she was used to Mama; and her father was no longer there to insist on filial obedience. She feared, however, that Mama, backed up by an imperious elder daughter, would decide with whom they made friends in Meols and Hoylake and with whom they did not. She would again find friends and acquaintances, if any, picked out for her.

With an effort, she answered Edna. 'Three double bedrooms and a little hall bedroom.'

A tired Dorothy had set the tea tray on a small table by

Louise's chair. She poured three cups of tea and handed them to the ladies with an embroidered table napkin under each, and then asked, 'Will that be all, Ma'am?'

Louise nodded, and Celia turned to ask the maid eagerly, 'Dorothy, when you were getting water from Mr Fairbanks this morning, you must have seen whether he had a tap or a pump?'

'Oh, aye, Miss. He's got hot and cold taps in the back kitchen. And he's got a water closet what flushes, by the back door.'

Louise forgot her tears immediately, and expressed great delight. She tucked her black hanky back into her sleeve, and said quite briskly to Celia, 'That will solve so many problems.'

'Yes, it will.' Though a good water supply could in future save her a great deal of work, there was doubt in her voice. She feared that there would now be two women leaning on her. As a girl, Edna had always found ways of pushing unpleasant tasks on to Celia, by saying, 'You are at home. It's your job to help Mother.'

Up to now, there had always been servants to do the physically dirty daily tasks, like emptying the slops from the bedrooms and washing out the chamber pots, the latter still used at night despite the advent of water closets. Celia knew that her mother would never do such jobs; she would bully Celia into doing them. She would, very likely, find herself, in addition, washing the dishes, doing the washing, scrubbing the floors and front steps, and Heaven only knew what else.

How much would Louise and Edna do for themselves, she wondered.

She wanted to walk out, run away. In her perturbation, she wished that she never had to face either woman ever again. And then she told herself that she was wicked, sinful, to even contemplate such ideas.

In any case, to whom could she go? She could think of

no one who would not simply scold her for being a fool and ship her back to her mother. Only her godmother, Great-aunt Blodwyn in Wales, who had not come to her nephew's funeral on the excuse that it was lambing time, but, in truth, had not come because she cordially detested Louise, a dislike which was heartily reciprocated. Great-aunt Blodwyn's reputation in the family as a battle-axe of the first water had scared Celia as a child, and she did not seem to be the right person to take in a runaway. Anyway, the farm she had inherited from her husband was far away in Pembrokeshire – and how would a penniless woman get there?

Penniless women could become like the harridan who had directed her to Lime Street Station, disgusting untouch-ables who slowly rotted to death. The idea, strongly held by her elders and whispered amongst the few girls she had known, was terrifying to her.

Louise was saying, 'That will be all, Dorothy,' and Edna announced that she would like to go to her bedroom to wash and change.

Edna asked if the gardener would take her trunks upstairs, to which Celia replied shortly, 'He comes only twice a week.' It took all her patience to persuade her sister that the trunks could be safely unpacked in the hall and the contents carried upstairs.

Louise said, 'Celia, get Ethel to help Edna carry the stuff up. Dorothy will be laying the table for dinner.'

While Edna fumed and fretted in the hall and looked in her handbag for the right keys and demanded a knife to cut the ropes, Celia ran downstairs to the basement kitchen. She was informed that Ethel had gone for an interview for a job as a nursery maid.

'Miss Phyllis's Lily heard about it and told her,' said Winnie, as she basted a capon in the oven.

Celia went slowly back up the stairs to tell her mother this. It immediately sparked an altercation. Edna said sharply that Louise should not allow the servants to go for interviews before she was ready to dismiss them – and, anyway, why wasn't she taking them to Meols? 'Good servants are never easy to find. In Salvador, I turned mine off on the day I was leaving.'

Bewildered, Louise told Celia to help her sister, and turned back into the sitting room, to pour herself another cup of tea and to weep.

The two of them cut the ropes and Edna unlocked the trunks. She then instructed Celia which trunk she should empty first, and went upstairs to her room.

As Celia appeared in the bedroom with a load of clothes and personal possessions, Edna told her which drawers to put them in. She herself took off her dress and went to the bathroom to wash.

Celia plodded wearily up and down stairs with long gowns swathed in tissue paper, with linen walking suits and straw hats, cotton petticoats, boots and shoes, tea gowns and dressing gowns, all finely made and embroidered – but all rather old-fashioned, thought Celia, with surprise. Edna would need to shorten all the skirts; even Celia who was used to looking frumpy had turned up her skirts, despite her mother's protests; they had, for a couple of years now, hung discreetly just above her ankles.

By the time the trunks stood yawning emptily in the hall, the dinner gong was being struck by Dorothy, for dressing, and most of Edna's dresses were still laid across her bed.

Edna hurried back from the bathroom, selected a black gown, shook it out and tutted that it needed pressing. She said to Celia, 'You might ask the maid to press the rest before they are hung up.'

With sudden spirit, Celia replied, 'You will have to do them yourself. Dorothy is coming out to the cottage with me tomorrow morning, to continue the cleaning of it. I have to meet the plumber there – and the building contractor's clerk.' She put down a winter coat, two umbrellas, a parasol and two pairs of walking boots, and added, 'That's everything, I think. I'm going to get washed.' And she went out quickly, before Edna could protest, to scrub her face, while she trembled with defiance.

Dinner was eaten in painful silence. Louise played glumly with the food on her plate. Edna did courteously praise the apple pie to Dorothy, and Dorothy conveyed the information to a depressed Winnie. Otherwise, almost nothing except the barest politenesses passed between them. Celia kept quiet, afraid that if she spoke, her resentment of the other two would show, and bring down upon her from her mother the usual accusations of ingratitude or bad temper.

After they had finished, they went in silent procession into the sitting room to sit by the fire and drink their coffee which Dorothy brought in on a tray.

Edna seated herself gracefully in her father's chair and, after the parlourmaid had left the room, she opened a little black evening purse, which she carried dangling on her wrist. She took out a pretty silver case and a matching silver tube.

As she opened the case, took out a cigarette and fitted it into the silver holder, she asked, 'Do you mind if I smoke, Mama?'

Aroused from her melancholic contemplation of a future without Timothy, Louise stared at her daughter in shocked disgust.

'Edna! You don't mean to say that you smoke?'

'I do, Mama. The doctor in Salvador recommended it when I was so upset at the loss of Rosemary. He said it would soothe my nerves – and it does.'

'The doctor must have been mad! No lady would surely ever smoke!'

'Tush, Mama. A lot of women do nowadays, especially Portuguese and Spanish ladies. I couldn't do without my cigarettes now.' She waved the cigarette holder with its unlit cigarette around, as if to indicate a big crowd of female smokers.

'I will not allow a woman to smoke in my house!' exclaimed an outraged Louise. 'I think it's awful. Even your dear father never smoked here in my sitting room. He smoked in the library or in the garden.'

Celia was both astounded and intrigued by the disagreement. How daring of Edna to do such a thing! With her hands folded neatly in her lap, she forgot her own woes and watched, fascinated.

Edna was nonplussed. Her mother had rarely refused her anything, and, since her Portuguese friends smoked, as did her mother-in-law, she was unprepared for the objection. She had forgotten that the upper classes in the north of England were much more conservative than those in the south.

Edna's lips were trembling. 'I cannot give it up, Mama. It would be quite impossible. I had my last cigarette in the train, and I badly need to smoke now.'

'Then you should confine such an unsociable activity to the garden or your bedroom.' Louise sounded absolutely frigid.

'Very well, Mama.' Edna rose, picked up her coffee cup, and left the room, a picture of offended dignity.

'This is horrible, Celia. Simply horrible.' Louise pulled her handkerchief out of her sleeve, and touched her eyes with it. 'I never dreamed of a daughter of mine smoking! I hope you never indulge in such a shameful practice.'

Celia swallowed. She did not really know what to say. She knew that Phyllis secretly smoked. 'Er – um, Mama. I don't think I would ever want to,' she finally said quite honestly, 'though it is becoming quite common.'

'I would never deny my daughter a home, but I must say I have always disapproved of women smoking. I cannot think what I shall do about it if she stays with us.'

'You could insist that she does the same as Papa did – smoke in the library or in the garden.'

Louise sniffed in disdain. She heaved a great shuddering sigh. 'I don't know, Celia. I really don't know. Our lives are all upside down, and I don't know what to deal with first.'

'I know, Mama. Just don't worry. Try to rest a lot tomorrow. It will help you,' Celia soothed. For a moment she forgot a lifetime of oppression and saw her mother as yet another casualty of the war and of pure bad luck. She felt sorry for the arrogant, selfish woman, suddenly brought low by circumstances which were not her fault. 'You should go to bed now,' she continued. 'I'll ask Dorothy to put a hot water bottle in for you.'

Chapter Twenty

Long before either Louise or Edna had stirred from their beds, Celia and Dorothy had left for Meols. This time, Dorothy carried only a shopping basket containing newspapers and a bottle of vinegar for cleaning the windows. As well as her handbag, Celia carried a neat brown paper parcel tied with string, which Winnie had pressed into her hand, saying, 'It's a lunch for you and Dorothy, Miss.' Dear faithful Winnie, she thought, and she smiled.

The news that Dorothy had given about Mr Fairbanks' water supply had finally lifted her spirits a little, and this morning, after a good night's sleep, she felt much more optimistic about her new home. Perhaps she could persuade her mother and Edna to share the domestic work, once they were in the cottage.

As they sat in the train, Dorothy, usually so silent, became quite talkative. She declared that, yesterday, Mr Fairbanks had been real nice. He had let her use his loo, as well as giving her hot water for her cleaning.

'At the back of his living-room fireplace, he says, he's got a hot-water tank just like we've got in the kitchen of your West Derby house. Hot water made everything easy for me, it did.

'And the sweep was a nice young man. Didn't make too much mess. He left his bill on the mantel shelf for you.' With her red, ungloved hands in her lap, she considered her young mistress, and then added, 'I promised as we would pay today. To tell truth, Miss, I think he's waiting on the money. He's only just set up after coming home from hospital. He says it's proper hard to get started again in civvy street – but his dad were a sweep, so at least he's got a trade.'

Celia promised to go into Hoylake and pay the sweep as soon as she had seen Miss Aspen and the plumber.

The fact that even a maid needed hot water to do her work properly had escaped Celia, and she was thankful for Eddie Fairbanks' consideration.

Feeling relaxed in the unusual situation in which she found herself, Dorothy felt able to advise Celia to order in from Hoylake a couple of hundredweight of coal and some wood chips, so that fires could be lit in the newly cleaned fireplaces. 'To dry the place out, like. Yesterday, it got proper cold what with the wind blowing in from the sea – and the damp.'

Celia agreed, and added a note to her list to find a coal merchant.

As they approached the cottage, they saw that Eddie was trimming his hedge. On seeing them struggling down the sandy lane, he laid his shears on the top of the hedge and came to relieve Dorothy of the basket. She simpered at him, as she handed it over to him. Real nice manners Mr Fairbanks had.

When he greeted Celia, he seemed to her to be an old friend, and she told him without a hint of shyness what Dorothy and she were going to do that day.

'I'll get me ladder and clean the outsides of the windows for you,' he offered. 'It'll be better than trying to reach them from the inside.'

Dorothy did not wait for Celia to answer. She accepted immediately. Then she turned to Celia and said, 'Sash windows, like your mam has got, I can manage, because I can sit on the windowsill and lower the window over me knees to hold me, so I don't fall. These here is casements

– they open outwards. Even if I chanced a fall, I couldn't get at them properly.'

Eddie Fairbanks, who had a daughter in service and knew the hazards of window-cleaning, said firmly that the last thing he wanted was someone around with a broken back. The women laughed, as they unlocked and went into the cottage.

'It looks so much better!' exclaimed Celia.

Dorothy beamed with pride. 'This is a first go. You wait till you've had it painted. It'll look real nice.'

Her words were echoed by Betty Aspen, who arrived soon afterwards and went slowly over the little building. Celia held the other end of her tape measure, as she carefully measured for two new boards for the floor of the small bedroom and suggested a new windowsill and new plaster below it, because the rain had probably got in between the brick and the plaster. She strongly recommended new window frames for the back windows. 'They're rotten,' she said, 'and beginning to let in the rain. Probably because they face the prevailing wind and have been soaked more often.'

When they entered the kitchen, she looked with mock horror at the heavily rusted old range.

'Miss Gilmore,' she exclaimed. 'While you have workmen on the premises, have it removed. It will give you much more wall space. Later on, you might be able to have a gas stove installed.'

Celia's first thought was of how much it would cost. She dithered.

As if reading her thoughts, Betty urged, 'It could be done quite economically – you'll never manage to get it clean and shiny again. It looks as if it has not been used for years and years.'

With visions of spending hours cleaning weighed against being indebted to Aspens' for months, Celia plunged, and ordered, a little breathlessly, 'Yes, please take it out.'

Betty knew Eddie Fairbanks, and, next, without hesitation, she asked if she could borrow his ladder. To Celia's astonishment, while Eddie held it for her, she climbed it fearlessly, her black skirt swinging round the calves of her plump legs, as she examined the roof, its gutters and downpipes and the chimneys. She announced, as she came down, after taking a final look at the back half of the roof, that someone had repaired the latter not too long before. 'And they did the gutters and downpipes. The chimney could do with repointing, but it's not too bad.'

'It would be Mr Billings, the agent, who saw to the roof, I think,' Celia told her. She felt glad that Mr Billings had, to a degree, watched over the fabric of the cottage for her mother. It reinforced the idea that he was a man of integrity.

Betty ploughed through overgrown bushes which had taken over the little flowerbed which ran along the walls of the house, to look at something she called the damp courses, and said that they, too, had been kept clear. Flushed and panting, she emerged near the back door.

As she paused to catch her breath, she looked down the length of the garden and spotted the outside lavatory. She sniffed disparagingly at it. 'Your biggest problem is that – and the water supply,' she announced. 'The rest is easy.'

Eddie was standing patiently near them, in case Betty wanted the ladder again, and he interjected with the information that he had his water from the mains and a good flush lavatory outside his back door. 'The earl got it done for me before I moved in,' he said proudly.

'A plumber's coming to look at the pump this morning,' Celia told them. 'I hope he can do the same for us.'

'Me dad could probably do that for you – and give you a better price,' Betty said promptly, as she took out a notebook and pencil and began to add to the notes she had made of her measurements. 'It pays to get more than one price.'

Celia saw the sense of this. In fact, later on, she often recounted the story of Betty's intrepidness at scaling the ladder, and said that Betty had, that very morning, taught her some of the basic principles of business.

While Eddie repositioned his ladder in order to clean the upstairs windows, and Dorothy came to the back door to tell him that she had the necessary paper, rags and vinegar to do the job, Celia was further surprised when Betty went outside the front gate and began to hunt through the foot-high grass and the straggling hedge.

She pulled out a clump of grass, and said with satisfaction, 'There it is.'

Celia squatted down by her, and watched as she cleared earth and roots from round a brass, embossed disc, like a small lid set in a ring of some other metal. 'You've got a water supply this far, anyway,' she said triumphantly. 'They'll know at the Town Hall if there's any piping into the house. I'm surprised whoever lived here wasn't connected at the same time as Mr Fairbanks was.'

'Maybe Aunt Felicity couldn't afford it – or Father wouldn't do it for tenants – he never wanted this house – said it was a nuisance,' Celia explained. 'But Mother can be very wooden when she wants to be, and she wanted it kept in the family. I can remember vaguely Father talking about selling it.'

'Get the water laid on,' advised Betty. She pointed to one of the upstairs windows. 'If you were prepared to sacrifice the back bedroom above the kitchen, Dad could probably put a bathroom and lavatory in it for you. A bathroom would add to the value of the house.' She turned to Eddie Fairbanks and inquired, 'Do you have a cesspool – or are you connected to the main drains somehow?'

'Cesspool. The earl had it dug when the lavatory were put in.'

'So the cesspool belongs to the earl?'

'Oh, aye. It will, no doubt, since he owns the land. He had it cleaned out recently.'

'So Mrs Gilmore would need to have her own dug?'

'Well, a flush lavatory outside, like mine, still has to be connected up to something!' Eddie Fairbanks took off his cap and scratched his head, while he considered this fact. Then he said doubtfully, 'You could ask the earl's agent if Mrs Gilmore's drains could be connected to it for the time being. There's a rumour in the village that some new houses are to be built just by; probably they will be connected with the main drains at the end of the lane – and if that's true, you and the earl could ask that these houses be connected at the same time. In fact, the Town Hall may insist on the connection to a drain. They don't believe in cesspools nowadays.'

'I'll find out from the Town Hall about the drainage and the water for you,' Betty promised.

'Would a loo and bathroom cost very much?'

'It wouldn't be cheap.' Celia's face fell, and Betty said cautiously. 'Me dad might be willing for you to pay by instalments – like monthly, and he might have secondhand bathroom fitments in stock which are still good – that would cut the cost a lot.'

Celia thought about this for a moment, as they walked towards the front door, and then she said, 'Once we sell our big Liverpool house, Mama should be able to pay all of the bill. I'll talk to Father's trustee about it.'

Betty nodded, and then Celia asked her, 'Would he mind telling me what it would cost for a bathroom, separate from the general repairs, even if we didn't have the work done?'

'He wouldn't mind. You don't get all the jobs you tender for. He'd give you two prices, if you like. One for a sink and taps and connections in the kitchen and an outside loo, and one for a complete bathroom with a loo in the house – and the kitchen taps the same.' She smiled, and added, 'And removing the range!'

Though she was worried at the possible cost, Celia was enchanted. 'Ask him, please,' she breathed. Then she inquired, 'Would you mind, since I have a plumber coming, if I got a price from him, too?'

'No. You would be accepting the advice I gave you just now!' She laughed, and Celia, finding her enthusiasm infectious, laughed as she had not done for weeks.

Delighted with themselves, they did some extra measurements and talked about painting the interior economically. Then, as Betty put her notebook back into her big black handbag, Celia told her about her mother's fine early nineteenth-century furniture – and that some of the pieces were too large to go into the cottage. 'Anyway, we have far too much of it – and china and curtains.'

'Will you sell it?'

'We'll have to. At first, I suggested to Mother that we get it auctioned, and she was quite miserable. Basically, I think both of us felt that we would not get good prices for it.' Celia paused to look at Betty's alert, friendly face, and then, gaining confidence, she plunged into a description of an idea she had had when visiting the Aspens' building yard.

'You remember, when I came to see you yesterday, you were cleaning out a kind of barn – where the car had been stored?'

'Yes, indeed,' Betty sounded surprised.

'I was wondering – I thought it might be easier for Mother, if we stored most of the furniture, so that she had a chance to consider what would look best in her new home – we need to vacate our present house fairly soon. I was thinking that we could sell piece by piece what we did not want and get a better price for it.'

Betty grinned, 'And you'd like to put it in our barn?'

'Yes. Do you think that Mr Aspen would rent it? I don't think I can pay very much.'

'I don't think he's any immediate plans to use it, to be honest. It was a matter of cashing in on the car more than anything.' The smile left her face, as, in her turn, she confided, 'Father thought that now is the time to sell it, while there's a possible market and it's still in good shape. He wants me to have the money as a nest egg, seeing as my hubby built it.'

She looked, for a moment, so desolate, that Celia instinctively put her arm round her shoulder to comfort her. 'Never mind,' she said pointlessly.

Betty bit her lip, and then, steadying herself, said, 'I'm so sorry. It comes over me at times.'

Celia smiled and, as if she had known her for years, hugged her gently. 'Of course it does. I do understand.'

'I'll ask me dad for you.'

'Thank you. I haven't talked to Mother yet, because my sister arrived from South America yesterday, and there has not been much opportunity. I believe that the idea would be agreeable to her.'

Betty had gathered up her courage again and had begun to move towards the lane, so Celia let her arm drop. 'And now I think of it, my sister may have stuff coming from Salvador that she may want to store, too.'

Betty paused to look again at Celia. 'My goodness! You'll have enough to stock a shop.'

Celia giggled. 'That'll be the day,' she said disparagingly. 'I'm not trained for anything.'

'Nonsense,' responded Betty with unexpected briskness. 'Women can do lots of things, if they have to. I never saw a woman ploughing, for instance, until the war began and there was no ploughman to do it.'

'That's true. I remember Great-aunt Blodwyn complaining that she had lost her ploughman to the army. His wife ploughed for her.'

'And Dad's training me to be a builder's clerk and maybe run the business one day when he feels too old – because it's going to take time for little Alfred to grow up and be able to do it.'

'Ah, but you're clever, Miss Aspen – and capable.'

'Tush, I didn't know anything much till Dad took me into the office, to fill in until he could get another man – and then found there were almost none left of the right age and experience. You could learn anything, if you set your mind to it.' Her eyes danced as she said this, as if she were suggesting something naughty.

'Well, thank you.' Celia felt hugely gratified at the compliment.

Although the plumber from the village, when he arrived, was shown politely round the cottage and asked for an estimate, Celia knew in her heart that Betty had impressed her so favourably that she would give the work to the Aspens. She already sensed that, in Betty, she had made a real friend.

That night, as they sat round the kitchen fire drinking their bedtime cocoa, Dorothy told Winnie, who was nursing Tommy Atkins on her lap, that she had never before seen Miss Celia look so happy.

'Then why is she up in her bedroom crying her eyes out?' asked Ethel in surprise. 'I saw her, when I went up to put the hot water bottles in the beds, just now. She were lying on her bed. But I could hear her when I were in the passage – and I didn't know what to do.'

'You shouldn't have gone in, Ethel. You should know that by now.'

'I thought maybe she hurt herself. Banged her head on something perhaps. How was I to know?'

'She was probably just tired out. It's not our business,

Ethel. In service, you got to keep your eyes down and mind your own business.'

'Yes, Ma'am,' Ethel replied sullenly, and returned to sipping her cocoa.

Dorothy said, 'Maybe her mam or Miss Edna has been at her again. It's a pity, because, you know, it were as if that Miss Aspen put new life into her,' she said.

'One of the few times she's been out of her mother's sight, I'd say. Most times, she's never had a chance to be herself,' responded Winnie dryly.

Chapter Twenty-One

❧

When Celia and Dorothy had returned from Meols at about five o'clock, Ethel had told them that the Missus and Miss Edna had gone to see how Mrs Woodcock was.

While Dorothy clattered downstairs to the basement kitchen, Celia took off her outer clothes and went into the sitting room, where a good fire blazed.

Though Celia would herself have enjoyed visiting Phyllis, she was relieved that her mother had kindly performed this duty, and that, though she should go soon, it did not have to be that particular evening. She badly needed time to talk over with her mother her ideas regarding their new home, and to hear what the bank manager had said to her.

She was also anxious to know what plans, if any, Edna had for her future. Would she want to live with her mother and herself?

Celia dreaded the answer to this question. Secretly, she chastised herself for not longing to share her home with her poor bereaved sister. You are supposed to love your sister – want to help her whenever she needs help, she told herself again and again. But, on Lime Street Station, she had felt the sting of Edna's remarks, though they were not much different from snubs she had received from Edna ever since she could remember.

Angrily, she asked herself, why doesn't she show me some affection? And promptly blamed the lack on her own shortcomings, that she was dull and stupid and not worthy of love. That Edna's attitude towards her might have been automatic, learned long ago from their mother, did not occur to her. She tried to comfort herself by remembering how Edna had held her hand in the taxi.

Without being asked, Winnie sent her up a tray of tea. It was brought upstairs by Ethel, who carefully put it down on a side table within reach of Celia. 'Dorothy's just getting washed and changed into her afternoon uniform, Miss,' she said, as she took the lid off the pot and gave the contents an energetic stir. 'So Winnie said to me to bring it up to you.'

'Thank you, Ethel.' Celia forced her thoughts away from Edna, and inquired, 'How did you get on at your interview yesterday?'

'I won't know for a day or two, Miss. The lady has one or two others to see – before she makes up her mind, like.'

Since Celia seemed interested, she felt encouraged to go on. 'You see, Miss, I haven't any official experience with children – that was the trouble. But I'm the second one in a family of thirteen.' She laughed. 'Coming to work for Mrs Gilmore was the first time I haven't been knee-deep in kids – and truth to tell, it feels lonely without them.'

'It might be a little different dealing with children in a house in West Derby,' Celia warned. It was a wealthy neighbourhood with a very different standard of living from that of Ethel's family in the north end of the city.

'Oh, aye. I'd have to bath the little terrors every night, no doubt – and be for ever changing nappies – much more than me mam and I could do for our kids. It took Mam all her time to feed them, never mind anything else.'

'How many children did this lady have?'

'Just had her second – she's got a two-year-old as well. She's hardly got started yet.

'And, Miss, there's a day nursery and a night nursery. And, you know, Miss, I'd sleep in the same room as the babies and it would be warm because there'd be a fire to keep the babies warm. And I wouldn't have to clean – other help is kept.' She paused for breath, and finished up by saying wistfully, 'I hope I get it, Miss.'

Suddenly aware, from Ethel's remark, that there was no heating in the bedrooms of the Gilmore servants, Celia said, 'I hope you do, Ethel. I am sure Mother will give you an excellent reference.'

Through the open door into the hall, Celia glimpsed a neatly uniformed Dorothy run to answer the front door. As soon as she opened it, there was a flurry of wet umbrellas being shaken and voices protesting a sudden shower.

Ethel turned guiltily.

'The Missus! And me talking like this!' She slipped out of the room as quietly as a cat, and Celia doubted if Louise even noticed her as she passed through to the basement stairs.

Celia smiled as she poured out her tea. She took a quick sip, and then went into the hall to greet her mother.

Both ladies were struggling out of damp jackets and hats; Edna was saying that the veiling and satin trimmings of their hats were ruined by spots of rain. Dorothy was putting their umbrellas into the umbrella stand. She promised, at the same time, to take the hats and coats downstairs to be dried in the kitchen. But Edna handed Celia her hat, and said, 'Put this somewhere to dry. Lay it on its crown to keep the crown flat.'

Celia looked at it, and said, 'I'd better take the veiling off and spread it out. I think it will have to be restiffened with a little gum water.' Her response to her sister's request had been automatic, and she immediately regretted it. She wanted to say, 'Do it yourself, when you are pressing your dresses.' But her courage failed her.

'I don't know how to do it,' Edna was continuing to Celia.

Her unthinking mother chimed in, 'Oh, Celia is very

good at such things. Would you iron mine at the same time, dear?'

The memory of her interesting and satisfying day was wiped out. Seething with indignation, she obediently took her mother's bonnet as well as Edna's hat, and said, 'I'll put them in the laundry room downstairs, and deal with them tomorrow.' And I'll deliberately forget about them, she thought angrily.

In the unlit laundry room, however, she stood and cried. Then she blew her nose and went back upstairs, to find her mother demanding more tea from Dorothy, and Edna saying that it had been a horrible visit; Phyllis's house looked positively unkempt and it stank of babies.

In the middle of the chaos, Phyllis had been lying on her unmade bed with a baby at her breast and a little boy howling beside her.

'And she didn't even get Lily to make a cup of tea for us,' added Louise. 'It's a good thing her mother is arriving tomorrow to help her.'

Celia was outraged. She forgot her tears, and said maliciously to Edna, 'I hope that you took little Eric up and comforted him and, at least, made her bed comfortable for her.'

Edna was seating herself by the fire and spreading out her damp skirt round her to dry. She froze for a moment, and then, as if she had not heard Celia's remark, she said, 'I think I had better go up and change immediately we have had tea.'

'Celia!' Her mother's voice held a warning note. 'If Phyllis needs more help, it is up to Arthur to provide it. It is not for us to imply criticism of the family's arrangements by offering to help.'

'But, Mama . . .'

'That's quite enough. I don't want to hear any more about it.'

'Very well, Mama.' Though the tea tray that Ethel had

brought her had been removed, her full cup still stood on the table next to Edna's chair. With trembling hands, she picked it up and walked over to the window, to stare at the rain-dashed panes while she drank the cold tea.

As she slowly put the cup and saucer down on a table crowded with family photographs in silver frames, Dorothy arrived with a larger tray, which she laid on the tea table beside Louise, and all three women remained quiet until she had left the room. Celia wondered if Louise and Edna had made up their quarrel over smoking the previous evening.

In the same strained silence the women sipped tea and nibbled scones, until Louise, anxious that her girls should not quarrel, introduced the reason for their visit to Phyllis, which was not really to inquire how the new mother fared.

'That awful estate agent man called this morning, to say he was bringing a lady from Manchester, who had need of a large house in which to set up a nursing home. He apologised for rushing us, but he wanted to add this house to the list of those he proposed to show her this afternoon.' Louise fumbled for her black handkerchief again. 'Of course, I said no. It was too sudden.'

'He's not a very easy man to deny,' interjected Edna reflectively. 'I didn't like him.' She ached to smoke, and wondered how soon she could run up to her bedroom for a quick puff.

As if they had never had a cross word between them, Louise turned to her gratefully, 'Neither do I, dear. He's too forward.' She turned back to Celia. 'He said, however, that your father's lawyer had impressed on him the need for speed. And he insisted that time and tide wait for no man – and that the lady was a very likely purchaser. But she had to return to Manchester tonight.' She dabbed her eyes with her handkerchief. 'So I gave in.'

'And we went to see your friend, to get out of his way.' Edna's expression as she looked into her empty teacup was sour, as if something unpleasant was passing under her nose.

'And because it was my duty to visit Phyllis, particularly as she is calling the baby after dear Timothy,' added Louise virtuously.

Celia realised that her mother was doing her best to keep the peace between Edna and herself, just as if they were still small girls quarrelling in the nursery. She picked up the olive branch. 'You were enormously kind to her, Mama, when the baby came so unexpectedly. I am sure she will feel a lifelong obligation to you.'

Louise actually smiled at her younger daughter. She said primly, 'I don't know what else we could have done.'

'Well, you did everything so graciously.' Celia felt she could say this honestly; and then she asked, 'When will the estate agent let you know what the result of the visit was?'

'He left his card with a note on it to say he would call on us tomorrow afternoon, just to give us the Manchester lady's reactions.' She sighed. 'On a Sunday afternoon!'

'It's not very nice, is it?' This from Edna, who had not enjoyed her practically smokeless day while enduring her mother's fairly constant laments.

'We shall have returned from church, at least,' said Celia, trying to comfort her mother about using the Lord's day for selling houses. She decided that the estate agent's insistence on speed opened the way for her to tell her mother about her discussions with Betty Aspen and the plumber. This she did, while Edna listened with some interest.

'A real bathroom? Like we have here?' exclaimed her mother. 'That would be wonderful. Oh, what a relief!'

'Well, perhaps not quite as grand as we have here, Mother. But Miss Aspen – I keep forgetting that she's a widow and her real name is Mrs Houghton – assured me that it would be quite nice-looking. And less likely to freeze up in winter than an outside water closet would. She has promised an estimate on Monday – she'll leave it at the cottage.'

'How shall we pay for it?' Louise asked helplessly.

'If Cousin Albert agrees, we might pay for it out of the money we'll get from this house. Otherwise, Mrs Houghton suggested that we could pay monthly to her father until we have paid it off.'

Edna opened her mouth to say kindly that she had a little ready money, but Celia cut her off by telling Louise about the barn, the rent of which Betty would also let her know on Monday.

'You see, Mama, if it does not cost much to store the furniture so close to the cottage, you can take your time in deciding, finally, what you would like to retain – and if something does not fit, we have somewhere to put it until it can be sold.'

Edna interjected that she had furniture coming from Brazil, which would arrive in about three months' time. It would be coming in on a freighter bound for Liverpool. 'I shall need somewhere to store it, if I remain up here – though Papa Fellowes has offered me a home with his family. The barn would be convenient for me, too.'

Louise leaned across the fireplace to take Edna's hand and squeeze it. 'My dear,' she said, 'you know that I would wish you to be with us.'

Celia dutifully echoed this, though she felt that life with Edna could be miserable. Her hands were clasped tightly in her lap, as she sought to control her feelings. She had, of course, no inkling of the turmoil of emotion through which Edna was going.

'Perhaps you and Mama could share the rent of the barn, and that would make it very inexpensive, I am sure,' she suggested.

While her mother nodded agreement to it, Edna considered the suggestion. Then she said reluctantly, 'I don't think I have to worry about small expenses. Papa Fellowes had the will which Paul made when we were married. He never changed it; he left me everything that he possessed. He was his father's junior partner and it means that money will come to me from the company.'

And thank God for that, she told herself; if she was never able to see Vital again, it was some comfort that she would be financially independent – simply because arrogant, self-centred Paul had never dreamed of dying young; he had made the original will only after his father had suggested it.

Her mother gave a sigh of relief. 'I am so thankful, dear, that Paul took care of you so well. We would have shared what we have with you. But it gives you much more freedom if you are independent.'

Celia opened her mouth to snap that she had absolutely nothing to share. She did not, however, want to upset her mother again, so she compressed her lips, kept her hands in her lap and said no more. A woman can learn, said Betty Houghton, who was well on her way to holding down a man's job. But where could she herself start to learn anything that would give her a chance of freedom?

Edna agreed dully that she was fortunate. She shifted uneasily in her chair, and sighed. She said slowly, 'I have no idea, as yet, what my income will be. Papa Fellowes has promised to send me a cheque each month until Paul's will has been probated. After that, I shall be considered a shareholder in the company, and I will be sent dividends according to the profits made each year.'

Louise nodded. 'It's a very big company,' she remarked. 'You should do well.'

'Papa Fellowes warned me that, though the company is doing extremely well now, sometimes such companies have huge financial losses, and there is no income for a while. He advised that I should save as much as I can in the good years and invest the savings conservatively, so that I will always have some income.' She thought for a moment, and then added, 'He said that he will be sending me enough until the will is probated for me to live on independently, if I am careful.'

'He really has your interests at heart, doesn't he?' Louise said warmly. 'He must be very fond of you.'

'Both Mama and Papa have always been extremely kind to me,' Edna responded. 'You'll remember them quite well, of course, from when they lived in Liverpool many years ago.' She felt a burst of guilt, as if the failure of her marriage had been her own fault and she was cheating her affectionate in-laws. She wanted to cry. Instead, she turned firmly to her sister, and said through tight lips, 'I would like to see the cottage.'

Celia, who had been listening with envy to the story of Mr Fellowes' generosity and good sense, was immediately alert. The request suggested that Louise had explained, as far as she was able, their financial situation and the grim necessity of selling the house. Edna had, therefore, presumably accepted the fact of her father's bankruptcy.

Celia had begun to think of the cottage as her own domain. But if Edna wanted to live with them, then she would naturally want to see the place. She said reluctantly, 'You could come with me – I shall go out on Monday to see Mrs Houghton and to discuss her estimates – and arrange with her for workmen to be let in. I was hoping you, Mama, would come with me – because you would have to decide if you wished the work to go forward.'

Louise's expression was one of nervous dismay. 'How on earth would I know what should be done – and how much it should cost?'

'Well, Cousin Albert is not here to advise you, so I don't know who else to ask – and it is you who will have to pay for anything which is done.'

Louise clutched at a straw. 'What about Mr Billings?'

'You could, of course, ask him to check the estimates,' Celia responded. Then she added doubtfully, 'I think he might make a charge for doing it – and I can't imagine his turning down estimates from a man he is obviously well acquainted with.'

Louise turned to Edna. 'What do you think, dear?'

Celia waited to be condemned, but Edna said absently, 'Me? I have been out of the country so long that I would not have the least idea. All I know is that everything seems terribly expensive, compared to what it was in 1913. I suppose it's because of the war.'

Celia agreed that her sister's observation was correct. She knew because she kept the housekeeping book for her mother and she had, as the war progressed, watched the butcher's and baker's bills go steadily up. Her mother had had to ask Father a number of times for an increase in housekeeping money. Then she thought suddenly, that's one thing I know. How to keep a simple account book and file all the receipts neatly, so that Father could look at them. She told herself not to be silly – anybody could do that.

Since they seemed to have silently agreed that there was no one to make the decision about repair costs, Celia knew she would have to plunge in and accept Betty Houghton's calculations. She deferred the debate about having a bathroom put in until Betty could tell Louise, on Monday, exactly what she envisaged.

It was agreed that all three ladies would make the journey to Meols on Monday.

Like a good chairwoman of the Knitting Committee they had belonged to during the war, Celia brought up the next subject on her agenda, by asking her mother to tell her what Mr Carruthers at the bank had had to say.

Except for payments to tradesmen, Louise had never discussed money with Celia, and she did not seem to be very keen to do so now. She did not immediately reply.

Celia urged, 'We need to know, Mama, whether we have any immediate money to pay workmen. I still have most of the five pounds you gave me, though I have paid the sweep.' She suddenly remembered the plumber, and told her mother how he had come and had also promised an estimate, on Monday, for the work he could do. 'That would be a way of checking at least part of Betty Houghton's estimate, wouldn't it?'

The information about the plumber was received by Louise with evident relief. In answer to the question, she said that Mr Carruthers had given her so much information about banking that her mind was quite in a tizzy. She was, however, clear that there was at least twenty pounds in her account and, in addition, she had paid in Mr Billings' cheque for nine pounds and eight shillings.

To Celia, nearly thirty pounds, together with the remaining bit of housekeeping Louise still had for the month of March, was a great deal of money, and she said so to Louise. Her own allowance from her father worked out at less than two pounds for an entire year. If there were only the two of them to maintain, and they could move into the cottage, she knew that the money in the bank would go quite a long way.

Edna simply wrinkled her nose and said nothing. She did not want to commit herself to anything much financially, until she knew what amount Papa Fellowes was going to send her.

'And was he able to give you the name of a solicitor?' Celia asked.

'Yes, indeed. He very kindly took me down the street to introduce me.' Louise's voice rang with approbation. 'Mr Little of Hart, Howard and Little. Such a handsome young man. Like George, he served in the navy and was actually once sunk by a submarine. He has only been home for a year. He was most sympathetic about dear George and Tom.'

Celia hoped that the young man's law was as good as his looks. I don't care if he looks like a Gorgon's head, she decided, if only he will keep us from falling into some unexpected abyss.

Her mother continued. 'He says I must never sign anything without first showing it to him.'

'Sensible advice,' remarked Edna to no one in particular.

'What does he charge?' asked Celia.

'Oh, I could never be so vulgar as to ask a gentleman, such as he is, what he charges! He will no doubt send us a bill.'

Though she felt that some snaillike progress had been made, Celia had a strong desire to scream. She was deadly tired from the long day; and her mother's silly attitude towards the lawyer added to her underlying fear that she would never manage to get her safely into a new home.

The silence which fell between the three women was broken by the sound of Dorothy banging the hall gong, to indicate that it was time to dress for dinner.

Edna rose with obvious relief. She looked down ruefully at her skirt, which, after being so damp, would certainly need pressing. She wondered if she could push her ironing on to the washerwoman, who, she had learned from Ethel, came to the house on Mondays; the woman could do it while they were in Meols. Ethel had murmured shyly that she would probably expect to be paid a bit more for the extra work, and Edna had accepted this suggestion.

Louise looked up at her and then at Celia, who had also risen. 'Will the estate agent expect tea when he comes tomorrow?' she asked, with a quaver in her voice.

'I have no idea,' replied Celia, who felt she could face no more.

Chapter Twenty-Two

੭৵৯

Three weeks later, a triumphant Ethel gave three days' notice, packed her small tin suitcase with her few belongings and, on the third day, went home to her mother, to spend a little while with her, before starting her new job as nursemaid.

Louise was very resentful of such short notice. 'Such impudence!' she exclaimed. 'She was smirking all over her face, as she told me. I felt like refusing to pay her her last week's wages!'

Amid the chaos to which the dining room had been reduced, they were carefully wrapping crockery in newspaper before laying it in wooden barrels ready for the movers. Celia paused, a huge gravy boat in one hand. Shocked, she exclaimed, 'You didn't actually do that, did you, Mama?'

Her mother bridled. 'No, but I threatened to – and it frightened her. I can't stand impudence.'

'Her mother depends on her sending most of her wages home,' Celia said unhappily. 'I am sure she was scared.'

'Well, I finally gave it to her. Good riddance to bad rubbish.'

Celia thought of the warm friendly youngster who had cheerfully done all the rough work of a big house. Was that all the thanks you got when people did not want you any more?

She shivered at the idea, and then slowly placed the gravy boat in a barrel, which would be stored in the Aspen barn until its contents were sold. What would three women do with twelve place settings of Crown Derby – in a cottage? she had asked her mother.

'We may have important visitors,' declared Louise loftily.

In despair, Celia expostulated, 'But we are already taking three sets of six with us!'

Louise agreed to the china being stored. 'But not sold, mind you!'

'It's a good thing we've got the barn,' Celia remarked. 'The workmen are still in the cottage, because they've yet to paint the parlour – though Betty persuaded Mr Aspen to do a fast job for us, specially.'

'A fast job sounds most unladylike.'

'That's what Betty called it.' Celia's lips compressed tightly, as she swallowed her irritation.

'And really, dear, I don't think you should be on first-name terms with a workman's daughter.'

Celia longed to snap back that Betty was proving to be an excellent friend, but restrained herself. It was useless to debate the matter; Betty was indisputably working-class.

As they packed, upstairs in her bedroom Edna wrote to her father-in-law in Southampton to notify him of her impending change of address. As she sealed the letter, she thought about writing to Vital. They had said farewell in the belief that they would never get the chance to meet again. It was wiser to leave it thus, she knew; and yet, the real pain inside her swelled at the idea of becoming lost to him for ever if he had no address for her.

She seized another sheet of paper and quickly scribbled a few lines on it to say that she expected to live with her mother for the time being and gave the cottage address. She added that she would be grateful if he would send on any letters addressed to her Brazilian home. That, at least, she thought, was a reasonable request, should anyone else chance to see the letter. She flung herself on to her bed; she did not cry – she was past that. She reached for her cigarettes.

While Celia strove to complete the packing of the best china, her thoughts turned to her old friends in the kitchen. Dorothy would not start her new employment as a cook-general with a family across the road for a day or two, so she had been glad, Celia knew, to stay on. She hoped that Louise would manage to pay any wages due to her, though the woman would probably be thankful enough just to be fed and housed until she started her new job.

It left only Winnie. What was the old cook going to do?

Perhaps she'll stay with one of her sons, Celia thought.

Long before the war, she remembered, Winnie, widowed when young, used to go on her days off to her own mother's house to see her boys. They were being brought up by their grandmother while Winnie went out to work to earn the money to feed them.

Celia made up her mind that when they had completed packing the contents of the china cupboard, which led off the dining room, she would go down to the kitchen to inquire what the elderly cook's plans were.

Winnie had been a tremendous help. She had picked out what she considered to be a reasonable set of kitchenware for a small kitchen, and it had been sent by carrier to the new home, together with boxes of food staples from the pantry. Large pieces of coarse crockery, like bread bowls, had been packed for storage, except for a few utensils for use in their final days of residence.

'Do you know if Winnie has found a position yet, Mama?'

Her mother was lifting a heavy silver basket out of the sideboard drawer. She said, 'I think we should take the silver out to Meols ourselves.' Then, in answer to Celia's question, she replied, 'I don't know. I haven't had time to ask her – I've been quite worn out.'

Though Celia answered in her usual gentle way, 'I know, Mama. The last few weeks have been very stressful,' Louise sensed a lack of sympathy, and, as she put the heavy basket of cutlery on to the table, she looked hard at her daughter.

Ever since dear Timothy had passed away, Celia had definitely not been herself.

Louise decided that the girl was getting above herself. That was it. Without her mother's permission, she had authorised all kinds of repairs to the cottage; she would never have dared to do that, if her dear father had been alive. And she had taken Dorothy down to the cottage for days at a time, so that there had been no one to answer her bell when she rang. Eventually – very eventually – she considered bitterly, Ethel or Winnie had come panting upstairs – but it was not the same. She had also been inconvenienced by the fact that Celia herself had not been in the house to do the innumerable small tasks that were required of her, as cupboards and drawers were cleared out. She had even found herself having to reply to late-arriving condolence letters, which had made her cry. It wasn't fair. And, though she had been told to do it, the girl had done nothing about notifying friends and relations about their change of address.

With the West Derby house not yet sold, the financial worry had been quite appalling – when she had written to Cousin Albert about it, he had replied by return of post that she could probably get a small loan from the bank on the strength of the pending sale of the house.

Ask Mr Carruthers for a loan? It was a shocking thought. Really, Cousin Albert was being no help whatever. What use was he as an executor? Nevertheless, pushed by Celia, she had obtained from Mr Carruthers a loan to help out.

Because she trusted him, she had blithely signed for it without first consulting her new solicitor and had never asked about the rate of interest that would be charged.

In her confusion she had no idea that Cousin Albert, terrified of a female invasion of his quiet home, was doing exactly what the law demanded of an executor – attending to the deceased's estate, or lack of it. He was determined not to become involved in Louise's financial troubles. As her husband's cousin, he had, he felt, given her sound advice; it was up to her to take it. He had, out of a sense of duty to his cousin's wife, set in train for her the sale of her house and would see that she bought an annuity from the proceeds. Other than that, he kept his head down and communicated only with Timothy's solicitor, Mr Barnett, and with his elderly clerk, whose salary he was temporarily paying himself, since he had to have someone in Liverpool to help him deal with angry creditors.

On top of Cousin Albert's callousness, here was Celia worrying about servants, thought Louise savagely – when she should have been concerned about her poor mother's dreadful state.

Her feeling of neglect surfaced, and she snapped, 'Servants are supposed to look after themselves. She probably has expectations somewhere.'

'Yes, Mother.'

After seven huge barrels lacking only their tops, which the removal men would nail on, stood in a neat line in front of the divested sideboard and china cupboard, Louise allowed herself to be installed in a chair by the morning-room fire to rest.

A troubled Celia slipped down to the kitchen to see her old friend.

Winnie was preparing dinner and was just putting a chicken into the oven to roast. As Celia edged round the big kitchen table to stand by the fire to warm her hands, grubby from the packing she had done, the cook straightened up and closed the oven door.

'I've got a big beef casserole at the back of the oven,' Winnie said. Her voice was strained and weary. 'It can go over to the cottage with the furniture tomorrow and be a good dinner for you. Your mam won't want to cook on her first day in her new house.'

She turned to the table and sat down by it. Swiftly, she began to peel potatoes which she had already washed.

'You are very kind, Winnie. That's most thoughtful of you.' Inwardly, she wondered if her mother would agree to cook at all. Then she explained the reason for her visit to the kitchen.

'Well, Miss Celia, I haven't got nothing yet. But I'm registered with Grey's Domestic Staff Registry and I've answered a couple of ads in *The Lady*. I'm hoping something will turn up.' She dropped a potato slowly into a pan of cold water, and then picked up another one.

'Do you have anywhere to stay while you're waiting?'

'Not really, Miss.'

'I thought you had sons?'

'Oh, aye, I had two. One emigrated to Canada. He's a miner in a place called Yellowknife. And the other one went to sea as a ship's cook.' She sighed, and her paring knife stopped its rapid run round the potato as she looked up at Celia. 'He married a Corpus Christi girl – an American – and sailed out of there for years. He seemed to forget about his old mam. Then, one day, I got a letter from his wife saying that he had been drowned when the Jerries torpedoed his ship.'

'Oh, how terrible! I never knew that,' Celia exclaimed.

The paring knife was slowly put back to work and another potato plopped into the pan, before Winnie could answer. She said, 'Your mam knew. It were a dreadful shock. I loved my boys and I always hoped he'd bring his girl over here to settle, and that I could live with them when I couldn't work no more.

'A good granny can always make herself useful,' she finished up a little piteously.

'Oh, Winnie. I had no idea! You poor thing.'

'Your mam probably kept it from you, so as not to upset you,' Winnie replied, putting the kindest interpretation she could on Louise's lack of communication.

Celia glanced round the kitchen, as if searching for inspiration. The big underground room already seemed deserted, its shelves practically empty. No Ethel at the kitchen sink patiently washing dishes. No sound of Dorothy's quick feet thudding down the stairs; she was out at the cottage, giving the kitchen a final clean and unpacking kitchenware already sent out. Not even a bell ringing for service upstairs.

'What are you going to do after you've done the final cleaning of the house? Mother said she had asked you and Dorothy to do this. This house'll be empty by tomorrow night, and she assumes you will have everything tidy by the day after – and be on your way.'

'I'll find a room somewhere. The Missus says she'll tell the removal men not to take the beds from me and Dorothy's bedroom – she says they can be abandoned – they're not worth moving. She wants Dorothy and me to clean up down here, after everything that's supposed to be moved is moved. She said that, if necessary, I can stay over a day or two to finish the cleaning. There's food left over for us in the pantry, and she'll pay me by the day.' She dropped another peeled potato into a saucepan. 'Is the house sold yet, Miss?'

'Not yet. There are two people considering it – a man who wants to make apartments out of it; and you saw the lady who wants to have it as a nursing home – she's still thinking about it. I believe the estate agent is bringing her tomorrow to look at it again – when it's empty.'

'Oh, aye. She can judge better then.' Winnie's voice seemed lacking in real interest. Then she roused herself to say, 'With so many wounded and not having enough hospitals, they got to have places to put them – those as will never get better, I mean.'

'Yes. It's very sad.' Celia paused, and then said wistfully, 'I wish you could come with us, Winnie. But now that Edna has come home, and one of the bedrooms has been made into a bathroom, the cottage won't hold anybody else.'

'I realise that, Miss. Our Dorothy told me all about the cottage.' She smiled slightly, and said formally, 'I hope you'll be happy there, Miss.'

'Thank you, Winnie. Will you write to tell me how you get on? I do hope you find a place soon.'

'Thank you, Miss.' The cook got up and took a small notebook from the mantelpiece. It had a pencil on a piece of string dangling from it. 'Could you write down your address, Miss?' she asked shyly. 'Because I may need to give your mam's name to a new employer. She's given me a good written reference to carry with me, but sometimes they like to write direct to your old employer – to make sure the reference is genuine, like.'

'Of course.' The address was carefully printed out. Then there did not seem to be anything more to say.

Celia put down the pencil, and turned to the cook. She bent over her and kissed her on the cheek. 'Goodbye, Winnie.' Then she put her arms round the old woman's shoulders and hugged her. 'We've been good friends, haven't we?'

Winnie returned the kiss and the hug. 'You take good care of yourself, Miss.'

As she reluctantly let Celia go, the cook felt that they both had their problems. She told herself that she wouldn't, for the world, like to have Miss Celia's worries. What's going to be left for her when she's as old as I am? At least I can cook. Somebody'll be glad of me.

Chapter Twenty-Three

෨෨

A long empty furniture pantechnicon backed cautiously away from the cottage's new front gate and, after its wheels had flung up a flurry of sand in all directions, it began its journey back to Liverpool to fetch another load which would, this time, be delivered to Aspen's Building Contractors in Hoylake.

In the Liverpool house, Louise and Edna were supervising the dispatch of the furniture, and in the Hoylake cottage Celia and Betty were dealing with its reception and the placing of each piece of furniture. By this time, Celia and Betty were fast friends, and Betty had begged a few hours off from her father, in order to help Celia.

All carpets, pictures and mirrors required in the new home had, two days before, been moved in a smaller van, and the carpets laid by the removal men, as directed by Celia. Much to Louise's horror, Celia had travelled in the van with them to the cottage. Later that day, Louise and Edna had come out to Meols to help to hang curtains and pictures, despite the fact that two men were still working in the bathroom and that the frames of the back windows would not be replaced for another week. A gaping hole where the old kitchen range had been awaited the attention of a plasterer. Such was Celia's fear, however, of the financial drain of the maintenance of the West Derby house that she pressed her mother ruthlessly to move without delay.

None of the women realised how much effort Betty had made to get the work done quickly. She had persuaded her father to give it priority, and had harried the foreman into putting their two best plumbers on the job. It was these two men who, in the late afternoon, came downstairs to say that everything was connected, and that the ladies could now have the water turned on.

This was solemnly done and the taps allowed to run.

As soon as the men had left, there was a rush to use the lavatory.

The plumbers had tidied up, but both sink and bath needed to be scoured.

'What shall we do?' wailed Louise.

'Clean them,' snapped Edna. She immediately went down to the kitchen to find rags and scouring powder and then, rather clumsily, went to work. The result was not very good. Her mother complained, and was met with pained silence.

Supervised by an irate Louise, who refused to actually do anything on the grounds that she was too heartbroken, Celia and Edna had spent the rest of the day inexpertly hammering nails into newly painted walls and hanging the pictures and mirrors wherever they saw fit; their mother, when asked, had gloomily refused to be interested in where they were hung, so, where possible, they hung them in the same rooms that they had been in in the Liverpool house.

Celia had remarked to Edna that it was a relief to be rid of most of the dirty old oil paintings that had graced the walls of the Liverpool house, and have only watercolours to look at. 'Except, of course, for the two oils I've just put here in the living room with the Landseer etching; Mother dotes on them.'

'Well, it's her home,' Edna replied. 'If that's what she wants . . .'

A little stab of fear went through Celia. The cottage belonged, indeed, to her mother – not to either Celia or Edna. She felt that, in future, she should never forget that fact.

Now, as the huge pantechnicon bumped safely on to the main road after delivering the furniture, Celia surveyed the little living room they had created, and declared to Betty, 'I don't think I would have ever been able to achieve this without your support, Betty. You've been such a help.'

Betty was tucking the dining chairs further under the table, to give a little more room for moving about. She made a mock bow. 'My pleasure,' she said. 'It's been the first fun I've had since the war. Even Dad's got interested in it, and he'll see the spare furniture properly stored so that it isn't damaged.'

'He's wonderful – so kind. In fact, everybody I've met in Hoylake has been so nice to me – and patient with Mother.'

'You're a pleasure to deal with – and your mam isn't any different from other women left in the same predicament – there are thousands of them – they just don't know things, that's all. If you can explain simply to them, they usually see the common sense of what you're suggesting. And your mam is no exception.'

'Well, you went far beyond the cause of duty, when you came over to Liverpool and went through the house with her to tell her what would fit here and what would not. She would never have accepted my word for it that you can't get a wardrobe built for crinolines into a cottage!'

Betty laughed. 'And the old-fashioned night commode that she had in her bedroom?'

It was Celia's turn to laugh. 'She only gave in because you could measure that the distance from her new bedroom to her new bathroom was less than walking across her present bedroom to use the awful old thing!'

Her mind turned to the dire need to sell some of the furniture, and she asked, 'Will your father mind, Betty, if I bring prospective purchasers into his barn to show them the pieces for sale?'

'Not him. The gates are open from 7 am to 6.30 pm,

anyway; and it will be a bit of an advertisement for him.'

'Let's sit down and have a cup of tea, while we wait for Mother and Edna,' Celia urged. 'They are bringing all the personal luggage that they didn't want to give to the movers.'

'Jewellery?'

'Yes – and furs and silverware.' She remembered something else for which she had to thank Betty. 'Remember sending me to see Mrs Jowett, in Liverpool – the lady with the antique shop?'

'Yes.'

'Well, once she heard your name, she was really helpful about pricing the furniture. At first, she wanted to come out and buy herself. But I did exactly as you advised me – I told her that I wanted to sell it myself, so that I made the most money. She didn't make fun of me – just said it was sensible. She's lent me a pile of magazines, and a list of Victorian furniture and what is a reasonable price for it – if it's in good condition. And two books on eighteenth-century furniture.' She patted the well-worn tomes sitting on the table in front of her. 'She said she was not an expert on eighteenth-century pieces; though since I know their origins – provenance, she called it – she assured me that I can probably get good prices for them.'

She smiled reflectively at the memory of the old Jewess, who had, in the course of an hour, tried to pass on to her a lifetime of experience in the trade. Then she went on, 'She told me that big pieces take time to sell these days – new houses – and flats – are smaller than pre-war ones – and there isn't the space for heavy furniture.

'She also said a lot of well-to-do people are closing their town houses and renting a flat instead, so that's brought more old furniture on to the market. But, you know, Betty, a lot of Mother's furniture is early Georgian and quite dainty.'

Betty nodded agreement. 'She's right. Dad's got one or

two jobs where he's making big houses into flats – houses like yours, in Liverpool, and the ones on Meols Drive in Hoylake.'

While the kettle for tea heated on the fire, they went slowly through the lobby and hall, both of which were newly painted cream; and the sunlight caught the glass door which Celia's grandmother had loved so much, and reflected the pretty design on to the wall.

In the hall hung some of her mother's favourite water-colours. Under their feet lay part of the good Brussels stair carpet from the West Derby house. The stone floor of the back room, to which they now slowly returned, boasted the Turkey carpet from the old dining room; it had been cut to fit the smaller room. Louise had said crossly that it was pure sacrilege to hack at such a beautiful carpet, but she had insisted on bringing it, so that was what Celia had arranged.

The red velvet curtains from the same room had been shortened by a local seamstress to fit the little windows. In the struggle to hang both pictures and curtains, the weary sisters had snapped and snarled at each other and argued with their mother.

In one case, Louise had suddenly decided she did not like the curtains in the front bedroom which was to be hers, and they had to take them down and put them in Edna's room. Edna did not like them either, but lost the battle.

It had been the most tiring two days that Celia ever remembered. Her shoulders and back had ached unbearably during the night.

By the time the three women had caught the train back to Liverpool, they were barely on speaking terms. The following morning, however, Edna, usually so silent, had asked Celia if she would rub her back with surgical spirit because it ached so badly. Celia agreed.

When she lifted her sister's shift in order to apply the

embrocation, she had been shocked at the incredible thinness of her. Her shoulder blades stuck out and her backbone looked like a knotted cord.

As she banged the cork back into the surgical spirit bottle, Celia asked, 'Are you well, Edna? You are too thin.'

'I am perfectly well, thank you. I am simply unused to having to work like a servant.' The tone did not brook a response, so Celia turned away; she herself had, in the previous month, done much more than either of the other two women, but she had not lost weight.

Now a fire, built by Celia according to Dorothy's careful instruction, blazed in the old-fashioned cottage grate which had been well burnished with black lead.

Dorothy is a professional when it comes to cleaning, thought Celia with a sigh, as she set out teacups on the table, and I will never be as good.

The division of domestic responsibilities had yet to be discussed, and Celia had automatically assumed that most of the work would be piled on to her shoulders.

'Dorothy's going to come in some time tomorrow, to clean out the garden shed,' she told Betty. 'It's got shelves on which we can store all the trunks.'

'That'll be a help,' Betty replied. She wondered grimly who would be the first woman to get up the following morning and make the living-room fire. Probably poor old Celia, she decided.

At that moment, Dorothy was busy cleaning the rapidly emptying house in West Derby, and Winnie was supervising the removers, while she also wielded a broom. Dorothy was not very happy about her new job as the only servant in a home, but she reckoned it would do until she got something better.

She had leaped at the chance of coming out to the cottage once more. She had always prided herself on knowing a good man when she saw one, and she had welcomed the possibility of meeting Eddie again. She had told Winnie that he was elderly – but not old – and a real nice fella.

Winnie wished her well, and wondered if the Missus would mind if she herself continued to sleep for a few extra days in her attic bedroom. After some thought, she decided that Mrs G. would probably never find out that she was there. If the estate agent called, she could always tell him that, in order to deter vandals, Mrs G. wanted her to stay until the house was sold. As she stolidly swept bare boards, ready for Dorothy to scrub them, she felt some relief at the idea of gaining a few more days' respite from wandering the streets looking for cheap accommodation while she continued her hunt for a job.

To this end, when packing up the contents of the pantry ready for transfer to the cottage, she had carefully segregated some of the large store of dry goods and hidden them in one of the cellars, where also lay at least a couple of hundredweight of coal which was not worth moving. If absolutely necessary, and if the house took time to sell, she could exist for a number of weeks, she planned, on porridge, potatoes, a little barrel of eggs preserved in isinglass, on bread she would bake for herself and on any scraps left over after the family had left.

Winnie had dealt honestly with the Gilmores during all the years she had been with them. But now, deeply resentful of Louise's indifference to the plight of her servants, she knew she must secure her own survival. If she could not get a job, her only resource would be the workhouse, and she shuddered at the very idea of being reduced to that.

In the Gilmores' new home, the removal men had placed the furniture under Celia's direction. It still needed a little adjustment, but the general effect was so friendly that Betty sank into a chair with a contented sigh, and said, 'It looks lovely, doesn't it?'

'Yes!' Celia did a small dancelike twirl round the centre

table, and came to rest by Betty. 'And you did it!' She put her arms round her new friend and kissed her.

Betty said firmly, 'No. I didn't. I simply encouraged you and Mrs Gilmore.' She smiled up at Celia. 'All the pair of you needed was confidence. Between the two of you, you put it all together; and Dad won't send his bill until the end of the month – I'll see to that!'

Celia laughed; she was worried about money, but was sure that, once the Liverpool house was sold, everything would be all right.

Betty asked, 'What about Mrs Fellowes?'

Celia sighed. Before she answered, she took the lid off the teapot and took down a tea caddy from the mantelpiece. As she carefully measured the tea into the pot, she said slowly, 'Well, Mother has encouraged Edna to come to live with us. So she's going to have the back bedroom, next to the bathroom – and we have put into it most of the furniture from the bedroom she had as a girl. Her own furniture will arrive eventually from South America – all beautiful and hand-turned, according to her – so, if Mr Aspen is agreeable, we'll put that into your barn until she is certain about where she will live.' She reached for the kettle which had come to the boil and poured the water on to the tea. Then, as she stirred it, she considered her sister.

She glanced at Betty, and went on, 'Edna's really very odd, Betty, and I worry about her sometimes. It is almost as if she is on the edge of a complete breakdown – and she's no flesh on her at all. I don't know whether she talks to Mother when I'm not with them, but I find it very strange that she never talks about Paul – or even generally about her life in Brazil. You would think that she would be eager to tell us all about it – because it would be very interesting – but she never says a word to me. It is almost as if it defeated her – if one can be defeated by a country.'

'Perhaps her loss is too great, Celia. Perhaps it is too

painful to talk about it. Not only has she lost her husband, but she has lost a country – which she may well have loved. And you said that her little girl was buried in Brazil?'

Celia nodded. She poured the tea and sat down opposite Betty. She offered her a plate of biscuits, and Betty took one. After they had eaten their biscuits, Celia continued her line of thought about Edna. 'I keep getting the feeling that she really didn't care much about Paul. He was a good match and she never complains about him – she just doesn't say anything about him. She's like someone patiently sitting in a railway station, waiting for a train to arrive.

'It puzzles me. It's as if his memory simply does not exist in her mind. Your David's always in your mind. I know, because you mention him with such love all the time, that I wish I had an equivalent memory to sustain me.' The last words were said with real longing.

Betty nodded, and then said lightly, 'You're young enough yet to meet someone.' She pushed her cup across the table, and asked, with the freedom of a friend, if she could have more tea. Celia quickly picked up the teapot and refilled the cup. She then pressed more biscuits on her.

As she settled in her chair again, Celia said, 'I don't have a chance, you know that. Besides, who will look after Mama?'

'She'll be young enough to look after herself for a very long time,' responded Betty a little tartly. She reverted to their discussion of Edna, and said, 'This little house will, unavoidably, make you and Edna live very close to each other – and she may open up, when she gets really used to you – and you to her. Be patient with her. She's obviously not well.'

'Betty, you're a saint, which I am not. But I'll try.'

Suddenly, Louise's voice could be heard raised high in complaint, as the new gate squeaked open. Behind her, Edna gave sharp orders to someone. A heavy weight was dumped at the open front door. There was a sound of men's voices, as Louise came down the passageway and into the little room.

'Oh, tea!' she exclaimed thankfully, and plunked down on a straight chair beside the table. The table had a plum-coloured velvet cloth on it and the pompoms which trimmed its edge got entangled in her handbag. She threatened to drag the cloth and the tea tray off the table. Celia sprang to her aid.

'Good afternoon, Miss Aspen,' she greeted Betty. 'Dear me! What a knot I'm in. No place to lay down a handbag in that poky little hall. I really don't know how we shall manage.'

Betty ignored her complaint. 'I'm Mrs Houghton,' she corrected her rather sharply.

'Of course. I am so sorry, Mrs Houghton.'

As her daughter untangled her handbag from the table-cloth, Louise ordered, 'Make a big fresh pot, Celia. We're exhausted!'

Outside, men gasped, and shouted encouragement to each other to 'Heave!' and Edna admonished them to be careful of her trunks, and told them to carry them straight upstairs.

One of them stepped inside to take a look at the extremely steep staircase, and there was a stubborn male refusal, the excuse being that they would scratch the obviously newly painted walls.

'Unpack 'em first, Ma'am. Then you can ease 'em up more careful,' they advised in chorus.

True Merseysiders who felt they were being pushed too hard, thought Celia with a smile. She herself had come up against such an attitude more than once during the previous month, and had discovered that the working class, no matter how poor it was, had a strong sense of self-preservation. She had learned to respect it.

Edna said something in Portuguese which sounded

derogatory, and the indignant men answered her in a united rumble of defence.

Celia, having unravelled her mother from the tablecloth, ignored her request for tea, and went to see what was happening outside.

Betty rose and said she must go back to work. She wished Louise happiness in her new home, and received a tired, resigned smile in return.

Outside stood a big railway station handcart with two trunks and a large suitcase still on it. Beside the cart lay three huge steamer trunks and a couple of packing cases. Edna was carrying, one in each hand, two large travelling jewellery cases.

Celia faced two red-faced porters standing by the trunks on the path, and a very cross Edna. She said placatingly, 'Don't worry, Edna. We'll manage. The trunks will have to be stored in the garden shed anyway.'

'I won't have handmade leather trunks stored in a place which is probably damp!' snapped Edna in response.

Behind Celia, Betty, trying to get out, edged round another big trunk which had already been dumped in the lobby. 'Hello, Freddy – George,' she greeted both men. 'Good afternoon, Mrs Fellowes.' She cast a critical glance over the trunks and said, 'With respect, Mrs Fellowes, the size of these really is too big for you to get them up the stairs, I am sure. They may get wedged – and almost certainly the staircase wall will be scratched. The men are simply being careful.'

The porters immediately relaxed and looked very self-righteous.

Edna had already met Betty on several occasions and had learned to respect her quick mind. She therefore accepted this professional estimate of size, and, with an effort, controlled her irritation. She said politely, 'Thank you, Mrs Houghton.'

She made way for Betty to get on to the pathway, and

then stepped round the trunks and into the house. Betty gravely winked at the porters and touched Celia's arm gently in acknowledgement, as the younger woman whispered a heartfelt 'Thank you.'

After Betty had marched down the red-tiled garden path, her black skirt swinging, her sensible shoes crunching the ever-present sand, the porters lifted the remaining luggage off their handcart. An unsmiling Edna thrust a sovereign into the hand of one of the men, and said, 'You may go.'

Without thanking her, the porters, wooden-faced, pushed the clumsy vehicle into the lane. After struggling in a muddy puddle, they managed to turn the handcart round. Celia watched them, as they followed Betty towards the main road.

Their good neighbour, Eddie Fairbanks, had cut the front hedge for them, and the cottage now had a view of a patch of rough green grass with a few trees and, at some distance, the thatched roof of the cottage where the fishing family lived. The whole area was so quiet that Celia concluded that the tide must be out. She had not yet had time to walk down to the sea.

The tiny front garden was a trampled mess after the constant comings and goings of workmen and movers, but, in an untouched corner, a rambler rose which Eddie had left unsnipped clung to the hedge and was putting out leaves.

Comforted by the sight of it and by a warm sun, Celia reluctantly turned to face the problems within the house.

Chapter Twenty-Four

❧

The first evening of the family's residence in their new home began peacefully, despite the muddle of clothes hastily unpacked from the trunks and dumped on to beds, and an argument about what to do with the trunks themselves. The trunks were eventually left by the front steps because no one could suggest where to put them, except in the garden shed, which was still awaiting Dorothy's ministrations. Tired out and aching everywhere, Edna mentally abandoned them; what were trunks anyway?

Since Edna and Louise both declared themselves exhausted, Celia laid the table for dinner. She had, some hours earlier, placed the casserole, which Winnie had made for them, in the oven of the range in the living room, to heat up. Now, she put out some bread and butter and made a pot of coffee.

Louise, who had given little thought to the need to eat that evening, looked at the single big dish in the middle of the table, and asked, 'Is that all that Winnie prepared? She said she was going to make dinner for us.'

'She put everything in one big dish, Mama – for simplicity.'

'No soup? No dessert?'

Celia pulled out a chair and sat down; Edna was already seated. She unfolded her linen table napkin and laid it across her lap.

'No, Mama. She simply made lots of meat and vegetables.'

Since her mother made no move to serve, though Celia had set three plates in front of her, she asked, 'Shall I serve?'

'Please.' The reality of her new life struck Louise forcibly. No one was going to cook for them or serve them; they would have to do everything themselves. She sulkily passed the little pile of plates to Celia.

Edna inquired, 'Shall I cut some bread, Mama?'

'Please.' Louise's little mouth was clamped closed. What had she come to? Looking round the cosy little room and then at the sparsely laid table, she again wondered bitterly why Timothy had had to die in the prime of his life – and leave her to rot in a place like this.

Edna sawed three thick slices of bread from the last loaf Winnie would bake for them, and then lifted up the wooden bread board with both hands, to offer pieces to her companions.

As she took a slice, Celia cast a quick, thankful glance at her sister. Now she was installed in the cottage, would she help her?

Louise ate slowly. The casserole was delicious. Celia knew it, but Louise grumbled throughout the meal. She felt terribly confined in the tiny room, she said – they could barely move around in it. She had banged her leg on the metal corner of one of her trunks and it was hurting. Going up and down stairs into freezing bedrooms had given her a chill, she was sure of it – everything was so draughty. 'Perhaps one of you girls would make a fire up there for me?' she whined hopefully.

Neither daughter answered because neither of them wanted to set a precedent. Most people managed without them – with hot water bottles in their beds, Celia finally reminded her.

Edna said wearily that she had a hot water bottle with

her, and that perhaps dear Mother would like to borrow it tonight. She could buy one for herself tomorrow in the village.

Louise responded savagely that, somewhere amid the furniture on its way to Aspen's there were probably umpteen hot water bottles. If not, she doubted if she could afford a new one after all the expense of setting up the cottage and moving into it.

Celia said soothingly that she would look for an old brick or a stone to put in the back of the oven to heat for her — wrapped in a towel, it would keep her feet warm in bed. 'Winnie used to have bricks in the back of the oven all the time, to heat the servants' beds,' she informed her mother.

'Servants!' exclaimed Louise. 'They take all kinds of liberties!'

'Well, you will be saved from that in future!' remarked Edna with unexpected acidity.

Louise's answer was icy. 'I am aware of it,' she almost snarled.

Edna helped herself to butter, and Celia asked if anyone was ready for coffee.

'We could have coffee in the front room,' Louise pointed out.

'There isn't a fire there, Mama. It may be rather chilly. And, as yet, there are heaps of boxes piled up in the middle of it. We have to get it tidied up by tomorrow, so that Mr Aspen's man can finish painting it.'

Celia hastily poured the coffee and handed her mother a cup, before she could reply. 'Would you like to sit closer to the fire, in here?' She pointed to her mother's favourite easy chair, carefully installed at the side of the fireplace so that she would be warm, and yet leave a little space to walk round the table. Louise squeezed round Edna's chair and plunked herself down in it.

She waited for Celia to hand her her coffee and then complained that she had nowhere to set it down.

'Mr Fairbanks always puts his cup down on the flat top of his brass fender,' Celia told her with determined cheerfulness.

'Humph.' Louise's grunt conveyed all too well her opinion of Mr Fairbanks' habits.

Louise's remark that she probably could not afford a hot water bottle had reminded Celia that they had to discuss money matters, and also domestic duties. And who was to care for the garden?

At the thought, she felt a little sick inside, but after she had served coffee for Edna and herself, she turned her chair so that she could see the faces of both the other women, and bravely opened up the subject, by saying, 'I imagine, Mama, that you and Edna have discussed what she should contribute as her share of the expenses?'

Without waiting for a reply, she added to Edna, 'When we were talking about your furniture being put in the barn, you told us that you will be receiving funds from Paul's company, so I imagine you will be able to help Mama – at least a little bit. Especially until the house is sold and Cousin Albert has arranged for Mother to have an annuity from that.'

Up to that moment, Louise had not thought that Edna should contribute to the household; she still thought of her as the dependent young girl she had been before her marriage.

'She's my daughter!' she exclaimed. 'I don't expect any money from her! Any more than I do from you.'

Celia's pale face flushed. She wanted to say indignantly, 'But I earn my food by running after you like a slave. And mighty little thanks, never mind money, I get for it. And ever since she came home, I've been at Edna's beck and call, too.' But wisdom prevailed, and she simply hung her head.

Edna stirred sugar into her coffee. 'Of course I shall contribute a share to the housekeeping, as long as I am living here,' she said indignantly. 'Now we're settled in the cottage, I would myself have brought the matter up tomorrow. I got a letter from Papa Fellowes yesterday, and he has arranged to send me a cheque each month. He has advised me to open a bank account nearby. The first cheque should arrive in a day or two.' She glanced resentfully at her mother. 'Up to now I have had only the money which Paul and I were carrying with us and a little which Papa Fellowes gave me – to help. He is very kind.'

She looked suddenly very forlorn. To comfort her, Celia impulsively put out her hand to cover her sister's shrivelled yellow one. She was rewarded by a wry smile, as Edna withdrew her hand to pick up her coffee cup and sip the cooling drink.

After she had dabbed her lips with her table napkin, Edna went on, 'There is also a thing called a letter of credit, which Paul used to transfer his savings from Salvador – but that's part of his estate, Papa Fellowes said, and it will be some time before that money comes to me. He recommends that, when he is able to cash it for me, I should bank it for emergencies.'

Louise had listened with rapt attention. 'It sounds as if you will be quite well off.'

'I don't know yet. I certainly won't starve.' Edna moved uneasily in her chair, as if agitated by the comment, and then added with real bitterness, 'As yet, I have no idea what I shall be able to do.' How could she say to this self-centred mother of hers that all she wanted to do was to be with Vital. Yet, if she went back to Brazil and married him, people would immediately begin to gossip – and they could both be ruined socially, even if they could find enough money to live on.

Louise was contrite. 'I'm sorry, dear. I should not have asked about your affairs. It is kind of you to offer to contribute to the housekeeping – and I must say that I shall be very grateful for it, since I have to keep two people.' She glanced towards Celia.

Celia flushed even more deeply with embarrassment. She summoned up a smile for Edna, however, and echoed Louise's thanks.

Louise heaved herself out of her chair, leaving her coffee cup resting on the flat surface of the brass fender. 'Well, I suppose I must go upstairs and put away my clothes,' she said wearily. 'It is going to be terribly cold up there. I must put on my velvet jacket.'

Celia got up, too, and mechanically went into the hall to find the velvet jacket and help her mother into it. As the cold silk lining touched her, Louise shivered dramatically, and said, 'Really, Celia, I think you should have lit more fires.'

'It has been a very busy day, Mama, and it *is* the end of April!' Dear God, how am I ever going to cope? she asked herself, and went back into the living room.

Edna had already piled the dishes together, and she said, 'You wash and I'll dry.'

Celia's spirits rose a little. She had earlier put the kettle on the fire, and when it had boiled, had set it on the hob to keep warm for washing dishes.

When she poured the water into the kitchen wash basin, set in a brand-new sink, she suddenly realised that it had two taps. She put down the kettle on the draining board, and there was an immediate hiss as its hot bottom scorched the wood. She snatched it off before it did any real damage, and with a laugh, said to Edna, 'I'd forgotten that, when Mr Aspen put the boiler in, it would be linked to the kitchen sink as well as the bathroom! Like an idiot, I've been running upstairs when I wanted hot water or I've been boiling it. Isn't it wonderful – we've got hot water upstairs and downstairs!'

'It will be a real help,' agreed Edna. 'Where are the tea towels?'

'I suppose Dorothy put them in one of the drawers.'

Though Edna was not very cheerful, she was at least company, thought Celia, and she had volunteered to help. As she inexpertly washed the dishes and handed them to Edna to dry, she ventured a question.

'Did you have many servants in Brazil?'

'I had six indoor ones, and two peons for the garden – and a housekeeper called Conchita.'

'That must have been nice.'

'It was in a way – but it could be terribly boring; they often quarrelled amongst themselves, and then I had to sort them out. And that wasn't everybody. Paul had a Brazilian live-in male secretary, Mr Vital Oliveira; he was very helpful, particularly when I first arrived and could not speak any Portuguese. He would translate for me, and he explained about local customs.' At the latter recollection, she smiled softly down at the saucer she was drying. 'Then there was a chauffeur who lived over the garage – there was a car for city use – these two men were company employees, not mine.'

She put the saucer carefully down on a side table, and took another one from Celia. She continued, 'Paul was away quite a lot of the time, up in the hills to see how the dam was going on – that's how they were going to get electricity, though I must say I don't understand these things. His senior works people and a translator – and the chauffeur – went with him. The chauffeur was in charge of the horses and stores that they had to take along.'

In the weeks that Edna had been at home, this was the longest response that Celia had got to a question, and she realised that it was the first time that she had been alone with Edna. Quite often, after a meal, Edna would vanish off to smoke in her bedroom or, if the weather was fine, into the narrow town garden behind the house. Conversational exchanges, when they occurred, had been between Louise and Edna; if Celia had been in the room, she had been ignored or sent away to do some errand for one of them. And, of course, she told herself, she had been away at the cottage much of the time.

'How did you fill your time?' she asked Edna, and Edna described a round of visits to other English women – and some Brazilians. 'When I first arrived, I had a Portuguese lesson each morning.'

'Can you speak it?'

'Yes – I think reasonably well now.'

'How clever of you!' Celia's admiration was genuine. 'What else did you do?'

'Sometimes there were festivals, like Christmas and Easter. And they were rather keen on saints' days. The churches had processions, which we used to watch from somebody's balcony. And there were musical evenings . . .' Her voice trailed off. 'I was ill a great deal – I seemed to catch every germ you can imagine, especially after little Rosemary died.'

'That must have grieved you very much.'

'It did. I refused to have any more children until we returned here.'

'How could you refuse? Phyllis says they come every year, once you're married.'

'There are ways.' Edna laughed a little cynically. 'And I just said no.'

The implications of the latter remark were lost on Celia, but she said, 'I wish you would explain that to Phyllis. She has already four little ones, and she looks so ill because the strain of it all is too much for her. I worry a lot about her – I simply must go to see her again soon.'

'Hasn't she ever heard of Margaret Sanger? She wrote a book at the beginning of the war on the need to limit families – and before her, there was, for years, a Malthusian League which spread information about how to do it. Really, Celia! English women should come into the twentieth century.'

Celia emptied and rinsed the washing-up basin. Then she sought a towel in the same drawer that had yielded the tea cloth, and slowly wiped her hands. She was blushing, as she admitted, 'I've never heard of any such thing. And I don't think Phyllis has.'

'Humph. A couple of years ago, a lady called Marie Carmichael Stopes wrote a very clear book about it. I am sure it must be available in Liverpool. Poor Phyllis should read it – she doesn't need to tell her husband!'

While Celia slowly digested this information, Edna folded the cloth she had been using, then realised that it was very wet and shook it out and draped it over the side of the sink to dry. With reference to Phyllis, Edna suggested diffidently, 'It might be a good idea if she first talked to her husband!'

'Him?' Celia's laugh was scornful. 'He's the most thoughtless man you can imagine.' Then she added anxiously, 'I've only seen Phyllis once since little Timothy was born. I wonder if Mother and you could manage, if I went over to Liverpool to see her tomorrow afternoon? I could tell her then. As you know, Dorothy will be here for a few hours to help you. And I should really go and see if the furniture has been put into the barn – and that it's all there.' Her voice was heavy with anxiety. 'And whether Winnie and Dorothy have cleaned the house properly, so that it is ready to be shown to the nursing home lady.'

'You had better ask Mother.' Edna relapsed into her usual melancholy silence, and wandered out of the kitchen and went upstairs, presumably to smoke and to put away the clothes lying on her bed.

Though Celia felt relieved that she had made some headway with Edna, she was overwhelmed with the work which would have to be done on the morrow. Could she, somehow, persuade her mother to go into Hoylake to buy food? The shops would surely send anything she chose – she had seen errand boys trailing around on their delivery bikes when she had been in the village before. And then someone must at least make the living-room fire and keep it up, so that they could cook, someone would have to wipe the mud from the lobby and sweep up the kitchen, make the beds; perhaps Dorothy would do those jobs just for tomorrow.

And we must decide what to do about the garden.

Every time she mentally went through the list and considered its long-term implications, however, the jobs came back to her.

Already tired to death with the effort of the previous few weeks, she wanted to scream.

Impulsively she yanked open the back kitchen door, stiff from new paint, and stared into the wilderness of the back garden.

Fresh sea air blew in upon her, making her skirt and apron billow. It caught at tendrils of her hair and blew them out of their confining pins. She thankfully lifted her tired face to it. A full moon in a sky empty of cloud gave good illumination.

In all her visits to the cottage, she had always walked towards Hoylake, never towards the sea – she had simply been too busy. And it was not cold this evening, she thought. Spring is here.

Left on the back of a chair was a shawl, discarded by her mother in favour of her heavy velvet house jacket. She snatched it up and whipped it round her shoulders. Her outdoor shoes lay, waiting to be cleaned, on a piece of newspaper by the kitchen door. She kicked off her house slippers and slid her little feet into them. Not bothering to tie the laces, she stepped out of the house and closed the kitchen door softly behind her. There was no back gate, so she ran round the side of the house.

When she reached the front gate, she turned right and

right again, so that she faced the sea. A narrower lane
continued before her. Bending to the wind, she joyfully
took it.

Chapter Twenty-Five

❧

Half stumbling over her loose shoelaces, she ran down towards the sea wall.

Between the cottage and the ocean, a huge dyke guarded the common land from the inroads of the remorseless sea, and she could hear the gentle slap of the waves rippling against the other side of this concrete embankment. The tide must be nearly full, she thought with sudden happiness.

Before climbing the embankment, she paused to catch her breath.

The moon lit up the coarse grass of the common and the rough surface of the dyke. A pair of oystercatchers, disturbed by her hurrying footsteps, fluttered out of the grass, to rise and then settle a little further away, to await the turn of the tide, when they would go hunting over the bare damp sand.

Faintly she could hear young voices calling to each other. It sounded as if a party had come out to enjoy a swim in the moonlit sea.

Feeling a little envious, she hitched up her skirt and climbed the steep land side of the embankment. The tide was coming in quite fast, she noted. Further out, towards the horizon, great waves foamed over the Hoyle sandbank.

She glanced to her right, where in the near distance, the Leasowe lighthouse, long disused, stood like a ghostly monument to forgotten seamen. The old castle beyond it was invisible, as was the new clutter of makeshift shacks, bereft of water or sanitation, which had, during the past year or two, been built by poverty-stricken homeless people on what was common land. A faint glow on the horizon marked where Liverpool lay on the other side of the Mersey Estuary.

About thirty feet out, a dozen or more people were cavorting in the water and splashing each other.

Holding down her skirts with one hand against the whipping wind and clutching her shawl with the other, she glanced to her left. Far on the horizon lay the dark hump of Wales pinpricked by an occasional light. Between it and her, she knew, lay the treacherous mouth of the River Dee with its infamous shifting sands waiting to drown the unwary.

A sharp shout from the water drew her eyes back to the bathers, and she was startled to realise that they were all naked.

She was immediately shocked and disapproving. She had swum many times herself at Rhyl, but always garbed, like other bathers, in a black woollen bathing costume, which, though it showed her figure, certainly covered her from neck to knee. And in Rhyl there were always bathing machines, drawn by horses a few feet into the sea itself, where one could change one's clothes and then slip discreetly into the water. Here, she could clearly see in the moonlight the bouncing breasts of women and the flash of male buttocks as men dived under the waves to tease the women.

'Come on, girl! Hurry up. Take your clothes off and come in,' said a male voice behind her, and someone gave her bottom a playful smack as if to encourage her to go down to the water.

She spun round.

A totally nude man was rocking on his heels in front of her. She was appalled, and her mouth fell open in a gasp.

She had never seen a naked man before, and his hairiness revolted her. A shock of black hair, a huge black moustache, a black doormat on the chest which tapered down over a protruding stomach to a bunch of hair out of which dangled, instead of the fig leaf on statues, the appendage which Phyllis had once tried to describe to her. Heavy hairy legs and huge ugly feet reminded her of an ape in the zoo.

As he snatched merrily at her shawl, he became, suddenly, a menace. 'Come on, now. Don't be shy,' he urged, breathing the smell of beer into her face, as he danced lightly in front of her to keep himself warm. 'All the other girls are in already.'

'How dare you!' she hissed frigidly, clutching her shawl close to her neck.

He was a little nonplussed. 'Well, what are you here for? You don't have to be such a prude. Come in and have some fun. Don't be silly.'

But, in panic, she dodged round him and was gone, slipping and sliding down the concrete slope towards the cottage, regardless of torn stockings or loose shoelaces, running along the shadowed lane, panting with fear.

For a moment, he stood watching her while he shivered slightly in the wind. Then he shrieked, 'Tally-ho! Tally-ho!' and, with arms waving, ran sure-footed down the slope after her.

His hunter's cry was apparently heard by other males, who answered promptly from the water side of the embankment. Two more men scrambled, dripping, to the top.

Regardless of the sudden cold of the wind on their bare skins, all three followed the fleeing figure down the lane, whooping joyfully as they went.

Celia glanced back and screamed in pure terror, her belief in the friendliness of her new neighbours gone.

O Lord! No back gate to the cottage garden. She shot round to the front, straight into the arms of another man.

In pure hysteria, she screamed again and again and

struggled in a pair of strong arms, while her shocked mother, who had heard her, pushed hard in order to open her bedroom window, stiff from its new paint.

Suddenly the window gave, and Louise was nearly precipitated out of it. 'Celia,' she shrieked. 'What on earth's going on?'

Chapter Twenty-Six

Strolling up and down in front of the cottages while he enjoyed a last smoke before bedtime, Eddie Fairbanks had hardly time to stuff his pipe into his jacket pocket before he caught the fleeing young woman in his arms.

'Jesus! What's up, luv?' he gasped, as three satyrs came tearing round the hedge, shrieking, 'View halloo!' as if they had sighted a hunted fox, to resolve themselves in seconds into three slightly shamefaced young men stopped in their tracks.

They shivered in the wind.

'What the hell are you doing?' Eddie demanded furiously of them over Celia's shoulder. 'Get out of here, you stupid bastards. Frightening a decent young woman to death!' He glanced down at Celia. 'It's all right, luv. It's all right.' He glared again at the young men fidgeting uncertainly before him. 'Now you get going and get yourselves covered, or I'll call the military police, I will.'

An exclamation from the bedroom window caused the men to look up. They were being viewed with horror by a portly lady in a nightgown and frilly bedcap. Behind her loomed another female, who was tittering loudly.

The titters did it. They turned and fled as quickly as they had come, while Celia clung to Eddie, her face buried in his shoulder as if he were her father. At the sound of his voice, she had ceased to scream, but she was still shaking with fright.

'Come on, luv. They've gone.' He felt behind his back,

to open the Gilmore front gate. 'I'll take you in to your mam. She'll make some tea for you. The boys don't mean no harm – they was just teasing you, I bet.' Holding her firmly, in case she fainted, he eased her up the garden path.

It was Edna, in a dressing gown, who opened the door to him, while Louise, wrapped in a quilt, stumped slowly down the staircase, saying crossly, as she descended, 'Celia! What are you doing outside at this time of night?'

Eddie ignored the older woman and said to Edna, 'She's had a proper scare, Ma'am. Take care of her.'

'Who were they?' Edna asked, as quite gently, she helped a weeping Celia across the threshold, and passed her to her scolding mother.

'They're probably ex-servicemen, Ma'am. There is a number of big houses round here as is nursing homes, so to speak – there's one full of blind, waiting to get into St Dunstan's. This lot was probably mostly shell-shocked or in for treatment for illness or gas in the trenches.' He sighed heavily. 'There's so many of them that it's easy for them to get out at night, and they come out to the pubs – and people stand them drinks – and they pick up the local girls.' He looked at the shrewd brown eyes before him, lit up by the oil lamp hanging in the hall. 'You know how it is.'

'I do have some idea,' Edna responded dryly. 'Though I cannot imagine what made Celia go out.' She gathered her dressing gown more tightly round her thin figure, and Eddie stepped back down the step. Then he hesitated, and said, 'Be careful of Miss Celia – she's gone through a lot lately. And done a lot.'

'It has been a difficult time for all of us, Mr Fairbanks.'

He was dismissed. He absently took his pipe out of his pocket, and looked at it. 'Oh, aye. It's a hard time for everybody. Good night.'

He plodded slowly down the path, carefully shutting the gate after him and went back to his empty house.

As he knocked the dottle out of his pipe on the top bar of the fireplace and then refilled it with fresh tobacco, he thought of the silly naked youngsters he had just told off.

'Half crazy with what they've been through,' he considered. 'Under twenty-five, I bet, but with four years of bloody war already behind them. Hell-bent because life don't mean much to them any more. Nerves shot; lungs ruined.'

As he tamped down the tobacco in his pipe, he sank slowly into his easy chair.

He was reminded suddenly of the earl in whose gardens he had served so faithfully. With three sons killed, when the old man died the earldom would probably die out – or go to some far-distant cousin safe in the Colonies. Proper cut up, the old earl had been. But maybe it was better than having them come back as crazy as the lads who had chased Miss Celia.

You could hate the aristocracy and the middle classes as much as you liked, he pondered sadly, but you had to admit that their families had paid a frightful price in the war – if you thought of the losses in proportion to numbers. And they were the educated, the future leaders – Eddie was very feudal in his outlook. In his book, rank had its obligation to provide leaders, as it had done since time began, and keep in line young louts like the men who had chased poor Celia.

There were thousands of working-class lads who never saw a battlefield, he ruminated – and thank goodness for that – safe in factories and works, they had been. And a tremendous number had been turned down by the army doctors as being physically unfit for service; rotten food, rotten housing, polluted rivers and air had wreaked havoc on the health of those who lived in the slums of the cities – and yet that very bad health had actually saved them from being flung into the furnace – it was strange how bad luck could become good luck, he mused.

But as long as he could stand up and walk, there was no excuse for an earl's son not to fight – or, come to that, for the boys who volunteered from Liverpool offices – the work they did in banks and insurance offices, shops and professions could be done by women. Likewise, the work of men on the farms. Boys like them simply answered the call to the colours and joined the Liverpool Pals – and knew they were going out to die, like Mrs Gilmore's boys next door, though one of them hadn't gone to France – he'd been drowned with Lord Kitchener, Miss Celia had told him.

The thought of young George Gilmore's drowning reminded him of the lads like his own son, merchant seamen who had drowned in thousands, sent to the bottom by submersibles – submarines, they called them now – the devil's work.

As he remembered the expressions on the faces of the scandalous young men he had chastised, his mood lightened and he chuckled. They had looked such utter fools. How Miss Celia had panicked – and her a brave little thing if ever there was one.

Then he told himself that it was no laughing matter; despite the cold wind on their damp naked bodies, they might have managed to rape her. They'd probably leave a few babies in the district before the military got round to putting them back into barracks or into better treatment in military hospitals.

But barracks and hospitals, wherever nurses and doctors could be found, were still full of the terribly wounded, unlikely to get better – or, if they did, with lives foreshortened by years in the trenches.

And their womenfolk – how were they managing? He knew a number of mothers and wives already harried to death by the need to care for helpless, crippled servicemen – and on miserably small pensions, to boot. Or widowed with young children and no man to help to look after them.

Betty Houghton was lucky that she had her father, Ben Aspen, to keep a hold on young Alfie.

He pulled himself up. 'Tush, man. You're getting morbid – it's too much being by yourself,' he chided himself. 'Maybe it's good that you've got some neighbours at last.'

He heaved himself out of his chair and went across the room to find his bottle of rum.

Chapter Twenty-Seven

✍

Followed by her mother, Celia stumbled into the living room and collapsed. She put her head down on her knees and sobbed helplessly, while Louise stood over her and continued to storm about stupid girls who went out at night and brought all kinds of trouble down on themselves.

When Edna entered the little room, she hesitated. The oil lamp on the mantelpiece still burned, but the fire had gone out and it would take time to rebuild it in order to boil water to make tea. She went to the sideboard and, with difficulty because of lack of space, opened the cupboard door and pulled out the first bottle she could reach. She managed, also, to open the matching cupboard on the other side sufficiently to get out a teacup. She had no idea where Dorothy had put the wine glasses.

With a little shrug, she filled the richly decorated cup with white wine.

She had almost to push Louise out of the way before she could kneel down by her sister. 'Have some wine,' she urged. 'It will help you.' She put her free arm round Celia's shoulders and pulled her a little upright.

Edna's touch was kind and Celia made an effort to stop sobbing, as she thankfully turned towards her. She obediently swallowed some of the wine, which was pleasantly sweet. Then she pulled her handkerchief out from her sleeve and blew her nose.

'I'm so sorry,' she gasped, and took the little cup and

finished its contents. 'I was just so frightened. They were naked. Lots of them, men and women in the sea!'

While Edna laughed at this, Louise stopped in the middle of her tirade, and exclaimed, 'Women?' Then she turned on Edna, and snapped, 'This is no laughing matter!'

Edna giggled. 'The men looked so funny!'

Celia put down the empty cup on the floor beside her feet. Still sobbing, she said defensively, 'They looked horrible to me. I was frightened to death.' She turned back to her sister, in whose eyes humour still twinkled.

'Haven't you ever seen a naked man before?' Edna asked.

'No! Of course not!'

'Really, Edna!' This was from Louise.

'Well, Mother, very few men look good in their skins.'

Louise's voice was icy. 'This is not a suitable subject for discussion. You are not to go out alone at night in future, Celia. You would never have done it in Liverpool, and why you should do so here is beyond me.'

Celia sighed, and continued to sniffle. 'I wanted to see the tide coming in.'

'Well, do it in the daytime – there are two tides a day on this part of the coast. Use your common sense, girl, if you have any.'

Louise pulled the trailing quilt closer round her shoulders. 'Now, let's get back into bed.'

Edna got slowly to her feet. She was taller than the other two women, and suddenly, although garbed only in a dressing gown, she seemed authoritative, as she said sharply to Louise, 'You are being too hard on poor Celia, Mother. It is not her fault if she doesn't understand much about men. I would myself have assumed that out here in the country I would be quite safe, even at night.'

Louise was shocked at being chided by a daughter. She opened her mouth to answer indignantly, and then thought better of it; as a result of their earlier discussion that evening, it seemed Edna was likely to be a source of much needed funds. She clamped her lips tightly. The quilt swished round her as she stalked out of the room and up the stairs.

Celia was dumbfounded at the sudden defence offered on her behalf. With her mouth half open in surprise, she slowly wiped her eyes and then rose from the sofa.

Edna said, 'I'll come up with you and see you into bed. You'll be fine in the morning. You don't have to be so frightened. I am sure they were only teasing you.'

At Edna's unexpected kindness, Celia wanted to cry again. Instead, she took Edna's outstretched hand and allowed herself to be led upstairs. Though the comfortable warmth of the wine was slowly spreading through her, her breath still came in small shuddering sobs.

In the bedroom, Edna quickly struck a match and lit the bedside candle. Then she shook out Celia's cotton nightgown from the small embroidered nightie case laid on her bed, and held it while Celia shyly undressed. As soon as she had taken off her camisole and eased the straps of her vest off her shoulders, she slipped the gown over herself and modestly completed her undressing under its voluminous folds.

Edna sat down on the end of the bed, and said quite crossly, 'I am not sure who annoys me most – Mother or my mother-in-law.'

Celia sat down by her, in order to peel off her black cotton stockings. She said in amazement, 'But I thought you loved Mother?'

'Well, of course I do – she's my mother. But that doesn't mean that she isn't infuriating. She forgets that I'm a grown woman married for years and used to my own household. She treats me like a little girl, and you like a companion-help, who must do what she's told or she'll lose her job.' As she shook her head in annoyance, her black plaits hanging over her breast swayed slightly as if they were in total agreement with her remarks. 'Although Mother has had enough grief to last her a lifetime, she is a very capable woman, and I'm fed up with her constant complaints; she isn't suffering any more than millions of other women. And she hasn't done anything much towards this move to the cottage. I am nearly as bad, because I've tended to sit and listen to her, partly because I am quite bewildered by my own problems and the strangeness of England. You've done all the work.'

Celia did not reply. She got up slowly and hung her stockings on the back of a chair with her other clothes. Edna, she thought, had been very kind this evening. As she pulled back the bedclothes, she said, 'Perhaps Mother will change, as she gets used to having you near her again as an adult.'

'I doubt it,' replied Edna gloomily. She rose from the narrow single bed, so that Celia could get into it. Her hands were clasped tightly in front of her, as she added, as if forcing herself, 'I am sorry I haven't been much help to you. I've also had a great deal to do which has involved a lot of correspondence with Papa Fellowes – and all the time I've had to think carefully what I am to do – because my life, like Mother's, has been reduced to chaos. There is nothing left of my married life – no home, no servants; and a very difficult change of country, with no one here to depend upon except Papa Fellowes – he really is doing his best to order my financial affairs for me.'

Her face pinched and white against her pillow, her fright forgotten, Celia was astounded as Edna looked down at her and asked, 'Do you think you will be all right now?'

'I think so,' Celia replied. She snuggled down under the bedclothes. 'Thank you, Edna. I'm so grateful. We'll talk some more tomorrow. I tend to forget your loss, but I am sorry about it; you must be feeling absolutely awful. And Mother is still very upset after losing Father – it takes time.'

Edna's responding smile was a little grim, but she bent

down to kiss Celia on her forehead. 'Shall I blow out the candle?'

'Yes, please. And I'm sorry, Edna, that I was such an idiot.'

Unexpectedly Edna laughed. 'It is not you who are the idiot,' she assured her, and went quietly to her own room, leaving a bewildered, but not unhappy, Celia to a night of disordered dreams.

Chapter Twenty-Eight

❧

Celia had forgotten to set her alarm clock and when, the next morning, she dragged herself out of bed, put on her grey woollen dressing gown and went downstairs, she found Edna ineffectually trying to build the living-room fire.

She was not having much success because she had not yet shovelled out yesterday's ashes from underneath the grate. Celia went through to the kitchen and brought a bucket and shovel and an old newspaper.

Still in their dressing gowns, they spread the newspaper over the hearth rug and side by side they kneeled down before the cold hearth, while Celia passed on the lessons on fire-making given her by Dorothy.

They sat back on their heels to watch the wood begin to crackle under the coal. Then, covered with dust from the removal of the ashes, they finally got up triumphantly, as the coal caught and began to blaze.

Celia went to fill the kettle. 'Better take Mother up some tea,' she said, as she turned the hob over the lighted coals and laid the kettle on it.

Though she agreed, Edna's voice held doubt. She said, 'Be careful what you do today, because you'll set the pattern for the future.' She paused, while, with her hands, she brushed down the front of her dressing gown. Then she went on firmly, 'Don't take Mother's breakfast up to her, for example. She's not an invalid, and there is no reason why she should stay in bed for breakfast.'

Weary as she was from her adventure of the previous night, Celia had taken it for granted that carrying her mother's breakfast up to her bed was precisely what she would have to do every day of her life. At her sister's advice, she gulped. 'I'm sure Mama will be awfully cross,' she said apprehensively.

'If you've any sense, Celia, she's going to be a lot angrier before you've finished.' Edna paused to look her sister up and down, and then went on, 'You look just about as ill as anyone could look and still be on their feet. You should see a doctor. I never could understand why you let Mother walk all over you.' Her voice rose. 'Your life isn't worth living – and it won't ever be unless you do something about it.'

This sudden outburst from her strong-minded sister surprised and confused Celia so much that she could not reply. She was trembling as she went back into the little kitchen to wash her hands again under the kitchen tap, before laying the table for breakfast.

Edna followed her, her own grubby hands held loosely in front of her, while she awaited her turn at the tap. She went on, 'Since coming home, I've been so upset myself that I've tried to keep out of things between you and Mother. But after being away for seven years and then seeing you, it hit me like a hammer. Though you're a grown woman, you still fawn around her – and cringe when she shouts at you. I know I'm tactless, and I've found myself ordering you around just as she does; then I feel so cross when you obey me, instead of telling me to get up and do it myself. But, as I said last night, my own life has been torn apart – and I'm not finding widowhood very easy.' Her lips quivered, and she sounded suddenly tired and dispirited.

'Even my servants aren't around me any more,' she continued. 'I've been used to having servants at my beck and call all the time – and I tend to expect somebody else to do everything for me. I don't even have a home of my own,' she finished up unhappily. She stood chewing her lower lip, as if she might say more about her predicament, but had thought better of it and remained silent.

Celia slowly dried her hands on the towel, while Edna washed hers. She was suddenly frightened by Edna's reference to seeing a doctor, but there was no doubt that her sister meant well.

Finally, she responded timidly, 'You're being so thoughtful of me, Edna, that I almost want to cry. Until last night, I had no idea that you felt like that. And the loss of Paul must be dreadful. I am so sorry – I've thought only of Mother, and not much about you.'

She handed the towel to Edna. At the same time, her old terror surfaced, that she was in some way physically handicapped or mentally ill and had never been told about it. 'Do you really think I'm ill?' she asked anxiously.

'I think you are probably very run-down – you look it. I think you need a good holiday – away from Mother.'

Celia laughed. 'That's impossible. Mother would never allow it – she would say she could not spare me.'

'Well, I'm here for the time being. And we could get a woman to come to clean the floors, to help out. I think it could be done.'

Celia sighed. 'I don't have any money to see a doctor – or go on a holiday.'

'Really?'

'Of course not.'

'I assumed Father had made you a reasonable allowance, since he kept you at home. Or had, at least, made some financial arrangement, like insurance, an annuity, or something – kept separate from his business debts – to cover you when he and Mother died. He must surely have thought about you.'

'He gave me pin money – the same amount as he paid Ethel.'

'The skivvy?' Edna asked, as they moved slowly back into the living room.

'Yes. Mother always bought my clothes – out of her dowry money.'

Edna made a face. 'They look like it!' she replied.

As she picked up a teapot and went to make her mother's tea, Celia glanced down at her old-fashioned black skirt, which lay on the back of a dining chair. She had brought it downstairs to sponge and press it. It was good wool and warm, she had always told herself. She had had it since before the war; it would never wear out.

While Celia made the tea, Edna laid the table, her mouth clamped shut very like her mother in a temper.

'I'll put some water on to boil eggs, and I'll make some toast,' she said. 'It's an easy breakfast.' And, as Celia carefully carried a cup of tea towards the hall and staircase, she added, 'And don't say anything to Mother about what we're going to do today.'

Celia paused. Mystified, she asked, 'Why not?'

'Because I'll make sure that Mother shops for food and cooks the dinner. It won't hurt her; she won't have to carry anything – the shops will deliver. She has to wake up and begin living again.' She shrugged a little hopelessly. 'You and I can't do everything. And it'll give you a chance to go this afternoon to see Phyllis.'

'Oh, Edna! Could you arrange that? I do want to see Phyllis. I must also go to Hoylake to see that the furniture in Mr Aspen's barn is all right. Betty says I should advertise it in the local paper.'

Edna said grimly, 'Betty's right. Getting all that collection sold is going to take time, too. You leave Mother to me.'

It was a fairly silent breakfast, except for a monologue delivered by Louise. When Edna had called up the stairs to say that breakfast was ready, Louise had descended slowly. She was still dressed in a bedcap and dressing gown, and her first complaint was that there was no hot water coming out of the bathroom tap. How was she to have a bath? And she felt almost too tired to get up for breakfast, she announced dolefully; Celia should know very well that she had to eat before she got out of bed.

A little scared, and anxious to placate her, Celia swallowed a spoonful of egg, and ignored the complaint about breakfast. She told her, 'The fire takes some time to heat the water in the big boiler behind the fireplace, Mama. In about an hour, you should be able to bath.'

'It was always hot when I was ready to get up in the old house.'

Before Celia could reply to this, Edna said smartly, 'And Ethel got up at five thirty to make sure that it was hot for you.'

'Humph.' Louise could not answer the implied reproof, so she ignored it. 'The toast is burned round the edge and you haven't trimmed the crust off it,' she fretted as she looked at it with disgust.

Edna picked up the toasting fork, and stuck a slice of bread on to its prongs. She handed the fork to Louise, and said with glacial sweetness, 'Make another slice yourself, Mother, and then you can be sure it is exactly as you like it.'

Celia closed her eyes in anticipation of an explosion, but her mother stared at Edna with shocked amazement and then, when she found her voice, responded with resignation. 'I suppose this will do.' She ate the offending toast with every indication of acute distaste. She then asked for another cup of tea and, with this in hand, once again retired to her bedroom.

As soon as her back was turned, Edna gravely winked at her sister.

'Oh, Edna, you are cruel!'

'Cruel to be kind,' was the unrepentant response.

When the sound of their mother's footsteps on the stairs

had died away, Edna said, 'You go and get washed quickly before she gets into the bathroom. And go to Hoylake. You could go straight from there to Liverpool to see Phyllis, if you like.'

'Would it be all right?'

'Of course it would, you idiot. These things have to be done.' Edna looked around the little room, which, by this time, was rather untidy. 'I'll wash up and make this room respectable, and each of us can keep our own bedrooms clean and tidy.'

Celia leaned back in her chair. 'You're wonderful,' she said. 'I wouldn't dare suggest that to Mother.'

'Well, if her room becomes a mess, that's her headache. I'm not going to make her bed or clean the room for her – and neither should you have to.'

Celia hastily wiped her mouth with her serviette, folded it and put it into the silver ring her Great-aunt Blodwyn had given to her at her christening. Then she eased herself round the table, planted a shy kiss on Edna's cheek and fled quietly upstairs, to get washed and to count her last remaining bit of pocket money to see if she had the train fare to Liverpool and then enough for a tram out to West Derby. She still had a couple of pounds given to her by Louise, to cover her various expenses while she had been travelling backwards and forwards from West Derby to the cottage; it never occurred to her to use any of it for a personal expedition, like going to see Phyllis.

She was so filled with hope and her wonderment at Edna's outburst that she forgot, for the moment, the sickeningly unpleasant encounter of the previous evening. As she quickly combed her hair into a neat bun at the back of her head, she said, in astonishment, to her reflection, 'Edna cares about you. I really believe she does.'

Less than an hour later, she was greeted enthusiastically by Betty Houghton, who slid down from her high stool behind the rough wooden counter of her father's office.

She closed an account book, before she took Celia's hand, and said, 'Everything looks all right. I don't think any of the furniture was damaged. The movers had it all wrapped in padded quilts. Come and have a look.'

She took down a key from amongst a number hanging near her desk, and together they walked briskly across the yard. It was busy, and Betty explained that her father had recently acquired a good sub-contract to build city housing in Birkenhead that summer.

'He's looking for skilled craftsmen, but they're hard to find. There's a lot of men looking for jobs, but they're not skilled – and it looks to me as if a lot of them ought to be in hospital still. He wants at least four brickies and some hod carriers.'

'Brickies?'

Betty laughed at her bewilderment. 'Bricklayers. He'd a nice young man here today, but he looked like a ghost. Though he said he'd done six months of bricklaying, before he joined the army. Dad couldn't even offer him a labouring job – he said he'd never stay the course, he was too run down.'

'Poor soul.'

'And as for hod carriers – you've got to be as strong as an ox to carry hods of bricks and mortar up to a brickie all day,' Betty informed her, as she unlocked the great barn.

The residue of Celia's home looked very forlorn. All the piled-up furniture had a veil of dust on it. Dismantled bed frames from the guest rooms had been leaned against the walls; their horsehair mattresses had been laid on the tops of tables and sideboards and against the fronts of chests of drawers to protect them from being scratched. Pictures of all kinds had been laid face to face on top of the mattresses. Rolls of rugs, barrels of china and ornaments and packing cases of unwanted kitchen equipment lay, as yet unopened, along the back wall.

Celia looked at the mighty pile in some despair, and

exclaimed, 'Phew! I'll never manage to sort it all out, never mind sell it.'

'I think you will sell it and at decent prices, if you advertise it in the Hoylake paper – and, say, in the *Evening Express*.' With a chuckle, Betty flung out her arms as if to a waiting audience and declaimed, ' "For Sale. Handsome fruitwood furnishings, many Georgian pieces. Sale includes fine china, ornaments, carpets, etc., also some kitchen equipment." That should do it.' She drew a happy face in the dust on what had been Timothy Gilmore's desk. 'What bothers me is how you are going to price it – I'm sure some of it is valuable – and I've no idea about the pictures, for example. Have you?'

'I've been worrying about that. Your friend Mrs Jowett helped me a lot – she was really sweet – but I'll still be guessing. I thought the first thing I could do would be to look in the very good furniture shops in Liverpool and see their prices for new things. I'm going over to Liverpool to see Phyllis Woodcock this afternoon. I could take a quick peep in that nice furniture shop in Bold Street, before catching the tram out to West Derby.'

'Well, at least you'll know that your price should be lower than theirs – though I'm not even very certain about that – those chairs are very fine; if they are antiques they may be worth more,' Betty replied, pointing to a neat line of refugees from the Gilmore dining room. She turned and smiled a little wryly at her friend. 'We're both out of our depths on this.'

'I have the books, of course, that Mrs Jowett lent me, as a rough guide to the age of what I have. She said to set the price at the most you feel you can get, and come down very slowly if someone is interested in a piece.'

'She would know.' Betty stared at the wild conglomeration before her. She herself did not know how to advise her friend. She suggested, 'I think there are one or two second-hand furniture shops in Berry Street, at the top of

Bold Street. You could go in and ask the price of anything that looks familiar to you. You might get some ideas.'

Celia agreed and, almost reluctantly, they locked up and went back to the office.

Celia looked worried. 'I could always get an auctioneer, I suppose,' she said.

Betty tried to cheer her up. 'An auctioneer will just get what he can for you. Out here, where there are so many high-class homes, such auctions always draw antique dealers and they bid low. Unless you're desperate for money, don't try to hurry the selling. Learn a bit first.'

'Mother is sure that we are poor as church mice, Betty. But Cousin Albert believes that we shall manage quite well once the house is sold. And I must say that I have been agreeably surprised at how much we have managed to do with what little money Mother had. And Edna has promised to help.' She stopped, and then said with a rueful grin, 'I'm the only one who doesn't have a bean.'

'Perhaps you could get a job.'

'Me? How could I? I don't know anything. Anyway, Mother wouldn't let me – I've got to sell that barnful first, because Mother's not going to stir a finger, as far as I can see. And it can't stay here for ever.'

'I don't see why your mother can't help you.'

'You have to remember that she's bereaved.'

'So is everybody,' responded Betty a little sharply, as she thought of her husband lying in a mass grave at Messines Ridge.

Celia bit her lower lip. 'Of course. I know, Betty.' Betty was so brave, she thought wistfully. She sighed, and said that she would come over in a couple of days, to make an inventory of the furniture, before pricing it. 'If I've got everything listed in a notebook I can put a likely price by each piece. So that I don't get flummoxed.'

Betty tried to pull herself together by concentrating on Celia's problems. Before she replied, she told herself for the umpteenth time that it was no good moping about David; it wouldn't bring him back. With forced gaiety, she teased, 'A notebook sounds most professional. We'll make a businesswoman of you yet!'

Celia laughed, and they stood talking for a few minutes amid the busy whirl of the yard, before Celia reluctantly said goodbye.

Chapter Twenty-Nine

❧

Holding young Timothy George against her shoulder, Phyllis answered her front door herself. Two-year-old Eric, his cheeks stained by recent tears, clung to her skirt. Phyllis's careworn face lit up as she saw Celia, and she stepped back to make way for her friend to enter the narrow malodorous hall. 'Come in – come in, dear,' she said. 'How nice of you to come such a long way. How are you?'

She opened the door of a tiny front sitting room, which had the dank airlessness of a room not much used, and, as Celia responded politely to her inquiry, she led the way in.

'Do sit down, Seelee. I'll ask Lily to make some tea for us.'

She hastened kitchenwards, while Eric, with his finger in his mouth, stood in the doorway and stared at the visitor.

Prior to taking a tram out to West Derby, Celia had walked rapidly down Lord Street, Church Street and Bold Street to take a quick look in the windows of the one or two furniture shops that she found; as she went along, she jotted down prices in her notebook.

Near St Luke's Church, she had found two second-hand furniture shops. She ventured shyly into both, and even more shyly asked the prices of one or two pieces amid their dusty stock, which were similar to those her mother owned; they had little of the quality of her mother's furnishings or of the style of Mrs Jowett's stock. She stored away the information that second-hand shop owners did not seem to mind if you just wandered round and looked at what they had. Her inspection made her realise that there was quite a difference between second-hand and antique shops.

She was both tired and late by the time she arrived at Phyllis's house, and she sat down thankfully in a pretty Victorian armchair. The room was familiar to her from many visits, when the friends had often shared their doubts and unhappinesses with each other – not many happinesses, thought Celia a little sadly.

She smiled at Eric and invited him to come to sit on her lap.

Eric refused to budge from the doorway until his mother returned to sit opposite her guest. As he moved close to Phyllis and rested his head against her arm, she laid Timothy George in her lap. He was awake, so Celia asked if she might nurse him.

'Of course you can,' Phyllis said and carefully laid the child in Celia's arms. 'And how is dear Mrs Gilmore?' she asked with brittle brightness.

Celia chucked little Timothy George under his chin and he kicked his tiny feet quite happily at the attention. Celia sighed at the thought of her mother. She replied, 'She's a little depressed at leaving her old home – and she misses Papa very much.'

'Naturally,' Phyllis responded politely, though she could not imagine that one would miss a husband very much.

The conversation threatened to languish. It was disappointing to Celia, who was used to Phyllis's pouring out the latest news about the small ills of her brood or about her husband's complaints. She never knew how to deal with the latter, but, in talking the matter out comfortably with Celia, Phyllis had always seemed to gain fresh courage. Today, however, she seemed absent-minded, as if she could not bring her thoughts to bear on what her visitor was saying.

Celia smiled down at the baby and inserted a finger into

his tiny hand. The child grasped it, and Celia laughed. Before the organisation of the move to the cottage had fallen on to her shoulders and absorbed most of her time, she had managed to run over to see the new baby only once. It did not seem to have grown much so she now asked, 'Is he gaining weight all right?'

'I think so. My milk isn't coming in as well as it should, and he doesn't like the cow's milk with which I supplement it.'

Celia made a face at the baby. 'Poor Timothy George!' Her eyes were on the child, and she did not see the fleeting despair of his mother's expression.

Lily, the Woodcocks' cook-general, pushed the door open with her backside. She eased Eric out of the way with a nudge from her bent knee, and set the tea tray down on a small table in front of his mother. The maid's apron was crumpled and grubby, and, as she straightened up, she pushed untidy bits of hair back off her face with her forearm. 'Will I be cutting the bread and butter for Christopher and Alison's tea now?' she asked, her accent sounding thick and ugly as if she had a cold. 'They'll be coming in from school soon.'

Phyllis replied mechanically. 'Yes, please. Open the new pot of plum jam for them.'

'When can Eric go to school?' Celia asked.

'When he is three – in September.'

'That should give you a little more time to yourself, with only baby Timothy at home.'

'I suppose.'

Celia wanted to bring up Edna's advice that it was not necessary to have babies one after the other. Though she felt that it was momentous news, she did not know how to open the subject; it was not something for a single lady to talk about. It savoured of wicked private subjects.

Instead, she said brightly, 'During the school holidays, you should bring the children out to visit us. We could have a picnic on the shore, and they could paddle.' Maybe Edna could talk more frankly to Phyllis and tell her exactly how a steady flow of infants could be brought to a halt.

Phyllis said, 'Thank you,' without expressing any particular enthusiasm for seaside picnics.

Celia looked at her friend uneasily. 'Are you all right, Phyllis? Do you feel recovered from having Timothy?'

Phyllis smiled slightly. 'Not quite. I am rather tired, Seelee dear. Timothy has not yet learned to sleep the night through, and Arthur gets so cross when I have to keep getting up to attend to the child.'

Celia knew only too well Arthur Woodcock's cold, whining voice. She had always wondered what had attracted Phyllis to him – and, in fact, Phyllis herself did not seem to know.

Celia had often thought that, fearing being single all her life, Phyllis had done what most girls did and had accepted the first offer of matrimony which she had received from a man with prospects. According to his wife, bearing in mind the number of bank staff who had been killed in the war, Arthur certainly had reasonable prospects of promotion. She had remarked, 'He was fortunate that his weak chest kept him out of the army.'

Phyllis had, during an earlier visit, mentioned that women who had served as bank clerks during the conflict were not being encouraged to stay on. 'I expect they will be glad to be at home again,' she had said idly.

It was a most unsatisfactory visit. Celia was unable to re-establish their usual freedom together. She told Phyllis how pretty the cottage looked and how kind Betty Houghton and Mr Fairbanks had been to her, about the shocking naked swimmers in the sea, and the putting in of a bathroom and hot water. It all came out higgledy-piggledy, and Phyllis listened politely and said, 'Indeed?' or 'How dreadful!' or 'How wonderful!' in all the right places, but there was no true reciprocation.

After twenty minutes and a cup of tea, a puzzled Celia gave up. She kissed the baby and carefully handed him back to his mother. She bent down to kiss a reluctant Eric, who turned his face away and clung to Phyllis.

'I must go. Goodbye, dear. Don't get up. I'll see myself out.' She put her arms round the little mother, and kissed her on the cheek. 'I'll come again soon.'

She was thankful to be out in the fresh air. During the train journey back to Meols, however, she worried about her old friend. That she herself had changed greatly since her father's death did not occur to her.

When she had gone, Phyllis leaned back in her chair and burst into tears. She was in a state of numb terror that she might be pregnant again. Arthur was not a patient man and he had forced himself upon her nightly for the past two weeks. It had hurt her physically; her pleas for a little longer to rest between babies had been ignored. His lack of consideration had hurt even more.

At home, Celia found Edna peacefully reading a novel in front of the living-room fire. The room looked tidy; the table was already laid for the evening meal. There was no sign of her mother, and as she took off her jacket, she inquired where she was.

Edna looked up with a grin. 'She's resting. She's had a busy day.'

Celia's conscience smote her.

'What happened?'

'Well, I persuaded her to go to the village and order some groceries and buy some meat, and so on. She was most put out, because she was refused credit – she's used to having weekly bills from the butcher and grocer, as you know.'

'Oh, dear! Didn't she have any money with her?'

'Yes, I gave her some – she would not believe me that,

as a stranger, they wouldn't trust her. I told her, also, that she must get her bank account transferred from Liverpool to the local branch here, so that she can easily draw money when she wants it. She didn't like the idea of having a strange bank manager to deal with – said she would prefer to go to Liverpool each time she needed money.'

'What did you say?'

'I didn't say anything. Let her learn how inconvenient it is going to be.' She saw the shocked look on Celia's face at this remark, and she sounded defensive as she added, 'It's no good, Celia, she simply has to change her ideas – we all have to. We are facing a new world, and we've nobody to help us, except ourselves.'

A sharp lance of fear of the unknown, the unpredictable, shot through poor Celia. She had already had too much of having to make decisions, of treading nervously along unknown paths, as she arranged for the cottage to be made habitable.

It had been a tremendous struggle for her. Her life had always been ordered by her parents, her slightest suggestion immediately crushed, and she had learned early to accept numbly all that they decided. Now her father was not there to order – and her mother had become a lamenting, pitiful heap.

She glanced round the cosy, crowded room as she sank down into her mother's easy chair. Suddenly, the room seemed to spread out its arms and offer her sanctuary – and she realised that she had organised it all herself. She had created this sense of comfort. A good odour of cooking had now been added to it by someone else.

Swallowing her fears, she said to her sister, with a nervous laugh, 'It smells as if everything fell out all right.'

'It did. The stuff she bought was delivered this afternoon by various errand boys, and she made a chicken pie – which is in the oven. And I managed to make a bread and butter pudding, which is also in the oven.'

Celia was dumbfounded. 'I would never have had the courage to push Mother into doing anything she didn't want to do,' she said flatly. 'Quite frankly, I took it for granted that I would have to do everything, now that we have no servants.'

Edna patted her knee. 'Oh, no. We'll try to share the work fairly. I've had enough of that kind of nonsense. I enjoyed tidying up this morning, and talking to Dorothy and to Mr Fairbanks when I saw him in his front garden. He inquired how you were, by the way. And Dorothy did, too. She made a good job of the shed, though I saw her hanging around talking over the hedge to Eddie Fairbanks for quite a while.'

At the mention of Mr Fairbanks, Celia felt a small twinge of jealousy. He was her friend, not Edna's or Dorothy's. She managed to respond by saying politely, 'That was very kind of him to inquire about me.' Her mind, however, quickly reverted to her mother, and she suggested that they must see that Louise got a rest each afternoon.

'Of course. But the busier she is, the less time she has to grieve.'

Edna put down her book and stood up. She took down a small brown business envelope from the mantelpiece, and dropped the missive into Celia's lap. 'Mr Aspen's yard boy came down on his bike to deliver this to you,' she said.

As she picked up the letter and looked at her name on it, Celia felt her nervousness return; nobody ever wrote to her except Great-aunt Blodwyn, who wrote meticulously at Christmas, Easter and on Celia's birthday.

Celia wondered why Betty could possibly need to write to her. She had seen her only that morning, and she had already received a statement from her with regard to the work done on the cottage; though the sum involved had seemed reasonable to her and there was a note on the bill that arrangements could be made to pay by monthly instalments, she had not yet had the courage to give the account to her mother.

She fumbled as she tore open the envelope.

Chapter Thirty

ॐ

As she read her letter, Celia's expression changed from trepidation to pleasure. She looked up at Edna, who was peeking into the oven at the side of the fire to see how dinner was progressing, and announced, 'A friend of Betty's, a cabinetmaker, has asked to see our furniture – he came in after I left this morning, and Betty mentioned it to him. She says he's interested in pieces that are dilapidated but made of good woods.' Celia's voice squeaked with excitement. 'He has a little furniture repair business – and she says he is knowledgeable about antiques because he does restoration work. He can alter heavy furniture to make it fit into a smaller home, and she thinks he might be interested in some of our heavier stuff.'

'That sounds very interesting.' Edna closed the oven door and turned round to face her sister, as she added, 'Not much of Mother's furniture is in need of repair, though.'

'Betty thinks that his knowledge of old furniture might be helpful to me.' Celia smiled down at the letter. 'In her PS she says he's a friendly type and that she's known him for years. She's arranged for him to come to their yard at eleven o'clock tomorrow morning, and she hopes this is convenient.'

Edna straightened herself up. 'It certainly is convenient. Away you go tomorrow morning.'

'What about Mother? She's not yet made up her mind about what she wants to sell.'

'Just tell her that someone is coming to look at it all. If they make an offer, she can then decide if she wishes to accept it.'

Though Celia nodded, her face fell. 'You know, Edna, it's going to take a terrible lot of time and running about, if I have to negotiate backwards and forwards between Mother and a buyer for every piece. Unless you want to help, I don't think I could do it. I imagine that people would want to take away immediately anything they decided to buy, wouldn't they?'

'They will, of course,' Edna agreed. She hung the oven cloth on its hook by the fireplace.

'And there's so much else to be done. The garden is a shocking mess – and just keeping the house going from day to day without servants will keep us all quite busy – I'm tired out already.'

Edna was suddenly curious. 'Is Mother going to give you anything for all the work you've done on the cottage? And for selling the furniture?' she asked.

'Give me something? What do you mean?'

'Well, er – um – pay you or buy you something?'

'I'm her daughter. She expects me to do what she wants – for love.'

'Look here, Celia. With a lot of work and a bit of luck, you're going to make hundreds of pounds out of that mighty pile of furniture, and you could find it less wearying, if you received a little money for the effort involved.

'If it were auctioned, she would have to pay the auctioneer, wouldn't she? Or if she asked a second-hand furniture shop to dispose of it for her, the shop would charge her a percentage on everything sold, probably a large percentage.'

Celia looked dumbfounded. 'I couldn't ask Mother for money!'

Edna could look quite ferocious at times. Now she did, as she snapped sharply, 'Are you going to be her slave for ever – until she dies? Well, I'm not and neither should you be.

'And another thing, Celia. As I said, times have changed. I don't have to worry, because Paul left me provided for. But you would be wise to learn how to earn a living.

'I know a lot of women are giving up their jobs to go home and be housewives again, now that the war is over. On the other hand, for a lot of us there is no chance of marriage – because the men who could have married us are dead, all the young businessmen, the professional men, the sons of county people – all gone!' She sounded bitter, as she went on, 'I'm told that, in the north-west here, there are whole villages without a single man left between the ages of seventeen and fifty. Do you know a single aristocratic or middle-class family without someone dead or dreadfully hurt?'

Celia looked at her, appalled. Her lower lip trembled as, in answer to her last question, she agreed. 'I don't know anyone, not that I ever had any hope of marriage. Even in Phyllis's husband's family, they lost two boys – Andrew had just qualified in law and the other one was an actuary in an insurance company.'

'That's exactly what I mean. There's hardly anybody left. We have to look after ourselves, particularly because Father left you nothing.'

Celia was silenced and filled with fear, as, with sudden perception, she looked down the years and saw herself, after Louise's death, an ageing, unpaid companion at the beck and call of some lady like her mother, not much better than a slave working for roof and food – because she did not know any other way of staying alive.

She was not given to self-pity, but, in her sense of shock, a tear ran down her face, and Edna said crossly, 'Don't start to cry – start to plan. Look, if Mother gave you ten per cent of everything you get from the furniture, it might be enough to pay for some training, though I can't suggest what for – and, at twenty-four, you are rather old to start.'

Celia was so agitated that at first she could not reply. Then she blurted out, 'I couldn't ask her, Edna. And, anyway, she needs me at home.'

'Rubbish. She's a perfectly capable woman, not quite fifty years old yet. I could broach the subject for you – or perhaps Cousin Albert could talk some sense into her next time he comes up to Liverpool.' Edna's expression relaxed, as she saw Celia's eyes fill. 'Cheer up, sweetie. You have to be at your best tomorrow – a business lady with something to sell.'

'It's almost too much for me, Edna – to face all at once, I mean.' She could feel panic beginning to overwhelm her again.

Edna sensed her real distress, and said firmly, 'Face one thing at a time. Go to Betty's yard tomorrow and if this man wants to buy something, simply set the best price you can and sell it to him – and don't worry about anything else. I'll keep the house going. And Mother has to learn that if she doesn't help you to sell the wretched stuff, she has to take the consequences. You are quite right that you cannot run backwards and forwards to consult her all the time.'

Celia got up wearily, Betty's letter still in her hand. 'Yes,' she agreed, and summoning up a smile, she added, 'It's good of you to care.' Then she said automatically, 'I'd better make a cup of tea for Mother and wake her up.'

Edna opened her mouth to object, and then thought better of it. 'That would be kind,' she replied. 'I've just to wash some lettuce which Mr Fairbanks gave me this morning, and dinner will be ready.'

Though still resentful at her elder daughter's sudden insistence, that morning, that she must actually contribute some effort to the establishment of their new life, Louise felt better after her nap, and accepted the cup of tea which

Celia brought upstairs to her. After she had taken a few sips and Celia had drawn back the curtains from the bedroom window, she inquired, quite amiably, how Phyllis was.

Celia expressed her unease at Phyllis's fatigue, and her mother responded that having one's family was the most fatiguing period of any woman's life, particularly if the household did not include a nanny.

Celia felt suddenly that she would rather have her own life than the hopeless one of trying to please Arthur. She did not think that it was the moment to broach the subject of her own future, so she said simply that Edna was making a salad and that dinner would be ready in a few minutes.

She left Louise drinking her tea, and went into their brand-new bathroom to bathe her face and tidy her wind-blown hair. The water ran hot, and she breathed a thankful prayer for such a luxury.

She felt refreshed after washing herself. As she ran downstairs, she began to anticipate with pleasure seeing Betty again.

Edna had refilled the kettle and put it on the hob. On the table steamed the chicken pie and by it lay a bowl of crisp green young lettuce.

The two young women sat down opposite each other and waited patiently as their mother plodded slowly down the narrow staircase and came to the table. Before sitting down, she gazed gloomily at the meal awaiting her, and sighed. Celia jumped up and pulled out her chair for her. Without thanking her, Louise sat down, and without a word proceeded to serve the pie. Obviously Edna was not yet forgiven for so ruthlessly driving her to action through the day.

Celia told her about the note from Betty.

'A strange man? How will you receive him?'

'In the barn,' replied Celia.

'By yourself?'

'I will have to, Mother, unless you want to come along.'

Louise looked very disapproving, so her daughter hastily added, 'Betty will be there. Would you like to come to meet him?'

'Certainly not. I don't want to have to talk to a workman, while I'm still in mourning.'

Edna interjected sharply, 'We are all in mourning. But you can leave it to Celia and Betty Aspen – I mean Betty Houghton – I keep forgetting that she was married; they seem to get along splendidly – and they are both very sensible.'

Then, without warning to Celia, she changed the subject, and said, 'Celia is going to have to work very hard to sell the furniture, Mother. I think she should have something for doing it. I would suggest fifteen per cent of all the money she manages to collect.'

At this suggestion, Louise's look of alarm was almost comical, her fork with a piece of chicken poised on it halfway to her mouth. But Edna went on ruthlessly, 'You are still very upset, I know – and naturally so. So I feel you should leave it all entirely to Celia how she does dispose of the stuff. It will all have to go – there's simply no more room in this cottage to put anything more.'

The silence grew and Celia's face flushed with embarrassment.

Finally, Louise asked, 'But what does she need money for?' She sounded genuinely puzzled. 'I keep her – and she will have her usual pocket money, as soon as Cousin Albert arranges my financial affairs.'

Celia opened her mouth to say that she should not worry about paying her. She felt she was simply being helpful to dear Mother.

Edna sensed this and quickly broke in again.

Her tone was sharp, as she said, 'I don't think, Mother, that you quite realise what a difficult position Celia is in, now that Father is no longer with us and has left her unprovided for.

'In the nature of things, she will not always be able to depend upon you. She needs to learn a way to earn her own living, as many other women out there will have to do.'

Louise looked bewilderedly at her elder daughter, as she slowly put the piece of chicken into her mouth. Then she said disparagingly, 'What can a girl like Celia do? She is not a working girl – she is a refined upper middle-class girl.'

'What do you expect her to do, when you die?' asked Edna icily, while Celia, shocked, murmured, 'Edna!'

'Well, I haven't thought about it. I have had enough to cope with since your father's sad passing, without thinking about Celia when I die.' She slowly put down her fork, and added with more certainty, 'I would have thought she could live with you. And she would have half the Birkenhead property from me, which would give her pin money. The other half would, naturally, go to you.'

'I certainly would not let her starve,' responded Edna tartly. 'But she does need a life of her own – as do I.'

The idea that Edna wanted to do anything other than stay with her shook Louise. She had just picked up her fork again and now she dropped it on to her plate with an alarming clatter. 'What are you thinking of doing?'

Edna found herself facing the surprised gaze of both Louise and Celia, and she said, 'I do not yet know.' Her voice was calm, but her eyes spoke of despair.

Since that seemed all that she would say, Louise, after a pause, chided her. 'I thought we would all live together?'

'Oh, Mother! We probably will. But you forget that I have been bereaved, too. I am simply in no state to make up my mind what I want to do. And Papa Fellowes has not yet settled Paul's estate. When he has done so, I must think what I am going to do for the rest of my life.' She sighed. 'With no children, I feel I need to plan. But not yet. In the meantime, I want to see you and Celia happily settled.'

Celia smiled at her sister. She was afraid to say anything, and she watched with some anxiety as Louise pushed her plate away, got up from the table, and marched back upstairs.

Chapter Thirty-One

That night, Louise lay on her bed and cried helplessly. She cried because her small safe world had already fallen apart and it appeared as if it might disintegrate even further. She had, she told herself, no one with any sense to turn to for help.

Even Mr Carruthers, her bank manager, was miles away. And cruel Edna had said that she must find a new bank in Hoylake, which meant dealing with a stranger. It was all too much for her.

Immediately after Timothy's death, she had assumed that Cousin Albert would secure a continuation of her life as she had always known it. She expected that widowhood would be very sad; she would grieve for the loss of her husband. But the pain would lessen with time, as had the agony of losing both her boys. Safe in her lovely home with familiar servants, in her usual circle of friends and acquaintances, with Celia to organise her social life, existence as a widow would be bearable. She had realised, a little guiltily, that it would also give her a certain amount of freedom to do as she pleased; she would not have to consult Timothy all the time.

Cousin Albert had soon disabused her of those expectations. Her cosy, wealthy world of 1914 would never return, just as her sons never would either. She and Celia would be lucky if they could make ends meet in this dreadful little cottage, round which the sea wind roared relentlessly.

The arrival of Edna, particularly an Edna with money, had cheered her up. If Edna's income was considerable, perhaps jointly they could afford a better house. With two daughters at home, she would not miss the servants so much; they could run the house between them.

But Edna seemed to be coming out of her own grief now and was proving to be quite awkward; she did not seem to be at all certain that she would continue to live with her mother. She was also putting ideas into Celia's head. Celia was a fool, but she might, with training, find a way to earn her own living – and leave home. A single woman living alone? She would be labelled a fast woman – a shocking idea.

At the latter thought, Louise cried harder. She herself could be left alone in this cottage, with very little money, with no friends nearby, no daughter or servant to make fires, do the washing, clean the house. For the first time in her life, she was terrified.

Loneliness gaped at her like a great, deep cavern, a future completely soundless, except for the remorseless crying wind. Not even the mewing of the cats would break the silence.

Celia had protested at Louise's abandonment of the household cats; Louise had simply shooed the animals out of the back door.

'They'll starve,' Celia had lamented.

'With all the mice and rats in Liverpool?' Louise had responded scornfully. 'They can hunt. They won't starve. And, sooner or later, someone will find them on their door-step and take them in. That's how we acquired them origin-ally. Don't you remember? They just arrived, at different times, at the back door, and Winnie took them in to deal with the mice.'

Louise was right. Celia, already disorientated, accepted their loss as yet another misery to be endured, and said no more.

Wrapped in her fine feather eiderdown on her bed in her new home, Louise cried on. Nobody cared about her. Nobody understood her. She admitted that even to have Tommy Atkins to cuddle would have been comforting. But big black Tommy Atkins was probably stalking mice down the narrow back alleys of Liverpool or learning to tip the lid off a dustbin to get at the contents.

Even cats knew everything about taking care of themselves, thought Louise angrily, as helpless grief gave way to rage at her predicament. Well-born women were not expected to be capable of facing the world outside the home.

Celia, left to herself, even if she could earn a living, might get entangled with a man – though she was, of course, quite old and plain – and make a fine mess of her life. Louise remembered the soldiers playing in the sea and had a horrifying thought of facing an illegitimate grandchild, if Celia was ever let off the leash. At all costs she must remain with her mother, no matter what Edna said.

With this determination and the justification that only Celia knew her taste in library books or could do all the mending and darning thrown at her, Louise stopped crying and, shortly after, fell asleep, exhausted.

It seemed no time at all before her younger daughter was gently shaking her awake and presenting her with early morning tea.

As Louise struggled to sit up, she noted that Celia was already dressed to go out, her hat pinned on her head. She lacked only her outdoor jacket.

As she took the teacup from Celia, she asked sulkily, 'Are you going to Hoylake to see Miss Aspen's man friend?'

'Mrs Houghton's,' corrected Celia nervously. 'She's a widow.'

'Humph.' Louise sipped her tea.

'Yes, Mother. I have to be there for eleven o'clock. I

thought I might walk over, because I haven't had any fresh air for days.' She stood uneasily by the bed watching her mother sip her tea, and then said anxiously, 'If he wants to buy something, I think I must agree immediately, don't you? If the price seems reasonable? I can't very well come all the way back here to ask you if you are agreeable to it.'

'No. You can't. I can see that. I am not stupid.'

Celia sighed, and assured Louise that she was far from stupid.

'How will you know what to charge people? We can use every penny, in case you've forgotten.'

'I do have some idea about prices, Mother.' Celia's voice held no hint of the indignation that she felt, and she continued firmly, 'You remember that I went to see a friend of Mrs Houghton's who owns an antique shop in Liverpool, and she gave me quite a lot of information on antique furniture and showed me round her shop and told me the prices she expected for each article. She was tremendously kind and gave me some idea of the likely value of our dining-room furniture, for instance.'

Louise was draining her cup and did not reply, so with a gulp, Celia added, 'Edna says that you do not have to shop for food today – there's enough in the house. And Mr Fairbanks is going to ask the fish and chicken lady to call on us every week – to save our having to go to the shops all the time – he says her stuff is very fresh – better than the shops'. Are you sure you don't want to come with me to Betty's office?'

Louise sniffed. 'I could not bear to,' she asserted forcefully. 'All my lovely things in a dusty barn!'

Celia's face softened, and she said with contrition, 'I'm sorry, Mother. It must be very hard for you to face.' She took her mother's empty cup from her. Then she leaned forward to kiss her cheek. 'I hope to be back by lunch time, but don't wait for me.' In a more cheerful tone, she said, 'I've had my breakfast, but Edna will have hers with you.'

Celia waited for an answer, but none came. She slipped nervously out of the room.

Downstairs, Edna, still in a dressing gown, was warming her backside by the fire which she had made. She inclined her head towards the staircase. 'How are things up there?'

'Not too good.'

'I can cope with her. You go now. Don't walk. Take the train to Hoylake Station – I think it puts you down quite close to Betty's place, doesn't it? Then you'll have time to take a quiet look at the furniture before he comes.'

Celia reluctantly agreed.

When she arrived, the builder's yard seemed full of lorries, two belonging to Mr Aspen; one was being loaded with bricks and another with lumber. A third vehicle was delivering large boxes. There was no sign of the car which Betty's husband had built. Celia presumed that it had been sold.

Celia now had her own key to the barn and she walked straight over to it and opened it up. She decided on a number of pieces which might benefit from being made smaller. Then she walked leisurely back to the gate and Betty's office. Betty was at her desk and looked up with a cheerful grin. 'Good morning, Miss Gilmore,' she said teasingly.

In a shadowy corner a man rose and, tweed cap in hand, emerged into the sunlight pouring through the doorway.

Nervously, Celia turned towards him.

He was much more gentlemanly-looking than she had expected. His black hair was neatly cut and, under heavy brows, eyes as blue-grey as the sea weighed her up. He was short, though heavy-set. Betty introduced him formally to her as Mr John Philpotts, repairer of fine furniture. Celia put out her hand and it was shaken firmly by a very strong one.

In a voice with a tinge of Welsh in it, he announced that he was pleased to meet her.

After a few pleasantries, the three of them went over to the barn. The building did not have any lighting, so they pulled the doors open as wide as they would go. The contents could then be seen clearly in the daylight.

'Phew!' exclaimed Mr Philpotts, his face breaking into a smile as he viewed the cornucopia within. He turned to Celia, and said, 'To look at this will take some time. Do you mind if I go through it rather carefully?'

With her hands clasped tightly in front of her, Celia assured him that he could take all the time in the world, if he was interested, and Betty said that, in that case, she would go and make some coffee and bring it over.

At Betty's request, the furniture removers had banked as much furniture as possible against the walls and then made a pile in the centre, leaving a narrow passageway through which Celia and John Philpotts slowly made their way.

The furniture repairer had brought a notebook and pencil, and after asking permission, he paused, from time to time, to carefully turn a chair upside down to examine it, or open drawers and cupboard doors, to gaze at finishings and joints and hinges or knobs. Once or twice, he asked the origins of a piece, and all the time he made notes. When he wanted to handle a piece, he tucked the pencil behind his ear and put his notebook into his side pocket, so that he did not mislay either of them amid the jungle of furniture. Celia kept her usual silence; she was anxious not to offend him in any way.

When Betty brought a tray of coffee, she suggested that they should all sit down and drink it while it was hot. Mr Philpotts gallantly undertook to lift down three chairs for them, so they sat in the sun in the doorway and watched the busy builder's yard. When they were settled and the women were politely sipping their coffee, Mr Philpotts sat down, and, cup in hand, chewed the end of his pencil as if it were a cigar which had gone out. He seemed deep in thought, but occasionally he would get up and go back down the passage to look again at something. Celia noted that he dragged one foot, as if he lacked strength to put it down straight on the ground.

Though Celia maintained her nervous silence bordering on reverence in the presence of a man, his old friend, Betty, asked him, after a minute or two, whether he had seen anything he was interested in. He replied unexpectedly promptly that he was interested in a lot of it, and he named several of the big pieces which Celia had earlier earmarked. He turned to Celia, and assuming that she was basically a dealer, remarked, 'You have a beautiful stock, Miss Gilmore.'

Celia smiled and replied, 'Didn't Mrs Houghton tell you? It's all from my parents' home.'

The man's rather grim, deeply seamed face broke into a surprisingly cheerful grin. 'Betty did say that, but looking at it, I didn't think it could have all come from one family home. There's enough to stock a shop.'

He went on to tell her that much of it was rather big for apartments and the smaller, lower-ceilinged houses of the present day. He could, however, often make sideboards, like the three she had, smaller by taking out the centre cupboard. 'And, of course, tables like the big dining table at the back can have all their extra extensions taken out and be shown as much smaller. I would like to buy the extension pieces and make them into hall tables, parsons' tables, et cetera. And there's another sideboard there that does not seem to match anything else – the big one made of oak. I could take out the centre cupboard and make a useful cupboard for odds and ends, and then join the two ends together to make a handsome, but small, sideboard again. I am sure I could find markets for them.'

'How clever of you!' exclaimed Celia.

'Oh, you'd be surprised what you could do with this lot. Betty said that you had some china, too?'

'Seven barrels of it.'

'Complete sets?'

'Oh, yes, Mr Philpotts. There is one service with twelve settings and all the bread and butter plates and vegetable dishes – and three different sizes of meat dishes. It's Crown Derby.'

'Well, well!' He surreptitiously rubbed his left thigh, as if it hurt – and, indeed, it did hurt. With an effort, he got up again, and asked of Celia if he might look further.

'Of course you may. Take all the time you want.'

Betty gathered up the cups and said she must go back to the office. Her father's lorries, gears grinding, went out of the gate, and suddenly the place was quieter. Celia continued to sit in the sunshine. She was excited, but tried not to show it. Mr Philpotts looked so respectable and the sunshine was so pleasant that she wished her mother had come with her. But Mother would have condescended so much to a tradesman that she would probably have offended him, so perhaps it was as well that she was alone, despite the awful responsibility.

Still carrying his empty coffee cup, Mr Philpotts eventually returned and sat down in front of her. He laid the coffee cup under his chair, and then took his notebook out of his pocket and laid it on his knee.

After a minute or two, he began, 'Before I make an offer for the articles I mentioned, may I ask you a personal question, Miss Gilmore?'

Celia nodded nervous acquiescence.

'Are you simply disposing of this surplus furniture because, perhaps, you have no room for it in your new house? Or do you need to really make a solid sum of money out of it? Or are you thinking, perhaps, that you will begin a business buying and selling second-hand furniture, with this as your first stock?'

Celia's surprise at the last question was apparent to the man before her. He said hastily, 'I hope you're not offended?'

'Oh, no. The idea of a business had not occurred to me.' She went on to tell him that the furniture was her mother's, and she was sure Mother would be grateful for as much as she could obtain for it. 'As for my running a business,' she finished up with a shy laugh, 'I have no experience at all – of anything.'

He smiled slightly, and then asked, 'May I tell you what struck me when I saw some of the pieces that you have?'

'Certainly.'

'They are beautiful,' he said flatly. 'But they will take time to sell. And those that are big will have to be shown in a way to indicate that they would fit into a modern home. Hence my interest in making small pieces out of larger ones.'

Celia nodded, and waited for him to explain further. Before he did so, he shifted uneasily in his chair, and inquired, 'Did Betty tell you anything about me – or my business?'

'Only that you repaired furniture.'

'Well. I've only recently been demobbed after serving for four years, and I don't have much of a business yet. But I did finish my time as a journeyman – and I worked for furniture makers subsequently. I always did furniture repairs at home on the side, even tackling antiques, which demands a fair knowledge.

'When I came home six months ago, I began to do repairs again, and I'm earning fairly steadily – but I've no capital.'

He looked at Celia slantwise. She was all attention. He said, 'I'm telling you this because I have an idea which may benefit both of us. But you should know my background first. I should mention, too, that I am still under treatment for the wound in my leg – and I can't stand for long. So I have to find ways to supplement what I can manage to earn at my old trade by selling pieces like parsons' tables which don't have an immense amount of work in them.'

Celia was suffering from nervous strain. Please, Lord, she prayed, let him come to the point. Aloud, she said with real sympathy, 'I hope your leg doesn't hurt very much.'

He shrugged. 'I have my good days and my bad days,' he told her with a grin. 'Do you want to know what I'm thinking?'

'Oh, indeed I do.'

'Well, you have a lot of fine furniture and need some money. I'm a skilled craftsman with a tiny shop just off Market Street – it's got a nice front window facing Market Street. Though I don't need the shop, except to show my tables occasionally, I need the work rooms behind it. I want to suggest to you that we team up. You have the shop and I'll continue in the back. We share the rent. It will mean that we both have low overheads.'

Celia's expression was rapt, as if she had suddenly seen sunlight after days of storm, but the word 'overheads' puzzled her and she frowned.

'Overheads means rent, taxes, lighting. Things like that.'

The frown cleared, and she nodded.

Emboldened, he went on. 'To give you some money to begin with, I would like to suggest that we sort out all the workaday stuff you've got in there – kitchen tables, older beds – anything that is not of much real value. Send the lot to a saleroom. An auctioneer will at least get something for it.'

'Yes?'

'The rest we move into the shed at the back of my shop. We put together sets and show them in the front window as complete rooms, as far as we can. I'll reduce the size of all the cabinets, sideboards, bookcases – the latter are too high to fit under the eight-foot ceilings in modern houses. Two of the five wardrobes you've got could have the drawers on which they stand removed and small feet put on instead – they're mahogany – lovely wood – only need polishing. I could probably make hope chests out of the drawers.'

Celia was thrilled. She forgot about her mother. She had her hands clasped together as if in prayer, as she said impulsively, 'What a wonderful idea!'

He laughed. He said, 'There's a catch in it.'

Her face fell.

'Anything that I've altered or refinished, you pay me half of what you get.'

She was silent, and he added persuasively, 'My work is very skilled work.'

'I do understand that, Mr Philpotts. I'll have to ask Mother,' she said with some anxiety, and then she asked him, 'Do you really think I can sell anything?'

'With your nice manners, Miss? With the kind of clientele I have, why you could sell anything with patience. You'd soon learn a trick or two for selling. With a bit of luck, you'd be dealing with high-class buyers.'

She smiled prettily. 'Thank you,' she said. 'I think that's the first compliment I've had in my life.' Then again anxiety clouded over. 'I've no idea what Mother will say about it.'

'Well, you should explain to her that, this way, she'll probably get the best return, although it'll be slow. There's a clientele round here who know good furniture when they see it. In addition, you should advertise as far as Chester and suchlike places. When they come to me for repairs, they'll see what you've got. And you could have your tables laid with your Crown Derby dinner services – it would look good.'

'What about the pictures? We seem to have quite a lot of them.'

'Now that's something I don't pretend to know anything about. You could get an art dealer to look at them, if you think they're good.'

Celia abandoned thought of the paintings, for the moment. She was more worried about her mother's reactions. It would not be the thought of selling the furniture that would strike her, but the dreadful indignity of a daughter, granddaughter of a baronet, becoming a shopkeeper. She would be horrified at the very idea.

Louise had always referred to Celia's father as being in commerce – not trade. Trade was vulgar. Celia wondered how she could even broach to her the subject of owning a shop.

Celia's sudden hope died. 'Mother will never agree to it – she'll send it all to an auctioneer first.'

Mr Philpotts rose slowly and stretched his sturdy form to its full height. 'Go – ask her,' he said. 'Nothing try, nothing have. I've a good name in this village – I'll not cheat her.'

'Oh, I'm sure you wouldn't. Betty would not have introduced us, if she had not felt that you would really help us.'

'Aye, I've known Betty and her dad – and her mam – since I was a little lad. Will you ask your mam?'

'I will,' Celia replied slowly, though the thought of doing so filled her with nameless terror. She put out her hand to shake Mr Philpotts' hand in farewell. He held it tightly for a moment, and then said, 'Don't be scared – I think we'll both benefit. Let me know how you get on.'

She licked her lips, and nodded agreement. Through her hand he could feel her trembling before he slowly dropped it.

She stood, framed by the open barn doors, and watched him drag his way across the yard, to pause a moment to

look in at the office door. She saw him wave to Betty and
then continue out of the yard. Then she sat down suddenly
on one of the chairs and cried from sheer nervous tension.

Chapter Thirty-Two

❧

When Celia arrived back at the cottage, Edna was seated by the living-room fire. She had a black skirt on her knee and a mouth full of pins. As Celia took off her hat and laid it on the table, she greeted her through her clenched teeth by saying, 'You are just in time to pin up this hem for me. All my skirts are too long for English fashions.' Then, after hastily removing the pins from her mouth, she inquired sharply, 'Have you been crying?'

'Yes, I did have a little weep.' Celia pulled her cotton handkerchief out of her sleeve and quickly wiped her eyes. Then she sat down opposite Edna, her hands clenched on her knees, and burst forth, 'I'm so scared of what Mother is going to say, Edna. I don't know how to ask her.'

Edna dropped the skirt off her lap and on to the floor and laid the pin cushion on it. 'What on earth do you mean? What now? Was the Philpotts man rude to you?' she asked.

'Oh, no, Edna. He was very nice indeed. He's not a gentleman; he's a skilled artisan. But I think you might like him.' She poured out the details of Mr Philpotts' offer.

'He's offered me a partnership in a little business, in effect, Edna,' she finished up. 'But it is Mother who will have to be the partner – because it's her furniture. But you know Mother. She'd burst into tears every time she looked at her furniture, and she'd be horrified at the idea of serving in a shop, and she won't want me there, either.' She shrugged her shoulders helplessly. 'Even if she agrees, she'll never do a stroke to help. It is I who will have to be at the shop all day, every day. And I can't do that and be here to look after her and help you with the house and the washing and the cooking and the cleaning – and do the garden.'

She wrung her hands in despair. 'What shall I do? I hardly know how to even begin with Mother.'

At that moment, the back door opened and Eddie Fairbanks called, 'Anybody home?'

Edna responded immediately that he was to come in. They heard his boots clomp as he kicked them off by the door and then he walked in in his socks. Celia's first thought was to thank heaven that Mother was not there to see a next-door neighbour in her living room without shoes on.

He beamed cheerfully at both sisters. He had been thinning out his seedlings and was carrying tiny fresh lettuces and some spring onions on a piece of newspaper.

'Thought you might like these,' he said. 'They're a bit muddy with the rain we had in the night, but they're real crisp. Where will I put them?'

He gazed at the two women seated by the fire, and realised that he had walked in at a difficult moment. Miss Celia looked as if she had been crying. Eyes and nose were red.

'I'll put them on the draining board,' he said hastily and prepared to retreat to the kitchen.

It was quick-witted Edna who insisted he stay and have a cup of tea. So the lettuces were disposed of in the kitchen, and Celia pushed a dining chair round so that he could join them by the fire.

Following her sister's lead, Celia said sweetly, 'Do sit down, Mr Fairbanks.' Then she turned to push the hob with the kettle on it over the blazing fire.

Edna was already getting teacups out of the small sideboard. She inquired brightly, 'Do you know a man called John Philpotts – lives in Hoylake?'

Eddie looked surprised. 'Sure I do – cabinetmaker and French polisher? Nice lad. Lost his fiancée in France – she was an ambulance driver or similar. He came back wounded, to be told about her death, poor lad. How is he – and how did you come to meet him?'

Celia answered him shyly. 'I was talking to him today, Mr Fairbanks. About Mother's furniture.'

'Oh, aye?'

Celia glanced at Edna inquiringly, and Edna said, 'Tell Mr Fairbanks about his suggestion. If he knows the man he can give an opinion.' She came, teapot in hand, to sit down until the kettle boiled.

Eddie nodded, and wondered what John Philpotts had been up to.

Celia's agreement sounded doubtful, and she evaded the issue by inquiring where Louise was. 'Is she napping?'

'No. She was complaining that she was completely fed up, so I suggested a walk on the promenade at Hoylake. She was going to take the train to Hoylake Station. I thought the fresh air would help her.'

Celia swallowed. She was going to have to go through her story three times, she realised. She sat slowly down on her chair and looked shyly up at the old man. He was smiling at her, so she went on to tell him about her morning interview.

She finished up by saying, 'Betty said it might lead to a very nice occupation for me – as an antique dealer.'

While Eddie stirred his cup of tea, he considered the matter carefully. Finally, he said, 'It depends what your mam thinks, doesn't it?

'The only piece of advice I would like to give you is to have a written agreement with John as to exactly what each of you is to going to do and how the money will be split. The family solicitor nearest to here is, I think, in West

Kirby – but that's only the next station after Hoylake – it's not far. He'd make it right for you. And being local, Miss Celia, he won't charge as much as a big Liverpool man might; it could save you a pile of trouble later on.' He wiped his mouth with the back of his hand, and then assured her, 'It's not that you can't trust John – he's a decent fella – but, as time passes, you tend to forget exactly what you agreed – or change things without thinking, like. Then you might quarrel. It's human nature.'

'Would you like to do what this Philpotts man suggests, Celia?' Edna asked with real curiosity.

Celia hesitated, and then said, 'Well, I don't know. I suppose I would learn how to sell things – and that might help me to get another job – though what Mother would say if I worked in a shop, I shudder to think.

'I can't do what Mr Philpotts suggests – that is, use our furniture as a basis on which to launch a continuing business – because I won't have the money, will I? It will be Mother's.'

Eddie had not worked for forty years for a lord without understanding to perfection the social gradations of his society. He said cautiously, 'It's no disgrace to work for a living, love, if that's what you want to do. And your mam might be prepared to share the proceeds of the sales with you – so you could save most of it and buy more furniture to sell. You'd never make a fortune, but there's others as make a living that way.'

Edna said, 'My furniture will arrive from South America in about two months' time. I shall not need all of it, even if I set up a home of my own. I'll give you what I don't need for your shop. It is handmade and carved very nicely.'

Celia looked at her open-mouthed. 'Would you really?'

'Well, of course I would. I don't have to worry about every penny, and you haven't a cent to bless yourself with. And, if truth were told, it wouldn't hurt Mother to let you have the proceeds of the furniture sale.'

Eddie studied a tea leaf floating around in his cup. And these people think they're hard up, he considered. They don't know they're born. Miss Celia was unlucky, now. He'd seen such women before. He'd heard that a lot of them like her, when their family didn't want them any more, had been shipped off to Canada or Australia to marry pioneers they'd never seen.

He felt very sorry for her, and there she was, looking at him with wide scared blue eyes as if she knew already what life had in store for her, poor little lass. Even her sister's kind offer did not seem to have taken the fear out of her.

Regardless of speaking in front of their plebeian visitor, Edna was continuing her tirade about her mother. She went on, 'If you are earning, you can eventually contribute to the household – so Mother will not have to keep you.'

'Oh, aye. That's true,' interjected Eddie. He took Celia's hand and said, as if to his own daughter, 'Don't be so frightened, luv. Your mam may be quite pleased at the idea.'

Celia seriously felt that her mother would never be pleased at anything she did or said. But this was her own special friend speaking, a friend she had made by herself, and she gained a little courage from him.

Edna smiled at the pair of them. She hoped that Eddie Fairbanks would still be with them when her mother returned. Louise was more likely to keep her temper, if an acquaintance were present. To that end, she asked him to give her his cup so that she could refill it.

Chapter Thirty-Three

❧

Louise walked slowly down King's Gap towards the sea. Though the tide was ebbing, there was still enough water on which the spring sunshine could dance, and a light breeze caught playfully at her widow's veil; the wind did not roar at her as it had done round the cottage.

She felt lonely and depressed. She had intended to call on Lady Tremaine, the widow of one of her husband's business friends, who lived in Meols Drive, Hoylake. She was one of the few women she was acquainted with on this side of the Mersey. When she went to the house, however, the lady was not at home, and she had had to content herself with leaving her card with the parlour-maid.

She could not immediately recall the address of anyone else in Hoylake with whom she could claim acquaintance, and she wished that she had, after all, accompanied Celia to her appointment with Mr Philpotts. She could not, she thought savagely, even go into a village shop to amuse herself by trying on hats. For a lady wearing a mourning bonnet to indulge in such frivolity would not be considered good conduct.

She turned along the promenade, and paused, one hand on the iron railing at the edge of the pavement, to look down at two children, as they sought sea shells on the shore. They reminded her of Tom and George when they were boys, and, also, that they had left no grandchildren to console her. What did widows do? she wondered. Nobody seemed to need them nowadays, perhaps because there were so many.

Except that she was temporarily drained by the stress of Timothy's untimely death and the consequential money shortage, she was a woman of excellent health and she had always kept herself busy, apart from running her home most efficiently, by planning elaborate dinners or soirées for Timothy's friends; she was well known as a hostess, and such efforts were very helpful to Timothy in keeping in touch with other businessmen; there was a point in arranging them. But such entertaining would not be possible on the small income she would have in future, even if it were a suitable occupation for a widowed lady. Aimless afternoon teas for other widows would be about the limit she could afford.

As she began to recover from the shock of bereavement, her sense of frustration was making her increasingly restless, and, in consequence, she continued her wanderings along the promenade until she was quite tired. Then she turned round to walk back the way she had come.

I can't live like I have been doing these past few weeks, she considered fretfully, as she watched the sea birds hunting over the wet sands.

Still deep in thought, she reached a bench on which, at the very end, sat a man. He held a walking stick clasped upright between his knees. He had rested his chin on his hands and looked as if he were searching the horizon for something. He wore a peaked tweed cap and a belted macintosh.

He looked respectable enough, so Louise sat quietly down on the far end of the bench to rest her feet. She nodded absently to the man as she passed him and said politely, 'Good morning.'

He ignored her.

She did not accept the rebuff kindly. As she arranged her skirts around her, she thought crossly that this was not

Liverpool where you would not talk to strangers. Hoylake was still small enough to be considered a village. Almost everyone would know everyone else, and she herself wanted to become casually acquainted with the local inhabitants. Once she knew the social standing of people, she would, as a result of moving so far away from her old home, have to make new, suitable friends from amongst them.

Really, some people were awfully rude.

While she rested her feet, her mind fretted on. She had received that morning a troublesome letter from Cousin Albert saying that he had had an offer for her house and that the price was being negotiated by the estate agent. He expected to be in Meols in the course of the next week or two.

'And where does he think he is going to sleep in a three-bedroomed cottage?' she asked herself crossly. Celia would simply have to give up her room and share Edna's bed. A male guest would be under one's feet the whole time. And such a lot of work.

There was also the dreadful finality of the sale. How was she going to face the fact that strangers would now have the right to live in her home? It was certain that Albert would not understand her grief over it. In fact it seemed to her that nobody, including Edna, herself a widow, understood what she was going through without dear Timothy to lean on and his needs to think about.

Her reverie was interrupted by a hoarse voice from the other end of the bench. It asked, 'Is someone there?' The accent was a Lancashire one.

The oddness of the question made Louise jump. She replied tartly, 'Yes. There is.'

It was as if the man had not heard her, because he went straight on speaking to her, and what he said shook her out of her irritation at Cousin Albert, out of her personal misery.

She turned to stare at him, her mouth open in disbelieving shock.

In a voice which seemed weakened by illness, he said, 'I hope I'm not disturbing you, but I get very bored sitting here. I'm deaf and blind. I can talk to you, but you can't talk to me – unless you would be kind enough to sit close to me and touch my hand once for yes and twice for no. Then, at least, you can say yes or no to me.'

She was alarmed by the unexpectedness of the request. She had been taught in childhood that nice women didn't touch strange men, unless they were first introduced – when a lady could politely allow her hand to be shaken.

For a second or two, she stared at the bent figure at the other end of the bench. Under the long, belted macintosh, she noticed that his trousers were hospital blue.

An ex-serviceman. Dear God! What dreadful thing had happened to him?

She knew from the newspapers about the number of blinded soldiers, who had, somehow, to be taught to read Braille and manage for themselves; she understood that the existing facilities were overwhelmed by their dire need. But that a man could be blinded and deafened had never occurred to her.

She was revolted at the idea. It was a revulsion equivalent to finding one of Tommy Atkins' half-dead mice in the drawing room, when her first instinct had been to call someone else to remove it – and dispose of it out of her sight.

But she was not without feeling. This was a young man, like Tom or George. A real man – not a mouse to be shovelled into the rubbish bin. Poor soul!

She swallowed nervously. Supposing George or Tom had returned to her smitten like that? What would she have done? How could she have coped with someone that helpless? How would she communicate with them? How could she convey to this man that she was grateful to him for going out to fight – sacrificing himself for king and country, as army generals were fond of saying.

The man had fallen silent, as she stared at him. She was suddenly filled with an immense pity, and what few motherly instincts she had ever had came to the fore. He didn't look more than thirty. Now that the war was over, how would he earn a living? Would he get a decent pension? Would his wife nurse him?

She forgot about Cousin Albert and all her other worries. Plucking up courage, she rose from her end of the bench, and bashfully reseated herself close to him. He felt the swish of her skirts against his leg, and asked, 'Are you a lady?'

She lifted his left hand from the walking stick, and he allowed her to turn it and open the palm. Very gently she touched his palm once. She saw him smile.

'Do you live here?'

Again she signalled yes. She allowed him to rest his hand, palm upwards, on her lap, while he told her how he had, in France, been blinded, deafened and wounded in the back. 'I'm with a lot of other lads in one of the houses facing the sea – I know by the smell of the wind that it faces the sea. All the lads are blind, but I believe only two of us are blind and deaf – and I don't think the army doctors know what to do with us.' His laugh was very cynical. 'If I had a family, I suspect they would just send me home and make the family work it out. But I have no close kin – which is why I joined the army in the first place.'

Louise was so shaken at the idea of such a decent-looking man, no gentleman but nevertheless very respectable-looking, being abandoned that she found herself trying to hold back tears, and one dropped on to his hand.

He felt it, and shifted round to face her. Very carefully, with two fingers he followed the line of her arm from his hand, up to the fur collar of her coat and then almost poked her chin as he found her face.

'Don't cry,' he said, as he felt the dampness on her cheek. 'It doesn't help.' He sighed, and then asked, 'Can I feel your face, so that I will know what you look like?' He felt her nod agreement.

As the fingers went gently over her skin, Louise was shocked to find herself sexually stirred. It was impossible with a strange man – indecent. But it was there, roused by a man young enough to be her son. Did he feel the same? She was a little frightened.

She held herself rigid, while the exploring fingers ventured over her curled fringe and then her bonnet and the veil thrown back over it.

If he felt anything, he gave no indication of it. He checked the veil again, and again he sighed.

'Forgive my asking, but are you a widow?'

She tapped yes.

'The war?'

She tapped no.

'Natural?'

He felt her sigh in her turn, and he did not probe further. A natural death made sense. The feel of the loose skin under her eyes told him that she was not young. And most war widows would be young and less likely to wear a veil.

He had held his stick between his knees, and after he had steadied it, he dropped his hands in his lap and tried another tack.

'I'm Sergeant Richard Williamson, 5th South Lancashire Regiment, and I was born in St Helens. I've been all over the world with the regular army. It's a miracle that I'm still alive, I suppose. What's your name?' He smiled suddenly, 'You could try spelling it out on the palm of my hand, if you like.'

Poor boy, she thought. Still so young, despite his rank – and trying so hard to communicate.

Totally absorbed by his terrible predicament, she ignored her own feelings, and again picked up his left hand. Very carefully she traced L, which he got immediately, and, after a couple of tries, he managed O and U. The rest of her name defeated him.

She saw the frustration on his face, and she squeezed his hand in the hope of conveying her understanding. Without thinking, she said to him, 'It doesn't matter. Louise is not a very common name.' Then she remembered that he could not hear.

He turned his hand round and clasped hers. 'Mrs Lou!'

She lifted his hand to her mouth, so that he could feel her laugh, and it made him chuckle, like a finger game would amuse a small child.

Their laughter ceased abruptly, as they were interrupted by the sound of footsteps behind them. Richard felt Louise freeze and then turn to see who was approaching.

He sat absolutely still, wary as a disturbed rabbit.

'Oh, Ma'am, I hope Mr Williamson is not being a nuisance to you?' A young woman in a nurse's cap and apron stood behind the bench. 'Sometimes they can be a pest – and that stupid.'

Louise rose. She noticed that the woman did not wear a nurse's pin. A servant dressed as a nurse did not impress her. She said frigidly, 'Certainly not. I am horrified by his predicament – and I was happy to try to communicate with him.'

The girl shrugged. 'Oh, aye. It's proper sad. Bad enough when they're blind. There's two of 'em here as is blind and deaf. Proper difficult it is looking after them.' She turned to Richard and tapped him on the shoulder.

He rose immediately, and held out his hand to where he thought Louise might be. She turned back to him and shook his hand. 'Goodbye, Mrs Lou,' he said, his voice formal.

Louise did not know what made her continue to hold his hand, but she did, while she asked the young woman, 'Where is he staying?'

The answer sounded a little impatient, 'In Mon Repos.

That's the house across the road. It's a nursing home now. Holds thirty men.' She put her hand firmly under Richard's arm and began to turn him away from Louise.

'Wait a minute,' Louise interrupted. 'May I come with you to the house? I should like to arrange to see Sergeant Williamson again. He tells me he has no relations – on whom he could call for help or advice. He might be glad to know a local family.'

Louise could appear very formidable when she chose. The girl hesitated. She looked carefully at her. Sealskin collar to her well-cut black coat, real kid gloves clasped in one hand, a hand with a huge diamond ring. A widow's bonnet and veil. A rich widow?

She smirked almost insolently, and Louise could have hit her. Then the girl shrugged. 'Very well, Ma'am. But I tell you, he's got a mind of his own, he has.' There was more than a hint of resentment at a man who would not do what he was told, because he could not hear, and therefore, instead, did what seemed to him to be best in the circumstances. She added reluctantly, 'You could talk to Matron if you want. He's got to come in now – it's lunch time.'

Still holding Richard's hand firmly, so that he would know that she was going with him, Louise repositioned herself, in order that the girl could guide him. Slowly, the three of them crossed the road, and Louise had to relinquish Richard's hand, so that he could use his stick to feel his way up a flight of steps to a lawn, where a number of abandoned lawn chairs suggested the existence of other residents in the fine, big house before them.

As they progressed, Louise's dislike of the young woman faded, to be replaced by some apprehension of the quandary in which she had suddenly placed herself. She knew nothing about the care or training of the blind or, even worse, the deaf and blind. She was about to offer help to a man who would surely be under doctors who, she presumed, already knew what to do for him. Or did they? That was a question to be asked.

But it might have been my George or Tom in such a desperate situation, she told herself passionately. In need of all the help they could get. At least I might be able to offer some entertainment to alleviate his boredom. Richard Williamson must be nearly out of his mind with simple, excruciating boredom.

And just what do you think you can do for this man, a working-class man? she asked herself.

The answer was that she had not the faintest idea, but she would try. It would give her something challenging to do.

She forgot her horrid cottage and her irritating daughters, as her far from stupid mind ground rustily into gear after weeks of disuse, and she began to think constructively of means of communication, of how to give Sergeant Williamson something to do other than sit on a bench.

Swept forward on a tide of overwhelming compassion and not a little of her own need, Louise entered the hall of the nursing home. She heard, in the distance, the rumble of young male voices and the clatter of knives and forks. Thirty of them, the maid had told her. How cruel war was.

It was the idea of two of them being both deaf and blind, however, which drove her upstairs to see an irate matron.

Matron was fed up with volunteers and other do-gooders whose enthusiasm, now that the war was over, waned within weeks; with a government which was simply muddling through and wished heartily that wounded soldiers would go home and get on with their lives; with a nursing staff with a marked tendency to get married and depart.

At first, Louise had some difficulty in persuading the matron, a very experienced army nurse who had seen more medical horrors than she cared to remember, that something more should be done for Sergeant Richard Williamson and his similarly afflicted comrade.

If Louise felt like doing something, she could be very stubborn. She was not stupid. She had some idea of planning and organisation. Her home and entertaining for her husband had both been well run. During the war, she had worked steadily for the Red Cross, and she understood the need to raise funds for charity.

But the dire need of an ordinary Lancashire man sitting on a seaside bench and an unknown number of others like him carried her far beyond the idea of charity. She sensed that it would take long-term dedication and, like the raising of Red Cross funds, endless patience. And, as she talked to the disillusioned matron, she realised that she herself would need to encourage others to help, just as she had when interesting herself in various charities.

A couple of hours later, when she finally left the nursing home, a bewildered matron, though very hungry for her forgotten lunch, had promised her cooperation in a scheme to find help for Sergeant Williamson and his fellow sufferer.

'As far as I know, there's nothing to help people like Richard, except I did hear that an American lady was once able to help a young deaf-blind girl,' Matron said flatly. Her grim middle-aged face was heavy with melancholy. 'The blind will be taught Braille, as soon as we've found teachers for them – the usual places are full, and the boys are having to wait. But I don't see how they can teach anyone blind and deaf.'

For the moment, Louise could not see a way out of Sergeant Williamson's dilemma either. She pushed the problem away for the moment, and inquired, 'Will they get a pension?'

'I suppose they will. There's supposed to be a bill going before Parliament this year, which, if it passes, will make the government responsible for all legally blind people. But you know government – they're as slow as snails.'

Louise nodded. 'Is Braille difficult to learn?' she asked. 'If we could find a way to teach him, we could communicate with Sergeant Williamson.'

'We could – Braille in itself is not that difficult – but the nurses and aides here are run off their feet. I don't think there is one of them who has the tenacity to learn something which won't be of much use when they return to general nursing. Braille would not be much needed by a civilian nurse.'

'I have time – I've all the time in the world,' replied Louise with a certain amount of bitterness in her voice. 'I wonder if I could learn it.'

It did not occur to her that her daughters would be thankful if she would use some of her time to help them. They did not need to earn a living like men did.

The matron smiled. 'You really want to help them, don't you?'

'I do,' Louise responded, with the same commitment with which she had said the same words when she had married dear Timothy.

Let her try, decided the matron; something good may eventually come out of it. But she had not much hope. Once a war was over, governments were not very interested in soldiers.

Nevertheless, she shook Louise's hand and assured her that she could visit at any time. 'The blind boys would probably be grateful if you could read to them occasionally – something light that would amuse them.'

Louise picked up her handbag. She rose and thanked Matron for her time. 'I'll most certainly come to read to them,' she promised. 'Do you think they'd like *Three Men in a Boat*?'

'I'm sure it would make them laugh – and that would be good for them,' Matron said.

Louise trudged slowly up to the station. She had felt drained and tired when she sat down beside Sergeant Williamson. Then she had been shocked out of her fatigue and her grief. Now she felt suddenly worn out, maddeningly frustrated because her tired mind simply would not work. Reading would help the blind boys, but it would not help Sergeant Williamson. And it was his predicament which touched her heart.

Chapter Thirty-Four

After three cups of tea, the conversation between Eddie, Edna and Celia languished, and he announced his departure because he had to cut his hedge.

Both ladies rose and ushered him out of the back door, with many thanks for the lettuce and spring onions. Just as he was about to vanish round the side of their house, however, Edna called him back to ask if he knew a young man who would clear their back garden and dig it over for them.

Eddie paused and scratched the back of his head. 'Do you mind a lad who's not all there?' he asked tentatively, while Celia tugged at her sister's sleeve and whispered that it would cost too much.

'Shush, Celia, it won't be that much.' Then she replied to Eddie. 'We don't mind who does it, as long as it gets tidied up,' she assured him.

'Well, I'll ask young Ethelred's mam if he could do it. He's a strong lad, though he's lost a few marbles.'

'That would be most kind of you.' She pushed a quietly protesting Celia back into the kitchen.

'We can't afford these things, Edna,' Celia argued. 'I was going to do it bit by bit.'

'Don't be a duffer, Celia. It needs real muscle, and you are not going to undertake it. I can manage the few shillings it will cost.' As they re-entered the living room, she added playfully, 'I have high ambitions for you. I'm very keen that you work with this Philpotts man and that it grows into a proper business and is a success.'

Celia smiled a little ruefully. She collected the tea things to take them to the kitchen sink. She said, 'It all depends on Mother. And she's going to be furious at the very idea.' She opened the back door and emptied the tea leaves round an anaemic-looking fern growing near the door. 'Edna, it is ferns that like tea leaves, isn't it?'

Edna came out to view the slightly yellow-tinged plant. 'I've no idea. I think we'd better buy a gardening book.'

Unexpectedly, Celia chuckled. 'What a useless pair we are! We don't know anything, do we?'

'Not much. I could try addressing it in Portuguese to find out if it likes tea leaves. It may not know English.'

Laughing, they turned, to face Louise, who had come silently through the front door and was astonished to see such levity in a house of mourning.

They greeted her, and Edna said she hoped she had enjoyed her walk.

Louise drew off her gloves and took out her hatpins. 'Well, yes and no,' she replied grudgingly. 'Have either of you done anything about dinner?'

Celia and Edna looked guiltily at each other. In one shot, their mother had put them in the wrong. 'No,' they admitted in chorus. When they followed Louise into the living room, Celia surreptitiously leaned over towards the fire and pulled out the oven damper, so that the oven would be hot if they needed it.

'I might have known it,' their mother said dolefully. Then, as she went to hang up her coat and hat, she asked Celia to make some tea and put some cheese and biscuits on a plate for her.

'I haven't had any lunch,' she explained. She made her request mechanically, however, as if her thoughts were elsewhere. 'I think I'll lie down for a little while. Bring it upstairs.'

'Yes, Mother.' Celia's response was equally mechanical. She had been gritting her teeth to keep down her sense of panic. She had been certain that her mother would open the subject of the furniture by asking how she had got on with Mr Philpotts. But she appeared to have forgotten all about him.

Celia was disappointed. The problem was weighing so heavily upon her that she was anxious to discuss it as soon as possible. Now it seemed that she herself would have to broach the subject, and she had no idea how to do it without, straight away, bringing Louise's wrath down on her head. She wished suddenly that Mr Philpotts could be with her to support her when she did so. He seemed such a calm, sensible person.

Chapter Thirty-Five

❧

Muttering irritably under her breath that she was old enough to know, roughly, what time dinner should arrive, Edna retired to the kitchen, to open the meat safe hanging on the wall and take out the remains of yesterday's chicken and see if she could make another dinner out of it. Celia pushed past her to fill the tea kettle at the tap.

Edna looked gloomily at the dried-out chicken remains. 'Better take Mother a lot of biscuits with her tea,' she advised. 'This bird is going to take some resurrecting.'

In spite of her inward qualms about facing her mother, Celia smiled. 'Cut lots of veggies up small, parboil them and then mix the chicken scraps with them,' she suggested. 'You can thicken it with a bit of flour mixed with water.'

'Aha! Wonderful! You can take over the cooking. Do you know how to make dumplings? They'd fill it out, too.'

'No. You could get down the cookery book which Winnie packed for us,' Celia suggested, and whipped the kettle away to put it on the fire.

After ladling tea leaves into the pot and putting it to warm by the fire, she returned to the kitchen.

'I wonder what has happened to Winnie. Has Mother said anything to you about her?'

'No.'

'Do you know if anyone has asked for confirmation of the written reference Mother gave her?'

'I don't think so.'

'I hope she has found a place. She was going to find a

room to live in, while she kept on looking. I'd write to her, except that I don't have an address. I gave her our address, because she told me that sometimes a new mistress likes to write directly to the old employer, in case the reference the servant is carrying is a forgery.'

With her finger poised over a recipe for dumplings, Edna asked idly, 'Did Mother do anything about trying to get her a position? She was with us a long time – since before I was married.'

'Not to my knowledge.'

Edna put down the cookery book slowly and said, 'I hope she did. I know I turned off my servants the day I left – but at least I knew that the next company man to be the tenant of the house would probably rehire them – and they knew it.' She shrugged. 'I expect she's OK. A good cook shouldn't have much difficulty in getting a place.'

Celia sighed. 'She was a good friend to me.'

'Was she? You knew her much longer than I did.'

Upstairs, Louise had taken off her dress and put on her brown velvet dressing gown. She had propped herself up on her bed with her writing case on her lap. She was chewing the end of a pencil, as Celia carefully edged the tea tray round the door. She looked up and inquired, 'Celia, do we have the address of the School for the Blind – I'm sure there is one in Liverpool?'

Astonished at such an odd remark, Celia put the tray down on the bedside table, and responded that she was sure they did not have it. 'I would have kept a record of the address, if you had ever contributed to it, Mama – but I don't think they ever solicited funds from us.'

'Hmm, I wonder how I can get it?'

Celia straightened up and winced as an unaccustomed pain shot up her back; carrying buckets of coal from the coal shed outside the back door was not very kind to backs, she decided.

In answer to Louise's query, she said, 'I'm not sure, Mama.' She stood staring at her mother's lap desk for a moment, and then said thoughtfully, 'I remember that I once got an address for you from the library – they have a number of reference books.'

'Is there a library in Hoylake?'

'Yes. I passed it yesterday.'

'Well, you can walk along to it tomorrow and see if the librarian can find the address. And also the address of St Dunstan's.' She added testily, 'Don't dawdle there. Pour the tea.'

Celia swallowed uneasily; it seemed as if her mother had revived the almost feverish activity which had always been a prelude to giving a party or organising the removal of the family to Rhyl for its annual holiday. She asked, 'Are you having trouble with your eyes, Mother?'

'No. But I want to learn Braille.'

Very puzzled, Celia exclaimed in surprise, 'But Braille is for blind people.'

'I know that.' Louise turned herself to face her daughter. She said, 'Do you know, Celia, in Hoylake there is a house full of blind soldiers waiting to learn it before being discharged. If I can learn it quickly I can help to teach them.' She sighed and turned to stare across at the open window. 'Even worse, Celia, two of them are both blind and deaf – and the matron says that no one really knows how to communicate with them at all.'

Celia handed her mother tea and biscuits and then sank down on the side of the bed. 'How dreadful. Poor things!' She was honestly shocked, and looked at her mother as if she had never seen her before, while Louise jotted something down on a list she appeared to be compiling. When her mother began to compile a list, it was certain that she was about to embark on, what was to her, a serious undertaking.

Louise flung her pencil down on the bed. 'Yes, Celia.

Poor things indeed. Can you imagine what it would be like if one of your dear brothers had been sent home to us in such a state? Where would we begin? What could we do?'

'I don't know, Mother. It would be terrible. How did you stumble on these soldiers?'

Eagerly now, Louise described her morning. She finished up by saying, 'I feel an urgent need to help if I can.'

Celia nodded. She did understand. It was yet another shocking revelation of young men's suffering in a merciless war.

She sat quietly for a moment or two. It looked as if her mother might be in the process of casting off the role of impoverished widow, which Celia had imagined she would play for the rest of her life. Was she reverting to that of a society woman who knew that rank had its obligations, a person who knew exactly how to plan a charity ball or banquet and had the strength to do it? Perhaps it would not be the best of roles, but at least it might put some life back into her. Most of her mother's acquaintances in Liverpool had a pet charity to which they contributed money or voluntary work.

Celia recalled that when Phyllis's baby had arrived so precipitously it had revived her; she had become the domineering matron who had been the scourge of less efficient Red Cross volunteers during the war. More shrewd than Celia, Edna had remarked only a few days earlier that their mother was a perfectly capable woman if she would only bestir herself.

And here she was, trying to bestir herself to some purpose on behalf of two ordinary soldiers, as if they were her own sons.

As she remembered her two brothers, Celia wanted to burst into tears. She had always recognised her mother's grief over the loss of them.

She made herself smile at Louise. Wounded soldiers in their helplessness could, indeed, be cared for as if they were

Tom and George. At least it was worthwhile giving them a hand, if it could be done; it would also make her mother focus on a definite goal instead of drifting miserably from day to day. Celia forgot, for the moment, her own problems, the greatest of which was the unexpectedly dedicated lady reclining beside her, and said with real enthusiasm, 'Mother, I think you're wonderful! I believe the library is open in the evenings. I can try to get those addresses tonight.'

Her mother's face glowed at the unexpected praise.

'May I tell Edna?' Celia asked. 'I should go downstairs to help her.'

'Of course.'

Chapter Thirty-Six

ॐॐ

Downstairs in the living room, Edna received the information with a very startled expression.

She slowly dropped a handful of chopped carrots into a saucepan on the fire. Then she grinned mischievously and gave a derisive hoot, as she stirred the mixture of vegetables and leftover chicken.

'You mean to say that Mother has found a cause, a real honest-to-goodness cause?'

'It looks like it.'

Wooden spoon poised over the pan, Edna stood rubbing her chin thoughtfully with her other hand, and left a long smudge of flour on her face. Then she said slowly, 'It'll be the making of her, if she can do it. I wonder if she realises what a huge undertaking it will be?' She looked disparagingly down at the chicken stew she had concocted, and added ruefully, 'She'll have no time for matters domestic – we'll get that job.' With a dripping wooden spoon, she gestured round the little room. Gravy flew from it and hissed as the liquid hit the hot range. The smell of burning was added to the stuffy atmosphere.

Celia laughed a little helplessly. 'I suppose we'll manage somehow. She doesn't do anything much now. Frankly, I think we should encourage her as much as possible – because it is a very real cause, Edna,' she said, and went to wash the lettuce brought in by their neighbour.

She felt very tired and wondered how many more responsibilities she could undertake. Edna had said that she would try to get the garden cleared of its overgrowth for her – but that was only the beginning. It had to be planted, weeded, raked, hedges cut. How could she do it? Tend a shop? Help Edna with the washing, ironing, cleaning, shopping, cooking, et cetera, and, on top of all that, do all the errands that Louise would now expect her to do in connection with this new interest. Edna could not do everything at home – and, in any case, Edna had hinted that she might set up a home of her own, once Paul's will had been probated. If she did that, the work for Celia would be overwhelming.

As she spread the cloth on the table, she wondered wistfully if she would ever have any leisure, even for a walk or to read a book. Or to visit Phyllis Woodcock.

It was almost certain that Louise would, indeed, use her as her secretary in her new endeavours, much as she had done during her father's lifetime – and how could she refuse when the need of the men her mother had met was so acute?

As promised, Celia went to the library that evening, and came home with a number of addresses of organisations which might help the deaf and another list of charities interested in the blind, but nothing in connection with those doubly handicapped.

Within the next two days, Louise wrote letters of inquiry to all the addresses provided by the librarian, seeking a clue to any charity which might know how the deaf-blind could be helped. Was there a form of signing, she inquired, for the deaf-blind, similar in principle to that used by the deaf?

She also received a further letter from Cousin Albert to say that he would arrive at the cottage on the following Monday and would stay at least three days, while he dealt with the estate agent selling her house and with the affairs of Timothy's estate.

It caused no little turmoil in the cottage, when Louise insisted that Celia double up with Edna. She was to remove her clothes from the small wardrobe in the hall bedroom and see that everything was clean for her second cousin.

'Mother!' wailed Edna. 'Can't he stay in a hotel in Liverpool?'

'Apparently not,' Louise snapped back. 'He's probably trying to save himself expense.'

Celia did not say anything. She did not want to offend her mother before discussing Mr Philpotts' offer with her.

She had not yet found an opportunity to broach the subject; it seemed as if Louise was either closeted in the tiny front sitting room writing, or had gone to Hoylake.

Much to Edna's annoyance, and adding to Celia's sense of being besieged by work, Louise had demanded that a fire be lit in the, as yet unused, front room, and that her lap desk be brought down and put on the tea table there.

Edna fought a noisy battle about the cost and work of making two fires each day – and lost. Louise was adamant that the work she was about to do was a priority over everything else.

Even Edna never considered telling her that if she wanted a fire in the room, she should make it and clear it up herself. Neither sister could visualise Louise doing such a menial task.

The same postal delivery that brought Cousin Albert's letter also brought two letters from Brazil for Edna.

Louise picked them up from the hall floor as she came down for breakfast, and she scanned the envelopes with some curiosity before handing them to Edna.

She seated herself at the table and began to open Cousin Albert's letter. 'Who are your letters from?' she asked. 'This one is from Albert.'

'Just friends,' Edna replied and slipped them both, unopened, into her skirt pocket. Inwardly, she steamed with irritation. Mother had no right to inquire who her correspondents were. She was a widow and entitled to her privacy. Celia was still a spinster and subject to her mother, but not Edna.

The inference of Edna's casual reply was not lost on Celia, who was quickly eating her breakfast egg, and she felt a pang of envy. It must be wonderful to be free, she thought.

'Edna, you'd better see that we have enough food in the house to feed Albert, in addition to us,' Louise ordered, as she put Albert's letter back into its envelope.

'Do you have any money?' Edna inquired quietly.

Louise looked startled. 'I think so,' she said. 'I've a little left over from the rents which Mr Billings sent me.'

Since moving into the cottage Edna had found herself paying for almost all their day-to-day needs and she felt that this was the moment to bring it home to Louise that she must pay her share. Her inquiry made Louise bite her lip and then promise to give her something for groceries.

The discovery that it would probably cost all Louise had in her purse to feed an extra mouth strengthened Celia's idea that, if permitted, she should try to earn enough to contribute to the housekeeping. She would delay no longer. She would, that evening, talk to Mother about it.

Chapter Thirty-Seven

❦

Carrying a brass coal hod of additional coal for her mother's fire, Celia knocked tentatively at the sitting-room door and was told in a querulous voice to come in.

Louise was running her hand along the large bookcase which took up one wall of the tiny room. She glanced round at her whey-faced daughter, and asked, 'Do you know where your father's books by Philip Oppenheim are? The boys apparently like his novels.'

'Yes, Mother. They're in a box in Betty's barn. We decided we would never read them again.' She squatted down on the hearth rug and, with the aid of a pair of tongs, added a few lumps of coal to the fire.

'Well, bring them back. I need them.'

'Yes, Mother.' The thought of carrying baskets full of books back from Hoylake made her back ache even more; Oppenheim was a very prolific writer.

As Celia rose stiffly from the hearth rug, Louise returned to the littered tea table. She sat down in front of it and scanned the list of things she felt she had to do, which seemed to be constantly beside her and never to grow any smaller. She did, however, now cross off Oppenheim.

Celia carefully placed the coal hod beside the end of the fender, clasped her hands tightly in front of her over her grubby apron and turned towards Louise.

'Mother, I need to talk to you about Mr Philpotts and the furniture.'

'Now?'

'Yes, Mother. I must let Mr Philpotts have an answer to a suggestion he has made.' Celia stood woodenly before her, hoping that she herself wouldn't break down with sheer fright. Two days' contemplation of Mr Philpotts' offer had convinced her of the common sense of it. And with a little money, she could be independent, even if she was a spinster.

Louise asked impatiently, 'Well?'

Celia had rehearsed very carefully what she would say, and she explained quite clearly what the idea was. She finished up by saying, 'The crux is that all the furniture is yours, not mine, and if we go into a modest partnership, such as Mr Philpotts has suggested, there should be some kind of written agreement that I may act for you – unless you would like to start a business yourself, of course.'

'Tut! I shall be much too busy. In any case it would be totally infra dig.'

Celia gritted her teeth. 'Very well, Mother. When I spoke to Edna about it, she suggested that you might allow me to own the furniture – as the capital, so to speak, to start a business in antiques and collectibles. I would hope, Mama, to make enough, in the long term, so that you did not have to keep me; I could contribute regularly to the household, and then you would reap a financial benefit from the investment.'

Too terrified to go on for the moment, she paused as she saw the gathering storm in Louise's expression. Then she added uncomfortably, 'Edna says it is essential that I learn to earn my living – because I shall be alone when you ... er ... pass on.'

'Keep a shop!' Louise was trembling with affronted dignity – and with an underlying fear that she would lose her hold over Celia, who would be most useful, not only at home, but as a general runabout in connection with the work Louise was undertaking. 'How insulting that this man should suggest it – and who is he, anyway, to interfere in our affairs?'

'He's just a small businessman. Basically, he has floor space to let in front of his workshop – and he'd like to share the rent with someone.'

Inwardly Celia prayed, God don't let me panic until I'm through this. She took a big breath, and went on determinedly, 'As I said, he's a furniture repairer and French polisher, and his kind of clients are likely to be people who appreciate good furniture; they may be interested in what we have for sale.'

Louise's chest swelled with indignation. She slammed down her pen and a blot of ink flew on to the carpet. She replied furiously, 'I'm surprised that you did not dismiss him on the spot. I won't hear of it. My good name – your father's good name – on a shop? A most repellent idea!'

Patiently Celia fought back. 'The shop does not have to have our name on it, Mother. We could call it something neutral, like Hoylake Fine Furniture.'

'I won't have it. Edna is quite wrong to encourage you. No girl of mine is going to serve in a shop. Anyway, you aren't capable of running anything.'

The latter remark stung.

The insult quelled Celia's panic. It was replaced by honest rage.

'Mother! You're most unfair,' she almost shouted. 'Who fixed up this cottage? Who found workmen and made it habitable? Who arranged the removal – and did most of the packing?

'I did, without much help from you. Who is going to have to plant the garden and make it decent? I shall – because you won't.' Her voice rose to a shriek. 'I know that the ex-soldiers need your help – but I need an atom of help, too. I know you're in mourning – and Edna and I have done our best to help you. But there's a limit.' She unclasped her hands and banged them flat on the table.

'You'd like to keep me tied to your apron strings until you die – and then you won't care what happens to me because you'll be dead and won't have need of me any more. Mr Philpotts and Edna have suggested a future for me and an investment of your discarded furniture – that's all.'

More shattered by this unexpected explosion than she liked to admit, Louise sat up straight and glared at the girl.

'Be quiet! You're behaving like a silly child. This idea of a shop is lunatic. I have no doubt that Edna will look after you when I'm gone – you're not capable of looking after yourself.'

At her last words, Celia's temper died. Reimplanted in her was the haunting fear that there was something the matter with her, that she was not normal in some way and was, therefore, incapable – and had been kept at home because of it. Since her father's death, she had done her utmost to cope with the many problems it had presented, and she had considered that she had, in the circumstances, done rather well, but perhaps other people would have done much better. She had no yardstick by which to measure her performance.

Now, she went a ghastly white, and clutched her arms across her waist as if she had been struck in the stomach. Then with bent head she stumbled to the door, opened it and went out into the hall. She hooked her toe in the door and slammed it behind her.

She nearly ran into Edna, hurrying from the living room.

'Hello,' Edna greeted her, obviously relieved to see Celia on her feet. 'I heard you shriek – thought you'd fallen down the stairs. Are you hurt?' She touched Celia's white cheek. 'You look absolutely awful!'

Celia looked into her sister's concerned face. She mourned, 'Oh, Edna, help me,' as she fell into her arms.

Edna gripped her stricken sister firmly, and said, 'Come into the living room and lie on the old settee. Shall I call Mother?'

'No,' Celia gasped, and stumbled to the settee, where she collapsed and curled herself into a tight knot.

Puzzled, Edna took one of Celia's clenched hands and chafed it, while she glanced over her face for bruises or some other injury. Then she pulled a knitted blanket down from the back of the settee and covered her. She turned and ran to the back kitchen for a glass of water.

'Here, sip this,' she ordered Celia and lifted her head so that she could do so. She eased the glass between Celia's chattering teeth, and water slopped over her. The shock of its icy coldness soaking through her black blouse seemed to ease the poor girl's rigor, and she gasped, 'Thanks.' Then she whispered pitifully, 'I'm so frightened, Edna. Mother's so angry.'

'Were you asking her about Mr Philpotts?'

'Yes. About my having the furniture. I don't think she cares very much whether or not I have the furniture – but she was so put out at the suggestion that we could start a shop, and that I should work in it. She was really shocked.'

'That's just like Mother.' Edna sounded slightly amused, as she leaned over to put the water glass down on the table. 'But that shouldn't throw you into a panic, dear. It could make you angry, of course – but you shouldn't be so upset just by that.'

Celia gave a big sobbing sigh. Through her chattering teeth, she said, 'It was what she said at the end that hit me – and she's said it so many times in my life – that I'm not capable of doing anything. And I wondered again if I'm kept at home because I'm mentally lacking – or because I've got tuberculosis – or something.'

'Ridiculous! Ever since I came home, you have steadily proved it. The only thing that is the matter with you is that you have never been taught anything, except to say, "Yes, Papa" and "Yes, Mama" like a talking doll. I am sure you could do very well, with Mr Philpotts to help you out to begin with.'

She still had her arm round her tiny sister. Now she hugged her close, while she considered the situation. Then she said, 'I think you need to be reassured by somebody outside the family. I noticed, when I was out, that there is a lady doctor who practises in Hoylake. You could tell a lady everything that has happened to you – much more easily than you could a male doctor. I think another woman would understand.' She smiled and hugged her sister closer. 'I am sure that she would reassure you that you are sane, though I don't think you're very well physically – we've all been under great strain and you have had to do a great deal – I simply don't know how Mother can say that you're incapable.'

She smiled down at Celia, and she could feel the younger woman's body beginning to relax. 'Let's go to see the doctor tomorrow,' she soothed. 'She probably has a morning surgery.'

'I can't pay her.'

'I know that – but I can. Between us, in case of emergency, Paul and I were carrying a fair amount of cash with us when we left Brazil. I changed it into English sovereigns when I arrived, and, thanks to Papa Fellowes, I have not had to spend much of it, except to help Mother out with her housekeeping. I can certainly afford a few shillings to pay for a doctor for you.'

As Celia began to protest, Edna stifled her objections by saying that she could accept the fee as an advance birthday present. 'Don't worry,' she added. 'My income will be quite adequate as soon as the will business is settled. If a doctor can lift this cloud from your mind, I think it will be the best birthday present I can give you.'

'It would, Edna. It really would. Do you think the doctor could? Could we go to her without telling Mother?'

'Certainly. She's going to read to her boys tomorrow morning and then help to take the two deaf-blind ones for a walk.' Edna laughed softly. 'We'll leave the housework – just forget about it.'

Celia struggled to sit up, and Edna loosened her hold on her. 'What am I going to do about Mr Philpotts?'

'Well, I think we should talk to Cousin Albert, when he comes on Monday. He may see how sensible John Philpotts' suggestion is – and understand that in the end Mother won't lose financially. If anyone can talk sense into her, I think he can.

'She has to realise that you're a human being, her daughter as much as I am. She must consider your future.'

'I never thought of Cousin Albert.'

'Well, at least he's a man, and Mother may listen to a man.'

'You're being wonderfully kind, Edna,' Celia said gently. 'I'm so grateful.'

Edna made a face. 'I'm making up for past sins. I never realised until recently what was happening to you. I was at school for years and you were just the younger sister at home. Quite honestly, I thought you liked helping Mother, and I was dreadfully self-centred anyway. For myself, I knew that to please Father I had to net a husband – a suitably well-off one. Then I was all excitement about meeting Paul – and then I went to Brazil. And, frankly, when I came back, I was quite distraught myself – my whole life seems to have gone to pieces, and England seems so different.'

Celia swung her feet carefully to the floor. She put one hand gently on Edna's shoulder. 'It must be dreadful for you, you poor dear,' she said with sympathy. Then she went on dejectedly, 'We didn't really see much of each other, did we?' She sat looking down at her slippered feet, and then, after reflection, said, 'I always thought Mother would bring me out and arrange for me to meet someone to marry, like you, as soon as I was old enough. Then the war came and both Mother and Father kept putting me off – and Father wouldn't hear of my becoming a nurse or anything. And that further convinced me that there must be something wrong with me, because a lot of untrained girls went to nurse the wounded.'

She looked up at Edna. 'You know, he threatened that if I left home, he would cut me off without a penny. And in the end, it was so ironical – he never did make any provision for me.'

'I think that was awful.'

Celia reverted to the question of her physical health. 'I've never seen a doctor in my life, not even when I caught Spanish flu,' she confided. Then she glanced apprehensively at the door into the hall. 'I'm so scared, Edna. I thought Mother would come after me – but she hasn't.'

'She must have thought that she has settled the matter with her refusal – and that you just had a childish tantrum which you will have forgotten by morning.' She began to laugh, and soon Celia was giggling, too.

In perfect imitation of their old nanny, Edna said reprovingly, '"Now, Miss Celia, no lady allows her temper to get the better of her. A gentle answer turneth away wrath, remember."' Then she added in her own voice, 'It can also make people think you are a doormat. Now, off you go to bed before she wipes her feet on you again.'

Chapter Thirty-Eight

After spending the tumultuous years of the war in a London hospital constantly full of wounded, Edith Mason came home to the village where she was born, to practise medicine with her father, who had had a family practice there for many years.

Though it was extremely difficult for a woman to obtain training as a doctor, old Dr Mason had given his only child every support and encouragement, and he was happy to welcome her home and to have such an experienced physician as his junior partner. Like many other medical students of the time, she had faced a constant flow of terribly wounded or very sick men, and, perforce, her experience during training had been much wider than it would have been in peacetime.

With her father as her partner, his patients tolerated her, though men often specified that they wanted to see old Dr Mason. When, in January 1920, he died, however, the old, ugly prejudice against women doctors surfaced and patients tended to drift away to any physician who wore a pair of trousers.

To Edith's relief, however, it became evident that women were glad to discuss their more intimate problems with her, and, at the time of Celia's visit, she was beginning to rebuild the practice, though she was still far from busy. Edna knew of her only from her business plate bolted to her front gate.

Edna felt that Celia would simply freeze in front of

a male doctor and that what her sister needed most was reassurance. Dr Mason seemed to her a sensible choice.

When the two young women arrived at the doctor's front door, they obeyed a cardboard notice hung on the door handle and entered her hallway. A further notice by an open doorway instructed them to Please Take a Seat, so in they went and shyly sat down.

Dr Mason's waiting room held only one middle-aged lady, who sat primly upright in a corner. In response to a small ting-ting of a bell, she immediately rose and went into an inner room to see the doctor. The sisters heard her being greeted with a cheerful good morning, and then the door was closed.

When Edna and a very timid Celia answered the bell and went in to face her, Dr Mason was able to give them plenty of time.

At first Edna did the talking, but when finally her description of her sister's fears about her health became clear, the doctor turned to Celia.

Celia said baldly, 'I want to know, Doctor, if I am quite normal and sane in my mind and that I am not physically ill in any way. My parents have always kept me at home and consistently said that I am incapable of looking after myself.'

Edith Mason saw much more in this request than Celia realised. She knew the type quite well. A daughter kept as a superior servant, no social life, no sex life, little education, few friends. Queen Victoria had set the fashion for this misuse of a daughter, and Dr Mason had seen a number like her, and, indeed, wives with the same crushed passive look. She knew that, in the case of the latter, sometimes their only escape was into a form of semi-invalidism which had little to do with real illness.

She suggested, first, that she take Celia's medical history and then give her a thorough physical examination.

Celia said she did not have any medical history. She had never been to a doctor before.

The doctor laughed and, after questioning her, ended up with a long list of childhood illnesses and, as an adult, recurring coughs, colds, unknown fevers, and Spanish flu.

When Edith saw the fear in her patient's eyes at the length of the list, she assured her that it was quite an ordinary list. Most people went through all these illnesses.

Celia agreed. 'It must be so, I suppose. Mother never called the doctor for any of them.'

Dr Mason took Celia behind a screen in a far corner of the spacious room, and asked her to undress and wrap herself in a white sheet lying on an examination table. While she did so, the doctor went to check that there was no one else in the waiting room.

Edna remained in the consulting room as chaperone. She was, however, seated at the furthest possible distance from the screen, and could reasonably be expected not to hear the doctor's quiet conversation with her patient.

It was Celia's first medical examination and her face went pink with embarrassment. While she was seated on the examination table, the doctor put her stethoscope to her chest and listened to her heart, turned her around and knocked carefully on her back, peered down her throat and down her ears, examined her throat and tongue and turned down her lower eyelids to check for anaemia. She took a little hammer and tapped her knees for reflexes. Then she laid Celia out on her back and took a good look at her, stark naked. She saw a short, small-breasted, perfectly formed, very white, reasonably nourished body that had obviously never been exposed to sunlight, hips of a normal width for her height. She was probably perfectly capable of bearing children and of feeding them. There was no apparent sign of malformation or ill health.

Anxious not to discommode a patient who, she guessed,

had probably never been stripped in front of anyone, never mind a doctor, she did not feel for breast cancer.

She gently covered the little body with the sheet, and pulled a swivel chair up close to the table and sat down herself, picked up her clipboard from under the table and began to make some notes.

'I should take your pulse,' she said, her worn face breaking into a smile. 'I forgot.' And, looking at her closely, Celia realised, with surprise, that this self-possessed, careful lady was not much older than Edna.

Celia returned the smile. She felt perfect confidence in the physician, and answered as carefully as she could the questions she was then asked. No aches? No bad accidents at any time? No pains? Headaches? Menses regular? Celia had to have the word 'menses' explained to her, having previously only heard polite euphemisms, including the curse, for the menstrual cycle. Her last curse had been two weeks before.

Dr Mason sat back and looked at the prematurely sad face before her, and said that she appeared to have normal health, except that she was a little anaemic, for which she would prescribe a tonic. 'And much more fresh air,' she suggested. 'Do you walk?' Yes. 'Can you swim?' No. 'Play tennis?' No. 'Ride a bicycle?' No. 'Church?' No. 'Mother goes, but I have not had time for months.'

The doctor leaned back in her swivel chair. 'What do you do with your day?' she asked in a friendly, conversational way.

Under the sheet, Celia squirmed uneasily. 'Usually I do whatever Mother wants doing. But now she's widowed, I have had to do all kinds of things.' Her voice sounded flat and tired.

'What kind of things?' The doctor's voice was soft and amiable.

The story of her father's bankruptcy and having to move to the cottage came out, at first diffidently, and then in a rush. 'Mother is so upset that she is not able to do much,' she finished up in polite defence of her surviving parent. 'So I had to make all the arrangements.'

'And what do you personally hope to do in the future?'

And Celia replied dully, 'Look after Mother and the house and the garden – and . . .' She tailed off.

'And?' The doctor prompted.

Celia looked her squarely in the eye. 'Do you really want to know?'

'Well, it is natural that you might want to do something you enjoy in your spare time. You don't have to tell me, but the more I know about you, the better I will be able to advise you. Did you lose someone in the war, my dear?'

'Both my brothers. There is just Edna, Mother and I left now – Edna's husband died of the Spanish flu.'

'No sweetheart?'

Celia laughed disparagingly. 'Me? I'm far too plain to have a sweetheart.'

Edith smiled inwardly. This, she thought, is where I begin the healing. 'I don't think you're too plain,' she assured her. 'You have a pretty, healthy body, and you are not at all ugly.'

'Really?' Celia had never in her life received a compliment regarding her appearance.

'Of course.' No need to tell her that most of the males of her generation were dead.

'Is there nothing that you would like to do, if you had time? Your mother is not going to live for ever. You need to have something else to do.'

Celia propped herself up on one elbow, and said almost eagerly, 'Well, yes, there is. But Mother has always assured me that I am totally incapable of doing anything. My father, too. That's why I came to you – to find out if I am sick in some way – or if I am mentally deficient. You see I get so frightened that I curl up into a ball and I can't do anything for hours until it passes.' Her voice faded into despair. 'You must think I'm awfully stupid.'

Panic attacks. 'You poor child. Because of these episodes you think you are mentally deficient?'

'I fear so. Edna doesn't think I am, but she doesn't know me very well. She's been in South America for years and has only just recently come home.'

The doctor again put her fingers round Celia's wrist. The girl's pulse was now racing. She grasped her hand and squeezed it. She smiled, and said, 'You strike me as a perfectly normal person, perhaps a little too dutiful a daughter, but, nevertheless, perfectly normal. Now, tell me what it was you wanted to do – it must be important since it apparently drove you to come to see me.' She laughed. 'Nobody knows better than a woman physician how difficult it is to become a professional – or do anything the least unusual.'

And while Edna fidgeted her way through a couple of magazines, Celia told Edith Mason about Mr Philpotts and the proposed furniture shop.

Edith Mason smiled. She said easily, 'People said things like that to me when I announced that I was going to be a doctor. Women are incapable, they told me, besides which it is vulgar – I might have to look at blood – and at naked men – shocking!'

Celia giggled nervously. Then she remembered the revolting characters who had chased her when she walked on the sea wall, and she felt slightly nauseated.

Her new-found doctor continued, 'Fortunately, my father was there to encourage me.'

'My father wasn't like that.' Celia's golden eyelashes closed over her tired eyes, as she remembered her dread of her father. The tiny movement was observed by Dr Mason. A lot of pain there, she considered. Had the man used her sexually?

She decided that it would only frighten her more if she

inquired. Instead, she said briskly, 'Perhaps you would like to dress, while I go to my desk and write this up. And then I hope I can suggest a few things to improve your health.'

She removed herself and went over to exchange a few pleasantries with Edna. She had noted Edna's mourning dress, but assumed that, like her sister's, it was worn because of her father's death. She sat down by her, and told her that Celia did not seem to have anything wrong with her, but she should get out and about, enjoy herself in the fresh air and get more sleep.

Edna's deeply lined, yellowed face broke into an unexpectedly pretty smile. 'I told her so.' She fidgeted with her black leather gloves, and then added, 'She's had a rotten life at home, and she's coped marvellously since Father died. But Mother keeps telling her she's a fool – and she isn't. She's just crushed.'

'I couldn't express it better myself,' Edith Mason replied softly, not wishing to have Celia hear herself discussed. 'You will know more about this business she wants to start than I do; but if it is worthwhile, it could be the making of her. A real interest.'

'And a way of maintaining herself after Mother dies,' replied Edna a little sharply.

'Oh, she didn't mention that. It must be an underlying fear, however.' She hesitated, and then said tentatively, 'She tells me that you have also lost your husband, and it must be trying for you to have to cope with Miss Gilmore's ills at such a time. Please accept my condolences.'

'Thank you,' Edna said. Then she heaved a big sigh. 'It's good for me to have Celia in whom to take an interest, since I have no children.'

The doctor took one of Edna's hands in both of hers, and said, 'Though you have not consulted me, the advice I am going to give Miss Celia may help you, too.'

She wrote a prescription for a tonic for Celia. 'Three times a day after meals. And I'd like to see both of you again in two weeks' time.' Then she advised them to take a long walk together every day or, better still, buy bicycles and go out and explore the Wirral. 'It's lovely at this time of year,' she said.

'Cycling in mourning? Mother will have a fit. She'll never permit it,' Celia protested.

'Tell her doctor's orders. Try to persuade her to ride with you,' suggested the indomitable doctor, and sent them home laughing at the idea of their mother in her long gowns riding a bicycle.

Laughing herself, Edith Mason went back to her desk, to write up her notes. Afterwards, she leaned back to stretch, and considered idly all the so-called stupid daughters and dumb maidservants who had hung up their aprons and gone out during the war to replace men on farms, in factories, in banks and offices. In France, she had seen them driving ambulances and nursing dreadfully hurt men in first aid stations on the front lines of battle. She hoped that now the war was over they would refuse to be treated ever again as nonentities, especially now that they had the vote – provided they were aged over thirty.

'Up with women,' she muttered with a grim smile, and went to put on her coat and hat and do her house calls – on a bicycle.

Chapter Thirty-Nine

As they went out of the doctor's front gate, Edna said with a gleam in her eye, 'I told you so, Celia. Nothing to worry about.'

Celia laughed a little shakily, and agreed. 'How kind she was,' she said warmly. 'I never thought of going to a lady doctor – and I simply couldn't have talked to a man – I don't think a man would have had much sympathy for me.'

Edna said, 'I think she understood the kind of life you have had, and that she really wanted to help. I liked her enormously; I'd enjoy having her as a friend.' She stopped, to fumble in her pocket for her handkerchief with which to dab her nose. Then she said, 'I don't really know anyone on Merseyside any more – and I miss my Portuguese friends in Brazil – and not having a place of my own.'

As they crossed Market Street, Celia replied with quick sympathy, 'I'm sure you do. I hope you'll make some new friends here, in time. I've already made a friend of Betty Houghton, though Mother thinks she's far too common.' She grinned mischievously as she said this, and then, as they regained the safety of the pavement, she asked, 'Would you like to meet Mr Philpotts? His workshop is somewhere near here.'

'Yes, I would.'

As they slowly made their way down the street, Edna went on, 'You know, Britain has changed so much in the years I've been away that I feel at a loss how to proceed in quite ordinary situations. Or perhaps I am so used to Brazil that I have forgotten what England is really like.'

Celia considered this for a moment, before replying. Then she said, 'Everything had to change because of the war. But we all thought that, once the war finished, we would go back to our old life – as it was in 1914.

'But we haven't been able to, Edna. Nothing is the same. The war's been over for nearly eighteen months, and we still seem to be in chaos. People are still distraught, still struggling because one of their number is either dead or wounded, and they have to make do in some new way. And when I do get a chance to read the newspaper, it is frightening: reports of unemployment and lack of housing – and huge war debts – and strikes threatening.'

They paused at the edge of the pavement, to allow a donkey cart out of a side alley, and the driver tipped his cap as he drove past them. Celia smiled at him, in response.

'I've felt the change myself,' Celia continued, as they crossed the alley. 'Mother was always saying that, when the boys came home, we would be busy again, as they established careers, got married, and she had grand-children; it seemed as if life would be more normal.' Her voice faltered, when she went on, 'But Tom and George never will come home, so she won't have any grandchildren – she grieved over Rosemary, you know, and so did I – poor little lamb. I would have so enjoyed her.'

As she mentioned Edna's daughter, she glanced at her sister. But Edna's expression was quite blank, as if she had retreated, once more, into herself.

Poor Edna, Celia thought contritely. She's had a rotten time, too. I shouldn't have mentioned Rosemary.

Anxious to keep the conversation going in spite of her blunder, she changed the subject. She said, 'Although Mother has, I believe, left a few cards with distant acquain-tances round here, she hasn't had one response, not even an invitation to an at home or morning coffee.' She stood aside to let an old crone wrapped in a shawl get by, and then said, 'I've come to the conclusion that ladies simply haven't the energy to re-establish their social life. Or perhaps, now she is a widow – not a couple – Mother will have to find entirely new friends amongst other widows.'

As a swarm of morning shoppers pushed between them, she paused in her chatter, and then said with a deprecating laugh, 'I doubt if anyone is interested in three impoverished ladies living together; no hostess would want to make the awful effort of finding three matching men for her dinner table.'

Edna bestirred herself to answer. Her mind had been diverted by thoughts of little Rosemary's lonely grave in far-away Brazil. At Celia's mention of the probable shortage of males at a formal dinner, she was reminded of quiet, cultivated Vital; he would be a pleasant addition to any dinner table; he belonged to a society where there was often a shortage of women, because they died young in childbirth. She wanted to whimper with the pain of it all.

Instead, she turned her attention firmly to Celia, and said, with a slight shrug, 'Our family is all upside down because we've had so many losses, and, as well, we've had to move. But you are right, dear. There are so many like us that I don't think home life will ever be the same again.'

As they walked slowly along, Edna lapsed into silence. Then she said suddenly, 'Eddie Fairbanks was telling me that the young men and women whom you saw cavorting in the sea with – er – nothing on – are not exceptional. He says that there is a lot of wild gaiety in London – even in Liverpool. Night clubs, drunkenness, and shocking things going on between the sexes. Not our kind of life at all. He says it's people trying to make up for their lost youth.' She smiled grimly. 'I don't seem to remember having much youth to lose myself. I was a mother at twenty-two.'

They had to stop to allow a flotilla of perambulators to pass them, and Edna made a small gesture towards the women hurrying towards them. 'So many people are still in mourning – it's all blacks and greys – you can see it. So many widows' weeds.' She moved swiftly aside again to avoid being bumped by a pram, and added, 'And an astonishing number of babies. Breeding troops for the next war?'

Celia was shocked. She stopped dead. 'Edna! How can you say such a dreadful thing – there will never be another war. It's too terrible to contemplate. We've finished with wars.' She did, however, see what Edna had pointed out. Not only were the women in mourning, but they looked carelessly dressed; they did not look elegant in their blacks and greys. There was a general air of dowdiness which, at this time of year in such a well-to-do district, would have been alleviated by the sight of new spring costumes in the latest fashion, and pretty hats trimmed with bows and flowers. Some of the few men about were still in uniform, and those in civilian dress looked generally older and wore unrelieved black, including black bowler hats.

Celia sighed, and eased her sister round a corner. 'Mr Philpotts' workshop is just here, I think,' she said.

The corner itself was occupied by an empty shop with windows facing both Market Street and the side road. Beyond the shop, on the side road, was a brick wall broken only by a single board door painted a dingy green.

The two women approached it doubtfully, but were reassured by a black notice board screwed to the adjoining wall, which stated in faded gold letters

J.D. PHILPOTTS,
UPHOLSTERER & FRENCH POLISHER.
COMPLETE RESTORATIONS UNDERTAKEN.

Celia swallowed nervously. 'I hope he doesn't mind our calling on him.'

'You're probably more important to him than he is to you at the moment,' Edna responded quickly, determined that the doctor's reassurance should not go down the drain immediately.

Celia's eyebrows shot up in surprise. 'I must say I never thought of it in that way.'

She smiled, and knocked at the door.

There was no response.

'Try again,' encouraged Edna.

There was a sound of slow movement within. 'Coming.'

The door swung open to reveal Mr Philpotts, looking rather different from his last meeting with Celia. He wore patched and stained overalls and his shirtsleeves were rolled up to the elbows to expose muscular forearms thatched with black hair. His wrists and hands were stained with a reddish-brown dye and he carried a grubby rag. On his head he wore an ancient peaked cap, and his face carried traces of the same stain as that on his hands.

He looked nonplussed for a moment – his clients usually sent for him rather than themselves descending on his smelly workshop, and he looked at the two women as if they were strangers. Then recollection dawned.

'Miss Gilmore!' he exclaimed.

Celia found her voice. She said apologetically, 'I'm afraid we have disturbed you when you are busy. Perhaps we can come another time. I wanted to have a look at the shop and to talk to you about one or two things.'

'Oh, that's all right, Miss. Come in. But mind your skirts don't brush anything. I've a grand piano drying out here. Follow me closely.' He dragged himself slowly down the side of the workshop.

The place was lit by skylights and was less dark than they had expected. The grand piano shone like a new one, and Edna, who played, looked at it enviously. They followed the polisher carefully, their eyes beginning to run from the sting of the rich mixed fumes of linseed oil, varnish, furniture polish and male sweat which assailed them.

He led them across a narrow corridor into another room,

carefully closing each door after they had entered. Here lay the bones of a set of dining chairs, their seats and padded backs ripped out. Rolls of material filled shelves along one wall. Beneath them were bales of cotton and horsehair, their contents protruding slightly along the seams of the sacks. A heavy-duty sewing machine and a large cutting-out table, with a pair of shears lying on it, occupied the centre of the room. Another set of shelves held what Celia supposed were woodworker's tools. On a wall hung several handsaws, two of them gleaming, the rest obviously rusty with neglect. A high old-fashioned bookkeeper's desk with a matching chair stood against a wall. Above it was a small shelf holding files and account books. On the desk itself stood a spike with bills or receipts impaled upon it.

In the middle of the workroom, Mr Philpotts turned towards them. 'I'm sorry I've only one chair at the moment. I'm really only just getting started again.' He pulled the bookkeeper's chair out from beside the desk. 'The place was locked up for the duration when I went away – me uncle owns the property, you know. He didn't charge me nothing in rent while I was serving. But now I'm trying to get everything on a proper footing again.' He glanced from Celia to Edna. 'Have a seat, Miss.'

Celia told him not to worry, that they had come only for a few minutes. As the elder sister, Edna automatically perched on the uncomfortably high chair. Celia then introduced her to him.

He immediately responded, 'Pleased to meet you, Ma'am.' Then he turned to Celia and asked, 'What was it, Miss, that you came about?'

She apologised for not giving him a quicker decision regarding a possible partnership, but said that she was waiting for her father's trustee to visit them on the following Monday. 'My mother, Mrs Gilmore, will naturally want to consult him first.'

'That'll be OK. And you wanted to see the shop?'

They both smiled and nodded, and he led them back through the workshops, again shutting doors carefully after him. 'I have to keep the furniture I'm finishing as dust free as I can,' he explained. 'If I keep the doors shut, I don't get much draught blowing it around.'

The shop was thoroughly neglected, dusty and badly in need of repainting, but it was quite large, stretching back a fair distance. It had very nice corner windows.

Mr Philpotts explained his idea of showing the furniture in the window as if it were in a room. 'Inspire them, like,' he said.

Celia remarked that she would not be able to show all the furniture at once.

'Oh, aye,' he agreed. 'There's some old stables at the back, though, with a good stone floor – and one wide double door. If you send some of the poorer pieces, like the iron bedsteads, to the salerooms, I think there'll be space for most of the good pieces, between the shop and the shed. Old Aspen may not mind if you continue to rent his barn for a bit, anyway. He's a very decent fella.'

In her mind's eye Celia saw the shop glittering with new paint and all her mother's best pieces set out to catch the eye of the passing shoppers. She saw herself receiving customers like honoured guests, and letting them admire the furniture even if they did not buy. Life suddenly seemed to be opening out.

'I been thinking about your safety in the shop by yourself, Miss. But I'll be on the premises most of the time, and you could have a little handbell to press if you were uneasy. And I'd be with you as quick as I could.'

Personal safety had not occurred to her. She had simply felt shy at being in the company of Mr Philpotts all day. Total plainness and self-effacement had meant that no man had ever approached her, except with distant politeness. And no self-respecting upper-class girl considered working-class men as anything but people who did the work you told them to do. So, in her view, poor Mr Philpotts was perfectly safe to be with. The idea of other threats to her person disturbed her; she recollected with nervous fright her encounter on the great dyke.

'Surely I would be all right, wouldn't I, Mr Philpotts? There are always lots of people in Market Street.'

'On the whole, I would say yes, Miss. I'd like to suggest that you keep the silver locked in some of the cabinets at the back of the shop though. Small valuable things, like silver, would attract shoplifters.'

'Oh, dear. Yes, we can certainly do that.'

'In fact, I was thinking, Miss, that if the silver is high quality, you might like to put it up for auction with a real classy auctioneer, like Sotheby's. And the same the oil paintings.' He stopped to rub his face wearily and left another brown smear on it, as he thought for a minute.

Then he went on, 'I got a client who might come and look at the pictures for you, if you would like. He's a teacher at the art school in Liverpool. I done some work on frames for him, and just yesterday, he brought a couple of real nice gilt frames to me, to ask if I could clean them. Which I'll do, of course. Now, he'd have some idea if the paintings were worth anything much.'

Edna had kept silent during the conversation, because she wished Celia to handle it, but she had paid attention. She said to Celia, 'I think it would be a good idea to let experts see both silver and paintings. Mother inherited nearly all of them from her grandfather, when he gave up his home – and he had an even nicer home than we did. Some of the paintings came from Father's boyhood home.'

Celia looked at Mr Philpotts, and said, 'We'll arrange it, as soon as we have Mrs Gilmore's permission. Thank you for the suggestion.' Then, remembering Eddie Fairbanks' advice, she said a little gaily, 'We have to find ourselves a solicitor to help us arrange a simple partnership with each other – just so that we are clear what we are doing.'

'I suppose you're right, Miss. I hope it doesn't cost much.'

She laughed. 'Me, too,' she agreed.

She thanked Mr Philpotts, and Edna rose. Neither lady offered her hand to be shaken; although he had dropped his dirty rag in the workshop, Mr Philpotts' hands looked too messy to shake.

He grinned cheerfully at them as he unlocked the shop door into the street, and let them out. She was a proper little sweetie, she was, and her sister seemed a nice lady – no side.

'See you next week,' he said. For a second or two, he watched them wistfully, as they paused to put on their gloves before proceeding down the street. Thanks to the bloody Huns, he was never going to be any use to a woman again, he told himself bitterly. Perhaps it was a good thing that Alison had died in France, because he would not have been able to marry her, anyway.

At the thought of Alison, he heaved a great sob which stuck in his throat until he thought he would choke. Sometimes life dealt you some rotten cards.

Chapter Forty

❦

Cousin Albert descended on the little house by the sea like a slowly rolling avalanche. None of Louise's excuses that she had to read to blind soldiers and go to Liverpool to talk to the director of the School for the Blind worked with Timothy's stout trustee. Albert was determined to wind up her husband's and her affairs without any unnecessary delays. He wanted to go back to his own gentle retirement of fishing in the Trent, painting water colours and being spoiled by his eager servant and friend who looked after him.

The problem had been in dealing with Timothy's debts, and making sure that no claims were made on his wife's income. This had not been as difficult as he had at first imagined. Louise's marriage contract made it quite clear that most of the contents of the house were part of her dowry, as well as the cottages in Birkenhead. And, in addition, when the house itself had long since been put in her name by Timothy, he had specified that he was transferring both house and contents to her, so that left no doubt as to her ownership of all the contents. He must have seen, over a number of years, the financial clouds gathering.

'The house is as good as sold,' Albert told her, 'although it will be a few weeks before the legal aspects are completed. The lady wanting to start a nursing home has made a reasonable offer. She wants immediate possession.'

'When shall I get some money?' Louise asked anxiously.

'Before the end of the summer,' promised Albert. 'As soon as I know the exact sum we shall have to invest, I will look for the best annuity I can get for you.'

On the principle of pressing him to waste no time in doing this, Louise said, 'Humph. I don't know how I shall manage until then.'

'Just have to manage on your rents,' Albert told her blithely. He was not going to offer to lend her anything; he had already paid his cousin's funeral expenses, and his expenses in dealing with the will were a loss to him – and that was enough.

Louise wept a little. She was lucky that neither of her daughters had yet had a private session with Albert; otherwise, she would have had the question of the shop unloaded on her that same evening.

As it was, she declared that life was too, too utterly hard, and took to her bed with a request that hot cocoa – and a glass of brandy, if they had any – be brought up to her.

Later, she also asked for her dinner to be brought up. Celia understood the considerable load of grief opened up by Cousin Albert, so she kissed her and promised to do this.

Her absence from the dinner table gave her daughters the opportunity to talk freely with Cousin Albert, as he sat, white linen table napkin tucked into his stiff, winged collar, and devoured the steak and kidney pie which Louise had prepared – like most middle-class women of her generation, she had, in her youth, been taught how to cook on the principle that, even if she employed a cook, the mistress of the house should be thoroughly conversant with all aspects of catering for a large family. Unfortunately, the custom had not continued into Edna and Celia's generation; more of their youth had been spent practising on the piano, or on reading, painting or embroidery or writing letters, rather than toiling in the kitchen. In school, Edna had also learned to play tennis and lacrosse and to ball-room dance, while Celia danced attendance on Louise.

It was Edna who now, almost gleefully, opened up the question of how to dispose of a barnful of furniture.

Despite the doctor's reassurance that she was quite well and capable, poor Celia was still scared, and she kept quiet.

As he wiped his mouth and leaned back to await dessert, Cousin Albert saw the common sense of Celia's attempting to earn a living. He was perfectly aware, from Louise's grumbling letters to him, what the young woman had, since Timothy's death, already achieved on her mother's behalf. In the back of his mind, he had been haunted by an uncomfortable premonition that, if he outlived Louise, he could, in his old age, have to maintain a penniless Celia in his contented male household. Here was a chance to lay at least that ghost to rest.

So Edna found the proposition received with rapt attention. Cousin Albert even smiled at silent Celia.

Just like the Cheshire Cat, thought Celia, though she did not understand the reasons behind his instant approval of the scheme.

As a dish of rice pudding and stewed prunes was set before him, he said, 'As I see it, there are two problems which must be clarified before you can do anything. One, the furniture belongs not to Celia, but to her mother. I presume, also, that the business, at least in its early years, would not produce enough return to pay Celia an adequate recompense for her work and at the same time show a profit which Louise could enjoy?'

'Exactly,' Celia blurted out, with her mouth full. 'If the furniture were mine, even from a small profit, I could give Mother something for my keep – I wouldn't cost her so much.' She swallowed, and went on more clearly, 'Of course, every time I sold a piece, I would have to save some of the money so that I could buy new stock, wouldn't I?'

Cousin Albert beamed. 'Yes,' he agreed. 'We'll make a business lady of you, I can see that.'

He was fortunately unaware that, because of his patronising tone, Edna felt a strong desire to tread hard on his toes under the table. She forbore, however, and instead smiled sweetly at him.

He carefully spat a prune stone out into his spoon and placed it on the edge of his dish. Then he went on. 'Two, you also need an agreement between yourself and this Mr Philpotts regarding rent and any repairs he may do for you. What do you know of this gentleman?'

They told him that he was well known locally as a decent, honest tradesman, who had recently been demobilised, wounded, from the army, and had just started up his business again. At this, Cousin Albert had a sudden hope that he might see Celia married off to such a person, which, from his own point of view, seemed even better.

'Obvious solution. Louise should give you the furniture, dear Celia. She won't ever need it again. The annuity I shall arrange for her, together with her rents, will give her an adequate income. She owns this house. Not bad at all.' He emptied his plate, put down his spoon and heaved a sigh of satisfaction. He beamed, and helped himself to a piece of cheese from a board proffered by Edna, while he continued to address Celia. 'Exactly what does the furniture consist of, my dear?'

Celia told him, and then added, 'There is some good china and her silver tea service, silver serving dishes and cake baskets, stacks of it – and all the old pictures that used to hang in the hall and in Father's study. Mother chose the nice ones she wanted to hang in this house.' She gestured vaguely towards the mantelpiece, over which hung an etching of Landseer's *A Stag at Bay*.

Cousin Albert glanced at the stag and grunted, 'Humph.' He looked round the room and found a couple of works featuring shaggy highland cattle standing in front of purple mountains. 'I imagine that you could sell the ones in the barn to local people,' he suggested.

'I expect so.'

'I wonder if dear Louise would, perhaps, like to have the silver auctioned by a good Liverpool auctioneer. It would give her some money to carry her through until I have bought the annuity. If you think she would like that, I am sure that it can be arranged.' He looked down at his dessert spoon and cheese knife. 'I see she has retained her tableware.'

Edna turned to Celia, and said, 'That's exactly what Mr Philpotts suggested; with regard to the silver he mentioned Sotheby's. I think it's a very good idea, Celia. The silver is probably the most valuable part of the whole collection. It may be out of date in design – but it is good – I seem to remember that it was very heavy.'

Celia agreed. She said shyly, 'I don't want Mother to give me anything terribly valuable – only the furniture she doesn't want. I would be very happy if the silver raised enough money to help her now.' She laughed a little rue-fully, when she added, 'I doubt if Mama ever thought about its value. She's always had it – the same as her friends had silverware. To her, it was simply too much clutter to store in this cottage.'

Edna interjected that Mr Philpotts felt that the silver in the little shop might attract thieves.

'He's right,' agreed Cousin Albert. 'I presume it is still packed up?'

'Yes, in barrels.'

'I'll talk to Louise about it.'

'Can you persuade her that it would be no disgrace for Celia to run her own shop?' Edna asked. 'I believe that her main objection is that it is improper for a lady to be in trade. And I also think she is shocked that Mr Philpotts, poor soul, will be in the same premises.' She suppressed a small chuckle behind her table napkin. The gesture, however, was not missed by Cousin Albert; he saw her twinkling eyes and then Celia's blush.

He replied carefully, 'Men and women are beginning to work together – in fact, they had to do so throughout the war. However much one may disapprove of it, a dignified young woman like Celia should have no problems.'

'Dear Cousin Albert,' Edna responded. 'You really are so wise and sensible. I hope you can convince Mother.'

The stout old gentleman beamed at her. He patted her hand and promised to do his best, as soon as Louise felt rested enough to receive him.

Because she was stifling a laugh, Celia kept her eyes down. Really Edna was without shame!

Chapter Forty-One

❧

It took time. But then women were so difficult to deal with.

With grinding patience, the following morning, Cousin Albert agreed to visit the nursing home full of blind soldiers and listened to Louise's belief that she should try, at least, to help them, particularly the two deaf-blind men.

Safe in his personal cocoon, the war had, largely, passed Albert Gilmore by. With no sons to worry about, his worst anxieties were concerned with the steady rise of prices. It was almost as much of a shock to him to see the young men in whom Louise was interested as it had been to Louise herself. He was not an unkind man and was genuinely touched at the sight of the helpless men.

In a vague way, he also understood her need for a reason to live, some honourable cause to work for in her lonely widowhood, and here were substitutes for her dead sons. The hugeness of her undertaking made him feel guilty that he had done nothing about the war, except be thankful not to be involved.

That evening, he sat with her in the front sitting room and after discussing the visit to the nursing home, he turned the conversation to Celia and the need for single women to work nowadays. He mentioned a well-educated young woman cashier in his bank, who had, throughout the war, dealt with his banking needs.

'Now, with demobilisation, of course, the men are

returning, and poor Celia would not stand a chance of such employment. In fact, she will have the greatest difficulty in maintaining herself once you are gone. And I believe she is now at least twenty-four so she has not much chance of matrimony. A tiny business of her own, however, could make all the difference.' He paused to sniff appreciatively at a glass of Timothy's brandy, thoughtfully provided by Edna. Then he continued, 'Beginning it in a very small way, with a small businessman to guide her while she learns to buy and sell, should mean that she won't make any major mistakes.'

He saw Louise stiffen in her chair, and before continuing in that vein, he said he wanted to speak to her about the silver.

'Silver?'

She listened open-mouthed while he suggested the plan he had already discussed with her daughters. Then she said, 'We could simply send everything for auction.'

'And spoil dear Celia's chance? No, Louise. You don't really need the furniture or the pictures or the china, or what they would bring in a sale. They would not fetch that much at auction anyway.

'Now the silverware is different. From what I remember, the silver is outstanding in workmanship and weight. It is probably worth much, much more. Give Celia the chance with the furniture. Let her try at least. She may, at worst, learn something which will prepare her for the new world we are facing – and it will have cost you very little. Since, after a while, she may be earning quite well, she can help you with the upkeep of the home.' He did not mention that he hoped she might marry – he considered that the idea of an artisan as a son-in-law would probably send Louise through the ceiling with an explosion of rage.

It wasn't that easy. Her old excuses that she needed Celia at home nearly defeated him. But he remembered that his own house was run by one manservant and a charwoman, so he suggested the employment of a daily woman to come in – that should be enough to keep a cottage going. Edna would have hugged him, had she heard him go on to suggest that she probably needed one anyway; Edna had for several days been putting off scrubbing the very dirty kitchen floor because she simply had not much idea of how to go about the job.

Afterwards, Cousin Albert felt that he had come through the equivalent of negotiating the post-war international peace proposals – but with greater success. He hoped that he had removed for ever the chance of having to endure women relatives in his home.

He stayed an extra week while he did his best to arrange everything so that Celia got legal ownership of the contents of Ben Aspen's barn and a shop sublet to her by John Philpotts. He also got the couple to sign a simple agreement regarding any repairs and refurbishing John did on the furniture for her; it was not perfect, but he thought that it would be workable.

He then took Louise to Liverpool to see her husband's solicitor regarding the legal details of the house sale and to meet the purchaser of her home, Mrs Dora Johnson, and the estate agent. Carried along by Cousin Albert's male self-confidence and the sense that he understood the sale of a house, she forgot completely Celia's warnings about her need for a solicitor to look after her own interests, and the charming Mr Little, to whom Mr Carruthers had sent her.

As she followed the grim-faced purchaser and the agent into Mr Barnett's office, she whispered to Albert that she hated selling the house to such a common woman.

Fearing she would make a fuss in the lawyer's office, Cousin Albert hastily whispered assurances into her ear that, though the lady did not sound her aitches, she was a very worthy, experienced nurse and one could respect the work she proposed to do.

Chapter Forty-Two

A veiled Louise and a businesslike Mrs Johnson signed their way through a sheaf of papers laid before them by Mr Barnett. Firmly guided by him, Louise put her name to every page without reading it or raising a single objection, exactly as Cousin Albert had taken for granted she would do.

The two ladies afterwards politely shook hands, and Cousin Albert shook the solicitor's hand. He breathed a sigh of relief that he would shortly have Louise off his hands. The house was sold.

Mr Barnett got up from his desk and bowed everyone out of his office.

In the outer office, Mrs Johnson paused, and said hesitantly to the other three that, if Mrs Gilmore could kindly spare the time, she would very much like to go over the house with Louise, while they were both in Liverpool. 'And you could tell me which chimneys smoke at times, like, and how long the hot water boiler takes to heat and how much water it holds – maybe I should have a bigger one installed. I am sure you could make some very useful suggestions regarding the adaptation of the house to nursing.'

Louise turned to Albert. 'Oh, Albert,' she wailed, 'I couldn't bear to look at the house.'

Over her head, Mrs Johnson mouthed, 'It would save me a lot of time if she would.'

Albert sighed, and said to the black veil, 'I know it would

be difficult for you, my dear Louise. We have to remember, however, that Mrs Johnson hopes to help men who have been badly wounded and need care until they can be admitted to a more permanent military institution. She naturally wants them to be as comfortable as possible.'

Mrs Johnson beamed at him. A sob came from under the veil.

He looked desperately round at the agent for inspiration, but before they could think of any way to persuade Louise, Mrs Johnson, a nurse with long experience, chimed in, in dulcet tones, to suggest that poor Mrs Gilmore might feel a bit easier if she had a nice hot cup of tea and a little rest in the tea shop across the road, before going to the house. 'It would set her up like nothing else would.' She smiled at the veil, and then added persuasively, 'I wouldn't keep her long at the house, but it would help to speed things up if Mrs G. would tell me a few details about it.'

Cousin Albert had put his arm round Louise's shoulders, and he could feel her cringe at being referred to as Mrs G. He felt that he should refuse and should take her home. But Louise, suddenly aware of cohorts of wounded in dire need of comfort, said, with a sniff, that if advising about chimneys would help our dear wounded, she would certainly make the trip.

Hugely relieved, Cousin Albert swept them into the lift. They were propelled down to the ground floor by an elderly, uniformed, one-armed lift man who, seeing yet another forlorn, veiled widow, leaning on Albert's arm, pulled the lift's ropes with care and brought them to a particularly gentle stop at street level. 'Poor dear!' he said to Albert. 'Lost 'er boys? I see 'em nearly every day.'

Slightly annoyed at this very personal remark, Albert merely nodded his head, and then eased the ladies out of the lift.

In the café, Louise lifted her veil back and silently ate a

petit four and drank a luke-warm cup of tea, while the philistine opposite her downed a rum baba and an equally chilled cup of tea. Cousin Albert, refusing tea, went to get a taxicab. The estate agent elected to go with him.

A widow herself, Mrs Johnson felt very sorry about Louise's grief, but did not know what to say. She rather wished, after all, she had not asked her to visit the house.

Finally, when she could endure the silence no longer, she asked tentatively if Louise would be kind enough to furnish her with the names of reliable local workmen.

Louise swallowed the last of the petit four, looked up and stared blankly at her.

'You see, Mrs Gilmore, I'm from Manchester, where I'm already running one little nursing home. I don't know Liverpool very well, so I'm anxious to know who to turn to. I also want to get reliable staff.'

Louise nodded, and Mrs Johnson, feeling the need of some further explanation, went on, 'Me hubby left me a thriving grocery shop and I ran it for a bit. But I'm no grocer. I'm a good nurse though, even if I says it myself – and I never gave it up altogether, even when I was married – so I sold the business and bought the Manchester nursing home – and it's done real well. A Liverpool doctor came to see one of my patients, and he gave me the idea that I could start another one here.'

She put down her cup and leaned back from the table. 'So here I am.'

By this time, Louise was diverted. She managed to remark, 'How interesting. How will you run them both?'

'Well, there's lots of army nurses out of work at present – and there's a real shortage of men for them to marry, so they've got to find work. I've a couple of real experienced nursing sisters workin' for me in Manchester – and the visiting doctors trust them. I can spend some time getting your house ready – and I'll see how we go.'

Haltingly, Louise began to tell her of her own work

amongst the deaf-blind. By the time Albert, puffing from his exertions, returned to tell them that a taxi awaited them and that the estate agent was already ensconced in it they were deeply engaged in conversation, and Louise was enduring the dropped aitches of Mrs Johnson with considerable fortitude.

Women! He would never understand them, Albert thought, as he paid the bill.

As they trailed up the unwashed front steps of the empty house and then waited while the estate agent, using his own key, unlocked the dusty front door, Louise wanted to cry. She was further distressed when they entered the vast emptiness of the hall.

'I thought I'd divide the hall up into me office and a reception area,' remarked Mrs Johnson prosaically as she looked slowly round it.

From behind the veil came a heavy sigh, and then a sudden shriek.

The service door at the back of the hall had opened silently, and, like a ghost, a white-haired woman clad in black stood before them. Her mouth agape with consternation, the woman stood transfixed as she faced the little group by the front door.

'Oh, Ma'am!' she gasped.

An astonished Louise flung back her veil with an angry gesture. 'Winnie! What on earth are you doing here?'

Albert was equally surprised. The estate agent, who had been putting his key chain back into his waistcoat pocket, looked up in absolute bewilderment. Both Mrs Johnson and he knew Winnie as the temporary caretaker of the house and neither could understand the fuss.

Sudden tears were running down Winnie's face. She glanced desperately to either side, as if trying to escape.

Louise repeated her question.

Winnie licked her lips. She hung her head and said

sullenly, 'When you left, I'd got nowhere to go – though I tried hard to get a job.'

'So?' Louise forgot her sorrow at having to look once more at her empty home. Her property had been violated, taken advantage of, and she was very annoyed.

'I thought you wouldn't mind, Ma'am. You never moved the furniture out of my room – wasn't worth it, you said. Likewise, the coal in the cellar.' She twisted a grubby handkerchief in her hands. 'I thought it would be useful to you if someone were in the house. It'd keep vandals from smashing the winders or even getting into the place. Till I got a live-in place, like.'

She fell silent.

The estate agent said hastily that he had been under the impression that that was exactly what Mrs Gilmore had intended. He had felt it was an extremely good idea. He had met Winnie on his first inspection of the home. She had said then that she was the cook and had served Mrs Gilmore for many years, and she had showed him round the kitchens and cellars. Mrs Gilmore might possibly recall that she was out when he came.

Mrs Gilmore did recall her unhappy visit to Phyllis's house on that day. She sniffed. It may very well have been a sensible idea, but Winnie had no right to take advantage of her like that.

'I still feel that her presence is very reprehensible. You had decent notice, Winnie, and you should have left on the day agreed as soon as the cleaning was completed.'

Winnie said shamefacedly, 'Yes, Ma'am.'

'You are to pack your bag and go, before we leave this house. You are trespassing.'

'Yes, Ma'am.'

Mrs Johnson had watched the exchange with fascination. The woman had held her temper admirably in the face of her employer's anger. And she was the cook? On her previous visits, Winnie had always discreetly withdrawn to her attic bedroom, and Mrs Johnson had thought her to be an old, trusted nanny, and had never really talked to her. The estate agent had explained that she was temporarily caretaking the house, which was the explanation of her presence given to him by Winnie.

Winnie slowly turned and went back down the kitchen staircase, where her straw trunk lay in a cupboard. It held everything she owned, and she had kept it downstairs so that she could move out quickly when the house changed hands.

In the vast, practically empty kitchen, she sat down on a solitary straight chair, put her hands over her face and sobbed aloud. She felt she had no friend in the world who could help her. Mrs Gilmore was a soulless bitch.

Meanwhile, Louise and Mrs Johnson went slowly round the house. Much of the curtaining had been included in the price of the house, and Mrs Johnson assured Louise that it would be a comfort to 'the boys' because it would keep out both cold in the winter and too much light in the summer.

In the bathroom, Mrs Johnson explained that each ward would have its own washstands, chamber pots and bedpans, and the invalids would mostly need bed baths. So one bathroom would probably be enough.

They discussed plumbers and painters and gas men and gardeners, until Louise became quite absorbed in the project, and Albert, finding an abandoned chair in a front bedroom, decided resignedly that he would sit there until they had finished.

As they descended to the basement kitchens, Mrs Johnson said she would make the servants' sitting room into another ward. It looked out on to the brick-lined area, a sunken yard alongside the basement which allowed light into the room. 'I could put some pots of geraniums out there, and it would be a nice place for men who can be lifted out of bed to sit in the fresh air. I believe in fresh air.'

'There is a large garden,' Louise reminded her.

'Oh, I'll grow a pile of fresh vegetables in that, though I'll keep a tiny lawn with flowers for the boys.'

Winnie heard the conversation as they came down the stairs, and she hastily wiped her face and picked up her hat from the cupboard. As they entered, she jabbed in her hatpins, and then glanced sulkily up at the ladies.

Mrs Johnson smiled kindly at her, and said, 'Oh, Winnie. I would like to have a word with you before you go.'

'Yes, Ma'am. Shall I wait here?'

'Please do.'

In that second, Louise realised that the house was truly not hers any more, and that Mrs Johnson now had every right to give orders in it. She wanted to expostulate, however, that Winnie was her servant and that she would say what she was to do. But she equally suddenly realised that this was no longer so; she had, long since, dismissed her.

She thought she would choke, as Winnie smiled suddenly at the new owner. Winnie sensed that she had just found herself a new job.

They inspected the area and the steps that led from it up to the garden.

Louise felt she had had enough. She pulled her veil over her face and said she must go home. They rejoined the estate agent patiently standing in the hall. He gave the entire collection of keys to the house to the new owner, with the remark that Winnie had additional keys to the back door and the back garden gate.

'I'll get them from her,' replied Mrs Johnson placidly.

Hearing the sounds of departure, Albert came slowly down the stairs. Farewells were said, and he escorted a very frustrated Louise down the steps to the waiting taxi.

'Tell the taxi driver to come back for me, when he's

finished with you,' Mrs Johnson shouted after them.

The taxi driver heard and tipped his hat in acknowledgement. Albert merely nodded.

In the cab, Louise exploded. 'So that's how Winnie was able to come and go. Celia never collected her house keys from her. Stupid girl!'

Albert sighed, and began the slow task of calming her down. To divert her attention, he spoke of the impending sale of the silverware which would, he was sure, do much to alleviate her present impoverished situation.

That evening, Celia got a resounding scolding for forgetting to collect all the keys of the old house, and subsequently wept silently in her bedroom.

A few days later, the silver was valued and a reserve price put on it prior to auction. Once it was sold, Louise had a respectable bank account – in a local bank, with a charming young manager, Mr Gwynn-Jones, who quite put Mr Carruthers in the shade – and Edna got her charwoman.

With regard to the proposed antique shop, Celia was, at first, frightened to death at the sudden realisation of the responsibilities she was taking on.

Supported by Edna's, Betty Houghton's and John Philpotts' encouragement, however, and a second visit to see Dr Mason to have her prescription of Dr Parrish's Food renewed, she began slowly to bloom. Dr Mason did not fail to notice a certain new liveliness in her, and took the time to discover the source of it.

She sat back in her chair, and told Celia, 'I know you can do it!' And privately hoped to God that she was right.

Chapter Forty-Three

❧

'Mr Fairbanks says to come to dig your garden – a shillin' for three hours.'

As Edna faced the blond giant standing on the back step, she dried her hands on her apron and stared at him – white knights sometimes arrive in strange disguises.

Absolutely calm pale-blue eyes stared amiably back at her. 'It's a right mess!' He gestured over his shoulder with a huge, grubby thumb. 'I looked at it. Want the bushes took out as well?'

Edna swallowed, and found her voice. 'Yes, please. And your name is . . . ?'

'Ethelred. What's yours?'

Though she was shaken by his impudence, she answered him, 'Mrs Fellowes.'

Ethelred smiled hugely and stuck his thumbs in his leather belt. 'Now we know each other, like me mam told me we would.'

Edna smiled a little stiffly, and asked, 'Do you have a spade, Ethelred?' She knew that some gardening tools had accidentally been sent to the barn instead of to the cottage. They had yet to be retrieved.

Ethelred's face crumpled up like a baby's about to cry. 'No,' he said sadly. Then he brightened as if enlightenment had dawned. 'Mam said if you didn't have one, Mr Fairbanks would lend us one.'

'Good,' said Edna, whipping off her apron. 'Let's go next door and ask him.' She walked round the outside of their cottage, Ethelred ambling behind her, like a friendly dog being taken for a walk. She thankfully handed him over to Eddie, who offered to instruct the boy in exactly what should be done.

Since Edna had no ideas about the garden, she readily accepted the offer.

Ethelred was not the fastest worker, but once a job was explained to him, he went at it steadily. He received with excessive pleasure a large mug of cocoa at mid-morning and quaffed it happily as he stood in the sunshine. Then he handed the mug back to Edna, and announced, 'I'm goin' to pee,' and strode straight through the wild hedge at the bottom of the garden on to the common behind it. Still buttoning his fly, he returned to removing the sod and bushes off the original garden beds before actually turning the soil over. At the very bottom of the garden a pile of rubbish began to grow.

'When I'm done I'll make a good bonfire of it,' he promised Edna cheerfully. 'We can roast some potatoes in it.'

Edna prayed that he would not accidentally set the house on fire.

Though Ethelred's mind might lack a tack or two, he proved to be wonderfully helpful when the two women began to fix up the shop. He was a gentle creature and became very fond of Edna. When she handed him a yard broom, to sweep out the shop, he kept on going right into John Philpotts' workshop and Edna had to persuade him that it was not her domain. She suggested that, perhaps, he would kindly sweep the pavement round the corner shop and also the front doorstep. This latter job took rather longer, since he knew absolutely everybody passing by, and some of them stopped to ask him what he was doing. He had a very sociable morning.

Urged on by Betty, Ben Aspen quoted Celia a very small

sum for lending one of his labourers for a couple of mornings to paint the interior of the shop. The price of the white paint was included. Since Celia did not as yet have any money, Betty simply added the charge to what the Gilmores owed for work on the cottage.

Ethelred helped to sort out from the barn the shabbier furniture which was to be sent for auction, and the auctioneer took it away in a lorry. After a closed van came from Liverpool to collect the barrels of silver, Celia was able to retrieve a couple of carpets which had been stacked at the back of the barn. She laid them on the newly scrubbed shop floor.

Edna and Celia had never been so tired in their lives. They found they worked quite well together, though they often disagreed about detail. As promised, Edna paid Ethelred for his work in the garden, and then lent Celia enough to pay him for his help in connection with the shop.

'We simply cannot function without him,' she said flatly.

Celia was glad to see Edna's complexion improve in the fresh sea air, which was inescapable in blustery Hoylake. She was naturally a dark woman, but she lost much of the unhealthy yellow look which life in the Tropics had given her. Because she smoked less, she was also eating better and her figure filled out. She seemed to enjoy helping Celia set up her little shop, and spent more and more time there.

She got on very well with John Philpotts, and sometimes talked to him about her life in Brazil.

Because Edna had been married, John felt more at ease talking to her, rather than to Celia, and, from a number of small hints, Edna guessed that he was impotent as a result of his wounds.

Neither woman would allow John to move furniture; they feared that he would damage his already wounded leg.

'I have to move pieces in the course of my own work,' he protested. But they laughed and told him they were not going to make a beast of burden of him. They did, however, borrow a small trolley cart, which he himself used for moving furniture round his workshop, and, since Ethelred had obviously become their devoted slave, John left the lifting to him.

Having Edna with her eased Celia's first days with John Philpotts, and her shyness slowly ebbed away. With regard to Ethelred, his almost childlike attitude made her protective of him; she never considered him as an adult male. He had, however, tremendous physical strength and was a real asset. He could lift almost anything.

Celia chose with care the first stock she wanted to show in her shop. When a small furniture remover from the village moved it over to the new premises for her, she got him to bring as much of the rest as could be squashed into the storage shed at the back of John's yard without damaging it.

There was still an alarming amount left in the barn, so she asked the furniture remover to stack it neatly to one side, and then went to see Betty about keeping it there.

Betty laughed, and said, 'Leave Father to me. It'll be all right for a while.' Then she recommended a sign writer to paint the name of the shop on the front of it. It was christened by the three of them, Celia's Antiques and Collectibles.

With over twenty-five pounds from the auction of the mass of everyday furniture from the maids' bedrooms, the kitchen, the servants' sitting room in the basement, the back hall and the back staircase, not to speak of a hefty stone angel which had stood in the back garden for years, she was able to pay for the remover and for the sign.

'I still owe you an awful lot, Edna,' she wailed. Then she added, 'You know, the angel drew the best bids.'

'Most appropriate, and don't worry about the money – I don't have many expenses. I can wait,' replied Edna cheerfully. 'Papa Fellowes sent me a cheque for this month.'

The outside of the shop got a good hose down from Ethelred and, when it was dry, Celia polished the front door and Edna cleaned the windows.

The day before she was to open, Eddie Fairbanks brought her, on a little trailer attached to his bicycle, two heavy white flowerpots crowded with red geraniums. He placed one on either side of the front door.

The whole place looked very pretty in the early summer sunshine.

Celia was overwhelmed when she saw the flowers. She thanked Eddie and then impulsively gave him a big hug. 'Everybody's been so kind,' she said, and took out her handkerchief and blew her nose hard.

Cousin Albert had also helped her with advice regarding a business licence, for which Edna had loaned her the money until the auctioneer paid her.

Altogether, Celia found herself surrounded by helpful friends and, in some wonderment, she said to Edna, 'I've never before had friends – or anybody – who did things for me; even Phyllis wasn't like this.'

Edna laughed. 'It's overdue,' she said. 'I don't think you've ever been out without Mother before. No chance to make any real friends of your own.'

Louise did not come to look at the shop. She said rightly that it would be too painful to see the contents of her old home up for sale. Though her visits to the soldiers in the nursing home often took her into Market Street, she always avoided passing the shop by crossing to the other side of the road.

Celia understood, and she sympathised. Because she was not so much under her mother's thumb, she was able to understand more fully her mother's efforts to come out of her grief and create a new life for herself.

One evening, after she had closed the shop for the night, she went over to the Aspens' yard, to rummage in the barn for more of the Philip Oppenheim books which her mother wanted. While doing so, she came across a little trunk of her own personal possessions.

Kneeling on the stone floor, she unstrapped it and looked at the curious collection of oddments which she had kept over the years. Wrapped in tissue paper and laid on the top was the dress she had worn for her Confirmation, together with the prayer book given her by Great-aunt Blodwyn. She smiled at the recollection of the excited four-teen-year-old who had worn it; she had felt like a bride. Underneath were letters, which she had lovingly tied together with blue baby ribbon, letters from both her brothers while at boarding school, and, later, when they went to war.

In the failing shaft of light from the setting sun through the great door of the barn, she held them in her hands and bowed her head and cried.

They had thought about their little sister consistently throughout their short lives, she realised. Perhaps, if there had been no war, they would have found amongst their friends some decent young man to marry her. At least she would never have had to worry about her future; one or the other of them would certainly have given her a home – and affection.

Outside, she heard Ben Aspen's workmen shouting good night to each other, and she hastily put down the letters and delved in the bottom of the box. Two battered dolls, some children's books, and at the very bottom the only toy which she knew had been given to her by her paternal grandmother, a wooden box of handmade building bricks. She had no real memory of her grandmother, but she lifted the box out and opened it.

Each little cube was about two inches in size and was grubby from much play. On all six sides of each brick, a letter of the alphabet had been carefully carved in relief, so that the letter stood out. She ran her fingers gently along the bricks, and remembered how her nanny had taught her the alphabet from them and how to spell simple words.

At the thought of Nanny kneeling on the floor with her and patiently spelling out words, she had a sudden inspiration about how her mother could, perhaps, communicate with the two poor deaf-blind servicemen about whom she was so concerned.

She bundled her other treasures back into the trunk and closed it. She would ask Ethelred, some time, to carry the trunk to the cottage. Her personal grief forgotten, she hurriedly pushed the barn doors closed and locked the padlock. She ran across the deserted yard to Betty's office to say good night before she left.

Betty had on her coat and hat, ready to go home. Her father was with her, so Celia simply paused to say that she had locked the barn up and wished them both good night. Then, clutching her box of bricks, she ran for the train to Meols.

Chapter Forty-Four

❧

Celia sat behind a little table which Ethelred had set across a corner at the back of the shop for her. It had a drawer in it in which to keep money, and, in that position, it would be difficult for a customer to ease round the table and open it. She had a brand-new account book in front of her, so that each day she could enter the transactions which had taken place. She also had a receipt book; a pen; a pencil box holding a pencil, India rubber and extra pen nibs; a piece of blotting paper and a cut-glass inkwell. On a corner of the table lay a number of books on antiques, which she was reading her way through very carefully.

All she needed was customers. Though a number of people walked in and looked round, nobody bought anything.

Occasionally, someone asked a price, and she would get up and walk round to them to tell them, and, perhaps, open a drawer to show the fine dovetailing of the piece's interior or remark that the wood was the finest mahogany and that the piece was over a hundred years old and, therefore, an antique. They invariably remarked that things were too expensive, but she refused to reduce the price.

She was very despondent, and made still more so when she discovered that some of the china ornaments she had put out for display had been stolen.

'It must have been when I was showing a dressing table to a woman, you know, John,' she lamented. 'Her friend was strolling round looking at things. I got distracted. Two really pretty shepherdesses and a pin tray just gone like that,' and she snapped her fingers to illustrate the rapidity of the theft.

'Oh, aye, it's a common enough ploy – two friends work together – and you'd better watch out if a woman comes in with children – the kids'll clear a display case while you're dealing with the mother at the counter.'

'The children would steal?' Celia was shocked.

'Yes.' John sighed and sat himself down on a wooden rocking chair. He was dressed in a suit and had a heavy portfolio of upholstery samples, which he laid carefully on the floor beside him; he had just returned from seeing a customer in her home. She wanted all her drawing-room furniture re-covered and repolished, a nice job which would help his finances.

He looked round the shop, and suggested, 'You could put your knick-knacks and – them four mantel clocks – in the big glass cabinet over there and lock it – I see it has a key. Keep the key in your pocket. And keep your eyes open, luv.'

She nodded, and sadly did as he advised.

'I must go and write up me estimate,' he said, and heaved the heavy samples into his workshop.

A week later, he knocked on the intervening door between his workshop and the shop, and, as usual, came in without waiting for her answer. He had brought her a rather grubby mug of tea, which he set before her on top of the closed receipt book. She thanked him shyly and put her cold hands round the mug to warm them, before drinking the tea.

He again sat down on the rocking chair, and said, 'I talked to Alec Tremaine last night. Met him in the Ship Inn. He's the teacher at the art school that I told you about. If it's all right with you, he'll come in on Saturday to look at your paintings. He says he's no expert, but he'd have a shrewd idea whether they were good or not.'

Acutely aware that the money left over from the auction was being rapidly eroded by the need to pay her rent and Ethelred's wages, she inquired anxiously, 'What would he charge?'

'Oh, he's not going to charge you; he's quite interested in old paintings. Paints himself, as well as teaching.'

'That's most awfully kind of you and of him. I shall be here all day, needless to say.'

As if he hadn't heard her last remark, he went on heavily, 'Him being a teacher and not owning a gallery, I think you're not likely to be cheated by him in any way – if there is something fairly valuable amongst them, like. A gallery might say they were not worth much and offer to buy them as a job lot very cheap. You could lose a lot of money that way.'

Celia sipped her tea and smiled, 'Oh, I'm sure you wouldn't recommend anybody who would be likely to cheat. And would a gallery really cheat?'

'Well, it can happen in any business, and more than anywhere in the antique trade. You can be had quick enough by anybody. When you need to buy stock, you ought to remember to decry whatever's up for sale, so that you give the lowest possible price for it.' He grinned slyly at her.

She knew that he was right. Her father's business adage, often repeated when his wife had been extravagant, had been buy low, sell high. And the value of second-hand furniture was, at best, uncertain; she was sure of that.

John got up and stretched himself. 'Haven't seen Miss Edna for a couple of days. Is she well?'

'Oh, yes, thank you. She's just catching up in the house. We've all been out so much that it's a mess.' She looked ruefully round the shop, and said, 'She can't do much here, at the moment – I'm not exactly busy.'

'No, that's for sure, luv.'

'Do you think I've priced stuff too high for people?'

'I doubt it. I think you're not getting the right kind of people into the shop. You need to do some advertising – and I need to do some, too – we could do it together, if you like. Let's talk about it when Miss Edna comes. Or Betty Houghton might have some ideas – there's a smart lady if ever there was. Maybe get a little article into the Hoylake paper or, better still, the Chester paper, about the opening of the shop.'

Although she had no idea what either Edna or Betty could contribute, Celia agreed enthusiastically, and John went back to his workshop.

The little bell on the front door tinged as someone entered. Celia turned towards it.

'Oh,' she exclaimed. 'Dr Mason! How nice to see you.'

Chapter Forty-Five

❧

Edith Mason came swiftly in, and looked round. 'How pretty it all looks,' she said, her eyes twinkling merrily behind gold-rimmed spectacles. 'Do you mind if I have a look?'

'Please do.'

Edith put down her doctor's bag by Celia's work table, took off her gloves and loosened a blue silk scarf which she was wearing. She proceeded to circle round, occasionally pausing to stare at a particular piece. She stopped in front of a bookcase in which Celia was displaying a collection of Victorian and Edwardian novels, many of them beautifully bound in leather, their titles in gilt. She laughed, and remarked, 'I see many old friends amongst these.'

'Are you looking for anything special?'

'I actually wanted a really large desk for my consulting room. But you don't seem to have one.'

'Oh, but I do. I have Father's desk. It's in the back shed, however. Would you mind coming through to the back?'

'Not at all.'

Celia shot the inside bolt on the front door, and then led her client through the back passage to the rear door.

'Phew!' exclaimed the doctor, as they passed the closed door of John's workshop.

Celia laughed. 'It's Mr Philpotts with his French polishing. I'm sorry – it makes an awful smell.'

'It can't be very good for him. I hope he has his work-room well ventilated.'

'Well, there are windows.'

They crossed the yard, and Celia unlocked and opened the double doors of the shed. In the poor light, she pointed out the desk.

It was rather dusty, so Celia pulled her little yellow duster from her pocket and ran it over the wood. She pointed out that it was double pillared with seven drawers, all with dovetailed corners. The pillars and the fronts of the drawers were elaborately carved. Round the top surface it was inlaid with mother-of-pearl in a pattern of lotuses. The writing area was covered in fine green leather embossed with a leaf-patterned edging in gold.

The drawer pulls were heavy brass, and Edith ran her fingers round one of them. 'Hand thrown?' she inquired.

'Yes. It is certainly beautifully made, although I don't think it is quite old enough to be classed as an antique,' Celia said honestly. 'My paternal grandfather brought it from Malaya.'

'How much do you want for it?'

'I am asking twenty-five pounds.' She knew that a cheap new desk could be bought for about five pounds, and she held her breath, while Edith considered it.

'It's rather expensive,' Edith said, running her fingers longingly over the exquisite mahogany. She sighed. 'I would like to see it in a better light, before I decide.'

'That could be arranged. If you would like to step in again tomorrow, I'll ask Ethelred to move it into the shop. You would be able to see it in a good light there.'

'Thank you. I would like that.' She shrugged, and confided, 'As you can imagine, I never know exactly when I will be free, but some time before you close, I'll come over.' She smiled at Celia, and added, 'I love beautiful things round me. I'm using Father's old desk at present. All the

350

drawers keep sticking, and the surface is stained beyond redemption. It doesn't give a good impression – besides which,' she said ruefully, 'I have to see an awful lot of it, and I would like to have something good. You know, Father never cared about possessions, and with no mother in the house, there was no one to suggest anything better.'

Celia laughed. 'People make do every day with things they don't like, don't they? And keep in store the really beautiful things they should be enjoying. Don't worry, I'll keep it for you until you come.'

The hint that it could be sold quite quickly was not lost on Edith. She thought that Celia was learning fast. She noted with some relief that the girl had lost the look of absolute despair which she had exhibited in her office.

The next day, the desk, in all its well-polished glory, stood in the window, its rich wood catching the afternoon sun, and when Edith saw it through the window, she knew that she wanted it very much, a fitting memento of a month when her practice had shown real growth. She dickered over the price, and Celia brought it down slowly to twenty pounds, agreeing reluctantly to a payment of ten pounds that day and ten pounds in fourteen days.

'You don't have to deliver it until I've paid the second instalment,' Edith said encouragingly.

Celia looked at this lady who had, she felt, given her new life, and had a strong inclination to give her the desk. Common sense won, however, when she remembered that she had obligations herself. She responded by saying that she was sure she could trust Edith to pay, and that Ethelred would deliver it on a handcart the next day. 'I'll wrap it well in a quilt so that it doesn't get scratched,' she promised.

The doctor gave her a cheque for ten pounds, and Celia carefully wrote her first receipt. For years afterwards, she said that this was the most exciting moment she could remember in all her life – with one exception.

After she had seen the doctor out, she ran through the shop, cheque in hand, to tell John Philpotts the good news.

Chapter Forty-Six

అని

After Ethelred had delivered the desk and while he still had the rented handcart, she closed the shop a little early, and together they walked over to the Aspens' yard, to collect all the pictures that she had. As Ethelred lifted them out of the barn, she arranged them carefully, back to back, on the old quilt which she had spread over the handcart. Betty came over from her office to look at some of them, and heard about the impending visit of Alec Tremaine.

'That's just like John,' she said. 'He'd help anyone struggling.'

'I hope his friend won't mind helping me.'

'I'm sure he won't. He'll probably be quite interested, if he's an artist, as you say. I wonder if he's Lady Tremaine's son back from the war at last.'

'I've no idea,' replied Celia. Then she said slowly, 'I believe that Mother is acquainted with a Lady Tremaine.'

It took three patient journeys with the handcart to transfer all the pictures to the shop, after which she sent Ethelred home and herself dusted them lightly with a feather duster, as she had seen Dorothy do, and then propped them up all round the shop, wherever they could be placed.

In order to save the train fare, she walked home.

As she crossed the road just before reaching Meols Station, she was nearly run down by a young woman on a bicycle. The woman swerved to avoid her, flung a laughing apology over her shoulder and continued merrily pedalling towards Hoylake.

Safely on the other side of the road, Celia, who had never ridden a bicycle in her life because her mother thought they were vulgar, watched her enviously.

With some of Dr Mason's money, I'll buy a second-hand bike, she promised herself. She said I should cycle. I won't tell Mother. I'll ask Eddie about it. She felt very bold and daring.

At home, Louise and Edna had already begun to eat dinner. They were both a little worried about her being late. 'You should tell us when you expect to be late,' her mother scolded.

'Yes, Mama,' she agreed, as she ran upstairs to wash her hands and tidy her hair before coming to the table.

As she snatched up her comb, she noticed the box of bricks she had earlier brought from her old trunk, and she picked up the box and took it down to the living room. She put it on the sideboard, and slid, breathless, into her chair.

She did not tell her mother about the sale. She thought it might distress her to know that her husband's desk had gone for ever. Nor did she mention the impending visit of Alec Tremaine to see the pictures. She had begun to feel strongly that it was her shop and her business, and was nothing to do with her mother, who would, anyway, only criticise anything she did.

While they were drinking an after-dinner cup of tea fairly sociably round the fire, she told Louise about the box of bricks. She got up, put down her cup, and then emptied the bricks on to the tablecloth.

'I thought, Mama, that you could spell a word or two by putting the bricks in a row, and then guide the men's hands round the letters.' She spoke eagerly, anxious to help.

'Both of them must be able to read already, and if their fingers were sensitive enough, they could recognise the letters. For instance, you could spell WALK, and they would possibly get the idea that they were going to go for a walk.

'You said that you had been able to tell them a few things by outlining letters on the palms of their hands – but the bricks would be steadier, and they could run their fingers over them more than once, if they were in doubt.'

She turned the bricks over quickly, and said, 'I don't think there is a question mark – or an exclamation mark – but somebody who could whittle could make two bricks with them on. Then you could ask a question, like WALK? and they could say yes or no.'

She stopped and looked triumphantly at Louise.

It was Edna who realised the possibilities first. She said, 'Celia! It's wonderful – it would be a crack in a wall of silence for them.' She stood looking at the little blocks, and then added thoughtfully, 'You could get them to identify the letter on a block and then guide their fingers to the same letter in Braille – and with a bit of luck they would understand the connection. You could really teach them, Mama.'

Celia nodded quick agreement. 'It would be awfully slow, I am sure. But, Mama, you could communicate quite a lot, if they can manage to read the letters.'

Louise was very tired; she was still shaky from the loss of Timothy and Paul. She did not answer immediately.

In addition, she had had an uncomfortable afternoon with the army doctor, when he had visited the nursing home. She had suggested that the two deaf-blind could be taken swimming, if an orderly who could swim went with each of them.

The doctor did not want to be bothered with wild ideas put forward by a stupid elderly widow, and had rudely quashed her suggestion as nonsense. He argued that all the men would then want to swim – and it would be impossible to ensure their safety in the water.

She had swallowed her anger, and had taken Richard and Charlie out for a walk on the seashore. As the tide retreated it left firm, damp sand on which they were not likely to trip up, and they walked quite steadily, one on either side of her, arms linked with hers. They seemed to enjoy it.

If only the pair could have read Braille, she thought, their own ideas on swimming might have been conveyed to the doctor and helped to win the battle. A knowledge of how to read and write Braille was, she knew, the first essential. Edna and Celia did not need to remind her.

Cup in hand, she turned wearily and without hope.

Her mouth fell open. She put down her cup and got up to look at the bricks. She realised immediately that here at last was a simple way to communicate with young Richard and Charlie until they could learn Braille. As Edna had said, it could form the actual link which would enable them to do so.

Through trembling lips, she said, 'Spell a word for me, Celia, and I'll close my eyes and see if I can read it.'

Celia arranged the bricks to read BLIND, and with closed eyes Louise allowed her hand to be guided to them. At first she spelled it out as BLINO, but Celia shook her hand and took her fingers back to the beginning again, and the second time she read it correctly.

Mrs Lou stood looking at the word and then she cried, and they laughed and cried together.

'I bet Eddie can carve you a question mark and an exclamation mark,' Edna assured her mother. Like Celia, she had a blissful belief that Eddie Fairbanks could do anything.

Chapter Forty-Seven

❧

When a very fit-looking man, trilby hat in hand, entered the shop, he found Celia on her knees sorting her mother's Crown Derby dinner service for twelve into two sets for six. She had noticed that, in the hardware store down the road, china services were being sold in sixes, and she thought it might be easier to dispose of smaller sets. She had come in early to do this, and now she rose hastily from the floor, undoing her apron as she turned to her visitor.

She smiled, and said, 'Good morning, Sir.'

'Alec Tremaine, Ma'am, John Philpotts' friend.'

'How nice of you to come,' she said, and held out her hand to be shaken. He took it carefully and shook it.

John Philpotts had told him, 'She's a little pet. So fresh and innocent. I don't want her to be cheated, if she has something good to show you. Take care of her.' And holding her hand and looking into a gentle pale face, Alec felt suddenly that he was going to enjoy helping her with her pictures very much. John was right – she looked like a real old-fashioned girl, and he astonished himself by thinking immediately that his mother was certain to approve of her. It was some time before he realised how quick a mind lay behind the calm blue eyes.

Unmarried, battle-scarred and weary after four years in the army, he had been thankful, at the age of thirty-three, to find a post teaching commercial art in a Liverpool college; it was a fairly new discipline. Before the war, he had been quite successful as a watercolour artist and book illustrator.

Now, he began to fret that his knowledge might not be adequate to judge Celia's collection of paintings. A quick glance round her showroom had told him that the contents were certainly not those of the usual second-hand shop, and this quiet little gentlewoman was certainly no ordinary second-hand shop owner.

Celia was equally unsure of herself. She turned a dining chair round for him to sit on, and then asked if he would like to take off his macintosh, since he was likely to be with her for some time.

He slowly divested himself of the garment and she fluttered to the back of the store to hang it up, nearly knocking over a pile of Crown Derby dinner plates. Then she realised that he would not sit down until she did, so she hastily got out another chair and sat on it.

Her hands modestly folded in her lap, she smiled shyly at him. He was a stolid, pleasant-faced man. His brown hair was close-clipped and had a few white hairs glinting in it. His face was clean shaven, deeply lined and ruddy from exposure. Military service had, presumably, given him his very upright posture. He spoke with the perfect pronunciation of a public school man.

She thought he was wonderful, a returned hero. As she carefully weighed him up, a wave of very odd sensations went through her. Though these made her feel a little unsteady, she led off the conversation like a good hostess, by inquiring how he would like to proceed.

Wrenching himself back from thoughts far removed from paintings, he said he would, first, like to walk round slowly and take a general look at the collection.

Not wishing to embarrass him by hovering behind him, she said she would finish sorting out the dinner service and put it away. He nodded, and, with hands clasped behind his back, he went slowly round the collection of paintings, most of which were oils in heavily carved gold frames. Occasionally, he took a picture down and carried it to the window to take a particular look at it. Despite his solid weight, he walked lightly, she noticed.

After half an hour, she brought him a cup of tea. She boiled the water on a gas ring in a tiny washroom at the back of the shop. He thanked her absently, and continued his promenade, teacup in hand. While she waited, she sat down at her corner table to drink her own cup of tea and draw faces on the blotting paper.

She did not know how to bear the suspense in silence, and was thankful when a girl of about fifteen entered and began to look round.

Celia put down her cup, and went forward to ask her if she needed help.

'I want a present for me mam,' was the reply. 'I thought you might have a nice ornament.'

Celia immediately opened the china cabinet and brought down a series of vases and small figurines. At two shillings each, the girl said they were too expensive. She could get similar ones down the road for sixpence.

'Well, this one and this one are early Royal Doulton,' Celia defended. But Royal Doulton meant nothing to the girl, and, after looking disparagingly at the various clocks in the shop, she walked out looking quite huffy.

A small burst of laughter from behind Celia, as she shut the door, lifted her low spirits.

Alec ventured a comment. 'Bravo,' he said. 'I can see from your stock that you don't need that kind of clientele. You need real collectors.' Then he immediately regretted his impolite intrusion into what was essentially her business, not his.

Unruffled, she smilingly agreed with him. His comments made him suddenly more human to her. 'I know, Mr Tremaine. You are quite correct. But I'm not sure how to let them know I am here!'

'Ah, well, if you would like to, we'll talk about that another time. I would be happy to make some suggestions, if you would permit it. Are you ready to talk about pictures?'

'Indeed, yes.' She went towards him eagerly, and they circled the shop together.

'Some of the paintings have been done by amateurs and I suggest that they were, perhaps, framed as gifts to loved ones. I think you could sell them for a guinea or two, to people who want good frames, say, for mirrors or other pictures.' He paused to look down at her, and asked, 'Shall I put them on one side for you?'

Fearing that she herself might make an error in sorting the pictures, if she did it when he was gone, she agreed, and he stacked them neatly against the back wall.

When that was done, he told her, 'Most of the others were done by local nineteenth-century artists – I recognise the names of some of them. They are not great paintings, but they were commissioned by someone with taste, and they are pleasant to look at. They are quite valuable, I think. Look at this one.' He lifted one down to show her. It was a peaceful scene of Raby Mere, which had hung in the dining room of her old home.

'It is nice, isn't it? Father was rather fond of it.'

He carefully put it on one side, and picked up the next one, which was painted in the style of the Impressionists.

'That's called *Sunday Afternoon*,' Celia offered. 'I can't think why. It's mostly blurred.'

He smiled down at her. 'It is, I think, quite good.'

They spent over an hour slowly going through the collection, until there were only two left. So that it could be seen particularly clearly, he propped up near the window the portrait of a young woman.

'I may be wrong,' he cautioned, 'but I have an idea that this is a Ramsay, though the frame seems to cover the signature.'

'Ramsay?'

'He was an eighteenth-century Scottish artist, noted for his portraits of Scottish gentlefolk. If I am right, it might fetch a fair sum, particularly if it were shown in Edinburgh.'

'Really? I think it's a painting of one of my ancestors.' Her pale-blue eyes had widened with astonishment. 'That would be a wonderful help! Cousin Albert says I must accumulate capital, so that I can buy good replacement stock when it is offered. At the moment I couldn't possibly buy anything.'

Alec murmured absently something about her having only just started out. Then he picked up the last painting, a seascape. 'I kept this one until last, because I am almost afraid to raise your hopes too much.'

Celia's heart gave a frightened thump. Then she realised what it was he was holding, and she said carelessly, 'Oh, that's the Turner. It's awfully dirty, isn't it? It's called *Hoylake Sands*.'

Alec was so stunned at her remark that he nearly dropped the precious work.

'You mean that you know it is a Turner?'

Fearful that she had said something wrong, she backed down and replied cautiously, 'Well, that's what I've always been told.'

Alec gasped. 'By Jove! I couldn't believe my eyes when I looked at it; I thought it must be simply a good copy.'

He went to the window and laid it in a clear shaft of light. Then he took a magnifying glass out of his pocket and studied it carefully.

Celia watched him, totally bewildered. She said, 'Mother didn't think much of it, but it fitted in in a spot by the breakfast room fireplace, and there it hung for years and years. That's why it's so dirty – from smoke and soot.'

Alec began to whistle under his breath. Then he asked, 'Have you any idea how it came into the family?'

'Well, when Great-aunt Blodwyn, my grandfather's sister, came from Wales to my sister Edna's wedding – she dislikes Mother, you must understand – I remember their quarrelling in the quiet, acid way that ladies sometimes do.'

Her laugh was rueful, as she glanced up at him. 'They were sitting in the breakfast room having a morning glass of sherry.' She stopped, and then said blankly, 'I remember the day so well. Great-aunt Blodwyn had her arm round my waist as I stood by her chair.'

Alec Tremaine looked at the small, dainty person in front of him, and remembered some of John's casual remarks about her. John had said cynically that she had probably been kept single so that she could care for her parents in their old age. It was a well-known custom much decried by the new Suffragette movement.

Celia realised that she had strayed a little from the question she was supposed to be answering, and went on quickly, 'Anyway, I remember Great-aunt Blodwyn baiting Mother by saying that such a good painting should not be left where it would gather soot.'

It was Alec's turn to chuckle softly, but he did not otherwise break into her story. In his mind's eye, he saw the kind of petty cattiness that occurs between women with not enough to do to really occupy themselves.

'Mother said it was a grubby old thing and she thought it was time it was thrown out and they bought something new. She never would throw it out, though, because Father was stuffy about these things – he liked old paintings and old furniture.

'Then Great-aunt Blodwyn flared up and said it was treasured by her grandfather as the gem of his collection of paintings. It had been painted by a man called Joseph Turner – she said that her grandfather had commissioned it, when he went to visit his friend, Mr Fawkes of Farnley Hall in Yorkshire. The artist was also staying with Mr

Fawkes, and he did the painting while they were both there. Simple as that.'

Alec Tremaine plonked himself down on his dining chair. 'Well, I'm damned!' he exclaimed, and then immediately apologised for his bad language. With a sudden thought, he asked, 'Do you know who Joseph Turner was?'

'Not really. He must have been an artist. According to Great-aunt Blodwyn, her grandfather was always buying pictures from artists whom he had met – it was his interest – the artist could have been anybody.'

'Turner was simply one of the greatest artists Britain has ever produced,' Alec told her. 'When I was studying, I spent a good deal of time examining his watercolours and engravings of them. I've seen many of his oils, too, of course.'

'Good heavens!' She hung her head and looked a little shamefaced. 'I'm so terribly ignorant,' she burst out. 'Edna might have known who he was – she went to school and learned to paint.' He sensed a bitterness in her tone.

He had noticed the pile of books on antiques amid the things lying on her work table. To comfort her, he made a slight gesture towards them and said, 'By the look of your desk, you seem to be making up for lost time now.'

She nodded, her face sad. 'I'm trying to.'

She looked so downcast that he said, 'Don't worry, Miss Gilmore. Both John Philpotts and I think the shop will be a success.'

What John had actually said was that the two sisters were unexpectedly enterprising. 'They know they don't know nothing, but they've got the guts to admit it – and they'll learn; they don't waste their time like so many are doing.'

'I'm sure I'm making all sorts of mistakes,' Celia said, almost as if she had read his mind.

He grinned, and got up briskly. 'We all have to learn,'

he replied. 'I never thought of teaching until this year.' Then he gestured to the two paintings which he had specially picked out, and suggested, 'If you would allow me to show these two to the head of my college, he might be able to suggest what their worth is, and the best way to dispose of them.'

She nodded, and smiled politely. 'Please do.' Despite the hopes he had raised of making some badly needed capital, all she could think of was that her ignorance had shamed her before this lovely man. After he had left, she spent some time sitting at her desk and going wistfully over every word he had said.

Also deep in thought, Alec walked over to his home in nearby Meols Drive to eat his lunch with his widowed mother. In the trenches, he and his fellow officers used to talk occasionally about being at home at their own fireside. Some of the men already had wives and small children, and they spoke longingly of the comfort of decent meals, warmth and affection. When they were very hungry, which was quite often, they planned their favourite meals, each man grinning and adding a bit to the feast until it became one enormous joke – and it was always homely meals that they longed for and for women, like wives, whom they knew well.

Lady Tremaine and her companion doted on Alec and were bent on 'feeding him up'. They were also bent on his paying court to his cousin, Daphne, a nice enough young woman, who would, they felt, be a suitable wife for a younger son who had not inherited much from his father. Alec had dutifully inspected the lady and played a few games of tennis with her. But that morning Alec had suddenly glimpsed something better, not just a woman who attracted him but a whole peaceful, orderly way of life, and his mother found him unusually silent at lunch time. She suggested a game of golf, but he said he felt like a stroll round the Liverpool Art Gallery, which he had not visited since he returned home, and took himself off to the railway station to catch a train to the city.

Chapter Forty-Eight

At home that night, Louise retired reluctantly to the sitting room to write a reference for Winnie, in reply to an inquiry from Mrs Johnson who was considering her for the post of cook in her new nursing home. Though still annoyed that a servant of hers should go so far as to trespass on her property, she had strict instructions from both her daughters that the reference should be an excellent one. Determined that her old friend should get the position, Celia reiterated to her mother Winnie's great ability to cook everything, from dinners for large parties to wine jelly for an invalid. 'Make it a really nice reference, Mama. Winnie is quite a wonderful cook.'

Being fundamentally a conscientious woman, Louise knew that Celia was correct, and in her best copperplate, she assured Mrs Johnson of Winnie's capabilities and her honesty. In her secret heart, she admitted that she wished she still had Winnie with her, and she quite envied Mrs Johnson her ability to employ a cook.

While Louise was safely occupied, Celia poured out to Edna the story of Alec Tremaine's visit and the Turner painting and her own dreadful ignorance.

Edna remembered the painting and said she had always known it as 'the Turner'. 'There were so many paintings of one sort or another in the house,' she said apologetically, 'I never thought of it as anything special. They all seemed to have been handed down to us from the year dot.'

'I felt such a fool, Edna, and he's what Winnie would

have called a loovelly man.' There was a yearning in her voice.

'You are smitten!' Edna teased.

Celia shrugged helplessly. 'Cats can look at kings.'

Edna smiled. 'Cheer up. What's he going to do with the two paintings?'

'We packed them up carefully and he's taking them to show the principal of his college.

'It was funny, Edna. He actually insisted on giving me a receipt for both the Turner and the Ramsay, and he promised not to let them out of his sight.' She sighed. 'Frankly, I thought he was overreacting.'

'Oh, no. They are probably valuable. It looks as if he will really take care of your interests.'

'Not mine. Mother's.'

'What do you mean?'

'Well, Mother let me have the pictures, because she thought they were old-fashioned and of no value. Morally, if I get any real money for them, I should hand it to her.'

Edna exploded. 'What utter nonsense! The paintings, the furniture and the china are all yours. Cousin Albert arranged it legally. And over the years, believe me, you've earned every cent of anything you get for them.'

She was truly angry. She got up off her chair, and spun round to walk up and down in the narrow space of the living room. 'I won't hear of it!' she almost shouted. 'It's absurd.'

She looked so like her mother in one of her rages that Celia quailed for a moment. Then she laughed. 'You're so good, Edna. I feel conscience-stricken, that's all.'

'Forget it. Mother's doing very nicely, what with the money from the silver and the annuity, which Cousin Albert is now arranging for her. Most of the time she's so absorbed with her boys that she forgets we exist, except to keep the house going.'

'Mother's certainly got a hold on life again,' Celia admitted. 'She's trying to get a committee together.'

'She is. She's already learning Braille and is beginning to get a grasp of it, and the Liverpool School for the Blind has been quite helpful with advice. Of course, they deal with civilians, whereas Mother's young men are still in the army. You forget her. She's fairly happy, and you enjoy whatever comes your way,' she ordered. 'Alec Tremaine sounds a dear. Be nice to him.'

'Yes, Edna,' Celia replied in mock submission.

Two days later, on his way home from the station, Alec dropped into the shop just as she was about to close up.

He whipped off his hat and told her in haste that her pictures were stored in his principal's office safe, until the principal could give more time to examining them. 'We're short of staff,' he explained apologetically. 'And there is a real rush of older students returning from the war. We are nearly run off our feet.'

She assured him shyly that neither he nor his principal should go to too much trouble for her. There was no hurry.

They stood looking at each other uncertainly, and then he said, smiling ruefully, that he must not be late for dinner – his mother didn't like it.

'My mother doesn't like it either,' she said with a small chuckle, and she held out her hand to be shaken.

He grasped it firmly, and said, 'I'll keep in touch. Goodbye.'

The feel of the warmth of his hand stayed with Celia, even after he had let himself out. As the sound of his footsteps on the pavement diminished with distance, she was flooded by feelings never before experienced. They seemed, somehow, to be connected with small unexpressed, unexplained longings that she had sometimes felt before; longings that no one else seemed to mention in conversation and which she had assumed, therefore, were vulgar, like talking about having the stomach ache or wanting to vomit.

Now, for a moment, she felt unsteady enough to think that she might faint, and she sat down suddenly in the nearest chair until it eased.

When finally she did lock the front door after herself, she walked home in an almost dreamlike state.

Some weeks elapsed without a word from Alec Tremaine and Celia began to think sadly that he had lost interest.

He'll post the paintings back to me, some time or other – with polite regrets that they are worthless, she told herself.

With a neat energetic Welsh woman as daily cleaning lady, Edna had more time to spare and she began to take a solid interest in the shop.

Small advertisements were put in local papers and in the *Liverpool Echo* and the *Evening Express*, which were read quite widely. Aided by Betty Houghton and John Philpotts, the two women emphasised the first-class quality of their stock and the fact that a French polisher and upholsterer was on the premises.

Betty also sent to see them an aggressive young woman who said she was the social reporter of the local paper, and that she would like to do a small article on the opening of the shop. Later, Celia described her to Edna as looking just like a ferret in a smart hat.

Notebook in hand, she breezed round the shop, admiring this and that, while John and Celia watched her as anxiously as if she were a ferret very liable to bite.

Behind her back, John quietly asked for the key to the china cabinet and a puzzled Celia gave it to him, eyebrows raised in silent question. 'Small gift,' he hissed. 'To mark the happy occasion of her visit.'

Celia was quite bewildered but she gave him the key. He quietly picked out a pretty cup and saucer and wrapped them in tissue paper. After about ten minutes and a few questions addressed to Celia, the lady announced that she had all the information she needed. Celia thanked her for coming, and John saw her to the door. As he opened the door, he handed her the parcel, and said they had enjoyed her visit and would like her to have the enclosed little memento of it.

All coyness and blushes, she accepted the present and they saw her lay it carefully in the basket attached to the handlebars of her bicycle.

John turned and laughed at Celia. He said, 'Write its value off in your account book as business expenses. It will be some of the best money you ever spent.'

He was correct. A very enthusiastic little article graced the column, next to a report of a local wedding. A number of ladies came to see this interesting new arrival on Market Street. They were a different breed from those who had come and gone at other times, and, as a result, Celia sold a pair of side chairs to one, and a number of delicate glass specimen vases to a collector. There was also an elderly man who bought a pair of pictures by a nineteenth-century local artist, whose work he admired.

Edna's furniture had arrived some weeks before from South America, and Celia began to show in her shop some pieces of it which Edna had given her when they first unpacked it and put it in the barn. It was very unusual to English eyes, and attracted a fair amount of attention. She wanted to give to Edna the money she received for it, but Edna would not hear of it.

She said, 'Celia, I am not sure how much I shall receive from the company, but I do know that I shall be quite a well-to-do woman. I don't even spend half of what Papa Fellowes sends me at present. Except for a few pieces, you can have it. I'm getting a lot of fun out of the shop – and that is enough for me.' She did not say that the furniture reminded her too much of great unhappiness for her to ever want to use it again.

'Have you decided about making a home of your own yet, Edna? You might need the furniture, after all.'

Edna thought of the tender letters going back and forth to Brazil. Because the liaison had originally been an illicit one, she had said nothing about Vital to either Celia or Louise. She sighed, 'Quite honestly, Celia, I don't know yet what to do. But you are not to worry. Let's get you launched first.'

Celia had almost given up hope of seeing Alec again, when he suddenly dropped into the shop late one afternoon, to tell her that examination of her pictures had been delayed, because the college principal was in hospital having further surgery on an old wound in his back.

'I'm so sorry for the long delay, but it cannot be helped, Miss Gilmore.'

'It doesn't matter,' Celia assured him. 'Is it very serious surgery?'

'Well, back surgery, I am told, is difficult, and he will need some time for recovery. But they hope to alleviate the nagging pain he has been enduring.' Alec frowned, and then added, 'They should never have called up men of his age.'

Celia sighed. 'I expect they were getting short of young ones.'

'They were indeed, Miss Gilmore.'

They spent a little time chatting about the war, and then a customer came in. Alec said shyly that he would be in touch with her, smiled and left.

With an inward sense of pure happiness, Celia reluctantly turned her attention to the lady who had entered.

Efforts at publicity drew other dealers to view their stock. They offered to buy pieces for ridiculously small prices. Both sisters quickly recognised them for what they were and sent them on their way.

It was not long, however, before more bona fide customers began to stroll in. Unlike many second-hand and antique stores, Celia and Edna took a lot of trouble to make the shop pretty and show off what they had in a good light. Everything shone with polish and the place smelled sweet with bowls of dried lavender.

It had been John's opinion that the hardest things to sell would be the beds, despite the fact that they were in good condition and had fine, carved bed heads.

'It's because folk are afraid of vermin,' he explained.

Undeterred, Edna got Ethelred to bring them, one at a time, from the barn, and, using some of the enormous amount of bed linen they had, she made them up as if ready to get into. She decked them out with a bunch of flowers or an old shawl or, in one case, a rose-trimmed summer hat laid on the counterpane, as if the owner had just come into the house.

In six months they had not a bed left. In two cases they had sold them complete with the bedding on them. They disposed of some of the others by agreeing to keep the bed until the cost was paid by weekly instalments.

'I suspect that couples setting up house are buying new furniture for the living rooms and economising when it comes to the bedrooms,' said Edna shrewdly.

A trip to buy furniture in Liverpool or Birkenhead involved either taking the electric train, which to many was quite expensive, or a complicated journey by bus and ferry. Celia undoubtedly benefited from the fact that hers was the only shop selling furniture between Hoylake and Birkenhead, at a time when private cars were few and there was, anyway, no tunnel under the Mersey through which to drive to Liverpool. She soon learned to stock some old, but good, furniture which was not as expensive as her genuine antiques, and this gave her a steady turnover.

They began early to look for advertisements of estate

sales, where they might purchase new stock. 'Before we buy, we'd better attend some sales,' Celia suggested. 'So that we understand what to do.'

They temporarily formed the habit of shutting the shop on Mondays and Tuesdays, days which seemed to bring the smallest number of clients. And off they went to country estate sales on bicycles which Eddie had obtained for them from a local repair shop.

It was as well they did go, because they learned how professional dealers joined up to keep the prices low at auctions, and yet outbid them. They also learned, sometimes by bitter experience, to examine with care every piece they wanted to buy, and not to be carried away by claims of antiquity.

Though Celia was learning fast, Edna was by far the more astute buyer. She had had much experience in South America of bargaining for everything, and she would pile in with great gusto, when Celia was far too polite to question an offer and would simply refuse it.

It was Celia, however, who really studied furniture as a subject. She read widely, and would shyly stand by a dealer at the showing before an auction and summon up courage to ask questions – and learn how to identify the work of famous furniture makers.

She found that there were second-hand dealers and antique dealers, and a third group which catered for collectors, mostly small things, like china, medals, coins or old toys.

'You'd be amazed what people collect,' one lady told her. 'I've a chap on my list who does nothing but collect corsets, the older the better.' She laughed. 'He's not perverted. He dresses exhibitions in museums, and to make the garments hang right, he needs proper underwear under them.'

Celia looked so innocent that, at first, it was apparent that the dealers assumed she attended sales for amusement rather than to buy. Until they began to know her face and heard her bid, they would talk quite frankly about fake antiques and cheap copies of better quality furniture.

She accepted any bit of information she could pick up, though she and Edna had had the advantage of living in a circle of people whose homes were invariably beautifully furnished, and had acquired, without realising it, an eye for fine design and finish. As a result, they could make a reasonable guess at the probable age of a piece.

After a while, the two women found themselves part of a fraternity of dealers, who, though often hostile to each other, tended to hang together at estate sales. As time went on, more than one client of Celia's Antiques turned out to be a person sent to them by another dealer, who did not have in stock what the client wanted. She took care to reciprocate.

While she waited with what patience she could muster for word from Alec regarding the two paintings he had taken away, Celia announced an art sale, everything one guinea, to get rid of those paintings which he had said were done by amateurs. She kept on the walls of her shop those which John had told her were done by local professionals.

On a fine October day, she set out the amateur efforts along the frontage of the shop. She herself sat in the doorway.

She discovered that pictures of flowers went very quickly, and two framed samplers were snapped up by an elderly lady who said she collected them. One street scene was stolen. Anything dark and gloomy failed to move.

John advised her to enter the stolen painting in her account book as one guinea lost by theft. 'It's an expense of doing business,' he explained calmly. Celia, who was learning about life almost too quickly, ruefully followed his advice.

It was news to her that people collected old samplers,

and she decided regretfully that she had probably sold her samplers far too low.

As soon as it was fairly apparent that the business was beginning to thrive, John also advised her to take out fire insurance, which she did. 'Fire's what I fear most,' John told her. 'It can wipe you out.'

Both Edna and Celia had begun to doubt that they would ever receive an opinion on the painting of Hoylake Sands, but, totally unexpectedly one Saturday afternoon, Alec came hurrying into the shop.

Celia was seated behind her little counter table and he saw how her face lit up at the sight of him.

Hat in hand, he bowed, and apologised. 'I am sorry to have left you so long in suspense. Getting the college back to a peacetime footing without our principal has taken up more time than we expected.'

Celia was so pleased to see him that the paintings seemed suddenly unimportant. She smiled, and said, as she pointed to a chair conveniently set near her, 'It doesn't matter. Do sit down and tell me what happened and how your principal is. Would you like a cup of tea?'

He refused the tea, as he seated himself and laid his hat on a sideboard at the back of him. Then he turned to grin at her cheerfully. The smile made her heart jump.

'Well, good news and bad news. The old boy is fine and was very interested, once he had a chance to really examine them. When I told him where I had got them from, he was cautious, however. He thinks they may be genuine, that is to say, not good copies, but is not sure. He has suggested I show them to an art expert.'

'Where do we find one?'

'I thought, first, of the Walker Art Gallery in Liverpool, and then I thought we might as well go to the Turner specialists and take them to London to the Tate Gallery. They have a whole Turner collection. And, in addition, they would probably know a Ramsay if they saw one. I am sure someone there would be kind enough to look at both of them.'

'Would they really bother with us?'

'I think so. After all, it was Tate of Tate and Lyle, the sugar people, in Liverpool, who founded the gallery. They owe something to Liverpudlians like us.'

Celia laughed. She was so happy, so glad to see him. 'Of course. Do whatever you think fit. It is most kind of you to be so interested.'

'Well, I spent the summer helping to plan a new curriculum and special extra lectures for ex-servicemen; and I never got an autumn break because of the absence of our principal – we're still so short of staff. But, as soon as the exams are finished, I'll get a few days' holiday – before Christmas – and I would be very glad to take them to London – if you'll trust me with them a little longer.'

'Of course, I trust you.'

By God, she really does, he thought, and he enjoyed the feeling it gave him.

Then he said, 'Well, you know, Miss Gilmore, it would be wonderful if we could announce the discovery of another Turner painting. If it happens to be true, it will give you enough capital to assure the continuation of the business, and enough to invest elsewhere for future use. I can tell you that it will put Celia's Antiques on the map.'

'Would it really? The lack of ready money to replace our stock has worried both Edna and me. And, by the way, do please call me Celia – John always does.'

His eyes twinkled, as he replied, his voice holding a little surprise. 'Well, thank you – I'm Alec. Now, keep your fingers crossed, Celia,' he teased. 'The Ramsay will be a nice find, too, if it is genuine.'

As he picked up his hat from the sideboard, he paused and, almost diffidently, asked her if, on the following Friday evening, she would like to go with him to the cinema to see a motion picture.

She blushed to the roots of her hair, and said she had never seen a film. He assured her that they were the coming thing in entertainment. 'The Birth of a Nation isn't a new film, but I am sure you would find it interesting,' he urged.

As a result, Celia entered a new magical world. She also enjoyed having her hand held during the more exciting scenes.

She did not tell her mother that she had sat in the dark holding the hand of a man she barely knew. She accounted for being so late home by saying she had spent the time rearranging the books in the shop for a sale the following week.

She decided that she would certainly never ever mention to Louise that, after the cinema show was over, they had walked along the shore and he had put his arm round her waist, while they watched the waves breaking on the distant sandbanks. And he had kissed her goodbye at the top of King's Gap, before they ran laughing across the road to the railway station and he had put her on the train for Meols. And she was going out with him again next week.

Sometimes you have to lie for peace, she decided after much quiet thought on the subject, and she felt so wonderful that she could not bear to have the feeling shattered by an angry parent. Nobody in the whole world, she knew for certain, had ever felt like she did; she was in love.

Edna laughed, when she confessed this to her, and said she was delighted. She had to have Alec described in detail to her, because she had, as yet, never met him. Celia spent about half an hour on the subject, without even stopping for breath.

Edna said wistfully that she wished she was as lucky as her sister. And Celia realised that the tables had indeed turned; Edna must be envious, much as she had been on her sister's wedding day.

She gave Edna a big hug, and said with conviction that Edna's time would come.

Edna nodded with a quiet smile, and went upstairs to her bedroom to smoke and to write to Vital.

Chapter Forty-Nine

❧

As winter crept on, the shop became quite busy, with fur-clad customers in search of ornaments, pictures and books for Christmas gifts. It was clear that Edna, just as much as Celia, had become a part of Celia's Antiques and Collectibles. She obviously enjoyed the battle of wits as they bought and sold, whereas Celia found it difficult to maintain a firm stance in the face of some clients who tried to force her prices down. It was Celia, however, who kept carefully the proof of the provenance of particularly good antiques, and, when they were occasionally asked to sell pieces on commission, it was she who kept note of the furniture's ownership. She also cleaned the store, polished the furniture and kept the accounts.

Despite her fear of bargain-hunting clients, she spent more and more time in the shop, while Edna bought at estate sales. If driven into a corner on the subject of price, Celia would say that she must consult her partner before agreeing to bring it down by more than ten per cent.

On occasions, clients would criticise a piece of furniture because it had minor scratches or chips or the upholstery was shabby. This gave the young women a chance to bring John Philpotts to the fore on the subject of repairs, and his salesmanship often clinched a deal.

They also went half shares with John in the purchase of a handcart and a better trolley to facilitate the movement of both his repairs and their stock. 'One day,' John promised, 'we'll buy our own van for deliveries.'

'Will you teach me how to drive?' Edna teased.

John was unexpectedly silent. Then he said reluctantly, 'We'll see when the time comes.'

It was only later that Edna was told by Eddie Fairbanks that John blamed himself for the death of his fiancée while driving an ambulance in France.

'You see, love, if he hadn't taught her, she'd probably never have gone to war. Not that the poor girl would have got much comfort from him if she'd stayed at home waiting for him.'

'Why not?'

'Didn't you know? The poor lad's so wounded he'll never be any use to a woman. You don't have to tell every Tom, Dick and Harry, of course.'

Edna nodded her head slowly. 'I suspected it from a few hints he dropped, though, naturally, I would never actually ask him straight out,' she said. 'But you do hear of men coming home disabled in every way, and their wives and fiancées stay with them and care for them.' She looked thoughtfully down at her feet, as if shy at discussing such a delicate matter, and then she suggested, 'I think, at times, that love can be an all-encompassing and forgiving emotion. And his fiancée might well have stood by him, even if the marriage could not have been consummated. He's a very nice man.'

'Oh, aye. It's possible.'

'Well, anyway, he's an excellent friend to both Celia and me – like you are.'

'Well, thank you, Miss Edna.' The old man grinned and returned to picking rosehips off the bushes in his front garden. What a fine, understanding lady Miss Edna was. He hoped she would find a nice man some day. He snipped three particularly lovely Christmas roses, and then called her back to give them to her.

*　　*　　*

Without Ethelred, the women admitted, they would have been lost. Much of the furniture was heavy, and, before it was sold, often had to be moved more than once. Eventually he became their full-time employee, at a very modest weekly wage, and he divided his time between their garden and the shop. As the newspapers reported an increased number of unemployed, his mother, knowing his limitations, was pitifully grateful.

'You've given him pride in himself, like nobody else would have bothered to do,' she told Celia almost tearfully, as one day she brought in the sandwich lunch which he had forgotten to bring with him to work.

'Well, he's the sweetest person to work with,' Celia replied. 'And he is so honest – I never have to worry about that. Of course, the shop isn't making very much yet – but we hope to improve his wages as time goes on.'

Alec Tremaine did not bother Celia with details of the convoluted situation he found himself in, as he sought to prove the origins of the two paintings he had taken away. Because he would not entrust them to anyone else, he had to wait for opportunities such as his pre-Christmas holiday to take them personally to show to various experts to hum and haw over.

The Ramsay was indeed a Ramsay, he was assured at the Tate, and the two women agreed, when asked, that it should be auctioned in Edinburgh.

During a weekend when Alec begged a Friday off he took the train to Scotland. He was armed with an introduction to the Director of the art gallery in Edinburgh. He was agreeably surprised when the gallery itself made an offer for it.

He made a long-distance call on a crackling telephone to his new-found friend at the Tate. His friend pointed out that the price seemed a little low. If he wanted to try for a better price, the gallery could bid at an auction.

Thoroughly out of his depth, Alec said he would consult the owner, and went back to Hoylake.

'Take it,' said Edna. 'We could get the finding of it written up in the Chester newspaper and even in the *Scotsman*, perhaps. It would give us wonderful publicity, that we made a find like that – and anyway, we need the capital.'

And so it was arranged. She was right about the publicity.

Instead of using the money for the Ramsay to buy stock, Alec suggested that it would probably more than pay a first-class specialist to clean the Turner.

'It would have to be done by a most reputable firm,' Alec warned. 'Because it could be easily damaged – it would have to be taken out of its frame, which nobody has tried to do up to now.'

He looked at Celia, and said, 'As I told you, the chap at the Tate is dead sure it is genuine. But he did say that to sell it on the international market – and it would be international – you'd do better if you had provenance to support the claim that it is a real Turner; otherwise, it is going to cost you a lot, with insurance and transport, while other experts nod their heads over it.' He paused to whistle under his breath, and then added, 'I suspect that, if it were cleaned, all the glorious Turner colours would come up and it would look more convincing.'

Celia was loath to chance losing what they had gained. She protested gently that they needed the money so badly.

'Tush, Celia. We take chances every day,' responded Edna. 'We make all kinds of blunders when we're buying and selling. Let's take this one big chance. It could be the best investment we ever made.'

Finally, they all crossed their fingers, and, once more, Celia packed the painting up very carefully.

The decision entailed two more visits to London, the first, a day or two later, to deliver the painting to an art restorer recommended by the Tate. The second, for which he took a day's leave one Friday some three months later, was to collect it after the cleaning was completed. Alec began to think that he was buying the London, Midland and Scottish Railway Company with his own small salary. 'The things I do for love.' He smiled at his predicament, and began to give earnest thought to engagement rings and to introducing Celia to his mother.

When the picture was finally returned to its owner, it glowed with colour. The man who had so painstakingly cleaned it had raved over it, and for the first time Alec was himself completely convinced that it was a genuine Turner.

While all three of them were in doubt as to what they should do next, Great-aunt Blodwyn became the unexpected source of confirmation of the picture's origins. When Celia wrote to her aunt for her birthday at the end of March, she mentioned her adventures with the shop and the good news about the portrait by Ramsay. She also said how much she wished the Turner was a real one.

She received by return of post a registered letter.

'I have preserved a lot of my grandfather's letters and papers, because he was an interesting man,' her godmother wrote. 'He did a considerable amount of writing about the state of the arts in his day. I always knew that Turner painted that picture – only Louise never seemed to realise that it was valuable and should be taken care of. I am glad you have more sense.

'Grandpa loved the picture – he said Turner did it from memory. I believe it was my grandfather's single biggest investment in a painting, though, as you know, he had quite a collection, some of which ended up in your house.'

Attached to her letter was another, rather crumpled epistle, in which in faded copperplate Joseph Turner acknowledged the safe receipt of a bank draft from Sir Thomas Gilmore in full settlement for an oil painting called *Hoylake Sands*.

Alec looked stupefied when he was shown the letter.

'Well, I'll be damned!' he exclaimed, and sat down, so flabbergasted that he forgot to apologise for using a swear word.

'This will do it,' he said with a satisfied grin. 'It will do it! You'll have plenty of capital to do whatever you want.'

Deeply moved, he got up and put his arms round Edna and hugged her, kissing her on either cheek. Then he smiled down at her little sister, and took her in his arms and did the same.

She blushed profusely as he held her for a moment before releasing her, and Edna decided that it would be very nice to have a brother again. As they discussed the moves they must make to put the painting on the market, she lit a cigarette and longed for Vital.

EPILOGUE

❧

Timothy George stowed his godmother's wheelchair in the back of his van, and drove her and her thin graceful companion, Rosemary, back home from the ceremony at the cenotaph to Celia's old-fashioned house in Hoylake.

All three of them were cold and rather dispirited.

Timothy George went straight upstairs to his apartment on the second floor. He thankfully turned on the electric fire in his bedroom and changed out of his uniform, which was a little tight around his waist. He hung the garments on hangers, and unpinned his medals and laid them carefully on the dressing table. He stood, for a moment, frowning down at them, and wondered if his son, a pillar of a London bank, would keep them after he himself was gone. He doubted it.

He went slowly downstairs to join Celia.

Celia's house, which she and Alec had bought on their marriage, had seen many changes.

After Celia's marriage, Louise and Edna had continued to live in the cottage at Meols, until, one day without warning, a glowing Edna had calmly introduced to Louise a small, neat stranger with charming manners. His name was Vital Oliveira, who had just arrived from Brazil to work as a translator for a big Liverpool fruit importer.

During the long correspondence with his beloved, he had not been idle; he had sought assiduously a post in England, by writing to every British company he had ever been in touch with. It was Edna who had suggested the Liverpool Fruit Exchange as a possible source of work, and through them he had finally reached a company which bought and sold fruit in Spanish and Portuguese-speaking countries. His excellent references, some of them from British companies, finally got him a decent post as translator. He would have to travel from time to time, but his base would be in Liverpool.

He had been in England two months, when he and Edna had announced to a startled Louise that they were to be quietly married within a month.

Since the couple wished to live in Liverpool in order to be near Vital's place of work, Louise had been thrown into a panic at the idea of being left alone in the Meols cottage.

Celia had wanted to offer Louise a home in her new house, but Edna would not hear of it. 'She'll start to bully you again, Celia, like she did when you were young,' she said forcefully. 'She could ruin your marriage. And, if I had her, she would probably ruin mine. Better by far that she should remain in the cottage.'

Through an employment agency, they found a penniless, cultivated lady to be a companion-help to Louise. Though Louise complained steadily about her, the arrangement actually suited them both very well. They lived out quite productive lives in the cottage by continuing Louise's interest in the fate of deaf-blind veterans.

In later years, as she began to interest others in the desperate plight of these unfortunate men, Cousin Albert became a fund-raiser for her, and did much to provide Braille lessons and teachers for them. Their joint compassion was a first step in a journey lasting nearly thirty years, to keep the deaf-blind army privates from being put into mental asylums and conveniently forgotten. Dear Mrs Lou won some battles, but lost many others. She became known to many of the men as a tender presence who smelled of lavender and was not afraid to hug them. She was a much loved lady.

Warned by the startling sensations caused by Sergeant Richard Williamson's gentle fingers on her face when she had first met him, she kept her personal feelings rigidly to herself, though, in her heart, she knew that probably the kindest thing she could do for any one of them would be to take him to bed. Upheld by Victorian principles of the nobility of self-abnegation, however, she never took advantage of their loneliness, and simply hoped they might find their own compassionate young women. And a few of them did. For herself, it was a bitter inward battle.

Louise made generous use of the cottage's spare bedroom by offering free seaside holidays for anyone who was both deaf and blind. They were specially good about this when they received requests to accommodate tiny tots who were so afflicted. At Mrs Lou's, a number of children, for the first time, explored the feel of sand in their hands and waves breaking over their tiny feet, and the lovely cosy lavender-scented comfort of being rocked in Mrs Lou's lap.

While she had the physical strength, Louise worked steadily to try to improve the lives of deaf-blind servicemen. In a country exhausted by the greatest war in history, however, there was a tendency to deal, first, with the greater number of men who were blinded but not deafened.

Over many years, poor Louise was to have considerable problems with the military's medical community, as she struggled to give a better life to her doubly disabled boys. Steeped in nineteenth-century attitudes towards medicine, abominably snobbish, they might bestir themselves for officers, but, as far as they were concerned, too often the other ranks were born unto trouble, as the sparks fly upwards, and must, like Job, patiently endure their suffering. She had discovered to her horror that the usual way of disposing of them, if they were deaf-blind and had no family to whom they could be sent, was to put them into lunatic asylums. If they were not insane when they went in, they frequently soon became so in their desperate confusion. This tragic information fired her with even greater determination to help them.

It was only years later, after another war, that she came into touch with the Perkins Institution for the Blind in Boston, Massachusetts, and was able to suggest to others interested that there should be special training for teachers to work with the deaf-blind, particularly in military hospitals. The names of Helen Adams Keller and her wonderful teacher, Anne Sullivan, became an inspiration.

Celia and Edna ran the antique business until Edna's marriage, after which Alec and Celia, helped by Ethelred and John and an art student or two, managed to run it, while, in quick succession, Celia gave birth to three healthy, mischievous boys, Peter, Paul and Bertram. They finally sold out in the second year of the Second World War.

The Second World War had brought them little but grief. When their last-remaining, third son, Bertram, was killed in Sicily, Celia and Alec offered part of their house as a home for his young widow, Margaret, and her twin boys. The second and third floors were made into a self-contained apartment for them. Celia and Alec occupied the ground floor, and, in later years, after Alec's death, the basement had been made into a living room and bedroom for a carer for Celia.

The grandsons were a consolation to Alec and Celia, as well as to Margaret. Alec had done his best to be a helpful grandfather to them, though he had not lived to see them grow into adulthood.

They were a cheery pair of young scamps, not in any way scholarly, and, in a country where jobs had become difficult to find, they had, after they left school, both joined the Navy.

To mitigate her loneliness after their departure, their

mother continued to share Celia's house. Celia, desperately lonely after her own widowhood, was very glad to have her continued company. It was the merest chance that both lads happened to be on the same ship when, while serving in the Falklands, it was hit by a missile and sank.

Although they were not the only family to suffer losses in all three wars, Celia had, at first, thought that both she and their mother would go mad with the remorseless grief which seemed to stalk the family. 'It's so often the same families who serve,' she cried out in her sorrow.

Though friends were kind, and Margaret's mother left the hotel she owned in Devon and came north to comfort her daughter, the two women could find no relief.

Celia felt suddenly very old and weak. She said to Margaret one day, 'My dear, you are still fairly young. On the other hand, I won't last long. You could make a new life. What about going to help your mother with her hotel? You would meet people. Begin a new life.'

So Margaret found Rosemary, an unemployed Trinidadian, to come to live with Celia, and then went down to Devon.

Unable to move around very much or go out without help, Celia thought she would die of boredom, never mind grief, though Rosemary became devoted to her and was happy in the small, private domain she had in the basement.

Then Timothy George was widowed. After his Royal Air Force service in the Second World War, he had run a small engineering firm in Birkenhead, and he and his wife used periodically to come out to Hoylake to visit his godmother. After his wife's death, he turned to Celia for comfort, the one person who had consistently shown him affection since the day he was born in her mother's house.

She persuaded him to move into the upstairs apartment.

'I shall leave the house to you, anyway,' she told him. 'I haven't anyone else to leave it to.

'Rosemary could look after both of us – she's a cheerful

person to live with. And here, in Hoylake, you would have one of the best golf courses nearby – lots of male company.' She had chuckled mischievously, as she added, 'And I wouldn't complain if you found a nice lady to share the flat.'

Though Timothy George doubted he would ever find another female companion, even if he wanted one, he felt that the arrangement would, at least, relieve him of the bother of housekeeping. He had, also, a great affection for Celia; he had, since boyhood, frankly shared his troubles with her, because she had often had more time for him than his own frail, harassed mother. She was not nosy, either – she wouldn't want to know every detail of where he had been or what he had been doing.

So he agreed.

Rosemary was consulted, and for a much bigger wage, she was willing to look after them both. It was a strange little household, but it worked extremely well.

This afternoon, the three of them were to share a cold lunch in Celia's apartment, and Timothy, with the familiarity of a son, knocked and then entered her room.

Before going to attend to the lunch, Rosemary had helped Celia into an easy chair. She was napping, and her new white wig was a little awry on her head. He went over to a side table, and poured himself a whisky and soda. The clink of glasses woke Celia and, as she straightened her wig, she demanded one, too.

As she watched him pour the whisky, she remembered the baby put into her arms so many years ago. It seemed fitting that, in lieu of her own darlings, this child should be her final consolation, and she smiled faintly.

Her hand was surprisingly steady as she took the glass from him, and he sat down beside her. She held the glass so that a stray ray of sunlight lit up its rich amber colour.

She was silent for a little while, twiddling the glass between her fingers. Then she said, 'You know, Timmy, what with an Empire and two World Wars plus the Korean War – and the Falklands – this old country of ours has been drained of male brains for a couple of hundred years.'

Timothy snorted. After all, he thought, he himself was still here.

To humour her, however, he agreed. 'Administering an Empire must have been pretty draining,' he said lightly. 'All the hundreds of bright young sparks serving from India to the Caribbean who got killed off by yellow fever, malaria, cholera – and the Khyber Pass.' He grinned, as he mentioned the famous Pass. 'When I was a lad, if you didn't have a great-uncle killed at Rorke's Drift, you almost certainly lost one defending the Khyber Pass.'

'True,' agreed Celia. 'My mother's brother was killed in India.' She sipped her whisky, letting it slide around her mouth to savour it. 'At the service this morning, I was thinking what a different place Britain would be, today, if we hadn't lost those men – and then two consecutive generations in the wars. So many of them were well educated or highly skilled. Just think, we might even have had a government of men and women who knew what they were doing!'

This was so close to what he himself had been thinking after the service that he burst into sardonic laughter.

'Well, we did produce Margaret Thatcher,' he reminded her.

'She came too late, and she wasn't clever enough to keep us out of the Falklands,' Celia replied, her eyes suddenly full of tears for the third generation. 'Poor Mike and Dave.' She held out her glass to him. 'Would you get me another glass of whisky please, dear? I feel a little low today.'

He was immediately contrite, and poured another drink for her.

She took the glass from him and stared absently into it, as if she saw in its golden depths the long procession of lost legions, taking away with them their own, unused, individual brilliance, their skills and their seed. Then she sighed; she knew that she would soon join them.

As she lifted her glass, she suggested, with forced cheerfulness, 'To all our beloved absent friends. May they rest in peace.'

He turned to look down at her. So tiny, so old, he thought, yet so indomitable. He touched her glass with his.

'Amen to that, my dear,' he said very gently. 'Amen.'